ACCLAIM FOR CHARLOTTE BINGHAM

The Kissing Garden
'A perfect escapist cocktail for summertime romantics'
Mail on Sunday

Love Song
'A perfect example of the new, darker romantic fiction
… a true 24-carat love story'
Sunday Times

'A poetic and poignant love story'
Sunday Post

The Love Knot
'The author perfectly evokes the atmosphere of a bygone
era … An entertaining Victorian romance'
Woman's Own

'Hearts are broken, scandals abound. It's totally addictive,
the sort of book you rush to finish – then wish you hadn't'
Woman's Realm

The Nightingale Sings
'A novel rich in dramatic surprises, with a large
cast of vivd characters whose antics will have you
frantically turning the pages'
Daily Mail

To Hear a Nightingale
'A story to make you laugh and cry'
Woman

'A delightful novel … Pulsating with vitality and deeply
felt emotions. I found myself with tears in my eyes on
one page and laughing out loud on another'
Sunday Express

The Business
'A compulsive, intriguing and perceptive read'
Sunday Express

'Compulsively readable'
Options

To Hear a Nightingale

Charlotte Bingham

BANTAM BOOKS

LONDON · TORONTO · SYDNEY · AUCKLAND · JOHANNESBURG

TRANSWORLD PUBLISHERS
61-63 Uxbridge Road, London W5 5SA
a division of The Random House Group Ltd
www.rbooks.co.uk

TO HEAR A NIGHTINGALE
A BANTAM BOOK : 9780553818420

First published in Great Britain
in 1988 by Michael Joseph Ltd
Bantam edition published 1989
Bantam edition reissued 2007

Mixed Sources
Product group from well-managed
forests and other controlled sources
www.fsc.org   Cert no. TT-COC-2139
© 1996 Forest Stewardship Council
FSC

Typeset in 10/11pt California by
Colset Private Limited, Singapore.
Printed in the UK by CPI Cox & Wyman, Reading, RG1 8EX.

4 6 8 10 9 7 5 3

To my beloved partner,
Terence Brady

She woke early
To his song
She had never heard
A bird sing
To her.
In each note
He wrote
The passing of time
And when it ceased
It was eternity.

PROLOGUE

Ireland
The Present

Cassie picked up her journal. It was bound in antique red leather, with her initials engraved in gold on the cover. But even though every page was now full, and she had long ago started on a new volume, she always kept it on her dressing table beside her silver hair brushes and the heavy old cut-glass bottles filled with her various scents. It seemed to her that she had only to pick it up at random and from its pages would fall some memento of her life – a picture given to her on her tenth birthday at the convent, a loving message written to her in haste from Tyrone, a Christmas tag gloriously misspelt in large childish writing from Josephine, a drawing of a monster from the leaky pen of Mattie, a piece cut from Tyrone's racing colours, or a birthday card from young Padraig.

Downstairs she could hear Erin her housekeeper opening the door to the man who had come to interview her.

Cassie stopped reading her journal for a moment and imagined him standing on the stone-flagged hall, perhaps looking up at her portrait. The painting had been commissioned by Mattie and given to her as a presentation from all the workers and stable staff at Claremore. It showed Cassie looking as they all liked to think of her but actually seldom saw her, wearing a saffron ballgown with a magnificent necklace of rubies, one hand resting on a sculpture of her husband Tyrone mounted on his trainer's hack Old Flurry.

She paused to put on a little more lipstick and then a last touch of perfume on each wrist. A nervous habit of hers, as ritualistic as the taking of holy water at the entrance to a church. She had lain awake half the night trying to think of original answers to the questions the famous J. J. Buchanan would inevitably pose. The most celebrated sporting writer in America, he was not exactly a noted feminist. And as the first woman to train an English Derby winner, Cassie McGann would be a prime target for his chauvinism.

Cassie looked at her watch. He would have been kept waiting fully five minutes by now. Enough time for him to be grateful for the delay which would enable him to take in everything in the drawing room, enough time to examine the graceful furnishings in the room, the paintings of past winners, the signed photographs from members of royalty and other famous and less famous owners, enough time to begin the journalist's ritualistic search for the keys to her character.

Erin was waiting for her in the hall, and as Cassie descended the stairs she moved in to pluck invisible pieces of hair from Cassie's shoulders and quite unnecessarily tug down the back of her perfectly cut jacket, her freckled face wearing the anxious look of a mother sending her child to her first party.

Cassie hesitated before entering the drawing room.

'Go on with you,' said Erin, as she pushed the door open for Cassie. 'I don't suppose he'll ate yer.'

Cassie lifted her small chin and walked determinedly past Erin, and into the room.

The man waiting for her had his back turned. He was well over six foot in height, and he appeared to be absorbed by the painting of Little Fred, Cassie's first winner trained under her own name.

'So you're the famous Mr Buchanan?' she heard herself say, aggressive as always in moments of doubt.

Buchanan turned to her. When he did, Cassie stopped. For she found that the tall man with the shock of white hair who was standing so seriously before her was someone quite other than J. J. Buchanan.

Part One

Chapter One

Cassie was six when she was sent away to school. She was enrolled in a convent in Pentland, New Hampshire, twenty miles from Westboro Falls where she lived alone with her grandmother. On her very first day there, when she walked down the long path which led to the playing fields, her clothes were so long and ill-fitting, and the turn on the hems of her shorts so deep, that when they saw her all the older girls laughed at her. Cassie laughed too, but only in the hope that the general merriment would make her accepted.

Later, when they were changing, one of the girls asked her why her mother didn't buy her clothes that fitted her.

'Because I don't have a mother,' Cassie replied. 'And Grandmother doesn't like sewing.'

Another girl with small bright blue eyes looked at Cassie sympathetically. Her name was Mary-Jo.

'My grandmother wears long drawers that keep falling down,' she said.

Cassie smiled, then stared at the sports clothes she had just taken off. How she hated them now. When she had seen them laid out, she had been so eager to put them on – the crisp white blouse, the smart blue shorts; they had seemed to hold such promise. And now they held only memories of ridicule. Cassie picked them off the floor and, bundling them all together, threw them into her cupboard.

'You're meant to fold everything up,' whispered Mary-Jo. 'You'll get into trouble.'

'I don't care,' replied Cassie. 'They're too big. They make me look silly.'

Mary-Jo carried on dressing. She did up her hair ribbons quickly and efficiently, while Cassie struggled hopelessly with hers. Hearing the bell ringing for class, Cassie tried to hurry even more and in her feverish haste pulled her ribbons into knots, unlike Mary-Jo's which were now like perfect butterflies. Mary-Jo, seeing her friend's difficulty and having got herself ready, helped Cassie out.

'Didn't you practise?' Mary-Jo asked her. 'My mother made me practise on the standard lamp for days. That's why I can do them so quickly.'

I bet that's what all mothers did, Cassie thought. They taught you how to do up your hair ribbons quickly. And they sent you to school with clothes which fitted you. And with store-bought jars of peanut butter. Not with great long shorts, and one pot of homemade spread, and not knowing how to tie your hair ribbons. That's what grandmothers did.

And mothers didn't forever tell you how wicked you were, like her grandmother was always doing. And how lucky it was that such a wicked girl was accepted by the good nuns.

Nuns were always good to Grandmother, but to Cassie, when she arrived at the convent, they had seemed terrifying, as they bent their wimpled heads down and stared with dark foreign eyes into hers. It seemed to Cassie as if they were staring right into her soul.

'Has she made her first confession yet?' one of them asked her grandmother. 'And if so, when? How long is it since she made her first confession?'

There seemed to be a great and general anxiety as to whether or not Cassie had purged herself of the burdens of her sinful six-year-old-soul, an anxiety of which Grandmother approved. To her Cassie was a sinner. She had been a sinner ever since the child had been left in her care, a fact of which she was forever reminding Cassie.

14

Her very first sin – and, according to her grandmother one of her very worst ones – was the day she wet her knickers in the shoe store in Westboro. In the excitement of going shopping, Cassie had forgotten to 'go' before they left the house, and by the time they were in the shoe shop, and Grandmother was trying on endless pairs of shoes, Cassie was afraid to ask. When Grandmother saw the stream trickling down Cassie's leg and on to her newly washed sock, she was outraged. So much so, and much to the horror of everyone in the shop, she beat her there and then. She turned her over on her knee and smacked her hard. And then she hit her again in the street outside the store and again and again on the way home, before she locked her in her room, where she was to remain until she learnt to control her 'functions'.

Young Cassie learned to control her 'functions' so well that she became adept at not going at all. She would leave going until the very last moment so that she would be wriggling and writhing by the time she shut herself in Grandmother's bathroom.

She dreaded going to the bathroom anyway, because Grandmother's bathroom was not a bathroom – it was a shrine. A place where before anything was done the carpet must first be rolled back, your sleeves folded and the basin filled with water; and care had to be taken so that not one drip would mark the shining chrome of the taps. Cassie was taught to spit her toothpaste down the plughole by her grandmother holding her face over it, and then, having soaped and rinsed herself with the wash flannel, she would be required to fold it, leaving it on the edge of the basin in a neat square. The carpet could then be rolled back, and the taps polished with a towel before Cassie was allowed to leave the room.

Not that life was any easier outside the bathroom. Every room of Grandmother's house was a model of cleanliness and tidiness. It was a mortal sin not to have all the long beige fringes on the rugs pointing in exactly the same direction. It was a sin not to step around the edges

15

of the room to prevent the carpets from wearing; and, climbing the stairs dozens of times each day when she was sent to fetch Grandmother's glasses or her Bufferin, or change her gloves for her, or whatever, she always had to tread on different parts of the carpet. Their life seemed very complicated, and Cassie's life in particular seemed to be one long round of fetching and carrying.

'Seeing as how you're my burden in life,' Grandmother would say constantly, 'you may as well be my donkey.'

But being a donkey brought no reprieves when it came to sins. To move at table meant a sharp slap on the legs. To cry out when Grandmother found a toy on the floor and pulled you down the corridors by your ears and beat you meant she would beat you harder. So Cassie learnt not to cry out. She also learned to remain silent when her grandmother, trying to provoke a response, would accuse her of lying, or of being deliberately disobedient, untidy or rude. Or simply of being ugly.

'You're the plainest child I've ever seen', she would tell Cassie.

And then on another day, 'No you're not, I'm quite wrong, you're not plain at all.'

Cassie looked up at her expectantly.

'I don't know how I could have thought you plain: you're not plain, you're ugly.'

The examination of her conscience was also done for Cassie by Grandmother. So there was no real need for her to be sent to the priest for this, but nonetheless sent she was, where she duly confessed to her lies, her disobedience, her failure to be pretty, her inability to grow curly hair, or have a nice straight nose, or nails that didn't need cutting, or to swallow the hard bread sandwiches wedged with fat that Grandmother dumped in front of her every night at supper.

Bedtime always came agonisingly early. So early that the light was of such a brightness that not even the heavy old blinds and the drapes combined could shut out the glow that would seep through from outside.

Outside was another place. Outside was another country. Outside was the world. As Cassie lay gazing at the ceiling, she could hear other children playing. She could hear the sound of their bicycle bells, of their bats and balls, and the inevitable delighted shouts of all the members of 'our gang'.

'Our gang' played together from the moment they came home from school. Cassie would watch them from her window, her hands pressed down on the sill the better to see the other children playing together. Each night was the same. They would bicycle or run excitedly towards each other and then, putting their heads together, arms around each other, they would arrange the evening game. Cassie never dared to pull aside Grandmother's clean white nets to watch them through just the window glass, and so she always viewed them through a film of white lace which made them seem heavenly and remote from her own sin-filled world.

Every evening Cassie would wonder what it would be like to be a child who was allowed outside on her own. A child who was allowed a bicycle, a bat and a ball, or a pair of grazed knees. She was never allowed to run anywhere. Walking was allowed, sedately beside Grandmother, but only once she had been washed and dressed and sat for what seemed like hours on a chair in the hall; there she watched the hands on the clock to see if she could spot them moving, for she felt, in some strange childish way, that if she could see them moving it would mean that time would be passing more quickly, and if time passed more quickly then it would become the future and might bring an end to the unhappy present.

When, rarely, there were visitors Cassie was made to sit in the dining room. The green velvet curtains made the room dark, and there was little to look at in the room except for one large painting: a painting of a fat man with hardly any clothes on holding out a bunch of grapes to an equally fat lady. The two were being viewed from afar by a man peering through trees. Even at the age of

17

four Cassie thought it a strange picture for Grandmother to possess.

Grandmother never excused the picture but she did make firm references to it having belonged to her late husband's father. It was a work of art. It was a source of admiration in the art world, she said; Cassie was very lucky to be privileged to sit in front of it. To Cassie it was horrible. She connected it with gathering gloom and the endless boredom of sitting in the dining room, while she could vaguely hear the voices of the people in the drawing room, usually commiserating with Grandmother and her 'burden'. Or sometimes the guests congratulated Grandmother on treating Cassie so nicely, in spite of Cassie being so different and such a nuisance.

'Being difficult' was Cassie's speciality, it seemed. Trouble was, it was easy to be difficult when Grandmother was around. Being difficult was making a mark on one of your white socks. It was speaking when you were spoken to by one of Grandmother's friends, instead of allowing her to answer for you. It was having a nightmare which woke her. It was being sick. It was being well. It was having a too white skin. It was having hair that was too thick. It was having hair ribbons that fell off. It was not being able to read. It was being able to read. It was going ahead of her on a walk. It was dropping behind her on a walk. It was being like your father. It was being like your mother. Being difficult was simply being alive.

Cassie was too good at being alive for Grandmother's peace of mind. No one imagined that she wanted Cassie to die; but when Cassie was ill she refused to look after her and sent Delta, her maid, in to check on her, or just stare at her from the door, so it was not unimaginable to Cassie that Grandmother might indeed be made a great deal happier if she was not there. On the bright days of summer when she lay in her bed listening to the other children playing she thought how it would be if God took her to Himself. He could not, stern as she knew He was, be any sterner than Grandmother, and since her body would undoubtedly be dead, then it followed, quite naturally, that she would at least be a little less irritating to God than she had been to Grandmother. She would not need to be fed by God. God would not need to worry about her hands being clean. God could have endless visitors without the need to find her a room in which to sit. It seemed to Cassie that she could be quite a favourite with God, and Grandmother could stay below and feel pleased that she was at last relieved of her terrible burden. So she used to pray every night to be allowed to die.

But God did not love her much, it seemed. Inching her way painfully through the months from four to five Cassie decided that God might need a little help. She had heard of something that was called 'pneumonia' that you caught from being cold, and so during the winter of her fifth year she would stand in front of the windows breathing in the cold night air and trying her hardest to 'catch pneumonia'. That she failed was something that she never understood, any more than she could understand why Grandmother had 'taken her in'. Grandmother did not like children. Children were a nuisance. Cassie's mother had been a nuisance. It was Grandfather who had wanted a child. Cassie felt sorry for Grandmother, and went on faithfully praying for death to come and relieve them both of the intolerable situation that both birth and death – Cassie's mother's death – had landed them in together.

Pneumonia did not come to her rescue, but measles did. She was satisfyingly ill with it. So ill that it seemed to her that even Grandmother thought she must be about to die. She knew this because she heard Delta asking the nurse. The priest came to visit her; and so did the doctor, who was a kind man. He gave her a peppermint. Cassie clung to the memory of his gentle smile all during her illness. All during the darkness, and the blinds being always down, and the tablets, and the spots, and the fever. She clung to it the way she clung to the memory of

19

being given a book about dogs by Mr O'Reilly who lived next door and who kept a spaniel, a spaniel that she was sometimes allowed to pat.

'I like dogs,' Cassie told him. 'But my grandmother doesn't.'

'Here's a book on dogs, honey,' Mr O'Reilly said to her one day. 'You choose which dog you'd really like to own before you go to sleep and who knows, one morning when you wake up you might even have one.'

Then he patted the top of Cassie's head just as she patted the top of his spaniel's head.

That book became everything to Cassie. The pictures were of dogs standing in fields or by trees, each one beautifully illustrated, delicately painted with watercolours. The pages were thick and the print clear and precise. It was an old book, published many years before the war, when covers were hard and leathery, and tissue paper covered the illustrations to keep them fresh.

Grandmother was soon on to the book. It never took her very much time to seize an opportunity to spoil someone else's happiness, and in Cassie's case it took even less. Sometimes it would be a hair ribbon. Sometimes it would be something that she liked to eat. But once Cassie had betrayed a preference it would not be long before that preference became a good weapon with which to punish her.

'If you had wanted to wear blue ribbons to match your dress,' she'd say, 'then you should have made your bed a little better.'

Or another time she would say 'Well, we were going to have your favourite baked custard, but since you forgot to clean your teeth I think now we'll keep it for tomorrow when Mrs Bennett calls.'

At first Cassie hid the book about the dogs, putting it under her bed, but then, some days having passed without punishment, she was lulled into a false sense of security and Grandmother found her looking at it at bedtime.

'Give me that,' she demanded, pulling Cassie out of bed. 'Where did you get this?'

Cassie remained silent.

'You tell me where you got this and I want none of your lies.'

'Mr O'Reilly gave it to me,' Cassie told her.

'Oh, Mr O'Reilly gave it to you, did he?' her grandmother replied, quickly flicking through the book. 'Mr O'Reilly gave it to you. An expensive book like this? You don't expect me to believe a lie like that?'

'I'm not lying, Grandmother,' Cassie protested. 'I promise you I'm not.'

'Of course you are. You're lying, and you will be punished for so doing. You just wait there until I've spoken to Mr O'Reilly about this book. Given it you indeed.'

While her grandmother went next door, Cassie sat on the end of her bed staring at her feet and wondering why God was so cruel, and why He had made her so unloveable.

Then she heard her grandmother return, and her footfall on the stairs. Soon she was by Cassie's bedroom door, still holding the book.

'You've been a very naughty child,' she said. 'You should have told me that Mr O'Reilly gave you the book instead of hiding it from me. Just for that I'm going to lock it away until you've earned the right to have it again.'

Cassie lay on her bed and stared at the ceiling. Darkness would not come. Her book, the source of her one moment of joy in the day when she could stare at those glorious creatures called dogs and imagine what it would be like to own one, was to be denied her. A tear fell down her cheeks, paused, and then slid on down her neck. She whispered the names she had made up for the dogs in the books, and then in her imagination she put her arms round their warm necks and buried her face in their fur. Trusted friends all of them, eyes liquid with love, looking at her the way Mr O'Reilly's spaniel looked at him.

'We'll come back to you, little mistress,' they told her. 'In your dreams we'll come back to you.'

21

But they didn't. Instead her dreams were all the kind that when she awoke in the night made her want to scream. But she caught her pillow in time and pressed it against her mouth so she could make a silent sound, which if it hadn't been silent would have been a sound something between a cry and a sob.

Weeks of running up and down the stairs for Grandmother's eye glasses and her book, and offering to help Delta didn't result in the return of the book – only in Grandmother becoming bored. Grandmother got very bored if you were too good because it gave her nothing for which to punish you. If Cassie's socks never had a mark on them, if she exiled herself to the dining room without being asked, if she ate up everything that was put in front of her no matter how much she hated it, if she was not sick, if she didn't speak unless spoken to, if she knelt for many minutes to say her prayers at night and at morning, if she played so quietly that not even a mouse could hear her, it was boring for Grandmother. It made her tired to be bored and she would fall asleep, even in the mornings sometimes, because she found Cassie so tedious.

'You're such a bore, child, go away,' she would tell her. 'You're such a boring child.'

Grandmother's friends agreed with her. Most of them had not her burden, but they pitied her, which was at least something. There was only one exception and that was Mrs Roebuck.

Mrs Roebuck lived across the way, and sometimes when Cassie was walking with Grandmother she would know without looking up that they were passing Mrs Roebuck's house because of the delicious smells that assailed her nostrils long before they passed her front garden. Mrs Roebuck's garden had all different kinds of flowers planted outside, with herbs growing down the sides and cats curled up on the front-door steps waiting for that magical moment when Mrs Roebuck would open the front door and allow them in to sit around the warm, wood-burning stove that was the centre of Mrs Roebuck's home. Like a priest called away from his church, Mrs Roebuck was never away from her stove for longer than need be. And if she was, it seemed to Cassie it was only in order that she could open the front door to friends and relatives and invite them in to sample the results of her efforts at the sacred stove.

'I have no idea why she should want to keep that old stove,' Grandmother would often say. 'She must have brought it with her from the mountains of South Carolina when she got married.'

Then she would sniff disparagingly about Mrs Roebuck as she always did, but Cassie would only sniff the smell of the home-baked bread and imagine what it must be like to be asked in to taste it. If they met Mrs Roebuck she would always have a basket full of something to eat: perhaps a bag of cherries, or a tin of cookies that she would announce loudly were going to accompany an ice cream that she was making. As soon as she saw Cassie she would peer shortsightedly into her basket and, seizing a cherry, polish it on her sleeve and pop it in to Cassie's mouth before Grandmother could utter.

'Cassie is not allowed to eat—' Grandmother would begin.

But Mrs Roebuck would ignore Grandmother, as she ignored everyone unless they were sitting quietly waiting for her to feed them.

'You're too pale,' she'd tell Cassie. 'Not getting enough fresh air. Tell your grandmother to send you over to play at my house.'

Grandmother would pretend not to look mortally offended by this remark and end up looking just plain sour.

'Cassie has to attend to her reading and writing,' she'd say to Mrs Roebuck, in an attempt to keep Cassie at home. 'She's a very slow child, very slow. She needs to be slippered just to learn her alphabet.'

'You're too strict with that child,' Mrs Roebuck would

retort, not afraid to let her feelings known, and all the more determined to invite Cassie over. She got her chance one day as they passed in the main street.

'I've got my grandchildren coming round next Thursday,' she said to Cassie. 'You'll come over and play, won't you?'

'Yes, please,' said Cassie quickly, and before Grandmother could open her mouth to say 'best not' Mrs Roebuck had smiled delightedly.

'That's settled then,' she said, 'Cassie can come and stay with us over Thursday and you can have a nice rest, Gloria – just what you're always saying you're so in need of.'

'I'm not sure Thursday's a good day,' said Grandmother.

'I am,' Mrs Roebuck answered, and turned away, but not before she had given Cassie a little friendly chuck under her chin. Grandmother stared after Mrs Roebuck's ample posterior wending its way back to her house and the beloved stove. She would have liked to have told Mirabelle Ann a firm 'no' there and then, but Mirabelle Ann was the head of the Women's Committee for War Veterans. She was the lead singer in the Church choir, sometimes even still doing solos when called upon. It was difficult to forbid Cassie to go over to Mirabelle Ann's for the night, seeing that the whole town held her in such respect; and there wasn't a man, woman, or child living there who hadn't at some time or another been privileged to sample her strawberry shortcake, and having done so would declare themselves prepared to service her old stove, brush her cats, or even listen to her singing, in exchange for just one more mouthful.

Thursday came, and Cassie, who had been waiting all week for Thursday to come, awoke so early that by the time Grandmother called to her that it was all right to get up, it seemed that half the day had gone already. Cassie leapt out of bed and going to her cupboard she chose her favourite blue dress and matching hair ribbons. Just the outfit for a hot summer's day.

But Grandmother had other ideas. She took the blue dress from Cassie and put it away, and instead she took a heavy brown wool dress with a lace collar from the closet. Cassie's heart sank. She hated the brown dress, even in winter. The brown dress would itch. Grandmother then chose some dull brown ribbons and a brown wool jacket.

'Must have you looking smart for Mrs Roebuck,' she said, smiling.

Cassie stared at the clothes in horror, but knew that to even try to refuse would mean that she would not go at all. And so she dressed in silence, and Grandmother watched her with visible satisfaction, nodding her head a few times as Cassie struggled with the back buttons and did up the buckles on her shoes.

By midday when her daily lessons with Grandmother had duly been completed – even though all the other children in the town were still on vacation – Cassie's face was bright red: two bright red patches burned on either cheek, and she felt her pulse racing.

'Why, child, look at you,' Grandmother said. 'The colour of you! We'll have to put you straight to bed.'

'I haven't a fever, Grandmother,' Cassie replied. 'I'm just far too hot in these clothes.'

'Nonsense, child. I know a fever when I see it,' her grandmother insisted. 'Now off with you to bed, and I'll call Mirabelle Ann to say that you won't be going over this afternoon.'

Cassie walked slowly up the stairs. The lump in her throat would not be swallowed away, any more than the tears that were welling up behind her eyelids. She pulled off the brown wool jacket, the brown wool dress, and then the heavy socks, and put her shoes neatly together under her chair with the fronts sticking outwards the way that Grandmother liked them to be.

Mrs Roebuck and her house now seemed as far away as Europe seemed when she looked at Grandmother's book of maps. She put on her night clothes and crept into bed.

25

She lay feeling more miserable than she had ever felt before. To play with someone else, to stay the night in someone else's house, had seemed like a dream, like part of a life that other children had. Like the members of the gang who daily played out there in the street beyond the lace curtains that guarded the room in which she was imprisoned.

But Grandmother reckoned without Mrs Roebuck, when she went to make her excuses for Cassie.

'My goodness, Gloria, I just can't believe what you're telling me,' Mrs Roebuck exclaimed. 'Why, I saw that grandchild of yours playing outside on the stoop only this morning. I'd better come right on over and see for myself.'

Before Grandmother could find a reason for her not to, Mrs Roebuck was not only in her house, but on her way up the stairs to Cassie's room. Cassie sat up quickly as she heard someone approaching, and wiped away her tears, afraid that it was Grandmother. When she saw it was Mrs Roebuck, she tried to smile.

Mrs Roebuck said nothing; instead she felt her pulse and put her rough-skinned hand against Cassie's flushed cheeks. Then turning to Grandmother who had followed her in, she laughed.

'There's nothing the matter with this child, Gloria,' she announced, looking over to Cassie's chair and to the clothes folded neatly on it. 'Except, no doubt, the clothes you put her in.'

Grandmother's mouth tightened and she glared at Cassie.

'Come on, Cassie,' Mrs Roebuck continued. 'You jump out of that bed right now and we'll go find you something pretty and cool to wear. How about this blue dress here?'

'That's far too skimpy,' Grandmother said.

'Nonsense, Gloria,' sighed Mrs Roebuck. 'The child will be fine in this. Why, the temperature's well in the eighties now.'

Grandmother watched helplessly as Mrs Roebuck

quickly dressed Cassie in her pale blue dress, and then turning her round she kissed her firmly on the cheek.

'There, child, cool as a cucumber again, aren't you?'

Cassie nodded, lost for words.

'Where's your overnight bag? Why there it is. Good. Now say goodbye to your grandmother and we'll be off.'

'Goodbye, Grandmother,' said Cassie dutifully. 'See you tomorrow.'

Her grandmother made no reply. She just looked at Cassie, her small green eyes staring at her, expressionless.

Cassie would never forget the feeling of freedom that day as she walked hand in hand with Mrs Roebuck down the stairs of Grandmother's house and out of the door, through the front garden, past the petunias standing planted in military rows, across the road and along the street to where Mrs Roebuck's house stood smiling a welcome, cats circulating round the steps, the smell of home-baked bread wafting gently out into the air and two small girls her own age running around the back yard without any clothes on playing with a hose.

Mrs Roebuck bent down and smiled at Cassie looking through the main hall and out towards this amazing sight. Cassie was never allowed to take all her clothes off, not even if she was undressing to take a shower. She had to remove each article discreetly, and only once Grandmother had left the room was she allowed to step into the shower without any clothes at all upon her person. It was a strict rule. Grandmother did not like bodies and said so frequently. She did not like Cassie's body in particular. She told her that too, just in case, Cassie felt, that Cassie might be tempted to show Grandmother her whole body and cause her a great upset.

'Do you want to take your clothes off like Gina and Maria?' Mrs Roebuck asked. 'You don't have to if you don't want. But it is awful hot right now.'

'Yes please,' Cassie replied. 'Except, can I keep my panties on?'

'Course you can, child.' Mrs Roebuck laughed. 'You

27

can keep your panties on, and anything else you want. Course you can.'

Cassie took all her clothes off, except her panties, then she walked into the yard. She smiled shyly at Gina and Maria who both looked at each other, then turned the hose on her. Cassie gasped and put her hands out in front of her; but even as she started to laugh with delight it seemed to her that Grandmother's eyes were on her, and any minute now she would feel her hand on her shoulder, or on her ear, pulling her back to the house and up to Grandmother's bedroom for a beating. But the spray of deliciously cold water didn't stop, and there was no tug at her ear. And Cassie suddenly realised that there wasn't going to be any punishment. Opening her arms and with her eyes still tightly shut, she let the water flow past her, and over her – it was wonderful.

'You can join our club if you like,' said Maria later. 'She can, can't she, Gina?'

Maria looked across at her elder sister for approval. Gina, who was lying on the grass, opened her large languid brown eyes a little wider and, looking at Cassie, nodded slowly.

'Sure,' she said, 'why not?'

Maria and Cassie gazed at her adoringly. Gina was so beautiful. Maria turned back to Cassie.

'It's called the Cookie Club,' she informed Cassie, lowering her voice. 'We go up that tree and eat cookies.'

They all turned towards the tree in question. It dominated the back yard. Cassie couldn't admit that she had never climbed a tree before. It looked a long way up from the ground to the nearest branch, such a long way that she couldn't help hoping that Gina and Maria might reverse their decision to make her a member of the Cookie Club.

'Let's all go up there now and eat cookies,' said Maria enthusiastically.

Again both the younger girls turned towards Gina and waited for a decision. To Cassie's relief Gina merely lay back, stretching out her lithe brown body in front of them.

'I don't feel like a cookie just now,' Gina announced.

Cassie gazed at her in admiration. Gina had long black glossy hair, which looked lovely against the green of the grass, thick black eyelashes and a tip-tilted nose. Cassie knew that Gina must be what her grandmother called a 'beauty'.

There was a long silence as Maria too lay back against the grass, and Cassie, anxious to conform, followed her example. She pretended to shut her eyes but in reality kept them half open, watching to see if either of the other two made some quick movement that she might miss. Sure enough Gina sat up suddenly. Maria and Cassie immediately did the same.

'Let's play weddings,' Gina said.

'Yes, let's,' Maria agreed. 'Who'll be the bride?'

Maria and Cassie both looked at Gina. They both knew that there could only be one 'bride'.

'I'll be the groom, and then I can wear those old horse-riding boots Grandma has in the closet,' said Maria with satisfaction.

Both girls got to their feet, and Cassie scrambled to hers, her heart beating uncomfortably. There was no mention of her role at the wedding. Wildly her mind raced ahead to the actual ceremony. Perhaps she could be the priest? They would surely need a priest? She followed them into the house and up to the attic. Instinct told her that if she mentioned herself in anyway it would only invite ridicule. If she kept quiet and said nothing Gina might turn round and suggest something that she could be.

Mrs Roebuck kept a great chest of old clothes for her grandchildren to dress up in on rainy days. Gina opened it slowly and carefully, and as the smell of old lavender filled the air, Cassie watched Gina carefully removing old shawls and evening dresses, patchwork spreads and lace veils, and then, at last, Mrs Roebuck's wedding

29

dress. The tissue paper fell from around it, and both girls looked at Gina with their mouths open in unbridled admiration as she held it against her and then walked to the mirror to gaze at her beautiful image. They all knew that this was how Gina would look one day on her wedding day.

'You're so beautiful, Gina,' sighed Maria, as Cassie nodded silently. 'shall we help you get dressed?'

'Yes, you may dress me,' Gina replied, turning slowly from the mirror. 'And then we'll find some bridegroom's clothes.'

Cassie held the wedding dress and helped Maria to do up all the tiny covered buttons at the back;. then she trotted after Maria as they tried to find her some boy's clothes from the trunk. They eventually unearthed a pair of old-fashioned short trousers, then an old silk shirt with lace at the wrists and throat, then Mr Roebuck's old horse-riding boots, which came so far up to the top of Maria's legs that not much of the trousers showed, but Maria didn't mind. It was just so good to be wearing riding boots, she told Cassie, as she walked up and down in front of the mirror, rapidly developing a boyish walk.

Cassie was still in just her panties. She shivered and looked longingly towards the dressing-up clothes. She knew there was enough still left in there for her to become a bridesmaid, or a funny kind of priest, but still nothing was said. She followed the sisters down the stairs and out into the yard again, where Gina pointed to the big tree.

'Let's be married under this tree,' she announced, tossing back her head of long dark hair. Maria clumped after her across the yard, with Cassie following at a discreet distance. They both knelt beneath the Cookie Club tree.

'You have to take my hand,' Gina said, 'and put a ring on it.'

'We haven't got a ring,' Maria hissed, turning to Cassie.

Cassie looked round and, plucking a piece of coarse grass, she quickly made it into a circle and handed it to Maria, who put it on Gina's finger. Kneeling behind them in her panties Cassie closed her eyes. She was a mother at the wedding, a mother in a pretend pretty hat. Gina and Maria stood up.

Mrs Roebuck came out of the house. She appeared not to notice Gina and Maria in their fine clothes, or the closing moments of the marriage ceremony. She held a yellow dress in her hand.

'Cassie?' she called.

Cassie went over to her.

'Bridesmaid's dress,' Mrs Roebuck announced. 'They can't get married without a bridesmaid.'

Cassie stared up into Mrs Roebuck's worn smiling face and swallowed hard. She knew that Mrs Roebuck was being kind – but why did people being kind make her sad?

'Thank you,' she whispered.

'No one decent gets married without a bridesmaid,' Mrs Roebuck muttered, pulling the dress over Cassie's head. It was made of stiff brocade with crisp organdie over the top.

'This was Gina's mother's dress when she was a bridesmaid,' she told Cassie. 'I had it made by Madame Celestine. She made all the bridal gowns and the bridesmaids' dresses round here in those days. She was a lovely woman. Didn't mind what she did for anyone.'

Mrs Roebuck stood back and put her hand under Cassie's chin.

'You're a very pretty child,' she went on, 'I always did love thick brown shining hair. Reminds me of my mother. She had thick brown shining hair. She brushed it one hundred times every night. Even when she was sick, she never forgot.'

Then she put a firm hand in the small of Cassie's back and steered Cassie back towards the Cookie tree where the newly married Gina and Maria were waiting for her.

They looked her up and down.

'Wedding's over,' Maria said.

'Doesn't matter,' Cassie replied, 'I don't really mind.'

'I suppose you could hold my train,' said Gina graciously. 'I haven't walked down the aisle yet.'

Cassie held the train. But the aisle was very short, because it was time to eat.

Lunch was a blissful affair. With their chins barely clearing the scrubbed pine table, the three of them waited for the freshly baked bread to be put on their plates. To Cassie's astonishment Gina and Maria's knives were allowed to dart in and out of the great slab of butter put in front of them. There was no food shortage in this house. The butter melted instantly into the springy speckled-brown surface of the warm doughy bread. Cassie felt that she could taste it before she even raised it to her lips. As they chewed silently on the hunks of bread Mrs Roebuck placed a large soup-plate in front of them, on to which she ladled her famous chicken and noodle bake – news of which had even reached Cassie's young ears, so famous was it in the neighbourhood.

Cassie, Gina and Maria chewed in reverential silence. Mrs Roebuck didn't seem to expect them to speak, and although she was a fervent churchgoer she had dispensed with grace before the meal – possibly because the bread had been at exactly the right temperature, possibly because the chicken and noodle bake had been at precisely the moment when it needed to be eaten. Whatever the reason, it was the first time Cassie had sat down to a meal without grace, at which she was encouraged to eat as much as she wanted.

'Everyone got enough?' asked Mrs Roebuck, turning from the stove every few minutes. 'There's plenty more.'

Her baked custard with fresh loganberries tasted as if it had been made in heaven, Cassie thought. Every spoonful melted in her mouth, and she had hardly begun before she found herself staring at an empty blue and white pattern on her plate.

'There's plenty more,' said Mrs Roebuck. 'You just pass me up those plates.'

The plates were piled up once again with fresh loganberries, their sugar-coated backs white against the creamy custard. Cassie looked at Mrs Roebuck with adoration. She must like children; and she must know what children liked, too.

'Thank you,' Cassie said. 'That was lovely.'

'Yes, but have you had enough, girls?' Mrs Roebuck said, smiling down at her.

The three girls looked at each other and then at Mrs Roebuck. They all nodded, then giggled and patted their small round stomachs.

'Rest time,' announced Mrs Roebuck as she undid the back of Gina's dress and lifted it carefully over her head.

'Off with those boots, Maria Rossetti,' she ordered. 'You're all going to have a rest in the hammocks while I do the dishes.'

At home Cassie helped with the dishes. Standing beside Delta the maid, cloth in hand, she would wait to polish each fork or each spoon until they shone. She was never allowed to touch the plates – Delta did those. But anything which didn't break was hers to dry. She wanted to do the knives and forks for Mrs Roebuck, but Mrs Roebuck didn't seem interested in anything except bedding them all down in hammocks under the Cookie tree.

'Back home, after our midday meal,' she told Cassie, 'our mother never let us move until we'd lain down in our hammocks.'

She piled comfortable old fringed cushions into the hammocks, and then helped the girls climb up into them. Well fed and already sleepy they did this with difficulty, laughing and swaying, and clutching on to each other, Mrs Roebuck and the sides of the hammocks. Gina stretched out on her own, a hammock to herself. Maria and Cassie lay looking up at the leaves of the trees with each other's feet beside their heads. Cassie half-closed her eyes. The patterns of the leaves became blurred. She could hear the distant sounds of the small town, but they were far away. She imagined that she was a bird, and

33

Maria was her friend and they were in a nest together. She imagined what life might be like if it was always like this day, and then she fell into the first happy sleep of her childhood.

'I just thought I'd call by and see if Cassie's fever is still in check.'

Cassie shrank nearer Gina and Maria. She could hear Grandmother's sharp voice from the hall. Cassie prayed that Grandmother would not come through and see that they were listening to the wireless. That would be enough for her to insist that Cassie be taken home.

'Cassie never had a fever, Gloria,' she heard Mrs Roebuck reply. 'I told you Cassie simply had on too many clothes.'

'Did she function at two as she should?' her grandmother demanded.

'I have no idea, Gloria,' Mrs Roebuck said. 'But to my way of thinking if you don't stop fussing the way you do, that child will grow up old before her time.'

'You have no idea what a burden she is to me, Mirabelle Ann,' her grandmother continued. 'You can have no idea of the burden of bringing up a child at my age on my own.'

'No, I have no idea, Gloria,' Mrs Roebuck agreed. 'But I have every idea that if you don't go away and leave that poor child here to enjoy herself with someone else of her own age you'll be making a rope to hang yourself. Too much attention is as bad as too little, Gloria. It makes a child feel unwanted. So now go back to your bridge and enjoy yourself in peace, and let me enjoy your grandchild in my peace.'

Cassie heard the front door shut, and she looked wildly round the room. The wireless was still on. The door was still firmly shut. Gina and Maria were laughing at the programme. There were no shadows; no one was coming in with the frown of an avenging angel. She felt like running up and down the room and shouting. Instead she fled to the bathroom.

To go to sleep in the same room as other children your own age, and to sit up all freshly washed in your night-clothes listening to Mrs Roebuck reading you a story, was yet another taste of heaven. Cassie sighed with happiness as she settled down into her bed and vowed that she would always remember this day as long as she lived. And when she was grown up she would buy Mrs Roebuck a diamond brooch.

Mrs Roebuck leant down and kissed Cassie. She kissed her as if she had always kissed her, and as if Cassie had always been used to being kissed. Cassie closed her eyes as she did so, and pretended that Mrs Roebuck was her grandmother, and that Cassie had always lived with her.

The light was turned off, but a night light was left burning. Cassie stared towards it from her bed. Deer played, and birds flew across its pink shade. Gina and Maria were already half asleep, but Cassie watched the light, her eyes unmoving. Normally she went to sleep in the dark, her eyes tightly closed against the terrible things that might happen if Grandmother found her awake. Tonight they were open, staring at the plastic lamp.

Grandmother called for her while they were still breakfasting. Cassie must come at once, Mrs Roebuck was told. Mrs Roebuck was adamant in her refusal: Cassie would not be going anywhere until such time as she had finished her waffles and syrup.

Grandmother pushed past her.

'She'll come this minute,' Cassie heard her say. 'She's late for her visit to the dentist.'

Grandmother in Mrs Roebuck's kitchen was the wicked witch from the west. She looked strange and dark against all the brightly patterned china on the dresser, and the flowers arranged in the middle of the white cloth, and Gina and Maria's red hair ribbons. By contrast Grandmother was a pool of darkness.

'Finish that up,' she said sharply to Cassie.

Gina and Maria stared up at Grandmother, and then

35

looked over to Cassie. Gina's large, languid brown eyes concentrated themselves on Cassie's equally large blue-green ones. For the first time a look of real friendship passed between them.

'Have another waffle,' was all Gina said, but they both knew what she meant.

'No thank you,' said Cassie, hastily cramming the last of the syrupy confection in front of her into her mouth.

She smiled at Gina as she quickly said her grace, and got down. It was nice of her to encourage rebellion.

'Grandma,' Gina called. 'Cassie's not being allowed another waffle. I don't think that's fair.'

'Fold your napkin properly,' said Grandmother to Cassie, pointing at it. 'And you shouldn't talk at table, young lady,' she added looking at Gina.

'We're allowed to talk at table,' Maria piped up. 'Our grandma's not sour like you.'

'Who said I was sour?' Grandmother demanded.

Cassie looked across at Maria. Cassie had never said anything about Grandmother being sour, but she would never believe her now.

'Did you say I was sour, Cassie?' asked her grand-mother. She bent down to Cassie, her horrid beady eyes staring hatefully into Cassie's large ones. 'I said,' she repeated, 'did you say I was sour?'

Cassie shook her head, too frightened even to speak. At that moment Mrs Roebuck came out of the pantry, where she had heard everything, and smiled at everyone generally.

'No, I said you were sour, Gloria, as a matter of fact. It was just kind of a joke. I said all old women like us were sour, and Maria picked it up – you know the way kids do? They're always picking things up either from grown-ups or the wireless.'

'Cassie is not allowed to listen to the wireless,' said Grandmother pointedly. 'And with good reason, it seems.'

A minute later, her bag packed, and having been given

barely enough time to be kissed by Mrs Roebuck, Cassie was marched from the house, back to Grandmother's house with all speed. Grandmother, she was told on the way home, couldn't wait to get her home, couldn't wait to get her up to her room, couldn't wait to punish her. She would be beaten, and then locked in, locked in until she learnt not to say bad things about her grandmother behind her back.

Cassie lay curled up on her bed in the dark. She didn't care about being punished now, and she never would again. Meanwhile she had her day with Mrs Roebuck to think about. It was the best day she had ever had in her life. It was a day that not even Grandmother could take away from her. Best of all, she knew now that life could be nice and kind, and full of warm things. One day, when she grew up, she would try and be like Mrs Roebuck, but until then she would just think about her. She had screamed hard when Grandmother had hit her, much harder than she had ever screamed before, because she had screamed so that Mrs Roebuck could hear. Of course Mrs Roebuck couldn't hear, but Grandmother hadn't liked it. She had stopped suddenly, sooner than she did normally, defeated by her own inability to administer pain and stifle Cassie's cries. She wouldn't be back for hours now. She never was when she locked the door. When Cassie was little she used to lock the door and leave her in her room until she got back from shopping, because taking Cassie shopping had been a bother. When she was tiny Cassie had used to knock on the windows and shout to her as she disappeared down the front garden to the road, but Grandmother would turn her back and never look at her. That also would have been too much of a bother.

It had been Mrs Roebuck's idea to send Cassie to the convent. Much better than being at home being a burden, Mrs Roebuck had said firmly. Grandmother had suddenly seemed uncertain about this.

'I don't know, Mirabelle Ann, I don't know so much.

I'm Cassie's only relative on this earth. I wonder, should I send her away?'

Grandmother's eyes flickered from Cassie sitting in her Sunday-best clothes to Mrs Roebuck pouring Grandmother an iced coffee. Gina and Maria were already at the convent, but Gina and Maria were one and two years older than Cassie.

'Of course you must send her to the convent, Gloria,' Mrs Roebuck argued. 'Why, it stands to reason – it'll leave you more time for the things that you enjoy.'

'There is that,' Grandmother conceded, but her eyes flickered once more towards Cassie, who was sitting carefully not swinging her legs.

Cassie stared at her stilled feet. If she said and did nothing perhaps Grandmother would be betrayed into thinking that she didn't want to go to school with Gina and Maria.

'It's not as if it's an ordinary school,' Mrs Roebuck went on. 'It's such a small school. The nuns, who are mostly refugees from the war, started taking girls of all ages, even five-year olds, when they felt there was a need, just as a favour to the neighbourhood. And then only those that – only those that they think will benefit in some way. It's a very special little school. I think it would suit Cassie.'

Mrs Roebuck put another piece of fudge cake on Cassie's plate.

'There's nothing special about Cassie,' Grandmother replied, 'except her wicked stubborn ways.'

Grandmother opened her purse, and took out her powder compact. As she powdered her nose, and then restlessly snapped the compact shut again, Mrs Roebuck winked at Cassie. Cassie quickly dropped her eyes. For one horrible second she imagined that her grandmother had caught sight of that wink, and that all would be lost.

There was a short silence. Grandmother looked at Cassie. Cassie's eyes were once more innocently focused on her white socks. Cassie tried to think of how much she would hate going to the convent with Gina and Maria. She tried to think that it was the last thing that she wanted, because she sensed that if she thought hard enough Grandmother would believe her thoughts and immediately want to send her there.

'I suppose it might be a solution to some of my troubles,' Grandmother reasoned. 'And her wretched father did at least leave her some money to provide for her education.'

Grandmother's voice always assumed a false piety when referring to money, as if it held no interest for her at all.

'Well, there we are then,' Mrs Roebuck concluded. 'That's all there is to be said about it, wouldn't you say?'

Grandmother continued to stare at Cassie a little longer.

'I'm not sure, Mirabelle Ann,' said Grandmother. 'After all there is Cassie herself. Will the good nuns accept someone like Cassie?'

'The good nuns specialise in taking the boldness out of children, Gloria, you know that,' Mrs Roebuck replied.

But still Grandmother hung out. It was as if she was aware that something was wrong, that no matter how much Cassie hid her true feelings from her, she nevertheless suspected her of wanting to go.

Day after day she would talk about the 'good nuns' to Delta, to visitors, sometimes even to Cassie, but it seemed that something always prevented her from going down to the convent and enrolling her irksome burden, until eventually, without telling Cassie she finally went.

Cassie held her breath as the suitcases came out. She still suspected that somehow, something would come between her and escaping from Grandmother to the convent. Only when she heard that Grandmother had acquired a new bridge partner did she feel safe to examine the possibility that escape to school might bring.

'Will you miss me?' her grandmother asked her, as Cassie lay in her bed that night, looking up into Grandmother's stern face. Cassie nodded slowly.

'You won't be tucked in by me at the convent you know,' Grandmother added.

Cassie nodded again. She knew that she must pretend to be sad at leaving Grandmother otherwise she would change her mind about sending her away.

'You'll probably enjoy yourself no matter, won't you?' Cassie shook her head.

'Of course you will. It's your positive duty to enjoy yourself. And I don't want any long faces on the first day, you hear? No nonsense and feeling sorry for yourself. You're six years old now and you should know better. I don't want any bad behaviour like that terrible evening when I went out to help with the sewing bee and you cried. I don't want that, do you hear?'

Cassie nodded. Grandmother leant forward and Cassie kissed her dutifully on her cheek which was always so surprisingly soft. She couldn't let her imagination encompass the idea of not seeing Grandmother, of not being with her, of not having to peck her cheek goodnight. It was unimaginable. She closed her eyes as the lights went out and darkness fell around her bed; for once the blackness seemed to be lighter.

Getting up and putting on her clothes for school made Cassie feel sick with excitement. The girls were encouraged to wear blue, Sister Joseph – Cassie's future housemother – had told Grandmother. Blue hair ribbons were encouraged on weekdays, and white ones on Sundays. Cassie stared at the silky blue ribbons in her hands, and then handed them up one by one to Grandmother. She mustn't wriggle or show excitement, she mustn't let Grandmother see how pleased she would be to be away from her. But deep down she must have suspected it, because Grandmother braided Cassie's hair so tightly that her head ached for the rest of the day.

'You be a good girl now,' she reminded Cassie when they arrived at the convent. 'And don't forget to keep your socks clean.'

Grandmother then bent towards Cassie.

'You may kiss me goodbye,' she said.

Then she turned away, and Cassie followed the other girls through the convent door. She didn't look back, and neither did her grandmother.

'Cassie McGann, you will be sharing with Mary-Jo Christiansen. Mary-Jo's already been with us one semester so she can show you the way we do things.'

Cassie looked up into Mary-Jo's blue eyes. She liked her straightaway. She knew she would always like her. She was tall and good-looking – not like Cassie who was small and had looks that Grandmother always described as 'plain Jane'.

'We wash our faces and hands like this,' Mary-Jo explained, taking a jug and pouring water into a bowl. They each had a brightly painted washstand, holding clean white towels on either side of them. 'And then we go to the bathroom, and we clean our teeth and do everything else there. OK?'

Cassie nodded. It all seemed so wonderfully exciting. Jugs, bowls and towels, and other girls, some of whom she could hear quietly saying the same things as Mary-Jo. She soaped her face flannel vigorously in imitation of Mary-Jo.

The convent smelled sweetly of flowers and wax polish. As soon as she'd arrived Cassie had noticed that if she pushed her shoes a little in front of her they slid beautifully on the shiny surface of the wooden floors. Now, as she followed Mary-Jo to the bathroom, she slid her new bedroom slippers a little, testing the surface. Obligingly her slippers carried her along. It was a little like pretending to skate.

She waited for Mary-Jo to finish cleaning her teeth. Mary-Jo spat vaguely towards the general direction of the plug hole, ran some water briefly, and then stepped aside to let Cassie do the same. Cassie stared amazed into the huge marble basin. Mary-Jo had left a mark on one of the taps. She turned briefly to look at her. Didn't she realise that she had committed a mortal sin by leaving

41

not just a mark on the taps, but toothpaste on the basin too? But Mary-Jo seemed oblivious of her trespasses.

Cassie followed her back to their room. If Mary-Jo had committed a sin, so had Cassie. What a wonderful feeling to be sinning with someone else for a change. Yet somehow she still couldn't believe that Mary-Jo had committed a sin, for if she had, how could she possibly be so carefree?

'Come on,' Mary-Jo said. 'It's my turn to read out aloud tonight.'

Cassie jumped into her bed. Her quilt was a deep maroon satin, very old-fashioned, from Grandmother's attic. Mary-Jo's was smart and new, with yellow checks and lace and ribbons. It looked as if it had just been newly bought from a department store, not thrown down from an attic. Cassie looked at her and it with admiration, and then lay back against her pillow. She had hoped that being at the convent would be good, but she hadn't quite realised until that moment, just how good being with the 'good' nuns was going to be.

'Come on,' Mary-Jo urged, as she looked at Cassie still struggling with her hair ribbons. 'We'll be late. It doesn't matter about your hair braids. Sister Joseph'll do them again for you.'

Cassie followed Mary-Jo to class. Everything was still new and lovely, despite her sports clothes being too big and everyone laughing at her on her first day. She started to half-run after Mary-Jo. Being taller she was always ahead of Cassie in seconds. But just so long as she never lost sight of her, Cassie knew she'd be all right.

Chapter Two

Cassie stared at her finished drawing. It was of her soul, big, and round, and coloured bright yellow. She bit her lip and frowned. There was a blemish on the drawing, where her pencil had overrun into the colour. Cassie wondered what to do, and then decided that if Sister Joseph asked her what the mark was she would say that it was a sin. Which indeed it was. It was the sin of carelessness, because she had allowed her pencil to slip.

But Sister Joseph didn't mention the smudge. Instead she just smiled down at Cassie.

'Very good, Cassie,' she said. 'Excellent. I can see how hard you've tried.'

Then she moved on down the line to Mary-Jo. Mary-Jo's drawing of her soul was a perfect and unblemished circle coloured purple, and surrounded with green leaves.

'How colourful, Mary-Jo,' Sister Joseph said, nodding happily. 'Very original.'

The quiet in the classroom was intense, as the children all looked at Sister Joseph in silent adoration. She was a very pretty nun, with clear blue eyes, a perfect complexion and a smile that lit up every inch of her face. All the children loved her, and had struggled in silence to produce their very best artwork for her.

'Now,' Sister Joseph announced, turning to face the class, 'several of you children are soon to be making your First Communion. Mary-Jo Christiansen, Rosella Savarese, Teresa Plunkett and Cassie McGann.'

The four girls all turned to each other. They were to be friends for life. That's what making your First Communion together meant. It was the closest you could be, besides actually being married.

'When Rosella, Mary-Jo, Teresa and Cassie ask those of you who have already made your First Communion what it's like, you can only answer wait and see. Because there are no words to describe it. But there is one thing you can do for them. And that is prepare your souls for your communion that day. And you can say that your communion is their communion.'

There was a silence as Sister Joseph looked down at her young class.

'Furthermore,' she continued, 'in the next few weeks we are all going to make sacrifices for the First Communicants. Which is why I want you all to rule a margin by the side of the pictures you have just drawn, to make a column for the stars you are going to win for all the sacrifices you are going to make for your four friends who are about to make their Holy Communion.'

In the playground after class, Cassie, Mary-Jo, Rosella and Teresa all linked arms. They were a band, friends for life, and Cassie was one of them. For the first time in her life she felt a sense of belonging, as she looked at the three shining faces looking back at her. Then quite spontaneously they all ran to the trees on the edge of the field and choosing the biggest they could get their arms around, encircled it, their fingers just hooking up, and their faces pressed hard against its bark. When they released their hands and stood back, they found the wood had made indentations on their faces. They pointed this out to each other and laughed. Then Rosella drew a hopscotch square in the earth with the heel of her shoe and they all started to play.

But despite their goodwill in the ensuing days it became very difficult not to cheat about the sacrifices they were all meant to be making. Cassie, like everyone else, desperately wanted to be able to claim as many stars as she could for her column. But she wanted to please Sister Joseph even more desperately and she knew she could not do that by cheating. Cassie knew she would be quite unable to look straight into Sister Joseph's clear blue eyes ever again in the knowledge that she had tricked the nun into awarding her one of the precious silver stars. But sacrifices were so hard to find when you were a new girl, and had to spend most of your time doing what everyone told you to do. Was it a sacrifice deliberately to lose a game when by so doing you disappointed Mary-Jo? Was it a sacrifice to push your chair in quietly when Grandmother had never allowed you to do otherwise? Was it a sacrifice not to think nice things about Sister Joseph?

Such was Cassie's indecision, and as a consequence her column was still bare of stars, while everyone else's were filling up rapidly. Sister Joseph was well aware of this, although naturally enough she made no comment, when at the end of the second week the time came to award the stars.

'And how have you done this week, darling?' she asked Cassie, bending down to hear her reply. 'What sacrifices have you made for your fellow communicants?'

Cassie looked at the floor long and hard before replying.

'None I don't think, Sister,' she said in a voice barely more than a whisper. 'No, none at all.'

'Well, I don't think that happens to be true, Cassie,' Sister Joseph replied. 'I see you making all sorts of sacrifices. But because they're things you usually do normally, you're too honest to claim them. So for that, for your honesty, I'm going to give you two silver stars.'

Sister Joseph picked the stars out of the box Rosella was holding and carefully stuck them in the margin on Cassie's drawing. Cassie stared at them silently, and swallowed hard to try and get rid of the lump in her throat.

Life was very full for the four First Communicants.

45

Not a day passed without there being something special for them to do, and something special to think about.

'When Jesus comes down to us from the altar in the form of bread, children,' Sister Joseph explained one day during their instruction, 'He will give us special strength. The strength to become more like Him, and like His Holy Mother; the strength to love our friends more, and to love and respect our parents more.'

Cassie wrestled with this one, but without much success. She tried to imagine loving her grandmother more, but it was not only difficult, it was practically impossible. How could you love someone 'more' if they didn't love you at all? And Cassie knew perfectly well that her grandmother didn't love her. She knew it not from her grandmother, but from her neighbours. From Mr O'Reilly, and Mrs Roebuck, and from Gina and Maria. She knew from the look of pity in people's eyes when they looked at her, and from the way they were always so kind to her. Too kind, almost. Gina and Maria were not in the same class as Cassie, but they went out of their way to come over and talk to her in the playground whenever they saw her. Mr O'Reilly had given her special permission to take his book to school and Mrs Roebuck had sent her some candy in the mail.

'I made enough candy for all three of you,' the note read. 'And when I was making it, I thought of you all in those hammocks that day. God bless you, little Cassie.'

'With love, Mirabelle Ann Roebuck.'

The candy was a double godsend to Cassie. Not only did it make her feel loved and wanted: better still, it meant that by giving it all away to the girls in her class and not having any herself she earned another silver star.

She didn't much enjoy practising receiving Communion though, when she had to stick out her tongue. Even with her eyes shut and her thoughts fixed on the meaning of ritual, Cassie still thought it hardly seemed a fitting way to receive the body of Our Lord. It made her feel awkward and embarrassed, even when they started

46

practising with tiny pieces of wafer on their tongues, morsels so small and light they seemed to disappear long before the children had closed their mouths over them.

Then there was the question of their dresses.

'Rosella's arrived today,' Mary-Jo told Cassie one evening. 'Wait till you see it. It's beautiful. Bright white with little white pieces of embroidery on the hem. Her veil is just like a real bride's veil.'

Cassie wriggled lower into her bed and pulled the maroon quilt up to cover her nose and her reddening cheeks. She had written to her grandmother several times about her own dress, but Grandmother hadn't replied. Every day she had waited in line as the letters and parcels were distributed, and every day there was neither a letter nor a parcel for her. Nobody said anything, but Cassie lived in a deep and silent fear that her grandmother would finally ignore her constant request for a dress of her own, and that Cassie, on her Day of Days, would have nothing special to wear.

Then Teresa's dress arrived. The class stood silently around the box in which it had arrived, and watched as Teresa lifted from a nest of snowy tissue paper a long dress with underskirts of net and white lace, and an overskirt caught up at intervals with exquisite handsewn flowers. Everyone gasped.

It was the most beautiful dress Cassie had ever seen. She was still staring at it while the other girls turned to look at her.

'So it's only Cassie's dress to come now,' someone said from the back. 'The other three have all got theirs.'

'It should have been here last week,' Cassie said. 'But Grandmother's had some trouble sewing the veil. She has bad arthritis, you see.'

Someone at the back of the group giggled as the class dispersed to discuss whose dress so far was the prettiest, and when no one was watching her, Cassie went outside and sat at the foot of the big tree the four friends had embraced that day, ashamed of the lie she had told.

47

Ashamed of the three lies she had told. She had lied about the dress arriving, she had lied about her grandmother having trouble sewing and she had lied about Grandmother having arthritis. She lay face down in the grass and prayed as hard as she could for God to let her die.

She wanted to die even more when the next day's mail brought no parcel for her, nor the mail the day after that. Cassie waited long after the other girls had collected their letters in the faintest of hopes that there had been some mistake. But there hadn't.

'Still nothing, I'm afraid, Cassie dear,' Sister John said, seeing the child standing waiting in silence. 'Maybe tomorrow.'

Cassie looked at the ground and said nothing, unable now even to raise a brave smile. Her First Communion was now only a matter of days away, and the possibility of her having a pretty dress to wear like the others was becoming more and more remote. She had written to her grandmother at least a dozen times, but had received no reply to any of her letters.

'Maybe it's gotten lost in the mail, Sister,' Cassie said suddenly, still staring at the polished floor.

'Why of course!' Sister John replied. 'That just has to be what's happened! Things do, you know. Things quite often do.'

Cassie looked up and the nun suddenly felt ashamed when she saw the light of hope her white lie had rekindled in the child's bright eyes.

'And just in case it has got lost,' Sister John added hastily, 'we'll say a special prayer to Saint Anthony to find it. Don't forget now!'

The nun called out after Cassie who had turned away to walk slowly down the long corridor.

'We'll both pray!'

Cassie stopped and looked back at Sister John.

'You bet,' she said. Then she walked away and disappeared around a corner.

You bet I'll pray, Cassie thought. I'll pray as hard as

48

anyone's ever prayed. Because there was no doubt at all in her mind that prayer was her very last resort.

So for the next two days she prayed. She prayed the moment she woke up, she prayed in between classes, she prayed as she played, as she ate, as they took their afternoon walks, and she prayed until the moment she fell asleep. But as the 29th of June approached, it seemed that her prayers were not to be answered.

'I guess I'll just have to wear my blue dress,' she said to Sister John, as she drew yet another blank in the morning's mail.

'You'll do no such thing,' Sister John retorted. 'Since your dress hasn't arrived, then we'll just have to borrow you one. I'll see you in white, darling, if it's the last thing I do. Don't you worry.'

'I don't know anyone with a white dress, Sister!' Cassie exclaimed. 'And I'm so much smaller than anyone else!'

'We'll come up with something,' Sister John assured her. 'Just wait and see. Now off you go to class. There's the bell.'

Cassie hesitated.

'You'll be late for Sister Joseph,' Sister John warned her.

But still Cassie didn't move.

'What is it, child? You'll have a dress, I promise.'

'Thank you, Sister,' Cassie said. 'But you see . . .'

'Yes?' Sister John prompted.

'Well you see, Sister,' Cassie answered, looking at the floor. 'It just won't be the same as having one of my own, you see.'

Cassie looked up at the nun, as bravely as she could, then turned and hurried away to class. Sister John watched her go, then hurried away herself, in the opposite direction, up the stairs to Matron's room.

Two days later, the day before the Feast of St Peter and St Paul, the day of the First Communion, Cassie nearly fainted when she heard her name called out by Sister

49

John for a parcel as she stood in line after breakfast. Mary-Jo squeezed her hand in delight, and Maria gave a cheer as Cassie hurried forward to collect the large box Sister John was holding up. Cassie looked at the writing on the covering paper, which was in large black block capitals. It certainly didn't look like her grandmother's usual careful but spidery hand, but then since it was a parcel, Cassie thought as she tore open the thick brown paper, perhaps it needed a different sort of writing. And besides, if the box she was now hurriedly pulling open contained what she hoped and prayed it would, who else but her grandmother would have sent it.

Cassie stared into the box as she folded back the tissue paper. Her prayers had been answered after all. She lifted out the dress almost reverently and held it up against her for the friends who had crowded round her to see. The group of children stood looking at the garment in silence, because Cassie's dress had to be the most beautiful of them all. It wasn't as ornate as Rosella's, nor did it have the exquisite handsewn flowers Teresa's dress had. And it was altogether much simpler than Mary-Jo's with its antique lace overskirt. But it was made of silk. Pure, expensive, heavy silk, which shone and caught the sunlight which was filtering through the corridor window as Cassie tried the dress up against her.

Mary-Jo leant forward and stroked it, as if the dress was a living thing.

'May I try it up against me?' she asked Cassie. 'It's so beautiful.'

The other children sighed and gasped in admiration, as Mary-Jo shook out her hair and held the silk dress up against herself. Edith, one of the youngest children, fought her way to the front of the group and snatched a handful of the precious material.

'Careful now, Edith,' Sister John warned her. 'That silk is – that silk must be pre-war, you know. And we don't want any grubby little handmarks on it now, do we?'

50

Cassie was busy searching through the box for a letter or a note from Grandmother. But there was nothing. Just tissue paper. She looked up and found SisterJohn smiling at her.

'Good for St Anthony, darling,' the nun said, 'wouldn't you agree?'

Cassie nodded emphatically and grinned, too happy to be able to express it, and as she turned away to claim her dress back from Mary-Jo, she was much too excited to notice the deep yawn of exhaustion Sister John was quite visibly failing to stifle.

As Cassie walked slowly up the aisle beside Mary-Jo and behind Teresa and Rosella, she thought she had never seen anything more beautiful than the way the chapel looked that day. The flames of what must have been hundreds of candles flickered and danced, and there was such a heady scent from the banks of white flowers that it seemed to Cassie she was walking into Paradise.

As they made their slow progress up the aisle, Cassie imagined that this must be how she would feel on her wedding day, dressed in a beautiful silk dress with a white veil and a headpiece of miniature white roses, and watched by hundreds of pairs of smiling eyes. She glanced to her side and caught sight of Mrs Roebuck, who was smiling at her, while dabbing at her eyes with her handkerchief. Grandmother was sitting next to her, but was looking not at Cassie but resolutely down at her missal. Cassie then noticed with delight that Mr O'Reilly was also there, in the row behind Mrs Roebuck and her grandmother. Cassie also noticed that he seemed to be frowning rather hard at the four communicants as they passed close by him, then he looked away and stared up at the ceiling, his chin puckering oddly, and one hand grasping the back of the pew in front of him. Cassie hoped that he was all right, and wasn't going to faint or something terrible.

The four girls then knelt at their flower-decked places,

and Cassie raised her eyes to the tabernacle. She closed her eyes and prayed, thanking God for sending her this wonderful day. Then she opened her missal and turned the thin crinkly pages over with her white-gloved hands till she came to the start of the High Mass. The nuns sang Ave Verum, and Cassie carefully read the words in front of her.

> I will go up to the altar of God –
> To God, the giver of youth and happiness.

Suffer the little children to come unto me. Maybe, Cassie thought as she looked up at the wondrously decorated altar in front of her, maybe it wasn't such a sinful thing to be a child after all.

After the Mass was over, the children went in search of their parents and relatives. Cassie stood on the edge of the hall trying to find her grandmother. Mrs Roebuck spotted the little figure standing in the doorway by herself and waved to her, then Gina and Maria ran over to her to collect her.

'Wasn't it a hoot when Rosella dropped her rosary?' Maria laughed, taking Cassie's hand. 'Gina had to stick her handkerchief in her mouth!'

Cassie smiled in return, but found it difficult. She'd just been through the most important moment of her young life, and all the time Gina and Maria had been laughing. For a moment, she couldn't help feeling hurt, and her smile masked her near-tears. Then she thought that perhaps if it hadn't been her special day, and someone had done something funny, because it was meant to be so solemn she'd have found herself laughing too. So she smiled genuinely now, as both girls started to rearrange her veil and stroke the wonderful silk of her dress.

Then she saw her grandmother, and the smile froze on her face. Grandmother was standing talking to Sister

John, but she was looking with a visible lack of affection at Cassie.

'I'd better go and say hello to Grandmother,' Cassie said to her friends.

'I shouldn't,' sighed Gina. 'She looks as if she's going to eat you.'

'I must,' Cassie replied. 'And I have to thank her for my dress.'

As Cassie walked away, Gina sniffed airily.

'It's not her grandmother Cassie should be thanking,' she said to her sister.

'What do you mean?' asked Maria.

'Don't be silly, Maria,' Gina replied. '*Everyone* knows that Sister John made Cassie's dress.'

Everyone except Cassie. Sister John watched the child approaching them and turned once more to her grandmother.

'Much the best thing, Mrs Arbuthnot,' she reiterated, 'not to say anything at all. You don't want the child disappointed now. Not on this her Day of Days.'

'You're surely not suggesting I tell a lie, Sister?' Grandmother replied. 'You're not seriously suggesting I should blacken my soul for the sake of a wretched child's vanity?'

'I'm suggesting no such thing, Mrs Arbuthnot,' Sister John answered very firmly. 'And well you know it. There's all the difference in the world between telling the truth, telling a lie, and sometimes remaining silent.'

Cassie's grandmother made a noise of distinct disapproval, but nonetheless did not further the argument. Which was as well, since Cassie now had reached where they stood.

'Hello, Grandmother,' Cassie said.

'Hello, child,' her grandmother replied, tugging Cassie's perfectly straight dress even straighter. 'And for heaven's sake put your shoulders back. You don't want to grow up a hunchback.'

Cassie did as she was told, even though she was standing quite straight.

53

'Thank you for my lovely dress, Grandmother,' she said. 'Everyone said it was by far the prettiest.'

'No doubt,' Grandmother replied curtly. 'But to my way of thinking a complete waste of money. Still, you can work off what it cost me in your holidays.'

'Of course I will, Grandmother,' Cassie agreed. 'And honestly, it wasn't a waste of money. I shall keep this dress for the rest of my life.'

'Of course you shall, Cassie,' Sister John said quickly, pre-empting any further remark from Cassie's grandmother. 'And please God who knows your own little daughter may one day take her own First Communion wearing the very same dress. Now off you go with your friends and have a good time.'

Sister John turned Cassie away and steered her off in the direction of Mary-Jo, Teresa, and Rosella, who were all having their photographs taken by Mr O'Reilly, who seemed quite to have recovered his old cheerful self.

Sister John turned back to Cassie's grandmother and gave her a very old-fashioned look.

'All I can say to you, Mrs Arbuthnot,' she said grimly, 'is if you intend to make young Cassie work off what we were going to charge you for making her little dress, then it would be a better thing were we not to charge you for it at all.'

Grandmother smiled to herself. That sort of arrangement would suit her perfectly.

'However,' Sister John continued. 'In these instances, rather than adding a small sum to the termly account, what is usually done is for the parent or guardian to make a contribution to St Anthony, for helping to find a solution to the problem.'

'That's as maybe,' Cassie's grandmother replied with a sniff.

'Indeed it is not,' Sister John replied. 'That's a fact. Perhaps you'd like me to include notice of your kind donation in the announcements I am just about to make. Shall we say twenty dollars?'

*　　*　　*

After the First Communion breakfast, Cassie and her grandmother were invited back to Mrs Roebuck's for a party. Cassie was seated at the head of the kitchen table, next to Gina on one side and Maria on the other. She had never felt so special, nor so happy, despite her grandmother's constant disapproving frowns and sighs.

'You really shouldn't have gone to so much trouble, Mirabelle Ann,' Grandmother said repeatedly through the lunch. 'It really doesn't merit it.'

But no one paid her the slightest heed, as they were far too busy laughing and talking, and cracking the shells of their prawns, or watching Mrs Roebuck carefully slicing the juicy pink beef.

The *pièce de résistance* was one of Mrs Roebuck's famous home-baked cakes, which everyone welcomed with delight. Everyone except Grandmother.

'None for Cassie,' she sniffed. 'That will be far too rich for her delicate constitution.'

'Oh what nonsense you talk, Gloria!' declared Mrs Roebuck. 'This is Dolce Alla Piemontese, and it's always been eaten by everyone in our family at First Communions. Everyone.'

And with that Mrs Roebuck cut an extra large slice for Cassie and served it to her with a grin. Cassie returned the grin happily. No one was taking the slightest notice of her grandmother, so for once she decided that she needn't either.

They ate the cake with long-handled spoons, which were designed, Mrs Roebuck explained, specially for eating soft puddings. The sponge inside was as soft as the meringue outside, and the home-made vanilla ice cream sandwiched in between just melted in the mouth.

Afterwards, while the coffee was brewing, and the men left the table to go outside in the yard to smoke cigarettes, Mrs Roebuck handed Cassie a pretty little white-painted basket with a bow on it.

'Almonds,' she told her. 'For luck.'

The basket was full of little packs of sugared almonds

55

tied into heart shapes. Gina and Maria jumped to their feet and helped Cassie hand them round to everyone, including the men who stood outside smoking. The men took the packets politely and thankfully, then left them on the wall while they continued smoking. Then after they had distributed the almonds, and while the womenfolk were taking their coffee, the three little girls went upstairs to Gina's room where they stood and watched as Gina sat in front of the mirror and brushed her hair into different styles.

'Thank you for my present,' Cassie said to them both, as she fingered the silver medal and chain Gina and Maria had given her. 'It's the nicest present I've ever ever had.'

'It's real silver,' said Gina.

'I know,' said Cassie, turning the medal round and looking at the marks.

'It was very expensive,' Maria added.

'I'll bet,' Cassie agreed.

Gina picked up Cassie's veil and headpiece of flowers and tried it on. Cassie and Maria stared at her mirrored image in awful silence. Gina was beautiful. But under a crown of tiny white roses and behind a pure white veil she looked like an angel.

'What did your grandmother give you?' Gina asked idly. 'Nothing, I bet.'

'No, she did give me something,' Cassie replied. 'She gave me a holy picture.'

Both the sisters turned and looked at her curiously.

'A proper holy picture?' Gina asked. 'In a frame? A painting?'

'No,' said Cassie, looking at the floor. 'Just a holy picture. You know.'

Gina and Maria looked at each other wide eyed, then giggled.

'Just a holy picture?' Gina repeated. 'Is that all?'

'I don't think she has very much money,' Cassie shrugged, all the same wondering why she felt the need to defend her grandmother.

56

'Sure,' Gina said, turning back to look at herself in the mirror. 'But she's always going to the beauty parlour. Least that's what our grandma says.'

'Yes,' Cassie agreed. 'But she has to go to the beauty parlour because it gets her out of the house.'

'I'd just say,' Gina said, with a look at her sister, 'that she has to go to the beauty parlour.'

Maria and Gina then collapsed in another fit of giggles, while Cassie, to cover her embarrassment, picked up her headpiece of roses and carefully readjusted the tiny flowers. She knew that it would soon be all round the school that her grandmother had only given her a paper holy picture on her Day of Days, and that all the girls would either laugh about it, or worse, feel sorry for her. Cassie just hated people feeling sorry for her.

'She's probably going to give me something else,' she added without much conviction. 'I think.'

And then she lay back and worried in case that was a sin, and if so would it cancel out any of her hard-earned silver stars, or leave a mark on the clear bright yellow of her crayoned soul?

Soon it was time to return to school, and the girls got ready to leave in Mrs Roebuck's car. When they came downstairs, Cassie's grandmother was still there, half asleep in an armchair, while the other women were clearing up around her. Cassie tiptoed past her, and hoped she wouldn't wake. No such luck. Just as Cassie reached the door she heard her grandmother call out behind her.

'Going without saying goodbye, child?' she asked.

'No, Grandmother,' Cassie dutifully replied. 'Goodbye, Grandmother.'

She stood looking back at her grandmother from the door.

'Haven't you forgotten something else?' Grandmother enquired.

Cassie frowned very hard.

'I don't think so, Grandmother,' she answered.

'You haven't said thank you for your present,' Grandmother informed her.

'Yes, I have,' Cassie protested.

'Not so as I can remember,' Grandmother persisted. 'Well?'

'Thank you for my present, Grandmother.'

'I should think so too, child. I don't know what children are coming to.'

Then she folded her arms again, settled back in the armchair and closed her eyes. Mrs Roebuck looked at her hopelessly and then took Cassie by the hand.

'Did anyone tell you how pretty you looked today, young lady?' she whispered to her as she bent down to re-do the sash on Cassie's dress. 'You looked a picture.'

Cassie sat in the middle of the back seat between Gina and Maria and all the way back to the convent they sang a song Gina and Maria had learned from the radio. Mrs Roebuck laughed and tapped her hands in time on the steering wheel, then made them sing it over and over again until she too had learned the song.

Cassie sang and sang until she was nearly hoarse. And while she sang she had her hand in the pocket of her dress. In her hand was her grandmother's gift of a holy picture; and as they turned into the drive of the convent, Cassie screwed the picture up as tightly as she could and, without anyone noticing, stuffed it down the back of the seat. It had been the happiest day of her life by far. Despite Grandmother.

Chapter Three

1949

Cassie and Mary-Jo were always the first in their house at the convent to be ready for bed. There was a good reason for this. Being first into bed meant you were also first into the bathroom, which meant you could use it when it was all freshly polished and shining and clean.

After they'd been to the bathroom, they would lie in their beds and talk about the one subject that had drawn them together into an increasingly deep friendship. Horses.

'Tell me about your foal again,' Cassie would ask Mary-Jo every night. 'Please.'

'I told you,' Mary-Jo would reply. 'He's brown. And he's got big black patches round his eyes.'

And then after lights out, Cassie would stare into the darkness and try to imagine what it must be like to own a horse, let alone a foal. Let alone a brown foal with black patches round its eyes.

One day a photograph of the recently born foal arrived from Mary-Jo's mother, together with a request for Mary-Jo to think up a name. Cassie and Mary-Jo in their every free moment pored over the photograph and racked their brains for exactly the right name. But it just wouldn't come to them.

Until one night, long after when they should have been asleep, Mary-Jo leant across to Cassie's bed.

'Prince,' she whispered.

'Really?' asked Cassie, leaning up on one elbow.

'Yes,' Mary-Jo answered. 'You're right. It is the best

name for him. And we've wasted all this time thinking up all those others. So I'm going to call him Prince.'

Cassie sighed and pulled her quilt up under her chin as she lay back. Prince. Mary-Jo was going to call her foal Prince, and she, Cassie, had thought of it. It made her feel in some way that part of the foal was now hers.

Then one Sunday Mary-Jo returned from a day at home and Cassie noticed that evening that Mary-Jo did everything one-handed. She washed her face one-handed, pulled on her nightdress one-handed, and even got into her bed one-handed. Cassie watched her curiously.

'Have you hurt yourself, Mary-Jo?' she asked.

'Of course not, silly,' Mary-Jo replied, holding up one hand. 'I'm just not going to wash this hand again ever.'

'Why not?' Cassie asked, half guessing the answer.

'Because Prince licked it,' Mary-Jo told her. 'He licked it all over, and then I rubbed my hand up and down his neck for you. So that you could smell him.'

Mary-Jo held out her hand in the dark, and Cassie reverently smelt it.

'Yes. I can smell him all right,' she frowned. 'At least I'm pretty sure I can.'

Mary-Jo took back her hand and held it close to her own nose, inhaling deeply and sighing.

'He's just gorgeous, Cassie,' she said. 'He's heavenly.'

'I'd give anything to see him,' Cassie sighed. 'Really anything.'

'Well, you probably won't have to,' Mary-Jo whispered, 'because Mamma says you can come and stay any time you like.'

Cassie lay in complete silence, not sure she'd heard right.

'Did you hear what I said, silly?' Mary-Jo hissed.

'I think so,' Cassie whispered back. 'But I just can't believe it.'

'Well it's true, so there!' Mary-Jo giggled. 'Mamma's going to write to your grandmother and tell her so.'

'Your Mamma must be an angel,' Cassie whispered.

'She is,' Mary-Jo replied simply. 'Goodnight.'

Then she turned on her side and placing her unwashed hand as close to her face as possible, fell into a deep untroubled sleep. While Cassie lay awake staring into the darkness and thinking of the adventure that might lie ahead.

She also lay thinking of how she could get her grandmother's permission to go and stay with Mary-Jo. She had never been away from Grandmother's, except for the magical night she slept at Mrs Roebuck's. But she wasn't going to be bested this time by her grandmother. She'd find a way of staying with Mary-Jo, even if it meant running away from home. There was no way Cassie was going to spend the long summer vacation shut up in Grandmother's stuffy house, with no one to see or to play with. Gina and Maria would probably be visiting Mrs Roebuck some of the time, but for most of the summer they were bound to be with their parents, like most normal children. Normal children. Why didn't she have parents? Why had Cassie been left in this world to be brought up by Grandmother? What had she done to make God so angry with her that He should punish her so?

Cassie tossed and turned in her bed, unable to sleep. Mary-Jo's invitation to go and stay with her had if anything made Cassie even more aware of her miserable existence, as she was frightened that her grandmother might refuse to allow her to go. In which case she would spend yet another endless vacation in the house that she had grown so much to hate. Grandmother would sleep a great deal, and Cassie would spend her day not playing in the sun but fetching and carrying, sweeping and tidying; then she would be sent to bed at a far earlier hour than she now went to bed at the convent, and she would have to lie there in her bed, night after night, with nothing to read, while the evening breeze blew at her dark blinds and carried the sounds of the gang of children playing below her in the street up into her lonely bedroom. In spite of all the joy the chance of seeing Prince and staying with Mary-Jo brought, that night Cassie cried herself to sleep.

Mrs Roebuck picked Cassie up from the convent at the end of term, together with her grandchildren. It appeared that Cassie's grandmother had gone to play bridge in Rochester, and wouldn't be back until the evening. So she had delegated her neighbour to collect Cassie from school. Most children would be sad if their own relative didn't pick them up at the end of term. Not so Cassie; she could hardly keep the smile off her face. Neither, for that matter, could Mrs Roebuck.

'You're to stay here with us,' she told Cassie, 'until your grandmother's back. And I've made you all a special walnut cake.'

The three girls yelled and hugged Mrs Roebuck, then, tearing all their clothes off, rushed out into the yard, free from the constraints of the convent. Within minutes the hose was running, and the yard was echoing with the happy unbridled laughter of the three children. They played all afternoon, dousing each other with the hose, climbing the big tree and tipping each other out of the hammocks, until it was time for tea and the walnut cake, then a massive collapse with jugs of homemade lemonade and the radio.

Then Grandmother returned, just as they were all having a bath, and as Mrs Roebuck was making up the spare bed for Cassie. She took Cassie home with her at once. There was absolutely no question of her staying the night again. Not on the first day of the vacation.

The next day at breakfast, Grandmother addressed herself to Cassie, having slowly and silently read Cassie's end of term report.

'Extraordinary,' she said, rolling up her napkin. 'The nuns seem to find no fault with you.'

She looked down the long table at the small solemn-faced child seated at the other end.

'I find that quite extraordinary,' she continued. 'Don't you?'

Cassie sat quite still and said nothing. She was sitting stiller than she had sat since last she was home, and she was keeping equally silent. At the convent they were allowed to talk and giggle within reason at breakfast, to push their chairs moderately noisily, and to run outside into the gardens and fields where there was always somebody to play with. But here, in Grandmother's house, you had to sit quite still, and silent, and push your chair in noiselessly, and there was never anyone to play with.

'If you can be patently this good at school, child,' her grandmother asked her in exasperation, 'then why are you such a trial at home?'

'I don't know, Grandmother,' Cassie answered. 'Can I get down please?'

'No you may not,' her grandmother replied. 'Not until I say so.'

And so they both sat there in silence for another quarter of an hour, while Grandmother re-read Cassie's report, sighing every so often as if it was the very worst document she had ever laid her eyes upon.

Later, up in her room, Cassie sat on the floor by her bed and read a book about horses Mary-Jo had lent her. It was the most beautiful book Cassie had ever read, even more beautiful than the book about dogs that Mr O'Reilly had given her. She had just reached an exciting moment when the door swung open and Grandmother came in.

'So here you are,' she said. 'Didn't you hear me calling you?'

'I was reading,' Cassie explained.

'What?' her grandmother demanded. 'What nonsense are you reading now?'

Cassie put the book down and tried to slide it under the bed.

'It's not nonsense,' she said. 'It's a book someone at school lent me.'

'If it's a book one of those girls at school lent you,' said her grandmother, 'then I want to see it at once please. Show me the book.'

Cassie pulled the book back out from under the bed, and handed it dutifully to her grandmother. Her grandmother stared at the picture on the cover as if it was something shocking, then she flicked through the pages.

'I suppose it makes a change from that ridiculous book all about dogs,' she said.

'It wasn't a ridiculous book,' Cassie said defensively.

'What do you mean, it "wasn't"?' asked her grandmother sharply. 'It wasn't? You haven't lost it or given it away, have you?'

Cassie looked her grandmother in the eye.

'Yes I have,' she answered. 'I gave it to the nuns to sell for the black babies.'

There was a terrible silence as Grandmother closed Mary-Jo's horse book and threw it on to the bed.

'I trust I didn't hear you right, child,' her grandmother said ominously. 'You gave away a book that Mr O'Reilly gave you? And not only that, you gave it away to help black children?'

'Yes,' Cassie said, not dropping her eyes. 'Yes I did.'

'That beautiful book poor Mr O'Reilly gave you. Which he could ill afford to do,' Grandmother continued, walking to the window. 'Why, that has to be one of the very worst things I ever heard in my life. You wait till Mr O'Reilly hears about you giving his book away.'

'It was my book, Grandmother,' Cassie argued. 'Mr O'Reilly gave it to me. And the nuns told us –'

'I don't care what the nuns told you, child!' said her grandmother, interrupting her sharply. 'It isn't your business to go around giving things away! Particularly things that mightn't properly belong to you!'

Cassie frowned in bewilderment.

'It was mine to give away!' she said.

'No it wasn't!' her grandmother retorted. 'And don't you dare to raise your voice at me! Now you're to stay here in your room while I go and see Mr O'Reilly! Who's to say that some day he wouldn't have wanted that beautiful dog book back?'

And with that Grandmother swept out, slamming and locking Cassie's bedrom door behind her. Cassie went to the window and saw her grandmother marching determinedly over to Mr O'Reilly who was standing contentedly watering his flowers. She watched for a while from behind the net curtains as Grandmother started talking to him, then as Mr O'Reilly looked up at Cassie's window, Cassie shrank back and went and hid by the side of her bed.

Perhaps Grandmother was right. Perhaps Mr O'Reilly had only lent it to her after all. Try as she might, Cassie couldn't actually remember him saying she was to keep the book. Here, this is for you, Cassie, he had said. But he hadn't said, as far as Cassie could recall, here – this is for you to *keep*, Cassie. But he had told her it was a very precious book, and that he had had it since he was a boy. And that it meant an awful lot to him. So perhaps he would some day have wanted it back. And now he knew that she had given it away, he'd think it had meant nothing to her, and he'd never be her friend again.

Why had she given it away? She had so few books of her own, and none which came anywhere near Mr O'Reilly's dog book. She gave it away because she had no money to give to Sister Joseph's charity. She had got up, after Sister Joseph had made the appeal, to help the poor black children, and walked quite spontaneously to the front of the class where there was a large box to collect the children's donations, and she had calmly placed the book at the bottom of the box. She was the first girl to go forward, and hers was the first donation. And Sister Joseph had praised her.

Perhaps that was why she gave away the book. Because she wanted Sister Joseph's approval. Because she craved Sister Joseph's special smile which she bestowed on you when she wanted you to know that she understood how you felt. But now it didn't seem worth it. Not if it was going to cost her Mr O'Reilly's friendship. Not if it was going to hurt Mr O'Reilly.

After what seemed like ages, Grandmother returned, Cassie heard her climbing the stairs and turning the key in the lock. She came into the room half-smiling, as she always did when she knew she had an extra chance to cause Cassie pain.

'Well,' she announced. 'Mr O'Reilly is very hurt. Very hurt indeed. So there you are. You're to be congratulated.'

'How hurt is he, Grandmother,' Cassie asked. 'What did he say?'

'He didn't say anything, child,' Grandmother replied. 'But I could see well enough from his eyes. You've rarely seen such a look of pain in a man's eyes.'

Cassie sat quite still on the carpet, trying to make herself as small as she could by the bed.

'Stand up,' her grandmother suddenly commanded. 'Stand up at once and tell me the truth. Tell me why you gave away Mr O'Reilly's lovely book. And I want the truth, understand? I don't want any of your lies! Or your fancy stories! Tell me why you gave that book away!'

Cassie stood up slowly and looked at her grandmother, who was staring at her in fury and loathing. There was a long silence as Cassie searched her soul for the truth of that moment, the moment when she had stood over that box with Mr O'Reilly's book in her hands, loath to drop it, loath to give up her adored picture of all the dogs who had become her closest friends, loath to sacrifice the only possession she had which she truly loved.

'I'm waiting,' hissed her grandmother.

Cassie looked up at her.

'I gave it away, Grandmother,' she replied, 'because I loved it.'

'What nonsense!'

'But I did, Grandmother!' Cassie persisted. 'I gave the book away because I loved it!'

'No you didn't!' shouted her grandmother. 'I'll tell you why you gave it away! You gave it away because you were showing off! Pretending you were some smart little

66

rich girl! Pretending you were somebody who could afford to give away books! Other people's books!'

At that, Cassie dropped her eyes and stared at the dark stained floor-boards of her room. Her grandmother went out, and for a moment Cassie thought the storm might have blown over. But she was soon disillusioned. Within a minute her grandmother was back carrying a chamber pot which she placed in the cupboard beside Cassie's bed.

'You're to stay in your room for the rest of the week,' she announced, then left, locking the door behind her.

Cassie stood stock still in the middle of the room, suddenly filled with feelings she couldn't understand, feelings which frightened her. She went over to the window and looked out on to the sunlit street outside where the other children were already playing. And then she stepped back from the window, almost as if she'd had an electric shock, as she realised what those feelings she was having meant. Because Cassie knew that at that moment she could have killed herself, had her single window not been barred and bolted.

By the weekend, when Cassie was allowed out of her room, Grandmother seemed almost cheerful. The incident with what was now referred to as Mr O'Reilly's beautiful book had apparently proved to her that Cassie was not as pure as the nuns had painted her. And now Cassie was to atone further for her crime, and also to pay Grandmother back for the donation she had been forced to make to St Anthony over the matter of Cassie's communion dress.

Cassie was made to slave. Up and down the stairs to fetch books, spectacles, medicines, more books, other spectacles, more medicines. She was sent to the mail and for the mail, to the baker's, the butcher's and the grocer's; she was made to run endless petty errands, and to sweep the garden path and the street in front of the house. There wasn't a moment of the day that Cassie had to herself. And if Grandmother ever caught her as much as drawing breath, a job usually even more demeaning than the last one was found at once for her. Other children went to summer camp, but not Cassie: Cassie slaved for her grandmother.

In the evenings, with all her chores done and yet another early night in prospect, Cassie used to long with all her heart to be back at school and amongst her friends. She would stand by the window and tears would roll uncontrollably down her cheeks. Before she had gone to the convent, she hadn't known that she was lonely; she hadn't understood the word. Now she knew that not only was she lonely, but that she was alone.

One morning, Cassie brought in the mail and noticed that there was a letter addressed to her grandmother postmarked Locksfield, Pennsylvania. Cassie's heart leaped. Locksfield was where Mary-Jo lived. Then she banished any further thoughts from her mind, lest her grandmother, already seated at the dining table, should read them. Cassie put the letters down in front of Grandmother and took her seat at the other end. Her grandmother studiously ignored the day's mail, as was her habit, preferring to open the letters once she had finished eating. Today she seemed to take longer than ever over her food, until finally she started to sift through the correspondence. She picked up the yellow envelope from Pennsylvania, with the unfamiliar handwriting, and held it up to the light, as if it might contain something distasteful.

'Who on earth can this be from?' she wondered out loud, before carefully slitting it open with a small ladies' knife kept especially for the purpose. Cassie kept her head bowed over her food.

Grandmother read the letter once, front and back, before turning it over and reading it through completely once again. Then she placed it on the table before her and looked at Cassie over her spectacles.

'This friend of yours, Mary-Jo,' she said.

Cassie counted to five then looked up as calmly as she could.

'Yes, Grandmother?'

'For some reason or other, her mother has invited you to go and stay with them,' she informed her, peering down at the letter. 'In Locksfield, Pennsylvania, wherever that may be.'

Cassie's face betrayed no emotion. She knew all too well that any enthusiasm on her behalf for such a notion would be enough for her grandmother to rule against it straightaway. It would be too expensive. Too difficult to arrange. Pennsylvania would be too far away. She would be too young to travel by herself. Or most likely of all, Mary-Jo's family would be declared as being 'the wrong sort of people'. So Cassie sat straightfaced and silent.

'I suppose you want to go, do you?' her grandmother asked her, without a trace of solace in her voice.

'Not especially,' Cassie replied as calmly as she could.

Her grandmother stared at her, trying, Cassie was sure, to read her thoughts.

'Not especially?' she repeated, unable to believe her ears. 'I thought this Mary-Jo was meant to be your best friend.'

'She was,' said Cassie carefully. 'But that was ages ago.'

'Then why is her mother inviting you to stay with her if you're not best friends any more?' Grandmother demanded.

Beneath the table Cassie crossed her fingers, praying silently to her guardian angel for forgiveness for all the lies she was telling and the lies she was about to tell.

'Because Mary-Jo still wants to be friends, I suppose.' Cassie replied.

The reply had the required effect. Grandmother removed her spectacles and glared down the table at her.

'You wretched, spoilt and ungrateful child,' she said. 'First of all you're forever complaining you've no friends, then when some poor child wants to be friends with you, and wants you to go and stay with her, you just shrug your shoulders and say "not especially". I really don't know what gets into you. And of course I suppose her poor mother's got nothing better to do than to invite ungrateful children down to stay with her poor lonely little girl, eh? Ungrateful spoilt little children who are too wrapped up in themselves to bother.'

Cassie kept staring down at the table and crossing her fingers more and more tightly.

'Not especially indeed,' her grandmother continued. 'You'll go up to your room this minute, child –'

At this, Cassie couldn't help but look up, to find out whether she had won or lost.

'You'll go up to your room,' Grandmother said, 'and you will sit down straightaway and write to this Mary-Jo's mother. And you will thank her for her kind invitation, and tell her you will be delighted to come and stay with her for as long as she'll have you.'

Cassie bit the inside of her cheek hard, to stop herself smiling.

'But Grandmother –' she began to protest.

'No buts!' Grandmother snapped. 'Upstairs this minute and write that letter, and thank God that with a character like yours you've any friends at all!'

It had worked. Cassie knew it shouldn't have worked – telling a lie in order to get what you wanted – but nevertheless the truth was that the deception had worked. Cassie was leaping up the stairs two at a time with excitement when she felt that the dining-room door was being opened quietly below her. So at once she stopped running and walked sedately up the stairs holding on to the bannisters with her eyes cast downwards, the way the nuns did. When she got to the top of the stairs and turned to go into her room, she saw indeed that her grandmother had been standing in the hall below, watching her.

'I want to see the letter written out in pencil first, mind!' she called. 'And then in pen when I've checked the

70

spelling! I don't want this Mary-Jo's mother thinking you're some sort of ignoramus!'

With that her grandmother walked off to the morning room to read the daily paper, and Cassie was free to skip happily across the landing to the privacy of her room. She was going to see Mary-Jo and Prince. Mary-Jo and Prince.

Cassie was just finishing her packing when her grandmother came into her bedroom. She saw the little box lying on the bed before Cassie had time to slip it down the side of her case under her nightclothes.

'What on earth, pray, is this?' Grandmother said, opening the box.

'Nothing,' said Cassie. 'Just a present for Mary-Jo.'

'So now you're buying things for girls you don't particularly like, are you?' Grandmother queried, taking a little china horse out from the tissue paper. 'I suppose it never occurred to you that it might be nice if you gave your grandmother something once in a while?'

Cassie bit her lip and continued with her packing. No, it never *had* occurred to her to do such a thing, and she couldn't in all honesty admit that it had. She gave her grandmother gifts at Christmas and on her birthday, presents she made herself since she had no money with which to buy anything, offerings which were sniffed at and soon discarded. But no, she'd never thought of buying something for her grandmother at any other time of the year. There didn't seem to be any reason.

'You can have that, if you like, Grandmother,' Cassie offered, watching as Grandmother examined the china ornament.

'Don't be absurd, child,' Grandmother replied. 'You know I can't stand horses.'

Cassie's grandmother put the china horse untidily back into its box, and dropped it on the bed. Cassie picked it up and lovingly repacked it in the tissue paper.

'Where did you get the money to buy such a thing

71

anyway?' Grandmother continued. 'I very much hope you didn't take it from my purse.'

'I got it with the money I saved from the bread,' Cassie answered. 'You said whenever you sent me for the bread I could keep the cents. So I have. Since last summer.'

'And now you've decided to waste it all on some cheap little gew-gaw.'

Cassie remained silent. She wasn't sure what a gew-gaw was, but from the way Grandmother had said it, she imagined it wasn't anything very nice. She packed the box containing the china horse, and was just about to fasten her case up, when Grandmother pushed her aside.

'Not till I've examined your packing,' she said. 'I'm not having you going off with a badly packed suitcase.'

Grandmother then proceeded to rifle through Cassie's carefully packed belongings, deliberately untidying them. Cassie watched helplessly as her grandmother then tipped out the entire contents of her case on to the floor.

'Disgraceful,' she announced, as she walked out of the bedroom. 'Do it all again.'

A cab took them to the station. That at least was a treat, Cassie thought, as she sat back in her seat and watched the town pass by.

'Will you miss me?' her grandmother suddenly asked.

Cassie frowned. Her grandmother hardly ever asked her such a thing.

'Yes,' she lied.

'No you won't,' Grandmother replied. 'I daresay you won't miss me one jot.'

Grandmother turned round and stared accusingly at Cassie.

'You never miss me when you're at school,' she went on. 'Whenever you deign to write to me, it's all about you and those friends of yours. But never a word about missing me.'

Cassie caught sight of the cab driver's eyes watching them both in his driving mirror. He gave Cassie a wink, and she looked down, anxious lest Grandmother should catch her smiling back at him.

'You really should think less of yourself, child,' Grandmother said. 'You should think less of yourself and more of what a burden you are to me. Can you imagine what it was like for me, being left to bring you up when your parents died? It's not as if I ever liked children.'

Cassie caught sight of the driver's eyes again. She'd often seen him driving through the town and they always waved at each other. This time as he looked at her in his mirror he crossed his eyes at her. Cassie had to bite her lip even harder to stop herself from laughing.

'You'll be sorry when you're older,' Grandmother sighed, looking out of the window as they approached the station. 'When I'm dead and buried. You'll be sorry you didn't buy me flowers, and thank me for all I've done for you.'

Cassie frowned and wondered why Grandmother was telling her all this. Particularly on this day, when she was just off to spend her first holiday away from home with her very best friend. Grandmother sighed deeply beside her, putting her hand to her chest and giving a small cough. Cassie looked out of her own window and instead of thinking of her grandmother lying dead and unloved, thought of Prince and his soft brown nose, which Mary-Jo had promised her was the softest and most velvety nose you'd ever touched in all your life.

The train was crowded with people, most of whom were a lot poorer than the people who lived in Grandmother's neighbourhood. Cassie, wedged where her grandmother had sat her between two ample spinsters, sat watching the poorer passengers watching the countryside go by. They watched it, Cassie reckoned, in the way people who seldom see it do. And soon Cassie was watching it that way too, because she had hardly ever seen anything except the streets and houses of Westboro Falls and the twenty miles of rather monotonous landscape that lay

73

between her home and the convent. The ladies she sat between took care of her, and asked her with real interest where she was going. When Cassie told them, they asked if she'd been there before, and when Cassie said she had not, they told her how pretty it was. Cassie then told them about Prince and, unlike Grandmother, they responded with real enthusiasm and interest, and one of the ladies told her all about the livery stable her father had run. At midday they rose and went to the restaurant car, and asked Cassie if she would come with them. But Cassie politely declined, pointing out that Mrs Roebuck who lived opposite had made her a special luncheon box of hot meat pie wrapped in a napkin, some fruit and a flask of homemade lemonade.

Cassie got down the luncheon box from the luggage rack and put it on her knee. Grandmother had told her not to have her lunch until she really needed it, lest she got hungry on the last part of the journey, and though her tummy was rumbling, anxious to please Grandmother even though she was a hundred miles away, she made herself wait until the very last moment before she tucked into Mrs Roebuck's picnic, with the consequence that she had barely finished eating as the train rolled into Locksfield.

It was a small station, set in rolling countryside. There were only six or seven people waiting to meet the train, and as Cassie was helped off with her luggage, she looked at once for Mary-Jo. There was no sign of her. Everyone else who got off the train met up almost at once with their friends and relatives, soon leaving Cassie standing alone on the platform beside her suitcase.

The porter, having safely delivered his last charge to the waiting cab, wandered back on to the platform and saw Cassie. He pushed his cap back on his head, sighed and walked up to her, hoping that she wasn't yet another child who had alighted at the wrong stop.

'You sure you got out at the right station, miss?' he asked her.

74

'This is Locksfield, Pennsylvania, isn't it?' Cassie replied anxiously, looking past the porter in case she missed Mary-Jo's arrival.

'This is Locksfield, Penn. all right, young lady,' the porter nodded. 'Any idea of the name of the people meeting you?'

'Yes,' Cassie said. 'Yes, it's Mary-Jo Christiansen and her mother.'

The porter suddenly roared with laughter, and took Cassie by the hand.

'Well, if it's the Christiansens who're meeting you, you'd better come with me and have a long, cold drink!' he said. 'The Christiansens are always late! That is if they don't forget you altogether!'

He winked at Cassie, and led her back to the station office, where he sat her down in front of the electric fan and poured her a ginger beer.

'If they're not here by next week,' he said with a twinkle in his eye, 'I might even give them a call on the telephone here.'

Cassie smiled at his teasing and drank her ginger beer. She looked out of the back window of the office and stared at a distant farm, with its perfectly tended fields of barley and corn waving gently in the summer breeze. Then she noticed faraway down the narrow road what seemed to be a ball of dust travelling towards them very fast. She stood up and stared harder. The porter stopped sorting out a new batch of rail tickets and came to Cassie's side.

'Looks like your friends have remembered,' he chuckled, as they made for the door. 'Not like one time last summer when they turned up the following day!'

Cassie laughed and ran out into the station yard, the porter following her with her luggage. She held on to her hat as into the yard amidst a cloud of white dust roared an old station wagon, with what seemed like a dozen children leaning out of its windows. Cassie waved and waved when she saw Mary-Jo, and long before the station

75

wagon had fully stopped, Mary-Jo and most of the other children had jumped out of the windows and were running towards Cassie.

One of Mary-Jo's brothers arrived first and stood in front of her grinning silently, twisting his cap in his hand. Mary-Jo arrived next, hotfoot, and, pushing her tongue-tied brother out of the way, grabbed Cassie by the hand.

'Hi,' she said. 'Sorry we're kinda late, but we had to pick up the horse food.'

Mary-Jo then ordered her still-grinning brother to pick up Cassie's luggage, as she took Cassie back to the car.

A very pretty woman at the wheel leaned out of her window.

'Hi, Cassie,' she said. 'I'm Mary-Jo's mother.'

Cassie smiled at her and held out her hand.

'How do you do, Mrs Christiansen,' she said.

'I'm fine, Cassie,' Mary-Jo's mother replied. 'How was the journey?'

'Very exciting,' said Cassie.

Mary-Jo's mother smiled back at Cassie then nodded backwards with her head.

'I should hop in and grab a seat, if I were you,' she advised. 'Otherwise you might end up running behind.'

Cassie got in by way of a door, while Mary-Jo and her brother tipped themselves back in through the open windows. Cassie, over-dressed as usual by her grandmother, felt like an old woman in this car full of check-shirted and blue-jeaned free spirits.

'Take off your coat,' Mary-Jo ordered. 'You'll boil.'

Cassie gratefully removed her coat and rolled her woollen socks down as Mary-Jo's mother engaged gear and roared out of the station yard at high speed. Everyone fell into each other, screaming with laughter. Cassie righted herself and pushed up the sleeves of her dress, and pulled the ribbons from her hair. Soon she was looking as dishevelled as the rest of the kids in the station wagon.

'How's Prince?' Cassie shouted at Mary-Jo over the noise of the engine.

'Great!' Mary-Jo shouted back. 'He's gotten enormous!' Cassie swallowed hard. It seemed as if in the excitement her heart had leapt right up into her throat.

The car then turned right at high speed into a dirt track and headed up through fields of corn. After what seemed to Cassie at least two or maybe three miles, they arrived at Mary-Jo's house, a large white clapboarded farmhouse, surrounded by barns and outbuildings. A pack of dogs of all shapes and sizes rushed out barking to greet the station wagon, and once again most of the children piled out of the doors and windows long before Mrs Christiansen had stopped. Cassie tried to emulate Mary-Jo by tumbling out of the rolled-down window at the back, but got hopelessly stuck, and ended up having her face washed from top to toe by a wildly friendly long-haired sheepdog.

'That's Erasmus,' Mary-Jo explained, helping Cassie extricate herself from the window. 'He's mad.'

Then still at the run, Cassie was taken into the old barn which was used as a summer dormitory for the family children and their friends. The top floor was lined with old double bunks, and the ground floor was a huge play area. Mary-Jo lifted Cassie's suitcase with her on to her bunk and opened it, to search for something more appropriate for Cassie to wear. They rifled through all the dresses and skirts and jumpers Grandmother had made her pack, but of course, as Cassie knew there wouldn't be, there were no casual clothes like everyone else was wearing.

'You need a pair of jeans, Cassie,' Mary-Jo said firmly. 'These clothes are no good.'

Mary-Jo ran off with Cassie as always running obediently some way behind her. Mary-Jo stopped in front of a large old closet and pulled open the doors. A pile of riding clothes, jeans, pants and check shirts tumbled out, all old, faded and patched, but washed and

77

cleaned and smelling of the same starch that Delta used back home.

Mary-Jo selected a pair of faded and patched jeans and held them up against Cassie, then chose a blue check shirt with long sleeves.

'There,' she said. 'They ought to do you.'

Cassie looked at the clothes, her eyes shining.

'Can I ride in these?' she asked.

'You can do what you like in them,' Mary-Jo replied. 'You can sleep in 'em if you want to.'

Cassie hugged the old clothes to her then ran back to the dormitory. She picked up all the clothes Grandmother had made her pack and crammed them back into the suitcase, and then looked desperately for somewhere to hide it.

'Shove it under the bed,' Mary-Jo suggested. 'You won't be needing anything from it.'

Cassie put the case on the floor, and was just about to kick it under the bunk, when she remembered something. She bent down and took the little box from the side pocket.

'Here,' she said, offering it to Mary-Jo. 'This is for you.'

Then while Mary-Jo carefully opened it, Cassie took off her dress and slipped into the jeans and shirt. Mary-Jo lifted the little china horse out from the tissue paper as if it was a living thing, then looked at Cassie.

'Oh Cassie,' she sighed. 'You're not going to believe it, but it's just like Prince!'

Cassie smiled shyly and pulled a belt through the loops on the jeans. Mary-Jo and Cassie didn't go in much for hugging each other and kissing. It was one of their many unspoken pacts that they would try and behave more like Mary-Jo's older brothers, who never hugged each other or did anything which could be construed as 'soppy'. But Cassie could tell from Mary-Jo's expression how much she loved the little horse. She could tell by the way she stroked the horse's nose and kissed the top of its china head.

Then once Cassie was completely changed, into her baggy blue shirt and jeans which were two sizes too big for her, but which were the most exciting clothes she had ever seen, let alone worn, the two girls ran downstairs and out into the late afternoon sunshine.

As she ran down behind Mary-Jo, to the pastures, Cassie could sense that this was a place where everything just happened naturally, just the way nature was happening all around her. She could sense the freedom, and the happiness, and the feeling that no one was going to call you in the middle of a game and send you somewhere where you didn't want to go. Here was a place where the days would go past helping with the horses, playing with the foals, paddling and fishing with worms on bent pins in the river that lay to one side of the house, lying chattering and sunbathing on the roof of the old station wagon, and hiding from each other in the branches of the huge trees.

And here was the place where Prince lived. Cassie stopped running and slowed to a walk the moment she saw him standing grazing by his mother. Mary-Jo called to him and he whickered, then cantered over in curiosity to the fence.

'Come on!' Mary-Jo called. 'Come over and stroke him!'

Cassie walked slowly up to the post and rails, anxious not to frighten the youngster. She put a hand through the fencing and Prince sniffed it. Mary-Jo was right. It was the softest nose she had ever touched.

'Hello, Prince,' Cassie said to him, her eyes shining brightly. 'Hello, boy.'

'Isn't he gorgeous?' sighed Mary-Jo. 'Isn't he the most beautiful foal you have ever seen?'

It wouldn't have been hard for Cassie to agree because of course she had never ever seen a real live foal before. But she agreed because it was true. Prince was quite beautiful.

'Come into the paddock,' Mary-Jo said, jumping down off the fence. 'It's OK. Prince won't mind, and neither will Bella his mother.'

Cassie slipped through the rails and did as Mary-Jo

79

did, plucking a handful of fresh grass and holding it out in front of her. The foal came back to them, lowered his head and blew at the grass held on the girls' outstretched hands. It scattered up into the air. So they plucked some more, and the same thing happened again. Mary-Jo laughed, her blue eyes crinkling with the joy of it all. Cassie had never seen Mary-Jo laugh like that. She had never seen anyone laugh like that. It was quite different from the sort of laugh girls gave when someone dropped their rosary during Mass.

Mary-Jo caught Prince by his slip and held him for Cassie to stroke. Cassie ran her hand down the foal's soft furry neck. The foal struggled against Mary-Jo's hold and butted Cassie in the stomach. Cassie stroked him again and laughed delightedly.

'He thinks you've got milk,' Mary-Jo said solemnly.

'Well I haven't, Prince,' Cassie replied. 'So there.'

Mary-Jo released the foal and he stood on his hind legs, waving his forelegs in the air, before running back to his mother's side. Cassie watched him canter away.

'He's the most beautiful thing I've ever seen, Mary-Jo,' she told her friend. 'Nothing bad must ever happen to him.'

'If it did,' Mary-Jo replied, 'I'd kill myself.'

'Me, too,' Cassie agreed, and they shook hands on it.

Then they just stood and watched Prince and Bella until the light started to fade, when they turned for home and walked back to the house side by side in silence, each with a long grass hanging from her mouth.

Mrs Christiansen was not the cook Mrs Roebuck was, but then she didn't have to be. The children spent so long out of doors that by the time they came in they'd have eaten the furniture. But what there was there was plenty of, and it was all homegrown. The pan-fried eggs were so buttery and soft that when they were slid on to the crisp french fries they seemed to be as good as anything Cassie had ever eaten at Mrs Roebuck's. Everyone talked as they ate, and no one was told to take their elbows off the table.

Cassie looked at all the sunburned faces round the table. It was easy to tell which were Mary-Jo's brothers, because they all had the same huge blue eyes and freckled noses, and the same serious way of looking at people. The other children were cousins, friends and neighbours' children. Cassie tried to count how many were seated round the huge table, and had just got to nine when her plate was whisked away and she was given a shiny red apple and a homemade cookie.

'Come on,' said Frank, the eldest of the brothers. 'We're going to play in the barn. You girls can come too.'

Cassie took her apple and cookie, like everyone else, and like them she jumped backwards off the long school bench upon which they'd been sitting, and ran out of the back door. What freedom, thought Cassie, never having to sit at table longer than the time it took to eat! Not having to ask to get down! And not having to eat things you didn't like which made you feel sick! Cassie ran deliriously after her new friends, her gang, and joined in the happy shrieking and shouting as they rushed to romp and play in the barn.

Later Cassie lay in her bunk, too drunk with happiness to think straight. Grandmother with her dark house and her cruel ways seemed as far away as the stars she could see through the skylight in the barn shining above her. Mary-Jo's face appeared upsidedown from the bunk above her.

'What time do you want to get up tomorrow?' she asked Cassie.

'Whatever time you think,' Cassie replied.

'Let's get up at five,' Mary-Jo suggested. 'Before everyone else. I'll set the alarm and put it under my pillow.'

But they were both so exhausted and they both slept so deeply that they slept through the alarm, and didn't manage to crawl out of their warm beds until just after six. They were the first up, nevertheless, and as the early morning sun started to climb its way up into the sky, they stood in the fields looking at the awakening world around them. Soon early morning would become another day, and the precise freshness of each drop of dew would have long disappeared. The diamond earrings which hung from each blade of grass would have gone, the dust that was now settled would be swirling and rising angrily in the air, and all the sounds would elide together, making a chorus of the single note of life that the children could feel pulsating quietly around them. Human voices layered between the shouts of children playing, the shouts of the children drowned by the sudden call of horses. The birds would no longer be heard calling their individual songs, some insistent, some joyous, but all would be blended into the orchestra of the day.

Mary-Jo broke the silence.

'Let's go and see Prince,' she said.

'OK,' Cassie replied. 'And on the way, you be Monarch, and I'll be Rainbow.'

They went on playing Monarch and Rainbow all week, except when Cassie was learning to ride the real Rainbow. With her legs straddled across the broad back of the patient pony, she was led round and round the outdoor school by Mary-Jo, and sometimes, while Mary-Jo was having a jumping lesson, by Mary-Jo's mother, herself an expert rider.

Sometimes as she bumped up and down at the trot, clinging in desperation to the pommel of the saddle, it seemed to Cassie that riding a pony was a sight more difficult than pretending to be one. But she stuck at it, sometimes falling off by sliding down the pony's neck, sometimes being tipped off backwards, and once or twice by being shot straight over Rainbow's head and through his furry ears.

At bathtime she would examine her bruises rather proudly. As the days passed, and Cassie grew more confident, so the bruises got smaller and fewer, until at last she was off the leading rein and learning to rise correctly and comfortably to the trot. By the end of the second week

Cassie had had her first canter, and so enthralled was she now with riding that she could hardly bear the hours wasted in sleep. By the beginning of the third week, she was riding out of the school, alongside Mary-Jo and her mother. They rode across the farm and down the sides of the huge cornfields, some of which were already being harvested, then back through the woods and down over the hills which rose behind the house.

One morning when they came back from their ride, they found an injured bird lying in the barn. From the look of it, it had broken its wing. Mary-Jo at once went and fetched the laundry basket which always served as a general hospital for abandoned or injured small animals, and together they laid the bird on a bed of cotton wool. They took it in turns to sit with him, trying to get him to eat the worms they had dug up, or to take warm milk from an eye-dropper. They sat up through the night with him, but the bird refused nourishment and by the morning, when Mary-Jo woke with a start, she found Cassie in tears holding the dead bird in her hands.

'We did everything we could, Cassie,' Mary-Jo told her. 'When they've broken a wing, they hardly ever live.'

'It's true, Cassie,' Mrs Christiansen told Cassie at breakfast. 'We've saved one or two, but they're the exception rather than the rule. You really couldn't have done any more.'

But as they dug the tiny grave, Cassie was still blaming herself, wondering whether or not the milk in the eye-dropper had been at the right temperature, and whether trying to give it worms had necessarily been such a good idea. Mary-Jo was busy carefully laying out the dead bird in an old soap box that still smelt of lavender which they then sealed down with sticky tape, and carefully placed in the ground. Cassie picked some flowers and placed them on the grave, while Mary-Jo went inside to fetch two veils.

'Lord, grant this bird eternal rest and let your perpetual light shine upon him,' Mary-Jo read.

'Amen,' said Cassie.

The boys all sat on the fence watching them, as Mary-Jo and Cassie sprinkled earth on the little box before covering it completely over. Mary-Jo put a little cross made from sticks on the grave to mark the spot, then both the girls closed their eyes and said silent prayers for the soul of a sparrow.

'On Saturday,' Mrs Christiansen announced that evening at supper, 'there's going to be a party.'

All heads turned to her.

'A barn dance,' she continued, 'to which you are all most cordially invited. Besides the usual fun and games, of course there's going to be a fancy-dress competition for you children, with an extra special first prize this year.'

Later as Cassie and Mary-Jo were getting ready for bed, Mary-Jo explained that they had a big barn dance every year once the main part of the harvest was taken in. Everyone in the neighbourhood came, and it was just the greatest fun in the world. The prize for the fancy-dress competition was always worth winning, thanks to the generosity of Mary-Jo's father, of whom Cassie had seen very little because he was so busy on the farm. And the rumour was that this year the prize was going to be a pony.

'You don't know which pony I suppose?' Cassie asked breathlessly. 'I mean, I don't suppose it's Rainbow?'

'I don't know,' Mary-Jo replied. 'Least I do, but I'm sworn to secrecy.'

Cassie lay back on her pillow and thought of winning Rainbow for her own. She had no idea at all what she would do with the pony should she win; she'd probably give it back to Mary-Jo, she decided, and just ride it whenever she came down and stayed. If ever she came down and stayed again. She couldn't tell Grandmother if she won, that was for certain. Grandmother would probably shoot it.

She turned in her bunk and stared out of the skylight which she could see by lying on her side. No, if she did

84

win it which wasn't really at all possible, Cassie suddenly decided that she would sell it and give all the money to Sister Joseph's charity. She turned back on to the other side. No she wouldn't, she thought. She couldn't. She lay on her back. Anyway, she wasn't going to win it, so what was the point of worrying? But there again, she thought dreamily as she turned once more on her side and started to fall asleep, there again, somebody had to . . .

The rest of the week was spent in feverish activity getting costumes prepared for the dance. There was tremendous secrecy, because no one wanted anyone else to know what they were going as, although heavy hints were dropped at mealtimes, and barely veiled questions were asked just in case any two people had alighted on the same ideas. Cassie had long decided on her costume. She was going to go as the Straw Man from *The Wizard of Oz*. It was the only movie she had ever seen in the cinema, and it had taken all her powers of persuasion to get Grandmother to allow her to go with Gina and Maria and Mrs Roebuck on Gina's last birthday. They had sat through the film twice, and Cassie could still remember the lines of dialogue and the songs as if it was yesterday.

So with a lot of secret help from Mary-Jo's father, who, having brought in a good harvest, now had some time to spare, and who had taken a great liking to Mary-Jo's serious-faced little friend, Cassie made her costume. One thing she knew they wouldn't be short of on the farm was straw, so she had chosen wisely, and well. Two days before the dance, when she got up very early to work in private on her costume, she saw Mr and Mrs Christiansen hard at work on it themselves, tearing up a more suitable old jacket, and reshaping one of Mr Christiansen's old hats. Cassie, unseen by them, backed away into the shadows and watched. She saw Mrs Christiansen smile at her husband and whisper something to him. Mr Christiansen smiled back and put the reshaped hat on himself. Then he took Mary-Jo's mother into his arms and together they danced around the corner of the old barn where Cassie had hidden her costume. Mr Christiansen then stopped dancing and kissed his wife, for, it seemed to Cassie, a very long time. Something, she didn't understand what, prompted Cassie then to slip out of the small barn and away altogether.

She went out by herself into the paddocks and whistled to Prince. Mary-Jo and she had spent hours teaching him to come to call, and now he trotted up obediently but still curiously every time they whistled him. Cassie sat on the rails and pulled Prince's ears. The foal tried to chew her foot, but Cassie laughed and pushed his nose away. Prince rolled his top lip back and bared his teeth in a grin. Cassie sighed and pulled his ears some more, and at that moment determined that even if she didn't win the pony on Saturday, one day she would have a beautiful horse all of her own.

With that happy notion in her young head, she jumped off the fence and ran back to the house when she heard the bell being rung for breakfast. She ran all the way, like she and Mary-Jo always did, and she ran into the kitchen. But she stopped in her tracks when she saw what was lying on a plate in her place. She knew what it was even before she saw the spidery writing on the blue envelope. It was a letter from Grandmother.

Chapter Four

Cassie read the letter for a second time, just to make sure she had read it right the first time. All around her all the other children were laughing and chattering, as the excitement of the dance and fancy-dress competition had built up. All the others, that was, except Mary-Jo, who knew from Cassie's eyes that something was the matter.

Nudging her brother Dick out of the way, she sat down on the bench next to Cassie.

'What's wrong, Cassie?' she asked. 'You've gone all white.'

'Grandmother's ill,' Cassie replied, putting the letter carefully back in the blue envelope. 'I'm to go home at once.'

'Not today?' Mary-Jo protested. 'You don't have to go today?'

'Yes I do,' Cassie said, getting up from the table. 'I'm to catch the eleven o'clock train.'

Mary-Jo ran after her to the barn.

'But what about the dance?' Mary-Jo said. 'And the fancy-dress competition! Surely you could go back on Sunday?'

'No I can't, Mary-Jo,' Cassie answered, climbing the stairs to the dormitory. 'Grandmother wants me home now. She says I've outstayed my welcome as it is.'

Cassie pulled out her suitcase from under the bunk and started to pack. Mary-Jo looked at her, then turned on her heel.

'I'm going to tell Mamma,' she announced. 'I'll try and

get her to ring your grandmother and explain.'

'It won't do any good!' Cassie called after her.

But the fleet-footed Mary-Jo had gone.

Cassie took off her jeans and blue check shirt, which she hadn't been out of except for the times they had been washed since the day she arrived. She folded them carefully and neatly and put them on the foot of her bed. It wouldn't do any good ringing Grandmother. She had said quite clearly that she had pains in her chest and a very bad cough, and that Cassie was to come home at once and help look after her, since Delta had quite enough to do keeping the house in order. Cassie went on folding her clothes almost ritualistically and putting them in her case. She thought of the wonderful time she had had with Mary-Jo and her family, and in order to stop the tears which were welling up behind her eyes from falling, she pinched the underneath of her arm so hard that the blood broke through the skin.

Mrs Christiansen drove her to the station. In the car there was just Mary-Jo, Erasmus, Cassie and Mary-Jo's mother. Everyone else was too sad to come with them, and when they had heard the news they had all silently disappeared to their various secret hiding places around the farm. Cassie had said goodbye to Prince, and Mary-Jo had given her a hair from his tail for luck. It had also started to rain, for the first time since she had arrived in Locksfield.

'Mary-Jo,' Cassie suddenly said, looking out of the rainswept front window. 'Will you do something, please?'

'Sure,' Mary-Jo answered. 'Anything.'

'Your little cousin Jeannie. I don't think she ever made a costume for the competition. Do you think you could give her mine? Your mother knows where I put it.'

Mrs Christiansen looked round at Cassie and smiled.

'That's real nice of you, Cassie,' she said. 'I meant to help little Jeannie, but I guess I never had the time.'

'She should fit into it all right,' Cassie told them. 'We're both rather small.'

After that, nobody spoke much until they reached the station and had escorted Cassie on to the platform.

'If your grandmother isn't *that* ill,' Mary-Jo said to Cassie, 'why don't you come back tomorrow?'

'I don't think Grandmother would let me,' Cassie replied. 'I don't think she could afford it.'

'We'll pay for your ticket!' Mary-Jo exclaimed. 'Won't we, Mamma?'

'Let's just wait and see how Cassie's grandmother is, shall we, Mary-Jo?' Mrs Christiansen answered. 'One thing at a time, dear.'

Then she bent down and kissed Cassie, and pressed something into her hand. Cassie looked to see what it was. It was a folded ten-dollar bill. The train was whistling its approach to the station as Cassie looked back up at Mary-Jo's mother, who shrugged in reply.

'You never know when you might need it, honey,' she said, and then she opened a carriage door for Cassie and helped her up and into the train.

As the train approached Manchester Station, Cassie made one last effort to dry her eyes. She had managed not to cry until a good half an hour out of Locksfield, then she had quite suddenly and, to the old gentleman sitting beside her unaccountably, burst into tears. The old gentleman had tried to comfort her, but his kindness only made matters worse, so Cassie spent most of the rest of the long journey shut in the washroom.

Now just five minutes from Manchester, she was back in the washroom, soaking her swollen eyes in cold water. She dried her face and looked at herself in the mirror. She looked simply dreadful. But then if Grandmother was really that ill, she could always say she'd been crying because the thought of her illness had upset her. She brushed her hair and tidied her dress, and then let herself out to go and collect her luggage.

The station was very crowded and, being so small, Cassie found it difficult to see if Delta had arrived to collect her. When the crowd thinned, Cassie could see no sign of her anywhere. So she did as she always did when nobody was there to meet her from school, she waited by the bookstall.

After half an hour, Cassie began to worry, and wonder what she should do. Perhaps Grandmother had been taken to hospital. Worse, perhaps she had died? She got up from her suitcase, upon which she had been sitting, and determined to go to the Station Master's office. At that moment she saw a figure in black striding towards her and her heart stood still. Grandmother.

'Your train must have been early,' she said as she arrived by Cassie's side. 'Come along.'

Cassie picked up her case and followed behind her grandmother to the cab which was waiting outside. It was the same driver, who doffed his cap to Grandmother, then winked at Cassie as he opened the rear door.

They drove in silence all the way home, with Grandmother offering no explanation and Cassie not daring to ask. The silence was interrupted only once when the driver started to whistle. Grandmother soon put a stop to that.

It wasn't until Cassie had done her unpacking and had been allowed down for tea that she dared raise the subject.

'How are you, Grandmother?' she asked.

'Perfectly all right, thank you, child,' Grandmother replied. 'Why?'

Cassie frowned. She couldn't have dreamed the letter.

'Why?' she said. 'Because you wrote to me saying you were seriously ill, and that I must come home at once.'

'That was that foolish Dr Fossett,' her grandmother announced. 'All it was was a summer cold. Bronchitis indeed.'

Grandmother stirred her tea and looked challengingly at Cassie. But this time Cassie refused to look down. For what seemed like minutes they just stared at each other, until Grandmother cleared her throat and Cassie looked away.

The following Wednesday when Cassie was sent out in the rain to collect the mail, she found there was a letter for her from Locksfield, in Mary-Jo's handwriting. She stood wet through and shivering in the porch while she read it. The dance had been a great success, the best ever, but they all missed her dreadfully. George Baxter from the neighbouring farm had danced all evening with Mary-Jo, Frank had got slightly tiddly on the punch, and all four judges had chosen Cousin Jeannie as the Straw Man as the outright winner of the fancy dress competition. The prize for the competition had been Rainbow.

Cassie was now fourteen, and had been attending the convent for eight years. She now regarded it as her home, much more so than her grandmother's house in Westboro Falls. Grandmother's house wasn't even a second home. Mary-Jo Christiansen's huge and rambling farmstead in Pennsylvania was that. Cassie's visits had become a regular feature. Grandmother viewed these vacational visits with undisguised displeasure, but she continued to allow Cassie to visit Mary-Jo, partly because it meant that Grandmother could spend a lot more time on herself, but more importantly because it saved Grandmother a considerable amount of money – money she preferred to spend on herself. Even so, despite this apparent indulgence, Cassie looked on the house in Westboro Falls very much as third best.

Her grandmother was well aware, however, that Cassie was growing up, and that with the increased visits to her friend in Pennsylvania she was also growing away from her. On the long afternoons which she would often spend alone, Grandmother would brood upon the changes that were coming over Cassie, and weigh up the pros and cons of allowing the child so much time out of her own company. When she was home, Cassie would

91

sometimes notice her grandmother staring down at her along the dining table during those silent mealtimes, or in the evening over her sewing as Cassie sat reading. And when Cassie went to bed, and gave her grandmother a dutiful kiss on the cheek, Cassie would notice that Grandmother turned away from her with a visibly scornful expression on her face, as if that was the best Cassie could do.

Unfortunately it was. Cassie had tried very hard and dutifully to love her grandmother, but she had always found it difficult because her grandmother showed her absolutely no affection in return. Now Cassie was growing older, she was even more aware of the impossibility of loving someone who seemed quite openly to despise her. In order to compensate for the lack of love she felt in her heart, Cassie tried to do even better at school, in an effort to please Grandmother, and to behave even better at home in an effort not to aggravate her. She needn't have bothered, because she was a little girl with healthy, high spirits, and little girls with healthy high spirits were anathema to her grandmother.

Happily they weren't to Mrs Roebuck. The moment her grandchildren came to stay with her she was across the road to invite Cassie over. Gina was growing prettier and prettier each day and was the most beautiful thirteen-year-old at the convent, and certainly, when she came to stay, in their neighbourhood. Cassie and Maria were still her devoted attendants, ready to indulge Gina's every whim, happy to watch her trying on clothes or brushing her hair, or simply just gazing back at them gazing at her.

Grandmother naturally thoroughly disliked and disapproved of Mrs Roebuck's grandchildren. She considered quite publicly that Mrs Roebuck over-indulged them.

'Anyone would think no one had ever had grandchildren before,' she would complain to Cassie, 'the way that silly woman carries on.'

Cassie longed to beg to differ, but rather than incur the wrath of her, grandmother through the defence of her friends, she would instead try to change the subject, usually to little avail. For once embarked on a subject, Grandmother never liked to let go of it until she had, like a dog with a rabbit, shaken it to death. She would go on and on about Gina and Maria's failings and weaknesses, and Mrs Roebuck's ridiculously indulgent ways. And the more she talked the subject over, the more satisfying it would become to her, because she would discover new and more pervasively dangerous influences that she imagined Gina and Maria and Mrs Roebuck to have over Cassie. Nothing in Mrs Roebuck's house was free from Grandmother's criticism. Why, it was a wonder that Cassie wasn't dead from diphtheria, the way Mrs Roebuck allowed that dirty, filthy cat to sit upon her dresser.

And then there was the matter of grace before meals. It had come to her attention that Mrs Roebuck and her granddaughters, and Cassie herself, often sat down to table without saying grace. This, to Grandmother, was the thin end of a very thick wedge, an obvious precursor of a state of utter ungodliness. And wasn't Mrs Roebuck always encouraging the children to help themselves to seconds as well? Wasn't Greed one of the seven deadly sins? As for the unkempt state Cassie was in whenever she returned from her visits across the road . . . Little wonder, Grandmother told Cassie, that she was beginning to have serious doubts about such friendships.

'You're getting above yourself,' she would admonish Cassie. 'Always answering back or thinking you've the answer. Is that what those nuns teach you? To be smarter than your elders and betters?'

Cassie would remain silent during these interminable harangues, and switch her mind to the days spent riding and playing on Mary-Jo's farm.

'Listen when I'm talking to you, child!' Grandmother said sharply one evening when Cassie had returned from Mrs Roebuck's. 'I have to tell you, I don't like the sort of child you're turning into. No, I most certainly don't.'

Cassie at that moment was imagining trotting a pony called Paintbox up the track which led away from the farm, prior to breaking into her first canter of the day.

'You're learning more bad ways than good, I can tell you,' Grandmother continued. 'And I don't like it. Not one little bit. Which is the reason I've decided to do something about it.'

Cassie snapped out of her reverie. There was something very different in her grandmother's tone of voice that evening, something considerably more determined. She frowned and looked up.

'What do you mean?' she asked. 'What have you decided to do about it?'

'Don't ask so many questions, child,' Grandmother replied, rising from her chair and going to the door. 'You'll discover soon enough.'

She went out of the room, leaving Cassie to wonder what new punishment was going to be inflicted upon her, for doing absolutely nothing worse than just being alive. Was Grandmother going to ban her from seeing Maria and Gina? Was she going to curtail her visits to Mary-Jo? Or what? It had to be one of these two things, because there were no other areas of any happiness and pleasure in her life. What was it going to be?

Cassie agonised for the rest of the vacation, but the subject was never ever raised again. She was allowed to continue to play with Gina and Maria, and her visit to Mary-Jo in Locksfield, Pennsylvania remained on as scheduled.

It wasn't until Cassie returned to the convent that she discovered her grandmother's revenge.

It was Sister Joseph who broke the news. She stopped Cassie one morning at break and took her down the long polished corridor which led to her study. Cassie thought there was nothing unusual in this, since the nuns often took you aside to one of their studies to have what they

94

called a little talk. It was never a talking-to, whatever your offence: just a good, sensible talk, to thrash the matter out. So Cassie walked quite happily with a spotlessly clear conscience, in step behind her favourite nun; and once in Sister Joseph's study she sat happily in the chair the nun pulled up for her, the other side of the desk.

Then Cassie saw the letter, and recognised the spidery handwriting. She went completely cold and all the happy thoughts which were in her head vanished. She knew it was bad news, from the way the envelope was lying so neatly on Sister Joseph's desk, and from the way Sister Joseph was standing looking silently out of the window. If it had been good news, Sister Joseph would have given her the letter to read and sat smiling opposite her. But the letter lay there, while Sister Joseph stood at the window.

'For some reason your grandmother intends to take you away from us,' Sister Joseph finally said, very calmly and without a trace of emotion.

Cassie didn't move and she said nothing. She just continued to stare at the letter. Sister Josepth turned from the window and came and sat down not opposite Cassie, but beside her.

'She thinks a change will be beneficial,' Sister Joseph continued. 'She considers that you have got everything you are going to get from here, and so you will leave at the end of this term and start at a new school in the fall.'

It was as cut and dried as that. Sister Joseph didn't even show her the contents of the letter. She just related her grandmother's intentions, then fell silent.

Cassie's head started to throb violently. Moments went by as she struggled to control the throbbing and focus her attention on what was happening. But she couldn't. She felt as if she was going mad. She imagined she could hear time passing, the very sound of time, from the time before she heard what Sister Joseph had to say, to the time now, and the time after. She wanted to stop it – to hold time back with her hand and push it away from her. But she couldn't. Time was closing in a tidal wave over her head, half drowning her, before throwing her gasping on to the strand of the present.

And then there was Sister Joseph, sitting beside her, unmoving, head erect, hands clasped. Cassie had loved Sister Joseph with all her heart, but now she hated her, because she had just sat there and told her what the letter said and was doing nothing about it. She wasn't telling Grandmother what a wrong and terrible thing she was about to do. She was just sitting there, looking calmly at Cassie. She needn't have done this, Cassie thought. She could have written back to Grandmother and told her how wrong she was, and persuaded her to change her mind. But she hadn't. She had just accepted what Grandmother wanted to do, the way nuns always seemed to accept the terrible things which people did.

Cassie looked at Sister Joseph once more and realised that the nun wasn't just sitting there looking at her hands doing nothing, but that she was in fact telling her rosary.

'I'm praying that you'll come back, Cassie darling,' Sister Joseph said, with a smile. 'I'm praying that you'll come back here and visit us just whenever you wish.'

'It won't be the same,' Cassie replied. 'All my friends are here – everyone I've grown up with, everyone in my class and you. And all the other nuns. I don't have any other friends. All my friends are here, and they'll be staying here, and I won't be. I'll be gone. And soon we won't know each other any more.'

Cassie felt the tears coming, but fought them back.

'You can write, darling,' Sister Joseph said. 'And there's always the vacations for seeing your friends.'

Cassie looked at Sister Joseph, who now dropped her eyes, because she knew that what the young girl was saying was true. Soon they wouldn't know each other any more, vacations or no vacations. The child's grandmother was doing a quite unnecessarily cruel thing. But despite all Sister Joseph's written pleadings to try and get her to change her mind, this latest letter of her grandmother's had spelt the sentence out quite finally. Cassie was to leave them at the end of term.

The nun looked back up at Cassie and saw the change in the young girl's eyes. There was a look in them of open hostility and even bitterness. Sister Joseph had seen that look many times before. She recognised it as the look in a person's eyes when they have given up the struggle to believe that the world could be a kind and loving place.

'Perhaps you'd like to pray with me, Cassie,' Sister Joseph suggested.

'No thank you,' Cassie answered. 'There's no point.'

'Perhaps that's how it seems now,' said Sister Joseph. 'Now it must seem to you like the end of the world has come. But it hasn't, Cassie. This is just a separation, not a severance.'

She offered Cassie her hand but Cassie turned away from her. Sister Joseph remained silent, as she knew she must, respectful of the struggle the child was having to make sense of her feelings, and mindful of the pain she was suffering in her young heart.

Instead she stood up and straightened out her habit.

'I'm going to the church to pray for you now, Cassie,' she said. 'You don't have to come with me, but I'd be delighted if you did.'

Cassie sat unmoving, staring out of the window across the playing fields and into the woods.

Sister Joseph waited a moment then turned and went out. Cassie remained sitting where she was.

Now the time flew by. Just when Cassie didn't want it to, the rest of the term seemed to go at the speed of the express train she took every vacation down to Locksfield.

Cassie tried to come to terms with the change which lay ahead. But try as she might she couldn't. She just couldn't imagine her life without her friends, at a different school. A quite different school, according to her grandmother. It wasn't a convent for a start. It was an academy for well-brought-up young ladies of good families. Cassie couldn't think what it must be like to be at a school which wasn't a convent. It seemed to be so alien for children to be taught by people who hadn't dedicated their lives to God.

She tried convincing herself that it would be better, that it would be freer, and so more fun. She also tried to convince herself that her time at the convent hadn't been everything she'd made it out to be and that the nuns, kind though they were, weren't really *that* special, and that there was every chance life at this new school could well be a darn sight brighter and better. In fact, she thought as she walked the corridors by herself in the late afternoons, the convent was really quite shabby and uncomfortable, despite its highly polished wood floors and the shining taps in the bathrooms. It was cold and damp in the winter, and the nuns weren't *always* kind and smiling. They were often pretty cross with the children: why, only the other week Sister John had put three girls outside the classroom door to kneel in the corridor for ten minutes, and that sort of thing quite obviously wouldn't happen at an academy for the well-brought-up young ladies of good families.

But this self-inflicted brainwashing had no real effect on Cassie. It was a glorious summer, and the roses in the convent garden smelled sweeter than ever. Even though everyone knew she was leaving them, her friendships, instead of fading, deepened even more. Every night Cassie would sit on her bed in the blue-flower-papered bedroom she and Mary-Jo now shared together, watching the groups of elder girls sitting in circles talking on the grass below, while Mary-Jo sat in silence, braiding her long dark hair and winding it round and round her head into a crown. She knew at those moments that the thought of leaving the convent was unbearable.

She did find some comfort in the hatred she felt for her grandmother, but it was short-lived, because, as Sister Joseph told her one day during one of their many heart-to-heart talks, hatred never warmed a loving heart. And she soon grew tired of trying to hate someone for whom she felt little more than duty anyway.

She was still going to be able to go and stay with Mary-Jo that vacation, even though she suspected that it would probably be the last time she would be allowed the privilege. Mary-Jo and she would spend every evening as the end of term approached discussing plans for the vacation: who was going to be there and what horses they were going to ride. And of course they talked endlessly about Mary-Jo's wonderful mother, and every time they did they sighed and their faces softened at the mention of her name.

'When I grow up, I want to be someone like your mother,' Cassie told Mary-Jo one midnight, as they lay whispering. 'But I don't suppose I ever will be. Not now I'm leaving here.'

They lay in their beds, silent at the thought of how different both their next terms were going to be. Mary-Jo knew how much she would miss her friend, and how her life would never again be the same. And Cassie knew how lonely and angry she would be at her new school, alone without her friends, and angry at the injustice which had been done to her.

'I wonder what my mother was *really* like?' Cassie suddenly whispered, although this was something the two girls wondered quite regularly, at least twice a week.

'I think she *must* have been dark like you, Cassie,' Mary-Jo said.

'She could have been red-haired like Grandmother,' Cassie replied.

'If she had been,' Mary-Jo countered, 'you'd have had the same sort of skin and eyes as your grandmother. White skin and small grey eyes.'

'I hope you're right,' said Cassie. 'I couldn't *bear* it if she'd been like Grandmother. If she'd been like Grandmother, I'd have hated her!'

'If she had, Cassie,' Mary-Jo whispered back, 'which

she obviously wasn't, it wouldn't have been your mother's fault. After all, your grandmother was her mother.'

Cassie lay staring out through the crack in the curtains at the night sky and gave this some thought. She had never really thought of her mother like that before, as the child of her grandmother – possibly because she could never have tolerated the thought: it would have clouded the vision Cassie had always had of the mother she had never known.

'I wonder if she loved me?' Cassie thought out loud.

'Of course she loved you,' Mary-Jo replied. 'Every mother loves her baby.'

'Do you really think so?' asked Cassie, looking across at Mary-Jo.

'Of course, silly,' Mary-Jo replied.

Cassie reached across the gap between their beds and took Mary-Jo's hands.

'We will always be friends, won't we?' she said.

'Always,' said Mary-Jo. 'We'll always love each other, always and forever.'

Cassie let go of her hand and pulled the sheet up under her chin. She stared hard at the ceiling, then closed her eyes tightly, hoping that sleep would come. But it didn't. Instead, tears rolled down her cheeks, warm, soft, satisfying tears; tears that were for herself and no one else.

Chapter Five

They gave her holy pictures. A holy picture was the largest gift one child was allowed to bestow upon another. Cassie put them all in her missal, where she would keep them for all her life. Whenever and wherever she opened the book, they would always bring memories of those shiningly happy days: days spent playing in 'paradise' woods, holding hands and jumping up and down on the lines cheering their teams, slip-sliding their shoes down the immaculately shining floors, jumping in and out of low windows on to newly mown lawns, painting pictures on rough grey paper and learning to dance waltzes to their precious collection of shiny black gramophone records.

The pictures were all placed lovingly at Cassie's place at breakfast on the last morning of term. Cassie read them all one by one and thanked every girl individually. She wanted to hug them all and kiss them, but she knew it wasn't necessary. She knew they loved her from the presents they had given her, just as they knew Cassie loved them by her smiling thanks.

They all knew also somewhere in their hearts, whatever age they were, that something was going to happen to them all, as it was now happening to Cassie. That life would change them, and none of them would remain the same; and that they would go their separate ways, until the chance moment they met in a street, or a shop, or in a friend's house. Then as they remembered each other any tiredness, or tedium, boredom, restlessness or disappointment they were feeling would vanish, and they would be young again, and children; they would once more be standing on the threshold between youth and childhood, and the blessed plot where the flowers of their childhood had been sown would once more be in bloom.

Cassie was to leave at the same time as everyone else, and it had been arranged that Mrs Roebuck would bring her home with Gina and Maria. But Grandmother changed her mind and sent a cab, early, instead, before anyone else had left. There was no explanation, since the driver turned up alone. Sister John summoned Cassie, who was just finishing her packing, and she went downstairs while the other girls were still busy running up and down the polished wooden corridors, shouting in excitement as they cemented their vacation plans and collected almost forgotten articles of clothing. Cassie paused at the bottom of the stairs wondering whether or not to call a last goodbye, but with the din coming down from above there seemed little point.

Sister John saw her to the door and out to the waiting cab. The driver took her case and put it in the trunk. Sister John squeezed her hand and Cassie thought she saw tears in her eyes. Then she shut the door on Cassie and the cab driver started the engine.

As the cab moved away, Cassie looked back through the rear window. Sister John had gone back inside. There was no one to wave to. Then halfway down the drive the cab driver looked in his driving mirror and stopped. He turned in his seat and grinned at Cassie, nodding his capped head back at the convent. Cassie turned round again, a frown on her face. At every upstairs window there were children waving. Cassie got out of the car and for a moment stood there, watching. It seemed as if the convent was a sea of waving white handkerchieves. Cassie pulled her own handkerchief from her pocket and waved back. Then as suddenly as it had started, it stopped and the children remained at the windows, silent and still, as Cassie got back into the cab.

The driver restarted the engine and drove off down the driveway. Cassie stared ahead. There was nothing else she could do.

Chapter Six

Miss Truefitt's Academy for Young Ladies,
Glenville, West Virginia

Leonora Von Wagner sat on the front of Miss Truefitt's desk, chewing gum and swinging her long, shapely legs. The other girls in the classroom were all watching her, silent except for the occasional unsuppressed giggle.

'As a result of the voting,' Leonora announced, 'Cassie McGann is once again voted the most unpopular girl in the class of '52.'

Every girl turned in Cassie's direction and grinned. Cassie was sitting in a corner at the back of the room, paying no attention to Leonora Von Wagner's baiting. Instead she was busy reading a book about the breeding of horses that Mary-Jo's mother had given to her at the end of her last vacation in Locksfield.

'Pay attention, Paddy McGann!' Leonora called.

Cassie ignored her.

'Whether you look up or not,' Leonora continued, 'makes little difference. I shall still pass sentence.'

Cassie turned over a page in her book and continued reading.

'Since Cassie Paddy McGann has been voted yet again the most unpopular girl in the class, she will not be spoken to by *anyone* until someone else is voted more unpopular than her.'

Leonora jumped down off the desk and pulled the chewing gum out of her mouth, tossing back her long blonde hair.

'And frankly,' she said, coming to where Cassie was sitting reading and slamming her book closed in front of her, 'the way things have been going, I see little chance of *that* happening.'

She stared down spitefully at Cassie. Cassie regarded her steadily, with complete disdain, then reopened her book and went on reading. Leonora snatched the book away and for one dreadful moment Cassie thought she was going to tear some pages out, or pour ink over it, like she had done with her book of the lives of the saints. But someone gave warning of Miss Truefitt's imminent approach, and Cassie took the chance while Leonora was off guard to snatch her book.

Leonora bent right down, level with Cassie's face, and hissed at her.

'I'll get you, Paddy,' she seethed, 'don't worry.'

Then she hurried back to her place.

Miss Truefitt came in, immaculate from head to toe as always, and the girls obediently rose to their feet.

'Good morning, young ladies,' she said.

'Good morning, Miss Truefitt!' the girls carolled back.

'I don't think we saw you say good morning, Cassie McGann,' Miss Truefitt called to Cassie, who had been the last to her feet. 'Good morning.'

'Good morning, Miss Truefitt,' Cassie answered, as flat and as dead as she could. 'Again.'

Miss Truefitt sighed and stared at the truculent youngster, before ordering the class, with the exception of Cassie, to be reseated.

'I know you're new here, Cassie,' Miss Truefitt told her, 'but it's no excuse for bad behaviour. You must follow the example of your classmates.' The headmistress smiled warmly at the rest of the class.

'That's what I'm trying to do,' Cassie replied.

Miss Truefitt frowned at her.

'I don't understand, I'm afraid.'

'I'm doing my very best, Miss Truefitt,' Cassie said, 'to behave exactly like the rest of my classmates.'

Cassie regarded Miss Truefitt evenly. As far as they were both concerned it had been hate at first sight. Cassie

McGann was precisely the sort of girl Miss Truefitt had always endeavoured to keep out of the Academy, a Catholic girl with a distinctly Irish-sounding name. But her grandmother had apparently impeccable connections, a lineage which could be traced back to old English stock, and an extremely generous hand when it came to writing a cheque towards the new library fund. So, much against Miss Truefitt's better judgement, she had accepted the McGann girl, considering that one swallow did not always make a summer.

The rest of the class, like the rest of the Academy, were angels. Miss Truefitt was especially fond of Leonora Von Wagner, whom she regarded as a particularly good influence on the rest of her young ladies. The fact that she was the only child of one of the richest men in America was neither here nor there. Leonora Von Wagner was a model pupil.

With this thought in her head she smiled at Leonora, who dimpled and smiled demurely back, all the time pinching as hard as she could the ample thigh of the girl sitting next to her.

'Good,' said Miss Truefitt, running her hand down one of her own soft cheeks. 'So today is poetry-reading day. If you recall, I asked you all to choose a favourite piece of verse and to prepare it for reading out loud to me. Since, Cassie, you are still on your feet, you may commence proceedings.'

Cassie picked up her book of verse and turned to a poem.

'What have you selected to read, please Cassie?' Miss Truefitt asked her.

'A poem by Walt Whitman,' Cassie answered, and then began to read with quite astonishing authority and conviction.

Come lovely and soothing death,
Undulate round the world, serenely arriving, arriving,
In the day, in the night, to all, to each,

Sooner or later, delicate death.
Prais'd be the fathomless universe,
For life, and joy, and for objects and knowledge
    curious,
And for love – sweet love – but praise! Praise! Praise!
For the sure-endwinding arms of cool-enfolding
    death.

There was complete silence, as all the class and the Headmistress stared at the defiant-faced Cassie.

Cassie stared evenly back at them all.

'Thank you, Cassie,' Miss Truefitt managed finally. 'Thank you. That was very . . . very interesting.'

Cassie sat back down and closed her book.

'Leonora?' Miss Truefitt said, and Cassie at once shut herself off from the rest of the class, and Leonora Von Wagner in particular.

For it was all Leonora's doing that she kept being voted the most unpopular girl in the class. Not that the other girls were much better, but Leonora Von Wagner was the worst of them all. She had picked on Cassie the moment Cassie had arrived on that miserable first day, and she hadn't let up since, over two months later. She had persecuted her so much that Cassie hadn't even had the chance to try to make any friends at all so she decided instead, to retreat into herself, and not bother with anyone. Mary-Jo still wrote to her twice a week, as did Cassie to her. Several times Leonora had stolen her letters from Mary-Jo and read them out to the class, mocking their friendship and the fact that Mary-Jo lived on a farm. Cassie had wanted to kill her at those moments, but decided instead that she would just hide her pain and anguish behind an expressionless mask. And wait for the moment when she could get her revenge on this stuck-up and spoilt little rich kid.

Cassie had hated the school from the moment she arrived. It made no difference to her that the rules were more relaxed and the girls were allowed much more time to themselves. It was a well of loneliness and unhappiness for Cassie, full of spoilt girls whose young lives were already dominated by social competitiveness. All they talked about was who they had been to stay with, which parties they had been to, which parties their parents had been to, where they were going on vacation or what new sort of car their fathers had just bought. Cassie had no desire to be in a social register, whatever that may be, and cared even less for the fact that, as Leonora kept telling her, there was little chance of her ever being in one.

One thing which made life easier for her was that, unlike the convent, she could do what she liked when she liked. So in order to help her endure the silence in which she was forced to live, Cassie started to read voraciously. But the subject matter was always the same: horses. She read and reread her book about breeding until she practically knew it by heart, and then she went systematically through the Academy library finding and reading every book which had anything remotely to do with *Equuo Caballus*. She learned about the points of the horse and its conformation. While other girls sighed over *Harpers* and *Vogue*, Cassie was reading up about stable management and stud care. And while her classmates discussed who and where they were going to get married, Cassie was making imaginary plans for the breeding of her first brood mare.

Without the loving friendship of her contemporaries at the convent, Cassie had to find an emotional substitute to carry her through these difficult times; and she found this in her growing determination to succeed. Once she set herself things to achieve, her isolation became less unendurable and, with no one speaking to her, she began to live more and more in her head, planning for the future, which had to hold more in store for her than the loneliness and utter misery of the present.

Cassie also decided that when she was grown up she was going to be rich. Grandmother may have determined to send her to a school which was intended to be a step up the social ladder, but without the enormous allowances the other girls enjoyed there was simply no way Cassie could hope to enter their world, even if and when they finally chose to speak to her. Whenever there was something extra planned at the Academy – an outing to a museum or a visit to the theatre – Cassie, because of her straitened circumstances, was forced to miss out, and so became the butt of a new set of jokes, based this time round on her poverty.

There was another way she could succeed at the Academy, however, a way which did not require considerable financial backing; she could become good at sport. She had always enjoyed games at the convent particularly tennis. But now she was determined not just to become better, but to become the best. Every morning, whatever the weather, she would get up an hour before anyone else and run two miles round the athletic track. Being small and not naturally athletic, Cassie knew that the only way she could beat the more gifted girls was by being fitter than them. So she worked out a fitness programme from books she read in the library, and from an instructional pamphlet for Air Force pilots which the gym instructor gave her. Her rivals all came from homes that employed private coaches for tennis, swimming and golf, but since these rich children had everything they wanted, none of them had the burning desire Cassie had to succeed. None of them had what the gym instructor used to call 'the killer streak'.

Cassie did. She would work with the dumb-bells in the gym until her sweat blinded her and climb the ropes until the insides of her thighs and hands were red raw. After her early morning run, she would swim fifty lengths of the full-size swimming pool, and then do a full half-hour of isometric exercises. Then in the afternoons, when the privately coached girls used to show off their tennis on the plentiful courts, Cassie would to all intents and purposes idly watch them, as if in admiration, but in reality

109

to note the fine detail of every properly coached overhead smash, or spun second service. Then she would go away and practise in private what she learned, working on low backhand volleys or passing shots down the line.

No one knew what she was up to, of course, since no one, except for the gym instructor, was the slightest bit interested in the silently defiant Cassie, whom Leonora had rechristened Little Orphan Annie. The gym instructor however, a retired marine called Burt Linowitz, understood Cassie's determination and ambitions without her ever telling him why. He grew both to like and really admire this young girl, for her spirit and her dedication. He saw she was blessed with neither a singular ability nor an outstanding physique, but under his private tutelage, harnessed to Cassie's fierce determination, she was developing into a highly competent all-round athlete.

He drove her hard, too – harder than he drove any of the other kids under his care. But this was because Cassie had requested him to do so, and sometimes after a particularly gruelling session on the wall bars, or the rings, Cassie would sit in the locker room, her face streaming with sweat, on the verge of giving up. Then she would catch sight of Leonora's self-satisfied face at breakfast, as she sat and held court, and every aching muscle and moment of utter exhaustion became one hundred and one per cent worthwhile.

'Oh my God, have you all heard who's in the basketball team?' Leonora asked the class one day. 'Little Orphan Annie McGann! The Academy must be *really* desperate if they're taking Irish!'

Cassie ignored the taunt and turned to a fresh chapter in her book on the thoroughbred.

'That's what my father always says, anyway,' Leonora continued. 'That's what he says about country clubs. They must be *really* desperate if they're taking Irish.'

It was Friday, the day Leonora always got sent a box of handmade chocolates from her grandfather. She bit into one, looked at what was in the centre, dropped it distastefully into the waste basket, then tried another one. Satisfied, next she handed the box round to the rest of the class, like she always did, until she stopped in front of Cassie, who was seated quietly in the corner, her head over her book. Leonora picked out the very worst chocolate and dropped it on the floor in front of Cassie. This, too, was part of the weekly ritual.

'Come on, Dobbin,' Leonora said. 'Eat up your treat.'

Cassie ignored her, as she did each Friday, and continued to read. The class laughed dutifully at Leonora's antics, and then again when Leonora whinnied in front of Cassie. But somehow the fun was going out of Leonora's constant persecution of the silent Cassie; most likely because Cassie refused to rise, always managing instead to maintain a dignified silence.

The girls all trooped out behind Leonora when she decided it was time to go and listen once again to her latest Frank Sinatra record. Cassie didn't look up until they had all left the room. Then she stared at the door, long after they had all left. Her moment would come. It was just a question of when.

By the beginning of her second summer at Miss Truefitt's Academy, Cassie was in a team for every sport except tennis. Not only that, she was the best athlete in whatever team she was in. Leonora, however, eschewed team games, considering them vulgar. She only bothered with tennis, which was the reason Cassie had never tried her own game in public. Leonora won at tennis whenever she played. She found the game singularly easy, having a natural talent for it. She was so superior to all her contemporaries that even in her competitive matches, she was hardly ever stretched. Her name was already engraved three times on the Academy Challenge cup and she was being talked of as a future American amateur champion.

In that second summer term, having practised her

game constantly in camera, but having played endless tough and no-quarter-asked-or-given games against Mary-Jo's older brother Frank whenever she had been down to Locksfield to stay, Cassie was ready to throw down the gauntlet. She had to be quite sure in her mind that when she made her move against Leonora not only that there was no chance of Leonora beating her, but also that Cassie would be assured of humiliating her and making Leonora the laughing stock of all her friends. Cassie was not going to play her until she knew Leonora would not be capable of taking one game, or even a single point off her.

Leonora smiled when she saw Cassie McGann's name entered in the competition for the Challenge cup. Cassie was drawn in the first round against Alice Williams, who was capable of beating everyone on a good day, except – naturally – Leonora herself. Leonora didn't, however, smile the next day when she saw that Alice was out of the competition in the first round, beaten 6–4, 9–7. Leonora tossed her blonde hair back petulantly and went in search of Alice, to find the reason for her shock defeat. But there was none – according to Alice, who was still in a state of shock: Cassie McGann had beaten her fair and square.

Not according to Cassie, however, who was only coasting. She could have beaten Alice to love, if she'd slipped up a gear. But she wanted Leonora to think it was a fluke, and that Alice Williams must have had an off-day. In the next round she played deliberately clumsily against the tall and powerful Lauren Benchley, apparently just scraping home with a few lucky passing shots 4–6, 8–6, 7–5. And then in the semi-final she sailed almost too close to the wind, having to go to 10–8 against Helena Franklyn in the third and final set, a game which Cassie knew she could have won as she liked in straight sets.

But it had the required effect. In the final, Leonora was a sure thing to beat Little Orphan Annie, whom everyone, thanks to Leonora's propaganda, considered to have had the easier passage through the competition. Cassie walked on to the court first, dressed in her old convent shorts and short-sleeved white tennis shirt. Leonora came on as if she was already playing in the final at Forest Hills. She had acquired a brand new tennis skirt, shirt, racquet and eye-shadow for the final, and her mother and other relatives had turned up in force to watch the walk-over. Everyone was there, in fact: the entire Academy and most of the pupils' parents. Leonora's sycophants cheered and clapped their heroine as she and Cassie knocked up. From the nervous way Cassie was knocking the ball back, either long, or usually netting it, the result was to all intents and purposes a foregone conclusion.

Then the umpire called for play, and Cassie made the sign of the cross with her Slazenger tennis racquet, which Burt Linowitz had lent her specially for the competition. The crowd settled in silence, expecting a one-sided contest.

They were not disappointed. The first ball served was an ace, which kicked up the paint down the centre line. The only difference was that it was Cassie McGann who served it. Leonora stared at her across the net and moved to the left-hand court. The next service kicked the paint up in the corner of the box, sizzling past Leonora's blonde head and crashing into the back netting. The crowd gasped, and Leonora threw her racquet on the ground and looked up at the umpire.

'That ball was out!' she announced.

'The ball was in,' the umpire replied. 'Thirty love.'

'It was out I tell you!' Leonora screamed. 'It was out by miles!'

'Thirty love,' the umpire insisted and ordered Leonora to take up her new position.

Cassie faulted her next service and carefully cut her second short of the line. Leonora ran on to it and hit a forehand hard at her opponent's face. Cassie just got her racket up to it, putting it back up to Leonora's overhand.

113

Leonora smashed it to Cassie's left, but Cassie, covering the ground at three times Leonora's speed, reached it easily and jinked it back high over Leonora's head. Leonora ran round and only just reached it, putting up a weak return for which Cassie was at the net waiting. Cassie reached up with all the time in the world and smashed it back so hard that the ball bounced high off the grass and out of the court altogether.

It was the only closely contested point of the whole match. Afterwards, all Cassie could remember was the extraordinary feeling of calm which came over her as the match progressed and as she watched Leonora start to sweat. Cassie gave her no chance. She passed her on both sides, she lobbed her, she aced her. She drew her to the net, then drilled her returns past her down the line. She forced her to the back of the court, then dropped her return shots tantalisingly just over the net. In her desperate attempts to reach most of Cassie's shots, Leonora fell over constantly. Her brand new tennis outfit quickly became stained with grass and sweat, and her blonde hair fell free of its restraining ribbons, plastering itself to Leonora's shining red face. Leonora questioned every call, until she realised from the silence of the crowd that she had long since lost any support, and that for the first time in her spoilt life, she was being utterly and completely thrashed. The final game was yet another game to love, and Cassie walked off the court, as composed as she had been when she first walked on to it, the victor at 6–0,6–0.

Miss Truefitt managed a polite little smile for Cassie as she awarded her the cup, but Burt Linowitz grabbed her arm and squeezed it tight as Cassie made her way through the crowds.

'Well done, kid,' he said. 'Well done. One for the little folk.'

Cassie grinned and handed him back his racquet.

'You crazy?' Burt replied. 'I don't need that dam' thing no more! You keep it! You know what it's for!'

Cassie twirled the racquet, then put it back in its press. She picked up her bag and made her way back to the locker room. One or two of the girls, members of some of the teams Cassie had played in, came up to her and rather shyly congratulated her, almost as if they were afraid that Cassie wouldn't speak to them. Cassie thanked them politely, and when the other girls saw that Cassie wasn't tearing everyone else's hair out, they all swarmed up to her and mobbed her. Cassie accepted all their changes of heart with the due grace she had been taught by the nuns and was escorted all the way back to the school buildings by her new friends. Cassie didn't look back in triumph. But in her mind's eye she could still see Leonora, sitting crying and dishevelled and soaking in sweat, being coldly grilled on her failure by her furious mother.

Cassie paid off the cab, then got out and looked up at Grandmother's front door. It had just been repainted, and the nets hanging at the windows were freshly washed and laundered. To any other child, it would look like the ideal home to return to after the long summer term. But to Cassie, who knew it, and hated it, it looked unwelcoming. It also, at this moment in her life, looked smaller, and far less imposing.

Cassie was growing up fast now. She was no longer the smallest girl in her class and, thanks no doubt to her obsessive period of training, she was very fit and strong. So when her grandmother opened the door, it came as a surprise to Cassie, who had not seen her all term, to see just how little she was. She was, however, just as unwelcoming as ever, and just as singularly uninterested in how Cassie had done at school.

So Cassie was glad she had chosen to leave the tennis Challenge cup behind in the Academy trophy cupboard. That way it could remain an untarnished triumph. Grandmother would only diminish her victory by some deliberately squashing remark; or would consider that

115

the trophy won by sweat and blood and determination was either a little on the vulgar side, or conversely not extravagant enough. She would also think little of Cassie's achievement, since to Grandmother, sport was of no consequence.

But the next morning, when Cassie came down a little late for breakfast having overslept, instead of finding her grandmother cross with her, she found her smiling broadly.

Cassie sat at table, more than a little apprehensive. When her grandmother smiled, it always heralded bad news. And to Cassie's mind, that morning's announcement was no exception.

'A girl called Leonora Von Wagner telephoned you, Cassie,' Grandmother told her.

Cassie at once felt uncomfortable, as she always did when on the few occasions her grandmother addressed her by her actual name.

'I said you were sleeping in,' Grandmother continued, 'and that you would call her back later.'

Cassie started to eat her cereal, wondering why on earth Leonora of all people should choose to telephone her.

'You never mentioned that there was a Von Wagner at the Academy,' her grandmother said, for once unaccusingly. 'Particularly one of the Philadelphia Von Wagners. They're an extremely distinguished family, you know.'

Cassie said nothing, but just finished her cereal and helped herself to some toast.

'Nor did you say that their daughter was a friend of yours.'

'She isn't,' Cassie replied simply.

Her grandmother ignored Cassie's contradiction as she shook out her linen napkin.

'Of course I knew the Academy would prove a step up for you,' she went on, 'which was why I chose to further your education there and take you away from that backwater of a convent. I knew the Academy would be a step up.'

Cassie finished the rest of her breakfast in silence, blocking out her grandmother's litany about how wonderful Leonora's family was and what a feather it was in Cassie's social cap for her to be befriended by the daughter of such rich and important people.

'May I get down please, Grandmother?' she asked.

'Why of course you may, Cassie,' her grandmother smiled. 'Off you go and ring your friend Leonora.'

Cassie left the room, without telling her grandmother that she had absolutely no intention of calling Leonora back. She went up to her room, and sat down instead to write to Mary-Jo.

'And what did your friend Leonora Von Wagner have to say, Cassie?' Grandmother asked her at teatime, which was the next time they met.

'I don't know,' Cassie replied, truthful as ever. 'Because I didn't call her back.'

'Why ever not, child?' queried her grandmother.

'I told you, Grandmother,' Cassie said. 'Because I don't like her.'

There was a short silence while Grandmother digested this information, but then instead of arguing with Cassie, she got up and left the room. For one brief moment, Cassie hoped that would be an end to the matter. But that hope was soon dashed as she heard her grandmother talking into the telephone in the hall. She was ringing the Von Wagner household personally.

Once again Cassie felt trapped by her childhood. The terrible thing about being a child, she had discovered, was that you were so dependent on other people. On grown ups; particularly in Cassie's case on Grandmother. She couldn't go anywhere or do anything without adult permission. And now Grandmother was out there in the hall making arrangements for Cassie to go and stay with Leonora Von Wagner, without even consulting her. And she, Cassie, was quite powerless to prevent it.

Grandmother came back into the room, a smile on her face, and sat down to pour herself some more tea.

'I explained that you had a slight sore throat,' she said, 'which was why you hadn't called back.'

'But that's a lie, Grandmother,' Cassie protested. 'I didn't call back—'

'That's quite enough, child!' her grandmother interrupted. 'You're not at an age when you know what's good for you.'

Her tone of voice changed, into something more silky, as she went on to explain the nature of Leonora's request.

'They want you to go and stay with them,' Grandmother told the silent Cassie. 'At least your friend Leonora does. I spoke to her. Such a nice girl. So refined.'

She hadn't been so refined when she was pouring ink over Cassie's classwork, Cassie thought. Or helping to hold Cassie's head down a lavatory pan while the rest of her court flushed it.

'They have a summer residence on Long Island,' Grandmother continued, 'and you're to go stay there next week.'

'I'm going to Mary-Jo's next week!' Cassie replied, rising to her feet.

'Don't you use that tone of voice with me, child!' Grandmother warned her. 'Or you won't be going anywhere! You can go to Mary-Jo's any time. But it's not every day you get asked somewhere like the Von Wagners'.

'I don't like Leonora Von Wagner, Grandmother!' Cassie pleaded. 'She's the most horrible bully! And she's stuck-up!'

Grandmother sighed and smoothed down her skirt.

'You really have to get rid of this quite dreadful social inferiority of yours, child. You only feel like that because you're not secure among people like the Von Wagners. That is why I insist that you go and stay with them.'

118

Cassie stood behind her chair and eyed her grandmother venomously. She was being sent to stay with Leonora as a step up a ladder, a ladder up which she had absolutely no desire to climb.

'I won't go,' she said, as bravely as she could muster.

'I think you will, child,' her grandmother replied. 'Because if you cause me any further displeasure, I shall simply never let you go and stay with Mary-Jo Christiansen ever again.'

Cassie lay in bed that night, clasping the ten-dollar bill Mary-Jo's mother had given her. Perhaps this was one of the times Mrs Christiansen had meant when she said Cassie never knew when she might need it. She could run away the next day, and catch the train to Locksfield with the ten dollars. But as she tossed and turned in her bed, wondering what to do, she knew in her heart that it would be but a short reprieve, because sooner or later she would be sent back to Grandmother, whether or not she had temporarily escaped from staying with the dreadful Leonora.

And so she duly capitulated, as she knew all children must do, when the adult world insists that they do something against their will. What was even worse and more despicable was that her grandmother took her on a shopping spree in Manchester, where she bought her six brand-new outfits for her forthcoming visit to the Von Wagners. Cassie found she wasn't in the least bit grateful for the expensive new clothes, paid for out of her grandmother's 'savings', since whenever she had asked her in the past for a pair of second-hand jeans or a cheap check shirt of her own to wear at Mary-Jo's, her appeals had always fallen on deaf ears. Yet because she was to stay with the Von Wagners, everything now had to be perfect.

Even worse, Leonora kept telephoning Cassie and gushing down the phone with excitement about her forthcoming visit. Her grandmother would stand by Cassie during their conversations, listening on the other

119

earpiece. Leonora would explain all about the house, with its twelve-automobile garage, its two swimming pools, its housekeeper's and chauffeur's cottages, and even its own ballroom with a marble staircase. If this was their summer house, Cassie wondered privately, what then was their normal residence like?

But Grandmother was visibly impressed and her smile would widen the more Leonora boasted of the Long Island house. And whenever she wasn't on the telephone to Leonora, her grandmother would rehearse Cassie through the required social niceties. But while Cassie complied, and learned what was expected of her, her heart was rebellious when she thought of the weeks she would be missing with Mary-Jo and her family in Pennsylvania.

Grandmother took the cab with her to the station to see her off to Leonora's. She had overdressed Cassie as usual, and even before the train drew out of the station, Cassie felt hot and stuffy. But her grandmother insisted she kept both her gloves and her coat on, because that was how people like the Von Wagners expected their guests to dress. As the train sped through Massachusetts, Cassie wondered, as she had so often wondered since that first fateful telephone call, why Leonora was so insistent that Cassie should come to stay with her. After all she now had as much reason to hate Cassie the way Cassie had so deeply hated her. She thought of every reason she could, but it never for one moment occurred to her young and open mind that the reason Leonora wanted Cassie to come and stay with her was because she was bored.

She changed trains at Grand Central with the help of a family who got talking to Cassie on the way through Connecticut, and who were also travelling on to Long Island. They were people very like the Christiansens, who lived on a large farm outside Hartford. There were three sisters, all with braces on their teeth, and one brother, who was bespectacled and very earnest. The father and mother spent the whole time laughing and joking both with their own children and with Cassie. When she had to bid them farewell at the end of their journey, Cassie stood for a moment on the station platform and longed even more for the chance to be a member of such a family.

A quite different child was waiting for her outside the station in the languid shape of Leonora Von Wagner. The first sight Cassie had of her was two long blonde legs draped out of the back window of a Rolls Royce, as Leonora lay on the back seat trying to catch the sun. The chauffeur put Cassie's bags in the trunk as Leonora waggled a foot at her.

'Hi!' she called from inside the car. 'Get in the front, will you? I'm trying to get my legs brown!'

Cassie did as she was told and got in beside the chauffeur, who started the car and drove them away from the station. The engine was so quiet at first that Cassie thought they must be coasting, until the chauffeur explained that the only sound you could hear in a Rolls Royce, besides Miss Von Wagner chewing gum, was the sound of the clock.

'Come on!' Leonora ordered Cassie. 'You can climb in the back now! I'm bored sunning my legs!'

Cassie asked the chauffeur if it was all right to climb over the seats, at which Leonora roared loudly with laughter. The chauffeur just smiled and glanced at Leonora in his mirror, but even so Cassie undid her shoes and removed them before climbing in the back.

Leonora also made her remove her coat and jacket and roll up the sleeves of her blouse.

'Christ – you must be boiled in all that!' she exclaimed, undoing another piece of gum. 'Jesus.'

Cassie bit her lip at Leonora's swearing, but even so did as she was told, because she was far, far too hot, even though all the windows of the car were down.

'Our other Rolls has air-conditioning,' Leonora

explained. 'But it's in the garage at the moment, being overhauled.'

Leonora sighed and pulled the pair of sunglasses she was wearing on top of her head down over her eyes. Then she stuck her legs out of the window again and blew bubbles with her gum.

Cassie watched the unfamiliar landscape of New York city flash by, before the Rolls joined the other traffic headed east on the turnpike. Leonora said nothing at all to Cassie for fully half an hour, until she suddenly turned and grinned at her.

'Did you bring me any chocolates?' she asked.

'I thought we'd share a room,' Leonora announced casually as they climbed up one side of the double staircase which swept up from the marble hall below. Behind them, two maids carried Cassie's luggage, one bag each.

'I hope you don't mind,' Leonora continued. 'But it being a strange house and rather large, I thought you might be lonely.'

She turned to Cassie for a moment, and popped another bubble with her gum. Then she shrugged and ran ahead of Cassie up the last of the stairs. But Cassie had seen in that one moment as Leonora had turned to her who the lonely person was, and why there was a need for Cassie to share her room. In fact she was beginning to see a similarity between Leonora and herself. For although the house was even more impressive than the way Leonora had casually described it on the telephone, it was as soulless a place as Grandmother's modest house was back in Westboro Falls; and both of them lived with grandparents. Leonora not all the time, because at least her mother was alive, but she was rarely home, because since her divorce, Leonora explained as she lay on her satin-quilted bed, she spent most of her time in Europe. In fact her visit to see the tennis competition had been the first time Leonora had seen her mother since Christmas.

Cassie listened as she started to unpack her case.

122

'Christ – what are you doing?' Leonora shrieked. 'Don't do that for Christ's sake! What do you think we have maids for?'

Cassie stopped her unpacking and looked over her suitcase.

'Do you have to say Christ all the time?' she asked. 'I'm sure you think it's awful grown up. But it isn't.'

And with that she continued to unpack. Leonora stared at her. No one had ever told her what not to do before. She blew the largest bubble she could with her gum, then got up and tipped the contents of Cassie's case on the floor.

'I said the maids will do that,' she announced. 'Come on, let's go have a swim.'

She got hold of Cassie's arm and started to drag her to the door. Cassie wrenched her arm free with ease.

'When I've finished my unpacking,' Cassie replied, and returned to where Leonora had spilt all her clothes on the floor.

Leonora watched her and sighed, loudly.

'It'll be quicker if you help me,' Cassie said.

Leonora stood leaning against the door and blew another gum bubble. Cassie looked up at her.

'I said we'll swim quicker if you come and help me.'

Leonora looked back at her, but Cassie could not only beat her hands down at tennis: she could also outstare her. Leonora clicked her tongue, and then went over to help clear up the mess she'd created.

'Let's annoy the maids,' Leonora suddenly announced, breaking off from the slow foxtrot she and Cassie were dancing to the latest Pat Boone record. 'Come on.'

She started to go out of the play-room, but Cassie held back, ostensibly to turn off the radiogram, but in reality to try and deter Leonora from making mischief. Cassie knew from the expression on her face that Leonora was up to no good. She'd seen that expression so many countless times before at the Academy.

'You still haven't shown me the horses,' she said hopefully.

'You can see the damn old horses any time,' Leonora retorted. 'I want to go and annoy the maids.'

She ran out of the room and Cassie heard her running and sliding across the hall. Reluctantly she followed, with little hope of diverting the headstrong Leonora. By the time Cassie reached Leonora and her shared bedroom, Leonora was sitting at her dressing table, smearing on a huge lipsticked mouth. She handed Cassie another lipstick and ordered her to follow suit, but Cassie just ignored the instruction and asked Leonora what she was intending to do.

'Annoy the maids, dummy!' she replied. 'I told you!'

With one last gleeful look at her huge red mouth, Leonora jumped up from the dressing table, and with the lipstick still in her hand, went into the adjoining bathroom. After a moment, Cassie followed her in, more from morbid curiosity at what was amusing Leonora so than from any desire to join in the sport.

Leonora was already busy, defacing the thick white fluffy towels with red lipsticked kisses. Whenever the paint ran thin on her mouth, she would at once repair the damage in a mirror, then start up once more, planting huge kisses all over the virgin towelling.

'Come on!' she screamed at Cassie through her convulsions of laughter. 'Don't be such a goddam wet blanket!'

She threw Cassie her lipstick, then continued with her vandalisation. Cassie watched appalled, then walked out of the bathroom and, picking up her book, lay on her bed reading, trying to block out the sound of Leonora's screams of laughter.

After a while, Leonora came back out, wiping off the final remnants of lipstick from her mouth which was now a blur of cosmetic. Then she picked up the house telephone and rang through to the housekeeper.

'Mrs Larkin?' she said, imperiously. 'This is Miss Von Wagner here. The towels in my bathroom are a disgrace, and unless you want me to tell my grandfather, and have you all dismissed, I suggest you send the maids up to see to it at once.'

She dropped the telephone back in its cradle, then lay back on her bed, hooting with delight, and waiting for the summoned servants to arrive.

Cassie said nothing, but just went on reading. She was aware every now and then that Leonora was staring at her, looking for some sort of reaction or approval. But Cassie had become very skilled at ignoring Leonora's attacks of delinquency, and she knew that rather than overreacting, if she made no comment Leonora would soon grow bored and find something else to do.

The maids came and silently changed all the lipsticked towels for a whole fresh set. After they had gone, Leonora turned on her side, and unwrapped two fresh sticks of chewing gum, chucking one at Cassie.

'Didn't you find that funny?' she finally asked. 'I mean they just daren't say a *word*.'

'I'd rather have gone to see the stables,' Cassie replied, still reading her book.

Leonora groaned and turned on to her back. For a good half-hour, she just lay there, chewing gum and blowing bubbles. Finally, she bored even herself, and jumped off her bed.

'OK,' she relented. 'Let's go and see the damned old horses. And on the way over, we'll go flirt with the chauffeur.'

The two girls walked through the immaculately laid out and maintained grounds, where an army of gardeners were hard at work. Cassie could see the stable block ahead and started to make for it, but Leonora caught hold of her arm and steered her towards one of what had to be the staff cottages.

'Lawrence is crazy about me,' Leonora told her as she led her up to the cottage. 'Didn't you see the way when we picked you up he kept looking at me in his mirror in the car?'

She pushed open the front door of the cottage without knocking.

'He's just crazy for me,' she whispered.

Cassie hung back on the porch, but Leonora grabbed her hand and pulled her into the cottage with her.

'Lawrence?' Leonora bawled. 'It's Miss Von Wagner!'

There was no answer, so Leonora called again. After a moment, a man stepped out from a room into the hall. He was wearing only a fresh white singlet and pants, hitched tightly up round his narrow waist with a thin belt. With his sleeked black hair, and cigarette stuck in the corner of his mouth, he looked to Cassie like somebody straight off a poster from the sort of movie her grandmother would never allow her to see.

'I didn't hear you knock,' the chauffeur said politely, but not without point.

Leonora ignored the nuance and, removing her gum, stuck it in an ash tray on the hall stand.

'We shall be wanting to go for a drive before dinner, Lawrence,' she ordered. 'In the Cadillac. And make sure it's polished.'

Then she turned on her heel and walked out. Cassie lingered for a moment, wanting to disassociate herself from her hostess's insufferable rudeness, but not knowing exactly what to say. So she just stared at the chauffeur in silence, who held the door open for her, then touched his forehead once with his index finger.

'Miss,' he said, before shutting the door behind her.

Leonora was waiting for her.

'How about that!' she hissed, catching Cassie's arm as they started to walk away. 'Did you see the way he looked at me when I pouted at him?'

Cassie hadn't. All she had noticed was the look of deep resentment in the man's brown eyes.

'I tell you, I'd just have to snap my fingers!' Leonora exclaimed, tossing back her mane of long blonde hair. 'He's just dying to do it with me.'

'I think you're terribly rude, Leonora,' Cassie said, her eyes firmly set on the stables ahead.

'Because I mentioned "it"?' Leonora asked, giggling.

'The way you treat people,' Cassie replied.

'People?' Leonora echoed disbelievingly. 'What are you talking about, dummy? They're servants!'

She kicked open a door in front of her and bawled down the stone corridor.

'Dex?' she shouted. 'Dex! It's Miss Von Wagner!'

Then she leant against the wall outside and chewed the edge of a fingernail.

'Dex is the assistant groom,' she explained. 'He'll show you the horses.'

Cassie was looking at the yard. It was modelled on the traditional pattern for a yard – boxes in a square, so that the horses could overlook each other and could also as easily be supervised. It was immaculately kept, from the unblemished paintwork to the perfect square of grass in the middle, which surrounded a large stone fountain. There were twelve boxes in all, four along each of three sides, while the last wall, through which they'd entered under an arch, housed tack and feed rooms and accommodation for the grooms. Cassie stared at the yard in disbelief. Every box was occupied with thoroughbreds, their names figured in gold lettering on wooden plaques which were fixed above their doors.

'Can we go riding now?' Cassie asked Leonora, trying, but for once not succeeding, to hide the excitement in her voice.

Leonora stared at her, already visibly bored.

'You can if you want,' she replied. 'I'm going to sunbathe. Christ, I hate horses!'

Leonora started to wander off out under the arch.

'I can't go riding by myself!' Cassie called after her. 'I wouldn't know where to go!'

'Dex'll show you!' Leonora answered back over her shoulder.

Cassie stood alone in the yard, looking at all the

127

magnificent heads, most of which were staring curiously back at her. She then walked to the nearest box and started to inspect each of the horses individually. What did Leonora mean, she hated horses? Did this mean that she didn't ride at all? And if she didn't, who did? Her mother was hardly ever here, she had no brothers or sisters, and her grandfather apparently walked on sticks. Cassie frowned as she stroked the head of a dark brown horse called Adventurer, running her hand finally down to his soft nose.

'Careful,' a voice said behind her. 'That one's not unknown to bite.'

Cassie wheeled round. She had been so immersed in her thoughts, she hadn't heard anyone approach.

'I'm Dexter,' said the serious young man standing now in front of her, touching his cap. 'The assistant groom.'

'How do you do?' Cassie replied, holding out her hand.

Dexter frowned at her for a moment, as if she was crazy, then quickly shook Cassie's hand.

'Wasn't that Miss Von Wagner calling a moment ago?' he asked her, dropping her hand as if he'd been scalded. 'I was down the end row, trying to get Rebel to stop windsucking.'

'Really?' Cassie said. 'Which one is Rebel?'

The boy pointed to a box facing them, where a horse was gripping the top of his door with his teeth and gulping in air.

'I don't know why he does it,' he said. 'Boredom, I guess.'

'Probably,' said Cassie, making her way across to the horse. 'Or a mineral deficiency.'

The young groom followed her.

'You know something about horses then?' he asked.

'A little,' Cassie nodded. 'Not as much as you, I'm sure.'

And she turned to smile at him, and noticed what he looked like for the first time, because the boy was looking back at her quite intensely, from under the deep peak of his cap. He couldn't have been that much older than

Cassie, say seventeen to her own fifteen years. But apart from Dick, one of Mary-Jo's brothers, he was the handsomest boy Cassie had ever seen, with his bright hazel eyes and his slightly turned-up nose. He also had the same look of determination in those hazel eyes which Cassie knew now burned in hers.

'I don't know much about horses, Miss,' he answered after a moment. 'But I'm learning. I know how to ride 'em though.'

He dropped his eyes, then bent down, to remove some hay Rebel had dropped over the top of his door.

'Miss Von Wagner said you might take me out riding,' Cassie ventured.

The boy looked up quickly, almost as if Cassie had startled him by her remark.

'Sure,' he replied, as calmly as he could. 'Any time you say.'

'What about now?' Cassie asked. 'Unless you're too busy.'

Dex shook his head, trying not to stare at Cassie.

'Now would be fine, Miss,' he answered. 'I normally exercise at this time as it happens.'

'Great,' said Cassie. 'I'll go and change.'

She started to leave the yard, then stopped and turned back.

'What can I ride?' she asked.

'How good are you, Miss?' the boy asked.

'I'm OK,' Cassie replied. 'I've been riding since I was seven.'

The boy turned towards the tack room.

'You can ride Missie,' he said. 'That's not her proper name. She's really called Funny Monkey. Missie's just her stable name.'

Cassie thanked him, and went. Dexter watched her go, for longer than he should.

Dexter may have been taken with the way Cassie looked, but he was no less taken with the way Miss Von Wagner's friend rode. Miss McGann had a natural sympathy with the filly he'd chosen for her and rode her as if the reins were made of silk. They hardly talked at all that first ride; Cassie was too shy to do so, and Dexter too aware of his place. But whenever they could, they stole glances at each other, when each thought the other wasn't looking.

Cassie was pretty impressed too with the way her companion rode. He was on a big bay called Windjammer, and when he hopped up on him in the yard, Cassie thought he'd overhorsed himself, maybe in an attempt to show off. The big bay jogged nervously around as Dexter tightened the girths, and half reared with him as he leaned forward to adjust the horse's neckstrap. But once on the move, there was no doubt who was boss. Dexter rode him firmly and with just the right amount of authority, so that within minutes of working their horses in, Windjammer was down on the bit, and listening to everything his rider was telling him.

They rode steadily, neither trying to impress the other, both simply concentrating on getting the very best out of their mounts. Dexter asked her halfway out on the ride if she could jump, and when Cassie told him she could, suggested they jump some fallen trees. Which they both did easily. Then they turned and walked their horses home, letting them down in a deeply contented silence.

Back in the yard Dexter took Cassie's horse from her.

'That's all right,' Cassie said. 'I'll put her away. If that's OK.'

Dexter looked a little apprehensive for a moment, as if Leonora was going to appear from out of the lengthening shadows to upbraid him. But seeing no one around, he nodded to Cassie and handed her back the reins.

Leonora appeared when Cassie was walking back to the tack room, carrying her saddle and bridle.

'What the hell are you doing that for?' she enquired angrily. 'Why do you think we have grooms? Dexter!'

'It's OK,' Cassie said, walking past her. 'I asked if I could do it.'

Leonora followed her into the tack room, where Cassie found three other boys all cleaning harness, under the supervision of an older man, who was the head groom.

The head groom looked up as Cassie struggled through the door with her tack.

'I'll take that for you, Miss,' he said hurriedly, seeing Leonora close behind.

'It's OK,' Cassie answered politely. 'Just tell me which is Missie's peg.'

There was an awkward silence, while the head groom looked at Leonora out of the corner of his eye.

'Miller will put that stuff away for you,' Leonora said tetchily, trying to take the tack from Cassie.

'I said it's OK, Leonora,' Cassie replied, hanging on to it.

Miller indicated a peg and rack on the wall, and Cassie hung up the tack. Dexter came in with his, and received a dirty look from Leonora, but to his relief nothing further.

'You haven't forgotten we're going for a drive, have you?' Leonora asked Cassie as they walked out of the yard.

'No,' Cassie said. 'It won't take me a moment to change.'

Then she ran into the house ahead of Leonora, and up the staircase into their bedroom, where she showered and changed – and for the first time in her life after she had been out riding found herself thinking about something else besides the horse.

Cassie was falling in love. At first, when she realised what was happening to her, she was frightened, and for two days running cancelled her carefully arranged afternoon hacks. Instead she swam up and down the pool, while Leonora lay sunbathing beside it, smoking and learning to drink gin and tonic. Then exhausted, she would lie on the opposite side of the pool, to escape from Leonora's cigarette smoke and try her best to think of other things – anything rather than Dexter Bryant. But it was quite hopeless. Even periods concentrated solely on remembering the great times at Mary-Jo's paled beside what was happening to her now, and she felt ashamed that she was in some way betraying the memory of her very best friend ever.

Occasionally Leonora, trailing one hand in the pool water, would ask half drunkenly why she wasn't riding that afternoon, and Cassie would simply reply that she didn't feel like it. Leonora would giggle and make some obscene comment in return, and then fall back into a gin- and sun-induced slumber. Cassie would ignore her and try once more to remember precise details of the horse rides she had been on with Mary-Jo.

But it was to no avail. From where she was lying by the pool she could see Dexter riding the horses out from the yard in the company of the other boys, and she knew how deeply she had been smitten when she found herself looking not at any of the horses in the string but just at the boy leading them. So soon she was back every afternoon riding Missie, jumping her more adventurously, and learning all about her young and very serious-minded companion.

'Do you really think you'll be a jockey?' Cassie asked him one afternoon, as they turned for home. 'I mean, don't you actually have to be very small to be one?'

'My cousin Don stopped growing when he was my age,' Dexter answered. 'I guess I'll just have to wait and see.'

'But your mother doesn't want you to be a jockey?' Cassie recapped.

'Jeeze, Miss McGann,' Dexter told her. 'There's only one thing my mom wants and that's for me to be President!'

Cassie laughed, and so did Dexter. As they laughed they turned and looked at each other.

'Couldn't you call me Cassie when we're out riding?' she asked.

Dexter hesitated, then nodded.

'Sure,' he said. 'Sure I can.'

Then he grinned delightedly and to celebrate jumped

his horse across a broad stream through which they had always previously waded. Cassie gathered her horse up and followed suit, wanting suddenly for some quite inexplicable reason to burst into song.

As they approached the yard, Leonora was sitting on the paddock rail, smoking a cigarette. She called Cassie to stop as they came abreast of her.

'Grandfather's coming home,' she announced, tossing her half-smoked cigarette on to the path and hopping down from the rail. 'You'll have to come in now and change.'

Cassie reined Missie back.

'I'll just put Missie away first,' she said.

'No you won't,' replied Leonora, catching hold of the bridle. 'Grandfather's one person you cannot be late for.'

Cassie dismounted and handed Dexter the reins.

'Thanks, Dexter,' she said. 'Sorry.'

'That's perfectly all right, Miss,' Dexter answered, but held the look he was giving Cassie a fraction of a second too long for Leonora's eagle eye.

'I never realised how sexy Dexter was before,' said Leonora as she lay in the bath, examining her fast-growing breasts. 'I don't suppose you find him sexy though, do you, Cassie?'

Cassie was busy cleaning her teeth. She looked up at Leonora in the mirror and reddened.

'He's a very nice boy,' Cassie replied. 'And a jolly good rider.'

'He's a very nice boy!' Leonora mocked. 'And a jolly good rider!'

She started slowly to soap her long legs, which she held up one at a time out of the water.

'But I wonder if he's ever done it!' she laughed.

Cassie dried her face and picked up her underclothes.

'Is that all you ever think about? Whether or not people have done it?'

133

'Sure,' Leonora replied. 'That's all I'm really interested in.'

'Well I'm not,' Cassie said tartly. 'There are other things far more important than whether or not someone's done "it".'

'I'd like to know what,' Leonora asked from the bath.

'It'd be a waste of time telling you,' Cassie answered before striding out of the bathroom.

> 'Don't throw bouquets at me!
> Don't please my folks too much!'

Leonora sang from behind her as she went.

> 'Don't laugh at my jokes too much –
> People will say we're in love!'

Cassie, struggling to put on her underclothes, noticed that she was visibly colouring all over.

Leonora let the bath water out, and came through into the bedroom, dripping water all over the white carpet. Her hair too was soaking wet, and as she passed Cassie she shook it out, soaking Cassie's clean underthings.

'You can't really be in love with a groom,' she stated categorically as she bent down and examined her face in the mirror. 'You could do it with one but you couldn't possibly fall in *love* with one.'

Cassie looked at Leonora's backside, sticking out invitingly at her as Leonora leant over the dressing table, and for once in her life giving in totally to temptation, kicked it as hard as she could. Leonora leapt upright, and turned round to Cassie, rubbing the place where Cassie's bare foot had landed.

'What in hell did you want to do that for?' she cried.

'For being such a disgusting little snob,' Cassie answered. 'I only wish I'd done it before.'

She went and fetched herself some dry underclothes, and started to get dressed all over again. As she put on her brassiere, she noticed Leonora staring at her contemptuously as she sat brushing her hair.

'You still haven't got very big breasts, have you?' she said.

'They're quite big enough for the moment,' Cassie answered, as she sat on the bed pulling on her stockings.

'Your legs aren't that great either,' concluded Leonora.

'At least I don't have your mind,' Cassie said. 'It must be really dreadful having your mind.'

Cassie looked back up at Leonora, who was watching her. Leonora suddenly threw back her head and laughed.

'Christ, you're great, Cassie!' she roared. 'Christ, you make me laugh!'

Then she turned back to her mirror and started to brush out her hair, still laughing, but, Cassie thought, knowing Leonora, probably privately thinking of something else altogether.

The butler showed Cassie into the drawing room, where she and Leonora were to wait for Leonora's grandfather. Leonora had sent Cassie down ahead of her, because she couldn't make up her mind what to wear: apparently her grandfather liked to see her really dressed up. She had helped choose Cassie's outfit for the evening, insisting she wear a dress which Leonora lent her, since according to Leonora all of Cassie's were far too plain and drab for the occasion. She had also helped her to make up her face. Cassie had protested, since she never wore make-up, except for the merest suggestion of lipstick, and that was only to humour Leonora. But Leonora was insistent. Her grandfather might be old, but he still liked his girls pretty.

Cassie stood in the drawing room and looked around her. It was a room she hadn't been in before, as there had been no call. It was enormous, and filled with foreign furniture and vast impersonal paintings; and it was also stiflingly hot, since all the windows were shut tight and a huge log fire was burning in the large stone fireplace.

Cassie stood there, uncomfortably warm, even in her

borrowed sleeveless dress. She looked at herself in a big gilt mirror and tried to pull the deeply plunging neckline of the dress higher up over her breasts. They may not according to Leonora be very big yet, but they were quite big enough for Cassie to be embarrassed by the amount of them displayed by her *décolletage*. As she was doing so, the door suddenly opened, and Leonora's grandfather appeared; a large man bent over almost double on two walking sticks, accompanied by his butler who held him securely by one elbow. Behind, bringing up the rear, was Leonora, demurely dressed in a baby-blue long-sleeved silk frock which was buttoned right up to her neck, with a sash at the waist, and net underskirts. She had tied her long blonde hair up and back and held it in place with matching blue ribbons. On her scrubbed pink face there wasn't a trace of make-up. She smiled sweetly at Cassie, looking for all the world like an innocent child of twelve, instead of a pubescent scheming teenager of fifteen. She was also acting the innocent too, helping her grandfather over to his big wing chair right by the fire and covering his knees with a rug, before sitting on the arm of the chair and holding his hand. Cassie stood going redder and redder, while wishing the ground beneath her would open and swallow her up.

'Leonora, you're an angel,' her grandfather said as she fetched him his whisky the butler had poured. 'If only all children were as good as you.'

Leonora kissed her grandfather on top of his white head, looking up at the same time with a malicious eye to Cassie.

'Tell your young friend to come over here,' he ordered his granddaughter. 'I want to see if she's as sweet as you. Though I very much doubt it.'

Cassie stood before Mr Von Wagner Senior as he slowly raised his head and looked at her.

'How do you do, sir?' she said. The old man, still astonishingly handsome despite the crippling nature of whatever disease had reduced him to such a state, simply

136

stared at Cassie and said nothing in reply. Then his head dropped to his chest again, as Leonora, with a smug smile, held his whisky glass to his lips and helped him drink.

After dinner, during which she entertained her grandfather with outrageous lies about how well she was doing at the Academy, Leonora helped take her grandfather to the library where she sat at the piano and played some simplified classics really quite passably. The old man addressed not one word to Cassie the entire evening, although there was nothing wrong with his conversation. Indeed, once he had had his two whiskies before dinner, he became quite loquacious, particularly on the decline of morals in modern America among the young. This was a subject very dear to his heart, for which he blamed Hollywood and the sale of cheap literature wholesale. Leonora, who did nothing but go to X-rated movies and read lurid paperback novels, agreed with his every word.

Finally Leonora yawned politely behind her hand, and eyeing Cassie, told her grandfather it was past their bedtime. She kissed the old man once again on his head and nodded to Cassie. Cassie wished him a polite goodnight, and once again he totally ignored her.

When they got upstairs to their bedroom, Leonora threw herself face down on the bed and started to laugh hysterically. Cassie, furious and ashamed with herself for being so easily duped, rushed into the bathroom, and slammed the door behind her. She grabbed a towel and removed the offending make-up, then ripped off the shaming dress. Then she washed and scrubbed her face clean, all the time conscious of Leonora's helpless laughter.

She came back out in her dressing gown, and collected her nightdress. Then she went to the door.

'Where are you going, Cassie?' asked Leonora in what seemed like genuine surprise. 'Hey, you're not cross, are you?'

'I'm going to sleep in another room,' Cassie replied.

'And yes, I am cross. OK?'

'You didn't have to make a fool of me,' returned Cassie, 'just because you don't like your grandfather.'

'I didn't mean to make a fool of you, Cassie!' Leonora protested. 'Honest! I guess I just wanted a bit of a laugh.'

She suddenly dropped her voice so convincingly that Cassie was almost taken in by the change to a note of what seemed genuine regret. Then she saw that familiar dark light in Leonora's eyes, and broke away from her to open the door.

'I'll sleep next door all the same, if you don't mind,' she told Leonora. 'Maybe I'll feel different about it in the morning.'

Leonora followed her out onto the landing.

'OK,' she said, quite unmaliciously. 'Maybe you will.'

Leonora wished Cassie goodnight and disappeared into her bedroom. Cassie went into the bedroom next door and for a moment leaned her back thoughtfully against the closed door, before getting into bed and settling down to sleep.

Cassie would have gone home at once if it hadn't been for Dex. She had long decided never to endure any further humiliations unnecessarily, but she knew if she got back on the train of her own volition, there was more than a strong possibility that between them, Leonora and her grandmother would see to it that Cassie never saw Dex again. But also, as it happened, Leonora seemed genuinely to regret her foolish prank, and tried to make up to Cassie in all sorts of ways. She stopped sulking whenever she didn't get her own way, encouraged Cassie in her relationship with Dex, and even gave what seemed to Cassie like some very sensible advice to her about boys and how to deal with them. Most surprising of all, Leonora even stopped being quite so high handed and arrogant with the servants.

They were also back sleeping in the same room together. Not that Leonora had pleaded with Cassie to come back, but more because she hadn't. Cassie couldn't help being aware all the time of how lonely Leonora really was, all alone except for Cassie's company in that vast house. Cassie never again saw Leonora's grandfather after the debacle of that evening, but then neither apparently did his favourite granddaughter. So Cassie moved back in with Leonora, and very soon they were lying awake into the small hours of the morning, discussing the sorts of things which girls like to discuss.

Cassie still loved horses, though, despite the growing strength of her feelings for Dex. She knew that maybe one day she might stop being in love with Dex, if that's what she indeed was, although she couldn't quite foresee such a time, but that she could never ever stop being in love with horses.

Which was probably what made Dex love Cassie quite so desperately. He hadn't ever before talked to a girl quite as pretty and as classy as Cassie, let alone one who could ride so brilliantly and who knew quite so much about horses. He could hardly wait until four o'clock each afternoon, for the pretty little dark-haired girl to walk into the yard, swinging her whip while quietly searching the row of boxes with her eyes to see which horse he was still 'doing'. Just as Cassie could really only think of him, so Dex could think of nothing beyond Cassie. And when he saw her, his young heart leaped with joy.

Cassie was even persuaded to ring her grandmother and ask if she might stay on with Leonora for a few more days, a request backed up one hundred per cent by Leonora. Grandmother naturally granted the request at once, because she fondly imagined that the reason was because Cassie had been accepted wholeheartedly into the bosom of the Von Wagner family. To Cassie's amazement, Grandmother even sent her some more money.

To celebrate, Leonora ordered Lawrence to drive them into town to do some shopping. Leonora wanted to buy some clothes, and Cassie wanted to buy Dex a present.

139

While they were browsing through the department store, Lawrence waited outside, polishing the Rolls. Leonora bought two sweaters, the sort June Allyson had worn in *The Glenn Miller Story*, which she and Cassie had been to see three times, and a blouse like Audrey Hepburn's in *Roman Holiday*. Cassie bought Dex a book called *The Art of Race Riding*. Before the assistant gift-wrapped it for her, Cassie wrote on the fly leaf 'To Dexter. With love, Cassie. Summer 1955.' Leonora looked over her shoulder without Cassie knowing, but refrained from comment.

She gave the book to Dex after they had come back from their ride that evening. Dex was hanging up the tack and the tackroom was empty, as the rest of the boys were out beginning evening stables. Cassie was sitting having a mug of hot tea under Missie's saddle-rack. Dex opened the present and stared at it.

'I wrote something in the front,' Cassie told him. 'Nothing special.'

Dex turned to the fly leaf and then stared at that too. Next he put the book back in the gift wrapping, and into his locker. Then he sat down beside Cassie, put his arm around her, and kissed her.

It was the very first time they had kissed. It was the very first time Cassie had been kissed. She didn't see stars, and she didn't faint. But when Dex stopped kissing her, all she knew was she wanted to be kissed by him some more. It was only the sound of someone approaching outside which stopped them sitting there kissing each other for the rest of the evening.

'I love you, Cassie,' Dex whispered, then grinned shyly.

'I think I love you too, Dex,' Cassie replied.

Leonora came in.'

'Oh Christ I'm sorry!' she exclaimed, when she saw the two of them side by side on the bench.

Dex rose, his face reddening.

'I was just sorting out some tack, Miss Von Wagner,' he said, picking up Adventurer's saddle.

'I couldn't care less what you're doing, Dex,' Leonora replied, actually smiling at him. 'I was actually looking for Lawrence, and George said he thought he'd seen him coming over here. Sorry!'

With that she was gone. But so was the moment. Cassie rose and brushed some straw off her clothes.

'I'd better go and change,' she said. 'We're going to a party in Patchogue.'

'Sure, Cassie,' Dex replied, swinging the saddle up over his head on to its rack. 'See you tomorrow, right?'

'You bet,' Cassie grinned.

'And thanks a million for the book, Cassie,' Dex called after her.

'It's OK,' Cassie said, putting her head back round the door. 'I'll see you at Arlington Park yet.'

'Sure you will, Cassie,' Dex replied. 'Bringing home one of your horses.'

They looked at each other, then Cassie blew him a kiss, and feeling very grown up, walked back up to the house.

Cassie surprised herself by enjoying the party. She had gone prepared for an evening of spoilt rich kids noisily having what they considered fun, but in fact it had turned out very civilised. Of course it helped that the Faverlys, the family throwing the party, were practically as rich as the Von Wagners, but even so, even to someone as young as Cassie, she knew that endless wealth was not a guarantee of a good party. She'd learned that from listening to some of the perfectly dreadful experiences recounted by the girls at the Academy when they returned from vacation.

Cassie just wished Dex could have been there, as she danced with a polite young man in a white tuxedo to a full-size swing band playing 'Satin Doll'. They could have danced all night, close in each other's arms, saying little or nothing. As it was, she danced with a succession of almost ruthlessly polite boys, who talked about practically anything and everything. On the one dance Cassie

141

sat out for the evening, by choice rather than by accident, Leonora came and sat down beside her to make sure she was having fun.

'Yes, I really am, thanks,' Cassie told her. 'It's a great party.'

'It's not bad,' Leonora admitted, tossing back her mane of hair. 'Let's have a drink.'

'I don't really want a drink,' Cassie told her as Leonora looked for a waiter. 'Unless it's a Coke.'

'Two punches over here!' Leonora called over the music to a passing servant. 'And hurry!'

Then she turned back and grinned at Cassie.

'It's OK, really. There's nothing in it.'

The waiter returned with two glasses with handles and set them on the cloth-covered table. Cassie sipped her drink while Leonora watched her. Leonora was right. It tasted completely innocuous.

'See?' said Leonora. 'Baby-juice.'

And downed hers in one.

For some reason the evening went even better from then on. Cassie became highly animated, and very soon the young men were queueing up to dance with her. Cassie found herself laughing at their every joke, and making what she thought were some pretty funny ones in return. And whenever she sat down to catch her breath, Leonora was there with some more punch.

Cassie was still laughing when they tiptoed up the stairs at two o'clock in the morning. Leonora, grinning, put a finger to her lips and opened the bedroom door. Cassie went in and the next thing she knew, she collapsed on the bed in another fit of helpless laughter. Then she turned round to see what Leonora was doing and saw that she was preparing to climb out of the window on a rope of knotted sheets.

'Where are you going now?' she asked curiously, as Leonora threw the sheets out of the window.

'I'm going to see Lawrence,' Leonora whispered in

142

return. 'It's all fixed. I'm going to lose it tonight.'

Cassie sat up in horror, then swung her legs off the bed. She rushed over to the window, and nearly lost her balance as she leaned out after Leonora.

'Don't be an idiot, Leonora!' she called down. 'Come back here at once!'

'Go to hell, Cassie McGann!' the reply floated up from below. 'Before you wake the whole household!'

Cassie watched helplessly as she saw Leonora duck away through the bushes, then she half-closed the window. But she didn't close it completely, so that Leonora could climb back up, when and if she wanted to.

She undressed slowly for bed and put her clothes on the bed. Then as she walked back across the room without any clothes on, she suddenly felt very ill and extremely dizzy, and only just made it to the bathroom in time.

At first Cassie thought she was dreaming when she heard the first tap on the window. She was sleeping so deeply, the sound seemed to be coming from the other side of space, so faint and distant was it. She turned over in her bed and, still asleep, gave a sigh. She was in Locksfield, with Dex and Mary-Jo, and they were all flying high above the farm, like birds, silent in the clear blue sky. Every now and then they would turn and smile at each other, and the people down below them would smile and wave up to them.

The tapping was louder now and more persistent. Cassie turned once more in her bed, still dreaming. Now she was on a train, moving very fast through a tunnel. Grandmother was sitting opposite her, but although she was smiling and talking, Cassie knew she was dead. Grandmother then put her hand on the window of the train compartment and started knocking on it. The glass broke and there was blood everywhere.

Cassie sat bolt upright in bed, her head pounding and her mouth as dry as dust. There was someone tapping on the bedroom window. Then she remembered Leonora, climbing down the sheets to go and see the chauffeur. So the noise must be someone trying to push up the bedroom window. Cassie got out of her bed and for a moment thought she was going to be sick again, as a wave of nausea overcame her. Then realising that she had no clothes on, she grabbed her dressing gown and, slipping into it in the dark, hurried over to the window to let Leonora in.

But it wasn't Leonora. It was Dex. Cassie stepped back in horror as she saw him climb through the window and then stand shyly before her in the bedroom, bathed in the still full moonlight.

'Dex!' Cassie found herself saying; barely in a whisper. 'Dex, what in heaven's name are you *doing*?'

'What am I doing?' the boy replied, fishing in the back pocket of his jeans and taking out a carefully folded sheet of paper. 'I'm only doing what you asked me to do, Cassie.'

Cassie backed away fearfully, pulling her dressing gown even tighter round her naked body.

'I must still be dreaming,' she said more to herself, putting the bed safely between her and Dex. 'I never asked you to come up here.'

Dex looked at her, and Cassie could see he was as frightened as her. He didn't say anything in reply. Instead he just handed the note to her, leaning across the bed, but making no attempt to come any nearer.

'What's this?' Cassie whispered, looking at the folded paper in her hand.

'It's your note,' Dex told her. 'The note you left in my locker.'

Cassie suddenly went ice cold all over as she began to suspect what may have happened. She sat on the edge of the bed and quickly turned on her bedside light. As soon as she did, Dex moved away from the window and hid in the shadows, also suspecting that something was going horribly wrong.

'Dear darling Dex,' the note started. 'I can't get to speak to you again this evening as we are going to a party.'

Cassie looked up at Dex, standing by the window with his back against the wall, looking sideways out of the window in case there was anyone below. Cassie quickly read through the rest of the bogus note.

'We shall be back just after midnight, I should reckon, and Leonora has arranged for me to be alone in the bedroom. Please, *please* come up and see me, because I have to go home tomorrow, and we may never ever have another chance to be alone! It will be perfectly safe. Leonora has fixed everything, and if you come, at last I will be able to show you just how much I love you. Cassie.'

She dropped the note on her bed, turned off her light and hurried over to Dex.

'Dex!' Cassie whispered to him, taking his hand. 'Dex – that's not *my* handwriting!'

The boy turned back to her, fear in his hazel eyes.

'But it has to be, Cassie!' he replied. 'I compared it with what you wrote in the book you gave me!'

'So I bet did Leonora,' Cassie said grimly. 'She's always copying people's writing at school and getting them into trouble. You'd better get out of here before it's too late!'

She turned Dex to the window and they both looked out from behind the curtains. There was no one out there in the grounds as far as they could see. Perhaps Leonora for once had been actually playing Cupid rather than the devil.

Dex turned back to her, still almost tearful.

'Cassie,' he pleaded. 'Please don't think less of me! I was only coming up here to tell you I loved you! I wasn't going . . .'

He looked her straight in the eyes and took both her hands.

'I wasn't going to do anything,' he finished lamely.

Cassie kissed him gently on his cheek.

'Sure you weren't,' she grinned. 'Anyhow, I wouldn't have let you.'

145

Cassie eased the window up a bit further and double-checked the grounds. She could see nothing below in the bright moonlight except the shrubbery and trees. Then she stood aside to let Dex make his escape.

Before he started to climb out, Dex turned to her for a moment.

'I love you, Cassie,' he whispered. 'Don't ever forget that.'

'You bet I won't, Dex,' Cassie replied. 'And I love you too.'

Dex took hold of the top sheet and prepared to let himself out of the window. The moment he did, the people waiting below hidden in the shrubbery turned on their flashlights.

Cassie gasped in horror and pulled Dex away from the window, flattening them both against the wall.

'Oh my God!' Dex cried. 'Oh my God, I have been seen! Oh my God, what are we going to do now?'

Cassie pulled him across the room to the door.

'Quickly!' she hissed. 'They might not have seen it was you! Let's try and get you out the back way!'

And then still holding on to Dex's hand, she opened the bedroom door and hurried them both out on to the landing.

As she did so, someone threw the lights on. Cassie blinked and instinctively put her hands up to her eyes, like someone trapped in the floodlights. Then as she got used to the sudden glare, she could see the figures waiting down below in the marbled hall. Leonora's grandfather in his pyjamas and dressing gown, seated in a wheel chair, with a nurse at his back, to one side of him Mrs Larkin the housekeeper, and to the other side, smiling back up at Cassie, Leonora.

Dex was kicked out there and then. Deaf to Cassie's protestations of their innocence, Leonora's grandfather had given orders for the boy's summary dismissal, and for Cassie herself to leave the following morning. Cassie pleaded with him and tried to explain the deception. But the old man ignored her and simply ordered his nurse to take him back to his ground-floor bedroom. Mrs Larkin was instructed to take Cassie upstairs and to lock her in the nursery until morning, lest she got any foolish notions, and to make arrangements for her to be on the first train back to New York.

Cassie recovered her composure and shaking off Mrs Larkin's grip on her arm, walked defiantly back up the stairs ahead of the grim-faced house-keeper. Leonora followed at a safe distance. Cassie said nothing to her as she turned away down the corridor which led to the nursery with its barred windows, but Leonora had something to say as she casually stood at the door before Mrs Larkin locked Cassie in.

'I'd say that made it one match all,' she grinned. 'Wouldn't you, Paddy?'

On the day of her sixteenth birthday, Cassie arrived back unannounced in Westboro Falls. When her grandmother discovered what had happened, she locked the front door, and taking a heavy walking stick from the stand, started to beat Cassie. She beat her on the back, and round the head, and on her arms as Cassie tried to protect her head. Then she beat her on the backs of her legs as Cassie ran bruised and bleeding and half-conscious up to her bedroom, and on her backside. She chased her up the stairs and along the landing, still raining blows on whatever part of Cassie's body she could, until Cassie reached the sanctuary of her bedroom and slammed the door behind her, leaning on it so that her grandmother couldn't get in. Finding the door shut against her, Grandmother simply turned the key which for Cassie's misfortune was still on the outside, and locked Cassie in.

At that moment Cassie didn't care. She was just supremely grateful to have escaped her grandmother and to be free of the vicious blows which she had landed on her. She fell on to her bed, and lay there holding the

147

bedposts tight with her bruised and bleeding hands, with her swollen face buried deep in her pillows.

Grandmother unlocked Cassie's door at six o'clock the following morning, after Cassie had been hammering on it for the best part of an hour. She stood outside on the landing, holding the heavy walking stick, while Cassie rushed past her to the bathroom. When Cassie came back out of the bathroom, a good twenty minutes later, she saw through her one open eye her grandmother standing in front of her holding up Cassie's bed sheets. Cassie watched her, as Grandmother threw them on the floor by Cassie's feet.

'I want those washed at once,' she told Cassie. 'I want every mark removed from them, and by that I mean *every* mark.'

'What do you think I was hammering at the door for?' Cassie cried through her swollen and bruised lips. 'I didn't have any towels! Everything's still in my suitcase down in the hall!'

'You should have thought of that,' her grandmother replied. 'You should have known when you were due.'

Her grandmother walked off back to her own bedroom, leaving Cassie to pick up the sheets and go down to the utility room, where she washed and scrubbed them by hand, in a pointless effort to shift the stubborn bloodstains. She now ached all over, inside and out, but even the worst of the bruises her grandmother had inflicted on her didn't hurt as much as the terrible dragging pain in her stomach. She tried once again to get the sheets clean, but with just soap and water it seemed a task of Herculean dimensions. Then the cramps in her stomach increased in their ferocity, and made her gasp out loud. Clutching at her stomach, and with tears coursing down her cheeks, Cassie slowly slid to the cold stone floor and surrendered to her emotions.

She must have fallen asleep, because when she reopened her eyes the sun was higher in the sky and there were signs of early life in the street outside. She remained on the floor

148

thinking for a while, and then decided what to do. There was only one person to whom she could turn, only one person who loved her enough to give her help.

Cassie stood in the hall for a minute, to make sure her grandmother's bedroom door was still tight shut. Grandmother had taken lately to sleeping in longer than usual, so since it was only just after seven a.m., not even Delta was up yet and going about her duties. So Cassie went back up to her room and threw some old clothes on. Then taking a scarf from her cupboard, in order to hide as many of the bruises on her face as possible, collected her still soaking laundry from downstairs before stealing out of the house and across the road to Mrs Roebuck's.

Mrs Roebuck had long been up and was already out attending to her plants. She saw Cassie crossing the road and pushing open her white-painted gate.

'Why hello, Cassie!' she cried, slowly straightening up. 'Mr O'Reilly said you were back from your trip! I thought from what your grandmother told me you were staying till the end of the week.'

Cassie muttered something thickly in return, but Mrs Roebuck didn't even have to see her face or hear what she said to know that something was seriously wrong. The pain and anguish seemed to radiate from Cassie. Mrs Roebuck put down her gardening things and held open the porch door.

'Come on, child,' she said, 'you'd best come inside at once.'

Cassie stood for a moment, smelling the heady fragrance of the herbs in Mrs Roebuck's garden, then she followed Mrs Roebuck in through her immaculate hall, and into the ever welcoming kitchen.

'I was wondering if you could do some washing for me,' Cassie said, standing in the shadow with her head well down.

Mrs Roebuck leant across and put her hand under Cassie's chin, to tilt the girl's face up to her. Cassie had done her best to conceal all the other cuts and bruises by

149

putting on a long-sleeved cardigan, her longest skirt and some thick stockings. But there was little she could do about the abrasions on her face. Mrs Roebuck looked at them in silence, then sat Cassie down at the table.

'Do you want to tell me about it, Cassie?' she asked as calmly as she could, 'while I make us some coffee?'

'I had a riding accident,' Cassie replied, her answer well rehearsed. 'It was my own fault. I was showing off on a horse which was far too good for me, and got hit in the face by a branch.'

Mrs Roebuck put on the kettle and for a while said nothing. It was perfectly possible of course that Cassie could have suffered a riding accident. But then why should that have brought her home early?

'When did this accident happen, Cassie?' Mrs Roebuck enquired.

'The day before yesterday,' Cassie answered. 'On our last ride.'

'You hurt your hands as well, I see,' Mrs Roebuck remarked, as she put the coffee cups out on the table.

'I guess I did that when I fell,' Cassie told her. 'I mean I really took a fall.'

Cassie tried to smile at Mrs Roebuck, but her lips were too swollen and the side of her face too deeply bruised.

'Well they do say, don't they,' said Mrs Roebuck, 'that you're no horseman till you fall off. Least that's what they told the folks round us when we were kids.'

Cassie sat at the table and drank her coffee, relieved that Mrs Roebuck had accepted her story.

'Now what's this laundry you want me to do for you?' Mrs Roebuck asked as she sat down opposite Cassie, putting a plate of home-made cookies in the middle of the table. 'That Delta gone on strike again or something?'

Cassie looked down, avoiding Mrs Roebuck's shrewd eyes.

'I had an accident, Mrs Roebuck,' she confessed. 'And I'm afraid Grandmother's a bit angry. I was early, you see. And – well. I guess I should have remembered I was nearly due.'

Mrs Roebuck clicked her tongue and shook her head. But the remonstration was aimed not at Cassie but at her grandmother. Mrs Roebuck stood up, took the bundle of laundry which also included some of Cassie's underthings, and disappeared to her utility room to put them all in to soak. Then she returned with a bottle of aspirin which she put in front of Cassie.

'Take two of those at once,' she ordered, filling a glass of water from the cold tap. 'Then I'll tend to those cuts and bruises of yours.'

Mrs Roebuck peered closely at Cassie's face.

'Most odd, I'd say, that no one put anything on them,' she added. 'And this cut by the side of your mouth – why, it's still bleeding.

Cassie remained silent, unable to think of a plausible excuse why her face still should be bleeding.

'Where else are you hurt?' Mrs Roebuck asked.

Cassie shrugged in reply.

'I asked you where else you were hurt, Cassie McGann.'

Cassie looked up at Mrs Roebuck, at the woman who loved her, at the woman she wished could be her mother, and her eyes filled with tears an she lowered her head on to the table in front of her.

After Mrs Roebuck had bathed her, during which time she made no remark about the multiple cuts and contusions to Cassie's body, and dressed and treated every mark, bruise and cut, she wrapped her up in a thick woollen dressing gown and sat the girl, who was obviously still in great shock, in front of her famous stove. Cassie sat drinking some hot milk and honey. There was nowhere she was so happy as she was in Mrs Roebuck's kitchen. Not even when she was staying on Mary-Jo's farm in Locksfield did Cassie feel this sense of tremendous warmth and peace. At the moment there were jars of bottled fruits waiting above the stove to be labelled, and beside them, hanging to dry, bunches of herbs for use in the winter. Cassie was never so aware of the seasons as she was in this kitchen. Whatever was happening outside was always reflected within this sanctum. And now because it was almost the fall, the rusts and fading greens of the landscape were present all round the room, colours once radiant but now fading, waiting to be preserved for the winter in jars or pots or muslin bags, making the approach of winter no less cheerful than the first buds of spring.

Mrs Roebuck came back into the kitchen from whatever she had been doing and ordered Cassie to bed.

'I have to go home, Mrs Roebuck,' Cassie protested. 'Grandmother will soon be up and wondering where I am.'

'Let her wonder,' Mrs Roebuck answered tartly. 'I've been doing a fair bit of wondering myself.'

She led Cassie upstairs and tucked her into Maria's bed.

'You're to stay there and sleep, do you hear?' she ordered Cassie. 'And leave any worrying and wondering to me.'

Then she tucked Cassie in, kissed her on the forehead, and went out, shutting the door.

Cassie lay quite still between the cool clean sheets, and thought she must be in heaven. The aspirin had eased the pain, particularly in her stomach, and soon she drifted off to sleep. She didn't hear Grandmother arrive unannounced and uninvited and order her return. And she missed Mrs Roebuck taking her through to the back porch and warning Grandmother that if she didn't let the child sleep for as long as she needed, and stay with her until she was better, she would call the doctor here to her house at once to hear his explanation of the cuts and bruises she had discovered all over the young girl's body.

She missed her grandmother's explanation too, of how they'd been caused by Cassie falling downstairs, and most of all she missed her grandmother's indignity of being asked to leave Mrs Roebuck's house this instant. She was too fast asleep, and too busy dreaming of Dex riding her first racehorse to a ten-length victory to hear her grandmother being chivvied out of the house, and the door slammed angrily behind her.

She did stir awake once, near midday, when Mrs Roebuck looked in on her to make sure she was all right, and to give her some more aspirin. She sat up to take them, then as she lay back on her pillows, Cassie's heart suddenly grew warm, as she realised that kind people could never finally be defeated. Not long after that, she fell again into another deep sleep.

Chapter Seven

Mary-Jo's hair was held back by flowers, a thick garland which crowned her beautiful face. The flowers held in place the veil which covered her long lustrous, dark hair.

Cassie walked up the aisle behind her best friend, chosen by her especially to hold her veil. Everyone's head in the chapel turned as Mary-Jo walked past, and it seemed to Cassie that she heard one or two of the congregation actually gasp at the beauty of the bride.

Her father stood waiting for her, to give her away. Cassie could see how rigid his back was, as he stared down at the floor in front of him. She wondered how her own father would have felt if he had been here, and it had been Cassie, not Mary-Jo. Mrs Christiansen turned and looked at her beautiful daughter when she stopped in front of the altar and smiled. Mary-Jo turned to her mother and smiled back, radiantly, then gazed to the front and lifted her eyes high to the tabernacle.

The organ stopped and Cassie made a small adjustment to the bride's veil. Mary-Jo's wedding dress was quite the most beautiful Cassie had ever seen. Her father had bought the material for it ten years before, when he had been out in Siam. It had lain at home in a bottom drawer, wrapped in paper and moth balls, waiting for the day his dearly beloved daughter was to be married.

And now this day had arrived. But still Mr Christiansen couldn't bring himself to look up from the ground and at the vision which was Mary-Jo. Cassie glanced at him, and felt a terrible pity for him, because she knew how hurt and bewildered he was at Mary-Jo's decision to become a nun.

'It's when they cut the hair off,' Maria said afterwards. 'That's the bit I hate.'

'I agree,' said Rosella. 'Mary-Jo had such gorgeous hair, and now it'll never ever be seen again.'

'It was only hair,' Cassie said, then found it quite impossible to believe what she had just heard herself say.

She couldn't get out of her mind's eye the image of Mary-Jo standing in the simple white shift; of the nuns whisking away her beautiful wedding dress and veil; of Mary-Jo prostrate on the floor in the sign of the Cross, in front of the altar; of the sudden sound of Mr Christiansen's sobs; or the image of him being comforted by Mary-Jo's mother, who stood behind him pale and silent. Why Mary-Jo? How did she know God had wanted her? How did anyone know? Did He appear to you one night and tell you that you were chosen? Or was it just some sort of internal revelation? And why, most of all, hadn't Mary-Jo told her?

Cassie had been staying with her only three months before, just after Christmas, and there hadn't been a word said about it. There'd been the usual tomfoolery, and there'd been snowball fights, and skating parties, but there hadn't been one word from any of them, least of all her best friend Mary-Jo, about the discovery of her vocation. Maybe, when Cassie came to think of it, maybe Mary-Jo had spent more time on her knees each night before they went to bed, but then she'd always been a very devout girl, so there didn't seem anything unusual in that. And then Cassie remembered waking briefly in the middle of one bitterly cold night, and imagining she heard the sound of someone crying. They all slept in the house in the winter, as the old barn was far too cold. Cassie had pulled her blankets up around her to block out the sound of this distant sobbing she had heard. Then being only young, and tired from the exertions of the

155

day, she had fallen back to sleep and forgotten all about it.

But now she knew who had been crying that night. When she heard those terrible sobs in the chapel, it carried her back to that night in Mary-Jo's house, and she knew now that the person crying then had also been her father. She looked around the room for Mr Christiansen, but could see him nowhere.

'He's gone home,' Maria told her. 'He wouldn't stay for the breakfast. It's broken his heart. Just as Grandma said it would.'

But Cassie could see Mary-Jo, wearing her new habit, and standing talking to her mother. She was a nun. One of the nuns. One of the nuns from whom when they were all so small they used to run, giggling. One of the nuns who later singled them out from class to give them a star, or a reprimand; one of the nuns who told them to sit up straight and to remember those less fortunate than themselves in their prayers. One of the nuns. Mary-Jo was one of the nuns.

Yet there was no doubting Mary-Jo's happiness. It radiated from her. No bride could have looked happier. It was Cassie's own happiness she was doubting, as she watched her best friend moving sweetly from group to group, accepting their congratulations, and their blessings. It was Cassie who was finding it unbearable, who could hardly look at the friend with whom she used to wrestle in the grass, chase butterflies, and ride helter-skelter over the hills and fields of Locksfield Farm, as she stood there now in the habit of a nun, her arms tucked up her voluminous sleeves, with all that wonderful lustrous hair which they used to plait together all gone, all shorn off.

Cassie couldn't help it, this feeling of overpowering resentment she felt when she looked at the person she loved most in the whole world, and who loved her back with all her heart. She knew it was the end of the first part of her life, of their shared age of innocence, and she wanted to turn the clock back so that she could try and persuade Mary-Jo not to take this momentuous step which was going to change both their lives so completely.

Mary-Jo came across to them and Cassie found herself looking at the ground. Mary-Jo took them all by the hand, one at a time and kissed them. Cassie looked in her eyes and Mary-Jo smiled back at her. At first Cassie thought her smile was as it had always been. Then she realised, the longer she looked at her friend, that Mary-Jo was no longer smiling with her, but for her. Her best friend was no longer Cassie. God was in her place.

Before they left, they gave her presents. Holy pictures inscribed with loving messages for Sister Teresa, which was Mary-Jo's newly adopted name. Mary-Jo had taken the name of the Little Flower, her favourite Saint. Mary-Jo had always prayed to Saint Teresa. And when Mary-Jo died, there would be the smell of flowers from her, too, as there had been from her patron saint. Cassie thought of these things, as she tried to stop remembering their races to be first to the bathroom, and their endless talks in bed as they waited for the blessings of the nun on duty. Always about horses. Horses, horses, horses. Who would Cassie talk to about horses now? Who would share her love of those wonderful animals? Where would she ever, ever find such a soulmate again?

Cassie was very silent for a long time as she drove away from the convent with Mary-Jo's mother, who was going to drop her back in Westboro Falls. Everyone was very silent: all her brothers and her mother. It was raining heavily.

Mr Christiansen had already left in his own car. On the journey back, as they passed through a town, Mrs Christiansen saw her husband's Dodge outside a bar. She stopped and went inside. After five or so minutes, during which time no one talked, she came back out again and called Frank out of the car. Frank was now twenty-one, and held a full driver's licence, and was obviously being instructed by his mother to bring his father home safely and in one piece. Frank went into the bar, and Mary-Jo's mother got back in the driving seat and drove off.

The rain fell more and more heavily.

'What's happened to Prince, Mrs Christiansen?' Cassie suddenly asked.

Mary-Jo's mother – Sister Teresa's mother – leaned forward and wiped the back of the windscreen with her glove.

'Mary-Jo gave him away, Cassie,' she replied. 'She gave all her possessions away, and Prince was the last to go.'

'I see,' Cassie said.

'He's gone to a very good home, Cassie,' Mrs Christiansen assured her. 'She made sure of that.'

They were talking about her as if she was dead, or as if she had become a totally different person. Yet Cassie remembered Sister Joseph laughing and telling Cassie about the last cigarette she had smoked on her way to becoming a nun, and Sister Margaret had told her about her last drink, and her last ride in her brother's supercharged Cord Roadster. So she knew they were still girls at that moment in their lives, and that underneath that starched and forbidding habit, they mostlike still were. It was just that instead of falling in love with someone called Tom, or Dick, or Harry, or Dex, they had fallen in love with someone called God.

Mrs Christiansen turned to Cassie, and Cassie could see that despite her smile, her eyes were sad.

'You'll still come and see us, Cassie, of course,' she said, taking her hand off the steering wheel for a moment and pressing Cassie's.

'Sure,' said Cassie, attempting a smile. 'Try and stop me.'

But they both knew that it would never and could never be the same again. Cassie would come and see them, as regular as clockwork, but then the visits would grow fewer as the distance between them all grew more.

158

Mary-Jo had been their touchstone, and with her gone the fabric of all their relationships would fall apart. There'd be no more sleeping in the bunks in summer, no more dare-devil rides in patched jeans and open-necked check shirts, no more barbecues out under the stars. Instead, as Cassie grew older, her relationship with Mrs Christiansen would grow more formal, and as they sat round the kitchen table, they would be finding other things to talk about, rather than their beloved Mary-Jo. Of course Cassie would ask how Mary-Jo was, and her mother would tell her fine, and in return ask Cassie how she was doing. And Cassie would tell her fine. But nothing would ever take away that ache in their hearts, nothing would ever fill that void that Mary-Jo's transformation into Sister Teresa had left in their lives.

Everyone in the car fell silent again, as they neared Westboro Falls. Cassie tried to imagine what that first evening was going to be like for Mary-Jo, for a girl so used to being outside, for someone who seemed to have spent most of her young life on the back of a horse. It would be an evening of prayers, as would every subsequent evening for as long as Mary-Jo lived. They would pray for people like her family and for people like Cassie, and for people who had never spared a second thought in their lives for those who had sacrificed everything they loved in life, except for their love of God, in order to pray for them. Then Sister Teresa would go to bed in a simple rough nightdress with a cross sewn on the back, and fold her arms across her chest in the sign of the Cross as she waited for the blessed gift of sleep.

Cassie leant her face against the car window, watching the rain run down the glass in incessant tears.

Chapter Eight

Cassie's life had changed in other ways as well, since that fateful day she was returned in disgrace from the Von Wagner house on Long Island. Her grandmother had promptly, to Cassie's great but hidden relief, removed her at once from Miss Truefitt's Academy, even though it meant the forfeit of the next term's fees. She had then found her a job in the town printing works, where Cassie toiled from nine to half past five every day for the next year to pay her grandmother back the money for the forfeited school fees. Once they had been repaid, Cassie was allowed to keep one half of her weekly wages, the other half going to her grandmother for board and lodging.

But most important of all, she had met a boy called Joe.

For a long time after she had returned from Leonora's, Cassie could barely eat or sleep, so much did her young heart ache at the thought of Dex, now lost to her. She had tried writing to Leonora for his address, but Leonora had never even bothered to reply. She had even written to the head groom, who had been so kind to her, but that letter was returned with a message scribbled on the back to the effect that he too had left the house on Long Island. So Cassie had no idea where Dex had gone, and Dex had no idea where Cassie lived.

Then gradually over the months the pain lessened, as it does in the young, and a year later, Cassie found herself now and then looking at some of the boys she was growing up with in Westboro, as she sat in the drug store on Saturday mornings having an ice-cream soda and listening to the jukebox. One morning when she was in the store with some friends from the printing works, she noticed a boy sitting by himself in the window, waiting for his date. One hour later he was still there by himself, but by now he was looking around. He noticed Cassie, sitting reading at the bar long after her friends had left, and he came and sat beside her. Cassie had never been picked up before, so she blushed, and wasn't sure that she should answer this stranger's questions.

But the young man seemed so very respectable, which he in fact was, as Cassie discovered when he introduced himself as Joe Harris, the son of the foremost solicitor in the town. As they got talking, Cassie soon found how easy it was to joke and tease with him, and for the first time since she had spent those wonderful afternoons riding with Dex, she once again found herself laughing and joking.

'So I'm second best, am I?' she asked him, as he bought her yet another milk shake. 'Since your number one choice didn't show up.'

Joe grinned and looked up from his straws.

'As a matter of fact I was waiting for my buddy Pete,' he told her. 'We were going to play some ball, but as usual he didn't show.'

Cassie was secretly pleased, though she couldn't imagine why, since she had only met this boy half an hour ago.

'May I call you tonight?' he asked her as he walked back home towards her grandmother's.

'Sure,' said Cassie. 'But call me between six and seven if that's OK, because I have to go out later.'

She didn't, but her grandmother would be out playing cards at that time, so she could spend as long as she liked talking to Joe on the telephone.

Joe shook her hand when they reached Cassie's house, and said he most certainly would call, right between

161

those times. Probably at twenty nine and a half minutes past six. Cassie laughed and went inside.

Grandmother was waiting for her, and called her into the living room the moment she shut the front door.

'Who was that you were talking to outside?' she asked.

'Just a boy,' Cassie replied. 'Someone I met down the drug store.'

'That was Fred Harris's boy, Joe,' Grandmother said, taking some of the latest pills Dr Fossett had prescribed for her.

'If you knew who it was, Grandmother,' Cassie replied, 'I don't know why you bother to ask me.'

She turned to go, but her grandmother called her back.

'And I don't know what's gotten into you of late,' she complained. 'You haven't a civil word to say to me.'

Cassie thought was it any wonder, but declined stating it out loud.

'If you'll excuse me', she said instead, 'I want to go and wash up and change. I'm playing tennis with Eleanor Greene this afternoon.'

'You'll miss me when I'm gone, mark my words!' Grandmother called after her as Cassie went upstairs. 'You'll miss me, don't you worry!'

Cassie went into her bedroom and closed the door. She wouldn't miss her grandmother when she was dead. Not one bit. In fact she could hardly wait for the moment.

Joe called her at exactly twenty nine and a half minutes past six o'clock, as promised, and asked her out the following evening. Cassie pretended she already had a date, so Joe asked her out the day after. Cassie made it sound as if that day was going to be pretty difficult too, then after a little more pleading from Joe, had second thoughts and agreed after all. After they had talked on the phone for half an hour, Cassie said she had to dash or she'd be late for her date, and hung up. She sat staring at the telephone for a couple of minutes, then ran upstairs singing. She stopped halfway up the stairs when she remembered that the last time she had sung had been the evening when she ran back to Leonora's house from the stables after Dex had kissed her.

Joe and she started dating pretty regularly. Joe had an old 1950 Packard Super 8 ragtop, whose hood took a year to put up if it suddenly rained, but which was enormous fun to drive around in when the sun shone. They dated the way kids always dated, going to drive-in movies, dancing to the touring big bands in the dance halls way out of town, and cheering on the home team at Joe's college ballgames. Joe was fun. He was tall, with dark hair, and Cassie didn't mind one bit that he wore glasses which he always removed whenever he was going to kiss her. Joe was a great kisser, too. As good a kisser as he was a dancer. He was also very attentive and loving, and he made Cassie feel safe, and wanted. He told Cassie that from the moment he had turned round from his window seat in the drug store and seen Cassie at the bar, that had been it. He had known that moment that Cassie was the girl for him.

Cassie hadn't been as sure as Joe was. Despite the fact that he made her laugh so much, and that he was so kind and gentle, Cassie took much longer to fall in love with Joe than he had with her. In a way she fought it. Not because she didn't want Joe, but because in the back of her mind she could always hear her grandmother's constant warnings.

'He's a nice enough young man all right,' she'd say, more than occasionally. 'But you'll never get his mother and father to accept you, not ever.'

Cassie would ask her grandmother what she meant by that, but her grandmother would just shake her head and repeat:

'Not ever.'

Cassie finally decided that this was just another of her grandmother's ploys to try and put Cassie off someone to whom she was quite obviously deeply attracted. With the result that very soon, Cassie became deaf to her grandmother's warnings. In fact, it was these prognostications which finally decided Cassie in the other direction. If Grandmother was so sure she was unacceptable, then Cassie would show her quite how wrong she was. And with her mind thus made up, she surrendered happily to her feelings.

And now she and Joe were going to the coming-out dance for Gina and Maria's cousin Jennifer, who lived in the small town of Ashburn, not far out of Westboro Falls. Cassie stood in front of her mirror and adjusted her new dress for the hundredth time, and turned herself around to check the hem for the hundredth and first. Cassie was a modest girl, but she had to admit to herself that evening she reckoned she'd never looked better.

Going downstairs, she went next door to show Mr O'Reilly the finished product. He had found the dress material up in his attic and had given it to her as a present for Mrs Laxman the town dressmaker to fashion into shape from a pattern Cassie had got from McCall's.

'She's done an excellent job,' Mr O'Reilly said, as Cassie twirled round and round in his living room. 'Better than anything you could get from Macy's, I'll bet. What does your grandmother think of it?'

'She didn't say,' Cassie answered. 'She's in bed, not very well at the moment.'

'Wouldn't she just be?' Mr O'Reilly said, relighting his pipe. 'Doesn't she always take to her bed when you're about to go out enjoying yourself?'

Cassie smiled but didn't reply, as she adjusted her hair in the mirror above Mr O'Reilly's cluttered mantelpiece.

'I don't know what I'd have worn if you hadn't found this material,' Cassie told him. 'Joe's seen all my other dresses, and I'm too broke to buy a new one.'

And with that Cassie turned and gave Mr O'Reilly a kiss on the cheek. Mr O'Reilly's eyes swam a little, and he blushed.

'Careful now, Cassie McGann,' he 'said. 'Or I'll propose to you myself.'

'Joe won't propose tonight,' said Cassie. 'Don't you worry.'

'If he doesn't,' Mr O'Reilly replied, 'I'll eat my hat.'

Cassie and Mr O'Reilly had become even closer friends since the incident with the dog book. Cassie had talked to him about it, and explained what she had done and why, and Mr O'Reilly had thoroughly approved, saying anyway if he hadn't approved, so what? He had given the book to Cassie, and it had been hers to do what she liked with. He was only too glad to think of it helping to feed black babies, rather than sitting gathering dust on a shelf. And he'd told as much to her grandmother.

'You're a beautiful young woman, Cassie,' he said to her as she stood at his window, waving to Joe who had just pulled up. 'Don't let anyone ever tell you different.'

Then Cassie kissed him again, and ran off down the path to Joe, who was standing by his newly washed Packard, adjusting his bow tie.

Mr O'Reilly watched her go, as proud as if she had been his own daughter. If he and his late wife had been able to have children, they'd have been more than proud to have had a little dark-haired girl as pretty and as personable and as popular as young Cassie McGann.

On the way, Joe stopped to pick up George West, Maria's beau, who got in the front of the car with Joe. Maria and Cassie sat in the back, giggling and trying to hold their bouncing skirts down. The yards of tulle underskirt made this practically impossible, and their skirts rose high in the air every time the Packard went over a bump. Both the boys, looking very smart in white tuxedos, talked seriously to each other about the forthcoming inter-collegiate ballgame; while Cassie and Maria talked excitedly about Gina, who was coming up from New York specially for the dance, with the promise that she'd be wearing the Paris original which she had just modelled for the fashion house where she was now working.

* * *

Back in Westboro, Grandmother had got out of her bed to watch Cassie, Maria and Joe leaving in the car, and had thought to herself how frightful the modern fashions had become, before settling down with a glass of warm milk and a copy of *Pride and Prejudice*. Feeling a twinge of pain in her chest, she slipped one of her new pills under her tongue, just to be on the safe side.

Jennifer's dance was fabulous. There were two name bands, one a sixteen-piece dance orchestra, the other a swing quintet. Rosemary Arlen had been booked to sing with the dance orchestra, and she wore a deep red sequinned dress which caught multiple reflections of the hundreds of fairy lights which hung from the trees.

As Joe and Cassie sat a number out, well away from the dance floor, Joe told Cassie how wonderful she looked, and Cassie gave him a present of a small gold heart on a chain, upon which she'd spent the last of her savings. Joe kissed her without smudging her make-up, and grinning, said he might have something for her later. Then they heard the quintet strike up 'Moonglow', which they had made into 'their' tune, since it had been playing on the jukebox in the drug store that Saturday morning when Joe had first come and sat down beside her.

Joe was a wonderful dancer. Cassie thought so every time he took her in his arms. He seemed to have a way of holding a girl so that she felt she was floating. He also held her hand in a special sort of way, tucked tightly into his and then resting on his shoulder. Cassie knew she wasn't as good a dancer as Joe, but by the way he held her and turned her, he always made her feel that she was.

As they danced, silently and cheek to cheek, Cassie knew that this was the moment for which she had always longed. It was no good pretending otherwise. Like most children who have had to endure an unhappy childhood, she had an intensely romantic idea of how life should be, and was determined that her dream of a better life should

166

be fulfilled. After she had lost Dex, and for the year which followed that unhappy incident, she had almost given up the hope that anything wonderful would ever happen to her again. She firmly believed while her heart was breaking that she had been given one chance to escape and be happy, and that it had been snatched away from her. Then she met Joe, whom she at once thought was wonderful, and who, miraculously, unbelievably, thought the same about her.

'It's not as if I hadn't heard about you,' he'd told her on their first or second date. 'I'd heard some of the guys discussing you, and Gina and Maria. But what I imagined was this mousey little girl, living all locked up with her wicked grandmother. Not a beautiful dark-haired girl, with blue-grey eyes and a wonderful laugh.'

Rosemary Arlen stepped back in front of the quintet to reprise the chorus of the song.

> I still hear you saying –
> Dear one, hold me fast –
> And I start in praying –
> Oh Lord, please let this last.

Joe held Cassie even tighter and kissed her hair. As she moved against him, Cassie could feel against her shoulder, behind the handkerchief in Joe's top pocket the shape of something small and hard. Like a little box. A little box which engagement rings came in. Her heart started to pound, and her mouth went dry with excitement.

> And now when there's Moonglow –
> Way up in the blue –
> I always remember –
> That Moonglow gave me to you.
> Yes –
> That Moonglow gave me to you.
> Yes –
> That Moonglow gave me to you.

167

The dancers all turned to the band and applauded. Except Joe and Cassie, who under the shadow of a large pine tree at the corner of the dance floor, stood kissing.

'Let's go walk by the lake, Cass,' Joe said. 'There's something I want to ask you.

Cassie held back, momentarily. She knew once she stepped off the floor and into the shadows of the tree-lined walk which led down to the lake, there would be no looking back. Joe was going to ask her to marry him, and she would answer yes for sure. Yet how could she be sure? How could anyone be sure? She was going to say yes to the rest of her life quite blindly. She was going to agree to spend what could be over fifty years with someone she had known for three months. For one brief moment she felt a flood of panic engulf her, and it was only Joe holding her hand so firmly which stopped her from turning and running away.

Then the moment passed, as she looked and saw Joe's handsome but serious face staring down at her.

'C'mon,' he said. 'This is important.'

Cassie smiled and tightening her grip on Joe's hand, turned to walk down to the lake and a future life with Joe.

'Cassie McGann?' said a voice through the microphone.

Cassie stopped at the end of the path and listened, unsure of what she had heard.

'If there's a Miss Cassie McGann here,' the announcement continued, 'would she please come to the bandstand where there's an urgent message for her.'

Cassie's heart sank right down to the new shoes Joe had given her to go with her dress, and she closed her eyes.

'I don't believe it,' she muttered grimly to herself, as she turned and started to walk back up the path. 'Not tonight of all nights. Please God, not tonight!'

Joe caught her up and took her arm.

'I missed what you said, Cass. What do you think it can be?'

'What do you think, Joe?' Cassie replied. 'It has to be Grandmother!'

Jennifer's mother was waiting for her by the bandstand. She led Cassie away from the music and into the house. Joe followed.

'It's my grandmother, isn't it?' Cassie asked her, unable to keep the bitterness and disappointment from her voice.

'I'm afraid so,' Mrs Gathorne replied. 'A Doctor Fossett rang, and said it would be best if you returned home immediately. Would you like me to drive you, dear?'

'I'll take her, Mrs Gathorne,' Joe volunteered. 'It's no problem.'

He drove very fast back to Westboro Falls, as if every minute spent on the errand was eroding into the happiness he had planned for Cassie and himself. Cassie said nothing for a long time, as she was doing her best to fight back the rage she felt.

'She's always doing this you know, Joe,' she told him finally. 'Ever since I was a kid. Always faking illness, so as I'd have to come home from wherever I was, particularly if she thought I was out enjoying myself. I even had to leave Jennifer's telephone number tonight. In case something happened. "My heart, you know".'

Joe turned and looked at Cassie. He was surprised by the anger and bitterness in her voice. He put his hand out and she took it for a moment, before laying her head on his shoulder.

'There's nothing wrong with her heart, you know,' Cassie said with a sigh. 'Doctor Fossett says these pains she's been having are just gastric.'

'Then why the emergency?' Joe queried, swinging the car left into the main street of Westboro.

'Because knowing my grandmother,' Cassie replied, 'if I didn't rush back at once, to spite me she'd kill herself.'

But her grandmother was still alive when Cassie got home, just as she thought she would be. Joe waited outside while Cassie talked to Doctor Fossett who was standing in

169

the living room when Cassie went in, examining the silver in Grandmother's corner cupboard.

He moved away from the small collection of silver when he saw Cassie, and picked up his overcoat, which he had left draped over the back of a chair. Cassie also noticed that he had helped himself to a drink.

'I should imagine it's only a chill,' he told Cassie, slipping his coat back on with the practised ease of someone used to putting it on and off many times during the course of a day. 'She has a raised temperature, and some congestion in her lungs. I've started her on a course of penicillin, which you're to administer every six hours.'

He picked up his bag and walked out to the front door. Cassie followed him.

'That means I have to stay home, I guess,' she said.

Doctor Fossett glanced at her party dress, then nodded.

'I'm afraid so, young lady,' he answered. 'At times like this there are more important things than going out dancing. I'll look in and see how she's getting on in the morning.'

Joe jumped out of his car when he saw Cassie standing so forlorn on the steps, and ran up to her.

'Everything OK?'

'I have to stay here, Joe,' Cassie told him, taking his hands. 'Grandmother's got a fever.'

'Can't the maid look after her?' Joe asked.

'Delta doesn't live in,' Cassie replied. 'I'm sorry, but the doctor says I really have to stay.'

Joe and Cassie stood on the porch for a moment in silence, looking out at the night, neither of them quite knowing what to say or how to pick up the pieces.

'I'll stay with you, Cassie,' Joe announced. 'Come on.'

Cassie stopped him by the door.

'And miss all the fun? Are you crazy?'

She turned him back towards the car.

'You go right back to the dance at once and enjoy yourself,' she told him. 'There's no point in us both being miserable.'

170

'That does it,' Joe said, turning back and taking one of Cassie's hands firmly. 'If you're going to be miserable, how in hell am I going to enjoy myself?'

He pulled her after him back into the house, and closed the front door.

Cassie went upstairs to see her grandmother. She was lying propped up by two extra pillows, half asleep, and Cassie noticed that her breathing did sound rather thick and rasping. But then whenever her grandmother had a cold, her breathing always sounded constrained.

She also looked pale, whiter than usual in fact. Cassie couldn't help entertaining the thought that, knowing her grandmother, she had probably powdered her face that colour specially, to frighten Cassie, and punish her for going out and enjoying herself. She also made herself a private bet that Grandmother's sixth sense had told her that Joe had bought an engagement ring and was going to propose to her that night.

Grandmother woke up just as Cassie was tiptoeing back out of the room.

'Is that you, Delta?' she asked.

'No, Grandmother,' Cassie replied, turning back. 'It's Cassie.'

'Go and tell Delta to make me a hot drink,' she ordered, still well enough to give her usual peremptory commands.

Cassie was about to tell her that Delta had long gone home, when she stopped. This was just another of Grandmother's bear traps. Always giving the credit for whatever Cassie might do for her to someone else. Cassie never did anything for her out of kindness, while everything Delta did was always altruistic and nothing to do with earning her salary.

Joe followed Cassie into the kitchen, and watched her as she made her grandmother a hot drink of milk and cinammon.

'How old is your grandmother?' Joe asked her, putting his arms round Cassie's waist from behind.

171

'Careful, Joe!' Cassie laughed. 'Unless you want me to get burned!'

'That's the last thing I want,' Joe replied, and turning her round to him, kissed her.

'How old is your grandmother?' he repeated.

'I don't know,' Cassie answered with a shrug. 'Not very old. Sixty-four, sixty-five. I'm not sure.'

'Right,' he said. 'About the same age as mine. That's no age.'

'Meaning?' Cassie asked.

'Meaning it's probably just the 'flu.'

Cassie took Grandmother up her drink, careful not to spill anything in the saucer, and thought that she'd never considered it might be anything other than a cold, or the 'flu. Her grandmother might be small, but although she was always complaining about her health, and carrying on like a semi-invalid, it had never affected her activities. She still went out three or four times a week to play bridge, and walked to the beauty parlour every Friday morning.

But she had fallen back asleep when Cassie went back into her bedroom, with her mouth wide open, and her right hand hanging out of bed. Cassie put the drink down, and gently replaced the hand under the bedcovers. She noticed her grandmother's breathing sounded slightly more congested, but then decided that if indeed she did have the 'flu, this was only to be expected. She turned the light out and closed the door, before tiptoeing back downstairs.

Joe had made them a jug of coffee, which he had taken through to the living room, where he was now fiddling with Grandmother's old radio set, trying to tune it in to some dance music.

'Not too loud for heaven's sake, Joe!' Cassie hissed with a backward glance up the stairs before closing the door. 'We don't want her waking up.'

'Too right,' grinned Joe, taking Cassie in his arms as a band on the radio played 'The Nearness Of You'.

'What are you doing, Joe?' Cassie asked, knowing full well.

'There's no reason why we have to stop dancing,' Joe replied. 'There's no reason I can't ask you here what I was going to ask you by the lake.'

Cassie looked up at him and smiled. Then she rested her head on his chest, loving him even more at that moment than she'd loved him before. He sang the words of the song softly to her, resting his chin on the top of her hair.

When you're in my arms, and I feel you so close to me –
All my wildest dreams come true –

They didn't hear the footfalls on the staircase, nor did they even hear the door opening behind them – most likely because they were fast in each other's arms and miles away. But they were rudely disturbed by the overhead light suddenly being switched on.

Cassie spun round in surprise to see the figure of her grandmother leaning against the doorway, her nightgown clasped around her.

'What do you think you two are doing?' she croaked, one hand at her throat. 'Don't you realise I am lying at death's door above your head?'

'I'm sorry, Grandmother,' Cassie said. 'We didn't think you'd be able to hear the radio.'

'Dancing indeed,' her grandmother continued. 'Smooching and dancing while someone lies waiting to meet their Maker. Have you *no* sense at all?'

Cassie went towards her grandmother as she grabbed hold of the lintel to stop herself slipping to the floor.

'It was entirely my fault, Mrs Arbuthnot,' Joe said. 'You mustn't hold Cassie to blame. It was entirely my fault.'

Cassie's grandmother ignored him, as she tried to catch her breath.

'Help me get her back upstairs, Joe,' Cassie said, taking

her grandmother by the arm. 'Then I must ring the doctor.'

Grandmother didn't seem to know what was happening to her as they almost carried her back up the stairs. She started to mutter deliriously, and sweat was running profusely down her face. They got her back into her bed, where she lay shivering with fever. Cassie fetched a cold flannel and wiped her grandmother's face and neck, then piled some more bedclothes on to the bed. They sat with her for a while, as she tossed her head restlessly from side to side on her pillow, all the time muttering dark and delirious imprecations.

Then she fell asleep, quite suddenly, and very deeply. Her breathing seemed more regular and much less congested, and under the welter of bedclothes, she had quite stopped shivering. They went quietly out of the room, and Cassie hurried downstairs to the telephone.

When it rang in Doctor Fossett's house, he was just sitting on the side of his bed, unlacing his shoes, having just returned from a good two hours in his regular poker school. He had also consumed the best part of half a quart of Jack Daniels.

Cassie, when she heard his voice on the telephone, thought the thickness of his speech was due to sleepiness.

'I know it's late, Doctor,' Cassie said, 'but she's really very feverish.'

'She would be,' Doctor Fossett replied, undoing his tie. 'It's a very nasty 'flu. Mrs Fossett had it, and wasn't at all well.'

'I still think you should come over and see her,' Cassie continued, prompted by Joe. 'She went really delirious.'

'Just like Mrs Fossett,' Doctor Fossett nodded, undoing the waistbelt of his pants. 'If she wakes up, give her three aspirin, and don't forget her penicillin. I'll look in in the morning.'

'It would only take you ten minutes to look in now,' Cassie suggested.

'Young lady,' Doctor Fossett said with unconcealed

174

impatience. 'I still have other calls to make. Your grandmother isn't the only victim of this influenza. We could have an epidemic on our hands.'

And with that he put the telephone back on its cradle and fell into bed, still in his underclothes.

Cassie and Joe kept a nightwatch. They took it in turns to stay awake, in case anything further should happen, but by four o'clock in the morning Grandmother was still sound asleep. While Cassie was upstairs checking her, Joe took the ring box out of his pocket and opened it. The stones on the pretty ring gleamed and shone by the firelight, but Joe knew that this was now neither the time nor the place to propose to Cassie. So he put it back in his pocket, and planned when next he could ask her.

Cassie came back down and told Joe that her grandmother was still asleep, and that he should now go home as the crisis seemed to have passed. Joe was reluctant to leave Cassie, but she insisted, as Joe needed some sleep before he went to work, as indeed Cassie herself did. They kissed on the doorstep then, turning once to wave at Cassie and blow her another kiss, he was gone into the dawn.

Cassie tidied up the living room, doused the fire down and prepared to go up to bed – when quite suddenly there was the sound of a heavy crash from her grandmother's room which was directly above her. At once Cassie dropped everything and rushed up the stairs, taking them two, three at a time. She flung open her grandmother's bedroom door to see her lying sprawled on the floor, face down, one leg still hitched up on the bed and caught under the bedding.

She didn't seem to be breathing as she lay with her face twisted sideways on the carpet. Her eyes were open and staring at Cassie, and from the side of her mouth ran a dark trickle of blood. Cassie stood for a moment, rooted to the spot with horror, before rushing to her grandmother to try and pick her up and put her back in bed. But even before she had lifted her light frame off the

175

floor, Cassie knew it was too late. Grandmother was dead. She had died before she had even hit the floor.

Doctor Fossett seemed more interested in the silver in Grandmother's cabinet than in the figure seated in black by the fireside behind him. His head was still throbbing from the amount of whisky he had drunk the night before, and already his internal mechanism was telling him it was time for a hair of the dog.

'There was nothing more you could have done, Cassie,' he assured the young woman, bending closer to look at a particularly pretty little silver cream jug he hadn't noticed before. 'With older people, there's just no telling where or when.'

'Or how,' replied Cassie, curious as to what had caused her grandmother's sudden death. 'It surely can't have been the 'flu.'

'No,' said Doctor Fossett gravely, taking the little jug out of the cupboard and turning it over to examine the hallmarks. 'No, no, I would say there must have been sudden and acute complications.'

'But not her heart,' Cassie persisted. 'You said there was nothing wrong with her heart.'

'As far as I could diagnose,' Doctor Fossett replied, clearing his throat, 'there was absolutely nothing wrong with her heart whatsoever. Nothing whatsoever. And as I keep trying to assure you, you really mustn't blame yourself.'

She wasn't, Cassie thought, watching the doctor replace the piece of silver he had been examining. She knew who was to blame, and so, in his heart, did Doctor Fossett. Cassie knew he should have called back during the night when she rang him. He might not have been able to save her, but his presence would have made sure that there could be no accusations of neglect levelled against either party. Grandmother must have known she was dying, and if Doctor Fosset had been there, and able to confirm this, she could at least have had the Last Rites.

176

Cassie knew she would mind about that. And she felt sorry for the dead woman, for missing her last chance to make her peace with God.

'I've made all the necessary arrangements,' Doctor Fossett said, buttoning up his coat. 'So there's nothing about which you need immediately concern yourself.'

'I want a post mortem,' Cassie said suddenly, as Doctor Fossett was just pulling on his gloves.

'I don't understand,' he replied, with the ghost of a smile. 'There's absolutely no need. Your grandmother died of influenza and complications. That's what I've put on the death certificate.'

'She didn't die of influenza, Doctor,' Cassie told him. 'As I think you probably suspect yourself. I called Joe Harris, who then spoke to his father—'

Cassie looked up, curious at what reaction that would bring from the doctor. She noticed with some satisfaction that what colour there was to his face was fast draining away.

'And he was of the opinion that there could be a misdiagnosis here,' Cassie finished.

'I think you'll find my diagnosis was perfectly correct,' Doctor Fossett faltered. 'They invariably are.'

'Probably because invariably they are never questioned,' Cassie answered calmly. 'Anyway, Doctor, it's not for me to find out if it was correct.'

Cassie rose to see him out. She wasn't demanding the post mortem for the sake of her grandmother, but for the sake of all the sick and dying people who were being treated by Doctor Fossett. Cassie had heard the tales about him, and in particular how all the old spinsters and widows lived in almost mortal fear of his predatory ways. She knew for a fact that he was always helping himself to valuable knick-knacks from his terminally ill patients; only last week, so the story went, he had helped himself to Mrs Edith Clarence's 150-year old silver fruit bowl, before the woman had drawn her last breath. In fact she had staged a late rally and embarrassed Doctor

177

Fossett, as she saw him putting the bowl in his bag. She rallied long enough to live another day and to tell her sister of the scandal when she came to visit her that evening.

So Cassie was determined that her grandmother was going to do one good thing in her life, even by the leaving it, and that was to expose Doctor Fossett's malpractices.

Doctor Fossett paused on the porch before leaving.

'I don't like to bring this up at a time like this, Cassie,' he said. 'But your poor grandmother's account is outstanding some three months now. And I thought perhaps in lieu of what is still owed—'

Cassie didn't allow him to finish.

'Grandmother's account has been paid up until these last two visits,' she replied. 'Anything outstanding will be settled once her affairs are in order.'

She then closed the door on him, and on any hopes Doctor Fossett might have nursed of getting his hands on the pretty little silver cream jug.

Cassie next turned her attentions to Delta, who was still sitting in the kitchen weeping copiously, in between taking slugs of Grandmother's brandy. Cassie knew that her tears were caused more by the fact that she was now out of a job, rather than by the sudden death of her employer.

'Pull yourself together, Delta,' Cassie ordered, 'and tell me what you're owed.'

'Two weeks and one half, Miss Cassie,' Delta sniffed. 'The Lord have mercy on her soul.'

Cassie opened her grandmother's purse, which she had been carrying around in order to keep it out of Delta's clutches. It was a strange feeling, opening the stiff clasp and rummaging inside. Cassie felt as if she was robbing a grave. She took out what Delta was owed and paid it to her, then put a piece of paper and a pen on the table in front of her.

'What's this for, Miss Cassie?' Delta asked, knowing full well.

'It's a receipt, Delta,' Cassie answered. 'Please sign it. Like you always did for Grandmother.'

Delta signed it, narrow-eyed. She never had liked Cassie, sharing her late employer's view that there would be far less work if there was no child in the house.

'I'm not sure as I can come back this evening, Miss Cassie,' Delta said on her way out, in an attempt to pay Cassie back for her lack of trust. 'My sister's coming over, do you see?'

'That's perfectly all right, Delta,' Cassie said, 'I shall be quite all right by myself'.

It wasn't as if Delta would be much company anyway. They were hardly going to become devoted friends just because Grandmother had died. Besides, Cassie wanted to be alone. She had even turned down Joe's offer to come round and sit with her that evening, because she had wanted to be by herself.

At first Cassie thought she would be nervous, left alone in the house where someone had just died. But she soon realised that she felt the very opposite. An enormous calm settled over her and, Cassie imagined, over the house itself. Cassie could now go where she liked in the house, and when she liked. She could go in and out of the front door a hundred thousand times if she wanted, singing at the top of her voice and slamming the door or leaving it wide open. She could invite her friends in and have a party. Or she could just ask Joe over and they could sit in the kitchen discussing their future. And there would never again be the presence lurking behind her, that shadow in the doorway, or that banging of Grandmother's stick on the floor, should Cassie raise her voice in laughter when she was napping in the afternoon, or play the radio too loudly when she was upstairs trying to read. Grandmother was dead. Grandmother was gone.

Cassie sat in her grandmother's chair, which the dead woman had treated like a throne, ruling her little kingdom with a rod of iron. Now Cassie stretched her own self out in it and tried to discover if she felt any grief at all. She had felt a terrible shock when she realised that the body on the floor was no longer a living body, and a kind of numb terror as she replaced the still warm corpse back as she found it, lest anyone should suspect her of what she understood to be called foul play. But once the body had been taken away, and Cassie had been left alone in the empty house, all she could feel was this extraordinary calm.

She looked over to the desk which her grandmother had always kept locked. Cassie had the key to it now, and access to all the dead woman's secrets. She wondered what it contained. Perhaps there would be letters, proving to Cassie that she had misunderstood her grandmother completely, correspondence which would reveal her in a totally different light, as a woman put upon by a child she had never wanted, who had consequently ruined her life. And perhaps there would be pictures of her mother, something Cassie had never seen, because Grandmother had never shown her photographs of either her late mother or her father. Cassie stared at the rosewood bureau, sorely tempted to open it there and then, but decided against it, in case she was not yet ready to deal with the information it could well divulge. It could wait. There was no hurry any more, and no need for privacy. Grandmother was dead.

It was Joe who telephoned her with the results of the post mortem, which had been carried out at Haven Hills hospital. Her grandmother had died from a massive coronary occlusion. The pains she had been suffering in her chest, diagnosed by Doctor Fossett as having their root cause in gastric disturbance, were quite obviously anginal. The state of her grandmother's arteries made this absolutely plain. Had her angina been correctly diagnosed, and had the usual nitroglycerin tablets been prescribed, instead of anti-indigestion remedies such as magnesia tablets and carminatives such as soda mint, her grandmother would have been able to live with her faulty arteries and enjoy a next-to-normal life. As it was, however, the post mortem revealed that she was lucky to have lived so long.

Cassie listened to all this calmly. Lucky for who? she couldn't help wondering. Certainly not for her grand-daughter.

'You still there?' Joe asked in the silence.

'Sure,' Cassie replied. 'I just got to thinking, that's all.'

'You want me to come round?'

'No, Joe, I'm fine. Really. Let's wait till after the funeral.'

'They're going to go for old Fossett, you can bet,' Joe said. 'A lot of people are going to thank you for this.'

'I don't want their thanks, Joe,' Cassie told him. 'It's just nice to know maybe there'll be a little less suffering in the town.'

She hung up, with a promise to see him again as soon as it was right and proper. In the meantime, she'd call him whenever and if ever she wanted to talk.

The Requiem Mass seemed to take forever. Cassie kept staring at the velvet-draped coffin in an attempt to find an eleventh-hour grief. But her heart remained unmoved, and her tear ducts dry. She didn't feel any hate, and of that she was glad. Mindful of what the nuns had taught her, she had cleared her heart of any hatred for her grandmother, even after the horrific beating she had received at her hands. Instead she had felt nothing. Nothing at all.

Before the funeral, she had taken the train out to the convent to talk to Sister Joseph.

'There's nothing in the Bible which says you *have* to love your parents, and I should imagine that goes for your grandparents as well, Cassie darling,' Sister Joseph had told her. 'Respect them, yes. Forgive them their trespasses, certainly. Honour them, of course. But there's nothing about having to love them, because it wouldn't make sense. Love is a special magic, and we can't expect to feel real love for everyone. Especially people who wish to do us harm.'

'What about the instruction to love our neighbour?' Cassie had asked. 'If we're expected to love our neighbour, then surely we must be expected to love our parents and grandparents?'

'I don't think so, Cassie,' Sister Joseph had replied thoughtfully. 'I think the instruction to love our neighbour is meant to make us think more carefully about him and his problems. And if people did that, and gave more thought to those who lived next door, who knows? Maybe we wouldn't be fighting so many wars.'

Cassie had thought about what Sister Joseph had said all the way back to Westboro Falls. She was grateful to the nun for her reasoned advice, because now and then, when she woke in the night and the death of her grandmother became more and more real to her, she had been frightened by her total lack of sentiment.

Now she sat in the church, before the coffin containing the mortal remains of her only known relative, while the priest for whom Grandmother had never had a good word read out an address in remembrance of the life of their sister Catherine. Cassie suddenly wondered why they had never heard from any other members of the family, at times such as Christmas when other people's long-forgotten aunts or faintly related cousins might suddenly send a card, or a greeting, or even stop by and call in. Cassie had only the earliest and vaguest recollections of any relatives calling or even just being mentioned. She dimly remembered a rather tall aunt who spoke with a most peculiar accent, and a cousin who once telephoned on his way up to Canada, wishing to call by and pay his respects. Cassie had been about twelve, and she remembered talking to this voice for a few minutes, with a mounting and inexplicable sense of excitement, before Grandmother, late back from the beauty parlour, snatched the telephone away from her, and explained for some peculiar reason that they were moving house and unfortunately would no longer be living in Westboro when he passed through. Cassie had begun to ask her grandmother where they were moving to, only, she now remembered, to be told to go up to her room and mind her own business.

After they had buried her, friends and acquaintances called back at the house to pay their respects. The friends of her late grandmother were frostily polite to Cassie, having always been fed the hand-out of what a difficult and impossible child she had been. While Cassie's friends expressed their sorrow for Cassie, but didn't pretend any false devotion to a woman whom they knew had been to put it mildly a little over-hard on the child. They didn't say her grandmother had always been so kind, because they knew she hadn't; and they didn't say they were sorry she was gone, because they weren't. They did say and mean that they were sorry for the small dignified figure in black who stood receiving their condolences. They felt truly sorry that Cassie had suffered so much, and that now, at the end of her childhood, she stood alone in the world, with no loving family behind her.

But then Cassie had Joe. Joe was beside her in the house, while her friends came and paid their respects, and Joe was the last to go when the visitors had departed, and Cassie was left with a half-drunk Delta to clear up the house. Once more, she wouldn't let him stay, lest people talked, finding such behaviour improper, but promised to meet him in exactly two weeks, when they would once more start walking out together, and would pick up exactly and precisely where they had left off.

But then one morning a month after her grandmother had died, Joe's father, who was her grandmother's lawyer, telephoned Cassie, and asked her most politely if she would be good enough to call at his office to see him. Cassie knew at once from the tone of his voice that there was something he had to tell her, and that that something wasn't necessarily to her benefit. She had met Joe's parents, naturally, and had been to lunch and dinner several times at their house, giving the lie to Grandmother's threat that they would never accept her. In fact Joe's parents liked Cassie and seemed openly delighted with the prospect that their much loved son Joe might be about to propose marriage to such a charming girl.

They were, however, Joe had hinted, just a little worried about Cassie's family background. Being pillars of the Westboro community, it was of course very important for them that if Joe was intending to get engaged, the family into which he was going to get married should be of good if not impeccable stock. Of course all the town knew how respectable Mrs Arbuthnot had been, even if most of them disapproved of her over-strict rearing of her grandchild. And there had never been as much as a hint of scandal about her. But for someone who claimed to be able to trace her lineage back to old England, whenever Mrs Harris attempted to glean a little more information, she ran up against a brick wall. Everyone could take her back to a certain point in Mrs Arbuthnot's history, namely the day she moved into Westboro Falls, but before that her life seemed veiled in mystery. Mrs Harris had in fact been intending to call upon Mrs Arbuthnot the very week she died, in order, she hoped, to learn a little more about her family and background.

So Cassie knew that it wasn't simply a matter of going through the motions of clearing up her grandmother's affairs when she called in at Mr Harris's office later in the day. Normally when Joe's father telephoned Cassie, he asked her to bring over some papers with her, or an account book, or some missing share certificates. On this occasion, he just wanted to see Cassie.

Mr Harris met Cassie at the door of his office personally and pulled up the very best chair for her. Cassie was wearing a new jacket and skirt; dark blue, with a white piqué collar to the jacket, it had seemed a suitable outfit for someone so recently in mourning. Mr Harris complimented Cassie on her appearance, and she thanked him, noting that as always Joe's father was himself impeccably dressed in an expensive and beautifully cut suit. He was a very handsome man, tall like his son, with a shock of white hair. Cassie wondered whether Joe's hair would go that colour early, and smiled to herself as she removed her gloves.

'I'll come to the point, Cassie dear,' Mr Harris said, 'because it's not good news.'

Cassie looked up but she was not surprised. Nothing to do with her grandmother had ever been good news.

'Your grandmother died leaving you no money,' he told her, sitting at his desk and cutting the end of an expensive cigar.

'I didn't expect she would,' Cassie replied very calmly. 'She didn't like me.'

'I know, Cassie,' said Mr Harris. 'I realise that, but even so. Even so. It's not as if she seems to have had any other family.'

'There's the house,' Cassie volunteered.

Mr Harris looked down at the end of his cigar before replying. Then he looked at her across his desk.

'Your grandmother left the house to Delta.'

That was a shock, a great shock. But Cassie refused to let it show. It wasn't what the house was worth that bothered her. It was the slap in the face from beyond the grave.

'She changed her will apparently,' Mr Harris explained, 'without me knowing anything about it. It was with those papers I had collected the other day. If I'd known about it, I'd have advised her against it, of course—'

'It wouldn't have made any difference, Mr Harris.'

'I'm sure, Cassie. But you never know. You never know.'

There was a silence while Joe's father swung his chair round and stared out of the window, carefully blowing out a slow stream of cigar smoke.

'There are also quite sizeable debts, I'm afraid,' he then continued, 'which will have to be paid out of her estate. When the jewellery, furniture and paintings have been sold, there's not going to be very much left.'

'I wasn't counting on a penny,' Cassie answered.

'Did you know your father left you a lot of money?' Mr Harris suddenly asked her, swinging his chair back so that he could face her.

Cassie hadn't known.

'It was to cover your schooling, which it did, and then there was meant to be a lump sum for you when you come of age. But I'm afraid your grandmother spent all that. All the extra. She was a very profligate woman it seems.'

'What did she spend it on?' Cassie asked curiously. 'She didn't seem to have very many expenses, besides her weekly trip to the beauty parlour. I mean, she never took vacations, and it's not as if we had a motor car.'

'I really couldn't say, Cassie,' Mr Harris replied. 'I've only just started trying to make sense of her accounts. All I can tell you is that she made a habit every month of drawing out a large sum of money in cash. Four hundred dollars to be precise.'

Cassie frowned and looked past Joe's father, through his window and out on to the street But she barely noticed the traffic passing by. What could her grandmother possibly have spent all that money on? And every month? Yet every time Cassie had asked her for something, like a new skirt, or a pair of shoes, which wasn't very often, her grandmother had refused, saying that, thanks to Cassie's school fees and keep, she hadn't any money.

'I'm sorry to have been the harbinger of such depressing news, Cassie,' Mr Harris said, rising in conclusion of the interview.

'Not at all, Mr Harris,' Cassie answered, pulling on her new gloves. 'It was very kind of you to take the time to tell me personally.'

'That was my pleasure, Cassie,' Mr Harris said, escorting her to the door. 'You mean a great deal to our family.'

Cassie smiled at him, and then shook his hand.

'Thank you all the same,' she said, and left.

She left with a spring in her step and with the lightest heart she had had since the day Joe had walked into her life. It wasn't bad news. On the contrary, it was great news. It meant that Cassie hadn't been wrong all her young years. Her grandmother had hated her, and so she had been right to close her heart to her in return. The only thing missing from the puzzle was why her grandmother had hated her. Cassie suddenly started to hurry on home. Perhaps the truth lay there, and had always lain hidden there, locked away in the rosewood bureau.

When she opened the front door and let herself in, the phone was ringing. It was Joe, anxious to come round and take her out to dinner. But Cassie pleaded a headache, and made a date for the following evening. Then she hurried upstairs to find her grandmother's purse, and in it, the key to the bureau.

By midnight it seemed that Cassie had got no further in solving the mystery. She sat on the floor surrounded by letters, every one of which she had read and sorted. But none of them told her anything beyond the fact that her grandmother had always moaned and complained about Cassie as a child to whomsoever she had written, since the answers to her letters reflected the constant dissatisfaction her grandmother had obviously felt with having to bring up a young child. It seemed from the correspondence that Cassie had ruined what life she might have had, and that she would never forgive Cassie for that.

But that still didn't seem to explain the depth of her grandmother's loathing for her. Other people she knew had been forced to bring up children that weren't their own, particularly, she had been told, after the war. And they hadn't hated those children just because of the fact they had been introduced by force of circumstance into their lives. She remembered the nuns telling her stories of families who loved their adopted children as much as their own. So why should a grandmother of all people take such a violent dislike to her own grandchild? Particularly to a child who had come to her as a baby, and not as a delinquent with ready-made problems.

Cassie stared at the letters on the carpet. There was something odd about the whole collection, yet she couldn't quite put her finger on it. Then she realised that there was no letter in all the carefully preserved correspondence which dated from before the year Grandmother had moved to Westboro, which had been in 1943, two years after Cassie had been born. And then there were the photographs, or rather the lack of them. Cassie had half expected to find some family albums: not of her and Grandmother, naturally, because Grandmother had never taken one single photograph of her, but of her grandmother's own and early life, before Cassie had been foisted on her, to ruin her remaining years on earth.

But there were none. Cassie found two fast-fading sepia portraits of a man and a woman she suspected must be her great-grandparents, but there were none whatsoever of her grandmother as a child, and none of anyone else at all. No unknown young men or women who could possibly be Cassie's own father or mother. Why had her grandmother taken and kept none of her own daughter? Did she hate her that much as well? The only other photographs which Cassie had found in a small locked tin were country views and pictures of a small town which looked as if it was in the far West.

And that was all. There were no diaries, or personal accounts of any nature. The only other items which her grandmother had kept locked away from her were a few board games, which Cassie remembered being allowed very occasionally to play on wet afternoons, usually after Sunday lunch, when Grandmother was sometimes, but not often, in a more benign frame of mind.

But nothing else.

A life had just gone, taking away with it a 65-year-old history. Cassie sat back, leaning on her hands, her arms stretched out behind her. Had her grandmother held out to the last, and carried the secrets of her hatred for Cassie to the grave?

Then she remembered the small key which hung by the large key which had opened the bureau. She took the ring out of the bureau's lock, and tried it in the tin which had contained the photographs, and which Cassie had easily forced open with a can opener. It didn't fit the box, so Cassie looked around for something else it might open. But as far as she could see, every drawer in the desk was open.

She saw the tiny keyhole quite by chance. She had been about to give up and go to bed, as it was now well past two o'clock, and if she hadn't been such a tidy-minded person she would never have discovered it. But rather than leave all the letters lying about on the floor until morning, Cassie had put them back in the order in which she had found them, preparatory to replacing them in the rosewood pigeon holes. It was as she was placing the last set of letters in the last cubicle that she saw it, a keyhole in miniature set up in the side of the woodwork inside the compartment itself. Once the letters were replaced there, it was invisible. But once removed, you could just see it if you bent down. Cassie was kneeling on the floor while she was putting the letters away, which is how she was able to discover it.

But she hesitated before trying the key in the lock. If there was indeed a secret drawer, then what it contained was meant to be secret, and therefore should remain undisturbed. But what if whatever may lie in there helped reveal to Cassie the truth? Was it not vital for her to try and understand the very nature of her existence? Could

189

she really live the rest of her life without opening the secret drawer and seeing what was within it? She knew at once she couldn't, because until she found out whether or not there was anything in there which might help her to understand what her life had meant so far, she would never rest easy.

She turned the little key, and immediately underneath the row of pigeon holes, a drawer held in place by a spring shot open. Cassie stared at it, transfixed. There *was* a letter, and there it lay, in a long white envelope, quite clearly and boldly addressed to Cassie.

Cassie took it out slowly, wondering why her grandmother had gone to this elaborate charade. If she had anything important to tell her after she was gone, then why not lodge the letter as most normal people did with their lawyers? But then of course, Cassie realised, as she turned the letter over in her hand, Grandmother was not most people, nor was she normal. She must have plotted it, and worked it all out: how Cassie, once Grandmother was dead, would inevitably go through her desk in order to try and find the meaning of her existence, and how at first she would find nothing. But knowing well Cassie's determination, she had obviously decided to prolong the game, and hide what must be the vital clue, in the hope of a bit more sadistic pleasure, albeit posthumous. But then Cassie had found it after all by chance, and not because of her determination, since Cassie had in fact given up, and was about to close up the desk for ever.

But now in her hand was a letter which could contain if not the answer, maybe at the least a partial explanation of her grandmother's attitude. Cassie sat down, and tore it open. Now she had it, there were no further reasons to delay. She would read it at once. And then as she read it, she wished she had never been born.

Cassie, (it started). Knowing you, you will eventually find this letter. And even if you do not, someone else will. Perhaps a stranger who will buy this bureau.

And if he or she may find it, then they will pass it on to you, once they too have read the contents.

You were forever curious about the conditions of your birth and the nature of your mother. I am going to tell you about these things now. You were born in a town outside Kerby in Oregon, where your mother had been touring in burlesque. Your father was the manager of a travelling group of players, who used to play the western towns, and sometimes some of the northern Californian ones. He was a drunk, and was having an affair with your mother. Then she became pregnant by him and once he discovered, which took him several months, he fired her from the troupe. This was a pity, because your mother was a wonderful singer and a consummate actress, and earlier in her career it had looked as if she might indeed have become a big star. But the business she had chosen for herself was a fickle one, and for many reasons which I won't go into, her career faltered and she was reduced to touring with third-rate outfits. Of course she and your father, although they had been cohabiting for several years, never married, so naturally you are what people like to call a bastard.

Your father left your mother out West to fend for herself while he travelled back to Chicago. She had no money, and was so ill while carrying you that there was no possibility of her being able to work. So it was in much reduced circumstances that you entered the world. However, your mother did not die giving birth to you, thanks to the ministrations of a young man who was at that time studying to be a doctor. Your mother survived, and soon was well enough to earn enough money to follow your father to Chicago, where he had become in those two years a surprisingly successful showman – no small thanks to a very rich woman he had seduced and consequently married.

Your mother did, however, manage to persuade

your father to part with a sizeable amount of money, since your mother knew he was already married and therefore a bigamist. He also agreed to settle on you, his child, a lump sum to cover your education and welfare. Your mother then moved on up east.

That is really all there is to the story of how you came to be. The only other fact which may interest you is that the young man who saved your mother's life finally qualified as a doctor and by coincidence settled to practise in the town where your mother was living. When he found where she was, and who she was, he tried to get her to marry him. But your mother didn't love him. She only ever loved your father. And as a consequence, the doctor became an alcoholic. However, he knew enough about your mother to cause a scandal in the respectable town in which she lived, so arrangements were made to pay him a certain amount of money regularly so that he should remain silent about these matters. But now that your mother is dead, such arrangements need no longer concern you.

Yes, Cassie. In case you have not yet arrived at the truth in your mind, I am not your grandmother, but in fact your mother. There was no problem in keeping up the deception, since I gave birth to you when I was forty-five, and when I finally settled in Westboro, I had made quite sure that all my past was well and truly buried. Until that is, Doctor Fossett, the young man who attended your birth, arrived in town.

I hope this satisfies your curiosity. Which is all I hope for you. For to my mind, it would have been a much better day had you never been born.

Mother.

Cassie stared at the letter and stared particularly at the word at the bottom. The word she had been looking for, the word she had been longing for. Mother. Someone to love her. Or someone whom she could have loved. And all the time it had been the person who had hated her and beaten her. Grandmother.

She began to tremble, and soon she was shaking. She didn't even hear the scream she gave as she consigned the letter to the flames of the dying fire, nor afterwards could she remember how she got up to her bedroom. But it was there she found herself, lying on the floor, with her fingers bruised from where she had been tearing at the carpet. Then she climbed into bed and, pulling all the covers over herself, lay beneath them in womblike darkness until long into the following day.

In the evening she vaguely heard the doorbell ring, and even though it was probably Joe she didn't bother to answer it. She just lay under the covers. Dead to everything but the truth. After some time, the bell stopped ringing and she heard a car drive away. Shortly after the telephone started ringing but she ignored that too.

By dawn she was sitting in front of the mirror trying to repair the ravages to her face. Then wearily she started to pack her case, and as the sun came up she left Westboro Falls on the first Greyhound bus which passed through the town. A small, lonely figure facing a future of uncertainty, a past of pain. The other passengers never looked at her, nor she at them. They were all just journeying on, but for Cassie anyway the road behind was shorter than the road in front.

Chapter Nine

New York
1960

When Cassie had arrived in New York, in the early hours of a late October morning, she made straight for the one and only address she had, which was Gina's apartment, two rooms shared with another aspiring model above a delicatessen in Greenwich Village. Gina, wearing a New York Giants sweat shirt and nothing else except for some night cream on her face, had opened the door to her almost as if she was expecting her, and immediately sensing that something was wrong, took Cassie into her apartment and under her wing.

Luckily for Cassie, Gina was on the way up. After a difficult eighteen months, she had finally been spotted on the catwalk by a scout for Richard Kanin, who was the latest most-important-up-and-coming fashion photographer. He had suggested Gina as the new Miss Angel Face, but although Gina didn't finally land the contract, Kanin was sufficiently taken with her to use her for a big spread in *Harpers*. Gina was on her way.

Cassie wouldn't have guessed it from the state of the tiny apartment, with its one barely double bedroom, and its cluttered living room, in the corner of which was also the kitchen area. There was no bath, just a shower, and the john was always a jungle of dripping hosiery and underwear.

But it was a haven for someone on the emotional run, and Cassie gratefully accepted Gina's generous offer for Cassie to share her bed until she found her feet and a job. For three months, in fact, rather than disturb Gina who because of the nature of her work needed her beauty sleep, Cassie slept on the floor, while working as a waitress in the diner on the corner of the block. Gina, having known Cassie most of her life, knew better than to enquire as the exact reason for Cassie's precipitous flight from Westboro Falls. Cassie volunteered a certain amount of information; that she had quarrelled with Joe, and that since her grandmother was dead, there seemed no reason for her to stay behind in such a one-horse town, where the most any girl could hope for was to get married to somebody 'suitable'. But the story didn't ring true, and Gina's doubts about its veracity were soon confirmed when Maria wrote to her and told Gina that Joe had gone completely to pieces when he discovered Cassie had fled Westboro without apparent reason.

But Joe didn't follow Cassie to New York, although he had found out easily enough where she was. And night after night as Cassie lay wrapped up against the cold, huddled on the draughty floor, she wondered why he hadn't. In her imagination, once she was over the first tremendous shock wave, she still thought of Joe as a kind of shining knight on a white charger, who would arrive back in her life and carry her off to the fields of Elysium, regardless of the fact that Cassie was a bastard and socially quite unacceptable. But he never showed up.

One day in December, though, he finally wrote. Cassie waited until Gina and her friend Barbara had left for work, before climbing into Gina's still warm bed to read his letter.

Dearest Cassie,
    I guess I should have written to you before, but I didn't because I was always just about to get into my car and drive to New York to see you and explain. But somehow I never got round to it, and when I tell you what happened after you disappeared from here, maybe you'll understand why. I don't go along with it

myself, but because you're so honest and understanding and sympathetic, I think you'll see the sense.

After you left, I guess I went a little wild. I'd never
gotten drunk before, but I did then. No one knew
where or why you'd gone. All we found in your house
were all those letters in the open bureau, but there
seemed nothing to cause you any great upset, unless,
as Pa said, you'd found something distressing and
taken it with you when you left. We did find the
remains of a burnt-up letter in the fireplace, but all we
could make out were the words 'much better day had
you never been born.'

Pa then reckoned your grandmother had left what
he calls a 'springer' for you to find, and you found it.
So God bless him, he ordered me to go at once and try
and find you and bring you home. But before I could
leave, Doctor Fossett called on us. He was pretty sore
because after the result of your grandmother's post
mortem had been made public there was a big move
made to have him replaced. He certainly lost an awful
lot of his patients overnight.

Cassie put the letter down and got out of bed. She
stopped reading deliberately to make herself a strong cup
of coffee, while she tried to stop herself shaking. She
knew what the rest of the letter was going to tell her.
Doctor Fossett had taken his revenge on Cassie by going
and blowing the whistle on her to Joe's parents. He'd
probably made the story even more unpalatable, if that
was possible, by exaggerating his own relationship with
her mother. Or maybe no exaggeration was needed.
However, whatever version of the story he chose to tell
Mr and Mrs Harris, it would be enough to put an end to
any hopes Cassie might have had of Joe climbing on his
white charger and carrying Cassie back in triumph to
Westboro and happy-ever-after land.

She sat and drank her coffee at the table, with the
letter still lying on the bed. Then when she had stopped

shaking sufficiently, Cassie collected it and finished reading it. She'd guessed dead right. Doctor Fossett had ridden in, shot up the Harris ranch, and ridden out of Westboro in a blaze of disgrace.

Please try and understand, Cassie dearest [Joe's letter finished], that there is nothing we can do about it. We all sat up all night – Pa, Mother and I – and talked about what to do. But we have no alternative. Due to the nature of my Father's position here, there is no chance of us ever getting married, let alone even seeing each other again. Were I a fully qualified lawyer in my own right, I'd come and get you right now, and we could go and live where no one would know about us.

Just like my mother, Cassie thought. No thanks, Joe. So she skipped through the excuses about money, and position, and responsibility, curious only to see how he had finished the letter.

So there it is. I know it's painful. It's painful for both of us. But if I came to see you, I'd only want to stay and we'd both be ruined. If it's any consolation at all, Cassie, I can tell you with complete conviction I will never again in my whole life love anyone the way I loved you. Joe.

Cassie read the last paragraph again and then lay back on her pillow. The way I loved you, he had written. Love in the past tense. He no longer loved her now, he had already finished loving her. She dropped the letter on the floor, folded her arms behind her head and stared up at the ceiling. She knew she wasn't going to cry, because her tears had long since ceased. Instead, she just determined to become even more determined. If people didn't consider her good enough, or acceptable, because she was a bastard and through no fault of her own, then she would

197

build the rest of her life in such a way that society would have no option whatsoever but to open its doors to her, come hell or high water.

That was nearly two years ago now, Cassie remembered, as she lay in the bath in Gina's new apartment in the East Fifties, recalling the morning she had lain in her friend's narrow bed, taking her new vow for life. And so far she had lived up to the promise she had made for herself. She had put Westboro right behind her, and Joe out of her mind. So much so that three months after her arrival in New York, when Gina and she moved in to share their new apartment, Cassie felt as if she had been reborn. Gina was now a successful model and Cassie, with a little help from her friend, had at last landed a regular job as a salesgirl in Bergdorf Goodman. It was in the lingerie department, and when Cassie summed up the rest of the girls working with her, she knew it wouldn't be very long before she had left them well behind.

The rent on the apartment was pretty high, a little too steep for Cassie's budget. But Gina, the languorous, cool-minded, even-tempered Gina, argued that since she was earning at least twenty times what Cassie was earning at present, then it was no hardship for her to pay more rent than Cassie. Cassie made up for it by waitressing three evenings a week, and doing all the cleaning and cooking, which wasn't Gina's strongest suit. And the two girls got along just fine. In return for Cassie slaving, Gina taught her how to make herself up properly and how to dress herself to the best effect. She taught her how to walk correctly, how to deport herself and, as Gina described with a lazy smile, how to use her gifts. It wasn't long before Cassie had been transformed from an obvious out-of-towner into what Gina described as one of New York's professional orphans.

For no one Cassie met in New York seemed to own up to having parents. It just wasn't chic. The 'in' thing was rather to surround yourself with an air of mystery, particularly with regard to your background. If you didn't have parents, you could be anyone. Particularly if you changed your name. With a different and more exotic-sounding name you couldn't be identified with some small town, or hick-farming community. Instead you could instantly become someone who could possibly be invited to lunch with Barbara Hutton, or to cocktails centred round a white piano being played by some celebrity, or someone who might even make it to Hollywood.

Fortunately Cassie was not in the least stage-struck, nor did she wish to change her name. Indeed part of her determination was to make her illegitimate name acceptable. She did, however, relish the anonymity of the enormous city, and was not one bit deterred by its apparent impersonality. Knowing Gina helped, sure it did, because without her Cassie would have been stuck for introductions. But once you'd been introduced to someone, you were once again on your own, and you had to make it on in there without any more outside help. And Cassie was learning how to do just that.

She had also made positively meteoric progress at Bergdorf Goodman's. From day one she made it quite plain that she wasn't interested in remaining just a sales assistant. She wanted to become a junior buyer, and in double-quick time. From that first day she determined always to be the first to arrive in the morning and the last to leave at night. In her lunch break, she didn't go and eat like the other girls, but stayed on to watch how the senior assistants operated, and how the display artists created their shows. She saw what lines sold at once and found out why, and she learned by watching how even a dud line could be pressed on an unsuspecting customer. And she asked questions. She was like a child – why this, why that? – annoying some of the more toffee-nosed employees, and intriguing others, usually the ones in more senior positions, who recognised in Cassie the sort of spirited and intelligent girl they generally never had the good fortune to find as their sales assistants.

199

Oddly enough, she was also popular with most of the other girls. One or two took exception to what they liked to think of as Cassie's 'vulgar ambitions', as there are few as snobbish as shop girls. But most of the others, girls either younger than Cassie, or even of the same age, liked the determined and bright dark-haired girl who had joined their ranks, attracted to her company as they saw at once, as girls often do about each other, something rather special in Cassie McGann.

So by the end of her first eighteen months in the lingerie department, Cassie was already one of their most valued sales assistants, and her supervisor had already marked her down as her top recommendation to make junior buyer. She'd even had a rise.

The rise was enough to allow Cassie off her extra waitressing work, which gave her more time to enjoy her growing social life. With Gina as a friend and companion, there was no shortage of dates. Gina was usually too tired after a long day's photography to want to do more most nights than lie on her bed with a face-pack on, watching TV. As a consequence, Cassie often acted as Gina's stand-in on certain dates, and her circle of acquaintances grew rapidly.

Her closest friend was Arnie, a young man born and bred in New York, who knew the city backwards. He was a jazz freak, and he introduced Cassie to a whole new world. Two or three times a week he'd take her to bars, and introduce her to the sounds of musicians, the like of Coleman Hawkins, Art Blakey, Stan Getz and the Adderly brothers. Cassie was at once taken with the music, although she had seldom heard any hard bop or East Coast jazz before at all. The hottest music she'd ever listened or danced to was the music of the late Glenn Miller, or at parties the swing music of Benny Goodman soundalikes. This music she was learning about now was much tougher and more determined, and altogether suited Cassie's emerging personality.

Arnie liked to think of himself as pretty cool, but he

found that stance hard to keep up when in the company of his new girlfriend Cassie. She was, as he liked to say, something else, and Cassie, making fun of his up-to-date slang, would seriously enquire what else was she? Whereupon Arnie would redden, and become totally tongue-tied when asked to explain his feelings in more conventional ways. He was, of course, falling hopelessly in love with Cassie, as most of her dates did. Cassie sometimes wondered why, when – as she explained to Gina – she did nothing whatsoever to encourage them. In fact, in most cases she positively discouraged their advances.

'Sure,' Gina answered, 'which just makes 'em queue up all the more.'

'I'm not sure I want them queueing up,' Cassie answered. 'I mean I don't want to go giving them the wrong impression.'

'You're not,' Gina assured her. 'These guys like you for what you are, or – in Arnie Puterman's case – love you for what you are.'

Gina grinned at her and then turned back to her dress mirror to see how her latest outfit was hanging on her lean frame.

'I don't want Arnie to love me,' Cassie said, somewhat, Gina thought, defiantly.

'That's OK, Cass,' Gina replied over her shoulder. 'I quite fancy him. So you can throw him back over here when you're done.'

'I don't think he'll go,' Cassie sighed. 'He's getting awful serious, and that's not what I want at all. But on the other hand, I don't want to hurt him.'

Gina threw the outfit down on her bed, and held up another one against her.

'Listen, Cassie McGann,' she said. 'You're going to have to sort out what you want. And fast.'

'I know what I want, Gina,' replied Cassie. 'And at the moment, there's not a lot of room for Arnie.'

Gina turned round and looked at her.

'What do you want, Cass?' she asked.

Cassie looked back at her steadily.

'What I want,' she replied, 'is for no one ever to call me a bastard.'

She had just walked out of her final promotional interview with the department supervisor when Cassie saw him. It was a sight she always dreaded seeing. A man in the lingerie department. Luckily, it wasn't a frequent occurrence.

Cherry, one of the new juniors, was doing her best to cope with him, but from the colour of her face, didn't seem to be succeeding too well. Cassie moved in to the rescue.

'May I be of some help here?' she enquired, in her perfectly trained manner.

The man, who was very tall, turned round and looked at her.

'That depends on whether you share the same objections as this young lady here,' he replied, staring Cassie right in the eyes.

Cassie had never seen such piercing deep blue eyes, nor did she think she had ever seen a man quite so handsome. Not off the movie screen, anyway.

'What's the difficulty, Cherry?'

Cassie turned her attentions to the young girl, who was still bright crimson.

'I simply wanted her to model some lingerie for me,' the man replied in her stead.

'I'm afraid we don't model garments in this department, sir,' Cassie replied. 'Perhaps if I could help?'

'You mean you'll model them for me?' he asked, without a glimmer of a smile.

Cassie felt the skin under her blouse begin to prickle, and she only hoped and prayed that she wasn't going to start blushing.

'No, sir,' she replied as calmly as she could. 'I meant if I could help by trying to help you find the sort of thing you're looking for.'

The man picked up in one of his strong, long-fingered hands, a frail wispy collection of undergarments.

'I've found what I want,' he told Cassie. 'Now all I need to know is if they'll fit. Which is why I asked this young lady to hold them up in front of her.'

'You don't know your wife's exact size,' Cassie essayed, trying to make it sound more of a statement than a surprised question.

'I'm not buying them for my wife,' the man countered.

'Your daughter then.'

'I'm not buying them for my daughter, either.'

'I see,' Cassie said.

'I'm buying them for—'

The man paused, quite deliberately, his eyes firmly on Cassie.

'I'm buying them for a friend.'

Cassie turned and dismissed Cherry, who as far as her colour went, was more than living up to her name.

'I'm the same size as Miss Garson,' Cassie told the man, who was now carefully laying out the flimsy underthings on the glass showcase in front of him. 'Perhaps if I held them up against myself . . .'

'Or perhaps if I held them up against you?' the man argued.

Then he sat down on the chair and crossed his long, elegant legs. Cassie thought she'd never seen such long legs since she'd first seen Gary Cooper in *High Noon*. Come to think of it, she thought, stealing another glance at him as she collected the underclothes, he didn't look at all unlike Gary Cooper, with his deep-thinking countenance and his slightly quizzical eyebrows. But his eyes were larger, and turned down at the ends, which gave him a funny sad look.

The man placed his hat on his crossed knee and nodded at Cassie.

'Let the floor show commence,' he said.

Cassie picked up the first garment, which was a black slip. She held it up against herself. The man just sat there

203

and tapped his hat on his knees. After a good two minutes, he nodded.

'Fine,' he said. 'Now the next.'

The next was a nightdress, in white silk crêpe de Chine, with a deeply plunging bustline. Cassie held it up.

'No, that's far too high,' the man told her. 'Nobody has bosoms on the collarbone. At least no-one I know does.'

Cassie knew she was blushing now, as she dropped the nightdress down to a lower level. But the man wasn't looking at the garment. He was staring at Cassie's face.

'You look rather hot,' he said. 'Are you all right?'

Had she not valued her job and career so highly, Cassie would have stuck her tongue out at him, and draped the stupid nightdress over his head. But seeing as she was one of Bergdorf Goodman's favourite girls, and was also on the verge of promotion, she endured the torment, and thanked God that so few men visited the lingerie department.

'Is that better, sir?' she enquired, holding the night-dress in the current position.

'Yes, that's better,' he replied. 'It's not good, but it's better. Now if I may see the panties.'

Cassie folded the crêpe de Chine nightdress carefully and replaced it on top of the equally carefully folded underslip, in order to give herself time.

'The panties are exactly the same size as the underslip, sir,' she told him. 'So there's really no need for you to worry.'

'That's very kind of you, miss,' he replied. 'But the lady in question isn't a regular size all over. She's more your shape. So if you don't mind.'

Cassie drew in a deep breath and then picked up the black panties. Then she turned round and held them against her.

'They're back to front,' the man informed her.

'Thank you, sir,' Cassie replied, wishing that he'd drop dead.

204

She turned the panties the right way round and waited for the man's verdict. He was looking at the panties, very seriously. Then he shook his head.

'I'm not sure about those at all,' he said. 'Perhaps you could show me others in black silk.'

Cassie collected some panties of slightly different cut and designs, and laid them out on the glass counter, inviting him to take his pick. She was trying to place his accent. From the way he was behaving, he should have been a Texan. But he wasn't. Anyway, his whole manner was actually far too sophisticated for a Southerner. He wasn't British, because she knew a British accent well enough. Lots of Englishmen and their wives came to Bergdorf Goodman's when they were in New York. And this lunatic certainly wasn't English.

It was the word lunatic that clinched it. That and those amazing eyes, and that deep musical voice. He was a mad Irishman.

And he was picking up the briefest of all the black silk panties which lay before him.

'I think I'd like to see these on you please, miss,' he said, without the hint of a smile.

Just at that moment the department supervisor walked past, having seen the odd charade from her office.

'Is everything all right, sir?' she enquired. 'Miss McGann?'

'Everything is fine, ma'am,' the man replied. 'We're just undecided about the panties.'

'The gentleman was insistent that I model them for him, Mrs Wellman,' Cassie explained.

'I see,' replied Mrs Wellman, in the tone she reserved for suspected sexual deviates. 'Well if you need any further assistance, Miss McGann, I'm right there in my office.'

She pointed out the proximity of her office for the gentleman customer's benefit, not Cassie's, then walked off.

'She reminds me of a mare I have back home,' the man said. 'Least from the back she certainly does.'

Later, Cassie was to decide that that was the moment she fell in love with Tyrone Rosse, because part of her burst into laughter. But the other part, and at that moment Cassie thought the better part of her gained control, and decided to ignore the remark altogether.

Instead she held up the tiny pair of black panties against her, by now almost inured to the ignominy. The man looked at her and shook his head at once.

'I really don't know how you could have recommended those,' he scolded her. 'They're most improper.'

Cassie sighed, but held her tongue. The man rose from his chair and pointed to an altogether more demure pair.

'I'll take those,' he said, 'and the nightgown, and the underslip. And I want a negligée as well. Like the one Grace Kelly wore in *Rear Window*, remember?'

'No I'm afraid I don't, sir,' Cassie answered. 'Can you possibly describe it a little more fully?'

The man rubbed his chin thoughtfully, then frowned down at her.

'Do you know I can't?' he said suddenly looking up at Cassie and catching her looking down at him. 'All I can remember is that it was very sexy. It's when Grace Kelly arrives in Stewart's apartment, and he's in a wheelchair, you see—'

'I did see the movie,' Cassie volunteered.

'The whole scene was very sexy, didn't you think?' her customer asked her, managing to sound not in the least provocative.

Cassie sidestepped the question with a polite smile, and pointed to a beautiful negligée which was on a dummy.

'Was it perhaps something along those lines, sir?' she enquired.

'You know, I think it was,' the man nodded. 'I'll take it, if you have it in your size.'

'You mean in the size I've been modelling,' Cassie corrected him.

'Yes. Which is your size,' he replied. 'Do you like that colour?'

'I think that blue is *very* sophisticated,' Cassie told him.

'Good,' said the man. 'Sold.'

Then he stood and taking from the front pocket of his pants a thick roll of dollar bills, started to count out some money, as Cassie collected a negligée in the correct size off the rail. She was glad it was sold, too, because it was the most expensive negligee in the store, and Cassie would earn a nice commission from it; besides the fact that Mr Know-It-All would feel the pinch in his pocket. Then as she glanced at him, flicking through the fat wad of bills, she wasn't so sure he would feel the draught: that looked like a big bank roll.

She returned with the negligée and started to fold it with the other lingerie. 'I want that wrapped and delivered separately,' he informed her, barely looking up. 'What's the damage?'

Cassie totted up the total on a pad, which she then showed to the man. He nodded and counted out the bills exactly.

'I'll take everything except the negligée, which I want delivered.'

'To what address would you like it sent, sir?' Cassie asked, as she carefully packed the gorgeous underwear away in thin tissue paper.

'Where do you live?' the man asked her.

'I'm afraid we're not allowed to give our addresses to customers, sir,' Cassie answered, as calmly as she could.

'Don't be absurd.'

'It's a store rule I'm afraid, sir.'

Cassie handed him the box of lingerie.

'So if you'd like to write down the address where we're to send the negligée.'

'I can't,' he replied. 'Not unless you tell me where you live.'

'I really don't understand,' Cassie said naively. 'I don't

207

see what where I live has to do with where you want us to deliver the negligée.'

The man sighed deeply, and shook his head.

'I want to know where you live,' he told her, 'because that's where I want you to deliver the negligée.'

Cassie stared at him, and just in time stopped her mouth from falling open. The man picked up the box containing the negligée.

'Better still,' he said, shoving it into her arms, 'let's save on the postage.'

Then he put his hat on and ambled out of the department.

Cassie heard nothing more from the man, which was all she knew him as, for what seemed months, but was in fact only three days. When she told Gina about the encounter, Gina, who was usually so bored with tales of guys meeting girls, really sat up and listened. She thought it was funny, and cute, and about the most romantic thing she'd heard since Grace Kelly upped and married that Prince Rainier.

Cassie contradicted her violently. After all, all that had happened was that this lunatic Irishman had come in and bought some lingerie, for somebody else, and then walked out again.

'No,' said Gina, lolling on her bed, waving her hands in the air in order to dry her freshly applied nail varnish. 'It's the way that you tell it. And the look in your eyes. He's run you over! And all this from the girl who was never going to have anything more to do with men, never ever!'

Cassie threw a pillow at Gina, who intercepted it easily with one long shapely leg.

'Let's see you in the negligée,' she ordered Cassie.

'No way,' Cassie retorted. 'It's just not me.'

'OK,' Gina laughed. 'So make me a present of it!'

'Sorry,' Cassie replied. 'I'm going to put it in my bottom drawer. I may grow into it yet.'

On the third evening, while Gina was soaking in the tub after a long day's work, Cassie, bathed and dry, tried the negligée on. It was simply gorgeous, and *very* sexy. She looked at herself in the full-length mirror and was astounded by the sudden rush of adrenalin through her veins. All she was wearing was a silk negligée, with a small run of swan-down at the collar and sleeves, but she suddenly felt as if she was a woman for perhaps the first time in her life. A woman who had the power to attract a man, to make love to him and to keep him in her thrall. She sat down on the edge of the bed and stared at herself in the mirror. It couldn't just be the lingerie that was making her feel that, surely? But if it wasn't, what else could it be?

There was a knock on the apartment door.

'That'll be Buck!' Gina called. 'Let him in, could you? And tell him some funny stories!'

Cassie grinned, and, without covering herself, went to open the door. The door was on the chain, so Cassie half-opened it, and when she saw the tall figure of someone she assumed was Buck Irvine, yet another American football player Gina had taken up with, she slipped the door off the chain and opened it.

'Hi, Buck,' she said, stepping aside to let him in.

The figure turned round. It wasn't Buck. It was the man.

'Tyrone as a matter of fact,' he said. 'Tyrone Rosse, Miss McGann. May I come in?'

Cassie drew her breath in sharply and gathered her clothes around her. It was then she remembered what she was wearing.

'I'm not dressed,' she replied.

'So I can see,' Tyrone nodded. 'But the little you have on certainly suits you.'

He walked past her into the apartment before Cassie could think of anything further to say. Cassie shut the door and breathed in deeply once again. Then she scuttled towards her bedroom.

'I won't be one moment!' she cried. 'I'll just go and get dressed!'

Gina came into the bedroom in a towel.

'Who's tall, dark, and handsome and helping himself to our whisky?' she enquired.

'That's him!' Cassie hissed, struggling into a wool dress. 'That's Mr Know-It-All from the Emerald Isle.'

'He looks like Gary Cooper's brother,' Gina said. 'Except of course much younger.'

'He's not *that* much younger,' Cassie opined airily. 'He must be well over thirty.'

Gina peered back through the crack in their bedroom door then came back and sat on the edge of the bed, drying her hair with another towel.

'Men are like wine, Cass,' she said. 'The longer they're around, the better they get.'

Cassie reddened and slipping into her shoes, went out to meet her destiny.

'How did you find where I lived?' she asked him, refilling his glass.

Gina always kept a stock of drinks in, now that she had so many what she mockingly called 'gentleman callers'.

'My closest friend is head of the FBI,' Tyrone replied with a perfectly straight face. 'I asked them to put a trace on a beautiful small dark-haired Caucasian, aged about nineteen or twenty, probably wearing Bergdorf Goodman's most expensive negligée, and hey presto.'

'I suppose one of the assistants told you,' she said, ignoring the jokes.

'Every man has his price,' Tyrone answered. 'And so does every woman. But hers is usually wholesale.'

Cassie had to laugh at that. Tyrone just nodded.

'I knew you'd be even prettier when you laughed,' he said. 'And I also knew it would take some doing.'

He drank his whisky quickly, and put the glass back down on the table.

'Right,' he continued. 'Now where would you like to go for dinner?'

'I'm afraid I already have a date,' Cassie protested.

'With whom?' Tyrone enquired.

'Well if it's any of your business, with a friend of mine called Arnie,' Cassie answered crossly. 'We're going to the Duke Ellington Concert at Carnegie Hall.'

'That's not until tomorrow,' Tyrone announced. 'So where would you like to go for dinner?'

'How do you know it's not until tomorrow?' Cassie demanded. 'You a Duke Ellington fan?'

'It's in your diary, which is open on the desk,' Tyrone informed her calmly. 'Tuesday the 25th, Carnegie Concert with Arnie. And it's Count Basie you're going to see by the way. Not the Duke. Now. Where would you like to go for dinner?'

Cassie was for once in her recent life rendered quite speechless.

Gina then came out of the bedroom, in a long black strapless sheath dress which clung to her like a second skin, her hair which was now dyed Titian swept and piled up on the top of her head, and a cultured pearl choker round her slender neck. Cassie found her heart sinking as she saw this vision of *Vogue* loveliness glide elegantly across the room. One look at Gina and Tyrone wouldn't spare Cassie a second glance. Then she frowned. Why was she so worried? This man meant nothing to her. She didn't even like this man.

'Hi,' her friend and room-mate said. 'I'm Gina.'

Tyrone took his eyes off Cassie for one moment to shake Gina's proffered hand.

'Hello there, Tina,' he said, and then looked back at Cassie. 'I'm still waiting to hear where you want to go for dinner.'

Gina regarded his back then hooted with laughter.

'How does the song go?' she asked no one in particular, pouring herself a Martini. 'But they all disappear from view –'Cos—'

'Shut up, Tina,' Cassie said, looking past Tyrone at Gina.

Gina smiled at her and winked. And raised her Martini glass. Cassie looked back at the man towering over her.

'I'd like you to take me to Harry's Diner,' she told him. 'Please.'

Harry's Diner was where Cassie had first worked when she had come to New York. It obviously wasn't what such an elegant and worldly man as Mr Tyrone Rosse would have been used to, but to Cassie's dismay, when they arrived and he saw where Cassie wanted to eat dinner, he didn't turn a hair.

In fact he behaved all evening as if they were dining at the Waldorf. He studiously consulted the extremely limited plastic-backed menu before deciding on Harry's home-made meat loaf with a double portion of french fries on the side, while Cassie chose what she always had eaten when working there herself, a straight hamburger with mayonnaise and a side salad.

Tyrone didn't even comment on the mayonnaise. Instead he sipped his 7-Up as if it was the best claret, and discussed what Cassie's interests were. Cassie told him she was very keen on modern jazz, and going to art museums. She made no mention of her love for and interest in horses, because since she had left Westboro Falls and changed her life, she had shut all her past and her past interests away, locking them up in a mental rosewood bureau. She told him she read a lot, particularly historical novels, and liked dancing. He told her he liked dancing as well, so why didn't they go and do some after they had eaten? Cassie smiled at this, but said neither yes nor no, until she had found out more about the man sitting opposite her – who never took his deep blue eyes off her all through dinner. She asked him what other interests he had; he shrugged, and replied this and that. Cassie thought either this or that could spell women, but it was not her place to ask. He said he didn't live in America, but in Ireland and only came over on business. Cassie asked him what was his business, and Tyrone said this and that again. Buying and selling. He also had friends over here, he told her. Rich friends who were also business associates. She laughed and said he sounded as if he was a member of the Mob, and Tyrone nodded quite seriously, and said in his line of business there were connections. Cassie didn't know whether or not he was pulling her leg. It was something she was always going to find difficult with Mr Rosse.

Over Harry's homemade ice cream and apple tart, he asked her if she liked working in a store. He asked her with no prejudice in his voice, nor with any innate curiosity. He simply asked her the question. Cassie said yes she did, and was it so surprising? Tyrone shook his head and said no, and there was no need to sound so defensive. He then asked her if she had any ambitions, and Cassie hesitated before replying. Then she turned the question back to him, before answering.

'My ambition is to be the best at what I do,' he told her, drinking his coffee.

'I guess that's mine too,' Cassie replied. 'I love my work.'

In the cab, he asked her where she would like to go dancing. She said there was a small club on 52nd Street where the music was always good, as long as he liked jazz.

'I like whatever you like, Cassie McGann,' he replied, and directed the cab driver where to go.

They danced until Pete the proprietor started stacking the chairs on the tables and the band packed up. Tyrone gave the pianist fifty dollars and a quart of bourbon and asked him to go on playing. The pianist laughed and said he'd have done it just for the whisky. Tyrone made Cassie choose all her favourite tunes, and she called them all, all except 'Moonglow'.

They walked home. Cabs passed them, but Tyrone waved them away, and with the snow beginning to fall around them, they walked all the way back to Cassie and

Gina's apartment. On the way they didn't talk at all. Instead Tyrone sang her love songs from Ireland.

He saw her up to her door, and waited till Cassie had unlocked it, and until she was safely inside, like the perfect gentleman he was – before he asked her to marry him. Cassie stared back at him through a door she was about to close.

'Excuse me?' she said, uncertain she had heard right.

'I said will you marry me, Cassie McGann?' came the reply. 'And please don't protest and say but we've only just met.'

'Why not?' Cassie protested. 'We have.'

'Because it's got nothing to do with it at all, that's why,' Tyrone replied.

Cassie stood staring at Tyrone and failed to think of a suitable reply.

'All right,' he nodded. 'You'll probably want some time to think. I'll ring you in the morning.'

He started down the corridor towards the elevator.

'It is morning!' Cassie called after him.

'Fine,' Tyrone called back. 'I'll call you later in the morning.'

The elevator doors closed and he was gone.

At eleven o'clock, Mrs Wellman called Cassie into her office and was pleased to inform her that she had won her promotion, and was now a junior buyer of lingerie for Bergdorf Goodman. There would be a considerable rise in her salary and furthermore there was every indication from her record so far that Cassie had a very promising future. Cassie was very pleased as well. It was exactly what she had been working so hard for, and yet she found herself only pleased rather than thrilled and delighted. Perhaps it was because she was still so tired after her night out dancing. After all, she had barely got in one hour's sleep before it was time to get up again and get ready to go to work. Maybe when she'd had an early night and slept on the wonderful news, it would have

214

had time to sink in and she'd feel the excitement she knew she ought to be feeling.

But deep in her heart as she turned to leave Mrs Wellman's office, Cassie knew the real reason for her moderate reaction to her promotion was that it was an anti-climax after the wonderful evening she had spent out on the town with Tyrone. When she had been called into her supervisor's office, her first thought was that Tyrone had telephoned her at the store, to find out the answer to his question. So she had hurried across the department floor, only to find that Mrs Wellman had news of quite a different nature for her.

Cassie thanked Mrs Wellman sincerely and promised she would do her very best to live up to the faith both Mrs Wellman and Bergdorf Goodman had in her. Then as she turned to leave, the telephone rang suddenly on Mrs Wellman's desk. Cassie hesitated, and then continued out of the office, dismissing the absurd notion from her head that it could possibly be for her. Besides, now that she'd had more time to think about it, she was sure that last night Tyrone Rosse Esquire had only been pulling her leg.

'Miss McGann?' came Mrs Wellman's voice, calling her back. 'It's for you.'

Cassie returned, a puzzled look on her face.

'It's a man,' Mrs Wellman informed her, 'a Doctor Rosse. He says it's very urgent.'

Cassie bit her lip to prevent herself from smiling, and Mrs Wellman took this as a sign of anxiety.

'I do hope everything's all right at home, dear,' she said solicitously. 'He does sound most frightfully anxious.'

Cassie picked up the telephone.

'Well?' said a voice in her ear, somewhat impatiently. 'Have you arrived at your answer?'

'No I'm afraid not,' Cassie replied. 'I didn't realise there was quite so much urgency.'

Hearing this, Mrs Wellman took off her spectacles and went to the office door.

215

'I'll leave you in private, my dear,' she said. 'I just hope everything's all right.'

Left alone, Cassie felt more at liberty to speak her mind.

'You shouldn't have called me here,' she told Tyrone. 'We're not allowed to receive personal calls during work hours.'

'Oh to hell with that!' Tyrone shouted down the phone. 'I have to fly down to Virginia today!'

'You'll be coming back, I'm quite sure,' Cassie answered, surprised at her coolness when in fact her heart was pounding in her chest.

'Of course I'll be coming back, Cassie McGann!' Tyrone exploded. 'If only to fetch you and take you home with me! Now is it yes, or is it no? Or do I have to come round to that wretched shop of yours and get down on my blasted knees in front of you and that horse-arsed woman you work for!'

Cassie took a deep breath, and closed her eyes, praying for both patience and guidance.

'Well?' Tyrone persisted.

'No,' said Cassie.

'What!' Tyrone roared back down the telephone, so loudly that Cassie was sure it rattled the windows in Mrs Wellman's office. 'What the hell do you mean, woman? No!'

'I mean I need more time, that's all,' Cassie said, not meaning it at all, knowing perfectly well that if Tyrone was there in the department rather than at the other end of a telephone she would be utterly unable to resist him.

'You have until the weekend,' Tyrone replied after an endless silence. 'Until I get back from Virginia.'

And he slammed down the telephone. Cassie waited for a moment, as she noticed Mrs Wellman hovering outside the door.

'I see, Doctor,' she said rather loudly. 'Thank you. Yes. Yes, I'll wait for your call this evening.'

Then she too replaced the telephone.

Mrs Wellman came back into the office and looked anxiously at Cassie.

'Not bad news I hope, my dear?' she enquired. 'I do hope it's not bad news?'

Cassie smiled bravely back at Mrs Wellman, instead of answering, unable to find a suitable reply as to whether Tyrone Rosse's proposal of marriage was indeed good or bad news.

'I'd best get back to my post,' she told her employer. 'I do apologise for Doctor Rosse ringing me here.'

'Nonsense, my dear,' Mrs Wellman replied. 'Anyway, very soon you'll have an office and a telephone of your own, and you won't have to mind who calls you.'

Cassie thanked her again and turned to leave the office. Mrs Wellman called her back, and looked at the pretty and determined girl who was staring back at her.

'You look most awfully pale, dear,' she said finally. 'You really do. I know it's none of my business, but something is quite obviously worrying you. So I insist you go straight home and take the rest of the day off.'

Cassie wasn't going to argue with that one, because even though she was young and strong, after ten hours out on the town, she was out on her feet.

So she thanked Mrs Wellman most gratefully and went to fetch her coat and change her shoes.

As she left the store, it was snowing more heavily than ever. So Cassie decided that what with the good news about her promotion, she'd splash out on a cab. There was one which had just pulled up, with a young woman in a fur coat leaning in the window paying off the fare, while an older and very glamorous woman was getting out of the back of the cab, holding a Bergdorf Goodman box by a neatly tied string handle. Cassie waited by the cab as the older woman strolled over to the store to gaze in the window, and puzzled to herself, because there was something familiar about the older woman, yet she couldn't quite place her.

A moment later she realised exactly who she was as the young woman paying off the cab extricated herself from the side window and Cassie came face to face with Leonora.

'Christ!' exclaimed Leonora with a grin. 'Christ Almighty, Cassie McGann!'

And she threw her arm around Cassie's shoulder and dragged her back to the store. Cassie looked hopelessly back over her shoulder and saw someone else purloining her cab.

'Mamma!' Leonora cried. 'For Christ's sake will you look who's here!'

Mrs Von Wagner turned away from her window shopping and looked without emotion at the girl in an inexpensive brown tweed coat whom her daughter was embracing.

'Jesus – you remember Cassie McGann!' Leonora continued with a wicked grin. 'The little bitch who beat me at tennis, and then came and stayed on Long Island!'

Mrs Von Wagner nodded.

'Sure,' she replied evenly. 'I remember all too well.'

'What are you doing in New York, Cassie?' Leonora asked, all the time leading her back into the store. 'Better still, don't tell me now. Let's go have a coffee, or even better a drink, and bring ourselves up to date.'

Cassie looked at Mrs Von Wagner who was looking back at her.

'It's all right,' Leonora's mother said. 'I don't bite.'

'Mamma couldn't stand Grandfather,' Leonora told Cassie. 'Anyway, he's dead.'

Mrs Von Wagner smiled at both the girls, rather automatically and without the slightest trace of emotion.

'Why don't you two girls go off and enjoy yourselves?' she suggested. 'I just have to return these items to Lingerie, and then I'm going on to lunch with someone anyway.'

She held up the string-tied Bergdorf Goodman parcel.

'OK,' said Leonora. 'I'll see you back at the apartment.'

Then she hailed another cab as her mother disappeared

inside the store, and bundled Cassie into the back for all the world as if she was kidnapping her.

They sat in the Plaza and drank champagne cocktails. The drinks revived Cassie sufficiently long enough to listen without any great interest to the recent story of Leonora's life.

'I've only just come back from the continent,' she told Cassie. 'Switzerland, where I was at this fabulous finishing school. By fabulous I mean fabulous for sex. We spent the whole time climbing in and out, and no one gave a goddam.'

She tossed back her blonde hair, which was longer and silkier than ever, and shouted at a waiter to bring two more champagne cocktails and quick.

Then she turned her attentions back to Cassie.

'I got laid so many times,' she said far too loudly for Cassie's comfort, 'I lost count. My last lover was a prince. He was dreadful. I reckon he was a fag.'

The waiter brought the drinks over and set them down. As he did so, Leonora lit a cigarette and blew smoke in his face.

'How about you, Cassie?' she grinned. 'You lost it yet?'

The waiter left, and Cassie went red, not with embarrassment, but with anger.

'That's none of your business, Leonora,' she retorted.

Leonora threw back her head and hooted with laughter.

'Jesus you're great! It's a wonder you haven't become a nun!'

Leonora took another pull at her cigarette then stubbed it out impatiently, lighting another one almost immediately as she yawned and looked round the room.

'You still haven't told me what you're doing in New York,' she said, her curiously cold eyes falling back on Cassie.

Cassie wondered whether or not to tell Leonora the truth, that she was working as shop girl in the store where they had re-met, and run the risk of more of Leonora's scorn, or whether this was an occasion for one of Sister Joseph's 'quite understandable and immediately forgivable white lies'.

She decided upon the latter.

'I'm a singer,' she said.

Leonora looked up from her cocktail.

'You're not?' she replied. 'No kidding. What sort of singer? You know, I mean nightclubs? Or what?'

'Opera,' Cassie corrected her. 'I'm at the Met.'

Leonora frowned, suddenly filled with a sneaking admiration for a girl she had always considered a dead-ender.

'Right,' she grinned. 'Back row of the chorus, right? In one of those fearful peasant costumes.'

'No,' Cassie replied calmly, the champagne cocktail giving her the necessary Dutch courage. 'Name roles. I studied for two years with Doctor Rosser, the famous Auscrian coach.'

'Oh Christ,' Leonora sighed. 'Even *I* have heard of Dr Rosser. You in anything right now?'

'Sure,' said Cassie. 'We're doing *Tristan und Isolde*, and I'm singing Gertrude.'

Leonora grabbed a copy of the *New York Times* which was lying nearby and turned to the Theater Guide. Cassie had to bite her lip for the second time that day to stop laughing as she watched Leonora running her finger down the list of entertainments. Cassie always knew what was on at the Met, because one of Gina's beaux, a rich stockbroker, was an opera buff, and poor Gina, who hated opera, was always being dragged off to see interminable productions of Wagner. Her latest torture had been *Tristan und Isolde*, only last week. Cassie wasn't at all sure about the part of Gertrude, but she could bet her bottom dollar that Leonora, who knew about as much about opera as Cassie knew about motor racing, was even less *au fait*.

Leonora looked up, almost for once in awe of Cassie.

'Christ!' she hissed, having found the listing. 'Can you get tickets?'

'Sure,' Cassie replied. 'Except I never knew you liked opera.'

'No chance for tonight, I suppose?' Leonora asked, without much hope. 'I'm only in town until tomorrow.'

Cassie sipped her cocktail, and took all the time in the world to answer. She knew from Gina how hot the tickets were for this production.

'As a matter of fact, you're not going to believe this,' she replied finally, 'but I had two friends from Newport coming tonight. But they've both gone down with food poisoning.

'That's tough,' said Leonora, barely able to contain her smile. 'So I could have their tickets?'

'OK,' said Cassie. 'But only because I don't want to let them go to waste.'

Leonora looked at Cassie, unsure how to take this. But Cassie was smiling so sweetly at her, Leonora thought she obviously intended no slight.

'I'll owe you for this, Cassie,' she said. 'There's this guy I really want to lay, and his wife's out of town. And he's a total opera freak. Jesus, I'll really owe you for this.'

'No,' said Cassie, 'I really owe you. I'll leave the tickets at the box office, in your name.'

Then she got up and walked out of the Plaza grinning like a Cheshire cat, already imagining and enjoying Leonora's forthcoming embarrassment.

Back in the apartment, still propped up by the champagne Cassie lay on her bed and thought about Tyrone. In her head she wanted to say no so badly to him, but in her heart she knew she felt quite differently. So which should she be ruled by? She so loved her life in New York, with all her friends. She loved going to hear jazz, or walking through Central Park with Arnie and their crowd, or late-night shopping with Gina, or just lying in her bed early in the morning hearing the sounds of the city waking up. She was free, and without any emotional ties. At least she had been, until that fateful day in the lingerie department of Bergdorf Goodman.

And yet here she was seriously contemplating accepting the marriage proposal of a man she barely knew, a man with whom she'd been out precisely once; who had sorely embarrassed her at her place of work, and then when she had asked for more time to consider his proposal, had given her until the end of the week! Cassie suddenly started to get angry, and punching her pillow into shape, turned on her side.

You've got until Friday indeed, she fumed. He had to be mad. And so did she, even to give such a notion a moment's serious thought. She knew nothing about him, nothing at all. She knew he lived in Ireland, in a large house called Claremore, but she didn't know what he did, or even what he had done. Who had he been buying all that expensive underwear for, for instance? A friend, he had said. Not his wife, not his daughter, but a friend. He had been buying the most intimate gift a man could buy for a woman, he had made Cassie model them for him, yet here she was, seriously thinking about whether or not she should marry him!

She was drunk. That's what the answer was. The champagne cocktails she'd had with Leonora at lunch had gone straight to her head, and she was drunk. Only a drunk would be lying there contemplating giving up everything she had worked and dreamed for over the last two years for a marriage to a complete stranger.

Cassie turned over on to her other side, then back again, as she realised with dread that she hadn't even considered the biggest obstacle to a marriage between them, even if she were to agree. Her birthright. If she really did love this man, for some peculiar reason, then she couldn't tell him in advance of their marriage and she couldn't tell him afterwards. And Cassie also knew there was no way she could keep it forever hidden from him. Someone would come into their lives, a Doctor Fossett, or somebody from Westboro Falls, or an acquaintance of the Harris family, and they would tell Tyrone with mock astonishment that he didn't know already, and she would be disgraced, and kicked out of Claremore. Cassie imagined the picture, like an illustration out of an old book, with Tyrone at the top of the steps, pointing the way for the forlorn Cassie to go off into her exile.

The telephone woke her up. Cassie sat up in the pitch darkness and for a moment wondered where she was, as the telephone rang and rang. Then she remembered, and realised that she must have slept all afternoon.

'Hello?' she said into the receiver. 'This is Cassie McGann speaking.'

'Well?' said the familiar voice.

Cassie sighed and stayed silent for a moment before answering.

'You said I had until the end of the week.'

'As your doctor, I have the right of an interim report.'

'There's no change in my condition,' Cassie said. 'None whatsoever.'

'Then I would say,' the voice replied, 'that you are in need of further and immediate attention.'

The phone went dead. Cassie lay back and stared at the shadows on the ceiling, when the telephone rang again. Cassie picked it up and spoke into it at once.

'If you want me to say yes to your proposal, Mr Rosse,' she said somewhat curtly, 'you'll stand a much better chance if you'll only leave me alone!'

'Who in hell is Mr Rosse?' asked Arnie. 'And where in hell are you? The concert starts in ten minutes!'

In the interval Cassie tried to explain to Arnie what had happened, but couldn't come up with another perfectly understandable and immediately forgivable white lie. If only Arnie had called for her, as he usually did. But this was the one night he couldn't, because on Tuesdays he had to work late and hadn't time to go home, change and come and pick Cassie up. She'd never have had to tell him about Tyrone otherwise. They could have just enjoyed the concert, eaten at Harry's, gone on and listened to a little jazz, kissed each other good night – end of story. But now here they were, with Arnie staring at the ground while Cassie tried to explain about this lunatic Irishman who'd burst into her life, and how it was all too crazy for words because even if she wanted to, she couldn't marry him anyway.

'Why not?' Arnie asked, without looking up. 'This guy married already or something?'

'I don't know!' Cassie answered helplessly.

'You don't know?' Arnie said, suddenly raising his voice. 'Some guy asks you to marry him, and you think about it, and you don't even know if he's married *already*?'

Some of the other Count Basie fans were beginning to take a great interest in the developing quarrel. Cassie tried to turn Arnie away, but he shook her arm off.

'That's not the reason I couldn't marry him,' she hissed, 'even if I wanted to.'

'You don't say!' Arnie retorted, as loud as before. 'Why? Are you married?'

'No!' said Cassie, still trying to drag Arnie away from their fast-growing audience.

'Then why?' Arnie shouted. 'If you wanted to marry this guy why the hell can't you?'

Cassie wanted to shout at the very top of her voice, because I'm a bastard! Because I'm a bastard! Because I'm a bastard! But she settled instead for something much less dramatic but unintentionally far more infuriating.

'Because I can't,' she replied.

Arnie stared at her, his eyes nearly popping out of his head.

'Because you *can't*?' he shouted in disbelief. 'Because you *can't*? The only reason you can't marry somebody you only met yesterday goddamit is because you *can't*? Listen, I tell you, I've heard some pretty whacky reasons in my time, Cassie McGann! But that has to be the all-time screwiest!'

Arnie shook his head at her disbelievingly as the bell sounded for the end of the interval.

'Come on,' said Cassie, taking his hand, 'we can talk about it afterwards.'

'The hell we can!' Arnie yelled, snatching his hand away, 'I'm going to get fried!'

He pushed his way out through the crowds going back in, and disappeared into the winter's night. By the time Cassie had fought her way through after him, he was gone.

When she came back from lunch on Wednesday and walked back on to the floor of the lingerie department to take up her post, Cassie failed to see the man who had been sitting next to the glass showcase – the very same showcase where Cassie had laid out on display the under-garments for Tyrone – get off his chair and drop to his knees.

What she did become aware of was some of her juniors, who were watching her and trying to contain their laughter. She was about to enquire what exactly was the source of their amusement, when she noticed the top of a man's head, the other side of the counter. Tyrone. She stood rooted to the spot, unable to think of either appropriate words or actions.

Tyrone knelt more upright, the better for Cassie to see him, and she observed through her mortification that he was holding a small bunch of violets. He offered them to her, but Cassie stood stock still, her hands by her sides. Tyrone laid them on the counter and nodded at her.

'Well?' he asked.

'Get up off your knees,' she hissed back at him, 'and then get out of here.'

'Not until you say yes.'

'You told me I had until Friday.'

'That was before I realised how stubborn you were.'

'Will you *please* – get up off your knees!'

'Will you *please* – say that you'll marry me?'

Cassie glared at him, then round at the juniors, who were all in various stages of hysteria. When they saw the look on Cassie's face, they at once regained their composure.

'Go into Mrs Wellman's office, Cherry,' Cassie requested her most responsible assistant, 'and ask her to send for the house detective.'

Cherry hurried across to Mrs Wellman's room, which didn't bother Tyrone one bit. He just watched her go, with that slow smile of his.

Then he looked back and up at Cassie, across the top of the glass divide.

'Are proposals of marriage against the house rules as well?' he enquired.

'Persistent worrying of the employees is,' Cassie replied.

'My dear child, you haven't an idea of how persistent I can be,' said Tyrone.

Cassie leaned across the counter, giving it one last go.

'Please,' she begged, 'get up off your knees.'

'You know the conditions,' Tyrone reminded her. 'One little word of three letters, beginning with "Y".'

'Not here,' Cassie said. 'Not in front of everyone.'

Tyrone looked round him and saw not only the girls, but some newly arrived customers all curiously watching the pantomime.

He got to his feet and Cassie closed her eyes in relief. Off guard, she was powerless to stop his next move. In a flash Tyrone had come round to her side of the counter and lifted her up easily into his arms. Cassie tried to struggle, but of course Tyrone was far too strong for her. With a broad grin on his face, he started to amble to the exit.

Mrs Wellman watched helplessly from her office and prayed that the store detective would arrive in time.

He didn't.

As Tyrone sauntered past Mrs Wellman's office, she thought that perhaps she'd best say something.

226

'Excuse me,' she ventured. 'But what exactly do you think you're doing, sir?'

'It's perfectly all right, madam,' Tyrone replied.

'It is not perfectly all right!' Cassie protested, trying to struggle free.

'I'm her physician, Doctor Rosse,' Tyrone continued regardless. 'And I'm afraid my patient here, Miss McGann, has been wilfully neglecting my instructions.'

He nodded pleasantly at Mrs Wellman and continued on his way. Mrs Wellman considered it best not to pursue the matter further if Miss McGann was indeed under the doctor's supervision. Besides, the man had a rather peculiar look in his eyes. She clapped her hands together for the juniors to return to their posts and went back into the safety of her office.

With Cassie still firmly held in his arms, Tyrone looked for a cab. He stood in the middle of the street, while the traffic hooted at him and slewed around him, but he didn't move until he saw a free cab. The driver, anxious to get home and out of the increasingly heavy snow, tried to ignore the tall man standing there with some dame in his arms, in the middle of the road and right in his path. He leaned on his horn, but the man didn't move. So he stood on his brakes instead.

Tyrone opened the back door of the cab and deposited the snow-soaked Cassie on the seat. Then he went round to the driver's door and opened it.

'Get out,' Tyrone demanded.

The traffic piled up behind the cab, and started to hoot angrily and monotonously, as the cab driver, who was a small man, got out and tried to measure up to the man towering over him.

'What's the matter, Mac?' he pleaded.

'The matter,' Tyrone informed him, 'is that it is bloody cold and wet out here! That's what the matter is! So next time you see a lady in distress, you damn well stop for her!'

Tyrone gave the driver Cassie's address and then got

into the cab. So did the driver. Tyrone apologised for the incident as if the driver's incivility was his own fault, and stripped off his jacket, draping it round Cassie. Cassie, who was cold, accepted it, but tried not to show her gratitude, staring out of the window instead at the blizzard which was beginning to rage.

'Some weather, huh?' the driver remarked over his shoulder.

Tyrone ignored him and brushed some snow solicitously off Cassie's skirt.

'It's OK,' said Cassie. 'I'm not going to get pneumonia.'

'Who said you were?' Tyrone replied, and then looking out of the other window started whistling *Peter and the Wolf.*

'Why are you taking me back to my apartment?' she asked him.

'I should imagine you'll want to get bathed and changed before tonight,' he answered. 'That's why.'

'Why? What's going to happen tonight?'

'It's going to get dark, that's what's going to happen.'

Tyrone then continued whistling, so rather than allow him to provoke her further, Cassie resumed her watch on the blizzard.

He dropped her off at her apartment, after telling her that he would send a cab back for her at six o'clock prompt. Before she had time to protest, he ordered the driver to take him back uptown. Cassie ran inside the building, more determined than ever to resist him.

Tyrone then went shopping and ordered what he bought to be sent around immediately to Miss Cassie McGann at her given address.

Gina collected the parcels from the driver who brought them round. There were several boxes, all gift-wrapped. She took them upstairs and put them on Cassie's bed.

'Father Christmas is a little early this year!' she shouted through the bathroom door, and then went back through to the kitchen to finish what she was cooking for dinner. Tonight was a stay-in night for Gina and Buck, and Gina was busy cooking some home-made pasta.

Cassie, wrapped in a towel, came through into the bedroom and saw all the boxes on her bed. She opened them, curiously, one by one. In the first square box was a pair of exquisite handmade Italian shoes, right in fashion. In the next was a set of silk underwear and stockings. In the third was a knee-length black voile dress with practically non-existent shoulder-straps. In the last was a white fur wrap.

There was no note in any of the boxes. Tyrone had obviously felt there was no need.

'I don't have a purse to go with all this!' Cassie remembered, as the ever-patient Gina re-did her hair.

'Stand still, will you?' Gina demanded. 'I'll lend you a purse! I have hundreds of the damn things!'

'I don't have any gloves either!'

'I'll lend you some gloves too! There!'

Gina turned Cassie round, and appraised her.

'You look great,' she said, beaming. 'Just great! You don't look at all like somebody who's just about to turn down a marriage proposal.'

Cassie pulled on the borrowed gloves and took the small purse Gina was offering her.

'Would you say yes?' she asked. 'To a mad Irishman? On just your second date?'

'I think,' Gina said, suddenly serious, 'if you get a chance to grab at happiness, you should grab it. This isn't a dress rehearsal, you know.'

'What isn't?' Cassie asked.

'Life,' said Gina, giving her a kiss. 'Life isn't.'

Cassie regarded herself in the mirror. The black voile dress fitted her perfectly, showing off her youthful figure to full advantage, the silk stockings flattered her shapely legs, and French underwear made her feel both excited and exciting.

'How do you feel?' Gina enquired.

'OK,' said Cassie, thoughtfully.

'OK,' grinned Gina. 'OK she says. You look like something on the front of *Vogue*.'

'You think so?'

'I know so.'

Cassie stared and stared at her new image, and then suddenly kicked off the handmade Italian shoes and unzippered the black voile dress.

'In that case—'

'Hey!' cried Gina. 'What the hell's going on here? What's the matter with you?'

'Nothing's the matter with me,' Cassie replied, stepping out of the dress. 'This is just not who I am, that's all.'

She was quarter of an hour late, as Gina had told her to be. She waited outside the swing doors for a moment, watching Tyrone pacing up and down the lobby, for all the world like an expectant father. He kept looking at his watch, and then raising his eyes to the ceiling. Obviously he wasn't a man to be kept waiting.

A party of middle-aged ladies with blue-rinsed hair and figures which indicated they'd enjoyed a lifetime of good living, made their way carefully through the swing doors. Tyrone looked round, but saw that Cassie was nowhere in their midst. He then returned to a chair where he'd been sitting, from which he could keep an eye on the main doors, and picked up his drink. He took a draught from it, flicked open the evening newspaper, and made a brave attempt at reading it. Cassie then made her way quietly through the doors.

She was by his side before he noticed her. But once he saw her, he was on his feet, dropping the paper and practically knocking over his drink.

'Cassie!' The way he greeted her, it was as if he hadn't seen her for a year. 'Let me take your coat.'

Cassie noticed the tone of his voice changing slightly, as he suddenly realised she wasn't wearing the fur. She turned her back to him and he removed her simple tweed coat in silence.

Then she swung back round to him and smiled. Tyrone looked at her. She was wearing a simple plain dark-blue wool dress, with matching-coloured court shoes, and round her neck a strand of costume pearls. Her shoulder-length dark hair shone lustrously, but she had left it down and unadorned. Tyrone, wanting to feel angry at the snub, couldn't, because dressed as she was, Cassie was a picture of innocent beauty.

'Do you know something, Cassie McGann,' he asked. 'Do you know that you're really quite beautiful?'

'*Quite* beautiful?' Cassie enquired back. 'Or quite *beautiful*?'

'And you've a lip on you as well, as we say back home,' he replied, taking her arm and leading her into the bar, where minutes later, for the second time in a week, Cassie sat drinking champagne. At first she had been a little taken aback when the cab Tyrone had sent for her brought her back to the famous hotel, afraid that she might once more bump into Leonora, who would try and revenge herself on Cassie for the trick she had played on her with the opera tickets. And then she thought, what the hell? What could Leonora do to her when she had Tyrone Rosse by her side? Looking at him, she wondered what the hell anyone could do.

Because there was no doubt about it at all. Tyrone was the best-looking and most attractive man she had ever seen, let alone met. He wasn't classically handsome, but then Cassie wasn't attracted to that sort of man, as she always felt that sort of man was so busy being attracted to himself, he didn't need anyone else.

Tyrone was, as Arnie would say, something else. Standing a good two inches over six feet, he was immensely strong-looking without being in any way heavy. And he was perfectly proportioned, with those wonderful long legs, and those oddly sensitive hands. Looking at them, Cassie wondered idly whether or not he rode. They looked like perfect horseman's hands.

But best of all were those eyes, large and doe-like, giving him, when serious, that oddly wistful appearance. But when he smiled, or at best laughed, his eyes danced and stole your heart away.

Tyrone knew he was being studied, and so for a moment, pretended to be absorbed in some distant thought. Then he signalled the waiter for more champagne.

'I thought we'd have dinner, and then maybe go dancing,' he told her. 'How does that sound?'

'It sounds like fun,' Cassie replied.

Tyrone stared at her.

'You are without doubt, Cassie McGann,' he said, 'the most beautiful girl I have ever seen. Slainte.'

With that he raised his glass to her.

'What's that?'

'Irish for good health.'

She raised her glass back to him, and they drank their champagne. Then Tyrone rose, and took her in to dinner.

Their table overlooked the park, but Tyrone had eyes only for her. Cassie tried to resist him, because she had made up her mind on the way over that she would try to remain detached and sophisticated. Gina had time and time again told Cassie in their endless conversations how possible it was to be loved and remain uninvolved. That's what sophisticated New York girls did. They took care of their emotions. They stayed cool. Getting involved was not cool.

But talking was one thing and doing was quite another. Now that Cassie was sitting opposite Tyrone, it was very, very different. When she had silently reminded herself in the cab about how uninvolved she was going to be, she wasn't being mesmerised by a pair of startlingly blue eyes and a wonderful baritone voice. She had been alone. But now she was there with him, and the two of them were talking and laughing as if they had always known each other, as if they had been made for each other.

232

'Is something the matter?' he asked her at one point, as Cassie suddenly looked away.

'No. No, not at all.'

'You look slightly flushed.'

'It's kind of hot in here.'

Cassie had held her glass of iced water to her cheek, but the burning had only momentarily ceased. As soon as she looked back at him, and was caught by his eyes, it started all over again. And she knew she was lost.

While Tyrone ordered dessert, Cassie turned away and stared out of the window, through the flurries of snow and into the darkness of Central Park. She wished suddenly to be a child again, staying with Mary-Jo, waiting for the dawn to break so that they could creep down and see the diamonds in the grass and the foals grazing rhythmically and gently as the sun rose. It was all so simple then. Everything was taken care of. Other people made all the hard decisions.

And marriage had been a game they played in Mrs Roebuck's back yard.

'Penny for them,' Tyrone said, touching her arm.

'I was remembering my childhood,' she said.

'It must be very fresh in your memory. The way you look tonight, you look fifteen.'

Cassie looked back at him. He was sitting staring at her, rubbing his mouth thoughtfully with a long slender finger.

'And you look like someone trying to decide whether or not to buy a horse,' she replied.

Tyrone laughed.

'Do I?' he said. 'Do I indeed? Now there's a thing!'

Dessert arrived, and was placed in front of them. They both made a pretence of eating it, but neither had a mind for food. Their first two courses had been taken away virtually untouched.

Tyrone drank some wine, then took one of Cassie's hands.

'Dear God but I love you,' he announced, rather too loudly for Cassie's comfort. 'Blast you anyway.'

Then he drained his glass and rose from the table to take her dancing.

There was something else about him which infuriated Cassie. He was an even better dancer than Joe. His right arm held her so lightly, yet so firmly, that she felt she could dance with him right through rush-hour traffic on Fifth Avenue without turning a hair. And with his left hand he held her right hand against his chest, occasionally lifting it to brush her fingertips with his lips.

'There's no good you fighting this, Cassie McGann,' he told her at one point. 'I'm very much afraid we were meant for each other.'

'No we were not,' Cassie said defiantly, but without any real authority.

'The moment I saw you in the store, I knew that was it.'

'You were buying lingerie for someone else.'

'For a going-away present.'

'She was leaving to go somewhere?'

'I was leaving her to go somewhere.'

He looked down at her, the smile in his eyes.

'I took one look at you,' he said, 'and that was that. Nothing else mattered until I saw you again.'

The band was playing 'Stardust'. Other people danced by them. Tyrone lifted Cassie off her feet, right in the middle of the dance floor, and kissed her.

'I love you, Cassie McGann, and you love me.'

'No I don't. I can't possibly.'

'Love isn't a possibility. It's a disease. For which there is no known cure.'

He turned her round and round, as the tune came to an end.

'That's how they treat it in India, you know,' he continued. 'They commiserate with you if they know you have fallen in love. They're very wise people. They know it's an illness. And you and I are both very ill.'

234

'I don't feel it,' Cassie said.

'Yes you do,' Tyrone contradicted her. 'And you know it.'

As the band started to play 'All The Things You Are', and they continued to dance, Cassie knew he was right. She did know it, but she didn't want to recognise it. And yet it was all so unlikely. He was so unlikely. And so was she. He was so much older than her, and genuinely sophisticated. And she was just out of her teens, trying to be a sophisticate. She was still looking for something, and was not sure what, while he knew exactly what he was searching for, and when he had found it.

But then it was so much easier for men. Men had more straightforward feelings, they knew what they wanted, and they knew how to get it. They were the conquerors, with a simple morality. Men didn't sit for hours talking to their best friend, wondering whether they should or they shouldn't. Because they wouldn't be men if they did. Men were expected to do it. Good girls weren't.

Tyrone tilted her face up to him and kissed her once more, gently. She sighed and buried her face in his chest, wishing he wouldn't keep kissing her. It was all right until he kissed her. She could keep a clear head. But then when he kissed her, all those freshly made resolutions just vanished. His kisses were intoxicating. Tyrone was intoxicating.

And now he was leading her out of the night club.

'Where are we going now?' she asked him in the cab.

'I thought we'd go back to the Plaza. For coffee. And a nightcap.'

She didn't have time to argue, because he was kissing her again.

At the hotel, he led her over to the elevator and stepped aside to let her in.

'Now where?' she asked a little late, as the doors were already closing.

'I have a suite,' he said. 'We don't want to sit in the bar at this time of night.'

They walked down the corridor to his rooms, Tyrone slightly ahead of her, the key in his hand. Cassie swallowed and determined to keep a clear head. She would have coffee, and nothing else, then thank him for another wonderful evening, and get him to call her a cab home.

Tyrone opened the door. Cassie went in and remarked on what a lovely suite it was without being able to see one stick of furniture. All she was aware of was the double bed which she could see through the half-open bedroom door. Tyrone closed the bedroom door, took Cassie's coat, then kissed her.

Tyrone's kisses were unlike any other kisses Cassie had ever experienced They were real kisses, searching kisses, kisses which asked for something else than just another kiss in return. They were questioning kisses. And they were demanding kisses.

Cassie tried to push away from him.

'Please,' she said, 'I can't breathe.'

'Good,' he replied, still holding her tight.

'I can't! I feel faint!'

'Excellent.'

And with that, he kissed her again. It seemed to Cassie he kissed her several hundred times.

She finally escaped, and stood by a wall, looking at him, seemingly bewildered by his passion. And by her response. He smiled gently at her, then took her coat and rang room service. Cassie tried vainly to hang on to her coat. But Tyrone took it from her quite firmly, saying he was not having her sitting around his suite in her overcoat. Then while they were waiting for the coffee, Tyrone produced a travelling flask and poured them both a drink.

'What's this?' Cassie enquired carefully.

'An aphrodisiac,' Tyrone replied, poker-faced.

'What's that?'

'Never you mind.'

He put the glass down in front of her.

'It's brandy,' he said.

'No thanks,' Cassie answered. 'I don't drink brandy.'

'Do you get a lot of opportunity?' Tyrone asked her.

'OK,' she admitted. 'I have never drunk brandy.'

'Then try some,' Tyrone encouraged her. 'It didn't do Napoleon any harm.'

'I wonder if the same can be said about Josephine?'

Tyrone smiled and raised his glass.

'Slainte.'

'Slainte,' Cassie answered perfectly.

'Good,' said Tyrone. 'We'll make an Irishwoman of you yet.'

Cassie wasn't sure she wanted to be an Irishwoman. She wasn't at all sure she wanted to be anything other than Cassie McGann.

She avoided drinking the brandy, but readily accepted the coffee which had now arrived.

Tyrone brought the cup over to her and looked down at her.

'Didn't you even wear the underwear?' he enquired.

'Pardon me?' Cassie faltered, almost spilling the coffee.

'I said. Didn't you even wear the underwear?'

'What underwear?'

'The clothes I sent you.'

'Oh yes. Those. No. No I didn't.'

'Didn't you like them? Most girls like silk underwear.'

Cassie didn't reply. She just looked down and drank her coffee.

'Most girls would have liked that dress as well. And the shoes. And the fur.'

'Perhaps I'm not most girls.'

'No,' Tyrone agreed. 'You certainly are not.'

He went back and sat in a chair, stirring his coffee and staring at her.

'So why didn't you wear the clothes?'

'Because they weren't me.'

'You mean they didn't suit you?'

237

'I mean they weren't me.'

'I'd like to see you in them,' Tyrone said. 'I think they would very much be you.'

'Perhaps you'd like me to model them for you sometime,' Cassie replied, with a fairly hopeless attempt at sarcasm.

Tyrone ignored it, and sighed, leaning back and sipping his brandy.

'And I really can't believe the underwear wouldn't have suited you.'

'Well it didn't.'

Cassie's reply was a lie, because it did. Worse than that, she still had the underwear on.

Tyrone looked at her quite suddenly, as if he too knew she was wearing it, because he was smiling. Cassie thought he was also smiling because he thought he had her enthralled. She could have got up and walked out there and then. But she didn't. So she knew he was right.

She was saved by the telephone, which suddenly rang beside Tyrone.

He excused himself and answered it, explaining he was expecting a call from someone. Cassie excused herself and went in search of the bathroom.

Before she closed the door she heard Tyrone talking back to whoever it was on the telephone. It was a woman, someone called Hélène. He was laughing and flirting with her, and calling her his love.

Cassie banged the bathroom door, and then leant against it, the way she'd seen girls do in the movies. And wasn't this just turning out to be like one of those movies she and Gina occasionally saw? Where the girl from the sticks nearly makes A Big Mistake with The Older Man?

She looked at herself in the mirror and tried to see if there were any visible signs showing from her close brush with disaster. She could still hear him laughing away on the telephone, so she eased the bathroom door open again to hear what he was saying. Now he was promising to fix up a lunch date with his Hélène my love! So that's what he was! Just a two-bit seducer. And she was just another two-bit shop assistant.

'You're a fool, Cassie McGann!' she said to herself in the mirror. 'A silly little fool! Who was just about to allow herself to be made into a great big silly fool!'

She reopened the bathroom door quietly and tiptoed back to the door between the bedroom and the sitting room. Tyrone had loosened his tie and collar, and was still talking on the phone. He had his back to her, and to the door. Cassie picked up her coat and purse without him seeing and was out of the suite before he realised.

She ran down the corridor, in the opposite direction to the elevator. She knew if he came after her he'd head straight for the elevator, and maybe catch her while she was waiting. So instead, with a kind of innate cunning, she made for the service stairs and started to race down them. Halfway down, when she realised there was no one coming after her, she stopped, and waited for a while. Just enough time for him, if he'd taken the elevator down, to arrive and find her gone from the lobby, and to return to his suite.

Then she continued on her way, going out of a side entrance of the hotel into the bitterly cold night.

When she arrived back at her apartment, having finally got a cab, she opened the door and found Tyrone waiting for her on the sofa. Cassie stood momentarily dumb-struck, then came in and closed the door.

'What are you doing here?' she asked him.

'Waiting for you,' he replied,

Cassie looked round for Gina, but Tyrone was alone. He sensed what she was looking for and told her that Gina had gone to bed. Cassie thought that made sense because Gina had a really early photocall the following morning. She looked at her watch. That morning.

Tyrone bought her back to the present with a jolt.

'You need your bottom smacked,' he told her.

Cassie's eyes flared, but she said nothing as she took off

her coat and hung it in the closet. He'd obviously out-thought her and come straight out of the hotel, into a cab and over here.

'Running out on me like that.'

'I didn't run out on you.'

'Really? Most people I know say thanks for a lovely evening and goodnight, before grabbing their coat and disappearing.'

'I bet,' Cassie said over her shoulder, going through into the kitchen to make herself some coffee. And to give herself time to think.

Tyrone followed her through and leant on the door frame.

'Well?'

'Well what now?'

'So why did you run away?'

Cassie heaped the coffee grounds into the percolator and didn't answer.

'Weren't you enjoying yourself? If anyone had asked me, I'd have said you were having a good time.'

Cassie nodded miserably, her back still to him.

'Sure I was. I was having a great time.'

'Then why did you run out like that?'

He was behind her now, turning her round to face him, gently. Cassie laid her head on his chest, without looking up at him, and Tyrone put his arms round her. They stood like that in silence, for several moments, then Cassie broke away, shaking out her hair and trying to find resolution.

'I'm not used to men like you,' she said, finally. 'I don't think I can handle you.'

'What are you afraid of?' he asked.

'You've obviously known so many women. You obviously still do.'

'Fine,' he said, turning the heat down under the percolator for her. 'Let's deal with first things first. The woman on the phone. She's an old friend, the wife of a very old friend, and they're business. Strictly business.

240

She's in New York, and I like to have lunch sometimes with my old friends. If you have no objection?'

He looked at her without malice, and asked her without sarcasm.

'Second, yes, I've known a lot of women. Quite a lot. Many women in fact. But none – not one – not one woman like you.'

'I'm not the type who has affairs,' she told him.

'I don't want to have an affair with you,' he replied.

'But tonight?'

Cassie looked up at him and bit her lip.

'Wouldn't you have taken me to bed tonight?'

'I wasn't even going to dream of asking you,' Tyrone replied perfectly truthfully. 'I was loving just being with you.'

Cassie stared at him and knew he was telling the truth. And then she felt ashamed of herself, because just before the telephone rang she had made up her mind to go to bed with him.

He took the coffee through into the living room, and Cassie hung behind for a moment, to wipe the tear away that had somehow found its way out of one eye. Then she followed, and sat in a chair opposite him, deliberately keeping her distance so that she could also keep her head.

'So,' he said. 'Is it yes then?'

'Tyrone—' she started to reply, but he interrupted her.

'I want no more excuses. I want you to marry me, and there's an end to it.'

'I've something to tell you, Tyrone,' she told him, looking down at her coffee. 'I'm illegitimate.'

There was a long silence, during which Cassie didn't dare look up. She just sat in her chair, staring into her coffee.

'Yes?' Tyrone finally answered. 'And?'

Cassie then looked up, sharply and in surprise. Tyrone was looking at her, but not with rage. More with a kind of quizzical surprise.

'I'm a bastard, Tyrone,' Cassie said, spelling it out. 'You can't marry a bastard.'

Tyrone just continued to stare at her, and then suddenly started to laugh.

'Who says I can't!' he roared. 'I'd like to see who'll stop me!'

'Everyone will stop you! I'm a bastard!'

'So what? So bloody what?'

'What do you mean – so bloody what?' Cassie retorted. 'I mean so bloody what, child! It couldn't matter less!'

Cassie leaped out of her chair and stood before him, hands on her hips, her eyes flashing wildly.

'It couldn't matter less, could it? Maybe not to you! but it bloody well matters to me!' she shouted, swearing for what was probably the first time in her life.

'You imagine it does, I'm quite sure,' Tyrone answered gently. 'But I assure you it doesn't.'

'That's all very well for you to say!' Cassie continued, infuriated that this man was trying to minimise what to her was the key aspect of her life. 'But you try being a bastard!'

'Back home, a lot of people consider that I am,' he replied, tongue in cheek.

'That isn't funny!' Cassie yelled, looking round for something to throw at him. 'There's nothing funny in being illegitimate!'

She threw one of her shoes at him, which missed. So then she threw the other. Tyrone caught it and looked at it.

'God – you've got lovely little feet.'

Cassie didn't know what to say. Life was so unfair, with its constant unpredictabilities. He shouldn't have reacted like that. He should have been aghast, he should have been horrified, he should have been too shocked for words. Then he should have taken her in his arms and rocked her, and she'd have cried, as they realised their future together was doomed. But instead he was sitting upon the sofa with a stupid smile on his face, nursing one of her shoes and telling her she had lovely little feet.

'Tyrone,' she finally said, through rather clenched teeth. 'You cannot possibly marry me if I'm a bastard.'

'Child,' he replied. 'I'd marry you if you were the child of the Pope himself.'

Cassie gasped in horror at the blasphemy. But when she saw the soft look in Tyrone's eyes, and the gentleness of his smile, she suddenly couldn't help smiling back. He held his arms open to her, and she came across to him, and sat beside him, in his embrace.

He held her tightly in his arms, and then Cassie started to weep, very softly.

'Blast you, Tyrone Rosse,' Cassie said, half-smiling and half-weeping.

'Why, Cassie?' he asked. 'Why blast me?'

'Blast you,' she answered, 'because I hadn't catered for you, that's why.'

Tyrone smiled at her and shook his head.

'No, God damn it,' he said. 'And I hadn't catered for you either, Cassie McGann.'

They sat silently for some time, and then Tyrone made sure she went to bed, before he let himself out to return alone to his hotel.

Tyrone stayed in New York until Christmas, making plans for their wedding. He wanted Cassie to fly back to Ireland with him for the holiday, and she was all set to go when Tyrone's favourite aunt died suddenly and he had to return early and without Cassie for the funeral.

He told her it would be no way to introduce her to his remaining relatives when they were grieving, and Cassie agreed. Instead she remained behind in New York, finalising all the arrangements for their wedding which was to take place in March. Tyrone hoped to be able to get back before then, but had warned her that once he set foot back home, he would be set upon to catch up on all sorts of business, and there was a very strong chance that he wouldn't see her again until the week of the wedding itself.

But love had become a strangely isolating experience for Cassie; and none of her friends, not even Gina, could cross back over that line. Cassie stood alone now, singled out by love, trying to learn how to cope with the helplessness engendered by great desire, as well as the dawning realisation that great love could, after all, exist.

In the time left before Christmas, and before Tyrone's aunt died, Cassie and Tyrone spent every moment of their free time together, Cassie worked out her notice at Bergdorf Goodman's, where Mrs Wellman, who was deeply romantic at heart, had quite forgiven Tyrone his indiscretions, and considered their whole romance just like something out of a Doris Day movie. Tyrone told Cassie all about Claremore, and showed her a photograph which he always carried around in his wallet when he was away from it of the house and grounds. It looked quite beautiful.

'*Quite* beautiful?' Tyrone had teased, 'or quite *beautiful*?'

They discussed their future together, and tried to guess how many children they would have, and what they would call them; and Cassie pictured herself seated by a roaring wood fire, surrounded by tousle-headed and laughing children. She imagined Tyrone coming back home from work, and the dogs running down the steps of the house while the children clung to her skirts, ready to welcome their father back. In her dreams the sun always shone, and the fires always burned bright, and the children which she was to bear Tyrone were always happy and healthy. Cassie was determined that the family life she was to lead in Ireland was in no way going to be anything like the life she had led growing up in New Hampshire.

And they had gone shopping, insisting that they should choose together everything Cassie was to have.

'No, not a bridal gown,' he'd told her, as she lingered

over white lace dresses. 'Bridal gowns are the biggest waste of money known to woman. You only wear them once, and then it's up in the attic with them, to be brought down later to be shown to your children. No, what you need is something beautiful and sophisticated, something you'll be able to wear over and over again, and remember your great day.'

He'd helped her to choose everything, from the colour of her stockings, to the hair ribbons bought to match her negligées. No detail was too dull, or too trivial. Hats, gloves, coats, dresses – everything was chosen with the utmost care and patience. Even her underwear, which was bought to the enjoyment of all in the lingerie department of Bergdorf Goodman. They went in there on Cassie's half day, and chose Cherry to serve them, whom Cassie considered most in need of the commission.

Tyrone had justified his tireless supervision of her wardrobe and trousseau by telling Cassie that he would be seeing her in what she wore more than anyone else, therefore she had to reflect his taste.

They were finally married in the following March, as planned, in a small church in the Italian quarter, which Cassie had made her regular place of worship. Gina supervised the making of the wedding dress, which was designed by Gina and sewn by a family of tiny Italian women all dressed in black and covered in so many pins that Cassie called them the hedgehogs. They worked in what had been an old sweat shop on Second Avenue, their once thick black hair now grey and tied back tightly into buns, and their teeth gleaming with gold fillings every time they removed a pin from their mouths to make an adjustment or to smile at the bride-to-be. They treated Cassie like she was a daughter, down to giving her advice on what she should do and what she shouldn't do on her wedding night. And what it would be like. They told her it would be painful the first time, but that she must be brave, and that making love would get better after she

245

had had a baby. They told her that the baby must be born screaming, but that she must not scream when it was born or it would not have courage. They told her the baby must be a boy, the first born, and if it wasn't a boy then her husband wasn't a man; that being a woman was all tears; and that not being married was worse than being married. And they made her a beautiful dress in pure white silk with white fur trimmings, which quite by chance echoed the famous negligée which Tyrone had bought for Cassie on the day they met.

As he had predicted Tyrone failed to return to New York until two days before the ceremony. He had telephoned Cassie two or three times a week, mainly to tell her he loved her and to find out what she was doing. When he arrived back in America he came with a man called Niall Brogan, a handsome red-faced fellow in a thornproof suit, who was to be Tyrone's best man. To the wedding itself he also invited several of his many American friends, all apparently rich, and all apparently devoted to Tyrone. Cassie asked all her new friends from New York. Even Arnie relented and consented to play some great jazz piano at the reception afterwards. Maria and Gina were her bridesmaids, and Mrs Roebuck journeyed down from Westboro the night before the wedding and stayed at Gina and Cassie's apartment for the very first time. Cassie was so nervous that the priest was forced to ask her to speak up a little, and when Tyrone kissed her, the ladies who had made the wedding dress and were sitting up in the gallery all cried and applauded.

The organist started to play the Widor Toccata and Fugue and Tyrone took his young bride's hand and wrapped it through his arm. As she passed Mrs Roebuck, Cassie gave her a special smile, a smile reserved for someone who had given her the happy days of her childhood in Westboro, and Mrs Roebuck smiled back, remembering the first day that a shy little child had arrived to play in her yard, and looking with love at the vision that was now the grown-up Cassie.

At the back of the church, uninvited and unnoticed in the crowd of well wishers, sat Mrs Von Wagner and her daughter Leonora. They both wore dark glasses and large hats. Leonora didn't take her eyes off Tyrone once as he walked down the aisle, and neither did her mother.

The reception was held in Tyrone's favourite Italian restaurant, which was the best in the neighbourhood. The gingham-clothed tables were a profusion of white flowers, and Andrea the owner presented Cassie with the traditional baskets of almonds which Italian brides always handed around. Cassie accepted the basket, which took her back to her First Communion when she had handed the almonds to the men smoking in the yard, and when Mrs Roebuck had baked them a beautiful cake shaped like a church. All her friends hugged her and kissed her, and Tyrone's friends shook him by the hand and kissed Cassie's hand; and one or two of them, emboldened by the wine, kissed Cassie on the cheek. She and Tyrone danced, while Arnie played the piano. Tyrone sang unrequested 'The Star of the County Down' solely for his bride, and once Andrea and his brothers discovered what a beautiful baritone voice he had, demanded an encore, which was followed by any other song which came into Tyrone's head. Tyrone, happier than he had ever been, or had ever thought he could be, sang them a selection of Irish songs, and then, with both Cassie's hands in his, he sang her his favourite ballad.

Well out of his knapsack he took a fine fiddle
He played her such merry tunes that you ever did
hear –
He played her such merry tunes that the valleys did
ring –
And then they both sat down together, love,
To hear the nightingale sing.
And they kiss'd so sweet and comforting as they
clung to each other –

They went arm and arm along the road like sister
and brother –
They went arm and arm along the road till they
came to a stream –
Then they both sat down together now to hear the
nightingale sing.

They had to cancel their Paris honeymoon at the last
minute because Tyrone told her he had to return at once
to Ireland because of his business. Cassie didn't mind,
because anywhere with Tyrone would be a honeymoon,
and besides, she was dying to see her new home.

On the plane back – Cassie's first time up in the air –
as Tyrone removed the final bits of confetti and rice from
his hair and suit, and as America disappeared in the cloud
below them, Cassie turned to the man who was now her
husband and grinned at him.

'Do you realise something, Tyrone?' she said. 'I know
we haven't known each other all that long, but even so,
I've never actually found out what business it is you do.'

'No you haven't, have you?' Tyrone replied, turning
those deep blue eyes on her and kissing her cheek. 'Not
that it's of any great importance. I train racehorses.'

Cassie said nothing in return, beyond expressing a
polite interest. But in her heart she felt her life was now
complete.

It was in fact only another beginning.

Part Two

Chapter Ten

Claremore, Co. Wicklow, Ireland
Spring, 1961

When they finally arrived in Dublin, Tyrone took her to tea at the Russell Hotel on the corner of St Stephen's Green, where they had platefuls of hot toast, with lashings of Irish butter. Tyrone then excused himself and said he had to go and do a few minutes' business. Cassie remained behind in the hotel, re-reading the magazines she had bought for the flight. Tyrone's few minutes of business turned into nearly two hours, so that by the time they left Dublin in Tyrone's new green E-type Jaguar, which had been delivered to him at the airport, dusk was falling.

Cassie caught glimpses of the charming old city as Tyrone hurried his way out through the traffic. She asked what certain places were and Tyrone told her: Grafton Street, the Bank of Ireland which used to be the old houses of parliament, the front gate of Trinity College, the rest of the university hidden from her gaze behind its high stone walls, the canal, and Fitzwilliam Square, where Tyrone had to stop briefly to have a quick word and a drink with a young bloodstock agent. Cassie was left sitting in the car.

She didn't mind because it gave her the chance to admire the beauty of the Georgian architecture. As she was looking with some wonder at the houses with their beautiful fanlights and elegant sash windows, some children tapped on the car window, since the hood was up and they couldn't talk to her direct. Cassie was appalled. They were filthy, with running noses, ragged clothes and

251

no shoes. There wasn't one of them either who could have been over seven or eight years of age.

She watched them through the glass as they tapped once more on the window. Then she wound it down.

'Give us a penny, will ya?' a boy asked her.

At first Cassie had great difficulty understanding what he was saying, so thick was his nasal twang.

'I said give us a penny, ma'am.'

'A penny!' Cassie said, smiling and opening her purse. 'And what do you want a penny for?'

'We're havin' a party,' the child replied very seriously. 'So give us a penny.'

Cassie looked in her purse. Tyrone had already given her some Irish money, just in case.

'I don't have a penny, I'm afraid,' she started to explain, but the little boy was leaning right into the car and looking in her purse.

'That's all right, ma'am,' he said, snatching a florin from her purse. 'This'll do fine.'

They fled down the street before Cassie could say another word. She turned and looked after them and saw them, as bold as anything, stop at the shop on the corner and go in. Cassie closed her purse and grinned, but decided to tell Tyrone nothing of the incident.

When Tyrone returned and drove out of the square, the kids were all coming out of the shop smoking cigarettes. Cassie saw them and was horrified. She looked over her shoulder and watched them as Tyrone turned right across Baggott Street, heading the car out of town.

'Something the matter, Mrs Rosse?' he asked.

'Those kids. They were smoking.'

'Those kids were born smoking.'

'That's terrible.'

'That's Ireland.'

Before long they had left the city far behind and were driving on headlights across a road which cut through the mountains. Even in the dark Cassie was struck by the majesty of the countryside through which they were driving.

'Not far now,' Tyrone told her. 'About another fifteen or so miles. The house lies just this side of the border with Kildare.'

Cassie sat back and watched as Ireland passed by.

They must have been waiting for them to arrive, because as Tyrone turned the last corner of the drive, bringing Cassie into view of the house, it was as if the house burst into flames. At every window candles suddenly spurted and flickered, and at the doorways, lanterns were lit.

'Don't tell me you don't have electricity?' Cassie laughed.

'Probably another powercut,' he replied. 'A couple of drops of rain and the whole damn thing goes phut.'

Cassie stared back at the house, which looked like something out of a fairytale. The moon had risen behind it, and Cassie could see by its light that the house stood against a backdrop of mountains. It was just as Tyrone had described it: the old stone, the tall chimneys, the long shuttered windows and the flight of steps up to the half-glassed double front doors, where a welcoming party waited with lanterns in hand.

Tyrone and his bride climbed out of the car. Something huge and hairy hurtled down the steps to greet Tyrone and nearly knocked him flying.

'This is Brian,' Tyrone told her as the wolfhound licked him all over his face. 'You'd best hold on to your hat.'

The dog then turned to Cassie on whose shoulders, since she was so small, he had no difficulty whatsoever in placing both paws. He sniffed her then licked her, smack on the nose.

'You're elected,' said Tyrone, and preceded her up the steps.

'So you've arrived at last, have you?' said an older man holding up a lantern. 'Six o'clock indeed.'

'I'd business in Dublin, Tomas. I'm lucky to be back at all tonight.'

'And what about your poor young bride?' the man who

253

was Tomas persisted. 'Have you no thought for her at all?'

Cassie had now climbed the steps and joined Tyrone and the white-haired man, who smiled shyly at her. Cassie could see by the lantern light that although his hair was shock white, his face was as smooth as a baby's.

'Pleased to meet you, ma'am,' he said, extending a strong gnarled hand. 'I'm Tomas.'

'How do you do, Tomas?' Cassie said as they shook hands. 'Mr Rosse has told me all about you.'

'Has he bedad?' Tomas wondered. 'Has he bedad?'

'Put the light up, Tomas!' someone called from the back. 'So we all may look at her!'

Tomas held the lantern to Cassie's face. There was a silence.

'Thank God!' another voice said. 'She's as pretty as a picture!'

A cheer went up as Cassie smiled, and Tomas led them to the front doors.

'They was afraid you'd be an ugly old hawk,' he said, grinning back at her. 'Most of 'em have never seen a Yank.'

Then he held open the doors and Cassie stood about to enter Claremore. But not on her feet. For Tyrone swept her up in his arms and carried her over the threshold.

'*Cead mile failte*, Mrs Rosse,' he said, setting her down in the candlelit hall. 'A hundred thousand welcomes.'

Then he kissed her, to further cheers from the assembled throng.

Cassie looked around her, at the beautiful hall with its sweeping staircase, at the wood fire burning in the huge grate, at all the faces looking back at her over their lanterns. Then a large woman in an apron stepped forward and introduced herself.

'I'm Mrs Muldoon, ma'am, Tomas's wife, and the cook. And this here's me daughter Erin, who works here with me.'

From the ranks behind her she pulled forward a

254

round-faced girl with a pile of frizzy hair brushed into a knot on the top of her head. She had so many freckles, Cassie thought, that she looked as if she'd been splashed by a paintbrush.

Cassie smiled at her, and Erin grinned and nodded, before dropping back in line.

'Well?' said Tyrone in that now familiar way of his. 'Are we just to stand here dying of thirst?'

Tomas grinned and, shaking his head, threw open the doors to the dining room and to the drawing room, both large rooms with fires blazing, and both set for a party. In the dining room there wasn't an inch of table space which wasn't taken up with food and drink, and in the drawing room every table was ablaze with jugs, vases and jars filled with spring flowers. Cassie gasped and took Tyrone's hand.

'There's been nothing but to-ing and fro-ing the last two days,' Tomas grumbled happily. 'You may have been wedded in America, Mr Rosse, but 'tis here at Claremore it'll duly be celebrated.'

'Will you just look at those wonderful flowers?' Cassie cried.

'Sure the women have been walking up to the house all day with the first of the spring flowers,' Tomas told her. 'I dare say there's not a daffodil left standing in the whole of the county. And as for the cooking, I don't think Mrs Muldoon has been in bed for a week. Least not so as I would notice.'

'It looks wonderful,' Cassie told Tomas, before Tyrone led her away to get them some drinks.

'All they did was grumble about our getting married over the water,' he said. 'So rather than have another civil war on my hands, I said we'd have a hoolie on our return. I hope you've no objection?'

Cassie, who on the drive to the house had secretly thought of curling up early in her wedding bed, quickly put aside such thoughts from her head as soon as she saw the joyous expectation on all the faces present.

She followed Tyrone to a sideboard, where he was making the drinks and, leaning up, kissed him on the cheek.

'You really don't mind, Cassie, love? About the party? They'd have murdered me otherwise.'

'Mind?' said Cassie. 'I've never seen anything lovelier.'

'I have,' Tyrone replied. 'It's standing looking at me.'

He touched her glass with his and drank his whisky.

When they had all eaten, the men first served by the women, and then the women themselves, the carpet in the hall was rolled back for dancing. Fiddles were produced, a side drum and an accordion, and an instrument which Cassie didn't recognise.

'Irish bagpipes,' Tyrone told her. 'You're to have them played at my funeral.'

Cassie turned and stared at him.

'That's a funny thing to say at a time like this, isn't it?' she asked.

'Good Lord no,' Tyrone replied laughing. 'Haven't you heard that the Irish are in love with death?'

Then he took her by the arm, away to watch the dancing. Cassie watched with fascination as the men and women danced Irish jigs, the girls with their arms held stiff by their sides, their feet weaving intricate patterns and movements, catching the reflection of the firelight in their shiny shoes, while the men danced likewise around them. Cassie watched it all, anxious to remember every moment of the celebrations. She knew tomorrow was already knocking on the door, but until it was formally here, she wanted to remember the candlelight, the faces and the flowers, and the sound of the celebrations, rising with the cigarette and pipe smoke, high into the ceiling. She wanted to remember the women from the village in their best black dresses and the handsome faces of the men, shining above their stiff white shirt collars and their unaccustomed neckties. And she wanted to remember all the beautiful children, dressed in their Sunday best, some of them dancing very seriously, others sitting in the corners of the hall just watching, their precious glasses of lemonade clasped in their two hands, or their empty dinner plates balanced on their stretched-out legs.

Halfway through the evening a priest arrived, who was greeted with due respect, and immediately given what Cassie heard described as a ball of malt. Cassie was led over by Tyrone to meet him.

He was a tall man, very tall, built like one of Gina's football players, with shoulders so wide you would swear they were padded. He was handsome, too. Not as handsome as Tyrone, but enormously good-looking, with a head of thick curly hair, and a very open expression to his face.

'I'm delighted to meet you, Mrs Rosse,' he said to her, 'even though you denied me the privilege of marrying you.'

Cassie made her apologies and explained the reasons why they had decided to marry in New York, but while she was doing so, she got the impression, as she always did with priests, that he wasn't really listening so much to her, but looking into her, straight into her soul, as if through a window. It took her back to her first day at the convent, when the nuns had frightened her so much with the intensity of their stares. Her excuses for not getting married in Ireland were beginning to sound feebler by the moment, as she faltered under Father Patrick's gaze.

Tyrone came to her rescue.

'If I'd brought this child back with me unmarried, I couldn't have taken the risk,' he said. 'You can see how beautiful she is, Patrick. Why, you might have forsaken your orders and run off with her yourself!'

Father Patrick nodded and laughed, and the ice was broken. Then Tyrone made his excuses and took Cassie out into the hall to teach her how to jig.

'They'll be gone soon enough, Cassie McGann,' Tyrone said in her ear. 'And once they're all gone I'll carry you to bed, and make love to you such as you never dreamed of.'

Cassie looked up at him and smiled. She couldn't

imagine what that would be like. Not just being made love to by Tyrone, but lying in her own bed. In her own house. With her husband. She couldn't begin to imagine any of it.

He didn't say a word to her as he carried her upstairs and along the corridor to what was to be their bedroom. He carried her easily into the darkened room, lit only by the one candle Cassie held in her hands. He put her down gently, and took the lit candle, placing it by the bed. Then he took both her hands and kissed her slowly and tenderly, then, putting his strong arms around her, more passionately, and for longer. She put her arms around his neck and his hand in her hair, and whispered to him softly to take care. And he murmured back to her that he would, that he would, as he undid the back of her dress, and let it fall down over her new silken underwear. He took her breasts in his hands, and a delicious shock ran through her body as he touched both her nipples. Then he carried her to the bed, as she undid his shirt. He laid her down, and took off the rest of his clothes, sliding under the cold linen sheets beside her. She could feel the softness of his skin against hers now, his arm around her back as he pulled her towards him; then she became aware of the whole of his body, as he explored the whole of her own. She shivered and groaned softly, very softly lest she might upset him, as he delicately searched her every area, anxious to find and to touch the places which would please her the most. And all this time they kissed, their lips against each other's, or against each other's necks, or chests, or breasts, or stomachs. Then gently, slowly, oh so gently he took her, and her back suddenly arched high and she gasped and cried; but he kept kissing her and telling her he loved her and to trust him. She found herself kissing him back with a ferocious passion, with a hunger she didn't know she felt, with a desire which suddenly inflamed her. She ran her hands through his hair and pulled hard, and his head came back as he was deep inside her. He laughed with delight and pleasure, putting his arm round her arching back and holding her suspended with this enormous strength of his, high above the bed. She gasped and cried and bit into his shoulder, hard, hard and ever harder when she suddenly became aware of him moaning and shuddering. His arm was now releasing her, and she found herself falling such a long, long way down, down slowly on to the bed far below and on to him as he turned and caught her endlessly falling body in both his arms, twisting her round to him but now so tenderly, so that their mouths met and kissed again softly in the dark as the candle sputtered and died. They lay there spent, he on his back and her face down on his chest, her arms under his shoulders, his arms round her body and the rest of her life.

Now the dim light of day crept under Cassie's tired eyelids, as she began to wake. She could hear the sound of steady rain, and the bed was empty and cold beside her. Tyrone was already up and gone. He'd warned her that this would be so, that this was his routine, up every morning at six to supervise the first string, and home for what he called a late breakfast at half past eight when the second string had returned and were back safe and, it was to be hoped, all sound in their boxes. Cassie sat up and looked about her, hugging the bedclothes around her as she suddenly felt the cold.

She looked towards the windows, thinking that Tyrone with his love of fresh air must have left a window open. But no, the two long windows were both quite shut. Cassie blinked against the morning light, and reckoned that the least Mr Rosse might have done was to leave the drapes closed. Then she saw that there were no drapes, just large wooden shutters which were already folded back. She pulled the bedclothes even more tightly around her and reached for her robe, then looked for something to put on, but her case stood still packed in the corner. Pulling the quilt from the bed, she wrapped herself up in

259

it, and ran over across the bare boards to grab her small overnight bag; then she ran back to the bed where underneath the already chilling linen sheets, with teeth chattering, she slipped into her nightgown and wrap. She looked again at the room, which was her first view of Claremore by the light of day. There was rain against the windows, and down the chimney came the sigh of the wind. The room looked very different from the room they had hurried up to by candlelight a few hours previously, when the last of their guests had staggered home singing their way down the long drive. It looked very bare and cheerless.

It was large, too large, much too large for comfort. It was hardly furnished either, for that matter. There was one big wardrobe, its doors open and revealing a mess of male clothes within it, one chest of drawers, an upright chair, and the bed. The bed was very grand, with its headboard of carved cherubs, and its ornate wooden scrolling, but it only helped to emphasise the vastness of the room. And not only was there no carpet, there wasn't even a rug anywhere.

She stared out of the window in front of her. There were cobwebs round the frames, thick and full of long dead insects. Beyond and outside there was a landscape which seemed all grass, and fields, and more grass and fields, with one hill distant, which seemed to be brown and green and mauve, all at the same time; and above that the sky, grey and dead, and full of rain.

Cassie swung her feet out of the bed on to the uncarpeted boards and hurried over to open one of the larger suitcases, in the hope of quickly locating a pair of socks, her slippers, and her tweed coat which she needed to fling over her thin wrap in order to stop her teeth from chattering. She found all three things and quickly wriggled her way into them, then made her way to the door. A bath would soon warm her up.

She found her way to the vast old-fashioned bathroom,

and started to run the water into the tub. It ran brown at first, then turned a normal colour, and was stone cold. Cassie sighed and went off in search of Mrs Muldoon. Along the landing and down the stairs there were still the remains of candles on saucers, and empty whisky and beer bottles seemed to fill every nook and cranny. Over the whole place hung a pervasive stench of stale drink and cigarette smoke. That didn't worry Cassie so much. A good airing and no doubt the place would be smelling as fresh as a daisy once again. What concerned her were the now visible patches of damp on the walls, and the peeling discoloured paintwork.

She crossed the flagstone hall and on her way peered into the drawing room. Although it was at least pretty fully furnished, in the grey morning light it looked as cheerless as the bedroom she had just left. The fire was out, which didn't help. Rooms with fireplaces always seemed to look miserable when nothing was burning in the hearth, but even so, Cassie thought, the *furniture* . . . It was all so old and worn, and the whole place was so dusty. The vases and jugs full of flowers left over from the party helped to cheer the room up a little, but not enough to help raise Cassie's rapidly sinking spirits.

She heard the clatter of feet and the clank of a bucket outside in the hall and hurried out to catch whoever it was.

It was Mrs Muldoon, who was surprised to see her, not because she was up but because she wasn't up and dressed. To her way of thinking, whatever hour they'd been a-bed, the lady of the house should be up and dressed by now, and about her business. But Cassie, now that she was a married woman and no longer had to rise every morning at a quarter to seven and fight her way to work across town on the subway, had decided that at Claremore she would sleep until she woke. She had told Tyrone, and Tyrone in his easy-going way had told her to please herself. She had no intention, however, of informing Mrs Muldoon of her planned daily schedule, because it was none of her concern. And they must start as they meant to go on – which, judging from Mrs Muldoon's expression of disapproval, was not going to be very well.

'The bathwater's cold, Mrs Muldoon,' Cassie informed her.

'And so it would be, Mrs Rosse,' came the answer. 'The boiler's only lit on Fridays for the weekend.'

'I don't understand,' Cassie said. 'How am I meant to bath in the morning?'

'If it's a bath you're after in the morning, ma'am,' sniffed Mrs Muldoon, 'then you'll have to be takin' it cold. Now if you'll excuse me, there's work to be done.'

She disappeared through a pass door at the back of the hall. Cassie, pulling her tweed coat even more tightly round her, stepped round what looked like a puddle of rain water in the middle of the flagstones, and followed her through, down into the kitchens.

If Cassie had thought the formal part of the house was in sad repair, the kitchens left her quite speechless. From the look of them, with the huge black iron stoves and hobs, the pots hanging above an open fire, the old black kettle sputtering constantly on a hob and the enormous stone sinks with their cracked wooden draining boards, Cassie reckoned they must have remained unchanged since the house had been built. As Mrs Muldoon had entered the kitchens, followed closely by Cassie, a cat had been sitting in the middle of the main kitchen table, helping itself to some liver. Mrs Muldoon had swiped at it with a broom, and protested to nobody in particular that the wretched cat had her annoyed.

'I really would like a bath this morning, Mrs Muldoon,' Cassie announced. 'We had a very long and tiring journey, with the flight, the drive from Dublin, and the reception.'

She tried a smile on her, but to no avail. Mrs Muldoon, standing there in a filthy dirty apron, with her sleeves rolled up over her elbows and her grey hair falling down from under her mob cap, was having none of it.

'The boiler is only lit,' she informed Cassie, 'with himself's own permission.'

'Mrs Muldoon, I am cold. Very cold. I need a bath.'

'The boiler is only lit with himself's own permission.'

'What about the fires?'

'The fires will be seen to later, Mrs Rosse.'

'The fires will be seen to now, Mrs Muldoon. I'm freezing.'

'Then if I may suggest so, ma'am, it'd be best for you to get dressed and go for a good brisk walk.'

'That won't make any difference to the temperature of the house, Mrs Muldoon,' Cassie argued.

'Ah sure, this place is always cold,' Mrs Muldoon replied, shaking out a filthy grey dishcloth. 'Sometimes in the winter it gets that cold you're better off standing outside.'

Then she turned away from Cassie and busied herself preparing what looked to Cassie like a side of bacon and cabbage.

But the new Mrs Rosse was not a woman to be defeated. She went through every cupboard in the kitchens until she found several large enamel jugs, which she somehow knew she'd find. Then she filled every pot she could lay her hands on with water, and set them all to boil on various hobs. Mrs Muldoon watched her all the time, never saying a word, and never lifting a hand to help her.

Then while she waited for the water to boil, Cassie helped herself to a cup of strong tea from the pot on the hob. Tyrone had at least been right about that. There was always a cup of tea to be had at Claremore.

He hadn't been right about much else concerning the house though, Cassie thought, looking round at the spiders' webs, and the cracked windowglass. A grand place, he'd described it as. Simply grand. Simple maybe; grand, most certainly not. But then Cassie wasn't to know when Tyrone said it that in Ireland grand didn't mean *grand* it meant lovely; and that lovely didn't mean beautiful, it meant grand.

Grand as in a grand cup of tea, which indeed it was, she thought gratefully, sipping at her mug and feeling the warmth flood back into her body.

'If you only have hot water at the weekends, Mrs Muldoon,' Cassie asked, 'what do you wash the dirty dishes in?'

'Cold,' she replied. 'We give them a good scrubbing in the cold. But if it's real dirty they are, then we'll boil up a jug or two. Then we hang them on the drainer, and polish 'em up with a rag after. That way you get a nice shiny look to everything.'

'It can't be very hygienic though.'

'Listen, if it wasn't, I wouldn't be standin' here arguin'.'

By now the water in the pots was beginning to boil, and Cassie leaped up to start pouring it into the enamel jugs, which she then carted singlehanded all the way back up to the bathroom. As Cassie went backwards and forwards, Mrs Muldoon kept an eye on her as she carefully chopped up cabbages, and skimmed the rind off the bacon. But she never offered to help, and Cassie was far too proud to even think of asking her.

Cassie was just putting her toe into the still deliciously hot water when Tyrone wandered into the bathroom, with not so much as a knock. There was no lock on the door and Cassie was stark naked.

'Who lit the boiler for you?' he asked, simply curious.

'No one lit the boiler for me,' Cassie replied, tying her hair up with a ribbon. 'I boiled up every inch of this water myself.'

'Every inch of it, did you now?' Tyrone laughed. 'Every inch?'

Then he came across and kissed her.

'Come on,' he said, unbuttoning his shirt.

'Tyrone,' Cassie protested, 'no, I'm just about to have my bath.'

'Are you denying me my rights, woman?'

'Tyrone, I am half dead from the cold.'

'What I have in mind'll soon warm you up,' Tyrone replied, lifting her up and carrying her back to the bedroom.

When Cassie finally made it back to the bathroom, the bath water she had boiled up so patiently had turned stone cold.

But by the time Cassie came down to the drawing room, Tyrone had lit a huge fire and opened a bottle of champagne. He was also wearing instead of his old riding breeches and jacket an impeccably cut tweed suit. Cassie had chosen a high-collared red silk jersey dress which she knew Tyrone adored. He should do, having bought it for her at great cost in New York. They both stood in front of the roaring fire, toasting each other in champagne, which Tyrone had poured into the finest Waterford crystal flutes. And incongruous as it seemed, as they drank and looked into each other's eyes, Cassie forgot entirely about the peeling wallpaper and sodden damp patches – and believed she was in heaven.

'To your first day at Claremore,' Tyrone said, raising his glass.'

Cassie strolled over to the window while Tyrone threw some more logs on to the fire. The rain was easing, and a faint sun was beginning to break through, lightening the grey of the skies, and brightening the lush green of the grass.

'So,' he said, coming to her side, and kissing the nape of her neck, 'what do you think of my ancestral home?'

Cassie didn't quite know what to say. From where she was standing, the rain was dripping steadily into the room, and she had just seen a mouse run under a sideboard and into the wainscoting.

But Tyrone had such love in his eyes, she couldn't bear to say what she really thought: that the whole place needed to be pulled down and rebuilt from scratch.

'It's wonderful, Tyrone,' she said, putting her hand up to his cheek. 'It's the most wonderful place I've ever seen.'

Which wasn't even a half truth. It was the whole truth.

Tyrone looked at her then smiled.

'Cassie McGann, I love you,' he said. 'And for that I love you even more. Claremore is the most wonderful place on earth, but as a house it's a disgrace.'

Cassie caught her breath, startled by Tyrone's admission.

'It's a midden,' he continued, 'and I should be ashamed of myself. I've been so busy with my horses, and there being no one in my life, no woman in my life – well just look at it. The whole place should be pulled down and rebuilt again from scratch.'

Cassie laughed, her hand to her mouth, then put the top of her head against his chest. Tyrone lifted her face up to look at him, holding a finger under her chin.

'What's the great joke?' he enquired.

'That was exactly what I was thinking,' Cassie admitted. 'Although I still do swear it's the most wonderful place I've ever seen. Because you're here.'

They lunched in front of the fire on smoked salmon and quails' eggs which arrived up from the kitchen. Cassie had been half expecting bacon and cabbage, judging from the smell, and expressed her surprise when she saw the delicate servings of pink fish and fluffy eggs, and thin brown bread fingers.

'Mrs Muldoon is full of surprises,' Tyrone said, and then asked her without much hope of an enthusiastic response if she'd like to wander over and look at the horses.

Cassie, still determined not to reveal the other true love in her life, lest she should encroach on her husband's territory, shrugged and said sure, that sounded like fun. Tyrone fetched her coat, and a pair of boots, and they walked hand in hand through the soaking grasses and under a watery April sun over to the racing yard.

The yard was in direct contrast to the house, and was quite obviously where Tyrone's heart was. It was immaculate, down to the shiny black paint on the hinges of the smart white stable doors and the carefully cross-mown square of grass in the middle. Like Leonora's yard, it was laid out in the traditional style, a square, but there the resemblance ended. The Von Wagner yard, albeit perfect, was an indulgence, but Tyrone Rosse's yard was a passion. As soon as the horses heard his voice and his step they were at their doors, stamping their feet and calling to him. Cassie knew it wasn't feed time. She knew from the noises the horses were making that they were calling to their master.

Tyrone took her round the yard, box by box, while Tomas and the lads swept down a yard which already looked as though you could eat your dinner off it. Tyrone informed her that he wasn't going to bore her with each and every horse's breeding, although Cassie wished fervently but secretly that he would. Instead he pointed out the horses with form, which had won races of note, and the horses which were expected to win their races this season which was just starting up. He knew the details and names of all forty horses in his yard, where they had come from and how much they'd cost. He never mentioned any of their owners once. Cassie asked him why, and Tyrone muttered something darkly about them being a necessary evil.

'Would I be a necessary evil, if I ever kept a horse with you, Tyrone?' she asked.

'You just stick to having babies, Cassie McGann,' he answered her. 'That way we'll stay friends for life.'

'Who are your best owners?' Cassie persisted.

'The ones who don't come near me,' Tyrone replied.

One of the lads came up and asked if he'd come and check a horse called Walkover, who'd struck into himself on the gallops the week before on both his forelegs, high up, just below the elbow.

'I've never seen it happen before,' Tyrone told Cassie,

pointing out where the vet had stitched the horse. 'Not that I was here to see it, of course, because we were in New York. But I've never seen a horse strike into himself that high up. And on both elbows.'

Cassie looked. At the back of both forelegs she saw the two deep cuts.

'He can't have done it with his hind legs,' she said involuntarily. 'Horses can't strike themselves that high up from behind.'

Tyrone looked at her underneath the horse, from the other side.

'And what do you know about it, Mrs Rosse?' he asked her. 'What exactly do you know about where and how a horse can strike into itself?'

Cassie straightened herself up, knowing she was small enough to hide her reddening face behind the horse.

'Common sense, I guess,' she countered, just in time.

'Well you're right, damn you,' Tyrone said, also straightening up. 'The blighter cut himself with his own front feet. Look.'

He flexed the horse's front leg, so that the toe of the horse's shoe was practically touching the sutured wound.

'You'd never believe the buggers' bend 'em back so high, isn't that right, Ted?'

The lad nodded to his governor and quietly agreed.

Tyrone and Cassie walked out of Walkover's box, and Tyrone sighed.

'That's a good month off work, which is a pity. I was going to win the Wills Gold Flake with that fellah.'

Cassie followed on behind, thoughtfully. From the little she'd seen of the horse just in his box, she reckoned that was no idle boast of Tyrone's.

One night, when they were dining, Cassie brought up the subject of the house. She felt it was a good time, because a two-year old colt Tyrone thought a lot of had run what he described as a nice race at Leopardstown to be second to a horse which had cost twenty times as much.

'If we could just redecorate this room – the dining room – and the drawing room and hall it'd be a start, Tyrone,' she said.

'If if and ands,' he grunted in reply.

'I'm thinking of your owners, not of myself.'

'The owners be blowed. All they want is to stand in front of the fire, with a large drink in their hands, telling you how damn clever it was of them to agree to buy the winning animal in the first place. Bugger the owners.'

Cassie grinned, getting well used to Tyrone's colourful way with words.

'OK, I'll come clean,' she confessed. 'For me, then. I'd like to do the bedroom. And this room. And the drawing room. I'd like to do them up so that you'll always have somewhere really warm and welcoming and comfortable to come back to, after a hard day.'

Tyrone looked across the table at her, chewing his bit of toast thoughtfully.

'And what'll it cost?'

Cassie shrugged.

'Whatever you can afford.'

'If Villa Maria wins her prep race tomorrow, you can do what you want.'

Cassie got up from her seat and threw her arms round Tyrone's neck from behind his chair. She kissed the top of his head.

'I just want to make this lovely place of yours even lovelier.'

Tyrone gave the palm of her hand a little bite and laughed. Then he got up himself, throwing his napkin down on to the table and addressed his next remark to his wolfhound, who'd been lying at his feet, but had now got up and was having a good stretch, in anticipation of his after-breakfast walk.

'Dear God – she's been here what a couple of weeks, Brian? And already she's talking like a native!'

He kissed Cassie, firmly, and squeezed her waist.

269

'You've made this lovely old place lovelier already,' he said, 'just by marrying me.'

Cassie walked the dog with Tyrone, as had become their habit. Or rather the dog ran, while they walked arm in arm. Brian chased in and out of the woods, putting up rabbits and startling the birds, while Cassie and Tyrone walked together through the long uncut grasses. The gardens and grounds of Claremore needed as much work as the house, but Cassie thought they could wait, because even in their wildly overgrown state, they were still charming. The daffodils, which had been allowed to run riot, were in full bloom, and on the edge of the first line of woods, there was a carpet of purple and yellow crocuses.

'Crocii, if you're going to be correct please,' Tyrone teased. 'Or didn't they teach you Latin at that American convent of yours?'

'Sure they taught us Latin,' Cassie replied.' I've just forgotten it all.'

As indeed she had. She'd forgotten all her Latin, except for two words: *Equo caballus*.

And there they all were, Tyrone's horses, looking out of their immaculate boxes, while the lads picked out and deposited on to lengths of sacking any droppings their precious charges had done since morning stables. The blacksmith had arrived and was hard at work, fitting racing plates, as Tyrone was at pains to explain to Cassie, on to the horses due to run at Thurles that afternoon. Then in answer to her request, he took Cassie over to look at the three-year-old Villa Maria, which was to carry the stable hopes and some of the lads' money in the Ransom Stakes at Leopardstown.

'She's a fine stamp of a filly,' he announced, as Cassie stroked the dark bay head over the stable door. 'She's by Ballygood out of a mare called Molten, who won the fillies' Triple Crown four years ago. That's the One Thousand Guineas, the Oaks, and the St Leger. She's in the Guineas, and she's certainly bred for the job. We'll just have to see whether or not she's good enough. I'll get Tomas to fetch her out of her box.'

Cassie stood to one side as the filly was led out for her. She was astonished at how big and well grown the young horse was, and how muscled up.

'When you think that strictly speaking she's not fully three years old,' Tyrone agreed, 'yes, I suppose it would seem surprising how forward she is. But remember, all horses have their official birthday on I January, and since there's damn few foaled before mid-February, there's damn few horses around as genuinely old as their race card age. This young lady wasn't foaled until the beginning of March.'

'But she's so big,' Cassie exclaimed, remembering the young Prince. 'And so strong.'

'We grow 'em that way over here, Cassie McGann. It's the grass. Good grass grown on limestone. That's what does it. That and having a genius like Tomas here, who knows how to feed.'

He nodded to Tomas to put the filly away, because she was beginning to show signs of impatience, and then walked Cassie over to his office.

'But you start racing them at two years,' Cassie said as she went in past him. 'Isn't it cruel to race them so young?'

'Diabolic,' Tyrone replied, shutting the door. 'But that's the business I'm in.'

Tyrone then busied himself going over the entries with his secretary Mrs Byrne, who was so in love with her job that she drove the long journey out from Dublin to Claremore five days a week, every week of her life.

While the two of them talked through the details of which horses were running where and why, Cassie stood and looked out on to the busy yard, and marvelled at what Tyrone had achieved in such an apparently short space of time. He had told her back in New York about the history of Claremore, and how he had been born and bred there, and Cassie had thought it a wonderfully romantic tale. But now she had seen the place for herself, and been shown the yard, the paddocks and the gallops, Cassie could form a much better idea of what it had taken to create a yard such as this.

Claremore had been left to Tyrone on his father's death twelve years before. Jack Rosse had always been a horseman, but had bred and trained horses really only for his own pleasure. Even so, during the twenty years he had indulged himself in what he called his pastime, he had trained the winners of over three hundred races. He won nothing of particular note, mostly point to points, Hunter Chases, and the odd seller on the Flat, the latter being always the medium of some pretty healthy and usually highly successful gambles. But, as Jack was always at pains to point out to his son, they may not have been Derby horses, but they were all 'homemade'.

As an amateur jockey, however, Tyrone's father was one of the very best, having ridden six times in the Grand National, coming third once, and falling at the second last on another occasion when well in the lead and going like the winner. His own favourite race, and probably the greatest he ever rode, was in the Kim Muir at the Cheltenham Festival, riding a horse owned by his greatest friend, Doctor George Grainger, one of the most sporting Irish owners of the time. A painting commemorating his famous victory hung over the fireplace in the drawing room at Claremore. Jack Rosse coming over the last on Dear Me, ten lengths clear of the odds-on favourite. The ensuing celebrations were, apparently, legendary.

Since as long as he could remember, Tyrone had worked under his father in the yard, which was then a row of just ten old wooden boxes. Having devoted his whole life since the premature death of his beloved wife to the study of horses, there wasn't anything Jack Rosse didn't know about them, and he passed all his great knowledge and horse sense on to his only son and heir.

Tyrone loved his father and the life he was teaching him to lead. He also loved all their horses.

'There's no damn good going into this game, Ty,' his father used to tell him, 'unless you love these creatures. The day horses become a business, as far as I'm concerned, is the day you can forget it.'

And as good as his word, if Jack Rosse produced the horse right on the day, and it ran what he liked to call a decent sort of a race, if it finished ninth or tenth, Tyrone's father enjoyed the experience as much as if the horse had won.

'The only difference between winning and losing, Ty, is there's no prizes for coming fifth.'

A lot of his critics said that because Jack Rosse had money, he wasn't 'hungry', and therefore he could adopt a more cavalier attitude to the racing game than those less financially fortunate than himself. But as Tyrone grew up, he learned his father's debonair attitude concealed what he truly felt, which was acute disappointment with himself and a sense of shame if the horse wasn't 'right' and failed to give its true running.

Then, when Tyrone was nearly twenty, his father realised that one of his 'home-cooked' youngsters was starting to show some promise late in his two-year-old career, and seemed to have the makings of a decent horse, maybe even one good enough to run in a classic. The horse, called By Myself, never actually won as a two-year-old, because although extremely fast, when produced to come and win his first race, he revealed an aversion to the whip. His tail went round in a fury, and he skedaddled across the racecourse sideways like a scalded crab. Then next time when his jockey rode him without a whip, he took fright when he saw the other horses being hit, and round went the tail again, and away across the course he flew.

So for his first race as a three-year-old, they fitted him with blinkers. He was a very nervous horse, and the blinkers frightened him so much that he dwelt at the start and lost a good three or four lengths, which is a critical amount over a seven-furlong trip. Then he suddenly got the hang of the blinkers and fairly flew past the opposition, which contained two Two Thousand Guineas candidates, to win by three lengths. Jack had entered him for the Guineas, more from hope than belief, but after that victory, Tyrone's father backed him to win £20,000 to £1,000 for the Newmarket classic, and the punters backed him silly, until his pre-race odds were reduced finally to 3/1. He was, according to one talkative Dublin bookmaker, the biggest loser on his books, laid to lose him over one million as the winner. On the morning of the Guineas, Jack and Tyrone found the horse doped and half dead in his box. He never recovered and died six months later. According to Tyrone, it broke his father's heart, and he followed the horse to the grave only three months later.

'Which is why I have to win the Derby,' Tyrone had told Cassie, when relating the story to her. 'For the old man. For By Myself. And for the bookmakers, God help them.'

Saturday was Cassie's very first visit to a racecourse. And she imagined that there could be few more charming places to enjoy such an experience than Leopardstown on such a fine spring day.

Tyrone had left her in the charge of the wife of another trainer while he went to saddle up Villa Maria. The woman was *en route* to the bar, and assumed that Cassie wanted to come along with her. Cassie politely demurred, preferring to stay where she was and take in the new sights all around her. For a start, she had never imagined seeing so many priests at a racecourse. They were everywhere, looking closely at the horses, reading up the form and scrutinising the odds. Cassie couldn't help it. She felt quite shocked.

She walked over to the paddock, into which the horses for the next race were starting to file. She found a place on the rails and looked for Villa Maria in her green and yellow Claremore paddock sheet. There she was, walking

274

out very keenly on the opposite side of the ring to Cassie, with Tony her lad jiggling her leading rope to stop her from getting too far ahead of him.

'She's looking well, number three,' said a man to his companion next to Cassie. 'I think I'll have a touch on her. The Rosse stable seems to be coming in form.'

He wandered away to place his bet and Cassie watched him go, before returning her attention to Villa Maria, contemplating her new life, with its undreamed-of connection with her beloved horses. Villa Maria was passing now, right in front of her, with the lad still having trouble holding her head. The filly's eye was very bright, and her big ears were pricked sharply forward, as she took in all the strange sights and sounds. Yet she wasn't at all hot, not like a lot of the other fillies who were beginning to break out in a lather of sweat. Seeing them, Cassie could understand now why it was called a lather, because the white foaming sweat on the dark skins of the horses looked for all the world like soap suds.

Then she saw Tyrone entering the ring, and her heart leaped. From afar, he looked even more handsome. As he walked to the middle of the ring, he was bending down slightly in order to listen to someone Cassie took as the owner, a small woman in middle age, dressed very smartly in a very expensive dark blue costume, with a matching hat. Tyrone was carrying his own hat behind him, and the wind ruffled his hair. Every now and then he would smooth it back nervously as he listened and nodded, and then as the horses were turned in towards their trainers and jockeys, Tyrone put his hat back on and set about the serious business of checking that all was well with the horse.

Cassie watched him intently as he folded the paddock sheet back over the filly's quarters and flicked the stirrups down from the tiny racing saddle. The jockey, in pink silks with a black crossband, stood half behind him, tapping his shiny boots with his whip. Tyrone checked the girths, and as he did so, the filly whipped round, pulling her lad with her. Cassie saw that it didn't bother Tyrone, because he moved with the horse as if he had been expecting such a reaction. Then seeing that all was well, he legged the jockey up so easily, Cassie thought, that it was almost like a move in a ballet. Last of all Tyrone removed the folded sheet from the horse's quarters as the jockey started to walk her away, then turned back to talk once again to the owner.

The racegoers were all making their way back to the grandstand now, or hurrying to the Tote to have a last-minute bet. Cassie had no idea how to bet, but she was dying to have what Tomas called a few bob on their horse. She went up to the Tote window and opened her purse, taking out two pounds.

'Can I have this on Villa Maria to win, please?' she asked. 'If that's all right?'

'You have to tell me the number, miss,' the man behind the grille replied. 'Sure the name's no good whatsoever.'

'Oh my, I am so sorry,' she replied, consulting her race card. 'Villa Maria's number three.'

She collected her ticket, carefully folding it inside her glove, then hurried over to the grandstand. She saw Tyrone standing high above her, his race glasses to his eyes as he watched the horses cantering down to the start. She wanted to be at his side, but he had made it quite plain that while she may be at the races for pleasure, he was there for business and must have no distractions.

So she stood some way below him and tried to focus her race glasses on the horses which were now down at the start. She just got them right as she heard the course commentator announce that the white flag was up, and a moment later they were off. Villa Maria broke in the middle of the pack, and Cassie could see the jockey settle the filly down behind the leading group as they covered the first furlong. She seemed to Cassie's untutored eye, to be running very sweetly and easily, while several of the fillies in front of her appeared to have taken a good hold and were running too freely. As they turned left-handed into the straight, a gap opened on the rails and Cassie saw Dermot Pryce, Villa Maria's jockey, pounce on the opening at once and kick for home. The field was fully two furlongs from the post, but the result was already a foregone conclusion. As soon as the dark bay filly with the big white blaze saw daylight, she flew. Cassie's race glasses started to shake up and down in her excitement, but she gripped them as tightly as she could so that she could see in close-up every moment of the finish. Pryce hardly moved on the filly once he had given her that initial command. She just quickened, lengthened her stride, and the race was over. Cassie shouted the horse home in her excitement, but there was no need. Villa Maria won by six lengths, with her ears pricked.

It was, as Tomas always had it, a handy win, and a popular one. Villa Maria had started 2/1 favourite, and the crowd were well pleased. They were already applauding the filly as Pryce steered her through their midst back to the winner's enclosure. As Cassie hurried after her, Tyrone passed her by.

'I could hear you shouting her home from the top of the stands!' he teased.

Cassie smiled happily and hurried after him.

When she fought her way finally through the crowd to the rail, the jockey was already off the horse and in the process of undoing the saddle. He was bending down under her to loosen the girth, all the time chatting sideways back up to Tyrone who towered above him. The woman Cassie thought was the owner was patting the filly's neck delightedly, while Tomas stood ready to throw a sweat sheet over the horse. The jockey touched his cap and disappeared into the weighing room. Tyrone saw Cassie and signalled for her to come through. Cassie beamed back at him and hurried round the crowd to join him.

'Well?' he asked her, in the same tone of voice he had used every time he had asked her to marry him.

'That was fantastic,' she replied. 'Well done.'

'The horse did it, not me,' Tyrone said, straightening the sweat sheet.

'You're too modest, Tyrone Rosse,' said the woman in the blue suit. 'It's always been your trouble. You know you're brilliant.'

Then the woman turned round and saw Cassie. She smiled at her and then looked at Tyrone.

'Introduce us, Tyrone,' she commanded. 'There are other living things on this planet besides horses, you know.'

'Cassie, this is Lady Meath,' Tyrone said. 'Sheila, my wife Cassie.'

'Congratulations,' Cassie said. 'What a terrific victory.'

'Yes, it was, wasn't it?' Lady Meath replied. 'But I don't own her, you know. No, no, I only bred her.'

'Only indeed,' Tyrone snorted. 'As if it was like boiling an egg.'

'I think it's far more clever to have bred her, Lady Meath,' Cassie said, 'than to have bought her.'

'Well said, Mrs Rosse,' Tyrone concluded. 'Well said. Now out of the way, or you'll get yourself killed.'

Cassie stepped back as Tomas wheeled the filly round and led her away from the enclosure. Tyrone gave the horse a loving pat on her quarters as she went past him.

'Well done, old girl,' he said.

To the members of the racing press, who were waiting to pick his brains, Tyrone simply said he was well pleased with the filly's performance, and that she would indeed be aimed at the English One Thousand Guineas. But to Cassie and Lady Meath, over a quick glass of champagne, he confided that provided she had no setbacks over the next couple of weeks, she only had one to beat at Newmarket, and that was Arthur Marshall's filly Time To Remember. Then he hurried off to saddle Needless To Say for the big handicap.

'Who does own Villa Maria, Lady Meath?' Cassie asked as they left the bar to watch the race.

'Do you know, I've completely forgotten?' Lady Meath laughed in return. 'But I've a feeling it's a fellow compatriot of yours.'

In the big handicap, Needless To Say finished last, having led for most of the way. On the journey home, Tyrone told Cassie the horse had swallowed its tongue. Cassie couldn't imagine such a thing, but then, as she herself knew, she still had an awful lot to learn about racing. As she peeled off her gloves and a tote ticket fluttered to the car floor, she discovered that she'd even forgotten to pick up her winnings.

Tyrone's percentage of the prize money came to less than £50, but happily she gathered from snatches of some of his telephone conversations she'd overheard in the house that he had also had a sizeable bet, so Cassie decided the time was ripe to bring up the subject of redecoration once again. After all, Tyrone had promised that if Villa Maria had won her prep race she could go ahead with her plans for redecorating.

She asked him after dinner, after he had drunk his whisky, and after she had taken him up to bed and made love. Tyrone lay on his back completely naked and roared with laughter.

'Cassie McGann I love you!' he cried. 'You're the complete woman!'

Then he had rolled over and stared at her lying beside him.

'I'd have said yes to you before dinner. Even if it had been a dish of cold potatoes and beans, and even if you'd denied me my rights.'

Cassie grinned back at him.

'You would?'

'Of course I would! I love you!'

Then he rolled a little further over towards her and they made love all over again.

* * *

279

Cassie's plans for Claremore were carefully considered ones. She made Tyrone give her a budget, and although the very idea of budgeting seemed totally foreign to Tyrone's spendthrift nature, Cassie was determined to stick to it. The local builders were invited to quote for the all-important repairs to the roof and for the replastering and painting of the main rooms. Cassie had decided on wallpapers for the drawing room, dining room and their bedroom, but after getting the initial estimates for the building repairs alone, she had to economise and get a price for painting the rooms instead. But she then discovered that by carefully mixing some of the suggested paints, she could get some wonderful pastel effects, which in the end could well prove, taking into account the size of the rooms, less overpowering than papered walls.

She also spent days going round country-house and auction-room sales, with Mrs Muldoon's daughter Erin in tow. Cassie hadn't yet got round to taking a driving test, but Erin could drive a pony and trap, so grudgingly her mother allowed her off her housemaid's duties on the occasions Cassie needed transport. She discovered that Ireland was a place of the most utter contrast: singularly beautiful countryside, the most lovely Cassie had ever seen, and utter poverty, at a level quite unknown to her. They would drive through the lanes, she and Erin, chatting and laughing past the green pastures, and distant blue hills, while the larks sang above them, and then would arrive at a drab little village, with a couple of dirty shops and about a dozen pubs. The houses all seemed to be painted grey, or brown, and everywhere Cassie saw the same sight; little children in tattered and torn clothing, usually without shoes, and invariably filthy. Their mothers would hurry in and out of the few shops, sometimes a black shawl over their heads, while the men, when not away inside the pubs, would be standing outside in idle gossip, propping up the walls, and smoking their pipes.

When they first went to a furniture sale, which was the contents of a large old house, Cassie had thrown poor Erin into a total confusion when she'd told her that she was so excited at the prospect of the sale, since most of the furniture was bound to be old.

'Of course it will,' Erin had replied. 'And sure what'll you be wanting with old things? If you've money to spend, you'd be better going into Dublin and buying yourself some fine new modern furniture. And maybe a nice radiogram.'

Cassie had started to laugh.

'You can't put modern furniture in an old house, Erin. It wouldn't look right. You need old furniture. Antiques. The kind of furniture that must have been in Claremore when my husband's father was a boy.'

'Sure I know the sort of thing, Mrs Rosse. There was lots of that old stuff. But it was so ancient, and a lot of it was falling to bits, so old Mr Rosse and me Da, they used to chop it up for firewood.'

Cassie remembered steadying herself, by holding on tight to the edge of the dog cart, as she tried to put out of her mind's eye what old Mr Rosse and Tomas must have warmed themselves before. Erin and she might see eye to eye about a lot of things, but furniture was most certainly not going to be one of them.

'For meself,' Erin had added with a sniff, 'I only really likes contemporary. And then only as long as it's not old-fashioned.

They had arrived at the sale early, with time enough to inspect the contents. Cassie's eyes were out on stalks when she saw some of the furniture, but Erin had remained totally unimpressed.

'You wouldn't pay more than five bob down the Quays for most of this auld rubbish,' she had kept whispering to Cassie.

It was the same at every sale they attended. While Cassie tried to educate Erin about antiques, Erin remained totally sceptical about them.

'Look, Erin,' Cassie would point out. 'This is a Regency commode. Don't you think it's beautiful?'

'It's got a great crack down its side!' Erin would point back triumphantly. 'Anyway, what do you want with a commode? There's toilets by the score in the house.'

Erin was greatly excited, however, by the glass and the linenware.

'That's fine cut glass, Mrs Rosse. You should buy what you can of that. And this linen's good linen. Mam would enjoy ironing that. And look at all those napkins! There's more table napkins there than anyone's a right to! You'll probably get all them for a few bob. A few bob, mind. For that's all they're worth.'

At the first sale Cassie had made the mistake of bidding herself. But as soon as they heard an American accent, up went the prices. So at subsequent sales, she got Erin to bid for her, and that way she came away with what she knew were some wonderful bargains.

'Neary's is where you want to go if it's a three-piece suite you're after,' Erin told Cassie one day after Cassie had bought a Victorian sofa and two library chairs. 'I was in Neary's with me mam last month, and they've a simply heavenly three-piece suite in a new sort of velvet crush.'

At one sale Cassie did so well she had to send Tomas in the horse-box to fetch the furniture home. That day she'd bought a Regency commode, a Georgian bow-fronted chest, a set of Victorian dining chairs with leather seats, a pair of Sheffield plate wine coolers, a picture of a lady sitting sewing with her little dog, five dozen linen napkins and six pairs of linen sheets – and all for well under a hundred pounds.

'What about that?' she asked Tyrone when he came back to the house that evening.

'What about what?' Tyrone replied, sitting in a wing chair Cassie had bought the week before that he had still not noticed.

'These things I've bought,' she told him.

'Very nice,' he said without looking up from his paper. 'Very nice.'

Furniture was not one of Tyrone's abiding passions.

Cassie sat in front of the fire, and imagined how the picture of the lady sewing would look hanging above it, and how elegant the Regency commode would look on the opposite side of the room.

'You wait till I have everything in place,' she sighed. 'You won't recognise the place.'

'Great,' said Tyrone, still reading. 'Well done.'

And then got up with some visible relief to answer the suddenly ringing telephone.

But Cassie was well content with her purchases. She knew enough about Tyrone by now to know that if he didn't say anything, he was happy. And if he was happy, then what she was doing to Claremore must be right.

Soon the Guineas was just over a week away. From what little Tyrone told her, it seemed that Villa Maria had pleased in all her work, and barring accidents, she had an outstanding chance of lifting the first of the season's classics for fillies. Her chance got even better when on Friday there was a very strong rumour in the sporting papers that all was not well with Arthur Marshall's filly, who was the firm pre-race favourite. Tyrone rang a scout of his in Newmarket, who confirmed that the 'on dit' was that the horse had pricked her foot on the gallops and was a doubtful starter.

Tyrone seemed to take it all in his stride. He slept soundly and didn't leave a mouthful of his food. Cassie, who was so excited she could hardly sleep, asked him how he managed to stay so calm, and he replied that it was only a race. It may be worth more money than other races, but in the final analysis, it was only a race, and as always there would only be one winner. And as always in racing, anything could happen: the horse could get boxed in, the jockey could mistime his run, or there could be an accident. Racing was entirely unpredictable. There was no such thing as a certainty.

Monday morning proved him tragically right. Tyrone had just returned on his hack from watching the second string work, when he saw the first of the horseboxes coming up the long drive. Cassie saw them too, as she walked Brian over to the yard as she did every morning. She saw the second lorry, too. And the third and fourth. When she saw what seemed like a convoy approaching the yard, she broke into a run, knowing instinctively that there must be something very wrong.

When she got to the yard, the first box was just drawing up. Tyrone was standing waiting for it, with an ashen face. Cassie ran to his side.

'What's happening, Tyrone?' she asked him. 'Whose are all those horseboxes?'

'Just go back to the house, Cassie,' he replied. 'This is no business of yours.'

'Something's going on, Tyrone. I can tell from your face.'

'Do as I tell you. Go back to the house.'

Cassie collected Brian, who was happily rolling in some fresh manure, and obediently started back to the house. She passed the office, and looking in through the window, saw Mrs Byrne crying. Tyrone had his back to them, engaged as he was in close conversation with the driver of the first horsebox.

Cassie opened the door of the office and went in.

'What's happening, Mrs Byrne? What have the horseboxes come for?'

Mrs Byrne looked up, and seeing Cassie's worried face, started to cry even more. But just as she started to pull herself together, and was about to tell Cassie the news, the telephone rang. Cassie glanced through the window as Mrs Byrne answered it, and saw Tyrone striding towards the office, his face black with anger. Rather than have him find her there, disobeying his direct orders, Cassie slipped out of the back door and ran with Brian into the cover of the nearby woods.

From there she hid and watched. One by one eighteen

284

of her husband's best horses were taken out from their stables and loaded into the horseboxes. Tyrone's staff stood around, silent to a man, as the cream of the yard disappeared up the ramps and into the lorries. Finally Villa Maria was led out from her stall, and Cassie, her hand to her mouth, saw Tony, the filly's faithful lad, overcome, suddenly run out of the yard.

Tyrone stood in the middle of the square of grass watching with his arms folded. Then when the ramp on the last box was up, and the lorries' engines were fired, Cassie saw him walk round the side of the yard, get into his Jaguar, and roar off ahead of the horseboxes down the drive.

Cassie had seen quite enough. She called Brian and ran all the way back to the house.

It wasn't until after ten o'clock that night that Tomas brought Tyrone home. He was upright, but far from sober. Too drunk even to speak. Tomas and Cassie took him upstairs, with Tomas bearing the brunt of Tyrone's weight. As they laid him on the bed, Cassie thought with amazement how heavy a man's body was when he was drunk. It was as if he was dead, as Tomas and she struggled to take off his jacket, trousers and shirt.

Down in the drawing room, with Tyrone safely asleep upstairs, Cassie offered Tomas a drink, which he declined, saying he'd already taken too much. Instead he elected to tell her of the terrible event which had just occurred.

Tomas shook his head and breathed in deeply.

'The bitch has taken all her horses away,' he said, 'saving your presence.'

'Who, Tomas?' Cassie asked. 'I mean who in the world would do such a thing?'

'Villa Maria's owner,' he replied. 'An American like yourself. By the name of Mrs Von Wagner.'

First of all, as she lay in bed beside the fast-sleeping Tyrone, Cassie blamed herself. She had to, for her habitual guilt told her it must be her fault. If Leonora's mother had taken all her horses away from Claremore, then it had to be Cassie's fault. Whose else could it be?

After all, it was Cassie who knew Leonora, and since Mrs Von Wagner was Leonora's mother, then that had to be the reason for the removal of the horses. It had to be part of Leonora's revenge on her, because of Cassie's last score with the opera tickets; perhaps Leonora had suffered such a humiliating evening that in her subsequent rage she had persuaded her mother to remove all her horses, all twenty of them, from the care of Cassie's new husband.

All twenty of them. The twenty best horses in the yard. They were ruined. In three brief weeks of marriage Cassie had ruined her new husband's life.

But then she thought, why? Why should Leonora's mother cut off her nose to spite her face for the sake of satisfying her petulant daughter? Tyrone Rosse was already being spoken of as the most promising young trainer in Ireland, and he had brought Villa Maria to her peak just at the right moment so that she was now quoted as co-favourite for the fillys' first Classic. Would Mrs Von Wagner seriously risk upsetting her horse by removing it at the eleventh hour? And if so, surely she would have ta¹ked it over with her trainer first, if they had quarrelled? It just didn't ring true that she should remove her horses, including the ante post favourite for the Thousand Guineas, the week of the big race itself. It just didn't make sense.

Tyrone must have known Mrs Von Wagner.

Well, of course he must have known her, Cassie corrected herself impatiently. She had twenty thoroughbreds in his keep. Of course he knew Mrs Von Wagner. But how exactly had he known her? And in what way? Cassie kept trying to push the thought out of her head, but back it kept on coming.

She must have been his mistress.

Then Cassie remembered the meeting in the snow outside Bergdorf Goodman. As Leonora was hijacking

Cassie into the cab, Mrs Von Wagner had been about to return some unwanted items. 'I just have to return these items to Lingerie.'

She remembered the words exactly. And she remembered the carefully wrapped box they were in. The box Cassie had herself packed for Tyrone four days earlier. He'd been buying lingerie for Leonora's mother.

Tyrone had been Mrs Von Wagner's lover.

Cassie turned round to the figure fast asleep in the bed beside her. She suddenly felt full of violent rage. She wanted to scratch his face, kick him, punch him, sit on his chest and hit him on his stupid drunken face until he was black and blue. That afternoon when they had met, when he said he had fallen in love at first sight with her, he'd been about to go back to Leonora's mother's house and make love to her, probably in her brand new Bergdorf Goodman lingerie.

Tyrone had made love to Leonora's mother.

It was horrible to think of. She must have been nearly forty.

But then, instead of attacking the sleeping Tyrone, which to her chagrin she realised was against her nature, she got out of bed, and pulling on her wrap, went downstairs to the drawing room, where she opened the shutters and the long french windows, and walked out on to the terrace. It was a cold, clear, moonlit night, but Cassie was unaware of the temperature. Instead, she just stood gazing out across the moonlit grounds, and wondered what she was to do, and what was the truth of the matter. Or of any matter?

It wasn't Leonora's revenge, the removal of the horses: it was her mother's. Tyrone had obviously told her about Cassie, and perhaps she had been civilised and gracious about it, as, it seemed, people like that sometimes were. And then maybe having been 'civilised', she had read about their wedding, and still done nothing – because all the time she was waiting: waiting for the moment when she could really hurt Tyrone. And when she had found it, she had made her move. She had taken away Villa Maria. She had removed in one dramatic stroke her ex-lover's greatest chance of success, even if it were to cost her the race itself.

Still Cassie stood staring out at the moonlit estate, listening to the sounds of the night. In the darkened woods the late-hunting owls screeched and a fox barked. Heaven has no hatred, like love to hatred turned, she remembered. Nor hell a fury like a woman scorned. Suddenly, reluctantly, with a pang, Cassie knew she'd grown up.

Tyrone was up at six and gone as usual before Cassie was even awake. She got up and dressed herself slowly, remembering the events of the day and the night, before going down to breakfast. When she went into the dining room, she discovered Tyrone already at table.

'I'm back early,' he explained, as if today was the same as every day, 'since there was only the one string to exercise.' Cassie kissed the top of his head as she passed him by, and then sat down next to him. He smiled at her, but said nothing, turning instead as he always did, to the sporting papers.

'They must have broken the story yesterday,' he said, showing her the headlines of *Sporting Life*. 'Guineas Favourite In Shock Move.'

Then he took the paper back from her to read the story, as detached as if it had all happened to somebody else.

'Won't it make a lot of difference to Villa Maria?' she asked him. 'Moving somewhere strange and new just before the race?'

Tyrone flicked the paper over to finish reading the story on the back.

'If there's a full manger in the corner of the stable and fresh straw on the floor it won't,' he replied. 'She'd have had to travel over to Newmarket from here tomorrow anyway.'

Cassie poured herself some black coffee, which was all

she wanted. She marvelled at Tyrone and his iron constitution. Dead drunk only a few hours ago, with his world in pieces round him, there he was, sitting eating a huge cooked breakfast as if he hadn't a care in the world.

'She's in good hands as it happens,' he announced, putting down *Sporting Life*. 'The bitch has sent her to Dick Longmann.'

Then he rose from the table and stretched.

'Are you all right, Tyrone?' Cassie enquired cautiously.

'Now I've had breakfast,' he smiled, 'and now I've seen you.'

He ambled to the door. Brian got up, yawned nervously, and followed his master to the door, anticipating a walk.

'Are you going out?'

'No, Cassie McGann. I am going to get a bottle of champagne.'

That was Tyrone. He had just suffered the heartbreak of having half his yard taken away on a whim, including the best horse he had ever trained, but he wasn't the man to sit down and feel sorry for himself. Instead, he opened a bottle of champagne. He called Cassie from the dining room, and she went and sat by his side opposite the wood fire Erin had just lit. They drank their champagne out of some exquisite old Waterford glass Cassie had bought at a house sale and for a long time said nothing. Because for a long time there seemed to be nothing to say.

Tyrone broke the silence.

'I'm sorry about last night, Cassie,' he said. 'I drove over to Leixlip to see a chum. But his wife was out so we didn't have anything to eat.'

'It doesn't matter about last night, Tyrone,' Cassie answered. 'But please tell me about yesterday.'

'Tomas said he told you,' Tyrone replied, rising to throw more wood on the fire. He remained standing, his back to Cassie.

'Tomas didn't tell me everything.'

'One of my owners took all her horses away. Owners

289

do that. Noel Collins once lost his whole yard in a fortnight.'

'I was at school with Leonora Von Wagner. I've known her since I was fourteen.'

'Now there's a thing,' Tyrone said, still not turning round.

'How long have you known Leonora's mother?' Cassie persisted, determined not to let him off the hook.

'Sybille Von Wagner and I were finished the moment I saw you that afternoon.'

Tyrone now turned back to her and stood in front of the fire, still in his riding breeches and old but highly polished leather boots.

'Actually, Cassie McGann, that's not strictly true.'

He looked down at her, and Cassie bit her lip. Of course it wasn't. He'd gone back to her house, hadn't he? And made love to her in her new lingerie.

'It had been over as far as I was concerned for months,' Tyrone continued. 'But she was my most important owner, so it was a question of gently, gently.'

'You were buying her lingerie.'

'It was the lady's birthday.'

'Do you always buy ladies you're no longer sleeping with lingerie for their birthdays?'

'Usually,' Tyrone replied with a smile. 'I think it's rather nice, don't you? I'm sure you'd find it very difficult to keep on nursing those hard feelings towards somebody who gave you silk underwear for your birthday.'

Cassie looked up at him and into his eyes. Then she held out her hands to him, and he took them, pulling her up in front of him.

Cassie remembered how much she'd hated him during the night, and for a moment despised herself for her apparent calm. Then Tyrone kissed her, and as always reason fled and hid its head in the passion of his embrace.

Cassie woke for the second time that morning, but this time Tyrone was still asleep in the bed beside her. Cassie kissed his shoulder, then grabbed her wrap and went and ran a bath. Since the first day, and the misery of the cold water, Mrs Muldoon had been forbidden ever to turn the boiler off again. Not even in high summer.

Cassie lay in the tub and thought of lots of things. She thought of the way Tyrone had made love to her that morning, as if he hadn't made love to anyone in a year. She thought about how when she had whispered in his ear how incredible he was and the way he had whispered back that he was always good on a hangover, particularly when topped up with champagne. Then she thought about his courage and resilience. No one would have known from his laughter and his lovemaking what he was really feeling. Even Cassie could only guess.

Over lunch he told her that Sybille Von Wagner's removal of her horses would only prove to be damaging in the very short run. Villa Maria was with what Tyrone considered the unrecognised best trainer in England, and provided the filly had travelled well, she should win her race. If and when she did, God willing, then in no time at all his own yard would fill up again, because as everyone knew, and as Dick Longmann who was a friend of his would also vouchsafe, he, Tyrone Rosse, had done all the donkey work.

And so they set off in apparently excellent spirits for Dublin airport the day before the race. Cassie had been pressganged by Tyrone into buying a brand new spring outfit, of hat, dress, coat and shoes, in very smart contrasting red and white. They stayed overnight in London, with some of Tyrone's racing friends, who took them out to dinner at a French restaurant called Chez Solange, and then on to see the hit satirical revue *Beyond The Fringe*, which Cassie thought was hilarious. What little she saw of London, she loved, and as she lay in Tyrone's arms back at their hotel, even though she knew that back home the yard was half empty, Cassie couldn't see one cloud on the horizon.

There were plenty in the night sky however, and when

they drove up to Newmarket with Ryan and Cath, two more of Tyrone's many friends, it was pouring down with rain.

'Does she like the wet?' Ryan asked Tyrone who was sitting up front beside him.

'If anything it'll increase her chances,' Tyrone replied. 'Her mother liked it up to her hocks.'

It didn't stop raining until half an hour before the big race, by which time the official going had been changed from good to soft. The mud-spattered jockeys who returned after the first race reportedly announced it to be on the heavy side of soft, and as a consequence even more money poured on Villa Maria, now the clear favourite since the overnight withdrawal of Arthur Marshall's Time To Remember.

As she climbed to take her place in the stands, Cassie was glad she had bought an outfit with a coat, and that the outfit was made of wool, because even though the rain had stopped, a sharp wind was blowing straight up the course and into the grandstand. Cassie thought it was peculiarly British to have the main stand facing down the straight mile, so that the spectator only got a headlong view of the horses, and trained her race glasses on the big dark filly that used to be at Claremore as she cantered easily down to the start.

She had looked for Leonora's mother in the parade ring before the race, but Mrs Von Wagner was notable by her absence. Dick Longmann came over and spoke to Tyrone after the horses had left to go down to the start, and after commiserating with him, and grumbling about the fickleness of owners, assured Tyrone that the filly was spot on and would take all the beating.

'I hope you're right,' Tyrone said. 'We've had a good touch.'

Cassie wasn't quite sure of all her racing terminology yet, but she suspected from the boyish smile on her husband's face that he had wagered a little more than a week's housekeeping.

Only one thing had really worried Tyrone, he told Cassie, as he legged it up to the owners' and trainers' part of the grandstand. Dermot Pryce had been jocked off Villa Maria, apparently on Mrs Von Wagner's express orders, and a young whizz kid jockey called Frankie West, the up and coming star of the English racing scene, had been booked for her instead at the last moment, once Time To Remember, whom he had been due to ride, wasn't declared to run.

'He's never been on the horse,' Tyrone grumbled, 'and I don't give a damn what they say. A horse you know is a horse you win on. I can't abide this blasted modern fashion of meeting your mount for the first time in the paddock. It's sheer nonsense.'

'She looks very well though,' Ryan said as he and his wife joined them. 'I reckon even I could win on her.'

'You couldn't win on her, Ryan,' Tyrone told him, 'if all the others fell down.'

The course suddenly went silent as the commentator called that they were under starter's orders. And what seemed an interminable time later, after several fillies had whipped round at the start, that they were off.

Cassie tracked Villa Maria. The jockey, riding very short and perched high on the filly's withers, or standing on her bloody head according to a mutter from Tyrone, had dropped her to the back of the field, hugging the rails. The field, which was a large one of over twenty runners, had all made their way to what was purported to be the best ground, on the stand side of the straight mile. Cassie learned all this from Tyrone's muttered running commentary.

Then Tyrone suddenly dropped his glasses and stared down the course.

'Jesus,' he announced, 'the idiot's hopelessly boxed.'

'There's another four furlongs yet,' Ryan replied. 'Christ but you're a pessimist.'

But Tyrone never raised his glasses again, because he knew he was right.

Coming to the bushes, Frankie West still had Villa Maria on the rails, four from last, and cruising, while he waited for the opening he felt sure would appear. Then suddenly, as they hit the rising ground, with a wall of tired horses coming back at him, West knew there was nowhere to go – except to pull out round the outside and go.

Which he did, but too late. Miracle, the much fancied French filly, had been kicked for home and was flying. West, having brought Villa Maria wide on the outside, set about the horse desperately with his whip, and despite showing her distaste for such unnecessary punishment by angrily swishing her tail, Villa Maria also showed her genuiness by finding top gear and fairly flying after the leader. But the post came too soon, and Villa Maria was beaten by a neck, while still catching Miracle hand over fist.

Tyrone was the first to commiserate with Dick Longmann, and to buy him a drink. Cassie didn't hear him recriminate once. Dick Longmann acidly remarked that Dermot Pryce would never have ridden such a cocky race.

'That's racing, Dick,' Tyrone replied. 'Drink up.'

On the flight back home, Tyrone said nothing. He held Cassie's hand and looked out of the window. It was then that Cassie knew he was ruined.

Chapter Eleven

By the end of May, a week before the English Derby, when the yard at Claremore should have been at its busiest, out of the forty horses Cassie had so admired on her first sight of the stables, there were only four left in training.

'Racing's a fickle auld business,' Tomas had told Cassie one morning when she walked the dog across by herself. 'Sure it's a world where words speak louder than actions.'

Which was something Tyrone in his optimism had not taken into consideration. Even after Villa Maria had lost her race, he had soon recovered his confidence and believed that no one could blame him even indirectly for the filly's defeat.

But they did.

The gossipmongers, and a certain section of the English racing press who loved gunning the Irish, hinted that the Rosse stable at Claremore was rife with dissension, that Mrs Von Wagner wasn't going to be the only owner to leave and that there were grave financial problems. These rumours had their required effect. The majority of Tyrone's remaining owners took fright and pulled their horses out, all except Tim Coughlan, the local butcher, who was having none of it and not only kept his three horses with Tyrone, but even went out and bought a fourth. The only trouble was that none of his horses were, according to Tyrone, any damn good.

There was truth in the rumour about financial difficulties however, as Cassie soon found out. The builders who had started work on the house in April, were summarily dismissed in May. And Cassie found a pile of recently delivered but unopened bills stuffed down the side of one of her rescued antique chairs when she was about to send it off to be re-covered. For days she dallied as to whether or not she should approach Tyrone on the matter of their finances, because she had already found out that he considered certain elements of his business nothing to do with a woman.

Then she opened the bills, and found out exactly how much they owed.

'They're my debts too, Tyrone!' she told him defiantly, as Tyrone stood glowering at her from in front of the drawing-room fire after dinner one night. 'It's my job to run this house, and I can't possibly be expected to do so on credit which seems to be drying up real fast!'

'Stop blathering away like a blasted accountant,' Tyrone told her, 'And leave the business side of things to the businessman.'

'I can't!' Cassie continued, 'and I won't! I can't be expected to try and run a place like this without knowing exactly how much I have or haven't got to run it on!'

Tyrone stared at her for a long time, in silence, which used to disconcert Cassie. But not any more. She stared back at him, good and hard.

'I'm owed a great deal of money,' he said finally. 'Your friend's mother didn't pay her training bills.'

'You mean for last month?'

'I mean for six months.'

'Tyrone – she had twenty horses with you!'

'That's why I'm owed a great deal of money.'

'You're going to have to sue her.'

'Oh, of course I am, Cassie McGann. But you know the old saying; possession is ninety-nine per cent of the law. And Sybille Von Wagner has all her twenty horses.'

Tyrone finished his coffee and walked over to the french windows. He stood looking out over Claremore, while Cassie racked her brains for what to do.

'You see, normally,' Tyrone continued, 'when owners owe you your fees, you hold their horses as collateral. That is standard and proper practice. Then if they still don't pay you, the horses become yours in lieu.'

'You shouldn't have let the horses go.'

'I know, Cassie McGann. I'm quite well aware. Come on, let's take Brian for his walk.'

They walked for miles, through the woods, across the fields, and out beyond the boundaries of Claremore. They walked along the lanes which led up into the hills, and then up into the hills themselves. All the time they made plans and talked of what they were going to do. By the time they had reached the highest of the hills, and stood where Cassie had never stood before, looking down at Claremore and the wonderful patchwork of the countryside which lay beneath them, Tyrone had convinced her he'd be back on his feet and in business, with a full yard, by the start of the following season, while Cassie had vowed she would undertake the restoration of the house personally, until such times as the builders could be recalled.

As they strolled back arm in arm, with the big wolfhound loping contentedly beside them, Cassie had only one remaining doubt.

'What'll you do for money until you're back on your feet, Tyrone?' she asked.

'What I always do when I'm stitched,' he replied. 'Go and see old Flann at the bank.'

'It's best not to look at the whole room when you're painting it,' Erin volunteered to Cassie. 'Least that's what me Mam says. What she says is just to look at one bit at a time. Otherwise you'll go bonkers.'

Cassie, taking a hard-earned coffee break with Erin, whom she'd roped in to help her with the decorating, could see the sense. Three days earlier, when they'd cleared the furniture out of the drawing room, she had been so excited at the prospect of repainting the lovely

297

room. Now it had become just sweated labour and Cassie couldn't wait for it all to be done.

She looked around her at the half-painted walls. At least they'd had the sense to do the worst job first, namely the ceiling, although when they'd finished Cassie had seriously wondered how Michelangelo had painted the Sistine Chapel without losing his reason.

And this was only the first of her undertakings. After this she had vowed to do the hall, the dining room, their bedroom, Tyrone's study, the landings and the corridors. Now, halfway through only the first room, Cassie suddenly could see herself painting Claremore for the rest of her life.

By the time she got to bed at night, she was exhausted, too tired even to make love. Tyrone was exhausted too, tired from traipsing round racecourses all over the country, buying drinks for and trying to chat up potential owners. So far he had managed just the one, a rather sharp and self-satisfied Dublin insurance broker, whom they had to entertain to dinner and feign intense interest in for the best part of four and a half hours while he told them in fine detail how he had succeeded in business.

Tyrone's lack of success in attracting new owners was demoralising. For a while he hoped for better things when the English Oaks were in prospect, for which Villa Maria was once again one of the favourites. If she won the race, he told Cassie, that surely would vindicate him, even though she'd been out of his yard for a month. Dick Longmann had persuaded Sybille Von Wagner to re-engage Dermot Pryce, but even though he rode her beautifully and produced the filly right at the prime moment, having tracked the leaders down round Tattenham Corner, all the time holding his place on the rails, Villa Maria didn't get the extra four furlongs, and dropped right out of contention in the last furlong to finish a well-beaten seventh.

So there was no great rush on behalf of owners to send their horses to Claremore. Consequently, by the end of

298

July Tyrone had just eight horses in full training.

But by the end of July Cassie and Erin had finished painting all the main rooms in the house. Fortunately, before the builders were dismissed, they had managed to mend the roof, and replaster the worst of the walls and ceilings. So now, with the drawing room a soft yellow, the dining room a deep red, Tyrone's study a dark green, and their bedroom a warm, fashionable maroon, at least things no longer looked as bad as they quite obviously were. The bank had granted Tyrone an extension on his overdraft, but Flann had warned Tyrone that he would have to call it in after a year if things had not improved dramatically. There was a long exchange of letters between Tyrone's and Sybille Von Wagner's solicitors, which resulted in no financial satisfaction for the innocent party, but yet another expense in the shape of legal fees. The only ray of sunshine throughout an otherwise bleak and rain-swept summer was the runaway victory of Tim Coughlan's 'no hopers' in a selling plate at Galway. Typical of Tyrone, even though he publicly considered the horse a joke, he had quietly sold his E-type Jaguar and put the proceeds of the sale on the nose at 6/1. The win allowed him breathing space, and meant that he only had to lay off half his staff. It also allowed him to take Cassie on a belated honeymoon.

He took her to Kerry. On the first night away they stayed in a small hotel just outside the town of Glenbeigh, run by a wonderful woman who fussed over Tyrone as if he was her son. From their bedroom window, they could see the long white stretch of Rossbeigh Sand, while underneath them in the lush garden exotic plants and palm trees bloomed in the sub-tropical climate.

Cassie couldn't believe the landscape.

'It's more like the South Seas than how you'd imagine Ireland,' Cassie told Tyrone with wonder.

'That's because it's on the end of the Gulf Stream,' Tyrone replied, 'which accounts for all this extraordinary vegetation'.

'And as for that countryside we drove through – I've never seen so many lakes. And those mountains!'

Tyrone looked out of the window with her, his arm round her waist.

'I always forget Kerry,' he said, 'the better to remember it.'

They went walking along the miles of white sand and saw only two people, a man throwing a ball for his dog, and a priest strolling by the water's edge, his head in the air, and his hands clasped firmly behind his back.

'Thank you for bringing me here,' Cassie said, looping her arm once more back through Tyrone's. 'This is heaven.'

'I brought you here for a purpose, Cassie McGann,' he replied.

'You rarely do anything without a purpose, Mr Rosse. What have you brought me here for exactly?'

'To make you pregnant.'

Cassie stopped walking, and pulled Tyrone to a halt by her action. He smiled round at her.

'Listen, Cassie McGann. You're making us a beautiful home, and I love you even the more for it. But a home isn't just fancy furniture, fresh paint and nicely arranged flowers. At least not to an Irishman it isn't. A home is children.'

'Well of course it is, Mr Rosse,' Cassie agreed. 'Sure. And we've agreed to have lots of them. But we have only been married six months.'

'We've been married six months, exactly. And nothing's happened.'

'People don't have babies in six months, Tyrone!'

'They get pregnant in six months, Cassie McGann. Maybe you should go and see Doctor Gilbert when we get back.'

'Maybe *I* should go and see Doctor Gilbert? Maybe – *you* should go and see Doctor Gilbert!'

'There's nothing the matter with me, Cassie,' Tyrone said rather too smugly, beginning to walk again along the beach.

'And there's nothing wrong with me either, Tyrone Rosse!' Cassie yelled after him, above the sound of the sea, and then ran to catch him up.

'You've been working too hard, that's what it is, Cassie. With all that painting and decorating.'

'So have you!' she retorted. 'And you've been worried about your yard!'

Tyrone stopped and looked out to sea, and then he turned and started to stride back in the direction of the hotel.

'Right!' he called over his shoulder. 'Come on! We've a good hour yet before dinner!'

As a consequence of the way they spent that hour before dinner, they both ate heartily at table. They dined off fresh salmon and lobster, and drank a bottle of the most delicious white wine Cassie had ever tasted. Then Tyrone introduced her to the delights of Irish coffee, before taking her for a stroll in the hotel gardens, where he kissed her in the shade of a palm tree, under a mantle of stars.

'I love you, Cassie McGann,' he told her, as he kissed her again.

'I love you, Tyrone,' she gasped, the breath squeezed out of her.

He then took her by the hand.

'Come on,' he said, and led her back towards the hotel. 'The night's still young.'

Because the hotel was full they spent the rest of the week in a rented house in the tiny village of Coumeenhoole, on Dingle, the beautiful peninsula opposite Glenbeigh that sweeps right out into the Atlantic. The weather suddenly relented and for that one week in September it could have been high summer, so cloudless were the skies. The plain white house they had rented was simply but very comfortably furnished, with bright-coloured rugs and bedcovers which had been woven locally. It stood high

on the hill practically at the end of the peninsula, opposite a set of almost deserted islands called the Blaskets,
which lay in the deep blue of the sea like enormous
whales. They walked, and fished, and ate, and slept, and
Cassie thought it had to be the most heavenly place on
the whole of God's earth.

One afternoon they hired a boat and went over to the
biggest of the islands, Great Blasket. They took a picnic
tea and sat staring out across the Atlantic, to the unseen
land where Cassie had come from. Then they explored
the rest of the island, which was totally deserted except
for a herd of sheep. They walked through the ruined old
buildings, and the deserted schoolhouse, while Tyrone
recounted to Cassie the history of the islands, and how
they had once housed a thriving community. Then as the
evening drew in, they took shelter in one of the old ruins,
reluctant to leave the wonderful and mysterious island.

As the sun started to sink behind the Atlantic which
stretched so calmly now before them, Tyrone took Cassie
in his arms and kissed her. Then he held her slightly away
from him and looked down at her.

'I don't know what it is about you, Cassie McGann,' he
said. 'But one kiss from you and I'm ruined. Other
women's kisses compared to yours are as ordinary as those
pebbles down there on the beach.'

'My kisses are no different,' Cassie replied. 'What's
different is the love I have for you.'

It was twilight now, as Tyrone gathered her again in
his arms, while the waves below them gently feathered
the shore with their ruffles of white. By the time they had
finished making love, darkness had completely enveloped
them.

Cassie started to feel sick on the drive back to Claremore.
She knew it wasn't car sickness, and she wasn't at all
surprised, because she knew she was pregnant when she
had finally fallen into her warm bed, the night of the
picnic on Great Blasket. There was something different

about the way they had made love, something indefinable, but something that was just very, very different. Tyrone had been so serious, and Cassie so passionate. Afterwards she had smiled and asked him why he had been frowning so deeply, and why he had kept his eyes closed for much of the time.

'Because a friend of mine once told me that if you want to have a beautiful baby,' Tyrone had replied, 'while you are making love, you must think beautiful things.'

Cassie had teased him and said he was probably thinking of winning the Derby, to which Tyrone took great exception, saying that when he had her in his arms, and was making love to her, all he ever thought about was her.

Which was why his daughter was going to be beautiful.

Cassie was astounded at that, since she had always understood that men wanted only sons. After all, that's what the 'hedgehogs' back in New York had told her, when they were pinning up her wedding gown. If the firstborn isn't a boy the husband isn't a man.

'Stuff and nonsense,' Tyrone replied to that. 'Old Italian wives' tales. I want my first child to be a girl.'

'Any particular reason?' Cassie asked, already half anticipating his answer.

'Of course,' Tyrone said. 'Girls look better on horses.'

Cassie had laughed and said she'd known it. It was just as Erin had told her. Nothing made sense to an Irishman unless it had a tail at one end and a mane on its neck.

She wasn't laughing now, as Tyrone's second-hand Ford which he'd bought to replace his beautiful Jaguar bumped its way up the long drive to Claremore.

'No one ever told me I'd feel this bad,' she groaned. 'And I can't be more than five days pregnant, if I'm pregnant at all. Why should something so normal make you feel so *ill*?'

'You'll feel better soon,' Tyrone told her, affecting to

303

feel sorry for her, but secretly triumphant. 'Perhaps Doctor Gilbert can give you something to stop the nausea.'

'No – there's nothing I can give you,' Doctor Gilbert told her, as she sat on the hard wooden chair on the opposite side of his desk from him. 'Nothing in the world whatsoever.'

Cassie swore that he was saying it with relish, gloating on the fact that in order to have children women had to suffer. Erin was right. He was a 'terrible auld stick of a man'. Once an obviously tall man, he was now permanently stooped, hunched in his back, with a dry skin, and a dry mouth clamped tightly over the end of a hand-rolled cigarette.

'The main thing is, Doctor,' Cassie repeated patiently, 'am I pregnant?'

'If you say you are, then that's enough for me,' the doctor replied. 'I always believe the woman in these cases, because as far as I'm concerned, in cases like these, she knows best.'

Doctor Gilbert sighed, and with the sigh blew a cloud of ash all down the front of his old tweed suit. He didn't bother to brush it away. He just looked up at Cassie over the top of his broken glasses.

'Besides,' he continued, 'if you go on feeling sick, and unwell, and start putting on a lot of weight, you'll not be needing me to tell you what's afoot.'

'What about a blood test?' Cassie asked, feeling bewildered but also feeling something more should be done.

'Blood tests indeed,' said Doctor Gilbert, relighting his cigarette, and saying nothing more.

Cassie rose, noticing how yellow-stained with nicotine even the lamp-shades in the surgery were.

'When would you like to see me again?' she enquired by the door.

The doctor looked surprised by the question.

'When there's something the matter with you, Mrs Rosse. When and if there's something the matter with you.'

Cassie walked the three miles back to Claremore quite

happily, as she had decided from the moment she thought she was pregnant to walk and exercise at every available opportunity. As she walked she considered Doctor Gilbert's matter-of-fact manner. And by the time she was halfway home, she thought he was probably very sensible not to fuss over her and make her out to be a special case. After all, she was now living in a country where four or five children was an average-sized family, and ten was certainly not unusual.

Like Tyrone, she discovered that she too wanted it to be a little girl, not because she'd look better on a horse, but because she wanted to make everything so different for her own daughter, so different to how it had been for her. She wanted to give her all the love and affection she could give, and buy her toys and dolls, and make sure she had a bicycle like all the other kids, and of course, being Ireland, a pony. And maybe even a foal called Prince. And when she was a growing kid, she wanted her to have masses of her friends to stay, all sleeping in bunks, and eating their meals round a big wooden table in one of the barns. And Cassie would buy herself an old car, a station wagon, so that her daughter and her pals could climb in and out of its windows when they went shopping, or to meet someone at the station, and it wouldn't matter a darn.

She neared the house and looked ahead up at it, standing silhouetted against its backdrop of mountains. Smoke curled from the tall chimneys, and she could see Tyrone and Brian running up the front steps two at a time as they went into the house for lunch. This was where her first child would be born. A big house. A grand house. Where everyone would love her, and there would never be a hand raised in anger against her.

They sat down to lunch, with Tyrone as solicitous towards her as if she was about to give birth that minute. Since her return from the doctor's, they had done nothing but discuss their unborn baby, even though Doctor Gilbert hadn't even bothered to examine her.

Then halfway through the pudding, Tyrone suddenly remembered something.

'Somebody telephoned for you,' he said. 'And you'll not guess who it was, so I'll tell you. Leonora Von Wagner.

He pronounced the name with a Teutonic relish, but for once his buffoonery failed to amuse Cassie.

'What on earth did she want?' Cassie asked, her heart filled with dread.

'She didn't say,' Tyrone replied. 'She just left her number. Apparently she's moved over here. She's living in Ireland.'

As Tomas drove her up the long tree-lined drive to Derry Na Loch, Leonora's newly purchased home, Cassie wondered for the tenth time in as many minutes what in heaven's name had inspired her to say yes to Leonora's invitation to lunch. Tyrone had said curiosity, and Cassie had been furious with him, probably because she knew it was true. She was curious. Curious as to what had brought Leonora to Ireland; curious as to why she wanted to see Cassie; curious as to what she'd be like now.

But she still felt nothing but contempt for herself for accepting the invitation. If the cat hadn't been curious, it wouldn't have got killed, she thought. Yet here she was, saying yes when she really meant no.

And she felt sick. She was little more than three weeks pregnant, and she had felt sick and nauseous every morning. God knows, she thought to herself, clinging to the handle on the inside of the car door. God only knows how I'm going to manage the nine months feeling like this.

The house was very grand, an enormous white Georgian mansion with a porticoed entrance. A butler in a black coat and striped pants opened the door to her, his hooded eyes flickering just once with quite visible contempt as Tomas drove off again in the old Ford, backfiring its way down the drive. The butler then showed

Cassie into the drawing room, where there was just Leonora.

She looked more stunning than Cassie had ever seen her. She'd lost the little bit of teenage fat she'd still had about her when they saw each other last in New York, and now had the figure of a model, perfect breasts, tiny waist and slim hips. Her blonde hair had been cut much shorter and expertly layered, so that however Leonora moved her head, her hair fell immaculately back into place. She was dressed in what Cassie guessed was a Chanel day dress, in white and blue, with a small matching jacket and dark blue shoes. Cassie came into the room, feeling very much the country mouse, even though she had put on her favourite red jersey dress.

Leonora sat for a moment, smoking a cigarette, which she then threw into the fire half-finished and got up to greet Cassie as if they were the very best of friends.

'Cassie darling,' she said, kissing her on the cheek, 'isn't this great?'

The butler poured them champagne, while Leonora took Cassie by the arm and sat her down beside her on the sofa, like one would a favourite child.

'Did you know I'd got married?' Leonora asked her.

'No,' said Cassie. 'I hadn't the faintest notion.'

'It was in all the papers.'

'I only ever get to read *Sporting Life*.'

Leonora grinned and lit another American cigarette.

'Pity Tyrone couldn't be here,' she said, glancing sideways at Cassie. 'He's gorgeous.'

'Who did you marry?' Cassie asked.

Leonora hooted with laughter before replying and nearly choked on her cigarette smoke.

'Christ I forgot how serious you could be!' she spluttered. 'So wait till you hear who I married! I married my faggy prince!'

This sent Leonora off into more gales of laughter, while Cassie looked round uncomfortably unless Leonora's husband should suddenly come in.

'It's OK, Cassie,' Leonora told her. 'He's not here. He had to go to Rome to see Mamma.'

'Are you happy?'

Leonora stared at Cassie as if she was crazy, then went off into more peals of laughter.

'I didn't get married to get happy!' Leonora hooted. 'Don't tell me you did?'

'What did you get married for then?' Cassie asked.

'Christ, because I was so *bored*!'

Leonora threw her cigarette away and dragged Cassie up off the sofa before she was halfway through her champagne.

'Let's go and eat,' she said. 'I'm starved.'

The dining room was even more magnificent than the drawing room. Or perhaps it seemed that way because at least Cassie got a chance to have a decent look at it, while Leonora wolfed an enormous lunch of thick homemade soup, beef in pastry and apple pie. The room was furnished with superb antiques, old paintings, chandeliers, Persian rugs, horse sculptures and a large collection of family miniatures which hung above the fireplace. It all looked so 'right' and yet Leonora had only been in residence for just over two weeks. It was amazing, Cassie thought, what money could buy.

Leonora said nothing at all while she ate, like she had always done. Cassie, still feeling slightly nauseated, toyed with her own lunch, and was amazed that Leonora managed to keep herself so slim if that was the way she was eating. Cassie chatted lightly about this and that, while trying to keep the amazement out of her eyes when she saw how much food was being stuffed into that thin frame which was Leonora, who was now eating a second helping of apple pie and cream.

As soon as she had finished it, she told Cassie she'd be back in a moment and left the room. A few minutes later she was back again, looking a little pale, Cassie thought but as bright in herself as she had been before she left the table.

'So how's this fabulous husband of yours?' she asked Cassie, helping herself to some fruit. 'What's he like in the sack?'

'That's none of your damn business, Leonora,' Cassie replied.

'Quite right, it isn't. I guess I'm just jealous because mine's so useless. He really is a fag, I swear.'

Leonora looked down the long table at Cassie, while the maid and the butler, privy to all their conversation, carefully cleared away. Cassie waited until they had gone.

'So why *did* you get married, Leonora?'

'I told you, darling. Because I was so bloody bored.'

Leonora finished her second apple and lit a cigarette. She blew the smoke up at the ceiling, then grinned at Cassie.

'And because although he may be a fag, he's also a prince.'

'Right,' Cassie replied. 'And there was I, forgetting to curtsey.'

'Come on,' Leonora said, yawning, 'I'll show you round the house.'

As they went round the house, which was impeccable in every detail, Leonora told Cassie about her sudden decision to say yes to her prince, shortly after Cassie had married Tyrone as it happened, and that the reason she had chosen to come and live in Ireland was because every one was 'so bloody bored with France'.

'You shouldn't have married a prince,' Cassie told her. 'You should have married into the Marines.'

'Oh Christ!' laughed Leonora. 'And you should be running a convent!'

Then she took her arm and led her into her own small sitting room for coffee.

'Why did you want to see me, Leonora?' Cassie asked. 'You can't be bored and lonely here already, surely?'

'Listen, Cassie. I'm never lonely, right? Not any more. If I think I'm going to get lonely, I pick up that telephone.

309

Bored? Christ, you bet I get bored. Don't you ever get bored in this rain-sodden country?'

'You've only been here a few weeks.'

'I can be bored in *minutes*.'

Leonora stubbed out yet another of her endless cigarettes, and poured herself more coffee. For a moment her face looked as black as thunder. Then when she looked up at Cassie, she was suddenly all smiles again.

'I wanted to see you again, because I missed you.'

'You don't even like me.'

'What are you talking about? I'm mad about you! You're my best friend! Sure we've had our misunderstandings, but you're the only person who's ever stood up to me. I really admire your style, you know that?'

'You still haven't told me why you wanted to see me.'

Leonora got up, restless as always, looking frantically for another packet of cigarettes. Finding them, she tore them open, lit one, and then stood gazing out of the window, smoking her cigarette very quickly.

'I'm going to buy some racehorses,' she suddenly announced. 'And I want your husband to train them.'

Cassie didn't know what to say. She wasn't expecting this, and was totally unprepared. All she could ask was why.

'Because he's the best racehorse trainer in Ireland, that's why.'

'Who told you? Your mother?'

'My mother can go jump. She's a stupid, selfish cow.'

'How many horses are you thinking of buying?'

'I thought I'd start with a dozen.'

'Why?'

'Because a dozen's a nice round number, I guess.'

'Why do you want to buy some racehorses?'

'I was told that's what one did in Ireland.'

'Are you serious?'

'It was my husband's idea at first. And I just thought what the hell? Then I don't know. I guess I thought it could be fun. You know. Why not? It might be a bit of fun winning a Derby.'

Cassie shook her head and smiled, and got up to leave. Quite wacky. It might be quite wacky winning a Derby. The trouble was, Cassie thought, with all her own vast wealth, and her new husband's even greater riches behind her, Leonora Von Wagner was the sort of person who might quite possibly do just that.

Tomas was waiting for her by the door. The butler handed her coat to her. Leonora strolled out from the sitting room and called to Cassie as she was leaving.

'You will ask, won't you, darling? Ask Tyrone and if he agrees, maybe he'll give me a ring!'

Because he had an appointment with Tyrone, Tomas drove far too fast on the way home and as a consequence, had to stop twice for Cassie to be sick.

Tyrone wouldn't agree. In fact he was quite adamant.

'I'm never going to rely on just the one big owner ever again,' he informed Cassie. 'Particularly one big owner by the name of Von Wagner.'

'Twelve horses,' Cassie pleaded. 'She's prepared to start with twelve horses, all of which you can find and buy, and she says she might even be able to persuade her husband to buy another six.'

'Over my dead body.'

'Leonora and Franco are great friends with the Mahmoud's son Tonan – who's just taken over his father's string of horses in France.'

'So?'

'So Leonora's serious. There's nothing she likes more than rivalry. She'd want to do better than Tonan.'

Tyrone paused before pouring his second whisky.

'She said she'll pay off her mother's debt to you,' Cassie said, pressing home her momentary advantage. 'You'd be in the clear again with the bank.'

'Until the moment your chum decides to move all her horses,' Tyrone replied, 'or give up the game altogether when she discovers how tough it is. When she finds out what the chances are of owning even the winner of a selling plate at Limerick junction.'

'Please. For me.'

'Why for you?'

'Because I want to see your yard full again.'

'Even if the horses belong to Leonora Von Wagner?'

'Even if they belonged to Khrushchev.'

Tyrone stood by the fireplace, drinking his whisky in silence and looking into the fire. Then he put his glass down and turned for the door.

'Over my dead body,' he said as he went out.

But, Cassie thought, with slightly less conviction.

By the beginning of December, there were nineteen horses back at Claremore, and eight of those belonged to Leonora. Common sense and Cassie had prevailed over the previously intransigent Tyrone. It would have been financial suicide, Cassie had told him, to turn away the blank cheque Leonora was offering Tyrone to go and buy her some racehorses. Not only that, a week after the two girls had lunched together, a cheque had arrived in the post from Leonora which effectively discharged all her mother's training debts. As a consequence, there was now no valid reason for Tyrone to continue to ignore Cassie's pleas.

It was not all plain sailing, however. As far as Tyrone was concerned, when he met Leonora it was hate at first sight. Leonora was far too vain to notice Tyrone's lack of interest in her as a woman, as she considered that she only had to get up in the morning for the world to fall at her feet. Tyrone was appalled by Leonora's manner and her conceit, and informed Cassie privately that the only way this new business arrangement was going to work was for Leonora to keep well out of his way. Fortunately, at least in the beginning, Leonora was not interested in travelling to horse sales, or visiting remotely situated studs in Ireland, England and America. Tyrone informed her what he was looking at on her behalf, but Leonora just waved a hand at him and granted him *carte blanche*.

'I can't tell one end of a horse from the other, darling,' she'd told him one evening when he and Cassie were struggling through one of Leonora's appalling dinner parties. 'All I want to know is when they're going to win.'

She then turned the conversation loudly and generally to her current favourite topic of conversation, which was the extremely indiscreet affair the British Secretary for State and War Mr John Profumo had engaged in with a girl called Christine Keeler, whom Leonora dismissed as nothing more nor less than a tart.

'I was there when it started,' she told her guests, whether they were interested or not. 'Franco and I were at the house party at Cliveden in July. This Keeler girl was taking a swim in the river in the nude, and Profumo couldn't take his eyes off her. Franco says the secret services stepped in and put a stop to it, because of some Russian connection or other. Isn't that right, Franco?'

She called down the table to her husband, who had not been paying the slightest attention to her, concentrating instead on an elegant young interior designer he had specifically invited for himself.

Tyrone and Cassie left early, Cassie pleading her pregnancy as their excuse.

'You're crazy,' said Leonora, walking them across the marbled hall to the door. 'This is going to be one hell of a party. Tristan, the guy you were sitting next to at dinner, he's brought some really good grass.'

'The only good grass I use,' Tyrone replied, 'is the stuff I give my horses. Oh and by the way' – he turned back to Leonora as the butler was helping him into his coat – 'I bought you a horse yesterday. A yearling, by the '54 Derby winner, Never Say Die. He's very small, which is why he failed to get his reserve at Ballsbridge. But he's decently made. And I only gave three and a half thousand for him.'

'Great,' Leonora replied with a singular lack of interest.

313

She then turned back to Cassie. 'Just stay for an hour. Come on. We'll have some fun.'

'Sorry,' Cassie replied. 'I get awfully tired, and then it's not fair on Tyrone.'

Leonora's eyes slid round to Tyrone and she stared at him for a moment. Tyrone wasn't paying her the slightest attention. Leonora threw her half-finished cigarette out into the driveway past them.

'Babies,' she said. 'Yuk!'

Then she turned away and walked back to her party.

At lunchtime on Christmas Eve, Tyrone threw a drinks party for all his old friends and one or two of his new owners. Fortunately Leonora and Franco had gone back to America for Christmas, so Tyrone and Cassie avoided having a row about whether or not to invite them. The party was enormous fun, and although one or two of Tyrone's hard-drinking friends lingered until nearly teatime, by dark the house was their own again.

The weather had turned very cold, and as Cassie dressed for dinner, she thought she'd never known the house so icy. The wind which had got up that afternoon seemed to be howling through the whole place. As she went downstairs, she found the reason. Someone had left the front doors open. Cassie closed them, shivered, pulled her cardigan even more tightly round her shoulders and went into the drawing room. Luckily there was a huge fire burning.

Tyrone wasn't down yet, as he'd only just finished supervising the stables, and was lying upstairs in the bath singing carols. Cassie threw another log on the fire and once again felt a draught that practically whipped her skirt up over her knees. She looked out into the hall once more and, sure enough, both the doors were once again open. She went and reclosed them, and this time shot the bolts, in case the wind blew them back open.

She had hardly sat down again by the fire when Erin was in the room.

'Begging your pardon, Mrs Rosse,' she said, 'but someone keeps shutting the front doors.'

'You bet they do, Erin,' Cassie replied. 'That someone is me.'

Erin frowned at her, as if Cassie was mad.

'But what about the Holy Family?' she enquired.

'What about the Holy Family, Erin?'

'We always leave the doors open for them, ma'am, and the fires well lit, and the kitchen table piled high with food, in case, as me mam says, this house'll be the lucky one.'

Cassie hadn't heard of this belief before, and as she looked into Erin's round green eyes, so full of childlike conviction, she suddenly felt envious, as if she herself had lost some of her innocence. Looking at Erin, she found her belief in a paradise renewed, and only hoped and prayed it was not a paradise that was lost.

'Our Donal still believes in Santa,' Erin confided, piling yet more wood on the already blazing fire, 'and he'll be fourteen next month.'

Cassie smiled as she read the warning in Erin's voice. Woe betide anyone who chose to try and disillusion young Donal. Or, for that matter, young Erin.

She pulled her cardigan round her and resigned herself to the draught.

As it happened, the Holy Family didn't avail themselves of the Rosse hospitality that year, but everyone else in the neighbourhood seemed to. By nine o'clock when Tyrone and Cassie finally sat down to dinner by themselves, it was as if the whole village had tramped through the house, most people bearing gifts, and all of them offered sustenance by Tyrone. The stable lads all called for their Christmas box, and for a drink; and Tomas, too, who would have stayed talking all night had Mrs Muldoon not physically dragged him away. Tyrone laughed over dinner at Cassie's exhaustion, and said the celebrations had hardly started yet. By the time New Year's Day had arrived, he warned her, she'd be ready for the sanatorium.

But Cassie loved it all, each and every moment: her first Christmas in her own house with Tyrone, and their

315

baby safely inside her. Tyrone took her hand and made her make a wish under the Christmas tree, which he had undertaken to decorate personally, in between tearing backwards and forwards to the stables, or dashing into Dublin for last-minute gifts. Cassie, although only three months pregnant, was treated as if she was expecting the following day, and not allowed to do a thing – particularly anything which involved lifting her arms above her shoulders. Even when she got undressed for bed, Tyrone was there to put her nightgown over her head and carefully pull it down.

After they'd been to Midnight Mass, and seen in their first Christmas together they came back to the house and turned all the lights off except those on the tree. Then they stood in the hall where the tree was, with their arms round each other's waists. They stood there in silence, just looking at the lights and smelling the wonderfully Christmassy smell of warm pine cones and log fires, and aware of the nativity they had both just celebrated. Then Tyrone led her up to bed and Cassie fell asleep with the side of his head on her stomach, listening for any signs of life from their own but as yet unborn baby.

After lunch on Christmas Day, when Cassie had happily sat at the large dining table with just Tyrone for company, peopling all the empty seats with the children they were planning to have together and trying to imagine what a huge happy family Christmas must be like, they opened their presents for each other in front of the fire, with a bottle of champagne.

'That's not all you're getting,' Tyrone told her, as Cassie opened yet another extravagance.

He took her upstairs to the nursery, which for some strange reason had been kept bolted for the past two weeks. Tyrone unlocked it and stood aside. Cassie stood silently in the doorway, unable to believe her eyes. It had been completely redecorated, ready for the baby, and in pink.

'One thing you're not short of, Tyrone Rosse,' Cassie said, hugging him, 'is confidence.'

'I know it's going to be a girl, and so do you,' he replied.

Then he pointed to something in the corner, a large shape made indistinguishable by the brown paper which was wrapped all over it. Cassie took off the wrapping. It was a beautiful old cradle, hand-carved in oak.

'Tomas and I restored it,' Tyrone told her shyly. 'It took us hours. It was mine, you know. I used to lie in that, would you believe?'

Cassie looked down into the empty cradle, and touched it, seeing the young Tyrone in it and now, after him, his daughter. She rocked it, and Tyrone laughed.

'They say that's why I'm such a good sailor,' he said. 'Because I was rocked for so long in that very cradle.'

And every day after that, until their baby was born, in her quiet moments Cassie would sit by the empty wooden cradle and rock it herself. She sat wondering, and wondering still more, what it would actually be like, having a baby.

The months sped by, as fast as the March clouds that had scudded across the sky, and as briskly as the April showers that came and went, suddenly rattling their raindrops against the windows, and then disappearing in a brisk blaze of early sun. Tyrone ran two of Leonora's horses before April was out; one was second at Leopardstown, and the other won a very hot maiden at the Curragh. Leonora was present on the second occasion and led in the winner. She posed for the photographers, who couldn't get enough pictures of the glamorous owner, and then disappeared with a supercilious English baronet she seemed currently to have in tow.

The win was all the encouragement certain owners needed to send their horses back to Tyrone. Leonora's colt, called Charmed Life, had beaten a Vincent O'Brien hot shot, and won on the bridle, so by May, the yard was once more practically full. Tyrone had no Classic hopes, naturally, because the horses he had bought Leonora were all now only two-year-olds, with the exception of a five-year-old handicapper called Slang. And besides, by now all the candidates for the Guineas and Derby had wintered with the trainers who were now busy preparing them for their all-important races.

But Tyrone was happy. His yard was full, the lads were back, and Charmed Life's victory proved he hadn't lost his touch.

The York Spring meeting underlined the strength of his young horses. An unraced two-year-old, Willowind, ran a blinder in a five-furlong sprint, to be caught just on the line by the odds-on favourite, who'd won his last three races. Leonora's handicapper Slang, off bottom weight, led from pillar to post, only to lose his race in the Steward's room, for coming off the rails and bumping the second horse so badly, it in turn nearly knocked the legs from under the third. Slang was disqualified and placed last, and Dermot Pryce was suspended for the rest of the meeting.

'It wasn't my fault,' the jockey told Tyrone after the enquiry. 'Taffy James fecked my whip, and I'd nothing to keep the bugger straight.'

Tyrone knew it wasn't Pryce's fault, because he'd seen the incident through his glasses, and also knew that Slang always hung badly to his right when tiring. But Leonora, although absent in the south of France, rang Tyrone the following day and banned Pryce from ever riding a horse of hers again. Tyrone tried to reason, explaining that he was possibly the most promising jockey in the whole of Ireland, and even the great Vincent O'Brien had his eye on him, but Leonora simply hung up the phone.

But Tyrone wasn't bothered. His horses were running well, and much more importantly, Cassie, in the final weeks of her pregnancy, was keeping well. As the birth approached, Tyrone turned the yard over to Tomas, and Cassie became his sole concern.

'You just watch him,' Erin said. 'The next thing he'll be

doing, at least that's what me mam says, the very next thing he'll be doing is nesting. Just like the birds, that's what me mam says. Tidying up something here, tucking up something there.'

And sure enough, as time ticked on towards the end of June when the baby was due, Tyrone, who was normally only concerned whether or not his dinner was ready when he came back from the stables, became totally pre-occupied with the state of the house. Cassie even found him dusting their bedroom.

'Look at this, Cassie, will you?' he cried. 'Look, Erin hasn't as much as moved these things! She's simply dusted all round them!'

Windows would be shut because of any possible draught, then the next day they'd all be flung open again because there was nothing so good for you as fresh air, then they'd all be shut again and newspaper would be stuck under the bedroom door. Blankets would be added to the bed, and then blankets would be taken away again. It was the same every night with the question of how many pillows Cassie should have. Or shouldn't. And every night there was an agony which Tyrone had to endure.

'I think I'll go and have a cold bath,' he'd say with a deep sigh. 'I think I'll have to.'

'Why, Tyrone?'

'God, because you're so beautiful, damn it! Look at you! I've never seen you look so beautiful! I'll have to go and have a cold bath.'

Then he'd turn miserably on to one side, and then back on to the other, until Cassie would find herself kissing him and smoothing his brow as if it was he who was just about to give birth.

'It won't be long now,' she'd say, as she started to fall asleep. 'Be patient. It won't be long now.'

Then she'd lie back on however many pillows had been allocated to her that night, and think of last September, and their honeymoon in Kerry.

It seemed so long ago, now that she was about to give

birth. Long ago and far away, too far away and too late now for anything ever to be the same again. She was glad that before she had left their little rented house on Dingle, with its plain wooden bed, its bright red bedcover and – and straw coloured drapes, she had touched every part of the bedroom, and lingered in every room in the place so that she could remember it forever, exactly how it had been. She had turned back at the door, before locking up, risking the bad luck that one last look was meant to bring, while Tyrone stood outside in a freshening wind, patiently waiting. She had looked long and hard, in order that her mind could photograph the whole place, and the memories it contained, so that now, as she lay waiting for the baby to be born, she could replay every golden moment of those sunlit far-off days.

Because now, as the birth approached, Cassie found she was frightened. She had been told that she would find tranquillity in the short time before the baby was born, but she had failed to do so. She dreaded the idea of pain, and the thought of how the child was to arrive seemed dreadful. Sometimes, as she lay in in the mornings, with Tyrone gone to the gallops, she wished desperately for someone more knowledgeable than Erin to talk to, or Erin's mother, Mrs Muldoon, who kept coming into her bedroom and regularly dowsing her with holy water.

They would then both stand at the end of Cassie's bed and look at her, as if she was a mare about to foal.

'You're a bit too large to my mind, Mrs Rosse,' Mrs Muldoon would announce. 'It's all that Guinness Mr Rosse has been forcing down you. I doubt if that'll do you any good unless the baby's going to be a publican.'

'Me mam says it might have got stuck,' Erin would volunteer. 'Sometimes they get their heads stuck, and then you have to go to hospital and they cuts it out of you. And you can never have a baby normally again. Isn't that right, Mam?'

Mrs Muldoon would nod, and refold her arms, and they

would both of them stay standing at the end of her bed, keeping their vigil.

It was the day of the Irish Derby. Tyrone had just come back from exercising the second string and was about to have his breakfast and get ready to leave for the Curragh when Cassie started. Tyrone had always lived in horror at the thought that he might be away racing when the birth began, and that Cassie would be by herself except for Erin and her mother. But as soon as Cassie told him, quite calmly, that she thought she was starting, Tyrone slung off his jacket and cap, and cancelled all other plans.

'You can't miss the Derby!' Cassie cried.

'To hell with the Derby!' Tyrone said. 'This is the event I wouldn't miss!'

Then he went to telephone the doctor.

Between the contractions, Cassie lay and stared at the trees outside, moving soundlessly in the breeze behind the closed windows. The sun was already quite high in the sky, and 29 June looked as though it was going to be another scorcher.

She tried to remain calm and practise her breathing, but she was still afraid. Afraid of the pains which had started, and the pain which was to come. She looked over to the door, and beyond it to the next room, which had been prepared for the home birth. But instead of feeling the intense excitement she had felt before in anticipation, now when she thought of the plain white bed and the rows of bowls, and instruments, and towels, she felt a terrible fear.

Tyrone ambled back into the room. He was still in his old breeches and polished riding boots, and looked more handsome and devil-may-care than ever. Cassie looked at him and felt a kind of helpless fury. It was so typical of a man, that all during her pregnancy he had fussed around her when she was perfectly all right, and now when she needed all his love and concern, he looked as though he hadn't a care in the world.

321

'The doctor's *en route*,' he announced, 'but I think we'll get you next door just the same. Just to be on the safe side.'

Mrs Muldoon was hovering in the background, doing her best not to look concerned but failing lamentably. Tyrone called on her to help get Cassie through to the next room.

'I don't need any help!' Cassie retorted. 'I can manage perfectly well by myself!'

But she hadn't gone farther than three or four paces when another and much sharper pain hit her, doubling her over. Tyrone and Mrs Muldoon caught her, and lifted her through to the bed next door.

'How often are the pains now, Mrs Rosse?' enquired Mrs Muldoon. 'Sure they seem to be coming thick and fast.'

They were, too. Much too thick and fast to Cassie's way of thinking.

'It's OK, Mrs Muldoon,' Cassie gasped, propping herself up on the pillows. 'My water's haven't gone yet, so we're OK for yet awhile.'

She saw Mrs Muldoon glance towards Tyrone, but his face remained quite impassive.

'How long did Doctor Gilbert say he'd be, Tyrone?' she asked anxiously.

'I told you, Cassie McGann. He's on his way.'

'You're quite sure?'

'Perfectly.'

'He'd better be,' Cassie groaned. 'It was all his idea for me to have it here at home. Like anyone normal, as he says.'

'Didn't I have all my six at home?' Mrs Muldoon announced. 'And wasn't I up that evening getting Mr Muldoon his tea?'

Cassie didn't bother trying to reply. She was too busy trying to cope with the pain which had hit her so hard that it had made her sit bolt upright.

'Jesus!' she found herself saying.

'That's right,' Tyrone said, 'Just try and relax.'

He laid her back on the pillows gently, while Mrs

322

Muldoon wiped Cassie's already sweating brow. There was a knock on the door and Tyrone went to answer it. Please God it was Doctor Gilbert.

It wasn't. It was Tomas. Cassie just glimpsed him through the door, before Tyrone shut it on them both. She heard their voices out on the landing, but couldn't make out what either of them was saying. The room seemed to be coming and going, and for a while she thought she must have passed out. Tyrone was back at her side, sitting holding her hand.

'Tomas is standing by with the hot water. We'll need plenty of hot water,' Tyrone joked, 'because old Gilbert's a great man for his tea.'

Cassie smiled up at Tyrone, who was squeezing her hand and smiling back down at her.

'Jesus God!' Cassie suddenly yelled. 'Jesus Christ Almighty!'

'That's it, my girl. That's the way. You have a damn'd good swear while you're at it.'

'I'm not swearing, damn you, Tyrone! I'm calling for His help!'

'Then call away. Call away, my love. You call away as much as you want.'

Tyrone's image was getting very blurred. The sweat was running down off Cassie's brow and into her eyes. Mrs Muldoon was wiping it away, but Cassie was drenched, as the contractions got sharper and sharper, and then suddenly she felt herself soaked, and the bed soaked, as her waters burst.

'Oh my God!' she cried. 'Oh my God! What is it! What's happened!'

' 'Tis your waters, Mrs Rosse,' Mrs Muldoon was saying. 'And your baby's on its way.'

The baby was on its way. The baby was being born. She was about to give birth and there was no damned doctor. Cassie yelled and cursed and swore, words she never knew she knew, words she'd never even thought. Mrs Muldoon was placing another cold flannel on her forehead, and for some reason Cassie was biting Tyrone's hand. She saw the blood. She tasted his blood in her mouth. The door was opening. It was the doctor! It wasn't the doctor. She could see it was Tomas. Very vaguely. He was carrying a steaming hot jug. She was going to have a bath. The boiler had gone out. She didn't want a hot bath. Not yet. She just wanted the pain to stop.

The baby was moving inside her. She could feel it. It was making its way down her, shuddering its way out to be born. She could feel its size, and the convulsions inside her as the child made its way down her, faster. And faster. And the pain was worse. It was tearing her apart. She was biting Tyrone again, and again she tasted his blood – or perhaps it was her own. She was being torn apart, and she was bleeding to her death.

Then she could see Tyrone suddenly more clearly and she knew it was a dream. He had on a sort of gown, some sort of gown like surgeons wear; it was a sheet, wrapped around him, and he had a mask over his mouth and nose. But she knew it was him because of those eyes.

'Anyone would think!' she gasped at him, feebly, 'that you were going to deliver the baby!'

The eyes smiled over the mask at her, and from behind it vaguely she heard Tyrone's voice contradicting her. All the same he was scrubbing his hands and arms in what smelled like disinfectant.

Cassie knew the doctor wasn't going to get there.

Of course the doctor was going to get there. Tyrone, thorough as ever, was getting himself ready in case he didn't. And why not? Cassie thought, somewhere in her mind. Why not? He'd delivered what was it? Over twenty foals in his time, and all without the vet. He'd delivered all those horses.

Cassie screamed.

'Jesus, my God, I'm going to die!'

Tyrone was bending over her, wiping the sweat off her face, and kissing her cheek.

324

'Breathe in and out, and in and out. And put your hands over your nose and mouth. It has an anaesthetising effect. That's why birds put their heads under their wings.'

He was putting her hands to her face, and Cassie felt her own breath against them, and heard it, deep and regular. She was still alive. She hadn't died yet.

Now Tyrone was talking to Mrs Muldoon. If he was talking, then there was nothing to worry about. They were talking and having a chat. Except Tyrone bent down. He'd gone. He'd disappeared.

'You're about to have it, Cassie.'

There he was. Cassie smiled at him. Oh my God the pain!

'You're just about to give birth. Now do exactly as I say. You can make as much noise as you like, but do as I say, and you'll be fine, my love. You just do as I say. Push when I say push. And stop when I say stop. Just do as I say and you'll be fine.'

Tomas came in with another steaming jug. Cassie bit her own hand. I'm biting my own hand. Someone's shouting to push. She pushed. Now to stop. Cassie stops.

'Christ! What a way to give birth! Dear God in heaven!'

She swore again. That's me. Cassie. What am I saying? Please dear Mary Mother of God! Please help me!

Push, damn you! I am pushing! Push again! Push! I'm being torn apart! Dear Christ, help me! Dear Christ!

Tyrone's shouting! That's Tyrone shouting, I can hear him! What's he saying? It's a girl! It's a girl! It's my little girl!

There was the sound of a smack, and she could see a baby, her baby, upside down and still attached to her. And then Cassie suddenly found she was laughing, and crying, and crying and laughing all at once.

'It's a little girl, Cassie McGann!' Tyrone was shouting. 'A little girl! We've just had a little girl!'

What she then remembered was Tyrone, with tears running down his face and the sweat pouring off him, kissing her and putting the little naked sticky wet baby in her arms for her to touch and hold. And then taking it away again. She remembered then the baby in her arms again, wrapped in a blanket, and she remembered, as she would for the rest of her life, the little fingers and the tiny, tiny features of the scrunched-up face which was the loveliest face she'd ever seen. She held it, not daring to hug it; she held her, her baby, as if she was made of glass, and looked with wonder on the new life which had suddenly entered theirs.

Doctor Gilbert arrived an hour and a half later. He was surprised that the baby had arrived so soon, but he had only got the message a quarter of an hour ago. His car had broken down and he had gone to the garage to pick it up. Unfortunately, he had neglected to leave word at the surgery where he was or how long he'd been gone. It had been one of those days, what with everyone bothering him for sick notes, so that they could get to the Derby. Still, judging from the outcome, Doctor Gilbert observed with a sniff, it seemed he hadn't been missed.

'Not only that,' he added, 'but that's the neatest umbilical I've seen outside the Rotunda.'

In the ensuing silence Tyrone suddenly got up, and walked to the window. Doctor Gilbert watched him with what Cassie thought was compassion on that old lined face. And then he turned back to take another look at the baby to make sure that all was well.

Tomas knocked at the door.

'More hot water!' he called.

'We've no need of any!' Mrs Muldoon shouted back. 'So off with you and turn it into some tea!'

Doctor Gilbert straightened up.

'Everything's fine, Tyrone. You did a grand job. So if I were in your shoes, I'd be off downstairs to open a bottle to wet the baby's head, while I have one more look at the patient.'

Tyrone kissed Cassie and was gone, taking Mrs Muldoon and Tomas with him.

Doctor Gilbert examined Cassie thoroughly, and pronounced all was well.

'I'd have done better to have been a vet,' he said, closing his bag. 'There's a lot more need for a good vet in these parts than there is a doctor. What's the baby to be called?'

'Josephine,' Cassie replied. 'Josephine Katherine McGann Rosse.'

'Good enough,' he replied. 'She's a nice strong infant. About eight, eight and a half pounds I'd say.'

He put his bag down and sat away from the bed, rolling himself a cigarette.

'And there are no complications, to yourself or to the baby. You'll be back to normal in no time at all.'

He lit his thin cigarette, drew on it, found it wasn't alight, and relit it.

'I apologise again for my absence. But then it really has been one of those days. Still, I shouldn't imagine you missed me. With a man who can cope like your husband.'

Cassie smiled, wearily but happily, looking at the baby which slept in her arms.

'Knowing Tyrone, Doctor,' she said, 'and his love of drama, I shouldn't be at all surprised if he hadn't had the whole thing planned. He'd probably have been extremely disappointed if you had actually shown up.'

Doctor Gilbert puffed on his cigarette, while he stared at the ceiling. Then he got up, collected his bag and went to the door.

'No,' he replied. 'No, no, no I don't think so. You see, what he did was remarkable. Agreed, at the best of times. But why I think you're wrong, and what is even more remarkable, is that this is the room, you see, where his mother died giving birth to him.'

Chapter Twelve

'If I didn't know you better, I'd say you'd strayed out on the balcony,' Tyrone said to Cassie, looking at Josephine's red hair as he kissed the baby and her goodbye. He was about to leave for America and the Keeneland Sales.

'Which according to Erin,' Cassie smiled in reply, 'means you think I've had a lover.'

For Erin had made precisely the same comment when she caught first sight of the baby, and Cassie had to ask her what she meant by it.

'It means a girl's done something she shouldn't with someone that she shouldn't, Mrs Rosse, and when she shouldn't,' Erin had answered. 'And usually at a hop.'

'What in heaven's name is a hop?'

'Sure it's a dance, isn't it? Like a *ceilidh* really. Except now they calls it a hop.'

Cassie looked at the baby lying fast asleep in her wooden cradle, and then held Tyrone tight once more, her arms round his waist.

'How long are you going to be away? I don't think I'll be able to live without you,' she whispered.

'You'll have Josephine.'

'I won't have you.'

Tyrone hugged her in return then kissed her softly.

'It's probably just as well I'm going,' he said. 'I couldn't live in this house waiting for six weeks until we can make love again.'

'Is that how long you're going to be away then?'

'Give or take a day,' Tyrone replied, buckling up his

battered old leather suitcase. 'After Keeneland, I've got some stud farms to visit while I'm in Kentucky, then I go to Maryland and Pennsylvania, then up to Canada to see some more youngsters, and back to Saratoga for the August sales.'

Pennsylvania, Locksfield, Penn. Mary-Jo and their childhood days. All the memories suddenly started flooding back. As if it was yesterday, Cassie could see the battered old station wagon pulling up in a cloud of dust in the station yard, and all the kids falling out of the windows in their rush to greet her.

'You didn't tell me you were going to be in Pennsylvania, Tyrone,' Cassie said, helping him pack the smaller of his two cases.

'I didn't know myself until yesterday, Cassie McGann.'

'Would you have time to pay someone a visit?'

'You know how big Pennsylvania is?'

'You bet,' Cassie smiled as she scribbled down the Christiansens' address.

She folded the piece of paper and tucked it in Tyrone's wallet.

'Just in case you're anywhere near Locksfield,' she told him. 'Or even if you're not, maybe you could just give them a call. It's Mary-Jo's family. You remember, I told you all about them.'

Tyrone looked at Cassie, and wondered how he was going to bear to be separated from her for the next six weeks. He found it hard enough when he had to go away from her for a day. But a month and a half! It was an intolerable notion. Particularly intolerable now they had their beautiful little girl.

'You take care of yourself, Cassie McGann,' he warned her, as they both stood by the front doors, trying to delay his departure.

Cassie had little Josephine cradled in her arms, and Tyrone kissed them both once again.

'And you take care of your mother, Josephine Rosse. I don't want her to get into any mischief.'

'And the same applies to you, Mr Rosse.'

Cassie watched until the car was well out of sight down the long drive, then turned to go back inside the house. Erin was waiting with arms outstretched to take the baby, as always, while Cassie took herself upstairs to do her exercises.

She lay on the floor of her bedroom, and tried to concentrate on what she was doing. It was still agony to raise each leg and hold them above the ground only ten seconds, but even the pain couldn't distract her from the great wave of sadness and loneliness which was rapidly engulfing her. She was going to miss Tyrone so much it was unthinkable. He'd only been gone half an hour, and yet already it seemed half a lifetime. As she tucked her feet under the bed and started to do her sit-ups, her eyes filled with tears. She pulled her aching body up from the floor, and let it back slowly again, but the pain she was feeling in her muscles couldn't begin to match the pain in her heart.

She lay back on the floor, staring at the ceiling, and let the tears slide sideways out of her eyes, down her cheeks and on to the bare wooden floor. She lay there for what seemed like hours, staring at the ceiling through a mist of tears, suddenly as unhappy as she had been when she was a child locked away by herself in her room.

It was probably just post-natal depression, she thought, as she wiped the tears from the corners of her eyes. She knew Tyrone had to go away to the sales: that was part of their life, that was part of his business. What she was actually crying for was herself. She hated what pregnancy had done to her young body. All those lines and wrinkles in the now sagging flesh across her stomach, which had been so taut and firm before. She had even made sure that there was a catch now on the bathroom door lest Tyrone should wander in when she was bathing and catch sight of her misshapen body. She was so appalled at what giving birth had done to her, that she would slip her nightdress on over her head before she had taken her underslip off, lest she herself would catch sight of her own body.

Tyrone would tease and cajole her, saying she'd be back in shape in no time, as if it was no more than having her hair cut too short. And she would get cross with him, as he paraded his long, lean, muscular body in front of her. How would he feel if his body had suddenly been changed when he was twenty-two? It was all right for men. Even God was a man. But Cassie was a woman, just twenty-two, and all she'd done was have a baby – albeit a beautiful baby, whom she loved passionately – and as a result she had lost her youthful figure, and not only that, she now felt dulled and depressed by the whole experience.

This inexplicable melancholia, which got worse the longer Tyrone was gone, made her feel ashamed as well as miserable. She should be so happy. She was married to a wonderful man, she lived in a beautiful house, she had people to help her, she had her health, she had a simply adorable baby. And she had lost her happiness. In desperation she wrote over-bright letters to her friends in America, to Gina and Maria, to Arnie, to Mary-Jo asking her to be a godmother, to Mrs Christiansen to give her all the news and to say that Tyrone might be calling, and to Mrs Roebuck. They all replied to her at once, thrilled at the birth, and delighting in Cassie's happiness. They told her how much they missed her and how they shared in the joy of Josephine's birth; and Mary-Jo wrote back to say how touched she had been at Cassie's request, and how honoured she would be to be young Josephine's godmother.

Cassie sat in her bed and read all the replies as she received them, but the love and humanity expressed in them only served to increase her despair. Mrs Roebuck was the last to reply, and her letter was over ten pages long. Cassie noticed how shaky her hand had become, yet nowhere was there a complaint nor mention of her obviously worsening arthritis. If only she hadn't had a

331

baby, Cassie thought, she could have gone to America with Tyrone and visited Mrs Roebuck, and perhaps found some way to help her. If only she hadn't had a baby!

Josephine suddenly started to cry for her food, and in a second Cassie was out of her bed and lifting her baby from its cradle. What can she have been thinking? she asked herself. Wishing the fact of Josephine's birth away? How selfish had she become? How vain? What was the state of her figure compared to the wonder of what she now held cradled in her arms? She hugged the baby closer, and kissed her – something Erin could never bear to see her do without taking Josephine from her on the pretence that she needed changing, or winding. She fed Josephine, and then walked round and round her bedroom, the baby falling asleep on her shoulder. Cassie remembered the first time she, Cassie, had been kissed. It had been by Mrs Roebuck. That was the first kiss in her whole life which she remembered. So she kissed her baby again, and again. And again. She vowed she would kiss her every day that they were part of each other's lives.

Then she sat in the rocking chair Tyrone had brought back for her from Dublin one day, strapped on the roof of the old Ford, and wished it was evening and that Tyrone was there, sitting rocking the wooden cradle and singing a lullaby to his daughter.

The October winds lament around
The Castle of Dromore,
Yet peace is in her lofty halls,
My loving treasure store.
Tho' autumn leaves may droop and die –
A bird of Spring are you.
 Sing hushaby loo la, loo la lan –
 Sing hushaby loo la lay.

Nearly one month after Tyrone's departure, Cassie and Erin were walking to the village, taking it in turns to wheel Josephine's pram. It was a hot August day, so they took their time, strolling leisurely and talking all the while. At one point, Erin stopped her gossip when she saw a cow down in a field they were passing. She left Cassie and ran at once to the nearby farm buildings, and then returned red in the face to take the pram from Cassie. When Cassie enquired what the matter was, Erin replied, still short of breath, that the cow had been about to calve, and that she seemed to be in difficulty.

'I was brought up on a farm, you see, Mrs Rosse,' she explained. 'We'd still have it, too, hadn't Da lost it all on the horses.'

'Your father farmed, then lost it all gambling?' Cassie repeated, unable to reconcile the gentle baby-faced Tomas with a man capable of gambling his family's livelihood away.

' 'Tis why we're all now in service.' Erin replied. 'We'd take enough off the land to keep the ten of us.'

'Your mother had eight children?'

'My grannie had sixteen. Then adopted two more.'

Cassie stopped and looked back at the field where the cow lay, now being helped in her labour by the farmer and one of his sons. The creature suddenly became to Cassie the symbol of the whole of Mother Ireland.

Then she felt her own stomach, as Erin strolled on ahead, cooing at the baby. If her stomach was like this after only one child, what would it be like after the five or six children Tyrone was demanding? By the time she was thirty-five or so, she'd be the same shape as the animals that were grazing in the field before her, their huge udders swinging between their legs as they ate their way slowly across the field.

'Women are made to have babies, Mrs Rosse,' Erin told her as they continued their progress. 'That's what God put us on this earth for.'

'Nonsense,' Cassie retorted. 'I'm not going to have a baby every year. At my age? By the time I'm forty-five, I could have had twenty.'

'And isn't that what Mr Rosse wants? At least a round dozen anyway, so he says.'

'He says he wants enough boys to ride out for him, that's what he says. But I hope it's only a joke.'

'Then you'll have to do what me mam did to Da after the last. She locked him out of her bedroom.'

Cassie smiled at Erin, but she wasn't really amused. The last thing she wanted was to be forced to lock Tyrone out of her bedroom. His lovemaking was something wonderful.

Erin parked the pram outside the village store, and taking the shopping list from under the cover, and unhitching the basket from the string on the pram handle, wandered inside the shop. Cassie remained outside, sitting on a small wooden bench, rather than expose herself to the cloud of pipe and cigarette smoke within, because, like so many small stores in Irish towns and villages, O'Leary's was a bar as well as a grocer's. And to Cassie's mind, the day was far too beautiful to be sullied by the smell of nicotine and porter.

Mrs O'Leary carried a box of groceries out from the shop and carefully laid it across the end of the pram. Erin followed with a full basket, which was duly hitched back on to the handle of the pram. Cassie and Mrs O'Leary exchanged a few words, Mrs O'Leary constantly pushing a strand of grey hair out of her eyes and wiping the sweat from her lined brow with the back of her hand. Then wishing them all good day, she returned inside the shop.

Erin insisted on pushing the laden pram back all the way, considering Cassie not strong enough.

'I feel sorry for poor old Mrs O'Leary,' Cassie said after a while. 'That's only the second or third time I've seen her since I've been here, but even in such a short space of time, she seems to have aged terribly.'

'She was pregnant when you arrived,' Erin answered, 'and she's had twins since.'

'Twins? Heavens, that must mean—'

'It means she's now blessed with nine children altogether. And every one of them bonny.'

334

'That'll be her last I hope, Erin. The poor woman must be nearly fifty.'

Erin stopped the pram and stared at her.

'Fifty, Mrs Rosse? Mrs O'Leary fifty? Sure she's not yet reached thirty.'

Cassie stopped in her tracks, horrified, remembering a tired woman in a black dress, with prematurely greying hair and a figure that had gone to middle age. Erin pushed the pram on ahead. If she'd wanted to shock Cassie, she'd succeeded.

Cassie followed on behind, slowly and thoughtfully. If Tyrone had his way, she too could be looking like Mrs O'Leary by the time she was thirty.

Rather than have that happen, she decided, she'd send to America for something.

Although Cassie had done nothing but live for the day of Tyrone's return to Claremore, she now began to fear it. When he was back, naturally they would resume their lovemaking. They had done little but talk of anything else prior to his departure, Tyrone even ringing the day on his office calendar when, as he teased her, normal service could again be resumed. But once he was back in her bed, the outcome would be inevitable. Cassie would get pregnant, and the whole cycle would start up all over again. Cassie knew it. She knew she could get pregnant just from looking at Tyrone.

It started to worry her, and it worried her so much that her milk started to dry up. She supplemented Josephine's feeds with a bottle, only to meet with stern disapproval from Erin.

'Me mam says you're to try beer,' she told Cassie.

'Tell your mother I have,' Cassie replied. 'I've tried beer, I've tried water, I've tried everything everyone's recommended. But I just can't produce enough.'

'Ah well then,' Erin sighed, 'sure there's nothing for it so. But don't worry about the nights. I'll get up to her meself.'

Erin made herself indispensable to Josephine, finally taking over her feeding completely, while Cassie's figure, helped by the rigorous exercises she put herself through, started to return to something like its original shape and size.

Tyrone was due back at the end of the week, and meanwhile Cassie was in a terrible confusion. Making love was one thing. But ending up looking like Mrs O'Leary was another thing altogether.

But she knew she couldn't deny Tyrone what he laughingly called his rights, nor in truth did she want to. She loved him far too much and she needed him. The only way of approaching the problem was to talk to him. Which would not be easy.

He arrived back from his long trip looking if anything even more handsome and attractive than ever. He had bought all sorts of presents for Josephine, from soft toys to a pretty little broderie anglaise dress which was far too big for her. He'd also bought a brand new dress in silver for Cassie, with a pair of sparkling silver tights to match.

They drank champagne before dinner, which was to be freshly caught salmon poached in herbs, accompanied by the white wine they had drunk that night in Glenbeigh. Cassie had rung up the hotel to find out what it was, then despatched poor Tomas off into Dublin to buy half a dozen bottles.

'Pully-Fumey?' he had muttered. 'I'll never get me tongue around that. Pully-Fumey indeed. You'd be far better off writing it down for them, Mrs Rosse.'

And she had put on Tyrone's favourite dress, her red silk jersey. By the time they had talked, and embraced, and drunk their champagne, and had their candlelit dinner, Cassie was quite convinced that she would be able to argue away all Tyrone's native superstitions about childbirth, and women being purely machines for reproduction, and bring him around to her way of thinking.

Happily, although he had missed Cassie quite terribly, a fact which was more than vouchsafed by the kisses with

336

which he greeted her, Tyrone's trip had been a great success. He had bought a dozen yearlings for a man called Peter Guthrie, and although they all remained in America to be trained, Guthrie was so pleased with his purchases, and the prices Tyrone had paid for them, that he had commissioned Tyrone to buy and train for him two horses in Ireland. He had also introduced Tyrone, on this his first visit to Keeneland, Lexington, to several wealthy and influential American owners, several of whom had expressed great interest in having horses in training in Ireland. He had also met at Laurel Park races a man called Townsend Warner, destined to become one of the most influential American owners of European horses ever.

After that he'd travelled up to Canada to see a horse by the great stallion Ribot, who had finished his racing career unbeaten. But he'd faulted the young horse, considering him too long in the pasterns, and so had rejected him. He did not return to America empty-handed, however, having been tipped off about another yearling standing in a field not twenty miles away. It was sired by an American stallion unknown to Tyrone called Drum Roll, out of a mare by Native Dancer, but the mare had failed lamentably on the racetrack. The colt, however, was a big strapping sort, to be described by the lads, when he finally arrived at Claremore, as a nice store sort, meaning that he could either race on the flat, or grow into a good jumping type. Tyrone bought him out of the field in Canada for a shade under $3000. The asking price for the Ribot colt was $30,000.

So he was in a very good mood as he sat down to one of his favourite dinners, served by Cassie, whom he thought he had never seen looking lovelier.

Cassie was about to broach the subject of Mrs O'Leary and her nine children when Tyrone smiled up at her.

'I saw your friends the Christiansens,' he said. 'I can see why you rate them so dearly.'

'You never told me!' Cassie answered indignantly. 'How were they?'

337

'Very well, and they sent their special love. I even bought a horse for John Christiansen's uncle.'

They talked about the Christiansens. It appeared that Tyrone had been welcomed into the family like a son, and had stayed for two nights on his way back to Saratoga. John Christiansen's uncle, James, had been staying, and was a mad racing man. He'd just lost his best horse, found dead in his box with a twisted gut, and so Tyrone took him to the sales at Saratoga and bought him a grandson of Nearco. The old man was delighted, and tried unsuccessfully to persuade Tyrone to move to America to train for him.

Cassie was thrilled with the story of Tyrone's trip, which took the whole of dinner to tell. He continued regaling her with anecdotes about America and the characters he'd met while they had coffee and brandy in the drawing room, by the ever-burning fire, and she was still laughing helplessly as he carried her up the stairs and started undressing her.

'Tyrone,' she said rather feebly, as her red dress slid to the floor. 'Tyrone, I have something to say to you.'

'And I have something to say to you, too, Cassie McGann,' Tyrone whispered, 'I love you. I love you more than ever. And I've thought of nothing but this since the moment I stepped out of the house six weeks ago.'

He then made love to her. And, as always, it seemed to Cassie like a totally new experience.

The end result of their lovemaking, however, was anything but a new experience. Cassie knew as she lay in bed late the next morning. She just knew that she was pregnant again. She didn't feel any physically different this time. She didn't feel sick. She just felt pregnant.

She laid her hand on her naked stomach, which she had worked so hard to get flat and strong once more, and she swore she could feel the new life that now lay within her. She stared up at the ceiling, and didn't know whether to laugh or cry. In the end she did neither. She just lay there in her bed all morning and stared at the ceiling.

Cassie waited for two months until she told Tyrone, just to make sure. Even then she hesitated, for the eight weeks since his return had been blissful. Because she knew she was pregnant, Cassie had become even more ardent and adventurous in her lovemaking, surprising even the worldly Tyrone. As a consequence, he became even more enthralled with his elf, as he called her – so much so that events outside Claremore seemed to have no reality or importance. But Cassie was afraid of telling him of her pregnancy, because even if he was excited by her news, as she felt sure he would be, she also knew it would be the end of an idyll, and with a second pregnancy, and ultimately another baby in the house, the end of the honeymoon of their lives together.

As it happened, it was an outside event which finally triggered Cassie's admission. The American-Russian confrontation over the Russian missile build-up in Cuba came to a head, and while the world held its breath to see whether or not it would survive the show-down between the two super-powers, Cassie, terrified at the possibility of a nuclear war, broke the news to Tyrone. It was on 24 October, the day the Polaris subs were instructed to begin their deep runs towards the USSR, and as the Russian ships carrying the missiles to Cuba were approaching the quarantine line. Tyrone switched off the news, and poured them both a large drink. Then he sat down beside Cassie, and she held both his hands.

'Tyrone,' she said quite simply, 'I have to tell you. Even though we might be dead at any time. I'm pregnant again.'

Tyrone turned and looked at her for a long time. Then he got up and stood looking down into the fire, the way he always did when something was preying on his mind.

'It doesn't seem too good a time to be bringing another child into the world,' Cassie continued.

339

'Every time is a good time,' Tyrone replied. 'Besides, babies bring their own good fortune.'

He stood still staring down at the fire, then coming and sitting back down beside her, smiled at her ruefully.

'Jesus, but you're fertile, my girl.'

He looked away, then took a drink from his whisky.

'Did you want this child, Cassie?'

'No,' Cassie replied quite truthfully. 'Not, that is, until I became pregnant. I didn't want to become pregnant again is what I mean. I was going to talk to you about it, but—'

Tyrone looked at her and she took his hand.

'Somehow I didn't get round to it,' she smiled.

'You should have told me, Cassie McGann. There are ways round these things, you know.'

'Not according to the Catholic Church there aren't.'

'There's a perfectly acceptable method approved by the Church.'

'Perfectly acceptable to whom, Tyrone?'

Tyrone fell silent again, and brooded into his whisky. Cassie leaned against the back of the sofa and stared upwards.

'This is ridiculous,' Tyrone said finally. 'We're talking now about one unborn baby, when any minute the whole world could be in flames.'

Cassie stared at him hopelessly.

'I'm sorry,' she said.

'What are you sorry for?' Tyrone asked, putting his arm round behind her and drawing her to him. 'You can't be sorry for getting pregnant.'

'No,' Cassie replied. 'No. I don't know. At least I don't know what I mean. I'm just – sorry, somehow.'

They sat for most of the rest of the evening in silence, holding on to each other, and staring into the dying fire. Then they went to bed and fell asleep in each other's arms.

*　　*　　*

As the prospect of nuclear annihilation diminished over the next few days, and Jack Kennedy, in one American columnist's words, 'won his manhood from the Russians', Tyrone and Cassie were able to get the expectation of another child into proper perspective. Tyrone was, he admitted, overjoyed, as long as Cassie herself was happy. Cassie said that of course she was happy. She was overjoyed too, as long as Tyrone was happy. The Russian ships were sailing for home, and even though winter was on the breath of the wind, there was a curious sense of rebirth about. So it seemed that with every day that the world and they survived, there could be worse times to be pregnant. It was a pregnancy to celebrate their continuing existence.

'I'll tell you one thing,' Tyrone said one morning when they were out walking. 'If it's a boy, we're not calling it Jack, or Nikita.'

'Or Fidel,' Cassie added, laughing.

Tyrone's happiness infused Cassie completely. She was so comfortably pregnant this time, with no terrible sicknesses or nausea, and she felt so fulfilled, that for the middle period of her new pregnancy she didn't at all dread the prospect of more children. In fact, when she saw how happy it was making Tyrone, as she watched Josephine growing bigger with each day, and as Tyrone walked the grounds with her, with his arm round her swelling waist, the thought of them both surrounded by six or seven children once again seemed the culmination of their mutual dream.

And then she fell in love.

Whenever she thought about it afterwards, she still didn't know what got into her. She could only explain that it must have been like the way Tyrone described his first meeting with her. A *coup de foudre*: a clap of thunder. Love at first sight. And once she was committed, just as Tyrone had explained how he felt about her, Cassie found there was no way out.

Besides the fact that it cost her a lot of money she could ill afford.

It happened at a horse sale. Not an important one, but one at which Cassie just happened to find herself. She'd gone with Tyrone, who'd concluded his buying then disappeared off on business, leaving her in the charge of Tomas. They'd stayed on at the sale because it was pouring with rain, and there seemed no point in getting any wetter slogging through the mud back to the car which Tyrone had parked miles away because the ground was so waterlogged.

So Tomas and Cassie sat in the leaky stand, watching the rain bouncing off the assembled umbrellas, which occasionally bobbed up and down when the owner decided to make a bid, and running down the backs and flanks of the horses as they were led in and out of the ring.

It was February, and the sale was of some very mediocre horses in and out of training. Tyrone had come to buy one, which he had done before disappearing, so to pass the time until the rain eased enough for them to get back to the car without fear of drowning, Cassie read through the rest of the catalogue. One or two of the few other women who were present eyed her curiously. Not because she was now well and visibly pregnant, but because Cassie most certainly was not one of their number. The other women were all well past their breeding years. They were large women, creatures which Tyrone delighted in calling 'the third sex', with sharp Anglo-Irish voices, thick tweed coats tightly buttoned up and odd hats pulled firmly down over their short hair.

Cassie stared at her catalogue and tried to make sense of the breeding of some of the horses which were passing in and out of the ring so quickly. She had started reading up secretly about horses and breeding again, knowing that since she faced another fairly inactive nine months, she needed another hobby or at least an interest. It was only natural that she should return to the first love of her life, although she kept the fact well concealed from Tyrone. Not that she was secretive by nature, but because she didn't want Tyrone to feel that she was trying to muscle in on his act.

The first thing she'd tried out was riding. One day when Tyrone had gone north, and the yard was slack because the season was over, she'd persuaded Tomas to saddle her up Old Flurry, Tyrone's hack which he rode when supervising work. Tomas refused point blank at first, saying it was more than his life was worth. But Cassie worked on him, and he finally allowed her up on the horse, but first only inside one of the barns they used for schooling the horses. Once he saw how competent she was, he agreed to allow her to hack out up into the hills, but only in his own company. And under a veil of total secrecy.

They rode across the estate, down the lanes, and headed for the hills. Along the side of one of the fields, there was a good, steady grass gallop. Cassie, although she hadn't ridden since she was last at Mary-Jo's, seemed dying to have a canter. So Tomas sent her on ahead, then kicked his horse on behind Old Flurry, who, belying his name, had got hold of his bit, and was galloping up the field like a two-year-old. Cassie was sitting on him well, and managed to pull the old boy up at the end of the gallop a little out of breath but none the worse for wear. They then walked the horses round the foot of the hills to cool them off, and returned home. Cassie thanked Tomas after she'd put Old Flurry away, said how much she'd enjoyed it, then walked back to the house where she drank a large brandy in one and then immediately after was violently sick.

She'd completely lost her nerve.

She'd read about it happening to girls, as soon as they'd had a baby, but she had never thought it would happen to her. She remembered it all now as she stared down at her sales catalogue. How as soon as she'd thrown her leg across the horse, her heart had started racing. At first she

343

thought it was just the old excitement. Then as they trotted up the lanes, she realised she was frightened. Frightened of riding. Frightened of Old Flurry. Frightened of falling off and leaving Josephine an orphan.

Cassie should have turned for home then, but she didn't, still hoping that as soon as she cantered the fear would go and the old thrill would return. But the horse had taken hold, probably knowing that the rider was fearful, and for one terrible moment as he galloped away with her up the side of the field towards the four-foot stone wall at the top, Cassie thought she wasn't going to be able to stop him, as the horse was pricking his ears and shaping up to jump. Cassie knew that on the other side of that wall was a good six-foot drop, because she and Tyrone often walked Brian up along this field. But she got Old Flurry back and stopped him, by sitting down and reining him back with all her strength, so that by the time Tomas caught them up, laughing about how the old horse was enjoying his day out, Cassie had recovered her composure sufficiently to deceive her escort.

But she had never gone back for more. Once or twice Tomas had winked at her and whispered should he get the old horse ready? But Cassie, pleading her new pregnancy, allowed the matter to drop. Instead she once more took up her interest in horse breeding, and spent the hours when Tyrone was out of the house reading everything on the subject in his library.

Besides the need for an interest to sustain her through her second pregnancy, she had taken it up again because she seemed to have nothing to do with her days. Josephine had more or less been taken out of her care, by Erin's subtle process of emotional erosion. Tyrone took a great interest in her, of course. Babies delighted him the same way that foals did. He took a studious interest in Josephine's growth in just the same way as he did with every youngster in his yard. He wanted to know if she was eating all her food, how her weight was, if she'd enjoyed her exercise, and how her teeth were coming on.

Sometimes, Cassie thought with a smile, she half expected him to ask if she'd started wind-sucking or crib-biting yet.

Erin and her mother were twice as bad. At least Josephine was Tyrone's child, but the way the Muldoon women went on, Cassie thought, you'd think she was theirs, too. Every aspect of the child was discussed and aired, so much so that Cassie felt overpowered by it all. She knew it was all well intentioned, but it left her with little say as to what happened to her baby, and consequently little to do with her increasingly inactive days.

Hence her interest in horse breeding, and her presence at the sales. The crowd was beginning to drift away now; the best of the lots had passed through and there were only a few odd mares in foal left now to be auctioned. Tomas stretched and asked Cassie if she was ready for the off, and Cassie found herself saying she wanted to stop and see lot 83. Tomas looked in his rain-sodden catalogue and shook his head in wonder.

'Whatever for, Mrs Rosse? We've seen the best of 'em, if that isn't over-describing what we've seen.'

'It's only the lot after this one, Tomas. I don't know why, but I just want to see her.'

Tomas breathed in deeply and for want of something better to do, restudied the breeding of the mare. She was a ten-year-old bay, by Le Levanstell out of a mare by Peeping Tom, a winner of eight races on the flat, and in whose pedigree – as Cassie well knew but Tomas did not – St Simon appeared three times in the first four generations. St Simon retired unbeaten in the 1880s, and he was to go on to be the leading sire of winners nine times, dominating, with his own sons, the list of winning sires for over a quarter of a century.

Which was why Cassie, who'd done her homework, was curious that a mare with such notable breeding should be the last lot in on a rainy day at a minor sale of horses in and out of training, Particularly as she was reported to be in foal by Facade. Curious perhaps, but quite unprepared for the *coup de foudre* she was about to suffer.

The mare simply walked into the ring and stopped in front of her. She stood just below Cassie and stared at her, with big genuine eyes, and twitching the largest and floppiest pair of ears Cassie had ever seen on a thoroughbred. The lad leading her round tugged on her lead-chain, but the mare stood rooted to the spot. Cassie was astonished and stared back at her, as if she too was hypnotised.

'Ah, these damn old mares,' Tomas sighed, 'saving your presence. Why can't they stale before they come into the ring?'

'She isn't staling, Tomas,' Cassie replied. 'She's just standing there.'

Cassie was right. The mare wasn't answering nature, she was simply rooted to the spot. Then she suddenly decided, regardless of her lad's promptings, that she'd walk round again, and ambled off round the rain-sodden ring.

'What am I bid on lot 83?' the auctioneer called, and half-heartedly tried to raise some interest by recounting the mare's breeding.

But what few spectators there were soon left the ring, once they'd caught sight of the mare. Cassie was surprised, because the animal looked well nourished, and well in herself. Yet there was no interest in her whatsoever. She asked Tomas why this should be so Tomas shrugged and said he hadn't the foggiest.

The only interest was being shown by a lean and tough-looking customer wearing an old riding coat and a cap turned round back to front to keep the rain from running down his neck.

'Meat,' said Tomas, rising. 'Come along, Mrs Rosse, we'd best be on our way.'

'Meat,' Cassie replied. 'They surely can't be buying that lovely mare for meat?'

'Sure there's no one else bidding.'

Cassie sat tight. The thin-faced man had answered the opening call for twenty guineas. The mare stopped again in front of Cassie. Cassie put up her hand.

The auctioneer looked at her slowly.

'Is that a bid, ma'am?' he asked. 'And if so, how much?'

'Two hundred and fifty pounds,' Cassie found herself saying.

'It'll have to be guineas, ma'am,' he corrected her.

The thin-faced man took off his soaking cap, slapped it on his leg, stared at Cassie as if she was mad, and wandered out of the ring. The mare was knocked down as fast as the auctioneer could drop his hammer to Cassie for two hundred and fifty guineas.

'It appears you've just bought yourself a horse,' Tomas told her, 'God help you.'

'Why should God help me?' Cassie enquired. 'I've just saved a horse.'

Tomas stood her up beside him and pointed below them to where Cassie's new purchase now stood.

'Saved her for how long?' Tomas asked. 'Sure the bloody old mare's a club foot! Savin' your presence.'

Cassie rang home and left Tyrone a message should he arrive back before them that Tomas's car had broken down. By the time she got back to the sales ring, Tomas had arranged transport for the mare with a farmer local to Claremore who was returning home with an empty lorry. There had been a small difficulty over the matter of payment, because of course Cassie was not carrying anywhere near that amount of money, and had no other means of securing the mare since, not having her own bank account, she didn't have a cheque book.

Tomas had come to the rescue, as always. He knew the auctioneer, and once he had quietly informed him of the identity of the buyer, credit was at once arranged. Cassie noticed, however, that Tomas slipped a few pounds to the auctioneer and touched the side of his own nose before returning to collect her.

'What was the backhander for, Tomas?' she asked.

'Sure you'll not be wanting Mr Rosse finding out, will you?' Tomas replied. 'So I told him to mark the sale down to cash.'

347

'You think of everything, Tomas.'

'I never thought we'd be walking out of here with a broken-down pregnant old mare, did I?'

On the drive back, ahead of the farmer's horsebox, Cassie wondered aloud why a well-bred mare who was obviously just about to foal, regardless of the fact that she had a club foot, should be sold at auction. Particularly since there were the necessary papers with her to prove that Facade was indeed the covering stallion.

'Her owner's just died, God rest her soul,' Tomas answered. 'So John Mulligan the auctioneer told me. And her family want nothing at all to do with her horses. She had ten, and they've all gone under the hammer. Three of them went for meat, and one of them a decent sort of hunter.'

Cassie looked back over her shoulder at the box following, and then round to Tomas, who as usual was driving very slowly and sedately right down the middle of the road.

'Tomas, are you sure you can keep her?' Cassie asked anxiously.

'You can hardly keep her at Claremore,' Tomas replied. 'Mr Rosse'd have a blue fit.'

'I could find a farm somewhere.'

'You could, you could. But won't she be better off tucked away behind me cottage where we can keep an eye on her? I've a decent little barn there, where she'll have room enough to foal.'

'I'll never be able to thank you enough, Tomas. You know that.'

Tomas just grunted in reply, and took both hands off the steering wheel to relight his pipe. Then he took a sideways look at Cassie sitting beside him, staring out of the window at her invisible purchase, and grinned to himself in the dark.

Tomas had the mare settled into the barn in no time. He made her a deep bed of fresh straw, and filled up a couple of large buckets with water. Cassie stood stroking the beautiful bay mare, pulling at her big ears, and rubbing her soft brown nose. The mare sighed, then shook herself, before deciding to rub the side of her face up and down against Cassie's tweed coat.

'I'll fetch her some hay now, which'll see her through to morning,' Tomas said, running his hand under her belly, 'then tomorrow I'll feck some feed from the yard, and get some Guinness for her from the village.'

'I'll pay you for all the feed and everything, Tomas,' Cassie told him.

'For what I don't get from the yard you can,' Tomas replied, carefully lifting up the mare's bad foot.

'Do you really think we should steal her fodder from the yard?' Cassie asked.

'Sure you're not stealing it!'Tis already your own and paid for!' Tomas snorted, then bent lower over the mare's food. 'And this foot's a damn sight worse then we first thought, saving your presence.'

Cassie bent down to have a closer look.

'Do you see there? Listen, half the foot's nearly off.'

Tomas put the mare's leg down, and patted the animal on her flanks.

'I'll get Kevin to have a look at it tomorrow,' Tomas said. 'He's coming to take Fairyglade's hind shoes off, so I'll get him to look in here before he goes on to Major Parker's. We'd a mare with a foot like this when Mr Rosse's father was alive, and we had her built a special shoe.'

Tomas bolted the bottom of the half doors, and turned to go back to his cottage. Cassie hung back, anxious to have a last look at her horse. Then she patted the mare goodnight on the neck and followed Tomas up the track.

'She'll be foalin' before you, Mrs Rosse,' Tomas said.

'Well before me, Tomas,' replied Cassie. 'I'm not due till the end of May.'

'And this'll be your first foal.'

'This is my first horse.'

349

'And may it not be your last,' Tomas wished her, as they arrived at his cottage.

Refusing his kind offer of tea, Cassie said she must get home, or Tyrone would be worried. Tomas insisted on driving her up to the house. On the way Cassie fell silent, remembering how when she was small every night she used to pray for God to send her a horse. And now she had one at last. She had a horse of her very own: a beautiful bay mare called Graceful Lady.

Leonora was just leaving Claremore when Cassie arrived back. They bumped into each other in the hall, as Cassie was hurrying into the drawing room to find Tyrone and warm herself in his arms by the fire.

'Leonora.'

Cassie couldn't keep the surprise out of her voice. She hadn't seen Leonora since the end of the flat, and when last heard of she was skiing in St Moritz – or rather, knowing Leonora, après-skiing.

'Cassie darling,' Leonora greeted her, kissing her on the cheek and at the same time exhaling the last smoke of the cigarette which she had just stubbed out on the floor. 'Congratulations. I hear you're in foal again.'

She hooted with laughter then looked back over her shoulder. Cassie followed her gaze and saw Tyrone wandering out into the hall, his tie half undone round his neck, pulling his old Aran cardigan back on.

'Cassie,' he said, 'I was beginning to get quite worried about you.'

Cassie looked from one to the other of them, and began to wonder if she'd even been missed.

'Leonora dropped by to discuss plans for the season. We thought we might run Slang in the Lincolnshire. He's thrown in at the weights.'

'Why not?' Cassie said, then with a tight smile hurried past Tyrone into the drawing room to get warm.

Leonora looked at Tyrone and shrugged, then walked away from the door of the drawing room.

'I'm on my way, Mrs Rosse,' she drawled, 'because I have a dinner party, and Christ – why didn't I ask you two! I must be crazy. It's going to be a hoot. We've got Peter Sellers, and hopefully, if he remembers, and if he's still alive, Brendan Behan, who's just back from New York. Jesus I'm going to be late. I'll ring you, Cassie. 'Bye.'

Leonora blew Cassie a kiss and was gone. Cassie heard Tyrone talking to her at the front doors, then the sound of her car driving away. Tyrone came back into the drawing room, and joined Cassie by the fire.

'I didn't know Leonora was calling,' Cassie said.

'Neither did I, Cassie McGann,' Tyrone replied, rubbing his hands together in front of the fire. 'She said she was just passing by, and dropped in on the off chance.'

'Passing by on her way where?'

'I haven't the slightest idea, Cassie.'

'Could I have a drink please?'

'Great idea.'

Tyrone poured himself a whisky, and Cassie a white wine, while she stared silently into the fire. She knew that what she was feeling was irrational and ridiculous, because Tyrone couldn't stand Leonora. But there it was. She was feeling jealous.

She took her drink from Tyrone and then went and sat in a chair by the fire rather than on the sofa. Tyrone looked at her, shrugged, then went and stretched himself out on the sofa.

'You're not very talkative, Mrs Rosse.'

'Sorry. I'm just rather cold and tired. I think I'll go and take a bath.'

'Did you stay till the end of the sales?'

'I had to. Tomas's car wouldn't start. Didn't you get the message?'

'Of course I got the message. I was just wondering if you had to stay till the end, how much that three-year-old of John O'Connor's fetched.'

'The chestnut by Merry Times? Four hundred guineas.'

'Not bad.'

'Not bad? He's got a bowed tendon.'

Tyrone looked round at her in surprise. Cassie ignored the look, finished her drink and went up for her bath. She lay soaking in the steaming water and thought how unfair life could be. She should at this moment have been feeling so good, excited about the secret purchase of her very first horse and happy to be safe at home, carrying the baby of a husband she adored and who adored her in return. Yet all she could think of was Leonora Von Wagner.

Perhaps Tyrone was attracted to her unknowingly because he had loved her mother. Perhaps he'd always been attracted to her, from the day he first met her. Men found Leonora irresistible. Even if they didn't fall in love with her, they inevitably fell for her. And it was perfectly obvious what Leonora felt about Tyrone from the way she looked at him.

The baby inside her womb suddenly kicked her and shifted position. Cassie looked down at her large rounded stomach, and ran both her hands slowly over it. Maybe she wasn't so much jealous, as afraid. Afraid that as she grew larger and larger in the next two months, and then struggled for another three months after the baby was born to regain her figure, that Tyrone would grow bored and impatient, and fall into Leonora's bed in a moment of sheer frustration.

She ran some more hot water until the bathroom was once more full of steam, and wondered if while she was lying in hospital having her next baby, Leonora would again pass by Claremore, and drop in, just on the off chance.

The Lincolnshire Handicap was now just a week off, and the yard at Claremore was back in full swing. Slang had gone so well in all his work that he was now, barring accidents, a definite runner, It had been a very wet March, so the going had come in his favour, and he was all set and expected to run a big race. Tyrone was so preoccupied that he didn't notice Cassie's increased absences during the day, and sometimes even when he returned to the house in the evening. He'd be by the fire with a drink in his hand, as Cassie would come in, her cheeks flushed from the fresh air, and her eyes aglow with happiness. Tyrone put her healthy look down to all the walking she seemed to be doing, and the look in her eyes to the thought of the impending birth. He was right on both counts, except that the birth Cassie was so eagerly anticipating was not yet that of their own offspring, but that of her now beloved mare Gracie, as she had since been nicknamed.

Tomas had told Cassie that it was any day now, and Cassie had insisted that she was to be told the moment the mare started. Even if it was in the middle of the night she was to be called.

'How?' Tomas had asked her. 'For if I telephones you, himself will be sure to answer.'

'Don't use the telephone,' Cassie had instructed him. 'Not if it's late. Send Erin up on her bicycle and tell her to throw a pebble up at my window. Mr Rosse is a very deep sleeper, and he won't even know that I'm gone.'

Fortunately, and Tomas put it down to the sudden cold spell that started in the weekend before the Lincoln, Gracie held on to her foal until after the raiding party had left for Doncaster. Tyrone was quietly confident about Slang's chances, particularly after he'd seen the horse's last bit of fast work. His only worry was that the cold snap would last and the ground would dry out. Leonora was to fly over on the day of the race.

The telephone rang at Cassie's bedside at half past ten, just as Cassie was about to put her light out. It was Mrs Muldoon to tell her that the mare had started. Cassie jumped out of bed, and dressed as quickly and as warmly as she could. She called into Erin's room to tell her that she was going to her father's, probably for the whole night, and then left. She hurried down the drive on foot, shining her torch all around her, and arrived at Tomas's cottage, which was about another half a mile on beyond the yard, just after eleven.

The mare was down, and Tomas, in his shirtsleeves, was kneeling in the straw beside her.

'How do you know when they're starting?' Cassie whispered, as she knelt in the straw beside him. 'It's not as if they can tell you. Not like us girls.'

'Restlessness is the first sign,' Tomas replied. 'The mare'll move about all the time, and her belly will sag as the foal gets ready to be born.'

'Not so different from us after all.'

'I wouldn't know, Mrs Rosse. Whenever Mrs Muldoon started her labours, I was away to O'Leary's.'

The mare scrambled to her feet again, and kicked at her belly as if she had colic. Then she started to wander round in an aimless fashion, sometimes stopping to gaze at her flanks. Once when she stopped, Tomas lifted the mare's tail to check if her vagina was relaxed, and if there was any sign of her water bag. Then with a shake of his head he dropped her tail and gently stroked the side of the animal's belly.

'You like horses more than humans I suspect, Tomas,' Cassie smiled.

Tomas nodded once, and sat back on his haunches to light a Sweet Afton cigarette. He stayed there, resting his buttocks on his heels, his back against the wall, cigarette stuck in the corner of his mouth, while they waited for the next stage of the birth. It followed after an unbroken succession of five Sweet Aftons.

'We're away now,' Tomas suddenly announced, deftly stubbing his present smoke out between finger and thumb and shoving the stub behind his ear, as the mare suddenly dropped to the ground and groaned. There followed a series of increasingly violent contractions until Cassie could see a bladder-like swelling appeared between the lips of the mare's vulva.

'Stand back now, Mrs Rosse!' Tomas ordered, 'unless you want to be drenched.'

354

Cassie did as she was told and was back against the wall just before the mare's water bags burst, and gallons of liquid poured out. Tomas ordered Cassie to throw down some fresh straw as he removed the wet material, then checked the mare's pulse in a vein under her chin. The mare, although breathing much faster, was now altogether calmer, and for a good twenty minutes to half an hour just lay there, seemingly at ease, even though Cassie could see what looked like the foal's forefeet and muzzle forming a kind of cone in the end of the animal's genital canal. Tomas relit his cigarette, and Cassie sat down on a straw bale enthralled, while they waited for the next and final stage of the birth to start.

Suddenly the mare whinnied and seemed to brace herself for the next stage. She had now rested sufficiently, and regained enough strength to deal with the powerful and violent pains which she must have known were imminent. Almost at once the contractions started again, exerting all the animal's strength upon the passive foetus as she tried to drive it out of her womb. Suddenly the foal's head appeared, and Tomas gave a great whoop of joy, although they were still a long way from the winning line.

'Come on, me old love!' he cried. 'Push! Push!'

Cassie watched, as the mare's back arched more and more in her efforts to give birth. The foal's head and forefeet remained sticking out, and for a while nothing seemed to be following. And then, after a contraction which caused the mare to whinny, the thorax and shoulders of the foal were driven through the horse's pelvis and out.

'Good, good!' cried Tomas. ' 'Tis perfection so far! Now come here, Mrs Rosse, and take hold of the foal's legs! Gently now! Towards the old girl's tail! But out behind – and now down!'

Tomas explained later that he'd asked her to do that so that the foal's withers could clear the mare's pelvis, and ease the rest of the birth – which it obviously did, for with only one more contraction, the rest of the foal appeared and it dropped to the ground, rupturing the umbilical cord as it fell.

'Perfect!' declared Tomas, patting the mare's sweat-stained neck. 'Perfect, you clever old article! But then I dare say this is not the first time you've done this!'

Then in a second he was down on his knees by the foal, checking that its nostrils were free of membranes, and that its breathing was unrestricted. Cassie stood staring down at Gracie and her foal, full of wonder and happiness. The mare was resting herself, lying breathing deeply and quietly, while she recovered from her agonies, while the foal was being inspected for its sex by Tomas.

"Tis a colt!' he looked up and said exultantly. 'Isn't that just fine and dandy? A beautiful, beautiful, bay colt!'

But Cassie hardly heard him. So that's what it was like, she wondered. That's how it is to give birth. She put her hands to her stomach, and was suffused with wonder and an odd terror. It was all so mysterious, so ancient a rite, so primal an event. And now the foal was up on its feet, standing on half-buckling legs, and staring at a world unseen and unknown to it only seconds ago.

Gracie suddenly raised her head off the straw and looked round for her young. Seeing him, she whickered and then got to her feet at once to start licking and cleansing her foal.

'He'll be on her any minute,' said Tomas, 'just you watch.'

And sure enough, it wasn't long before the foal had found his mother's teat and was beginning to take his first drink of milk.

Afterwards, they sat and drank strong tea in Tomas' kitchen. The rest of the proceedings had passed smoothly and without hitch, the mare expelling her afterbirth in due course, and Tomas cleaning out the box and laying fresh bedding. By half past three in the morning, they had left a proud mother with her son, both doing well.

'By Facade out of Graceful Lady,' said Tomas, rubbing his stubbled chin. 'I'd be stuck to find a name now for that one.'

'I thought of Celebration,' Cassie ventured.

'I'm damned if I see the connection,' Tomas replied, 'savin' your presence.'

'There isn't any. It's just I like the name, and I feel that that's what it is, the birth of the foal I mean, any birth I feel it's a celebration, don't you? Of life. And it also fits in with what Mr Rosse has to say about Derby winners.'

'Ah it's the Derby he's to win now, is it?'

'Of course. And Mr Rosse says that the name has to fit in with the sentence: the year so and so won the Derby. And I think the year Celebration won the Derby kind of works, don't you?'

Tomas looked at her, sniffed and rubbed his chin once more.

'The year Celebration won the Derby,' he repeated. 'The year Celebration won the Derby. You know, you're right there. It does have a sort of ring about it.'

Cassie thought so too, as she repeated it to herself all the way back up the drive in the cold March dawn.

The year Celebration won the Derby. The year Celebration won the Derby. The year Celebration won the Derby.

He'd have to have a stable name as well, though. But Cassie'd already decided on that as she watched him being born. She may have christened him Celebration, but to her he'd always really be known as Prince.

Chapter Thirteen

She learned of Slang's victory in the Lincolnshire the next morning in the *Sporting Life*. She read all about his pillar-to-post victory, and how Dermot Pryce had slipped his field to make the most of his light weight, long before the telephone rang in the hall. As she made her way slowly out to answer it, she wondered why Tyrone hadn't rung her at once from the course. Or failing that, from his hotel in the evening.

'It's Tyrone.'

'Hi, Mr Rosse. And well done.'

'Wasn't it great? He won on the bridle.'

'I've just read all about it in the *Life*.'

'Listen. I tried to ring you from the course—'

'Yes?'

'I couldn't get near a blasted telephone.'

'There must have been one at the hotel.'

'There were plenty. But we couldn't get a line. There was some problem with our local exchange. As always.'

Cassie thought for a moment, trying to remember if anyone had phoned the night before. Yes of course. Tomas had.

'And then when we did get a line,' Tyrone continued, 'just after half ten, there was no answer. Where were you? Out dancing with Tomas?'

'Almost,' Cassie answered. 'Actually I slept in Josephine's room, because she was very restless. I can't have heard the phone.'

'Oh,' said Tyrone. 'Anyway. Isn't it great?'

Cassie was about to ask him what flight he was catching home, when she heard him ask her to hang on. Then Leonora came on the line.

'Hi there, Cassie Rosse!' she said. 'What about this husband of yours then?'

What about him? Cassie thought. But didn't say so.

'I know,' she replied instead. 'Congratulations.'

'Congratulations? Jesus, Cassie, we've just won the goddam Lincolnshire Handicap! You should be dancing on the table!'

'I would, except, if you remember, I'm over seven months pregnant. Is that what you're doing? Dancing on the table?'

'It's what we've been doing, sweetheart! This husband of yours is a genius! I just love him! We're coming back on the midday flight, and we're going to pour champagne all over you! Here's Tyrone.'

Cassie thought this was a good time to practise her deep breathing, so she did, holding the telephone away from her ear until Tyrone had called her name at least three times.

'Cassie – where did you go?'

'Nowhere, Tyrone. There must still be a fault on the line.'

'Cassie McGann. You sound cross.'

'Sorry. I guess I'm a little tired. After dancing all night with Tomas.'

And she put down the receiver.

She found she was shaking. Shaking with an inner rage. And burning with that dreadful, gnawing jealousy again. Where were they ringing from? Tyrone's room? Leonora's room? Their joint room?

And they both sounded still drunk.

Cassie took her coat from the hall cupboard and, calling Brian, walked out into the brisk March morning.

Tyrone arrived back at the house early in the evening. Cassie was ready and waiting for him in the drawing room. What she wasn't prepared for was him still to be drunk. He threw the doors open, then ran over to Cassie, lifted her up in his arms, and kissed her passionately.

'Cassie my darling!' he cried. 'We've won our first big race!'

'Put me down, Tyrone!'

'Never! I shall never put you down again for a minute ever!'

'The baby!'

'I have you quite safe, never you fear!'

He kissed her again, then lowered her gently to the ground, taking her by both of her hands.

'We've won our first big race,' he said softly.

'Tyrone—' Cassie started.

'Never mind with your Tyrones!' he replied. 'Upstairs with you and get changed! We're going into Dublin to celebrate!'

And he waltzed out of the room, singing 'The Wild Colonial Boy' and taking off all his clothes as he went.

Cassie, who had been all prepared for a showdown about Leonora, and quite determined to walk out on Tyrone if what the showdown revealed made it necessary, instead started to laugh quite helplessly – initially at Tyrone for being such a fool, but really more at herself, for being such a damned fool.

Then she followed the trail of Tyrone's discarded clothes upstairs, and changed for the evening, after dancing a tango round the bedroom with her stark naked husband.

They ate at Jammets. And they also drank at Jammets. Cassie didn't know half the people in the party, and she was quite sure Tyrone didn't either, even though he was picking up the bill. Leonora looked absolutely ravishing, although she was well and truly gone, as Tyrone called it, and kept telling everyone in Jammets, whether they were with the party or not, that Tyrone Rosse was the best bloody trainer in Ireland, and that she was mad for him.

'I'm mad for your husband, Cassie,' she shouted down

the bar to Cassie. 'If he's as good in the sack as he is with horses, Christ – let me know the minute you're bored!'

Cassie ate only some white fish, and drank no wine. Even so, she suddenly felt terribly sick and faint at the end of the meal, and excused herself to go to the washroom. Leonora was in there when she came in, sticking her fingers down her throat and being quite openly sick in the basin. She barely took any notice of Cassie when she saw her.

'Leonora!' Cassie exclaimed. 'What on earth are you doing?'

'Making myself sick, darling,' she replied. 'What does it bloody well look like?'

'*Making* yourself sick?'

'How do you think I keep this thin, the way I eat? This way, I can eat as much as I like, when I like, and never put on a goddam pound.'

Cassie sat on the chair and bent her head down between her own knees, now feeling fainter than ever. Leonora took no notice. She just washed her face and carefully remade up her face. Within minutes she looked as fresh as she had the moment she'd walked into the restaurant.

Then she turned round and saw Cassie still bent over.

'What's the matter with you?' she enquired.

'The matter with me is, I'm pregnant,' Cassie answered.

'So you keep telling me, sweetheart,' Leonora replied, turning back to run a final check on her make-up. 'If I were you I'd go home.'

Cassie did, but not in response to Leonora's advice. She told Tyrone how unwell she was feeling, and he immediately agreed to take her home, not quite disguising his disappointment. The party was all now on the move to Bailey's, where, it was rumoured, Brendan Behan had been barred, and was fighting all and sundry to get back in.

'I don't think I'm quite up to it, Ty,' Cassie said. 'But I

361

don't want to spoil your fun. I can drive myself home.'

Tyrone wavered. Cassie'd had a licence for six months now, and was a very good driver. Besides, if she stayed, the way he was going she'd be driving home anyway.

'No,' he said, weakening. 'I won't hear of it. It isn't fair on you.'

'It isn't fair on you, Tyrone. This is a big night for you.'

'To hell, Cassie McGann! It's only a horse race!'

'It's the biggest one you've ever won. I can see you don't want to go home yet.'

Tyrone took her in his arms and gazed at her, half stupefied.

'As long as you'll be all right,' he said.

'As long as you'll be all right,' Cassie countered. 'If I were you, I'd stay the night at the club.'

'You're on!' Tyrone said, pointing a finger. 'That's a damn good notion if ever I heard one!'

Cassie put Tyrone in the charge of the nicest of his friends, Maurice Collins, and made him swear to keep an eye on Tyrone for the rest of the night. Maurice swore that he would, and so Cassie left him in Grafton Street, and made the long drive along the Military Road and across the mountains back to Claremore for the first time ever by herself.

A chauffeur-driven Bentley returned Tyrone the following day at tea-time. Cassie was out walking Brian when the car came up the drive. And by the time she got back to the house, Tyrone was fast asleep in their bed, still in his clothes.

Two weeks after Slang's victory in the Lincoln, there wasn't a box left empty in the yard. In fact, Tyrone was so inundated with requests from owners to take horses into training for them that he applied for permission to build an extra ten boxes. Leonora's Never Say Die colt Charmed Life, now a not very tall but an extremely burly three-year-old, won his prep race for the Guineas in good enough style to bring his ante-post price

362

tumbling down from 25/1 to 6/1, while the other stable hot-shot, Willowind, on his initial outing led every inch of the way for six of the seven furlongs, and promised to look unbeatable over shorter distances. The couple of two-year-olds Tyrone had bought for James Christiansen ran well enough first time out to indicate that although well short of classic standard, it shouldn't be long before they both won their first races; and even the best of Tim Coughlan the butcher's no-hopers was showing marked signs of improvement on the gallops.

'Ever since he got his nose in front at Galway,' Tim said, 'sure he's developed a taste for it.'

Tyrone certainly thought the old horse's surprise win had been a contributory factor to the animal's renewed interest in racing. But most of all he knew he owed the bonny health of all the horses in his care to Tomas' inspired stable management. All in all, Claremore looked set for a bumper season.

Until, that was, Charmed Life started coughing. By the end of that week, three quarters of the horses had a 'nose', and by the middle of May most of the best ones were still only walking. Charmed Life had missed his tilt at the Guineas, and although he was at least in work and cantering, it was touch and go whether or not Tyrone could get a decent race into him before the English Derby.

Cassie was devastated at Tyrone's misfortune, but Tyrone endured it with his usual good humour.

'That's racing, Cassie McGann,' he said. 'There are far, far more disappointments in this game than there are celebrations.'

Leonora did not view the setback quite so philosophically as her trainer. She blamed him for not quarantining her horses in time, and she blamed Bill Hutchings, Tyrone's vet, for not getting the horses back to work quickly enough. She was told by both parties that, with an epidemic such as this one time was the only healer, but Leonora would hear none of it, and insisted on flying over two vets from Newmarket, which cost her a lot of money to hear exactly the same advice. Leonora stormed out of Claremore and got on the next plane for the south of France, from whence she rang daily for updates on the condition of her horses.

'God but she's an awful woman,' Tyrone sighed one evening, after half an hour on the telephone with her.

'I thought you two were getting on much better now,' Cassie replied, without looking up from the little jacket she was knitting for the new baby. 'After the Lincoln, I thought I was going to be a divorcee.'

It was the first time Cassie had mentioned Tyrone's night out on Dublin with Leonora, but Tyrone paid it slight attention, simply throwing his head back and roaring with uncomplicated laughter.

'Can you imagine Leonora and me?' he exclaimed. 'God I don't know who'd strangle the other first!'

Cassie still didn't look up at him, until Tyrone came and sat down beside her on the sofa. He put a hand under her chin and turned her face towards him.

'Cassie McGann,' he said, as he saw the look in her eye. 'Cassie McGann, what can you have been thinking?'

'Only what most pregnant women think, I suppose,' she replied, 'when they see their husbands with beautiful blondes crawling all over them.'

'Cassie McGann,' was all Tyrone replied, 'I'm ashamed for you!'

Fortunately Cassie's foal, being well away from the main yard, escaped the virulent infection which had decimated the majority of Tyrone's string. Cassie visited him every day, and marvelled at how strong the colt was growing. Gracie was the perfect mother, patiently enduring her son's violent attacks on her teats, and barely even scolding him when he decided to try out his teeth on her neck.

'She's a nice stamp of mare, Mrs Rosse. Notwithstanding the old foot,' Tomas said to her one afternoon, as they leant on the old post and rails of the field in which Tomas had turned out the mare and her foal. 'You thought well having her covered by old Major Parker's stallion, Bright Spring.'

'I thought a little extra speed mightn't go amiss,' Cassie replied. 'After all, he won the Cork and Orrery pretty quickly.'

'Sure he did. And since there's abundant stamina in the mare's pedigree, we could be right. A little bit of speed won't go amiss.'

Cassie smiled to herself. Between Tomas and her it was all 'we' and 'us' now, whereas before it had been very much 'you'. Tomas had fallen for Graceful Lady in quite the same way as Cassie had. It had just taken a little bit more time.

As they walked back to Tomas' cottage, Cassie was aware of Tomas appraising her.

'It'll not be long now,' he said, 'before you'll be foaling yourself.'

'Do you reckon?' Cassie had asked. 'It's meant to be at least another ten days.'

'Savin' your presence,' Tomas replied, 'but I'd say you've dropped. Sure you've the softening of the bones, as we say about the mares.'

Doctor Gilbert confirmed Tomas' diagnosis.

'It looks as though you might be early,' he told her, for once brushing the cigarette ash off the front of his suit, 'which of course is not unusual with the second child. But then I'm not altogether happy with your shape. You look quite the wrong shape to me. It could be a breech.'

Whereupon he picked up the telephone and asked to be connected to the hospital.

Cassie was on her feet in a moment.

'I'm not having it in hospital!' she told him. 'I'm having it at Claremore, just as I had Josephine!'

'First,' Doctor Gilbert replied, blowing his nose, 'we'll just make quite sure that everything's as it should be.'

Tyrone drove her to hospital that afternoon. They took

a suitcase with Cassie's overnight things on Doctor Gilbert's instructions, just as a precaution. As they drove across the mountains, Tyrone gave her an update on all the horses to try and get the frown off Cassie's brow. But Cassie was not to be diverted. Dr Gilbert was not a man to send someone to hospital unless he had the strongest suspicions that all was not well.

The doctor who attended her was young and brusque. He examined her thoroughly, and then regarded Cassie for a moment in silence, sucking the inside of his cheek.

'Your doctor was right,' he said finally. 'The baby's turned itself round, and I'm afraid it's a breech.'

Cassie lay on the couch, not knowing what to say. Not understanding the implications fully.

'It's very simple,' the young doctor told her. 'You know what a breech presentation is I'm quite sure. The baby's going to come out feet first. I've tried turning the baby but it seems stuck. Which is why I'm going to operate. By Caesarian section.'

The doctor opened the door to the examination room and called in Tyrone who'd been pacing the corridor outside.

He told him what he planned to do to his wife.

Tyrone came to Cassie's side and took her hand. For once he was at a loss for words, as was Cassie. Tyrone squeezed her hand hard, and smiled. But Cassie could see in those ever-expressive eyes the terrible deep concern which lay behind the smile.

'I don't want to be cut open, Ty,' she whispered. 'Ask him if there's not something else he can do.'

'Of course there's something else I can do,' the doctor replied, without waiting to be asked by Tyrone. 'I could let you have the baby by the normal process and risk losing the child, and probably you as well, Mrs Rosse. But as you know, our duty lies to the unborn child.'

Cassie bit her lip to stop herself from crying and held on tightly to Tyrone's hand. She didn't want to die to save her child. She knew that was what she was meant to do, as a good and responsible Catholic. She was meant to be prepared to offer up her life for that of her unborn child. A child who could be born dead.

But Cassie didn't want to lose her life. Because she didn't want to lose her life with Tyrone. It wasn't her own life she was protecting. It was the joint life they had made together. They could always make another child, Tyrone and she. But they could never ever make another life between them, if Cassie were dead and gone.

'I want to talk to my husband,' Cassie said.

'By all means. But please be quick. I have to make the necessary arrangements.'

The doctor left them together. Cassie sat up, releasing Tyrone's hand, and straightened her clothes.

'Well?' Cassie asked Tyrone, for once challenging him. 'Am I to die for this baby?'

'There's no saying you'll die, Cassie,' Tyrone replied, sitting on the chair by the side of the couch. 'But you both might if you have it the normal way.'

'So I'm to be cut open.'

'You're to be operated on, Cassie. In order to give you both the best chance.'

'In order to give the baby the best chance.'

'There isn't an alternative.'

Cassie got herself slowly down off the examination couch and walked to the window. There was nothing to see. The window looked out on to the black windows of one of the hospital blocks.

'If during the operation, it's a question of saving your child—'

'Our child,' Tyrone corrected her.

'If it's a question of saving your child or me, who do you *really* think the doctor should save?'

'We've talked about this before, Cassie.'

'We've never mentioned it once.'

'We have indirectly. It's not my choice. We're bound by the rules.'

'The rules?' Cassie exclaimed, turning round sharply.

'What rules? This isn't the goddamn Jockey Club, you know! This is a matter of my life or my death!'

'Yes,' Tyrone nodded. 'And of the baby's life. Or death.'

'Tyrone,' Cassie said, as calmly as she could. 'I love you, Tyrone. I don't want to die for a baby. I want to live for you.'

Tyrone stood and took her in his arms.

'You won't die, my love,' he told her. 'God will take care of you both. He'll see you don't die.'

They were due to operate on Cassie first thing the following morning. Cassie was woken up from her drug-induced sleep that night by a sharp pain and a sudden discomfort. For a moment she thought she was starting to give birth, and she lay there, waiting for the next contraction. But no subsequent pain followed, so she shut her eyes and drifted off, thinking it must have been a false start.

They gave her a pre-med at dawn, and she vaguely remembered being wheeled to the theatre. Then someone asked her to count some numbers, and that was that.

She woke up briefly in a large white room. She was dimly aware of other people being there, and looked for Tyrone. But he wasn't present.

When she awoke the next time, she was lying behind green screens, pulled all around her bed. She looked at him and frowned. Tyrone smiled and stood up. He bent low over her and kissed her on the forehead, then he sat again, his hands stretched out to hers, clasping Cassie's over the carefully folded sheet. Cassie felt the warmth in his hands, and she grasped them, feeling her own move when she asked them. And her head turn when she bade it. And she could smile. She smiled at Tyrone. She was alive.

'How's the baby?' she asked. 'What is it? Where is it?'

She tried to sit up, but the pain across her stomach made her gasp, and she lay back.

Tyrone was still smiling at her, but Cassie knew he wasn't really. She knew at once by his eyes that the baby was dead.

A nurse pulled back one of the curtains on the screen with a sudden rattle and stared at Cassie.

'Ah yes,' she said. 'Mrs Rosse. You'd be the one who's lost the baby.'

Tyrone was on his feet in a flash, grabbing the nurse by her shoulders so violently that the medicines she was holding spilled all over the bed. He barked something at the girl and then he spun her round and hauled her out of the curtained cubicle with him. Cassie lay there stunned. It was a nightmare, some terrible nightmare. Soon she'd be thankfully awake.

Then Tyrone was back in the cubicle, and at Cassie's side. 'Jesus Christ!' he gasped. 'Jesus Christ!'

Then he collapsed on a chair, buried his head on the bed, and sobbed. Cassie tried to put out a hand to stroke the back of his head, but the tubes in her arms prevented her.

'The baby,' Cassie said slowly. 'Our baby. Tyrone—'

'The baby's dead, Cassie,' Tyrone whispered. 'He was stillborn. Strangled by the cord.'

'He, did you say? You did say he?'

'Yes, my darling. Yes. It was a little boy.'

It was Tyrone junior. It was their boy. It was Michael, the name which he was to have been called. And Michael was no more.

Cassie wept. She turned on her pillow and wept into it. She now realised that she would much rather Michael had lived and that she had died.

At some time she must have fallen into a deep sleep. Because the next thing she knew it had got dark. And Tyrone was standing at the opening of the cubicle, talking in low and urgent tones to another nurse, a nurse in a different uniform, whom Cassie then recognised as Sister.

'I will not have my girls spoken to in such a manner,'

369

Sister was saying, albeit without much authority. 'Nor will I have them manhandled.'

'She's lucky she's still alive,' Tyrone answered. So quietly that only Cassie knew how angry he was. 'And I strongly advise you, Sister, to think before you say anything more. About anything. That nurse is not to be let back in here, you understand?'

He looked at the woman challengingly. She shifted uncomfortably under his gaze and dropped her eyes almost at once.

'If that nurse goes near my wife again,' he warned her, 'I shall have her sacked. And you too.'

'Mr Rosse—' Sister began.

'Two of your governors are personal friends of mine,' Tyrone interrupted. 'One word from me, and you're without a job. Now where can I find Doctor Rigby?'

'Doctor Rigby is off duty, I'm afraid, Mr Rosse.'

'Probably just as well for him. But you can tell him, when he comes back on duty, that I'm filing a complaint against him. For negligence.'

'Doctor Rigby did everything within his power to save the child, Mr Rosse.'

'Except operate early enough. He should have operated yesterday. As soon as he discovered it was a breech, and while the baby was not yet engaged. Even my vet could have told your Doctor Rigby that.'

Tyrone then dismissed her, and came back and sat by Cassie's bedside again.

'Tyrone—' Cassie whispered.

'Sshhhh, now,' he ordered. 'You just go back to sleep. I'll be here.'

'I should have died, Ty. I should have died, and you should have had your son.'

'Nonsense. That's nonsense, Cassie, do you hear me? You're never to say that again. You're not even to think it. I can always have another child. I can never have another you.'

Then he leaned over her and kissed her gently on her cold forehead.

'I mean it,' he said.

There was a girl in the next bed to Cassie, waiting to have her child. She must have sensed the moment Cassie felt like talking, because for a day she said nothing to Cassie at all. She just read her paperback novel, and chain-smoked. Then in the evening, although Cassie didn't turn towards her, or make any indicative move, the girl suddenly spoke to her.

'Are yous all right?' she asked her, with that now familiar Dublin twang. ' 'Cos I heard what happened.'

'Yes,' Cassie answered. 'Yes, I'm fine, thanks.'

'Do yous smoke?'

'No thank you.'

'Do yous mind if I do?'

'Not at all.'

That was their entire first exchange. The girl obviously knew instinctively that Cassie didn't feel like talking so she just left her alone. Now and then when Cassie shifted position in the bed, she'd find the girl smiling at her, and she'd do her best to smile back, although all she actually felt like doing was crying.

The next morning, after Tyrone had reluctantly returned to Claremore, Cassie sat herself a little higher in her bed and pretended to read a book. The girl in the next bed took this as a cue for further conversation.

'I'm Kathleen,' she said. 'Kathleen O'Donnell.'

'I'm Cassie Rosse.'

'Was this your first?'

'Second.'

'Jeeze that's rotten. It's always rotten, whatever they tell yous. This is my second as well.'

Kathleen then had a bad attack of coughing, which enabled Cassie to take a better look at her. She was, as Tyrone would say, but a slip of a thing. To Cassie she appeared no more than seventeen or eighteen years old.

371

Even through her advanced state of pregnancy, it was quite clear that she was badly under-nourished and, by the time she had finished coughing, that she wasn't very well, for she was as white as the hospital sheets, and had dark grey rings under her eyes.

'What's your other child?' Cassie asked. 'A boy or a girl? I've got a little girl.'

'Mine's a boy,' Kathleen answered. 'Sean. Sean Patrick, and yous wouldn't think it, but I miss the little divil. Me auntie's lookin' after him, the bitch. God she's cruel. She's the cruellest woman in the world. I should know 'cos the bitch brought me up. She'd beat yous so hard yous couldn't get out of your bed except be crawlin' on your hands and knees. But I couldn't leave Sean Patrick with his father. Jeeze his father'd have him fallin' in the firė. Or runnin' under a bus. The stupid old man.'

'Your husband's older than you, is he?'

'Isn't yours?'

'Yes. But not that much older.'

'Mine is. God he's damn near sixty. Me auntie married me off to him for a few quid. And all to inherit his stinkin' old farm.'

She suddenly stopped talking and Cassie realised that even though she'd turned away ostensibly to light another cigarette, she was in fact crying.

She waited a few moments before asking the girl what the matter was.

'I shouldn't be sayin' this to you,' she answered, 'God forgive me. But you see, Mary Mother of God, I don't want this baby! I never did! I don't want this wretched child!'

'Why not?' Cassie asked carefully.

'Ah because!' Kathleen sobbed. 'Because I was going to leave the old bastard! But with another child, jeeze how the hell can I? How the bloody hell can I?'

Kathleen started going into labour at ten o'clock that night, but by the time Cassie was woken the next morning at half past six, the bed next to her was still empty.

The nurse whom Tyrone had expelled from Cassie's cubicle was on duty. And despite Tyrone's warning, she still delighted in tormenting Cassie whenever the opportunity arose. Now she came to the bottom of Cassie's bed and smiled at her. But as always the smile was on her lips only.

'And how's Mrs Rosse this morning?' she said, shaking down a thermometer. 'Feeling a little less sorry for ourself, are we?'

She put the thermometer in Cassie's mouth as she opened it to reply, and lifted her wrist to check her pulse.

'It's hardly the end of the world, you know, what happened to you. You're married and can have more babies. Can't you? Because *you're* still alive.'

She stood above Cassie, by the side of her head, so that Cassie couldn't quite make out the expression on her face. She left the thermometer in her mouth for far too long deliberately, while she called across the ward to another nurse.

'Mary? You remember the woman who lost the little boy a couple or so days ago? Mrs Rosse here? Well, you can please come and strip her bed. Over here, please.'

Then she whipped the thermometer out of Cassie's mouth and shook it down without even looking at it.

'Out of bed then, Mrs Rosse,' she ordered, moving away, only to stop by the door and look back.

'Oh and better luck next time!' she added. 'That is if there *is* a next time!'

Cassie hadn't even the strength to walk. She slowly swung her weakened legs out of bed and sat on the side. The other nurse came over to help her up.

'You don't want to pay any attention to Nurse Riordan,' she whispered. 'Everyone hates her, and we're all only too happy she's been dismissed.'

Cassie smiled as the nurse helped her dress, realising suddenly that Tyrone had obviously been as good as his word.

'Any news of the little girl in the next bed?' Cassie enquired. 'Kathleen O'Donnell?'

'The poor soul had a terrible long labour,' the nurse replied, doing up the back of Cassie's dress. 'But thank God she was safely delivered half an hour ago. She's another little boy.'

Cassie thanked the nurse for her help, and sat on the small wooden chair by her bed to wait for Tyrone. Across the ward, two women lay chatting, with their newborn babies at their breasts. One of them caught Cassie's eye, smiled shyly, then looked away in embarrassment.

They'll be taking their babies home with them, Cassie thought. They'll be taking them home, and putting them in the cots that have stood waiting for them, and dressing them in the little clothes they've been knitting during their long and often boring confinements. They'll be taking their babies home. The cots will be filled. The clothes will be worn.

But the blue room back at Claremore will be empty.

They'll be taking their babies home.

But my new blue nursery full of all those handmade clothes will be empty.

Cassie sat on the plain wooden chair, then suddenly dropped her head into her hands and sobbed publicly.

Chapter Fourteen

She heard voices in the study down below her, but she couldn't make out what they were saying. Not that she was greatly interested. She was really only interested in staring at the walls and the ceiling, and thinking how much she hated maroon. She couldn't imagine why she had painted the room that colour. It was like dried blood. It was like a womb.

That made her laugh. It was funny to think of her lying in a womb. Lying staring at the walls of a dark maroon womb, while outside she could hear the voices of the people as they waited for her to be born. Well, she'd make them wait. They could wait as long as they liked. As long as she made them. Because she wasn't coming out of this dark maroon womb. And they weren't going to take her out either, by some brute force. Because she could stop them doing that. She could lock herself in. Then there was no way they could make her be born.

Tyrone found her by the door as he opened it.

'Where's the key?' Cassie asked him.

'There isn't a key,' Tyrone replied.

'There used to be a key.'

'There wasn't ever a key.'

'Then will you get me one, please?'

Tyrone had her back in her bed now, and was tucking her in. Cassie was crying, as she begged him for a key. But Tyrone just kissed her head and said there was no need for one.

'But there is, Ty!' Cassie pleaded. 'There is! I must be

locked in here, you see! Then they can never take me away from here!'

He was giving her something to drink, something pink, that fizzed. Cassie smiled because she liked it. Because she knew she could go floating again. The key stopped being so important, as she felt her body lighten, and she knew that she could smile at Tyrone again.

'Erin's going to come in and read to you while I'm out,' someone was saying. It was Tyrone. Cassie smiled at him.

'I won't be out long, and Josephine's sleeping. So Erin said she'd come in and read.'

Yes, it was Tyrone. She could see him now. He was so handsome. Cassie smiled at him again.

'Doctor Gilbert's just been.'

You remember that smell of tobacco, Cassie? That must have been old Doctor Gilbert.

'He says you have to stay in bed.'

Cassie, are you smiling? Yes, yes of course you are. You're smiling because the doctor understands. He's making you stay in bed because he knows you don't want to leave this room. Your womb.

Tyrone watched Cassie as he sat on the edge of their bed. She was looking at him, smiling in that still vague way. Smiling at him without seeing him, as she had been doing now for nearly three months.

He left her sleeping and went downstairs, where Doctor Gilbert was helping himself to some more whisky.

'There has to be something else we can do, Doc,' Tyrone said, taking the decanter and helping himself to a drink. 'She's not showing the slightest sign of improvement.'

'There's the electric shock business I told you about,' Doctor Gilbert replied, looking out of the study window and across the newly mown lawns. 'But – and quite wisely so to my way of thinking – you've said no to that. So there we are.'

376

'And that's it?' Tyrone said, knowing full well that it was. Either they let time take its course, or they risked Cassie's finely balanced sanity by a course of electric shock treatment.

'That's the size of it, I'm afraid, Tyrone Rosse. Now tell me which of your two horses is going to win at the Curragh on Saturday.'

As it happened, they both did, thus breaking Tyrone's sequence of thirty-two successive losers. James Christiansen's horse The Walker duly obliged, finally, in a nursery stakes, and Willowind recovered her form to win the big five-furlong sprint by three lengths. But it had been a terrible season otherwise, disastrously so for one which had begun in such fine style. The virus had taken far more out of the horses than even Tomas had predicted, and although the horses worked sweetly and strongly at home on the gallops, as soon as they were in a race they collapsed. Tyrone got sick of the sight of his good horses trailing in last behind greatly inferior ones.

He had managed to get Charmed Life to the post for the Epsom Derby. But he was uneasy in the market, drifting from 5/1 out to 10/1 on the morning of the race, and finally starting at 12/1. Two furlongs out, Tyrone and Leonora thought they had the bookmakers proved totally wrong, but once again the bookies' information service had done them proud, as Charmed Life, from looking every inch the winner, suddenly blew up and finished next to last. He did the same thing in the Irish Derby, so Tyrone decided to give him a short holiday and bring him up again for the Champion Stakes in October.

It was a totally frustrating summer, particularly since all the tests they ran on the horses came up one hundred per cent negative. It was, as all his other training friends told him, the long-term effect of a particularly nasty virus.

So it was with great relief that he watched his two winners being led in, especially since The Walker had been the last horse to go down with the virus, and now he was the first one back in the winner's enclosure. Tyrone did have one further worry, however. He was due to take two horses out to race in Milan the following week, but since Cassie was showing no signs of any improvement whatsoever, he was extremely doubtful about leaving her, even in the capable and caring hands of Mrs Muldoon and Erin. Fate, however, in the shape of Lady Meath intervened.

Tyrone saw her in the bar after Willowind's victory. She came up to him, and congratulated him warmly, saying how delighted she was to see Claremore back in the frame again. Tyrone mentioned he hadn't seen her on the course for a few weeks, and wondered if she'd been away.

'No,' she told him, 'I've been ill. I've had a cancer, but thank God it doesn't seem to have been malignant. I'm completely recovered, so there's no need to pull any long faces. How's that pretty young wife of yours?'

Tyrone told her of their troubles, while Sheila Meath listened to him intently. Halfway through, she stopped him.

'This is far too important to talk about on a racecourse,' she said. 'Stop in for a drink on your way home.'

By the time Tyrone left Sheila Meath's house that evening, he felt better than he had done for weeks. Sheila had liked Cassie on the several occasions they had met and Cassie had reciprocated her feelings. So it was agreed that while Tyrone was away in Italy, Sheila would stay at Claremore, and see what, if anything, she could do for Cassie.

'I know a thing or two about these problems, Tyrone,' she'd told him over their whiskies. 'I won't go into details now, in case I'm proved wrong. But I think I may know how to get to the bottom of this one.'

And so Tyrone left for Milan, safe in the knowledge that Cassie was in good hands. Cassie had brightened up considerably when Sheila had arrived, and the two of them had sat talking for nearly an hour. The longest coherent conversation Cassie had managed previously since coming out of hospital was about ten minutes. Sheila moved into the bedroom next door to Cassie's, where Tyrone had been sleeping, in case she needed her in the night.

Which in fact she did. The first night Tyrone was gone, Cassie suffered one of her terrifying nightmares, and Sheila found her down the end of the bed, under all the covers, screaming that she couldn't find her baby. Sheila calmed her, and got some tranquillisers into her, but Cassie couldn't get back to sleep, so the two women sat in Cassie's double bed and talked until dawn.

'I have to find my baby,' Cassie kept saying to her. 'You do know I have to find my baby.'

'Yes, Cassie,' Sheila replied, 'I do. And I agree. You must find your baby, and tomorrow we'll talk a little more about it.'

Cassie had seemed settled by that assurance, and she suddenly fell asleep. Sheila went back to her own room, and exhausted by the events of the night, she too fell into a deep sleep. She was awakened two hours later by Erin who told her that Mrs Rosse had disappeared.

At first Cassie couldn't find the farm. She had the address, because it was in her bag. But whenever she stopped someone to ask them where it was, once she was driving again, she couldn't remember what they had told her. Finally a boy hopped in the car beside her, all too anxious to get a ride, and took her right to the door.

Cassie sat in the car and stared at the farmhouse, which wasn't much bigger than Tomas' cottage. It was nowhere near as clean, however. Even Cassie could see that, Cassie thought, as she brushed some stray hair from her eyes. The front door was open, and chickens were busy wandering in and out, pecking everywhere they went in the constant quest for food. There was an old pram outside the door, rusting, but obviously in use, judging from the blanket and sheet which were carelessly tossed over the side. It'll be all right if that's the case, Cassie thought as she walked to the door. If that's how it is, then it's going to be all right.

Kathleen didn't know who it was at first as she looked up from the stove. She had her baby on her hip, and was busy cooking some chicken feed, when she looked up and saw the woman at the door.

'Yes?' she said. 'Can I help yous?'

'It's me,' the woman replied. 'Cassie Rosse. From the hospital.'

Even when she stepped into the kitchen and she was no longer silhouetted against the morning sun, Kathleen would scarcely have recognised her. Cassie looked so gaunt, and unkempt, with her usually lustrous shining hair all lifeless and unwashed. And underneath her smart blue wool coat, she was still in her slippers and long cotton nightdress.

Kathleen pulled a kitchen chair out from under the table and offered it to her. Cassie smiled at her vaguely, then stared at the baby which was still on Kathleen's hip.

'I'll just put the nipper in his pram,' she said. 'There's tea in the pot.'

She disappeared outside and Cassie sat at the table. But she didn't help herself to any tea. That wasn't what Cassie had come for.

Kathleen came back in, pushing back her hair, and peeling off her apron. She sat down opposite Cassie and poured herself some dark strong tea.

'That's the sort of tea Tomas likes,' Cassie informed her. 'Or rather "tay" as he calls it.'

'Is that right now?' replied Kathleen, wishing her husband was home. He'd know what to do. 'And who's Tomas?'

'Tomas is Tomas,' Cassie said. 'He delivered my Prince. How are you?'

'Jeeze I'm fine, Mrs Rosse, just fine. A little surprised to see yous all the way out here. But no, I'm great.'

'Tomas is my husband's head lad, and please. You

must call me Cassie. If we're still to be friends.'

'Cassie. Right yous are, Cassie.'

Kathleen sipped her tea and watched Cassie as Cassie slowly looked around the room. She'd begged her husband to put a telephone in, but he was too blasted mean. If ever there was a time she needed a telephone, this was surely it.

'Where's Sean?' Cassie suddenly asked.

'Sean's got the croup, Cassie,' Kathleen answered. 'So I left him be in bed.'

The girl offered Cassie a cigarette, forgetting that Cassie didn't smoke. But Cassie took one, and Kathleen lit it for her, and then lit her own. Cassie sat there puffing at the cigarette, while staring at the ceiling. Kathleen, feeling more and more frightened, prattled conversation at her, talking about anything and everything. Finally she fell to silence, disconcerted by Cassie's remoteness.

'I think I should explain,' Cassie suddenly said, out of the blue. 'I think perhaps I should explain why I'm here. You see, I'm here, because I have to find my baby.'

Kathleen stared at her blankly. Cassie looked back at her.

'You don't understand, Kathleen, do you? If you remember, I lost my baby. And I must find it again. Now I remember that you had a baby.'

Kathleen nodded, and relit a fresh Woodbine from her nearly finished one.

'Of course I had a baby. You've just seen him, Cassie. That was my baby I put in the pram there.'

Cassie opened her purse, as if Kathleen hadn't even spoken, and took out her wallet. Then she closed her purse again and put it on the table. She held up her nearly smoked cigarette.

'Where shall I put this?' she asked.

Kathleen took it from her and stubbed it out in her saucer.

'You did say, if I remember, Kathleen, in the hospital,' Cassie continued, 'that you didn't want your baby.'

'Well now, I might have done,' Kathleen replied, wondering whether she should make a run for the door and take her baby with her. Then she remembered Sean sleeping in his room upstairs.

'Yes,' she said nodding and drawing on her cigarette, 'yes, I might well have done. But then hospitals are funny places, aren't they now? And besides, I hadn't had the baby then.'

Cassie looked up sharply.

'You haven't changed your mind, I hope, Kathleen?'

'Changed me mind about what, Cassie?'

'About not wanting your baby.'

Kathleen didn't reply. She knew instinctively that this was a time to keep silent, or at worst, not to say anything that might annoy or upset this crazy woman who was sitting across the table from her.

'OK,' Cassie said. 'Then if you haven't changed your mind, I'll have it. I'll have your baby.'

'But it isn't yours, Cassie. I thought you said you were trying to find your baby.'

'I don't think I'm going to be able to, Kathleen. But if you don't want yours, and I have it, then your baby could be mine, you see. I'd have your baby and it would be mine.'

'Yes,' Kathleen nodded slowly. 'Yes, I see.'

Cassie opened her wallet.

'So how much do you want for it, Kathleen? I can give you a hundred and fifty pounds.'

Kathleen saw a way out.

'That's nowhere near enough, Cassie,' she said. 'I want a thousand.'

'A thousand,' Cassie repeated thoughtfully.

'No – no, two thousand,' Kathleen announced. 'My baby's very dear to me, you see, even though I didn't want him in hospital. So it'll cost you two thousand pounds, Cassie!'

Cassie sat nodding slowly and repeating the new sum of money over and over again. Then she rose and smiled so tenderly at Kathleen, that if she wasn't so frightened, Kathleen could have cried.

'Thank you, Kathleen,' Cassie said, doing up her coat over her nightgown. 'I'm so glad I met you in hospital. You're such a dear girl. And I'm so glad we can help each other. Thank you. Two thousand pounds. I'll go home and get the money now.'

Kathleen watched her speechlessly as she turned and walked out of the kitchen. Then she jumped up after her, remembering her baby.

Sure enough, Cassie was bent over his pram as Kathleen ran outside. She wasn't stealing him. She was just stroking his head and smiling at him.

'There we are,' she was saying. 'Mummy won't be long now. She'll be back in a minute. As soon as she's got the money, you'll see. You just wait there and be a good boy now, Michael.'

Doctor Gilbert was all for sending Cassie to a clinic in Bray, what with Tyrone away in Italy.

'I'm not sure otherwise how I can be responsible for his wife's mental health,' he told Lady Meath.

Cassie was lying upstairs in her bed, heavily sedated. She had driven safely all the way back to Claremore and, when everyone had returned from their initial fruitless search, Erin had found her in Tyrone's study, on the telephone, trying to locate Mrs Von Wagner.

'I have to find her, Erin,' she explained, 'because she's got so much money, she's the only one who can help me buy my baby.'

Sheila Meath saw Doctor Gilbert's point of view, but persuaded him to stay his hand. After all, she reasoned, she'd been making great headway with Cassie in at least getting her to talk, and except for the unfortunate but finally harmless incident with Kathleen O'Donnell, there had been no real harm done. Doctor Gilbert agreed, once Sheila Meath assured him she would be entirely responsible.

She waited a day before she even brought the subject up once more with Cassie; who, having slept for nearly twenty-four hours as a result of the sedating injection, seemed in much brighter spirits.

'Do you feel well enough to get up, Cassie?' Sheila asked her. 'You must be getting sick and tired of this room.'

Cassie looked round it, and instinctively pulled the sheet up tighter under her chin.

'Don't if you don't want to. But it's such a lovely day, I thought we could stroll across to the yard.'

'Why?'

'Look, dear, don't if you don't want to. I'll go by myself.'

Perhaps it was the thought of seeing the yard again, or perhaps it was just the kindness in Sheila Meath's voice. But whatever, Cassie found herself getting out of bed once more, but this time taking great care to get dressed. They then strolled very slowly with Brian bounding good-humouredly beside them, through the now culti-vated gardens and down the track to the yard.

Tomas greeted her as if he'd seen her every day instead of not for nearly three months, and then escorted Lady Meath round the boxes. Tomas told Cassie how well Prince was doing, and she said she'd drive down and see him tomorrow. Tomas and Sheila Meath exchanged a hopeful look between them, and then it was decided it was time to stroll back to the house.

'I lost a child, you know,' Sheila told Cassie as they paused by a large fish pond Tyrone had dug himself. 'I was about your age, and rather like yourself, the child was stillborn.'

Cassie looked at Sheila as if she'd been hit in the face. For a moment Sheila wondered about her shock tactics, as Cassie's eyes seemed to flash first in anguish then in rage. But Cassie remained silent, instead just turning away again to throw food to the fish.

'I also had a breakdown,' Sheila continued. 'In fact I

384

took to my bed for the best part of a year.'

Cassie threw the last of the food to the fish, then started to walk back towards the house, ahead of her friend.

'Then an old chum from Trinity came to stay,' Sheila said, having caught Cassie up. 'She was a doctor, specialising in this sort of problem. Particularly with the loss of babies.'

Cassie stopped dead, and Sheila could see her painfully thin body beginning to shake. She wanted to take the girl in her arms, and hold her, and comfort her. But she knew if she did, her last chance would go. So she resisted the temptation, and continued.

'The problem was,' she said, 'and still is, in allowing the hospital to bury the child. It seems the right thing to do, but it's not. And by not burying a child we have lost, we deprive ourselves of the proper mourning process. Which in turn leads to this sort of breakdown. So she got me out of my bed, and we found where the hospital had buried my baby, and she made me give it a proper funeral, and that was that. I mourned the child naturally, and I regained my sanity. Which is why you're right in what you're saying. You must find your baby. And you must then bury it accordingly.'

For minutes, Cassie stood staring away from Sheila, out into the skies above her and beyond. She put a hand to her lips, and just stood there, looking at the universe. Then she turned to her friend and adviser and, putting her arms round Sheila's waist, buried her head on her shoulder and held on as tight as she possibly could.

They had to wait until Tyrone was back, of course, both to get the necessary permissions ratified by both parents and, more importantly, because Sheila Meath told Cassie that Tyrone too must mourn. On the day of the funeral, Cassie was unable to get out of bed. Tyrone and Sheila sat and talked to her for two hours, until they got her up and dressed her, in a simple black dress and a hat with a veil. Tyrone drove them to the church where, in the company of Tomas, his wife, daughter and Sheila Meath, Father Patrick held a service in memory of a life that never was. The tiny coffin, with a simple wreath of pure white flowers, stood on a trestle in front of Cassie and Tyrone. Tyrone couldn't look at it, nor for a long while could Cassie. Then having prayed to God for the strength, she lifted up her head and made herself look; and as she did so, she took Tyrone's hand. Tyrone's face was streaked with tears and his body was shaking with the sobs he could hardly contain. Cassie grasped his hand even more firmly and Tyrone, at last, but only because of Cassie's great courage, also lifted up his head and looked at their dead son's coffin.

They laid him to rest in the graveyard of the village church which nestled in the shelter of the blue-green hills beyond. As Father Patrick wished him eternal rest, a single bell tolled in the church behind them, and a lark gave song high above their heads.

By a coincidence, on the day Tyrone and Cassie buried their baby son Michael Joseph McGann Rosse, a man unknown to them personally, but known to all the world, was also burying his infant boy. He too was deeply affected by the loss of his son Patrick Bouvier, so much so that he had to be restrained by Cardinal Cushing, who was presiding over the funeral mass, and reminded that God was good. Three months later, on 22 November, the same man was shot and murdered while driving in a Presidential motorcade through Dallas; and Cassie and Tyrone sublimated their personal sorrow and joined in a world grieving for the loss of its prodigal son.

Chapter Fifteen

Claremore
1966

It was at Leonora's annual pre-Derby dinner and dance that the idea of an adoption was first mooted. Cassie, one of the last to arrive, as usual, thanks to Tyrone's appalling sense of social punctuality, was standing in the enormous marbled hall while Tyrone, again from custom, closely scrutinised the 'placement' for dinner, which was always left on display for the illumination of Leonora's guests.

'Jesus God,' Tyrone groaned, 'she's really done you this time. You're between not only the two biggest bores in Ireland, but probably in the whole bloody universe.'

Tyrone immediately altered Cassie's placement so that she would be seated between two far more entertaining and attractive gentlemen, and then asked Leonora's butler to go and alter the place cards in the dining room. The butler was only too pleased to do so, since Tyrone was often in the habit of tipping him off about the stables' 'certainties'.

Leonora seized Tyrone and whisked him away from Cassie the moment they stepped in the drawing room. Cassie took a glass of champagne and looked carefully for someone to whom she could talk. She was well used to Leonora commandeering Tyrone on these occasions and, by not letting it bother her, Leonora was the one who became increasingly infuriated.

Very soon Cassie was in conversation with a circle of people, all of whom were well known to her, with the exception of a tall, intellectual-looking Frenchman, who had broken off his conversation to stare at her.

'Allow me to introduce myself,' he said, leaving the woman he was talking to and coming over to Cassie. 'Jean-Luc de Vendrer.'

'Cassie Rosse.'

'Enchanté.'

The Frenchman fetched them both fresh glasses of champagne from a passing footman, and handed Cassie her glass.

'Beware what you say about the wine,' he warned her.

'Why?' Cassie asked, sipping some more. 'It's very good.'

'I know. I made it.'

He nodded seriously at Cassie, who looked up at him. He had a very high forehead, accentuated by the recession of his hair, and a very bright, interested eye. Cassie found herself smiling.

'Something about me amuses you?'

'I'm sorry. That was very rude. It's just – well, I guess I see too many horses. I was looking at what we call your finer points.'

'And how did I rate? Would I fetch a high price at the sales?'

'Do you know about horses then?' Cassie asked, deflecting the direct flirtation.

'Nothing at all,' de Vendrer replied. 'But if I am to be a horse, then I do not wish to be *bon marché*.'

Cassie frowned at him, forgetful of her French.

'Cheap,' he translated. '*Et puis.* What would you like to talk of? Myself, I find there are only two subjects worth the discussion. Women and love, and not necessarily in that order.'

He shook a Gitanes from a packet and lit it. As he did, Cassie laughed.

'Not bad for openers.'

'Pardon me?'

'Most people start in with the small talk. But not the French.'

'You know a lot about the French, Mrs Rosse?'

'About as much as you do, I guess, about horses, Monsieur de Vendrer.'

De Vendrer drew on his cigarette thoughtfully and stared at her.

'Perhaps you would prefer to talk about your children,' he said.

'Why did you say that?' Cassie asked, looking down into her glass.

'Oh, every American woman *loves* to tell you about her children! Do you have children?'

'No,' said Cassie, 'I don't. Not at parties.'

'*Ah bon*,' said de Vendrer, smiling. 'Perhaps at last France and America may have an *entente cordiale*.'

Cassie smiled back at the implacable Frenchman, who was watching her closely. He was definitely most attractive, and sophisticated. But there was something about him, something in this initial meeting which Cassie couldn't quite define.

As he walked her in to dinner, Cassie identified the portraits about which de Vendrer enquired. She knew them all off by heart now from her many visits to Derry Na Loch, so much so that she felt like a guide as she identified the splendid paintings of beautiful women in their carefully arranged clothes, posing with their backs against trees while their grooms held their horses; or surrounded by adoring-looking knee-breeched husbands and children; or sitting in a garden under a parasol with their lap dogs; or posing somewhere in their houses dressed in their finest ballgown and jewels. And none of them had anything to do with Leonora Von Wagner or her husband whatsoever.

But Cassie gave Leonora her due. She had bought Derry Na Loch lock, stock and barrel. Nothing in the grand house had belonged to her previously, and yet she had made it all now somehow look a part of her; most probably, Cassie thought, because wherever Leonora roamed, and however much she complained about Ireland and its terrible climate, she always came back to

389

the beautiful white mansion that was Derry Na Loch, because it was her home. Cassie would have been quite happy had it been otherwise, because since Leonora's arrival in their lives she had without much apparent difficulty relegated Cassie to the role of the 'wife', the chattel, the person who got pregnant, and often the person who stayed at home, while Leonora had very often and quite successfully promoted herself to the woman seen socially most often by Tyrone Rosse's side.

Happily this was no longer a cause for jealous worry in Cassie, because since the loss of their child, and the poignancy of their mutual grief, Cassie knew that Tyrone and she loved each other more than even life itself. The strength of their love was there to be felt by them both, more, much more than could ever be put into words. While they mourned their dead baby, they grew ever closer together, so much so that often their two identities would merge into one. Tyrone could be the other side of the world and Cassie would know when he was thinking of her, and what.

He had once telephoned her from America, in the middle of her afternoon, and at the break of his day.

'I can see you,' he'd said. 'I suddenly saw you in my mind. You're sitting in our bed, in that peach silk nightshirt. And you're reading a book of poems, thinking of me.'

She had been. And she hadn't been surprised by his call.

At dinner, Tyrone had reseated her between Dan Kelly, a painter and set designer whom Tyrone knew Cassie adored for his droll humour, and his sudden mad streak; and, on the other side, Seamus O'Connor, an old friend of Tyrone's who had started life as a sports commentator and was now one of the biggest and most popular figures on British television. Cassie loved Seamus as well, because, contrary to his public image as a man of straw, he was in fact a very kind and deeply concerned man.

390

As they ate their first two courses in the magnificent candle-lit dining room, with over a hundred guests dining at five large round tables, Cassie spent her time delightfully between the two men, as they gossiped and joked, and teased one another. Then as they were eating pudding, and Dan turned to his right to flirt outrageously with the wife of the Irish Ambassador, Seamus asked Cassie how she was.

'Do you mean am I over it?' she enquired lightly.

'I do not,' Seamus told her. 'It's not something you'll ever get "over". But we have a responsibility to life itself, you know. To our own lives. To live them fully, whatever tragedies may befall us. Otherwise I'd say we're wasting that precious gift of life itself. We have to learn to live with what happens to us. To pass through the experience and live with it. It mustn't overshadow the rest of our lives.'

'I think Tyrone and I have come to terms with it now,' Cassie answered carefully. 'We haven't buried it away. We talk about it now and then, and the more we do, the less it seems to hurt.'

Seamus nodded and drank some wine.

'What about more children?'

'Well now,' Cassie replied, putting down her fork, 'that's not so good. Something went wrong somewhere along the line during the Caesarian, at least that's the theory. Scar tissue in the womb maybe. Anyway, I don't seem to be able to conceive.'

'Have you thought of adopting?'

'No. I mean, yes, of course we have, but no. We really want to go on trying to have a child of our own.'

'That's perfectly understandable, Cassie, but if I may make so bold. First, supposing you can't conceive? You're wasting all the time you could be giving some child a wonderful home and family. And second, as is often the case, people adopt a child, and something happens. God knows what. Anyway, whatever it is, once they've adopted, they find they can conceive again. It's happened to three friends of ours.'

Seeing the look in her eyes, Seamus tactfully changed the subject. 'That's enough of that,' he said. 'Tell me what's going to win tomorrow.'

The conversation opened out to the chances of various fancied horses in the big race the next day, but Cassie gradually slid out of her involvement in it and looked around the vast room instead. She wanted to remember it all, exactly as it was at that moment, because although it didn't seem possible, one day in the not so distant future everything here could be gone. The sense of permanence which seemed to pervade the rooms and the inhabitants could well vanish overnight, leaving future visitors to wander through the once magnificent house and wonder how it had all actually been on nights such as this.

But they would never be able to imagine it, because they would have nothing in their minds with which to compare such splendour. They wouldn't be able to see how the flickering candles in the vast silver candlebra sent waves of warm light scudding across the table to reflect themselves in the women's jewels; and how their colour in turn seemed to reflect in the heavy crystal glasses, until the whole room seemed to be a cavern alight, permanently aglow.

Nor would they be able to imagine the stiffness of the liveried footmen's backs, and the white and gold of the porcelain off which the hundred guests dined; nor hear the strains of music from an orchestra playing unseen in another room throughout the dinner; nor see the waves of tail-coated gentlemen rising and sitting as the ladies left the room, the formality of their evening dress giving distinction to even the most ordinary of the faces.

As she danced with Tyrone after dinner, Cassie remembered too for all time the tune of the Strauss waltz and the rustle of her golden dress as Tyrone danced her across the ballroom. She remembered that the windows

392

were open on to the gardens, and the terrace outside looked cream-coloured in the bright clear moonlight. She knew as they danced that for most of the people circling around her this night was a night like many others; like last night, or tomorrow night, an everyday night, part of the social routine. They wouldn't be looking round them, trying to capture and hold the moment fast. Some of them were probably bored tonight; some were probably bored every night. But for Cassie, dancing featherlight in Tyrone's strong arms, every scent and sound was etched on her mind, to be remembered at will. A place from long ago. A place filled with everything you know.

As they drove back in Tyrone's month-old Aston Martin, it was almost dawn, and the Derby runners would already be awake in their boxes, kicking the doors for food or stamping the ground for attention.

'I think we should adopt a baby,' Cassie said as they turned up the drive to Claremore.

'Great,' answered Tyrone. 'Just what I was thinking.'

Sodium won the Derby, and the following Monday Tyrone and Cassie went to see the Adoption Society. It was decided that their cause was a proper one and a worthy one, and if Cassie's medical reports confirmed her history, they would be placed on the list of suitable parents. On the way home, Tyrone was very silent and thoughtful, so much so that Cassie was afraid he might have changed his mind.

'No, Cassie McGann,' he replied, 'you should know me better than that by now. I'm just not sure about this process of adoption at all. No, no. No, that's a lie. I'm an impatient man, and when I've made my mind up about something I don't like being told I might well have to wait a year. Or more.'

'I don't see the alternative, Mr Rosse,' Cassie ventured.

'Neither do I,' he agreed, scratching his head. 'But I'll find one.'

He did, too. Cassie met her one evening when she came back from visiting her now three-year-old colt, who was now in training with one of Tyrone's friendly rivals in Kildare. Tyrone had hooted with laughter when Cassie finally confessed to him what she had done a year after Celebration was foaled, but when he went and was introduced to Cassie's foal, and saw what a strapping youngster he was, he told her at once that she must put the horse in training for the next season. Cassie was thrilled, until Tyrone announced that he would not have him in his yard, because he wished to stay married to Cassie and, if she remembered, he had refused ever to let Cassie be 'one of his damn owners'.

So with perfectly good grace he advised her to send her colt to Willie Moore, since he was the second-best young trainer in Ireland. Which is where Cassie had been the afternoon she returned to Claremore and met the mother of her next child.

Antoinette was a tall, handsome English girl, possibly, so Cassie thought, not yet twenty-one. She was extremely nervous, constantly tossing back her mane of long dark hair and twisting a small white lace-edged handkerchief between her long elegant fingers. She was very well dressed in the traditional upper middle class English fashion, which flatters a pretty young woman by dressing her in slightly too severe clothes, deliberately designed to look a little too old for the wearer, who consequently looks younger. Thus Antoinette was wearing a pleated blue linen skirt, a crisp but plain white blouse, flat shoes and a dark blue cardigan draped around her shoulders. Tyrone was sitting talking to her on the window seat, a tray of tea in front of them, doing his best to put the girl at her ease. He rose and introduced Cassie to Antoinette, then poured Cassie her first cup and them a second cup of tea.

'Antoinette's been over here working for Alec Secker,' Tyrone informed Cassie as she pulled up a chair. 'You remember Alec. Head of Irish Bloodstock Incorporated.'

'Actually I've really been working more for Mr Secker's son Gerald,' Antoinette volunteered. 'He's learning the business, and I was attached to him as a sort of dogsbody.'

Cassie knew the son well enough, too. A dashing, devil-may-care young man, with thick curly hair, and a famous seat on a horse. They'd attended his twenty-first birthday only the summer before, where his father, to celebrate his son's six successes in his first proper point-to-point season, had given him a retired steeplechaser which Tyrone had been instructed to find.

The three of them had tea and indulged in small talk, Cassie having no idea at all of the purpose of the girl's visit. Tyrone gave no clue to Cassie either, and it wasn't until after the girl had left to drive herself back into Dublin and Cassie and Tyrone were having dinner that the mystery was solved.

'Well?' said Tyrone.

'Well what?' Cassie replied.

'Well, what did you think of her?'

'What am I meant to think of her? What is this, Tyrone? Some sort of audition for your new mistress?'

'I haven't had an old mistress, Cassie, so I can hardly have a new one.

'You had an old mistress before you met me.'

'What did you think of the girl?' Tyrone repeated emphatically, positively demanding an answer to his question.

'She seemed a little nervous,' Cassie replied.

'Did you think she was pretty?'

'This is some sort of audition.'

'All right,' Tyrone agreed, 'it is. But not for what you think. She's a pretty girl and, when she's not shaking with fright, a very nice bright one, too.'

'I could understand this if this was years later and she was a possible fiancée for a son of ours,' Cassie said. 'But I don't get what or why I'm meant to be approving right now.'

Tyrone got up and cut himself some more cold meat from the sideboard.

'She's pregnant,' he told Cassie with his back to her.

'Not by you, I hope,' Cassie replied.

'I'm not joking, Cassie McGann,' Tyrone said, sitting back down. 'The silly young thing fell for Gerald's charm, of course, and now she's gone and got herself pregnant.'

'Gerald must have had something to do with it,' Cassie answered with a straight face.

'Will you please take this seriously? You don't seem to understand. The girl is nearly four months gone.'

'Well?'

'Yes. Well. She says we can have her baby.'

Cassie looked down the table at Tyrone, who was sitting there staring back at her, his knife and fork resting on the table beside his plate. At first she didn't know what to say, but then she thought that rather than get herself confused or excited, she'd just take it slowly and calmly.

'Well?' Tyrone was asking her again even more impatiently.

'OK,' Cassie argued. 'So why doesn't she want the baby?'

'Cassie – you saw what age she was! She's a slip of a thing!'

'She's older than I was when I met you.'

'The point is her father will kill her. Alec told me all about it, because the girl's been crying on Maureen's shoulder for the last six weeks. She was practically suicidal.'

'Surely her parents will find out anyway?'

'Not necessarily. They're abroad. Her father's in the Army. And he doesn't get posted back to England until January. Antoinette's meant to stay over here for a year. Till March.'

'How do you know once you've had it you won't want to keep it?' Cassie asked the girl quite cold-bloodedly when they took proceedings one stage further.

'I can't, Mrs Rosse,' the girl replied. 'I mean even if one wanted to.'

'It can all be done perfectly legally,' Tyrone said. 'Antoinette will be twenty-one in September, and the baby's not due till the end of November. The adoption will be legalised through an English court, and there's very little chance of anybody even remotely connected with this young lady here ever hearing a thing about it. Besides she'll be a major by then.'

'Sorry?' Antoinette enquired.

'You'll have achieved your majority, and can legally allow the adoption.'

'She can have the baby here,' Cassie said to Tyrone, after she'd been into Josephine's room to read her a story and tuck her up. 'She should have it here. If we're to adopt it. Then we can always say to the child, when it's grown, that it was born here. That it really is part of the fabric of Claremore.'

'Great,' Tyrone replied. 'Very sound. In fact she'll have to stop working soon, so she can come and stay here and help out. And old Alec, if anyone asks, can say I'm helping with her equine education.'

'One thing occurs to me, Ty. One rather important thing. It's never been discussed – least not in my presence – why she and Gerald don't want to get married.'

'We don't love each other, Mrs Rosse,' the girl told her. 'And anyway, you see, there's somebody else in England, in Hampshire.'

Cassie stared at the girl. It was all so alien to her. The girl had slept with Gerald and got pregnant by him, although they weren't in love, and although she had someone else whom she did love back in England.

'Didn't you take any precautions?' Cassie enquired.

'Yes. But – well. You know what Ireland's like. I don't think I can have had enough left of the sort of . . . well, of the cream really.'

Cassie suddenly felt old. And out of touch. Being tucked away in Ireland, in the folds of its luxuriant countryside, it was easy to forget that they were now living in an age the papers had christened the Swinging Sixties, and that promiscuity was all the rage. This was the age of the Rolling Stones and cannabis, of Hair and the mini-skirt; of the Trial of Lady Chatterley, of Unisex clothing, of Mandy Rice-Davies and Christine Keeler – an end to censorship and a time when people had never had it so good. As a result, there were a lot of excited but bewildered people who wanted to jump on the bandwagon, even though they were unsure as to whether they genuinely liked the music the band was playing.

And here was one result sitting on the sofa in front of her, still pulling and twisting at that same small lace handkerchief, pregnant with an unwanted and unintended child, the result of an act carelessly undertaken quite possibly because everyone else she knew was carelessly undertaking the self-same act with exactly the same lack of good reason.

'What would you have done had Mr Rosse not found out and offered to take your child?' Cassie asked her.

'I don't know, Mrs Rosse,' the girl replied truthfully. 'But I'd have had to do something.'

Cassie felt sorry for her, yet at the same time was irritated by her reply. Why, when there were so many people who wanted to have babies but couldn't, people like herself who would love them and give them good homes, and bring the children up properly, why was life so unfair that the most unsuitable people got pregnant? Girls who didn't want children, girls who didn't mean to have children, girls who would rather abort them, girls who would rather give their children away, girls who didn't know, who hadn't thought.

Nevertheless, the mother of Tyrone and Cassie's child-to-be moved into Claremore for the final weeks of her pregnancy and helped Mrs Byrne in the racing office efficiently and with quiet good humour.

Cassie was in the office one Monday morning, looking

at the week's entries, when she noticed that Value Guide, a potentially useful three-year-old of Leonora's, was entered in three races, one of them the same maiden for which she and Willie Moore had been preparing Celebration. Celebration had finally not run at all as a two-year-old, because Willie, though thinking highly of the young horse, considered him too big for his own strength, so had put him away until he was three. He was still backward at the beginning of the current season, so they hadn't given him his first race until July, when he ran very encouragingly at Phoenix Park, finishing a close-up sixth of fourteen. He ran again a month later and improved two places, and Willie declared he was at last coming to hand, and if they could find the right race, he should win.

They'd finally settled for what looked like being a moderately contested maiden at Gowran Park, only to find that Leonora's impeccably bred Value Guide was still in at the four day declarations.

As Cassie was looking at the other races for which Leonora's horse had been entered that week, to try and guess the likelihood of them both chasing the same prize, Tyrone came in from the yard. Cassie asked him what the chances were of Value Guide running against Celebration, and Tyrone said he didn't even know that the horse had been entered at Gowran.

'He's much more likely to run at Navan on Wednesday,' he told Cassie. 'Least that's where I've been aiming him.'

But it rained north of Dublin from midday: so much so that the going was reported heavy on Tuesday by the Clerk of the Course when Tyrone rang. He had no alternative but to take Value Guide, who didn't act on the heavy, out of the race, and leave him in at Gowran and Leopardstown. The race on Saturday at Leopardstown, however, was very hot, too hot for the novice Value Guide who was still a maiden. And so it was that Cassie's Celebration came to take on Leonora's much fancied horse in a £352 maiden race down at Gowran Park.

'If he were mine,' Tyrone said to Cassie as they drove south to the races, 'I'd have taken him out and waited till the Curragh next week. And if it had been any other owner, they'd have listened and done as I advised. But Leonora wasn't having any. She insisted on the horse running. And I wonder why.'

Tyrone grinned at her, then flicked the Aston up through the gears as they hit a straight stretch of road to see if he could, as he was wont to say, get her off the clock. They'd reached 125mph before Cassie cried enough.

'Couldn't we wait to kill ourselves until after the race?' she yelled over the roar of the engine. 'I quite fancy my horse's chances!'

The afternoon had turned fine and sunny by the time they arrived at the course and the official going was good. Cassie rushed off to find Willie Moore, because the three-year-old maiden was the second race on the card, and the horses would already be in the pre-parade ring. Tyrone always loved to cut things fine.

Celebration looked a picture. Even in the pre-parade ring he was dancing around on his toes, and snorting with what Cassie hoped was excitement. Leonora's horse, in direct contrast, looked half asleep. He was a big sort, dark brown, with a thin white blaze, and huge quarters. Like all the Claremore horses, he was turned out to perfection. The rest of the opposition looked moderate; and this was reflected in the betting. Value Guide was on offer at 6/4 against, Celebration 2/1, and it was 8/1 bar. Cassie stood by as Willie saddled him up in his box. The young horse always did a 'jelly', as it was called, as soon as he was put in to be saddled. He stood quaking and shaking, with his eyes rolling round his head, and his flanks heaving. But as soon as his number cloth was on and his mouth and bit had been given a squirt from the sponge, he calmed right down and walked out into the parade ring like a seasoned performer.

400

Dermot Pryce was riding for Willie Moore, and Tyrone had put up Dirk Norton, a young Australian who was fast making a name for himself in his first season in Ireland. In fact it was Leonora who insisted that Norton should ride, because not everyone, Tyrone included, altogether approved of the young man's racing tactics. There was no doubt as the two jockeys were legged up that the Rosse horses were the pick of the paddock. Celebration was right on his toes, and beautifully behaved, while Value Guide, always a very nervy horse, reared with Norton and very nearly went over. But the Australian settled him down well before they left the paddock, and cantered down after Cassie's horse to the start.

Willie Moore and Cassie went to the rails to see what price they could get for their horse. Value Guide was now 5/4 against, and Willie managed to pick up the only 2/1 still on offer before Celebration shortened to 7/4. Cassie had her five pounds on with the Tote, forgetting as always her horse's number, and giving his name instead, then hurried to stand by her trainer in the grandstand.

'They're joint favourites now, Cassie,' he told her, scanning the boards with his race glasses. 'In fact two of the buggers have us now clear favourite.'

Cassie put her glasses up and looked to where Willie was looking. Celebration was now 5/4, and sure enough Value Guide was drifting in places to 6/4.

'I think the devils are just after late money,' Willie said and put his glasses down. 'We've no right to be favourite. And certainly not at that price. I don't think any horse has a right to be a short-price favourite in a maiden.'

Even so, it was a two-horse race from start to finish, with the favourites drawing right away from their field in the final two furlongs of the ten-furlong race. Pryce rode exactly to Willie Moore's orders, and tracked Value Guide on the rails to the furlong marker. Then he feinted as if to go through the gap Norton had deliberately left for him between his horse and the rails, but as soon as he did so, Norton moved Leonora's horse across and

401

effectively closed the gap. But Pryce had read the tactic in advance, and as Norton moved across him, he had already switched Celebration to the outside where he had always intended to make his run and kicked for home. The young horse, finding that vital extra gear which singles out the winners from the also-rans, fairly ate up the ground, and fifty yards from the post had his head in front and looked as though he was going away. Then quite suddenly, with both jockeys riding for all they were worth, and with Norton really beating his horse up, Pryce seemed to lose his rhythm, bouncing awkwardly in the plate, and as a result, Celebration changed his legs. In that vital moment Cassie's horse lost his momentary advantage, and the two animals crossed the line in what seemed like a dead heat.

'Photograph,' the course commentator announced. 'Photograph.'

While the punters rushed to take the ridiculously cramped odds on offer for the result of the photo finish, Cassie ran behind Willie, who, although he was an ex-jockey and even shorter than Cassie, was already half-way to the unsaddling enclosure.

'That was terrific, wasn't it, Willie?' she asked him anxiously as she caught him up. 'He really ran one heck of a race.'

'He did,' Willie replied. 'A race he should have won.'

'You don't think we got up?'

'We were beat a short head, as well that bastard Norton knows.'

Willie was eyeing the Australian jockey as he confidently steered Leonora's horse into the berth reserved for the winner. Pryce on the other hand was standing Celebration in no man's land, the space between the place for the first horse and the second.

'Yes?' said Willie, helping the jockey off with the saddle. 'So what did the bugger do this time?'

'He kicked me bloody foot out of the iron,' Pryce replied, grinning toothlessly at his trainer. 'Just as the post was coming up. Just as we was galloping all over them, he kicks me bloody foot out of me iron.'

'That'll teach you to try riding like Piggott,' Willie muttered. 'Do you want to object?'

'What's the point?' Pryce answered, swinging the saddle and girth over his arm. 'He'd have to admit it voluntarily, because the others were all somewhere in the next country.'

The jockey disappeared into the weighing room, while the lad led the horse round and round, waiting for the result of the photograph.

Leonora suddenly appeared at Cassie's side, and grabbed her arm. Cassie hadn't even noticed she was there until now. She was dressed as if she was at Royal Ascot, and most of the punters were staring at her rather than at the waiting horses.

'What do you think, Cassie darling?' she said. 'I reckon you won.'

'No you don't, Leonora,' Cassie replied. 'If you did, you wouldn't be speaking to me.'

Leonora found this hilarious and hooted with laughter. The she grabbed Cassie's arm again as the commentator announced they had the result of the photograph.

'Sshh!' she whispered. 'Here goes!'

'First number four, Value Guide.'

Leonora gave a great and unladylike whoop, as did several happy punters.

'And second number nine, Celebration. The third horse was number thirteen, Lecturer, and the distances were a short head and a distance.'

A short head and a distance. The shortest and the longest winning margins in racing. Leonora still had hold of Cassie and she was dragging her away from the enclosure.

'Come on, darling!' she was shouting over the noise. 'This calls for a bottle!'

'I'll join you in a minute,' Cassie answered, detaching herself from Leonora. 'I want to see Celebration put away first.'

But Leonora didn't care, nor was she listening: because

she'd just spied Tyrone coming towards them and was flying towards him, one hand on her hat, the other ready to grab Tyrone's arm. Cassie watched them go, Leonora prattling excitedly and Tyrone listening patiently, with that grave expression he always saved for garrulous owners.

Cassie smiled to herself and turned to pat and comfort her unlucky horse. Willie'd got him so fit that, even after such a hard race, he was barely blowing.

'Can't we do anything about what happened, Willie?' Cassie asked her trainer as they took their horse back to be hosed down and put away.

'Yes,' Willie replied. 'We can. We'll bury the bastard next time we meet.'

The next morning, when Willie walked him out, Celebration was lame in his off fore. A group gathered as usual round the horse, the 'Leg Committee' as Tyrone called it at Claremore, while Celebration's tendons and ligaments were carefully inspected. But there was no swelling or puffiness in the lower leg and the tendon was still sharp, to the Committee's great relief. There was, however, a little heat in the foot and the pastern, enough to suggest that the horse had jarred himself, probably as a result of having to change his legs in those few final and fateful strides. Niall Brogan, who was Willie Moore's vet as well as Tyrone's, was of the opinion that the damage was very slight and one hundred per cent curable, but preferring to be safe rather than sorry, advised roughing him off and turning him away after a couple of weeks in his box, particularly since so little of the flat season now remained. Cassie was disappointed, but not dismayed. She had learned from watching Tyrone that as far as racehorses went much valuable energy could be wasted in venting your frustrations.

As for Claremore, the season ended on a high note. Value Guide franked his form by trotting up in a valuable three-year-old handicap at the Curragh in mid-

October; and at the same meeting a colt Tyrone had bought and was training for the American tycoon Townshend Warner, whom he had met at Laurel Park on his 1962 American trip, upset the odds laid on the hot favourite in the Champion Stakes to win nicely by a length and a half. Warner had flown in specially to see his first runner in Ireland, and was so pleased at the winning result that he immediately commissioned Tyrone to buy and train him two more horses.

Tyrone had also flown to Paris for the Prix de l'Arc de Triomphe a fortnight earlier, for, although he hadn't a runner, there were two French-bred yearlings he was anxious to see. Cassie was to have accompanied him, but three days before they were due to leave Josephine developed measles, so Cassie remained behind to nurse the very sick four-year-old. Tyrone had also insisted on staying, but Cassie said there was nothing for him to do except fuss and worry, so persuaded him to fly over to France after all. On the Saturday night, Josephine's temperature shot up to 104° and she became delirious, seeing large rats and spiders all over her bed. Cassie sat up all night, changing her daughter's soaking pyjamas half a dozen times and holding her burning head while she was constantly sick. She was so ill through the night that Cassie was quite sure that she was going to die. But by dawn on Sunday the child suddenly fell into a deep and peaceful sleep, and by midday the crisis was over, her temperature having dropped to just under 100°. Cassie remained in her bedroom, sleeping fitfully throughout the day on a mattress on the floor. Tyrone telephoned constantly from Paris, although Cassie never let him know for one moment quite how ill his daughter was, or had been. By Monday, before he left the French capital to go and see the yearlings, Josephine was able to talk to him on the telephone and for his part he was able to depart in great relief.

He was due back from France on Thursday, but telephoned on Wednesday night to say he'd suddenly been offered another half a dozen horses to look at, and so he wouldn't be home again until after the weekend. Cassie, used to the vagaries of Tyrone's work, thought nothing of the delay, and returned to the nursery to finish Josephine's bedtime story.

On 30 November it became evident that Antoinette was about to give birth to her child. She had been a model mother-to-be, and she and Cassie had become close friends. The girl had revealed in full the circumstances of the conception. It had been after a wild party in Dublin where some rich idiot boy had made some hash cookies and thought it hysterically funny to hand them round to all the girls without telling them what was in them. Gerald had been smoking all evening, as had most of the boys at the party, and the last fully coherent memory Antoinette had before waking up the next morning in Gerald's bed was playing cards and taking all her clothes off. The first excuse she had given Cassie for her pregnancy about an ill-prepared contraceptive was a lie. She had been in no fit state to remember to take any precautions and neither had Gerald. Antoinette did however vaguely remember some people at the party discussing birth control, Gerald included, saying that it was wrong to use contraception, because it was against the natural order of things, and therefore impure, coming as it did between the individual and his or her search for certainty and absoluteness.

Cassie said what absolute rubbish. Unsurprisingly Antoinette agreed.

Antoinette went into labour at six o'clock in the evening, and by quarter to eight she was delivered of a son, who weighed just under eight pounds. Cassie and Erin attended the midwife, who declared that she wished all births were as easy. Antoinette in fact managed to half sit up and see her baby actually enter the world. The midwife held the baby up, gave it a good slap, cut the cord, and handed it to Erin to wash. Once this was done,

Cassie took the infant from Erin and went back to the bed.

'Here,' Cassie said, offering the girl her baby.

Antoinette looked at her and frowned.

'But why?' she asked. 'I don't understand.'

'Because you must hold it,' Cassie told her. 'You must hold your baby in your arms, or you'll never know. You'll never be sure of what you're about to do otherwise.'

Cassie placed the newborn baby gently in the girl's arms and stood back. It took all her mental strength and willpower to do so, because she knew that the chances of being able to remove the baby from the mother once it was in her arms might be very remote. But she had to make the gesture. Not only that, but Cassie herself also had to be sure.

The girl looked down at the tiny squawling baby in her arms, at her son, her firstborn, and Cassie saw her eyes fill with tears. At that moment she was sure that she had lost the child to its mother, but she made no move and showed nothing on her face of the turmoil she was feeling inside. Instead she just turned and smiled to Erin, who was standing anxiously biting her lip.

The midwife, however, was totally unaware of the drama which was being played out before her and went about her duties, prattling away about what a straightforward delivery it had been, thank God, and what a beautiful little baby he was. All the time Antoinette just looked down at her child, rocking it gently in her arms, and slipping one of her fingers into the baby's tiny hand.

'Come on with you, Erin,' the midwife announced. 'It's time for that tea you promised.'

She shut up her medical bag and smiled at Antoinette.

'We'll leave you in peace with your baby for a while,' she finished. 'Then I'll pop up and make sure everything's tidy and back in its right place before I leave.'

Erin and the midwife left, but not before Erin had cast one of her long, soulful glances back at Cassie, who remained standing by the side of the bed.

After they had gone, Antoinette looked up at Cassie and smiled. Cassie read it as the smile of maternity, and though her heart was breaking, smiled back and touched the girl on her arm. Then she turned and walked to the door.

'Sorry,' Antoinette called after her.

Cassie turned, to see the girl holding out her baby to her. She swallowed hard as she saw the tears in the young girl's eyes.

'You do still want him?' Antoinette asked.

'Yes,' Cassie replied. 'As long as *you're* quite sure.'

'I am,' the girl said, lying. 'Yes. Absolutely.'

And she handed Cassie the baby who was now to be Cassie's and Tyrone's son.

'How's the boy?' Tyrone would demand, leaping up the stairs two at a time every evening on his way to see Mattie, as the child was now named.

Cassie would follow behind laughing and Erin would be waiting as always in the nursery, holding the baby and ready with the same response.

'You can hardly expect him to have grown now since lunchtime, Mr Rosse.'

'Nonsense,' Tyrone would laugh. 'There's always something different about him! A bit of a new tooth! An even bigger smile for his Dad than he gave him at breakfast!'

'Dear Lord,' Erin then grumbled, jealous as always of the attention Mattie was taking away from 'her' Josèphine. 'Anyone would think this was the first in the nursery.'

Cassie would try to arbitrate, and make sure that nobody's feathers got too ruffled and that everyone got the same amount of love and attention, including Erin. It wasn't easy.

Tyrone would hit the roof if he found that Erin had started to bathe his son before he got home, and in reply Erin would colour deeply and start to sulk, which was

408

what she always did when she was found out in one of her little possessive practices – habits which she imagined nobody else was noticing.

'You were twenty minutes late, Mr Rosse,' she'd say. 'We can't have the baby getting tired.'

'Erin Muldoon, this is my son, and I'll tell you whether or not he's tired!' Tyrone would announce. 'Now is that understood?'

Which was where Cassie would step in, placating the glowering Erin while making pleading faces at Tyrone. Tyrone would resolutely ignore them, although quite well aware that he was skating on extremely thin ice. Then Erin would down tools and disappear to her mam below in the kitchens, from where Cassie would have to coax her back up to the nursery once more with apologies, flatteries and promises.

Even when Erin was persuaded to rejoin the bathing party upstairs, she couldn't help opening that big mouth of hers and starting it up all over again.

'You haven't dried his feet properly, Mr Rosse.'

'Be careful of the top of his little head now.'

'You can't sit him like that! Sure his poor little head'll drop off!'

'Make sure that towel's dry now, Mr Rosse. You don't want your baby catching the pneumonia.'

Sometimes things would reach such an *impasse* that Tyrone would closet Cassie in their bedroom and hiss at her that either Erin went or he did. Cassie would reason with him, since she knew full well that his son's welfare was no joking matter to Tyrone, and Tyrone would finally come off the boil and troop back along the corridor after Cassie to the nursery for storytime, which he firmly maintained was his favourite moment of the day.

Before going in for that final magical half-hour with their children, Tyrone and Cassie would both pause on the threshold of the nursery and look in, both of them still quite unable to believe their good fortune in having two beautiful children. Josephine, so dark and serious, with

409

huge almond eyes, and Mattie with a bubble of blonde curls and already the sweetest of dispositions. When Cassie and Tyrone peeped round the nursery door, Josephine would look up very seriously from whatever book she had chosen for her parents to read and smile, while Mattie would be lying gurgling in his cot, waving his little chubby arms up above him.

Tyrone would then read to them both – *Peter Rabbit* usually, or some other Beatrix Potter story. He would read the story, turning to them both as he did so, even though Mattie was barely four months old. Erin would sniff, and say that she couldn't imagine what he could be thinking of, reading a book out loud to a baby. And Tyrone would look up at her very seriously and say that she would be surprised how much babies understood, even when they were in the womb. Then he would continue to read, in that wonderful baritone voice which never failed to thrill Cassie, even though she heard it every day of her life.

While he read, Cassie would sit and sew a button back on one of Josephine's little cardigans, or put away a pile of Erin's immaculately washed and ironed diapers, reluctant for the moment when Tyrone put the book away and kissed his children goodnight. Then they would both take a last look round the nursery, which was filled with the toys, clothes and children's furniture which Tyrone had brought back for them whenever he was away for any length of time, be it a day in Dublin, or a week in America. He'd even had two little chairs handmade in London, engraved with the children's names, which he'd brought back with him for Mattie's first Christmas.

Cassie knew that he was indulging himself and his children, but at this stage of their development it didn't seem to matter, and Cassie had no wish to diminish the joy it gave him.

'Money's there to be spent, Cassie,' he'd tell her. 'There's no damn point in working this hard and earning

410

the stuff if you can't spend it and enjoy it. We only pass this way once, remember.'

Then he would scoop her up in his arms and dance her down the corridor and, if Erin wasn't snooping, into their bedroom and straight into bed.

At some times of the year it seemed to Cassie that they were never out of bed. Tyrone would come back to the house for lunch, and if he wasn't going racing, they'd have a bottle of wine and then spend the afternoon making love. If he was racing, he'd be back at the house as quickly as he could after the horsebox was back and the animals unloaded and, after pouring himself a pipe-opener, he'd carry the laughing Cassie up the stairs as if she was swansdown and drop her on the bed. She'd lie there, silently, while Tyrone stood above her, smiling, and slowly getting undressed.

When he was away abroad, Cassie would dream of these and other such moments. And sometimes when she did so, the phone beside her bed would ring, and Tyrone's voice would whisper things in her ear from far away. Cassie would smile and weakly try to make him stop, in case anyone was listening, but this always only made Tyrone even more bold so that by the time Cassie was forced to hang the telephone up on him, in fits of laughter, she felt as if he'd been there in the bed, making love to her.

She'd surprise him too. Sometimes, on their stroll back from the stables on a hot summer's day, she'd take his arm and lead him into the woods, silently, through and under the branches of beech and oak and ash. She'd take him to an old folly deep in the woodland, a place they shared with no one. And there they would make love alone except for the wild life outside.

At other times, on cold dark and damp winter evenings, they would lock the drawing-room door and make love in front of the fire. Sometimes someone would call, and while Erin was opening the front doors, there'd be a mad scramble to get back into whatever clothes they'd taken off and get the door unlocked before Erin had hung up the visitor's coat and knocked on the door. But usually they were left undisturbed, and would end their evenings sitting on the floor in front of the dying fire, talking backwards and forwards through their lives.

Cassie would make Tyrone tell her over and over again about his childhood, which to Cassie seemed totally idyllic, living as he did in this wonderful old house and being brought up in Wicklow's magical country-side. And always surrounded by animals: dogs, ponies, horses, a tame hare – once even a pet fox which Tyrone had saved from a poacher's snare. All Cassie had enjoyed in the way of animal company, until she had started staying at Mary-Jo's, were the dogs so lovingly drawn in Mr O'Reilly's book.

But while Cassie could never hear enough about Tyrone's childhood, he in turn was so appalled by Cassie's that he could hardly bear her to speak about it. Yet he knew she had to try and talk it away, so he would sit and listen, and become even more shocked as new details of her childhood surfaced. And the more he heard, the less he understood. How could anyone do such things to a child? How could anyone beat up a little girl? Why should anyone want to lock their daughter up in a room for days on end? People were meant to love not hate their children. As Cassie told him these things he would watch her, frowning uncomprehendingly.

Cassie felt envious of him. She compared their two upbringings and found herself wondering over and over again what it must have been like to reach up to a door handle and enter a room where someone waited for you with a smile, and with love in their hearts – someone who had delighted in your birth, and was glad you were alive.

'No child of mine will ever have a hand raised against it,' Tyrone had said one evening. 'No child of mine shall ever be aware of anything except the love in this house. Even when they do something wrong, they shall know that we scold them from love.'

Cassie had sighed, and looked up at him from where she lay, her head in his lap.

'Dear Ty,' she'd replied. 'I do love you. Sometimes you're so Irish.'

It was then that the telephone rang out in the hall. At moments like these, Cassie was always all for letting it ring. But Tyrone kissed her on the forehead and rose to answer it.

'Probably some damn owner,' he said, leaving the room.

He was back a moment later, telling Cassie that it was for her.

'I think it's the Principessa's old man,' he added. 'At least it sounds like Franco.'

Cassie went out to the hall, wondering what on earth Leonora's husband could want with her. She soon found out.

' 'Allo, Cassie darling,' Franco said down the phone. 'I do 'ope this is not the bad moment.'

'No, it's OK, Franco,' Cassie replied. 'What can I do for you? Is everything all right?'

'Ah. That depends what you mean by all right, Cassie.'

'Is anything wrong? With Leonora?'

'Well. I do not know 'ow to answer this. If you ask Leonora, I am sure she say everything it is all right.'

'Would you mind coming to the point, Franco? I happen to have guests.'

She said this as she was aware of Tyrone standing in the doorway, cranking her up as if she was an old wind-up gramophone. She stuck her tongue out at him, and he clasped his hand to his chest, and slithered down the doorway, as if he'd been shot.

'Oh! Forgive me! Then perhaps I should ring back when you 'ave no guests,' Franco apologised.

'I'd rather you said what was on your mind now, actually,' Cassie said. 'I mean if it's something social—'

'Nope,' Franco cut in. 'It is nothing social, Cassie. I want to know if you know something.'

'What do you want to know if I know?'

'I want you to tell me if you know your lovely 'usband is being unfaithful.'

Cassie's blood ran cold. She had never fully understood that phrase until that very moment. Now she did, as everything in her seemed to die, turning to ice. She held on to the side of the telephone table and took a deep breath.

'I don't think I can have heard you right,' she said very quietly.

'I think you can. I can tell by the silence. The very shocked silence,' Franco replied.

Cassie could just see him smiling.

'Even so,' he continued, 'I will repeat it. Your 'usband is being unfaithful. And you will not be surprised when you find out with who. With my wife. Leonora. With your friend.'

'That isn't possible,' Cassie said. 'That's just not possible.'

In the mirror in front of her she could see Tyrone standing up again and frowning at her, puzzled by the change in her tone perhaps.

'I'm afraid, dear Cassie, it is very possible. First when he go racing in Milan. Remember? That's when it started. They spent two days in the south of France together. Since then, who knows? Ask your 'usband about Paris. The Prix de l'Arc de Triomphe. Ask 'im why he no come home till one week later.'

The last sentence was hissed almost venomously down the telephone, then Franco hung up, leaving Cassie to stare uselessly at the dead receiver. She put it back slowly on its cradle, then remained standing with her back to Tyrone.

He came to her side at once, full of anxiety.

'What's the matter?' he asked. 'Has something happened?'

'That was Franco,' Cassie replied.

'I know who it was. But you look so upset,' Tyrone said. 'Has something happened to Leonora?'

414

'Why don't you ring her yourself and find out!' Cassie suddenly shouted.

Then she picked up the whole telephone and threw it at Tyrone. He was completely wrong-footed by her action and dropped half the instrument on the floor.

Cassie ran across the hall and started to flee upstairs. When she got to the landing, she stopped and screamed down at Tyrone, who was picking up the body of the telephone from the floor.

'And while you're at it, ask her how was the goddam Prix de l'Arc de Triomphe!'

And with that, she disappeared inside their bedroom and slammed the door shut behind her.

Tyrone carefully replaced the receiver back on the telephone before putting it on the hall table. He waited a moment, then dialled Leonora's number.

She answered the call herself.

'What's going on?' Tyrone asked her.

'Oh nothing much,' Leonora replied. 'Except we're getting divorced.'

Chapter Sixteen

'You were in the south of France with her!'

'Yes.'

'So you weren't in Milan!'

'I was in Milan.'

'You just said you were in the south of France with her!'

'I was also in Milan. When I said I was.'

'And what about Paris!'

'What about Paris?'

'What do you mean – what about Paris! What about Paris!'

Cassie was screaming hysterically, the black from her eye make-up streaming down her face, a handkerchief held to her mouth. Tyrone stood at the end of the bed, his hands on the carved wooden footboard, trying to calm Cassie down, trying to reduce the level of hysteria, trying to keep the dialogue rational.

'Rational! How the bloody hell can I be expected to be rational! You! You *bastard*!'

'You must try and be rational, Cassie. On the strength of what Franco told you on the telephone—'

'You've just *admitted* you were in the south of France with her! You've just admitted it, you pig!'

'I haven't admitted that I've slept with her.'

'You don't have to! Franco told me! You've been sleeping with her ever since you were meant to be in Milan—'

'I was in Milan.'

'So what's the point in admitting it! You've been sleeping with her for three bloody years!'

Cassie suddenly gasped and put her hands to her face. Tyrone, afraid for her, moved away from the end of the bed and came quickly to her side. But Cassie saw him make the move and, picking up a large book that was by her bedside, hurled it at him, catching Tyrone on the side of the head.

'Get away from me!' she screamed. 'Don't you *dare* come near me!'

And she scrabbled panic-struck across the bed, still trying to make sense of the terrible truth that was just dawning.

'What is it? What's the matter, Cassie?'

'You bastard,' she hissed. 'You cruel, thoughtless bastard.'

'What *is* it?'

'You were in Milan, you were in the south of France, while I was lying in this bed going mad! You were sleeping with that whore while I was lying here going out of my mind! When I was lying here mad! Mad from losing my baby!'

'Cassie. I have never once—'

'I'll kill you,' Cassie said, suddenly quite calmly. 'I'll kill you for that.'

Tyrone came back round to the end of the bed, while, wild-eyed, Cassie crouched up against the corner of the headboard. They watched each other in silence.

'When you're ready to talk sensibly,' Tyrone said.

'I'll kill you.'

'When you're ready to talk sensibly. And listen.'

'I will. I'll kill you.'

Tyrone breathed in deeply, then turned his back and walked to the large window. He'd make one more effort to try and get her to see sense, and if he still failed he'd ring Dr Gilbert and they'd have to get some Valium into her. Once she was calm, he knew he could get her to see sense.

By this time, Cassie had slid open her bedside drawer and silently pulled out her large pair of sewing scissors.

417

Tyrone heard nothing until the very last moment, when he was suddenly aware of something or somebody hurtling through the air. He turned and saw Cassie practically on top of him and caught the glint of the silver scissors in her hand. He put up both his hands to protect himself and to grab Cassie as she flew at him. His right hand caught the hand with the scissors, but not before they were deeply embedded in the top of his left arm. Tyrone roared with the sudden pain as the instrument tore into his flesh, and before he could even think of how much it was going to hurt him, he wrenched the scissors out and clasped his right hand to the wound.

Cassie stood in front of him, frozen with horror. Between Tyrone's long, slender fingers, dark red blood was oozing out, staining his torn white shirt. Tyrone's head was back and he was moaning with pain. Cassie sobbed once, and sank slowly to her knees, stuffing the knuckles of her fist into her mouth. Then, moaning and rocking backwards and forwards on her knees, she put both her arms around Tyrone's legs, and hugged herself to them.

Tyrone discharged himself from the hospital after he had been stitched up, having telephoned Tomas to come and collect him. Tomas drove him home, as fast as he dare, with Tyrone urging him on.

'I daren't now,' Tomas said. 'Not with the state you're in. Not with your arm slung up like that.'

'For Christ's sake do as you're told for once, Tomas!' Tyrone roared. 'I'm stuffed full of God knows what and I can't feel a thing!'

It wasn't true. They'd given him a shot of morphine, but that was three hours ago, and the effects were beginning to wear off. But Tyrone was so anxious to get back to Cassie's side that he couldn't have cared if his whole arm had fallen off.

'Faster, you silly ass!' he exhorted Tomas. 'And get over your own side of the road just for once!'

When they got back to Claremore, Doctor Gilbert was in the drawing room and at the whisky. Tyrone poured himself a large one, in direct contradiction to the old doctor's advice. He drained it in one and then made to go upstairs.

'She's asleep, Tyrone Rosse,' Dr Gilbert informed him. 'And she'd best be left sleeping.'

'I have to get this straightened out, Doc,' Tyrone told him.

'You'll get nothing straightened out until morning. The sedative I've given her'd lay out one of your horses.'

Tyrone glared at him, but from frustration, not anger. He poured himself another whisky, then went to the door and bellowed for Tomas, who was down in the kitchens.

'What's all this about anyway?' Doctor Gilbert enquired, hand-rolling himself a smoke.

'My wife thinks I'm being unfaithful to her,' Tyrone replied, finishing his second whisky.

'Indeed,' the old man nodded. 'And are you?'

'Christ, I'd cut out the heart from every one of my horses before I'd even *look* at another woman, Doc!' Tyrone cried, then sank to the sofa.

'That's what I thought,' Doctor Gilbert concluded, as he struck a match for his cigarette.

Tomas appeared at the door and Tyrone pulled himself to his feet.

'You're to take me to Derry Na Loch, Tomas,' he ordered, 'this minute.'

Behind him, safely out of sight, Dr Gilbert slowly shook his head. Tyrone drained his glass, and pulling his tweed jacket around him, made for the door. He was nearly as far as Tomas when he blacked out.

'You were in the south of France with her though.'

'I was in the south of France with her.'

'Why were you in the south of France with her?'

'I was in the south of France with her and several others. If you remember the horse won—'

419

'I don't remember.'

'Well it did, Cassie. Soyaze, Terry Colebourne's good horse, yes? It won the big race, and as a result of the ensuing celebration, we missed our plane. Leonora *and* Franco were at the race, and she persuaded us all – that's Kim Shaughnessy, Peter Willis, Michael Prior-Parker, and myself – to return via Nice where their yacht was moored.'

'You were going to boat home?'

'One of their millionaire friends had flown down in his private plane and she promised us all a free flight back to London. There was a party on the yacht that night, and the next night, and then we flew home.'

'You stayed for two parties.'

'I had no alternative. I had to wait for the millionaire to leave.'

'Why didn't you tell me?'

'You were far too ill. Anyway, what was there to tell? That I was bored silly, and only wanted to get back to you?'

'Why did you go in the first place? You could have got another flight home.'

'I was legless. I got legless every chance I had. Ever since we lost the boy.'

Cassie fell silent. She was sitting propped up in bed, pale but calm. Tyrone took her hand. This time Cassie let him keep holding it.

'How do I know what you say is true?' she asked.

'Easy,' Tyrone replied. 'Because I've told you so.'

'What about Paris?'

'Paris was just as I said. Leonora came for the Arc, and we had dinner at her hotel afterwards. She was as determined as always to get me into her bed, and I was as determined as always not to let her.'

'You mean you had to make a conscious effort not to sleep with her?'

Her eyes suddenly flashed dangerously as Cassie turned to look at Tyrone.

'Cassie McGann,' Tyrone laughed. 'Show me a man worth the name who doesn't have to make a conscious effort not to go to bed with a beautiful woman when she asks him? It doesn't mean he wants to go to bed with the woman. But it does mean he has to make a conscious decision between saying yes or no.'

'And you've always said no.'

'You know I can't stand the woman.'

'Then why do you let her treat you like – like . . .'

'Cassie. She has sixteen horses in training with me. Sixteen. Nearly half my yard. The least I can do is smile at her. Laugh at her jokes. Dance with her.'

Cassie spread her hands out in front of her on the bed, and looked down at them. She adjusted her wedding band and looked at the light dancing in the diamond of her engagement ring.

'Have you ever kissed Leonora?'

'Yes.'

'When?' she asked, looking up at him. 'And how often?'

'On her yacht. Rather she kissed me. The night of the second party. We were dancing, and I was pretty drunk. And she kissed me.'

'And you let her.'

'Yes.'

Tyrone stroked the side of his face, and Cassie could hear stubble rasp against his fingers.

'Some people say that kissing is more intimate than actually going to bed with someone.'

'It isn't. Not with Leonora. She kisses you as if she's been very well coached.'

Cassie suddenly smiled. That's exactly the way Leonora would kiss you. As if a kissing coach had taught her the best and most effective way. Just like her tennis game.

'But you didn't go to bed with her,' she puzzled.

'No.'

'Even though I was a couple of thousand miles away. Lying here and pretty crazy.'

421

'Yes.'

'Why not?'

'Because I didn't bloody want to, Cassie McGann! It's you I love, dammit!'

'But yet you kissed her.'

'Yes.'

'Why?'

'Jesus, why do you think! Because I was pretty damn crazy too!'

Cassie put both her hands up to his face and kept them there. Tyrone looked down into her eyes, then bent over and kissed her. Cassie wrapped her arms round his neck and gently pulled him down on to the bed, where they lay for what seemed like hours wrapped in each other's arms.

'What I don't understand,' Cassie said to Tyrone over lunch the next day, 'is why Franco, as they say, fingered you.'

Tyrone stopped eating and glanced across the table. He shook his head.

'I don't think you'd want to know, really.'

'Try me.'

'Franco doesn't like me.'

'Sure. But why?'

Tyrone took a long time before answering, then, putting down his knife and fork, he pushed his plate to one side and lit a cigar.

'You remember Tony?' he asked Cassie. 'The good-looking Cork lad who was in the stables a few seasons ago? A very nice and talented youngster. Could have gone right to the top.'

'He wasn't here very long,' Cassie recalled.

'No. Franco saw to that.'

Cassie frowned and stopped peeling her apple. 'I don't understand.'

'Franco took a fancy to him. Set him up in a very nice flat in Baggot Street. Bought him some expensive clothes, took him abroad, introduced him to a lot of very rich people. But while Franco could have lots of – how shall we say – lots of friendships, Tony had to wait in for Franco. One day, he didn't. A man he'd met on Franco's and Leonora's yacht was in Dublin and started taking Tony around. Franco came back from abroad, heard about it, and that was that.'

'What was what, Tyrone?'

'I was in Jammet's one night. Tony came out of the back bar. I didn't recognise him at first. But he saw me and made a dive for the door. I caught him outside, and we went and had a quiet jar in Davy Byrnes. He looked as if he'd been in a road accident. But he hadn't.'

'Franco?'

'Friends of Franco. They beat him up, taking particular care to break both his hands. So even if he'd wanted to get back with horses—'

Tyrone paused and blew some cigar smoke to the ceiling.

'What did you do? You must have done something to Franco for Franco to hate you.'

Tyrone grinned. 'You remember how pretty Franco was?'

'Well – right. Until he broke his nose.'

'No,' Tyrone replied. 'Until I broke his nose.'

After that, Cassie never gave Franco's accusations another thought. She had known Tyrone was telling the truth from the first moment he had come into the bedroom and stood at the bottom of the bed to protest his innocence. He was so utterly honest that Cassie suddenly knew he was incapable of deception. When Tyrone announced he was telling the truth, that truth literally shone from his eyes.

And as events proved, it was as well that Cassie trusted and believed so much in Tyrone, as it emerged that Franco, about to be sued for divorce by Leonora, was calling up all Leonora's girlfriends and insinuating that their husbands or lovers had been having affairs with his wife. In some cases it was probably true, but his accusations were so indiscriminate that it became a running joke in Dublin society. Anyone who was anyone was rumoured to have been found at some time or other in Leonora's bed, and even anyone who wasn't anyone. Bishops and cardinals were reported to have been seen joining the queue outside Leonora's bedroom door; and certain of the racing fraternity, when asked to dinner at Derry Na Loch, would turn up with their pyjama jackets on under their dinner jackets, with a razor and toothbrush clearly visible in their breast pocket.

Franco, realising he had become a laughing stock, fled back to Mamma in Italy, as Leonora prepared her divorce case. She, on the other hand, had a mountain of very real evidence, as she was at pains to tell Cassie and Tyrone.

'OK,' she sighed. 'The waiters, the actors, fine. Those I could turn a blind eye to. Even the hairdressers and the stable boys. But when I came back early from the States once, and found this but I mean enormous bricklayer sleeping in my bed, in my best satin sheets, I reckoned enough was enough.'

She had hooted with that derisive laugh of hers and made as light of these incidents as she could. But Cassie noticed that she was beginning to drink more heavily, and despite her ritualistic self-induced vomiting after every meal, was also beginning to gain weight. Tyrone later expressed the opinion that he felt sorry for her, and Cassie concurred. It was terrible, they agreed, that someone who had been given everything should be quite so utterly miserable.

But then Leonora disappeared out of their lives, as she did every winter, taking herself off to St Moritz, Rome and finally New York before returning to Ireland in the spring. Tyrone was usually vociferous in his relief once Leonora was gone and the telephone stopped ringing at all the wrong hours, but this year Cassie and he were so busy and enthralled with the new addition to their family, and with making all the preparations necessary for his legal adoption, that neither of them really noticed Leonora's annual departure from their shores.

The adoption procedures were made more complicated by the fact that Antoinette had British nationality, Tyrone had Irish, and Cassie American, although she had applied to become a naturalised Irish citizen. They could only therefore apply in the English courts for the grant of a provisional adoption order, which would enable them to keep Mattie in Ireland while they then applied to the Irish courts for a full adoption order. Luckily, Seamus O'Connor was familiar both with the Irish legal system as far as non-native adoptions went and with several of the top lawyers who advised in such cases, so with his and his lawyers' help and direction Cassie and Tyrone's path was made considerably smoother. At the end of March they flew to London to attend a High Court hearing, which, as is the custom, was held *in camera*, with only the Rosses' solicitor and the social worker, who had been detailed to make sure that Claremore was a suitable home for an adoption, present in front of the judge. Antoinette was absent, as was perfectly permissible, but had granted her full consent in writing. Gerald Secker's consent, since he was not legally regarded as a parent, was not needed. The judge read the social worker's report on Tyrone and Cassie as potential parents, and Claremore as a potentially good adoptive home. He then asked the prospective parents to give their own accounts of their reason for wanting to adopt Mattie, carefully considering their answers before turning to Cassie's medical report. Seamus O'Connor had warned them that there was a possibility that Cassie's breakdown after losing her second child could work in their disfavour, and had advised an independent psychiatrist's report, which happily declared Cassie to be 100 per cent mentally stable and an ideal adoptive parent. Under the circumstances, the judge declared that he had no hesitation whatsoever in granting them a provisional order.

To celebrate, Tyrone took Cassie to lunch at the Caprice. But they were both far too elated and excited to eat, and were only really marking time until they could board their flight back to Dublin. On their return, their Dublin lawyers informed them that, anticipating such a good result, the application was ready for submission to the Irish courts, and if all went as well here as it had across the water, they could expect finalisation by September at the latest. Tyrone protested that this was just not good enough. If the English courts had been able to grant him an adoption order in three months, then why not his native law courts? He rang Seamus O'Connor at once, and Seamus promised to see what he could do.

Even so, because of the advice they received, Cassie and Tyrone quietly fancied their chances on being granted the final and full adoption order.

Tyrone also quietly fancied Cassie's horse in his second run of the new season, which was a competitive stakes to be run at Leopardstown the second week of May. Celebration had already run a copybook race first time out at Thurles, lying up with the pace until the lack of a previous outing showed in the way he tied up in the last half furlong, to finish fourth, six lengths off the winner. It was a good enough run, however, to make sure he started favourite at Leopardstown, particularly since he had pulled up completely sound after his first outing, indicating that the injury sustained in his race against Value Guide had healed totally.

But although everything came good for the horse – his preparation and even the weather itself, with the rain easing the day before and a good drying wind making the going good to soft, just as Celebration liked it – the race itself unfortunately did not go to plan. Dermot Pryce had the horse lying second approaching the final turn into the straight and the horse in front of him was beaten. The jockey was already seriously at work and his horse was visibly tiring, rolling away from the rails and leaving

Pryce just the gap he wanted. Pryce took a quick look over his right shoulder and saw that the rest of the field were also hard at work just to keep in the contest, and from the feel Celebration was giving him, he knew he had the race sewn up.

The next thing he knew he was on the ground.

He was on the ground and rolling himself up into a ball as the other horses galloped over and round him. One hefty kick in the back knocked all the wind out of him, and another hoof landed right on his knee. He stayed absolutely still on the ground until he was quite sure the last horse had galloped by, and then he gingerly started to try and sit up, wondering what had happened.

Which was when he saw the horse lying dead on the other side of the broken running rails.

From the stands Cassie and Willie could see quite clearly what had happened. As Pryce had slipped Celebration through on the rails turning into the straight, Tim McGrath's horse Caunoge, who had been leading, but was quite obviously already beat, suddenly nosedived to the left right in front of the accelerating Celebration and crashed through the rails. Pryce had snatched Celebration up in time to miss a full-scale collision, but Celebration had braked, then swerved so violently that Pryce had no chance of staying aboard and had shot out the side door and was thrown into the path of the oncoming field. He was lucky to escape serious injury, and so too was Cassie's horse, who galloped home with the reins tangled around his forelegs. Caunoge, on the other hand, must have been dead before he even hit the rails, killed, it later transpired, by a massive coronary.

Celebration's lad caught him some way past the post and led him back to his owner and trainer, who were anxiously awaiting both him and the ambulance bringing Dermot Pryce back. Pryce was despatched at once to the hospital for an X-ray; Celebration, other than being badly shaken up, was fortunately none the worse for wear.

Willie took Cassie to the bar for a stiff drink. At a table in

427

one corner Cassie spied Sheila Meath, who was just getting up to go to the bar to fetch more drinks for herself and the woman she was with.

'That was desperately bad luck, Cassie,' she said as they waited their turn. 'Celebration would have trotted up.'

'I'm sorry about Caunoge, Lady Meath,' Willie said. 'Can I buy you a drink?'

'Thanks, Willie,' Lady Meath replied, 'but I'm looking after poor Joyce O'Sullevan. She's devastated.'

'Of course, you bred Caunoge, Sheila, didn't you?' Cassie remembered.

'I did indeed, which is hard enough,' came the reply. 'But that gorgeous horse, he was the love of poor Joyce's life.'

The barman set Sheila Meath's drinks on the bar before her, for which Willie insisted on paying. Cassie glanced at the woman in the corner who was sitting white-faced and very upright, smoking a cigarette.

'He was a lovely horse, too,' Willie told Cassie. 'Though Tim told me he'd a dodgy ticker. Apparently he'd been spun by two vets before Mrs O'Sullevan bought him.'

'But he'd won a fair amount of races, Willie,' Cassie argued. 'Besides running fourth in last year's Irish Derby.'

' 'Tis a funny thing about thoroughbreds, Cassie,' Willie replied, after downing his whisky. 'You'd be amazed how many of them have something wrong with their hearts. Ailments which'd have you or me six feet under. Yet it often makes them a better horse for it. That is,' he added, 'until the day they drop stone dead under you.'

Tyrone had missed the race, as one of Leonora's two-year-old hot-shots had bolted on the gallops and broken a leg trying to jump a ditch. Tyrone had stayed for two hours with the young horse until Niall Brogan arrived to shoot it, so by the time Cassie returned and told him her news, they were both in fairly reflective moods.

'You'll still win next time out, don't worry, Cass,' Tyrone assured her as he poured them another drink. 'That was a good field he had strung out behind him, make no mistake.'

'Sure,' Cassie replied. 'It's not him getting beat that's bringing me down. I just can't get the look on Joyce O'Sullevan's face out of my mind.'

'No,' Tyrone said, coming back to sit down next to her. 'I just wish I'd a few owners like her. She's the stuff of racing. Here's to her. There are few like her. And most of those that are, are dead.'

They drank a silent toast. And then Tyrone, having glanced at the clock, suddenly jumped to his feet.

'My God, Cassie McGann!' he announced. 'We're missing the children's bath time!'

Claremore was planning its biggest raid ever on Royal Ascot. Altogether Tyrone was intent on sending eight runners. He had a double handful in the Cork and Orrery, with Stagmount, one of Leonora's new purchases, and Annagh Bridge, whom Tyrone had bought on behalf of Townshend Warner. It seemed, from the price on offer in the pre-race betting, that Annagh Bridge was home and hosed. Claremore's other two hotly fancied raiders were a horse called Turnispigody owned in partnership by four doctors and well fancied for the Ribblesdale, and Value Guide, which had been trained and entered especially for the Hardwicke Stakes.

Value Guide had done nothing wrong since he first set foot on a race-course that season, winning all his three races in a manner which suggested he had improved out of all proportion over the winter. Tyrone had adopted a new winter routine for his outstanding horses, sending them over to the more temperate climate of middle Italy, rather than turning them out for a few hours daily to stand in the Wicklow rains. It had certainly worked wonders with Value Guide, who returned looking well and contented, and came to hand much more readily than he had the previous season.

Willie Moore had just the one runner entered at the hugely prestigious meeting, namely Celebration, who, none the worse for wear after his near-accident at Leopardstown, was popping out of his skin and ready to run a big race. Tyrone made no apologies to Cassie for taking her on again with Leonora's champion, and Cassie in return looked for none. She was eager to do battle once more, to prove that Value Guide's victory over her beloved bay at Gowran Park had not been a true result. Dermot Pryce had recovered completely from his fall; except oddly enough he was found now to be deaf in one ear, although there was no sign of him having been kicked on the head in the accident. Dermot put it down to years of being ear-wigged by 'the Guv'nor'.

By the last day of the Royal Ascot meeting, the Friday, when the Hardwicke Stakes is run, Tyrone had notched up four winners and was carrying all before him. Both Annagh Bridge and Turnispigody had duly obliged, the former at 4/7 and the latter at 6/1. Townshend Warner's other runner at the meeting, who was not greatly fancied either by the stable or the owner, won the Coventry Stakes in a photo-finish at 25/1, and Leonora won the Waterford with Easy Does It, a very expensive horse Tyrone had thought he had paid far too much for on her behalf at Keeneland.

So with Value Guide quoted in advance at even money for the Hardwicke, Princess Leonora Hochfeiler stood every chance of her horses pulling off a notable double, while Tyrone's place at the top of the trainers' table was already assured.

On Thursday evening Cassie and Tyrone dined early and were in bed by ten. Tyrone had to be up at dawn and Cassie wanted to be on the racecourse when Willie Moore pulled Celebration out of his box first thing to make sure everything was all right with her horse. She barely slept at all, while Tyrone hardly stirred once

430

throughout the night. Even when Cassie put on her light at three o'clock, to read through the runners and their form for the hundredth time, Tyrone never moved. Cassie finally fell into her only patch of deep sleep some time after half past four, with the consequence that she missed Tyrone slipping quietly out of bed one hour later.

By the time he woke her, he was shaved and dressed. Cassie cursed him good-naturedly.

'Why in hell didn't you wake me?' she asked, struggling into her slacks and jumper. 'You knew I had to get up.'

'And you know how I always hate waking you,' Tyrone smiled back. 'You look so pretty when you're asleep.'

Cassie rushed to the window to see what the weather was like.

'It's raining!' she exclaimed happily.

'It is,' answered Tyrone. 'Just the job for your fellow.'

They had already pulled Celebration out of his box when Cassie arrived. She only had to take one look at her trainer's face to know something was wrong.

'He's given his old head a bang,' Willie told her. 'Nothing to worry about, but he must have given it a knock in the night.'

Celebration's lad was holding a cold water compress to the horse's eye, so Cassie couldn't yet ascertain the damage. Celebration was standing perfectly still while the compress was being applied and Willie ran his hand expertly up and down the horse's legs.

'There's no sign of any other knock, thank God,' he said. 'But something must have frightened him, because he's got a very nasty cut just over his right eye.'

Willie told the lad to leave off the compress, while he showed Cassie the cut. The bleeding had been staunched, but Willie told her that the cut was going to need stitching; but she was not to worry because the vet was on his way. Cassie waited until he had arrived and sutured the wound, rather than return to the house where they were

431

staying and come back after breakfast, as Willie had suggested. If it was bad news, she wanted to know straight away.

'I'm afraid it is bad news, Mrs Rosse,' the vet informed her. 'Your horse is blind in his right eye.'

'You mean permanently blind?' Cassie asked, as her legs seemed to turn to jelly.

'That I couldn't say,' said the vet. 'All I can tell you now, is that at this moment, he can't see a thing out of this eye.'

To demonstrate, the vet moved his hand sharply up to the horse's blind eye, and Celebration didn't move. He did the same to his good eye, and the horse at once threw his head up.

'He must have banged an optical nerve. It's a not uncommon occurrence.'

'Will he be able to race this afternoon?'

'That, Mrs Rosse, can only be answered by your trainer.'

The surgeon excused himself with a doff of his old brown hat, then moved along the row of boxes to attend to a much sicker animal, whom it was rumoured had been 'got at' during the night.

'Maybe that's what frightened him,' Willie said. 'Maybe there were strangers in the yard.'

Willie's lad was instructed to get the horse ready for his early morning exercise, while it was determined whether or not to race him. Dermot Pryce arrived and was told the news.

'Christ,' he grinned, 'We're a right old pair. Me half deaf and the poor old horse half blind. I'd better carry a white stick instead of me whip.'

'Can he race, do you reckon, Willie?' Cassie asked as they watched Dermot hop up on him and start walking the horse round.

'If it had been his left eye, Cassie,' Willie answered, 'I'd have said there wasn't a problem. Ascot's a right-handed track and he'd at least have been able to follow the rail round with his one good eye. But with the poor old fellow's right eye out of commission, we'll have to rethink the whole race entirely.'

They watched Pryce give Celebration a canter, and were moderately encouraged by the result. The horse seemed to run in a true line, although of course Pryce had been instructed not to try turning him right in case the animal panicked. One thing, however, was patently clear to anyone watching: the horse was fighting fit.

Over black coffee laced with brandy, drunk in Willie's unbelievably untidy old Jaguar, Cassie, her jockey and her trainer examined the problem from every angle.

'I'm all for pulling him out,' Willie said. 'He's a cracking good horse, and if the eye's only temporary, he'll come out and win again for you.'

Cassie agreed and was on the point of pulling her horse out, when a voice spoke up from behind her.

'He could do a leg next time, guv'nor,' Pryce said. 'Or drop down dead. You're forever tellin' us all there's no such thing as a next time in racing. That it's the race you're in that counts. And not only that, I've never known the horse so fit.'

Willie fell to silence and poured himself some more coffee.

'Right,' he said. 'We're on. But – and make sure you've your good ear turned this way, Dermot – you're going to have to ride an entirely different sort of race.'

'I'm all ears,' Pryce replied. 'Even me bad one.'

They agreed to tell no one of the incident, not even Tyrone.

'Particularly Tyrone,' Willie reiterated. 'If he finds out, he'll stitch us.'

'He's my husband!' Cassie protested.

'He'll still stitch us,' answered Willie, 'and all the more so.'

Nevertheless, rumours flew around the course that all wasn't well with Willie Moore's runner. Willie saddled him up last, and led him late into the paddock, so that his eye would get as little a public airing as possible. Fortunately, horses always parade clockwise round the ring, so, it being the right eye which was damaged, at least nobody on the rails could get a close view. Willie had skilfully trimmed the gut on the stitches right back, and applied a good coat of Vaseline and brown shoe polish to the wound, with the result that someone would have to know what they were looking for to spot anything wrong at a distance other than close. And Celebration behaved himself perfectly, not fussing, or wheeling round or swinging his head at all. To all intents and purposes he looked a worthy second favourite – which he had been in the pre-race lists. But now he was drifting ominously in the betting, as the word got stronger and stronger that all was not well with the horse.

'That doesn't mean he still won't trot up,' Willie hissed at Cassie as he checked the horse's girths. 'As long as Dermot here has heard what I've told him—'

'Just put the champagne on ice, guv'nor,' Dermot grinned down at them from atop the big bay horse. ' 'Cos if we don't win, we'll only have yourself to blame.'

Pryce avoided slipping the horse in behind one of the outsiders, a French challenger who was kicking out at everyone and everything in sight, and elected to follow Value Guide out of the paddock – which gave Cassie and Willie a chance to see the horses together for the first time since the previous season.

'He looks to have done better than ours,' Willie muttered. 'Will you look at that neck on him?'

'But he's always been a big sort,' Cassie countered. 'You said exactly the same thing down at Gowran.'

'I did. And didn't we get beat?'

'No we didn't, Willie. And you know it. Now stop being such a Jeremiah and let's go and watch our horse bury the favourite.'

But Cassie's optimism was only skin deep. Even on the way down to the start, Value Guide looked as if he could win if he ran the race backwards. The big horse was taking such a hold with Dirk Norton, who as usual had the ride, that by the time the field was under the starter's order Leonora's horse had shortened to 2/1 on, while Listen Willya, the second favourite, could be backed at shades of 3/1 against. Celebration had drifted right out to 8/1.

On her way to the grandstand, Tyrone caught her up and kissed her, knocking her hat back on her head.

'Good luck, Cassie McGann!' he called as he hurried on to catch up with Leonora and her party. 'Even if you win, I'll still love you!'

He disappeared into the crowd, leaving Cassie to straighten her hat.

Willie appeared at Cassie's side in the portion of the stand reserved for owners and trainers, bright red in the face. He was holding a clutch of bookmaker's tickets which he stuffed in his top pocket.

'He's at eights all over the shop!' he told her. 'One stupid ejeet has him at ten, and we'll never get that price about him again!'

He handed Cassie a single ticket, with the name Honest Joe Brady.

'In case you haven't had a bet,' he told her. 'Christ he'd better win now, or be tomorrow I'll have nowhere to live!'

Cassie didn't have the time to ask him how much he'd had on for her as the course commentator called the field off.

It was a good-size field of fourteen runners, and as Cassie trained her race glasses on the runners she could see that the French outsider Histoire was determined to earn his fare over by setting a blistering gallop. By the time the field reached Swinley Bottom, the pace was starting to tell, and the runners were beginning to get stretched out. But as they turned right out of the back straight, Histoire was off the bridle and falling back quickly, the lead now being taken by Tonan, the

Mahmouds' son's horse Chirador, which to Cassie's way of thinking was the horse both hers and Leonora's had to beat. Listen Willya was not at the races and was already tailed off at the back of the field. Meeting the rising ground, Chirador's jockey, hugging the rails, kicked on, and opened up a gap of two to three lengths between him and the second horse Scales of Justice who was having to be pushed along to keep in touch. Then third and fourth and making up ground fast were Value Guide, going exceptionally well, and Celebration, right on his tail, but apparently beginning to hang away from the rails.

As they turned into the straight, the bell rang as it always does at Ascot, and the race was suddenly on in earnest. The run-in at Ascot is barely over two and a half furlongs, so for a horse to have a chance in a true-run race, as Tyrone had repeatedly told Cassie on the journey over, it is vital for it to be in the first half dozen as the field swings for home.

Value Guide and Celebration both were.

Then Celebration suddenly swung very wide on the final part of the turn, coming right away from Value Guide, behind whom Pryce had carefully tucked Cassie's horse so that he'd have something to follow since he couldn't see the rails. As Norton pulled Value Guide off the rails in order to attack Chirador in line in front of him, Celebration for the first time in the race must suddenly have become aware of his blind eye, and as a result started to wander across towards the middle of the course, losing a good three or four lengths in the process.

Willie swore under his breath and took a deep breath.

'He's got nothing to run against now!' he shouted over the noise of the crowd to Cassie. 'Our only hope was to track Norton and take him on the rails, so as the horse could see him with his good eye!'

Now, with less than two furlongs to go, Celebration, with the leading three horses all on his blind side, apparently had nothing to race against, and began to idle. Norton, on the other hand, forced his way through on the rails and kicked for home, as Scales of Justice tired, and now had only Chirador in front and to the left of him. Scales of Justice, under heavy pressure from his rider, also began to wander, and as he did, Pryce saw his chance of saving the day. He took a pull at Celebration and in a couple of strides switched Cassie's horse to the right of Scales of Justice.

Now Celebration could see a horse and had something to race against. Pryce sat down and started to ride a finish. Celebration, as soon as he could sight the horse on his left, picked up and began to gallop in earnest. So too, ominously, did Scales of Justice again, whose jockey, having pulled his whip through to his left hand and managed to straighten the horse out, was now producing a magnificent rally.

All four horses were now flying and locked together in a line of four, with Norton, his whip in his right hand, hitting his horse on every stride. But Chirador was the first to crack, dropping away beaten at the furlong pole. Celebration now became the meat in the sandwich as Value Guide, under the merciless beating he was getting from Norton, began to hang badly away from the rails, as the gallant but tiring Scales of Justice began to lean in to his right. Norton made no attempt to pull his whip through into his left and straighten his horse up for fear of losing a vital moment of impetus, so with one horse bumping Celebration and the other leaning in on him, Pryce himself had no room to give his horse the one reminder he thought Celebration might need to get home.

So instead he could only ride the horse out to the best of his ability with his hands and heels, kicking and pumping, driving and urging the horse on until Celebration, responding to Pryce's inspired riding, found that extra something that distinguishes great horses from the simply good, and stuck his half-blind head out, forcing his way up between the two horses who were closing in on him ever tighter on either side.

'Photograph,' the commentator called. 'Photograph.'

'They seem to like havin' their picture took, these two,' Willie said, as he and Cassie fought their way through the buzzing crowds.

'What do you think?' Cassie asked him anxiously.

'What do I think?' Willie replied. 'What I think at times like this is that me mother was right and I should have gone into the Church.'

Leonora passed them by ashen-faced – and without a word. Tyrone hung back and took Cassie aside.

'A head, I'd say,' he informed her. 'Not even a short head. And if I'm wrong, which I'm not, you'll win it in the Steward's Room.'

Tyrone was right on both counts. Celebration won the race by a head and a neck, and there was also a steward's enquiry.

Surprisingly, there was also an objection, lodged by Norton against Pryce for bumping and boring and taking his ground. Unsurprisingly, Norton's objection was quickly overruled, and he lost his deposit. The result of the enquiry took a little bit longer to be announced. When it finally was, the racegoers learned that Norton had himself been found guilty of bumping and boring, and of excessive use of the whip. For the latter offence he was fined £25, and spat at by certain angry punters who saw the angry weals on Value Guide's quarters when the horse was led in after the race. For his appalling race riding, Norton was later suspended for two weeks.

Tyrone looked everywhere for Cassie and finally found her walking her beloved horse around to cool him off down by the stables.

'Look at the two of you,' he said. 'Isn't that the prettiest sight in the world?'

'Isn't this the bravest boy in the world?' Cassie replied, stroking Celebration's neck. 'You didn't know he'd lost the sight in his right eye last night, did you?'

'No I didn't,' Tyrone confessed. 'The rumour was he'd been cast in his box and had jarred himself up. Talking of which, I've a bottle or two on ice in Leonora's private box.'

'I'm not going to drink the boy's health in Leonora's company, thank you,' Cassie replied, handing her horse over to his lad.

'You won't have to,' Tyrone grinned. 'She left straight after the race in high dudgeon. She waded in a little too deep for her liking on Value Guide, I'm afraid.'

'And what about you?' Cassie enquired.

'Oh I had a good touch as well,' Tyrone confessed, nodding. 'On yours.'

While they were drinking champagne in Leonora's almost deserted box, overlooking a fast emptying racecourse, Cassie suddenly remembered her bookmaker's ticket. Willie Moore, who was celebrating with them, told her not to get anxious because he'd collect her winnings for her the following day, the first day of the Heath Meeting. For once in his life, the lugubrious Willie Moore was actually smiling from ear to ear, so Cassie knew he'd been serious when he said he'd had a tilt at the ring.

'Aren't you going to give us even a rough idea of what you took off the bookies?' Cassie pressed him.

'For you, because it's you, maybe,' he replied. 'Just don't tell the missus or she'll be after wanting a new dress or something daft.'

'So how much was it?'

'All told, Mrs Rosse,' Willie said, closing his eyes blissfully, 'all told that grand horse of yours has won us over twenty thousand pounds.'

Cassie stared at him, but Willie just laughed.

'You have to be kidding.'

'I am not. Between us we've picked up twenty grand. And that's not counting the prize money.'

'Oh. Sure. That's what you mean by "us". I'd forgotten the prize money.'

439

'That's not what I mean by us. By that I mean I also put a hundred pounds on him for you.'

He turned her betting slip over, and there on the back the sum £100 at 10/1 was written.

'Why, Willie?' Cassie asked him. 'After what happened last evening, how could you be that confident?'

'Listen, Cassie,' he replied, refilling their glasses. 'That horse of yours, if he'd lost the sight in the both of his eyes, he'd have won even farther. That's the sort of horse he is, God love him.'

He raised his glass. Cassie touched it with her own. 'To Celebration,' she said.

Tyrone came across and joined them.

'Well done again, Willie,' he said. 'It couldn't have happened to a more committed trainer. Nor to a more compassionate owner.'

He smiled at Cassie, and kissed her, then raised his own glass.

'And that's the toast I'd like to propose. To the three things that matter most in this life. Compassion. Commitment. And Celebration.'

As they lay talking, back in their own bed on Sunday morning, Cassie turned to Tyrone and laid her head on his chest.

'Can I ask you something, Ty?' she said.

'Supposing I said no?' he laughed. 'You'd still ask me.'

'I know. I just like to have your permission.'

'My permission is granted.'

He stroked her hair, which Cassie had grown till by now it fell round her shoulders.

'You know what you said about the three things in life? Compassion, commitment, and celebration?'

'I do.'

'Well. What with my horse winning, and you being the top trainer, and having Josephine and Mattie, and each other . . .'

'Yes, woman? Come to the point.'

'I think it's high time we celebrated. Do you realise we've never had a party? I've never had a party.'

Tyrone turned her round so that he could look at her.

'You've never had a party?'

Cassie shook her head.

'You must have had a birthday party.'

'Never.'

'Jesus God!' he said, leaping out of bed. 'Then I will throw you the greatest damned party ever!'

And he did. For Cassie's twenty-seventh birthday, which fell on 20 July, Tyrone, with Cassie's calm approval, invited nearly five hundred guests. Three marquees were erected on the lawns and the nursery paddock which ran down one side of the house, and everyone was instructed to wear white – all except Cassie, who was expressly forbidden by Tyrone even to think about what she might wear. He told her she would find out just before the party.

She found out something else just before the party, too. At the beginning of the week, Seamus O'Connor called them to tell them that he'd managed to get the adoption hearing brought forward, and could they present themselves in court that Thursday. Tyrone and Cassie couldn't believe their luck, but Seamus quickly dampened their enthusiasm by telling them the presiding judge was not wholly sympathetic to cases such as theirs, with a split nationality parenthood. It was, he agreed, a quite unreasonable bias, but the mitigating circumstance, besides the glowing report the supervising officer had prepared on them as potential adoptive parents, was the fact that Cassie had applied for Irish nationality. On the other hand, if they wanted to wait for a more sympathetic judge, then they could take the other date which had been offered to them in September.

Cassie was all for waiting, but Tyrone would have none of it.

'We're to be judged for what we are, Cassie,' he said.

441

'For the sort of people we are. For the kind of parents we are. Not for the colour of our damned passports.'

And so it was with a certain amount of trepidation that Cassie sat in the chambers with their lawyers, the supervising probation officer and the stern-faced Judge Kenneally.

The judge read the report out loud to them, making all the good points which the officer had made about them sound like criticisms. He then turned to Tyrone.

'You're a racehorse trainer I see, Mr Rosse.'

'I am, your honour.'

'Are you a gambling man?'

'Only where horses are concerned, sir.'

'Isn't racing a rather suspect activity?'

'Only where dishonest humans are concerned it is.'

'Is it a proper world in which to bring up a child, would you say?'

'No, sir.'

'Then why are you applying to adopt this child?'

'Because I intend to bring this child up in my home, your honour. In my house. Not in my stableyard. Nor on the racetrack.'

The judge looked over his glasses for several seconds at Tyrone, then turned his attention to Cassie.

'Mrs Rosse. You have one healthy daughter, you unfortunately lost a son, and at present you are unable to conceive another child. Am I correct?'

'Yes, your honour.'

'I gather though that you once tried to buy someone's child.'

Cassie looked at Tyrone, who took her hand and nodded for her to answer the question.

'How did you know that, sir?'

'Please just answer my question, Mrs Rosse.'

'Yes. Yes, sir, I did once offer to buy the child of someone I mistakenly believed didn't want her baby.'

The judge nodded and made a note.

'I was not very well at the time.'

442

'You were suffering a severe nervous breakdown, I gather.'

'That is quite correct, sir. I was. It was immediately following the loss of our son.'

'Your mental health since this incident.'

The judge looked over his glasses at her, making the statement into a question.

'Perfectly fine, sir. I believe you have two independent reports in front of you which will underwrite my mental stability.'

'I have.'

The judge opened them and flicked through them.

'But oddly enough,' he said, closing the folders, 'neither make mention of the time you made a murderous attack on your husband with, I gather, a pair of scissors.'

Cassie fell silent.

'Do they, Mrs Rosse?'

'No, sir.'

'I wonder why.'

'Because that was my fault, your honour,' Tyrone interrupted. 'My wife thought I was being unfaithful.'

'So I understand.'

The judge removed his glasses to wipe them carefully with a spotless white handkerchief, before looking slowly up at Tyrone.

'But of course you were not.'

'No, sir. I was not.'

'Do you have many such violent misunderstandings, Mrs Rosse?'

'That is the only misunderstanding we have ever had, your honour.'

'I see. You believed your husband when he told you he was not being unfaithful.'

Again a statement, not a question.

'Yes, I did.'

'Why?'

'Because my husband never lies to me.'

443

'Ah. Rather like George Washington, I suppose. He is quite incapable of telling falsehoods.'

'I am perfectly capable of lying like the rest of us, your honour,' Tyrone announced. 'But not to my wife.'

'Good. I was beginning to think you might be a little bit too much of a paragon, Mr Rosse.'

The judge smiled, but not very warmly, then turned back to Cassie.

'You are an American, Mrs Rosse, but have applied to become an Irish citizen.'

'Yes, sir.'

'I wonder why that is now.'

'Because I intend to spend the rest of my life here.'

'It's not because your parents were perhaps Irish?'

He paused and looked at her, tapping his pencil on the desk in front of him. Cassie bit her lip and looked at Tyrone.

'Well, Mrs Rosse?'

'It's not because my parents were Irish.'

'What were your parents?'

Cassie swallowed then looked up.

'My father was a theatrical producer, and my mother was once a singer and an actress. Before she gave birth to me.'

'And were you ever an actress?'

'I'm sorry,' said Tyrone, his eyes beginning to flash dangerously, 'but I fail to see what relevance this has to our suitability as adoptive parents, your honour.'

'It has every relevance, Mr Rosse,' the judge replied. 'I am considering the sort of backgrounds you have both come from, in an attempt to assess what kind of characters you may be. In which case, you would do well to control your temper. Now then, Mrs Rosse, you were going to tell me the sort of career you were pursuing when you met and married Mr Rosse.'

'I was training to be a fashion buyer in Bergdorf Goodmans in New York, sir.'

'That is a department store, I take it.'

'Yes, sir.'

'You were working as a shop girl.'

'I was training to be a buyer, your honour.'

'In which department were you working?'

Tyrone was on his feet.

'Your honour—'

'Not another objection, Mr Rosse?'

He stared up at Tyrone, who for once bit his tongue and sat down again, as bidden.

'I was working in the lingerie department, your honour.'

'Thank you. If I may return to the matter of your parents.'

There was a silence, then Cassie slowly looked up, straight into Judge Kenneally's eyes.

'They were unmarried. My father was a drunk, who used to beat my mother, then he abandoned her when she became pregnant, quite late in her life, with me. My mother then moved from the West Coast to the East Coast and pretended I was her grandchild. I didn't find out until after she was dead what the truth was. That she was my mother. And that I was a bastard.'

'And your grandmother. Or rather your mother. How did she treat you?'

Cassie fell silent again, and searched for Tyrone's hand under the table.

'Her mother beat her constantly, publicly humiliated her, locked her in her room for days, starved her, and did everything she could to make my wife's childhood as wretched an experience as possible,' Tyrone informed the judge. 'My wife won't tell you that, your honour. She won't tell you because she's too proud. And she wouldn't want you feeling sorry for her. That's the sort of person my wife is.'

'Thank you.'

The judge nodded, and closed the folders which lay open in front of him. Then he removed his glasses and stared up at the ceiling.

'This would have been a fairly straightforward case upon which to have ruled,' he said, 'and I could have made a far speedier conclusion had it not been for this eleventh-hour opposition from the father, Gerald Secker.'

Cassie and Tyrone exchanged an astonished look.

'But the father has no rights, your honour!' Tyrone protested.

'His consent isn't needed, certainly,' the judge replied. 'But that doesn't mean that he is prevented from putting his point of view to the court. Unfortunately, after we received this letter from him, we were unable to trace him, and we have since been informed that he has left the country on some sort of pilgrimage to India.'

'May we be told what the letter contained, your honour?' Tyrone enquired.

The judge took some papers out from his folder, and pushed them across the desk to Tyrone. Cassie and he read through them quickly. The typewritten letter contained all the salient facts about Cassie's upbringing, her mental breakdown and her attack on Tyrone. It ended by asking whether or not this really made her a suitable adoptive mother for his illegitimate son.

Tyrone returned the letter to the judge.

'You realise that letter couldn't possibly be from Secker, don't you?'

The judge nodded.

'Even if it had been, what's to say it's nothing but a pack of lies anyway?' Tyrone added.

'This letter is quite palpably not from the child's father,' the judge replied. 'Young Secker disappeared off to India two months ago. This letter is dated three days ago. The point is, however, that it contained certain allegations which had to be examined. And from my examination of Mrs Rosse, it seems that whoever wrote that letter, a person who quite obviously wished Mrs Rosse harm—'

Cassie looked at Tyrone once more and saw from his

446

face that he'd already guessed the identity of the writer.

'It seems that the sender of the letter is indeed extremely familiar with Mrs Rosse's history and is of the opinion that she would not make a suitable adoptive mother.'

Tyrone gripped Cassie's hand even more tightly under the table.

'Indeed, were I to consider a case such as yours just on paper, on its face value, I would have no hesitation whatsoever in refusing to grant you an adoption order. Which is why these hearings have such a value. If I had not met and talked to you both, I would have had no idea of your characters. I would have had no chance to witness Mrs Rosse's truthfulness and courage, and I would not have been able to witness the strength of your love for each other. In other words, I would never have been able to conclude that there is no doubt in my mind whatsoever, particularly after seeing the way you have faced the tribulations of this hearing, that you will both make ideal parents for this child whom you wish to adopt. It is therefore without any hesitation or qualification whatsoever that I am happy to grant you the adoption order for which you have applied.'

Cassie remembered the drama and exhilaration of the day before yesterday as she now sat in her dressing gown, waiting in her bedroom as instructed for Tyrone to return from Dublin, while downstairs she could hear the caterers and organisers frantically putting the finishing touches to their preparations. Then she heard Tyrone's Aston Martin roar up the drive, and from her window she watched as he unloaded several boxes from the rear seat.

Tyrone looked up, and seeing Cassie standing at their bedroom window, grinned, poked his tongue out at her and hurried inside the house.

'Where on *earth* have you been, Ty?' Cassie asked him as he burst into the bedroom, barely visible behind the boxes piled up in his arms.

'I had to go to the blasted airport!' he replied, arranging

the boxes on the bed. 'And would you believe it? The bloody flight was nearly an hour late!'

'Who were you meeting?' Cassie enquired. 'I didn't see anyone with you.'

'I wasn't meeting anyone, Cassie McGann,' Tyrone answered. 'I was collecting this.'

He tapped the largest of the boxes on the bed.

'May I open it?' she asked him.

'No you certainly may not,' he retorted. 'What you have to do is to stand there and close your eyes.'

Cassie did as she was told. She heard Tyrone walk up behind her and felt his lips brush the top of her shoulders as he took off her robe.

'Not now, Tyrone,' she sighed. 'Our guests will be here at any moment.'

'Ssshhh,' he ordered, and for a moment the room was quite silent.

Then Cassie felt the silk of one of her scarves as Tyrone tied it into a blindfold round her eyes.

'What are you *doing?*' Cassie gasped.

'Sssshhh,' came the reply.

Cassie stood there in nothing but the silk scarf. She started to laugh, but was at once hushed into silence again by Tyrone. She heard him undoing one of the boxes, and then the rustle of thin tissue paper. More silence.

'Which way round does this damned thing go anyway?' Tyrone muttered to himself.

'May I help?' Cassie asked.

'No you may not,' Tyrone replied. 'Ah.'

Tyrone put his arms round her waist, and kissed her neck as he fastened something round her waist. Cassie knew what it was from the feel of the satin straps which hung loosely against her thighs.

'Now lift up your left leg, Cassie McGann.'

She did as she was told.

'And now your right.'

Likewise.

She felt the silk of another garment as Tyrone gently pulled it up over her naked body. Over her hips, until the elastic rested just below the line of her stomach.

'What about a bra?'

'No bra.'

'No?'

'No.'

Next Tyrone pulled on to her legs a pair of silk stockings. He'd given her silk stockings previously, but he'd never rolled them on and up to her thighs before – particularly not when she was standing there helplessly blindfolded. Cassie was so happy that she wanted to turn round and take hold of Tyrone and make love to him there and then. But there wasn't time. Besides she didn't, because she knew that her present submissiveness would make the love-making they would later enjoy all the more enthralling.

So she just stood there silently as Tyrone carefully attached the top of the stockings to her garter belt.

'I'll bet you've got your tongue stuck in the side of your cheek,' she said laughing.

'You'll get a smack on that wonderful backside of yours if you don't keep quiet,' he replied.

'May I look now?'

'No you may not.

'I'd love to see what I look like.'

'If you look, I'll make you go downstairs and greet your guests just as you are.

There followed a longer silence while she heard Tyrone undoing what Cassie imagined must be the largest of the parcels. She heard the sound of more tissue paper being removed, then the soft swish of material, coming nearer and nearer.

'Left leg.'

'It would be easier over my head, surely.'

'Left leg.'

Cassie lifted her left leg.

'Right leg.'

Right leg.

Left arm, right arm. Long sleeves. Cassie plunged her arms into them, sleeves that softly clung to her. And then the dress was on. Except for something draped round the front of her waist which she was aware that Tyrone was now lifting up over her head, and arranging behind her. Silence, while Cassie imagined Tyrone standing back to appraise his handiwork.

'May I look now?'

'No.'

'When may I look?'

'When I say so.'

The dress was very soft and clung to Cassie like a second skin from the tops of her thighs, up her stomach and over her bare breasts. There seemed to be no back to it, at least not until dangerously far down. Then there seemed to be a sort of bustle, which must have been the swathe Tyrone had lifted over her head and arranged behind her. Finally she felt him lifting each of her silk-stockinged feet and fastening them into what she guessed must be latticed evening sandals.

'Now?' she asked.

'No,' he replied, taking her by the hand and sitting her down on a chair. 'I said I'd tell you when.'

'I have to do my hair.'

'You've done your hair.'

'I'll need to check it.'

'No you won't. I'll check it.'

Cassie felt his hand and her hairbrush on her hair, carefully reshaping any strand which might have fallen out of place.

'It looks fine,' Tyrone told her. 'Now sit there and don't move until I come for you.'

She heard him go out of the room and close the door. And she just sat there, totally enthralled. Outside, she heard unseen cars arriving, and then below, the voices of their guests as they began to arrive.

And still Cassie sat there, her hands in her lap, totally ignorant of what she was wearing and how she looked.

She could quite easily have removed the blindfold, looked at her dress and replaced the blindfold again, but she didn't.

She had no idea how long she must have sat there, as car after car rolled up the drive and parked in the field opposite. She heard raised voices, laughter, feet on the gravel and an increasing swell of noise from below. She didn't hear the bedroom door reopen and Tyrone come back in.

All she knew was that suddenly someone was at her side. And that someone was Tyrone.

'Ty?'

He said nothing. He just put one hand under one of her arms and lifted her gently from the chair. Then he led her across the bedroom and stopped her by the door.

He took off her blindfold.

'May I look now?'

Tyrone shook his head.

'No.'

'Why not?'

'I want you to see how beautiful you are from the way everyone will look at you.'

He touched her hair, rearranging it where the scarf had been.

'Happy birthday, Cassie McGann,' he whispered. 'Happy birthday, my love.'

He took her hand and opened the door. Below, the hall was full of their friends and guests, everyone dressed in white suits and dresses. They all looked up as Cassie appeared at the top of the stairs, hand in hand with Tyrone, and fell silent, as if on cue. Cassie frowned round at Tyrone, but he wasn't looking at her. He was nodding to somebody across the hall, who was nodding back to someone else, out of sight to them.

Suddenly there was an explosion of music, as a twelve-piece swing band, hidden away under the fold of the staircase, burst into the Glenn Miller arrangement of Pennsylvania 65000. Cassie burst into laughter and hugged Tyrone's arm. She'd always told Tyrone that when they were rich and famous, or just rich, or just famous maybe, they'd have a party, just like the one in one of her all-time favourite movies, *The Glenn Miller Story*; and Tyrone and she would walk down the staircase just as they did in the movie, while a band played 'In the Mood'. And now here she was, walking down the stairs towards a sea of smiling faces, in what she now saw was a vivid scarlet silk dress, through a throng of friends who caught her hands, kissed her and wished her happy birthday, while Dublin's top swing band played Glenn Miller. Tyrone took her in his arms and started to dance with her.

'Isn't this what they did in the film as well?' he asked.

'I guess so, Mr Rosse,' Cassie sighed, looking up at him. 'But just don't get any funny ideas about taking up flying.'

'Who needs to fly,' he replied, 'when I can dance with you?'

The guests who had filled the hall all started dancing, unable to resist the music of the band. Tyrone steered Cassie into his study and shut the door behind them.

'Thank you for this wonderful present, Ty,' Cassie said, smoothing down her dress. 'Where on earth did you buy it?'

'I had it sent from Paris,' he replied. 'And it's not your present. That's just part one.'

'But it must have cost a fortune.'

'Jesus. You Americans. Sometimes you're awful vulgar.'

'It's the most beautiful dress I've ever seen.'

Tyrone laughed with delight. 'And you're not to see it either,' he told her. 'Not till the party's over. If I catch you looking in a mirror once, I'll take the dress off you in front of everyone.'

'Don't worry,' Cassie replied. 'I won't. I wouldn't dare.'

Tyrone took something out of a drawer in his desk and

handed it to her. It was a small box tied up with a scarlet ribbon.

'Here's part two of your birthday present,' he said.

Inside the box, Cassie found a gold locket in the shape of a heart, with her initial engraved on one side and Tyrone's on the other. Inside – when prompted by Tyrone, she opened it – there were two photographs, one of Josephine and one of Mattie.

'In celebration of our family,' Tyrone said.

He promised her part three of her present after they had eaten. The food was stupendous: an enormous buffet of fresh Irish salmon, lobster, chicken and beef, served against the music of a Palm Court Orchestra. Cassie and Tyrone sat side by side at a round table in the middle of the main marquee, Cassie a splash of vivid red in an ocean of white. The flowers were lilies and white roses; the musicians were in white tie and tails; and the solo violinist who stood behind Cassie, serenading her through dinner, played a white violin. Afterwards they danced again to the Swing Orchestra, who were all dressed in white tuxedos, and whose black singer had to everyone's delight made her face and arms up blindingly white.

Cassie danced every dance with Tyrone, who looked resplendent in a perfectly cut pair of white tails and white patent-leather dancing pumps. Cassie still had little idea of the whole look of her dress, as she had been true to her promise and only seen it through the eyes of her guests, all of whom had admired it unequivocally. She had also, of course, looked down at it as she sat, or as she danced; and besides being enthralled by the sensuality of the brilliant colour against her pale skin, could see even from such a difficult angle and feel when she moved and danced how perfectly cut it was.

The only person Cassie had failed to spot was Leonora. She and Tyrone had talked long and hard in the first place about whether or not to invite her, and it was Cassie, forgiving as always, who had pointed out the

453

diplomatic necessity alone of not witholding an invitation to her.

'She represents over one third of your yard,' she reminded him. 'You told me yourself.'

But after the discovery of the letter at the adoption hearing, Tyrone became quite adamant that Leonora's invitation should be rescinded. Cassie was for once inclined to agree, not from a sense of revenge, but because she wasn't sure how she would be able to deal with Leonora now that she knew how far Leonora was prepared to go to spite her. Finally discretion overcame both their valour, when they realised that if they banned Leonora from Cassie's birthday party, she would dominate the proceedings even more by her enforced absence. It would be the talk of Dublin society, and consequently of the party.

As it was, it seemed that quite voluntarily she was not going to appear at the party after all. But Cassie liked this even less. She would rather have known definitely one way or the other. She couldn't believe that Leonora would stay away from her party unless she had a very good reason for it.

She didn't. Leonora was just timing her entrance.

Tyrone had called a halt to the dancing and ordered the lights to be lowered completely. Once they were down, a spotlight came on, trained on the far corner of the huge marquee. Into the light a gigantic birthday cake was wheeled, a confection Tyrone had ordered to be made in the old Hollywood proportions. It was huge, and quite obviously phoney, but was so wonderfully constructed and decorated that it brought the party to its feet, as it was wheeled across to Cassie's table amidst wild applause.

The drummer rolled a long crescendo roll. Then to a fanfare from the band the top of the cake flew open. But instead of an actor dressed as Al Capone with a toy machine gun loaded with ping-pong balls, as Tyrone had intended, out stepped Leonora, armed with the toy gun which she pointed at Cassie and fired. Cassie put her arms to her head as she was peppered with the plastic table-tennis balls, and Tyrone got to his feet. Leonora saved the last round for him and, aiming the toy gun carefully, popped the plastic ball at him so that it bounced off his forehead. All the guests roared with laughter, and applauded even more, thinking that Leonora's appearance was all part of the act, while Leonora, incredible in a brilliant white full-length Courrèges cape and bonnet, and quite obviously drunk, blew kisses and took a series of bows from the top of the cake.

Two waiters, in answer to her imperious command, helped her down out of the cake and on to the table, where she stood for a few moments more so that the party could fully appreciate her stunning but vulgar outfit. The bonnet was deliberately absurd, fashioned like Bo-Peep's, but in the same heavy material as the dress, and held together by an enormous white bow, practically concealing her mouth. The cape itself was ankle-length, with gold bobbles running from either side of the collar down to the hem, and was also fastened by a bow, across her half-exposed breasts. Underneath the cape she wore nothing else other than a pair of skin-tight glittering gold pants, tied enticingly at the waist with another large white floppy bow. She swung round once, so that the air lifted the cape away from her body and revealed her state of half-nakedness beneath.

Some of the younger but more of the older guests wolf-whistled before Tyrone held up his hand for silence.

'On behalf of us all,' he announced, as the noise subsided, 'I would like to thank the Principessa for taking us so completely and dramatically by surprise. But then, that is fast becoming a habit with her.'

Tyrone turned and gave her a little ironic bow. Leonora ignored the irony and blew him a kiss in return instead.

'However, I would like to point out to the Principessa,' Tyrone continued, 'that the invitation states quite clearly this was to be an all-white party. And that by the wearing of a colour, in the Principessa's case her gold pants, as I believe she calls them, the rules of the party have quite clearly been transgressed, and retribution must follow, just as surely as night follows day.'

A buzz started round the marquee as some of the more forward-thinking guests anticipated what might well be in store for Leonora. They weren't to be disappointed.

'Therefore I invite whichever of the Principessa's friends who may feel like it to help her to divest herself of the prohibited item of clothing.'

Tyrone had barely finished issuing his invitation before Leonora, unable to escape in time, disappeared under a scrum of both men and women. Soon there was one almighty and joyous shout, as Leonora was debagged and her gold pants hurled high into the air above the scrum.

Everyone who had been involved returned roaring with laughter to their tables in search of immediate refreshment, while Leonora got slowly to her feet. Standing there in her crooked Bo-Beep bonnet and shiny plastic boots, with just a brief pair of white bikini knickers showing under her cape, her expensive and once outrageous outfit now just looked absurd. The cape was cut in such a way that it was impossible to close it over completely at the front and thus cover Leonora's embarrassment. So she stood by Cassie and Tyrone's table, half-dressed and looking murderous. Then she turned on her heel and walked quickly out of the marquee.

Tyrone blew a kiss to her departing back.

'I'm not sure that was the wisest thing you ever did, Mr Rosse,' Cassie said after a moment. 'Funny, you bet. Diplomatic, I don't think.'

'Nonsense, woman,' Tyrone laughed. 'She's so legless I doubt if she'll even remember it. Anyway, I'm not having her upstaging you at your party. Now come and dance.'

Later he danced her out of the marquee and on to the

lawns. It was a warm, balmy night, and the gardens were lit with old-fashioned flares. He danced her away from the house until the music grew faint, and when it could barely be heard, he sang softly to her instead, until he had danced her away down the path to the yard.

'Where are you taking me now?' asked Cassie, with the starlight reflected in her eyes.

'Part three of your birthday present,' Tyrone whispered in her ear.

He led her by the hand to the row of new boxes. They went very quietly so as not to disturb the sleeping race-horses. Tyrone stopped by the end box, which had a huge pink bow nailed on the door.

'Happy birthday, pilgrim,' he said.

'Why pilgrim?' Cassie asked, staring at the bow.

'Because one man loved the pilgrim soul in you,' Tyrone answered, 'that's why. Go on now. Aren't you going to open the box?'

Cassie smiled, bit her lip, and quietly opened the top of the closed box. For a moment there was silence, then she heard a horse scrabbling to get to its feet, and a moment later a head came over the door. Round and through its head collar was another huge pink ribbon.

Cassie turned and frowned at Tyrone.

'Well?' he demanded.

'You and your "well's",' Cassie sighed. 'Well, what is this?'

'What do you think it is, you lunatic? A motor car?'

Tyrone opened the doors completely and led the horse out.

'This is for you, Cassie McGann,' he said, handing the horse over to her. 'Happy twenty-seventh birthday.'

'I have a horse, Tyrone. I have two in fact. No, three now, with the yearling.'

'You haven't a horse to *ride*, Mrs Rosse. This is a riding horse.'

Cassie looked at the horse she was holding. He had the kindest face she'd ever seen on an animal, with big liquid eyes and large ears that flopped forward over his brow. From what she could see, he was a light bay, and probably no more than five years old.

'Four actually,' Tyrone corrected her. 'And he's a Christian. Sheila Meath bred him, and she backed and broke him specially for you. He's perfectly schooled for a youngster, like all of her horses. And he's only half-bred, so he's not going to play silly buggers. He's out of that lovely Welsh mare of hers, by None Better whom I used to train. And you could put a baby on his back, even on the day he was going racing.'

'Tyrone,' Cassie said. 'He's beautiful. Really. But why do you want to give me a horse?'

'So as we can ride together.'

'I can't ride.'

'Yes you can. You've just lost your nerve. Girls do, once they've had babies.'

'How do you know I can ride?'

'For crying out loud, Cassie! I stayed with the blasted Christiansens, didn't I? And all I heard was how brilliant you were with horses! And not only with them, on them, too!'

'Why did you never say?'

'Because if you didn't tell me, Mrs Rosse, I reckoned you didn't want me to know.'

At that moment, if it were possible, Cassie loved Tyrone more than ever. He'd never once mentioned her riding, nor asked if she did ride, and if so why she didn't. He'd just waited till he felt the time was right for her to start again, and then quietly and patiently set the whole thing up with Sheila Meath, down to finding the right horse for her and making sure it was broken the right way.

She put the horse back in his box and stood for a moment looking at him, before once more shutting him away.

Then she turned and hugged Tyrone, her heart full to bursting. 'You know you've made me the happiest person in the world?' she said.

458

'You mean you've been going around asking?' Tyrone laughed.

One or two of the other horses in the boxes further down started to stir, so Tyrone led her out of the yard and back up the path towards the house. Once in sight of the house, he held back and took Cassie in his arms and kissed her. Cassie put her arms around his neck and kissed him back.

'When can I see my dress?' she pleaded.

'When I take it off you,' he answered.

They rejoined their party and started once more to dance. The main band finished its last set, and then for an hour the Dubliners performed a cabaret. After that there was dancing in the two main marquees to two quartets, both consisting of tenor saxophone, piano, bass and drums. People started leaving about three, although most weren't gone till well after. For those who stayed, Erin and Mrs Muldoon made scrambled eggs and bacon, with eggs laid that day. When Cassie and Tyrone had bid their last farewell, and the band were packing up, Tyrone asked the pianist to play 'One For The Road' before they went. He duly obliged, and Cassie and Tyrone danced slowly round the empty dance floor, with Tyrone quietly crooning the words. Then the house was empty of guests, but full of memories of the best night Cassie had ever had.

'Except, that is, for the first time we went out,' she said. 'When we danced while they were putting up the tables and you sang to me as you walked me all the way home.'

'It has to have been the best party you've ever had.'

'Far and away,' Cassie laughed. 'Far, far and away.'

Tyrone fetched her a wrap, then took her outside to watch the dawn break. They walked down the long avenue between the trees, and past the woods where they sometimes secretly made love. Tyrone suddenly stopped, and cocking his head like a dog, bade Cassie to listen. From deep within the woods she heard a sound she would remember for the rest of her life. A bird song. The song of a nightingale.

Tyrone whispered the one word, the name of the bird to her, then pressed a finger to his lips as they both stood motionless. The song was surprisingly loud, and very clear as it echoed round and through the woods. There were deep, full notes, surprisingly rich and powerful for such a shy, timid bird; and then there were trills, and warbles, of such beauty and clarity that Cassie could feel the hair on the nape of her neck prickle, and the tears well up in her eyes.

The bird sang on and on, its wondrous song floating on the early morning air. It was so heavenly that Cassie thought she must be dreaming. She had never in her whole life heard such astounding music from such a tiny creature. Tyrone was transported with the delight of it, his brow furrowed deeply, and his eyes full of amazement.

Then he turned to her, and taking her hand in his, sat down together with her to hear the nightingale sing.

As they walked back to the house, dawn had broken.

'What do you want to do now?' Tyrone asked her.

'I don't know,' Cassie answered. 'It's such a wonderful morning. It's been such a wonderful night.'

'If we go to bed now, we won't get up again.'

'I know. Are you tired?'

'Not in the slightest, Cassie McGann. Are you?'

'No. You know me,' she said as she leaned her head on his shoulder, 'I won't be tired until tonight. Then I'll sleep for a week.'

'In that case,' Tyrone said, 'let's go and try out that new horse of yours.'

Cassie had a few butterflies in her stomach, as she followed Tyrone, who was running up the stairs in front of her. But she also felt a buzz of that old excitement: the thrill she used to feel at Mary-Jo's when they would get

460

up at dawn and run out through the dew-soaked pastures to catch their ponies.

She kicked her shoes off in the bedroom then suddenly stopped when she caught sight of herself for the first time in a mirror since she had been dressed by Tyrone the night before. The dress was indescribably beautiful, so superbly cut, and such a vivid colour, that she could understand why she had won quite so many compliments. She half-turned, so that she could see the back, and saw that it was scooped out very low, and that the bustle Tyrone had carefully draped over her head was a wonderful swathe of silk which fell in a fold at the back of the gown. She turned herself round once, then twice, and felt she was still in Tyrone's arms, and dancing.

Tyrone appeared from the bathroom in a cotton polo neck jumper, doing up his breeches. Cassie was standing, still in her black silk stockings, buttoning up a dark blue wool shirt. Tyrone pinched her bottom as he passed her on his way to the wardrobes.

'I'll see you later,' he grinned.

Then he sat on her dressing-table stool and watched her, while he pulled his highly polished old riding boots on to his long, elegant legs.

They got the horses ready themselves, as the yard was barely awake. Tomas was in the feed room, mixing the first meal of the day, and the lads were beginning to make their way in to muck out and get their own horses done. Cassie pulled her new horse out of his box and ran her hand down his neck and back. He was perfectly made, not much higher than 15.2 hands, and quite lightly framed. He regarded her steadily with a very kind eye while Cassie started to groom him, and hardly fidgeted at all until she found a ticklish spot on his stomach.

Tyrone brought her over a brand new saddle and bridle.

'He's been fitted for the saddle,' he said, 'and it's perfect. Don't worry if it squeaks a bit. It'll need to be ridden in.'

461

Soon both the horses were ready and tacked up. They looked a picture in the early morning sun, their coats gleaming and their manes and tails watered and brushed. Cassie checked her girths and Tomas arrived to give her a leg up.

'How does he feel?' Tyrone asked her as they walked round the yard. 'You look absolutely right for him.'

'Don't worry about him,' Cassie replied. 'You should be asking how I feel.'

'You look a picture!' Tyrone laughed. 'You were made for each other!'

Then he squeezed his horse on ahead and led her out of the yard.

'We'll go back up towards the house,' Tyrone said dropping Old Flurry back alongside her, 'so that you can get a good feel of him. Then you can give him a trot in the paddock.'

They walked up the avenue of trees on the two horses, where they had walked so many hundreds of times on foot. Cassie's new horse was impeccably schooled, as Tyrone had promised he was, coming down on to his bit once Cassie asked him correctly, and walking out as soon as she squeezed him lightly with her leg.

'Like I said,' Tyrone smiled. 'You look a picture.'

They trotted in the paddock, the young horse throwing her up a little higher from the saddle than Cassie had expected.

'He's got a very bouncy trot!' she called to Tyrone.

'Perhaps that's what you should call him then!' he replied. 'Bouncer!'

'Why not?' Cassie agreed, changing rein and trotting him in the opposite direction. 'I think it suits him!'

Gone were all the butterflies now, as Cassie suddenly felt her confidence return. The little horse moved so beautifully and so obediently that it was hard for Cassie to believe she wasn't riding a ten-year-old dressage horse.

'Sheila certainly knows her business,' she said, as she slowed the horse to a walk.

'Nobody can make a horse like her,' Tyrone agreed. 'We'll see you at the Dublin Horse Show yet.'

They decided to go up into the hills, up the gallop cut along the side of the field where Cassie had been run off with on Old Flurry, and then beyond the stone wall and right up on to the ridge, where they were to rest and look back down at Claremore. When they got to the foot of the gallop, Tyrone asked Cassie whether or not she wanted to canter.

'Of course!' she replied. 'Why? Don't you?'

'No racing now!' Tyrone warned her. 'You tuck yourself in behind us, and we'll just give him a bit of a stretch.'

Tyrone kicked on Old Flurry, and the horse set off straight into a canter. Cassie steadied her youngster, and trotted him a few strides first, before sitting down and asking him to canter on. The response was immediate, as the horse tucked his hocks under him and set off after Old Flurry. Cassie steadied him, and to her delight the horse came back. For a moment she'd been afraid. Not frightened, she found, but afraid that the horse wouldn't listen to her and take off after Tyrone's. Now she had him nicely settled, and let him out a notch so that he could stride up the hill and enjoy himself.

She was catching Tyrone's horse hand over fist as they pulled up, long before the high stone wall.

'Well?' he asked her.

'Well yourself,' Cassie grinned.

'He seemed to go sweetly enough.'

'He's – how do you say? He's a dote.'

Cassie patted her new horse's neck.

'You're quite a sight on a horse, Mrs Rosse,' Tyrone said. 'Remind me not to let you out hunting unaccompanied.'

Then they swung their horses through a gap in the wall and cantered easily up the rise until they reached the ridge. Tyrone reined back, as did Cassie, and they turned their horses around so that they could see the beauty that was Claremore spread before them, bathed in the early morning sunlight.

'I doubt if there's anywhere on God's earth as lovely as this place on a fine summer morning,' Tyrone said. 'What do you think?'

'Tomas says this is the spot God rested when His work was done in the Creation,' Cassie replied. 'That fold in the mountains there! That's where Tomas says He laid His head!'

'Tomas was taken to kiss the Blarney stone when he was a day old,' Tyrone grinned. 'Now what's the matter?'

Cassie was frowning, with her hand to her neck.

'My locket,' she said.

'What about it?'

'The locket you gave me. It's gone.'

'It can't have gone, Cassie. It must have fallen down inside your shirt.'

Cassie looked.

'It hasn't, Ty. It must have come off when we started cantering. I know I had it on before we got into the field, because the chain was caught on a button.'

Cassie looked around her hopelessly.

'I don't know what I'll do if I've lost it.'

'We'll buy you another one.'

'It won't be the same.'

'Didn't you do up the safety chain?'

'I thought I did.'

'Come on then,' Tyrone sighed good-humouredly, 'let's go and find it.'

'Tyrone – it could be anywhere!'

'Then say a prayer to St Anthony!'

Cassie did so as they slowly retraced their steps, both of them bent over the sides of their horses and searching the ground. They turned back into the field, and walked slowly towards the end of the gallop, Tyrone ahead of Cassie.

Cassie was on her fourth or fifth Hail Mary when she heard Tyrone give a cry.

'Here it is!' he called. 'I've found it!'

He reined his horse back as Cassie trotted hers up to join him. She saw the sun catching the locket as it lay in the short grass at the very end of the gallop. It must have fallen off as she pulled up, maybe still caught up round a button, and coming undone as she sat back to rein the horse back.

'Oh thank God!' she cried. 'Thank God, Tyrone! I don't know what I'd have done if I'd lost that!'

'Did you say a prayer to St Anthony?' Tyrone asked as he kicked his feet out of his stirrups.

'You bet!' Cassie laughed. 'I said more than one!'

Tyrone was on the ground, behind Old Flurry, as he bent down to pick up the locket.

'There you are!' he called up. 'God is kind!'

Which were the last words Tyrone spoke. As he started to straighten up, something vicious must have stung Old Flurry because the horse suddenly and totally uncharacteristically stamped and kicked out violently. His hoof caught Tyrone on the side of his head, spinning him round completely, and knocking him off his feet and on to his back in a second. Cassie leaped from her horse and rushed over to where Tyrone lay on his face in the grass. She was aware of someone somewhere calling his name over and over again and screaming, but she wasn't aware that that person was her.

Then she was down on her knees, pulling at Tyrone. The noise of the someone who was screaming Tyrone's name was louder now in her ears, louder and louder as she turned Tyrone over and saw the dead stare that was in those deep blue eyes. Above one eye his temple was kicked in, and there was a dark trickle of blood running from his nose and the side of his mouth. The noise of the person shouting stopped and there was sobbing now, a deep breathless sobbing, as Cassie cradled Tyrone's head in her arms and tried to call to him through the sound of the person crying. But he didn't reply, and he didn't move. His blue eyes looked back up at her, unwaveringly, unblinking, with all the laughter gone from them. Tyrone, the voice was crying. Tyrone, Tyrone, speak to me. Speak to me, Tyrone. Please say something. Please. Please please, my love, please just say something.

But his voice was silent now. The voice that had sung to her and wooed her, that had laughed and teased, that had roared horses home and whispered to her as he loved her in the night, that deep and wonderful voice that had thrilled her every time she heard it speak or call or sing – that voice was gone now, gone now and silenced for ever more.

And when she realised that, the sound of the person who had been calling his name stopped, and the sound of the person who was crying became louder and louder as Cassie put both her arms around her own love's beautiful crushed head and cradled the terrible silence to her.

Interim One

The Present

Early on a Tuesday morning in June, a small group of
people stand high up on Epsom racecourse, at the top of
the back straight, half a mile away from the Derby start. It
is a fine, clear morning, with the dew still on the grass.
Below them, on the heath and in the enclosures proper,
preparations are already under way to accommodate and
entertain the anticipated record crowd of racegoers; but
this is of little or no interest to the group of people standing
by the rails, just above the point where the course begins to
fall away to the world-famous Tattenham Hill. Their eyes
are trained on the two horses which are coming towards
them at a good swinging gallop.

At the front of the group stands a woman, dressed in a
well-worn but still smart three-quarter-length fawn
gaberdine with a faded sheepskin lining. She is hatless,
and the early morning breeze ruffles her long dark hair.
Beside her stand two men, one white-haired and with a
back rounded from years of riding strong horses at work,
the other a small, dapper man, in a brown trilby and a
short overcoat similar to the one the woman is wearing.
The rest of the group consists of a man with a lightweight
television camera, another with a microphone and a third
with their ancillary equipment.

The woman and the man in the brown trilby are watching the horses through their race glasses with intense interest, while the white-haired man, ignoring his binoculars,
stands appraising the approaching animals, smoking a
cigarette.

It takes the horses approximately a minute to cover the uphill four furlongs. Even after the hundreds of horses the three people at the front of the group have watched gallop over the years, they still thrill as much as they ever did as these horses race by them, their hooves pounding the turf, their nostrils flaring and their jockeys perched in perfect balance high on the horses' withers.

Every one of the group swings round as the horses gallop by, and watch as the jockeys ease them carefully down to a canter, then a trot, and finally a walk, lest they should jar their precious charges' legs.

The man in the brown trilby takes his hat off and runs a hand over his now almost hairless head.

'Well?' he says to the woman. 'Do you think we've just seen the winner of tomorrow's Derby?'

The cameraman swings his camera into position to record the woman's reply.

'It will take an exceptional horse to beat him,' she answers.

'Like yours.'

'Like mine.'

'So you're quietly confident?' the man enquires, with a charming smile.

'I'm quietly terrified,' the woman replies, very seriously.

'The name of the horse,' the interviewer continues. 'He's by your own stallion Commitment, a grandson of your foundation stallion Celebration, out of the mare Last Waltz who was by Song. So why was he called the Nightingale? I understand it has some rather special significance for you.'

'It will have,' the woman agrees. 'It will have a very special significance, John, if tomorrow afternoon I hear the Nightingale called home first.'

Chapter Seventeen

Claremore
1969

The sweat streamed down off her forehead and into her eyes, stinging and half-blinding her. Beneath the four layers of clothing she was wearing, she could feel the it coursing down her back and between her breasts. But her breath was coming good and strong and regular, and her legs and arms, despite the one-pound lead racing weight she had clasped in each hand, were still pumping rhythmically. So Cassie kept on running.

She turned for home, up the last hill with the gates of Claremore in her sights. Only the hill and the drive now. Four hundred and sixty strides up that hill, which had seemed an endless mountain when she'd first started running it, and then the last eight hundred and ninety paces up and round the pot-holed drive.

Turning in the gate Cassie raised one lead-weighted arm and wiped the river of sweat from her eyes. It was March, and everywhere there were daffodils, waving in the stiff wind which blew in Cassie's face as she headed up the private road between the home paddocks. She was aware of the myriads of yellow flowers either side of her as she ran, but they no longer heralded spring and warmth and happiness. Spring was now just another of the four seasons, bringing with it yet more hardship and, for all Cassie knew, yet more heartbreak.

The first thing she heard as she ran into the house and up the stairs was Mattie coughing. She paused on the stairs, sweat-soaked and weary, and wondered why on top of everything else her beloved little boy should have

469

been found to have had asthma. It had started quite suddenly, so suddenly and so violently one night almost exactly a year ago that Cassie thought he would be dead before she could get him to the hospital. Tomas had driven them there as fast as he could, but as Cassie sat cradling the child in her arms, the breath seemed already to have left his body.

But they saved him. It was touch and go for two days, while Cassie sat by his side in the hospital, watching while he slept, and treasuring every visible breath, but they saved his young life. Now Cassie stood outside the nursery door, and braced herself, while she stood listening to the cough which was racking her son's little body. Sometimes in the night, when Cassie was exhausted from the day, but because of her grief unable to sleep, Mattie would be coughing and Cassie would block her ears, begging him silently to stop. Then she would stumble out of bed and go into the nursery, and lift up her son, who would be lying on his pillow white-faced with black-ringed eyes, clutching the sheets tightly in his little hands in an effort to stop himself coughing. Cassie would take him back to her bed and he would put his small arms round her neck, and they would finally fall asleep together.

Now she stood about to go into the nursery and see what she could do for him, knowing in fact that there was nothing. Doctor Gilbert had been wonderful, never failing her when she called him out, arriving at all hours in his battered old Ford, to bring comfort to Mattie and usually to Cassie as well. After he had attended the child, he and Cassie would sit in front of the kitchen stove and drink a whisky each from his hip flask.

'It's probably an inherited weakness,' he once told Cassie. 'We can only guess, because of course we don't know the medical history of his parents proper. And the weakness might not even be in this generation. It could be TB either side of the family generations ago. No wonder they call it the Devil's Disease. It's a devil to treat, and the very devil to have.'

Of course they did everything they could for Mattie. Everything they could afford to do. Cassie and Erin dusted his room twice or three times daily with a wet duster; the carpet was removed from the nursery and replaced with oiled lino; his woollen blankets were replaced with cotton ones; an extra half length of sheeting was sewn on to the top bed sheet; and all the woolly furry toys were removed, until it seemed to Cassie that what had once been such a warm and welcoming room now looked like a prison cell.

And still he coughed. When he had a bad attack, he coughed day and night, and Cassie would sleep on a mattress on his floor. Most nights the child would have trouble sleeping, so Cassie would sit beside him on the bed, both of them propped up by his pillows, and she would read to him until finally in the early hours he would fall back into an uneasy slumber, while Josephine slept next door in Cassie's bed in the spare room.

Cassie had moved out of the main bedroom, unable to face the memories which were locked fast within it. She had taken all her things out, leaving Tyrone's clothes still hanging in his wardrobe, with his shoes and boots in neat rows underneath. Then she had turned the key in the door and moved herself into the spare room next to the nursery.

Erin was already in there when Cassie opened the door, sitting reading to Mattie, who was lying in his bed like a little white ghost. He smiled when he saw Cassie, and his large brown flecked eyes lit up.

'Hello, Mattie,' Cassie said. 'Another rotten day, my poor darling?'

And she came towards his bed, only to be intercepted by Erin.

'Now away with you and out of those wet clothes,' Erin ordered. 'We don't want you down ill in bed as well now, do we?'

'Just time for one big bear hug, surely, Erin?' Cassie asked, picking up her son.

'Sure you're soakin' wet! You're wet right through! You hold that child to yous and it won't just be you down with the pneumonia!'

Erin took Mattie back from Cassie and rubbed his back.

'Go along now,' she chivvied, 'or you'll catch your death.'

Cassie leaned forward and kissed her son, then went, wiping the sweat from her still soaking brow. Erin was right, of course, as usual. Already her clothes felt damp on her, as her body began to chill. So she went, as she always did after her training session, and showered herself off under cold water. She took the shower in the children's bathroom, unable to face the memories sealed in what was now her bathroom, but which just like the main bedroom had once always been known as theirs.

The bitterly cold water coursed over her, but Cassie shut out the sensation, as she had shut out most other sensations for the past twenty months. Father Patrick had once hinted that God had sent Mattie's asthma to deflect her attention away from the memory of Tyrone, and Cassie had to restrain herself from attacking him physically. He had further hinted that her son's asthma might also be due to her professional activities with her horses: that it was a child's call for attention and that a mother's place was in the home. Cassie had listened to him in silence, refusing to enter an argument, and point out that the children would have no home if she lingered too long in the nursery, and that there would be no point in her business if there were no children to feed and clothe.

When the priest had left, fortunately Doctor Gilbert had called on his rounds, and he and Cassie sat into the small hours talking the problem out. Cassie was so glad for Doctor Gilbert, and so ashamed of her previous mistrust of the old man, for at the times of her worst stress, he had been a rock, turning up sometimes as if he instinctively knew when she was teetering on an emo-

472

tional precipice. Poor Doctor Gilbert, whose smoking and old-fashioned attitudes used to drive Cassie to distraction. He was now her St Peter.

Then there was the worry about Josephine not eating, Cassie thought, as she reached for a towel still damp from yesterday's shower and stood shivering on the children's faded Mickey Mouse bathmat. Josephine had stopped eating about the same time as Mattie suffered his first asthma attack, and Cassie thought it was probably also about the time her daughter had finally realised that her Daddy really wasn't coming home any more. Now she just picked at her food, and sometimes would go two, maybe three days without actually eating anything at all.

'If you ate yourself,' Erin would volunteer, 'then your daughter would eat. What sort of example are yous setting her anyway?'

'She sees you eating,' Cassie would counter. 'And your mother. She has plenty of examples.'

' 'Tis not the same as the mother eatin',' Erin would answer. ' 'Tis not the same thing at all.'

Erin would sigh and sit with her eyes raised to heaven. Cassie would want to scream in return, but didn't, instead retiring to her little bedroom and lying on the bed with her teeth sunk deep in her wrist to stop herself from crying. When she had recovered, she would go in search of Josephine, and take her outside for a walk if it was fine, or sit and play a game with her if it was raining, and try and find a way to reactivate her daughter's appetite. But nothing she could say, nor anything anyone of them cooked, aroused the slightest interest in Josephine, and plate after plate of specially prepared food would be taken and thrown away.

'Listen, Mrs Rosse,' Tomas would tell her. 'Sure dogs and childer. They never starve themselves.'

He advised Cassie to leave well alone, and Cassie knew it was good advice. But she couldn't. It preyed on her mind to see her little girl pushing away everything which

473

was put in front of her, rejecting even biscuits and the occasional bar of chocolate with which Cassie would try to bribe her. And then, which Cassie found even harder to bear, she started to eat a little, but not for her. She would eat for Erin, or for her mother Mrs Muldoon. But as soon as Cassie came into the kitchen where they were all sitting, Josephine would push her plate away and refuse point blank to eat anything more. It was as if she was blaming Cassie for her father not coming home any more.

When she'd dried herself and changed, Cassie went back into the nursery to say goodnight to Mattie. She kissed the pale-faced little boy, who put his arms up round Cassie's neck and kissed her in return. Erin was seated by his bed, knitting, as she did every night until Mattie fell asleep, when she would creep across the corridor into her own room, and go to sleep herself, fully clothed and lying under only the eiderdown, in case of an emergency. Cassie then went to Josephine's room, but Josephine was sound asleep, her face turned to the wall, a little tear-stained handkerchief grasped in one hand.

Watching her daughter in sleep, Cassie suddenly felt more lonely than she had ever felt before in the whole of her life. She had her children, she had Erin and Tomas and Mrs Muldoon, she had Doctor Gilbert, and she had friends. But she also had no one. There was no one in her life who understood what it was like one moment to have been standing in full sun and the very next moment to have been plunged into the darkness.

Later, in the spare bedroom, in her bedroom, in her own single lonely bedroom, she wearily turned off the light and, lying back on her pillow, talked to Tyrone.

'I'm so tired, Ty,' she told him, 'so very tired, I really don't think I can go on. It's so hard without you. And so pointless. What's the point, Ty, of all this pain and anguish? I can't bear it, I promise you I can't. I can't bear coming home, with your hat not thrown any old how on

the hall stand any more. And no race glasses on the chair.
no crumpled race card. Not hearing your voice. Oh how
I miss your voice, Ty. Oh Ty – how I miss you. I die a
little more each day when you don't come home. I die a
little more each morning, every morning when I wake up
and know you're gone.'

She just managed to cover her face with her pillow to
stifle the sob she had cried which was now turning into a
howl. She wrapped both her arms tightly around the
pillow, pulling it against her face until it almost suffocated her. But she held it there until she stopped crying.
No one had seen her cry yet. No one had heard her. And
no one was going to.

Turning on her side, she stared into the darkness of the
small room, and thought about tomorrow. Tomorrow
she had to go and see the bank manager. She had to go
and see 'Old Flann at the Bank', as Tyrone had always
laughingly prefaced his own visits. Tyrone's premature
and tragic death had left his affairs in a terrible state, a
confusion which was only now beginning to be
unscrambled by his lawyer and his executors.

The debts had been collossal. For every pound Tyrone
had earned or won, he had spent five. Cassie naturally
had never queried whether or not everything was paid
for, because since Tyrone had been doing so well, she had
naturally assumed he was managing his affairs respon-
sibly. Even when he showered her with expensive
presents, which he did with increasing regularity whenever he was on a winning streak, despite her delighted
protests that he really shouldn't be so extravagant, never
for one moment did it occur to Cassie that he couldn't
afford them. Everything had been going so well and so
successfully that it never crossed Cassie's mind to doubt
their solvency.

It never crossed Tyrone's either.

So the more he earned, the more he spent. New stables,
better stables, new gallops, new machinery, new tack,
new clothing for his beloved thoroughbreds, better

475

conditions for his lads, better wages, new horseboxes, expensive yearlings bought on spec to be sold on, new cars, new clothes, the best food, champagne and presents. Always presents. Happy day presents, Tyrone would call them, when for no apparent reason at all he would return laden with surprises for Cassie and the children. Even sometimes for Erin and Mrs Muldoon. Not forgetting his beloved Brian, who was constantly bought new beds, leads, chewy bars and rubber bones. Life with Tyrone had been like one long birthday party. But now it was over. The balloons had burst and the moon had been taken away.

And the piper had to be paid. No income tax had been paid for what Cassie's lawyer called a considerable period of time, which when decoded meant over four years, not counting the year of Tyrone's death. And a good eighty per cent of the new machinery, plant and equipment that had been bought for the yard had been purchased so on credit. So the goods had to be either returned or paid for. The yearlings were sold off at absurdly low prices in order to satisfy the most impatient creditors, and Cassie was finally reduced to selling off silver, paintings and even her jewellery to meet other less pressing but equally unavoidable debts. By the time probate was granted, what Cassie still actually owned could be hung and stored in one small wardrobe.

What she didn't own, the bank did. She was only still at Claremore because the bank hadn't foreclosed on the mortgage (which Tyrone had taken out to cover his debts), due simply, as the manager Mr John Flannery put it, to 'an old and happy arrangement'. The old and happy arrangement emerged to be extended credit at prohibitively high interest rates.

For the first year, Cassie had met the mortgage payments with some difficulty, but met they had been simply because of the loyalty and generosity of some of Tyrone's owners, who had kept their horses on in the yard, to be trained nominally by Tomas for the remainder of the season subsequent to Tyrone's death. Luck for once was also on Cassie's side, because two of Townhend Warner's horses won four more good races, with Annagh Bridge who had won at Royal Ascot topping it off by running third in the Prix de l'Arc de Triomphe. But the second year had been a disaster, with the defection of the majority of Claremore's owners, and with a simple attack of a virus which decimated the rest of the yard.

Leonora had started the defection, naturally. And in true Leonora style, she had picked her moment perfectly.

The funeral had been extraordinary, even by Irish standards. Cassie had at first wanted family only, but Tomas had been quite astonishingly adamant on the subject.

'You'll have a riot on your hands, Mrs Rosse,' he warned her, 'if you deny the people the chance to pay their last respects. Mr Rosse was Claremore. And Claremore won't be denied its farewell.'

He was right. The day before they buried Tyrone, the whole village and surrounding community walked up the drive to shake hands with Cassie, who stood alone dressed in black at the top of the steps of the house, alone except for Brian, who lay silent at her feet. Each and every person from the vicinity climbed the steps and shook Cassie by the hand, old men, young men, young and old women, and even children.

'I never knew my husband was so loved,' Cassie said afterwards to Tomas.

'There wasn't a man to touch him,' Tomas replied. 'There's not a man born.'

On the day of the funeral it rained: a fine light summer rain that barely dusted the mourners with its damp. They laid Tyrone to rest in a grave dug next to that of his infant son, and the earth Cassie threw on to his flower-strewn coffin was the earth from a graveyard where Tyrone had once played as a boy. Josephine stood beside Cassie, her hand in her mother's, looking with bewilderment at a

477

box which she had been told contained the mortal remains of her father. Everyone who had brought flowers with them, and there were many such people, filed past the open grave and dropped their flowers on the coffin of a man they were all going to miss grievously, while a young boy from the village, with cheeks like peaches and a thatch of black hair, played a lament on his bagpipes.

Nobody said a word, and the graveyard seemed silent except for the piper's lament. As the women filed by, Cassie saw that they were weeping.

Nobody said a word, except Leonora. As Cassie was leaving the graveyard, Leonora appeared at her side, dressed in black velvet with a lace veil over her blonde hair, and touched Cassie on the elbow.

'I'll take the horses away, of course,' she'd said, as if she was relieving Cassie of an enormous burden, rather than taking away her major source of income.

'There's really no need—' Cassie began. 'Tomas is going to carry on.'

Leonora laid a small and heavily ringed hand on Cassie's arm.

'I wouldn't hear of it,' she said. 'I mean it. Not even I could be that heartless. I'll make arrangements for them to be moved next week. Now you're not to think another thing about it.'

Cassie turned and looked up into Leonora's eyes. Even under her veil they still glittered with malevolence. Cassie knew at that precise moment what bitterness really was.

'I won't forget this, Leonora,' Cassie whispered. 'Not ever.'

'That's all right, darling,' Leonora said, giving her arm another consolatory squeeze. 'If there's anything else I can do, call me. Anything.'

She moved off to her waiting Rolls Royce, with Cassie's eyes and her silently uttered curse following her. Cassie asked God to forgive her, because she truly had cursed Leonora: not with a swearing hopeless kind of curse, but

478

with a deep and fully intentioned one, the sort of curse which people make and intend to keep, and which follows the accursed around forever, until they are avenged.

'May she know no peace,' Erin suddenly said from behind her, as if she had been reading Cassie's thoughts.

Then they both stood and watched as Leonora's chauffeur settled her into her seat, before closing the door on what to anyone else would seem like a sweet and deeply sympathetic smile.

For once Cassie was glad of the almost suffocating heat in Mr Flannery's office. It seemed that the gas fire was kept on throughout the year, regardless of the weather, and usually Cassie found the temperature of the room overpowering. But now, having been forced to turn the heating off in every room in her own house save the children's, Cassie found the warmth very comforting, having just stepped in from a particularly vicious March wind.

Mr Flannery offered Cassie a dry sherry and a biscuit, as was his habit, and enquired how she was.

'I'm just fine, thank you,' she replied, crossing her silk-stockinged legs and sending up a prayer of thanks to Tyrone for always buying her such expensive clothes, because they lasted. Even so, she was careful which leg she crossed on which, lest a run had appeared without her knowing.

'You always look most attractive, if I may say so, Mrs Rosse,' Flannery told her, 'in that fur coat of yours. Most attractive, yes indeed.'

He leaned over her to top up her sherry glass, and Cassie tried her best not to move away from him. The last thing she wanted was him guessing how repulsive she found him, with his soft rounded almost female body, and his smooth white unlined face and little cherry-red lips.

'You wanted to see me,' Cassie said, unbuttoning her coat and allowing it to fall open, revealing her figure-hugging blue cashmere dress.

479

'Yes indeed,' Flannery replied, eyeing her slyly, 'yes indeed I did, and who wouldn't? No, no it would be a very strange sort of person who *didn't* want to see someone as pretty as you. Yes? Yes?'

Cassie laughed politely with him as he enjoyed his own joke, and thought how wise Erin had been to make her keep all her fine clothes.

'You'll get nothin' for them, Mrs Rosse,' she'd said. 'Nothin' at all. And you'll get nothin' for Mr Rosse's either. Sure you'd be better off keepin' them, and sellin' somethin' you'll not be needin'. 'Cos if yous intend stayin' on here in Claremore, please God, then yous is goin' to have to keep that dirty old man down at the bank happy for a start.'

And Erin had been right. As long as Cassie looked smart and, as Erin coyly called it, dead sexy, then Flannery, besides enjoying the company of a well-dressed and quite visibly attractive woman, was also deceived into believing that Cassie was coping and surviving better than she indeed was.

In fact Flannery had now broken out into a mild sweat as he enquired whether or not Cassie would like to remove her fur coat.

'Do you know I think I will, Mr Flannery?' Cassie agreed. 'Your office is so lovely and warm.'

Flannery helped her remove the coat and took the chance to run his hands down the sleeves of her dress. Cassie noticed in the mirror above the fireplace that he also buried his face momentarily in the fur of her coat before hanging it on the hatstand.

'Now then,' he said, his white face for once quite flushed as he sat down. 'To business.'

'You know, Mr Flannery,' Cassie interrupted, 'for a man who works as hard as you do, you look amazing. You look as if you haven't a care in the world.'

Flannery looked up at her, pursing his little red lips into a smile.

'That's very kind of you, Mrs Rosse,' he replied, 'but

480

I'm really no chicken, you know. I shall be fifty-two come Michaelmas.'

'Never,' Cassie said, clasping one hand to her breast and hating herself deeply. 'I just don't believe it.'

'Fifty-two come Michaelmas.'

'I'm still amazed that no woman in the town hasn't snapped you up, you know.'

'Ah. Ah well perhaps now. Perhaps I'm waiting for the right woman – for a very particular woman to come and snap me up. Yes? Yes?'

He looked over his glasses at her and did his best to get his beady eyes to twinkle. Cassie smiled demurely back, and lowered her own eyes, while her stomach turned over at the thought of even eating dinner with him, let alone sharing his bed. She made a private bet with herself that he was the sort of man who'd keep his singlet on under his pyjamas, at the same time hoping she would never be in a position to find out.

'Anyway. To business, Mrs Rosse. I'm afraid it's time for us to review your position.'

And review it he did, hardly able to keep the crow from his voice. Tyrone had often remarked that 'Old Flann' wouldn't be happy until he himself owned Claremore, and that he had been wildly jealous of Tyrone ever since he had first taken Tyrone on as a client. Of course, Claremore was totally out of Flannery's financial reach. Unless, of course, the bank foreclosed, and the estate was sold off at an absurdly low price in order to pay its remaining creditors, namely the bank. At which point, no doubt, 'Old Flann' would be the first and the very last to bid at the auction.

'So even though as you say, Mrs Rosse,' Flannery was concluding, 'that your prospects are improving, and your hopes for the forthcoming race season run high – I have to say it appears to me, and please don't misunderstand me, because you know that I am only here to help you – but it does appear to me you may well be requiring some further help from the bank.'

Cassie deliberately fingered the large emerald brooch she was wearing, in order to draw Flannery's attention to it. It was worth well over a thousand pounds, and Cassie hired it from a pawnbroking cousin of Tomas' every time she had an interview at the bank. The pawnbroker charged her five pounds for the day, which was exorbitant to say the least, but invaluable as visible collateral.

And sure enough, Flannery now had his eyes fixed on the beautiful brooch.

'I have no need, dear Mr Flannery,' Cassie replied, 'to avail myself of your very kind offer. In fact, I'm in the happy position of being able to pay off a lot of what I owe you.'

While she spoke, Cassie had opened her purse, and had started to lay wads of notes on the desk in front of her. She glanced up to find that Flannery, as she had hoped, had immediately transferred his gaze from the brooch to the two thousand pounds she was laying on the desk.

'Gracious. How much do we have there?'

'I'm not sure. Around two thousand pounds, I imagine. A hundred pounds at 20/1. Yes, that's two thousand pounds, isn't it?'

Cassie looked up at him, as she took the last elastic-banded bundle of notes from her purse. Then she put both hands below the desk and crossed her fingers tightly.

'This was the result of a flutter then, Mrs Rosse?' Flannery enquired.

'This, Mr Flannery,' Cassie replied, 'is no flutter. You're looking at an almighty gamble.'

Which indeed it was. Cassie and Tomas had hatched the plan together, in the hope of buying more time, the time they needed either to prepare a horse to win, or to back someone else's certainty. But with the season only just about to start, it would be a good month if not longer before they could be certain of finding a 'good thing'. So they had persuaded the ever-affable Joe Coughlan to lend Cassie two thousand pounds in cash, just for the afternoon. If the gamble paid off, Cassie promised Coughlan he could have a week's free training for his four horses. Joe Coughlan had laughed and dismissed the notion.

'For what?' he'd said. 'What do I have to lose?'

'Two thousand hard-earned pounds, Joe,' Cassie had warned him, 'if Flanelly Flann decides to take the money off me.'

'He won't,' Tomas had stated quite categorically. 'For he wants you out of Claremore. And if he thinks you've started gambling, then he'll want you to keep the money for you to go away and lose it. Which if you were a gambler, you most surely would.'

And now the chips were down. Flannery was staring at the piles of money, while making his conclusions. Then he looked up at Cassie who was busily pretending to repair her make-up with the aid of her lipstick and powder compact. She smiled blithely at him, as if the money didn't mean a thing, then continued carefully to lipstick her mouth.

Flannery stared back at the money, and then picking it all up, stacked it in front of him.

Cassie's blood chilled, but she barely glanced away from her handheld mirror.

'No, no,' Flannery suddenly said, tapping the bundles into better shape, 'no, there's no reason at all for you to pay the bank back early. That's not the reason I wanted to see you at all. No no, while your position, financially, is still a little precarious, I wouldn't hear of such a thing.'

'Dear Mr Flannery,' she protested, 'you must take it. We don't want head office getting cross with you. That would never do at all.'

Flannery hadn't thought of that. But this reminded him. He remembered that the annual audit was coming up, and he had already received a letter from Dublin to the effect that he must review all outstanding overdrafts, and call in those over a certain limit. Cassie's was well over that limit.

483

'Besides,' Cassie continued, 'if you don't take all this money, I could go and lose it all. I could. Just as easily as I won it. And just as quickly.'

Flannery hesitated. People who gambled were fools. Women who gambled were even bigger fools. Cassie, like her husband gone before her, was quite obviously now a gambler. He pushed the money back to her.

'You wouldn't be such a silly girl,' he said with a little smile. 'Now come along, and I shall buy you lunch at the hotel.'

Cassie put the money back in her purse with as much reluctance as she could muster, while Flannery fetched her fur coat. This time as he slipped it back on her, his hand brushed one of her breasts.

He held the office door open for her, his puffy white cheeks once more slightly tinged with pink.

'In the midst of death,' Cassie thought to herself, 'we are in farce.'

'He almost proposed to me over lunch!' Cassie told Tomas as they did evening stables. ' "Now I'm aware this is neither quite the time nor the place, Mrs Rosse, to be telling you this. But sooner or later it may occur to you that in a big house such as Claremore, you're going to get maybe a little bit lonesome." Can you imagine, Tomas?'

'I cannot, Mrs Rosse,' Tomas replied. 'I'd sooner see you marry into English royalty.'

'It's as bad as *that*?' Cassie laughed. 'Gracious, I thought *my* dislike for the dirty old man at the bank was bad enough!'

They finished their round of inspection, which nowadays took less than a quarter of the time it had taken when Tyrone was alive, because now between them they had only ten horses in their charge. Leonora's defection had left the yard almost half empty, and then ten months ago a mystery virus had finished off where Leonora had started.

Cassie had determined to take over the running of the

yard shortly after Tyrone had been killed. But since under the rules of racing, as a woman Cassie wasn't allowed officially to train, the licence had to be taken out in Tomas' name. Cassie had made her decision known to Tomas some time after the funeral, at the time of year when they were usually beginning to rough the horses off for the winter. Tomas hadn't argued, or queried her reasons. He had just nodded, and quietly gone about his work as if it was the most natural decision in the world, and even though the Jockey Club was showing no sign of relenting their Men Only training rule.

'I know nothing at all about it, you understand,' Cassie had warned him. 'Nothing whatsoever.'

'Who does when they start, Mrs Rosse?' Tomas had replied. 'The main thing is you know how to feed 'em. And that's a good head start for you.'

'*I* know how to feed them?'

'No. But I do.'

Tomas had then touched his old cap and disappeared into the feed room to weigh out his secret recipes.

But then one morning the following May, when Cassie was first in the yard in the morning as always, in the first box she opened up she had found a horse dying. It was a big three-year-old chestnut colt called Interim, and the day before he had been in such apparent high spirits he had bucked his work rider off on the way to the gallops and had taken all the catching. Now he was standing with his head hanging down by his knees, his eyes sunk back into his skull with a ribbon of white showing, and his breathing was fast and shallow.

'At least he's not gone down,' Tomas muttered, inserting the thermometer in the horse's rectum. 'That's the good news. The bad news is this fellah's not our only invalid.'

'Who else?' Cassie asked, with an urgent look.

'Mr Toad, Whirlybird, Rockin' in Rhythm and Annagh Bridge.'

By dawn next morning, four of their best horses lay

dead in their boxes. Their vet, Niall Brogan, was baffled, saying that he'd never seen horses drop down dead so quickly. He'd come out the instant Cassie had called him, and shot the horses full of antibiotics. But the moment he inspected them, he told Cassie that it would be touch and go. Interim, who was apparently the worst case, survived, but more by luck than judgement. Cassie had sat up with him in his box, since he seemed the most likely to die, and, tiring of sitting on an upturned water bucket, she'd pulled in a bale of hay. After a couple of hours, the horse had suddenly started nibbling the hay, and didn't stop for the next eight hours, the crucial hours, as Niall Brogan had warned them they would be, and as a consequence of his greed the horse didn't go down. Instead he kept wearily nibbling while Cassie stroked his neck, and kept squeezing a soaking sponge into his mouth to stop him dehydrating completely. By midnight the horse had turned the corner.

So too it seemed had the star of the yard, Annagh Bridge. His temperature hadn't hit the frightening heights that Interim's had, staying steady around about 104° for twenty-four hours, and then slowly descending. But two days later, seemingly over the worst, his temperature again shot up, this time to 106° and twenty-four hours later he too was lying dead.

All told, out of the twenty-two horses still in training, five died, and ten more contracted the virus. Fortunately Niall Brogan had given every horse a covering antibiotic as a necessary precaution, and those that then contracted the virus subsequently were much less severely stricken and survived. The seven horses who remained uninfected were put at once into isolation, before being removed, once the vet had given them the all-clear, to other yards, and by the end of the season, following a period of convalescence, eight of the remaining ten horses had run in over twenty-four races and all had come nowhere.

When training started for the following season, the string had been reduced to eight horses. Two of

Townshend Warner's, one of the few owners who had stood by Claremore regardless, Moviola, a new horse of James Christiansen's, Celebration, whom Cassie had taken back for the winter from Willie Moore, and who due to a sudden attack of ringworm was fortunately in isolation when the virus struck, running out in the home paddocks all by himself, and of course the ever-loyal Joe Coughlan's regular foursome.

And somewhere, from this depleted string, Cassie and Tomas had to find their racing certainty.

'If it has to be within a month, six weeks,' Tomas said, scratching the back of his head, 'then forget about Celebration, for he'll not be ready, Moviola's too big and backward still, all of Joe's are dogs anyway, so that leaves us Mr Warner's.'

They walked first to one of Townshend Warner's horses and then back to the other. One was Tootsie, a very nice filly by the French stallion Mainspring out of the Irish mare Night Club Girl, who had won eight good races on the flat, and run a close second in the Irish Oaks, and the other was a big strong colt, with all the makings of a fine horse, called Reverse. His dam was a Canadian winning mare called Goody Two-Shoes, and he was the second crop of a barely known North American stallion standing in Maryland called Northern Dancer.

'This could be our boy,' Cassie said finally, after they had walked hither and thither between the two boxes half a dozen times. 'When Mr Warner sent him over, he said the agent who found him and bought him said he could be a classic horse.'

'Ach,' said Tomas dismissively. 'These fancy-bred American bloody horses, savin' your presence. What's it my old sergeant-major used to call it? That's it. They're all mouth and trousers.'

'We'll see about that, Tomas Muldoon,' Cassie replied, 'when he does his first serious bit of work.'

In the office, Cassie looked at her work chart, and saw that Reverse was down for a spin the following Friday.

She pinned Pat Ward's name next to Tootsie, Liam Docherty's next to Gearhan, one of Joe Coughlan's 'dogs', and Tomas's up next to Moviola.

'So who's to ride the big boy?' Tomas asked.

'I am,' Cassie answered.

Tomas ran out of the office after her.

'Have you taken leave of your senses, Mrs Rosse?' he cried. ' 'Tis riding work we're talking about! Not hacking out on Bouncer!'

'I have been doing riding work, Tomas,' she told him. 'I've been doing riding work three times a week for Willie Moore.'

'And who taught yous?'

'Willie.'

'Willie! Willie Moore taught yous? And what was wrong with me?'

Cassie turned and smiled at Tomas, who was practically hopping up and down with rage.

'I thought if I was going to make a fool of myself,' she answered, 'much better to do it away from home.'

'And who's to say you'll be able to handle Reverse?' Tomas persisted.

'Willie Moore does, Tomas. He put me up on Fly In Me Eye last evening, and he said if I could pull him up before Tipperary then I could ride anything.'

Cassie grinned. 'I pulled him half a furlong from the end of the gallop. Willie said I'd rewritten history.'

Cassie had only been able to do so thanks to her winter of preparation: thanks to the six months she'd spent pounding the roads and running up the hills, the weeks she'd spent doing sit ups and press ups and lift ups, to tighten and tauten every muscle in her arms and legs and stomach, and the hours she'd spent crouched, as Willie Moore had shown her, in the proper 'riding out' position.

'Until you can stay like this,' he'd said to her, demonstrating what he meant, 'until you can remain motionless like this for fifteen minutes, forget about riding racehorses. That's if you want to ride them properly.'

The 'riding-out' position meant adopting the orthodox jockey position, but without the benefit of saddle, irons, or horse. You simply stood crouched, with your legs bent at the knees, your thighs parallel to the floor and your hands holding invisible reins. Cassie thought it looked easy until she first tried it, having to straighten up with cramp after only one minute.

It took her a fortnight before she was able to hold the position for two and a half minutes without moving, six weeks before she was strong enough to hold it for ten and six months before she finally could do it for fifteen minutes. And all this time she was riding. First on Bouncer, whom she would canter for three or four miles with her leathers pulled up four holes and her hands turned over on the reins; then on one of Willie's school-masters, an ex-racehorse he used to school all his lads; and finally the day came when he put her up on her first two-year-old.

'Remember, Cassie,' he warned her, 'what you have under you is even more frightened probably than you.'

'Is that possible?' Cassie asked, as she felt the colt begin to prance under her.

'You've got to give him the confidence, Cassie,' Willie went on. 'And that'll come through your hands. If he feels frightened hands on those ribbons, he'll cart you into the next county.'

'Why am I doing this, Willie?' Cassie cried, as the horse bucked and then ran sideways out of the gate with her. 'I could be in bed, reading a book!'

Willie had ridden alongside her that morning not only to give her confidence, but also to watch how she went. The young horse gave Cassie a terrible time on the way to the gallops, trying to climb banks and hedges, and shying at everything from a drain cover to his own shadow. Then when they got on to Willie's gallops, he plunged and tried to run off with her before they'd even settled and checked their girths, and Cassie did well to hold him in check.

By then her terror had passed. As they walked towards the point where they would start their serious work, Cassie realised that the worst that could happen to her was that she could get thrown and killed, and if that was the case there was nothing to be frightened of because it meant she would be seeing Tyrone again. So she forgot her fear and concentrated on settling the horse under her, whose sole intention at that moment was either to throw her or bolt with her.

She relaxed her rein and dropped the horse. He was taken completely by surprise and, finding nothing to fight against, he too relaxed, and started walking round in the circle which Cassie was asking him to do. Willie nodded, and circled after her. Then he reminded his lads of his instructions and called to Cassie to lead off. Cassie collected her horse up, squeezed him on and forward, and as soon as he was cantering nicely she was up in the correct position without a bump. The horse tried to seize hold of his bit now that he realised he was being asked to go, but Cassie fooled him again by refusing to fight him. Instead she softened her hands and tightened her legs, shortening the horse's stride and bringing him back on the bridle.

By the end of the first furlong Cassie had him striding out sweetly. Willie was upside her, and he called across to her as they passed the second furlong pole to let him stretch for the last two of the five furlong workout. Cassie did as she was told and as soon as she asked the horse, he quickened nicely, and left Willie's horse for dead.

It was then a matter of stopping him, and of doing so without jarring him, or hurting the young horse in the mouth. But he had a good hold of his bit now, and was doing his level best to cock his jaw so that Cassie would lose control of him. But his jockey had done her homework, and rather than jab him in the mouth, she kept herself perfectly balanced in the saddle and slackened her rein off almost completely. As soon as she felt the horse drop his bit, she gathered the reins up again, but so smoothly that the horse didn't even notice, and having got him back, began to pull him up gradually by tipping her weight further and further back from his centre of gravity, at the same time letting out more rein.

The young horse came down correctly through the canter, into a good long trot, then finally a walk, as Cassie turned him round at the end of the straight.

Willie finally ranged alongside once more, pulling his horse up sweetly and carefully. He turned his horse round and walked back in silence with Cassie. Cassie patted her horse's neck, flicked his mane over, and let out a notch on his girth. What she didn't do was ask her trainer what he thought. Instead, as they headed the string home, she observed the total silence he was keeping.

Finally, after they'd hopped down off their horses in the yard and untacked them, Willie deigned to speak.

'OK, Cassie,' he said, as they headed for the tack room, 'if they ever let you girls ride under rules, you'll be the first one I'll ring.'

That Friday, an hour after dawn had broken, Reverse with Cassie on board did everything that was asked of him in his first serious piece, and more. Cassie didn't make him take on the three-year-old filly who was galloping upside him, in case the more experienced horse headed him and disheartened her youngster. All too often she had heard Tyrone say that a young horse's heart could be broken on the gallops by letting him get beat by older and sometimes faster animals.

'The whole point of galloping a horse, Cassie McGann,' she could hear him saying to her as she steadied the horse halfway through his work, 'is to keep him sweet. Sweet and enthusiastic. Good horses don't like getting beat. So why bury them out on the gallops?'

So she let Reverse just lob along by the side of Tootsie, and when she called to Tomas to let out a reef just for the final hundred yards, she could feel the big horse quicken so immediately under her that she knew for certain he was a Ferrari and not a Ford.

Back in the office they checked through his entries, and found that he was in at Naas in three weeks, and the Curragh in four. Cassie opted for the Curragh, and Tomas agreed, albeit reluctantly, being of the opinion that even a month might be a little bit soon for him.

'We'll play it by ear, Tomas,' Cassie said.

'We'll need to be certain, Mrs Rosse,' Tomas replied. 'That race at the Curragh's usually a pretty hot one.'

'I have a feeling Reverse's a pretty hot horse.'

'He will be by July or August, certainly. By the look of him, he's going to need time. Maybe we should slip little Tootsie in a modest little race out in the country. She's still a maiden, remember.'

'Let's play it by ear, Tomas,' Cassie repeated.

Tomas nodded, touched his cap and went to make up his feeds. But Cassie knew his walk well enough to know that he was not in full agreement.

That evening Cassie was too tired to go running, and too tired to face Erin in the kitchen, who, from what she'd seen of her that afternoon was in one of her 'sighing' moods. Instead she thought she'd sit in the study and put her feet up in front of the television.

She sat not watching or listening to the programme but staring at the row of ledgers which remained undisturbed since Tyrone's death above his desk. Cassie had felt at first as if she was trespassing sitting in the study by herself, because this had always been what Tyrone had called his dug-out. She had only ever disturbed him in here if there had been a crisis, and they had never once sat down in this room together to discuss anything. Whenever they had something to say to each other, Tyrone would lock his desk with the ledgers in it, rise, take Cassie by the hand and lead her across the hall to the drawing room.

And now the ledgers he had always so carefully locked away were up on the shelf where Cassie had replaced them when she had forced herself to go through the heart-breaking process of sorting through all Tyrone's papers. She had found notes she had written to him, little billet-doux she had sometimes slipped into his pocket on the racecourse or at a stuffy dinner party, for him to read when she wasn't at his side to remind him of her love for him. And there was a drawer full of all the birthday cards she had ever written him, and all the gift tags she had attached to her presents to him. He had kept every one, secretly, unknown to her. There were photographs too, pictures she still couldn't bear to look at, and probably, she thought, never could. And there were the letters she had sent him from America just before they were married, which he had tied up in a pink ribbon, in the exact order in which he had received them.

But she had never once looked in the ledgers. Now, however, she found herself rising and taking them down and putting them in a pile on the desk in front of her. They were each gold-stamped with a year, starting back in 1948, when Cassie had been in her second year at the convent. Nineteen forty-eight. She had been seven years old when Tyrone had started his first ledger. So what did it contain? What did they all contain? Were they diaries? A detailed journal of his life? Or what? Cassie hardly dared open them.

When she did, she found they were records of all Tyrone's wagers. They contained a near twenty-year history of every bet Tyrone had ever struck. The entries were all in his wonderfully neat hand, and in the same coloured inks: black for the name of the horse, the meeting and the odds, blue for his winnings, red for his losses. As she progressed through the volumes, Cassie was staggered by the size of the wagers. She had known that Tyrone liked what he called the odd tilt or touch, but she had never realised that it was a full-time occupation. Nor had she realised what a totally reckless man he had been, gambling heavily at times such as when they were first married when he could ill afford to do so.

493

But he seemed to have won more than he lost, particularly when Leonora sent all her horses to him, when the size of his bets increased, and also their frequency. But even at that time he didn't confine his bets to his own horses, with whose chances and form he was most familiar. He had wagers everywhere, including France and even America. He had regularly made and lost fortunes. No wonder he had sent to Paris for model gowns for her, and lavished presents on them all at crazy times. When he was on a winning streak, he spent.

'You old devil,' Cassie said out loud with a smile. 'You're a rogue. You never said a thing about it. Even when you were down and losing thousands.'

She had thought he had made all his money just from training and selling on young horses. Now she was entering the game herself, she realised quite how impossible that was, to make a rich living from training other people's horses. Obviously if you wanted to strike gold, you gambled.

So was this what she was going to have to do all the time? Rather than just the once to try and get her finances on an even keel? That was naïve for a start, she suddenly realised – putting all her eggs in one racing basket. But what else could she do to stop Flannery foreclosing on the mortgage? She was going to have to gamble. She was going to have to follow in Tyrone's footsteps. She was going to have to study not just form, but the form of the form, and find out on the grapevine which horses were 'on' and which were 'off'.

When she'd first become really interested in racing, Cassie had been confused by the two terms, believing wrongly when she heard a certain stable was 'off' that they were 'on', and vice versa. Now she understood that when the word was out that a certain horse was 'on', it meant that it was expected duly to win. And if these tips were horses running in selling plates, or claiming races, or moderate handicaps, the chances of them obliging, as Cassie learned winning was called, were pretty short.

She sat back in Tyrone's chair. It was too large for her, so much so that she felt as if she was wearing one of his old sports coats. She sat back and stared at the books in front of her, and wondered whether she would have the nerve and the daring of her dead and beloved husband.

Then she went upstairs and tucked up her children, even though they were both fast asleep, Mattie for once sleeping quite quietly and peacefully. She kissed them both, and they barely stirred from their deep, innocent sleeps, before retiring to her own little room.

How she hated the dark now! Before it had never worried her, not even in her mother's house. But now she practically always slept with her bedside light on. When she slept. Sleep was now something to be fought, lest it took her into that strange land of terrible and frightening dreams. She hadn't started dreaming about Tyrone for months, probably because of the heavy sleeping tablets Doctor Gilbert had prescribed. But now it seemed that every night she dreamt some black and ghoulish vision, and she would wake soaked in sweat and numbed with a grievous fear. Then she would get up and go down to the kitchen to make herself a cup of tea, and sit by the still warm stove until dawn broke, and the birds started singing once more. When she wasn't riding work, which seemed to be now about only one day a week, sometimes she would creep back to bed for an hour, but usually once it was light she would change swiftly and silently and leave for the yard before anyone else was awake.

Sometimes on fine mornings, she would stop by the woods at the exact point where she and Tyrone had heard the nightingale. She would sit on the old tree trunk and pray to God to make the little bird sing again, as a sign that Tyrone was there, somewhere, anywhere. It didn't matter where. Just that he *was* still, that somehow he still existed if only now in spirit, and that he was looking down on her, and making sure that they were all, all three of them, going to be all right until they met again.

495

But the woods were filled not with the throbbing luscious sound of the nightingale's song, but with the rattle and prattle of the dawn chorus, the sharp cries of the starlings and the flapping of the bigger birds' wings. And Cassie would rise, weary and disheartened, not even cheered by the sound which before had never failed to raise her spirits: that of the horses calling and shouting for their breakfasts.

It was decided to run Reverse at the Curragh, or rather Cassie decided the horse was to run. Tomas said he still had too much fat about him and Cassie, looking at the horse, was inclined to agree. But two things forced her hand. Firstly, Tootsie came heavily into season, and lost all interest in her work, and secondly, despite still being a little on the tubby side, Reverse did a piece of work in the week before his intended race which even nearly convinced Tomas he was ready to go. Cassie galloped him over the full six furlongs, leaving Tomas on the ground with the stopwatches. Reverse's split times for the last two furlongs, when he was no way fully extended, were the fastest times Cassie had ever seen recorded at Claremore.

'What sort of speed will he go when he's asked, eh Tomas?' Cassie asked as she hopped off his back and gave him an easy. 'Jeeze, he was barely out of a canter!'

'He's having a bit of a blow, Mrs Rosse,' Tomas said doubtfully. 'I'd like to see him easier in his wind.'

'He will be after his next piece of work,' Cassie retorted. 'He's a bit of a stuffy horse, I reckon, and one more piece of fast work should have him spot on.'

Tomas picked a handful of grass and offered it to the horse, who ate it with relish. Then he stuck a Sweet Afton in his own mouth and, lighting it, thoughtfully watched the smoke drift up to the sky.

Cassie asked him for a leg back up on to her horse, and as she walked him home, wondered what on earth she could do to convince her very own Doubting Tomas.

*   *   *

Everything went in copybook fashion until the Claremore team arrived at the Curragh itself. Reverse had continued to improve in condition, and pleased even Tomas in his final bit of work. The two horses Cassie and Tomas most feared didn't stand their ground, leaving from an original entry of over thirty horses, a field of only eight runners, six of whom according to their spies could more or less be discounted. There was only one other strongly fancied runner, from Tim Curley's yard, a well-bred grey called Blazes Man, but Tomas bought his lad a large drink on his arrival at the course and came back with the information that the grey was only out for a school in public, an activity frowned upon by the authorities but widely practised by most trainers, whereby their horses' first run in public was, as it was said, something in the nature of an education. Reverse was the short-priced favourite in all the newspapers, so once they had digested all the evidence, Tomas grudgingly admitted he could well be their 'good thing'. He still had the last word, however, advising Cassie not to plunge until the horse was saddled and on his way to the start. Tomas was a firm believer in the amount of slipping which took place between cups and lips.

Unhappily he was to be proved right, and all too soon.

Dermot Pryce was involved in a car crash on his way to the racecourse, and was rushed to hospital with multiple injuries. Cassie called the hospital at once, to be told that Pryce was in no danger, but had sustained a broken pelvis, three broken ribs and multiple lacerations, while Tomas rushed around to find another jockey. They had very little time, because Reverse's race was the second on the card. Tomas' first three choices were all booked, and two other jockeys who would have made able substitutes only had rides in the last two races so hadn't yet arrived at the Curragh. Finally and sixth best, Tomas offered last season's star apprentice the ride, a cocky little Dubliner called Brendan O'Dowell. He was a very talented lad, of that there was no doubt; but the the the more orthodox trainers and horseman strongly disapproved of his style of riding, considering that for a tall boy he rode far too short.

'Just tell him to drop his leathers a couple of holes then, Tomas,' Cassie said, throwing the saddle up on to Reverse's back.

'You tell him,' Tomas retorted, 'and Christ you've only forgotten the number cloth!'

Tomas yanked the saddle back off and looked round for the missing article of tack.

'I'm going to go and have a word with O'Dowell,' Cassie said. 'Because you won't. Liam will help you finish saddling up.'

Cassie left Tomas and Liam to it, and went in search of her jockey. She saw him standing just inside the door of the weighing room, having a cigarette and a gossip with some of his fellow riders.

'Now listen, O'Dowell,' Cassie said taking him outside, 'you haven't ridden for Mr Muldoon before, and he wants you to know that while he reckons you, he also thinks like a lot of people that you ride too short.'

O'Dowell turned round and pulled a very open face to one of the jockeys in the doorway behind him. Then he turned back and looked Cassie coolly in the eye.

'There's plenty of other jocks, ma'am,' he replied, stubbing out his cigarette.

'You're booked, O'Dowell,' Cassie told him. 'You've accepted the ride and you're to ride to orders.'

'Whose orders would these be, ma'am?'

'Mr Muldoon's, and the owner's – who unfortunately isn't here.'

'I see.'

He gave another backwards look to his chum, and slapped his whip down on top of his boot.

'I have to get mounted now, ma'am,' he said, touching his cap, 'if you'll excuse me.'

Cassie followed him towards the paddock, seething quietly. The boy hadn't been directly discourteous, but his every question and reply had been heavily tinged with recognisable sarcasm.

'Mr Muldoon says you're to ride the horse two holes longer than you normally do,' Cassie instructed as they made their way across the grass to where the horse had been pulled in.

'I'll check that with Mr Muldoon, ma'am,' O'Dowell replied. 'Just to make sure there's no misunderstanding. You know – too many cooks and all that.'

The jockey touched his cap to Tomas and then ran his eye over the horse.

'Nice sort of animal, sir,' he said to Tomas, his back now to Cassie.

'You're to hold him up until a furlong out, O'Dowell,' Cassie instructed. 'He's got a lot of speed, and if you tuck him in third or fourth, just off the pace until the distance, once you let him down you'll bury them.'

Tomas legged the boy up and checked the girths. The boy immediately started shortening his leathers.

'Leave those be now,' Tomas said. 'That's the length you're to ride him.'

O'Dowell nodded, and settled into the horse, while Liam tugged the number cloth, one side of which had got rucked up under the girths and saddle.

'Let that thing alone,' Tomas said. 'And get the horse out of here, O'Dowell. He's beginning to get warm.'

Warm was an understatement, Cassie thought, looking at the lathers of sweat which had broken out between the horse's hind legs, down his neck and under his saddle. Reverse was also becoming visibly upset with the pre-race activity, and was beginning to prance and roll his eye.

Liam grabbed the lead chain in an attempt to get the horse quickly out of the paddock, but the horse suddenly stood upon his hind legs and sent Liam flying. Tomas grabbed the bridle as the horse came down, and Liam scrambled back on to his feet, a bit shaken but luckily unscathed.

'Go on now!' urged Tomas. 'Get the beast out of here! And take him down easy, O'Dowell!'

The jockey tried to settle the horse as Liam led him towards the paddock exit, but Reverse's blood was up, and he jinked and pranced and practically knocked another horse flying as he crashed sideways out of the exit.

'Come on,' Tomas said grimly, taking Cassie by the elbow. 'We'd best see how he goes down.'

'But I haven't placed the bet yet!' Cassie protested.

' 'Tis just as well I'd say,' Tomas replied. 'By the look of him he's already run his race.'

They stood at the bottom of the enclosure, right by the rails, and watched intently as Reverse came out first onto the course.

'My God, Tomas!' Cassie exclaimed. 'That little so and so's only shortening his leathers!'

Tomas took a look through his race glasses and saw that Cassie was right. Instead of steadying and calming the very anxious horse he had under him, the boy was quite coolly and openly yanking up his irons.

'Stupid little bugger,' Tomas muttered, 'savin' your presence. Ah well. All we can do now is pray he rides as good as they all say he does.'

Moments later, Reverse cantered right by the two of them on his way down to the start. Another moment later, the horse shied violently away from the rails as a newspaper blew across the track in front of him, and half a second later, O'Dowell was lying on the ground. Cassie clapped a horrified hand to her mouth and Tomas let fly some fearsome oaths in Irish, as the now 2/1 favourite galloped off across the vast expanse of the Curragh.

They caught him after five minutes, down by the mile-and-a-half start. O'Dowell, perfectly unhurt, was reunited with his truant partner, and having to walk him the best part of three quarters of a mile back to the six-furlong start, the race was delayed a further five minutes.

'That's him cooked,' Tomas sighed. 'You can save your money.'

'I don't think so,' Cassie replied. 'He's such a strong horse. It won't have taken that much out of him.'

'He's cooked,' Tomas said succinctly, and wandered off to the bar.

Cassie hesitated and, taking her purse from under her arm where she held it tight, opened it and looked at the money she had been due to lay. One thousand pounds in her purse, and the other thousand in the lining of Tomas's old tweed jacket. The entire two thousand pounds Joe Coughlan had lent them before and had willingly lent them again for what seemed now a crazy gamble. Seeing what she had just seen, and knowing what she did now, Cassie doubted her own sanity for a moment. That people could willingly be prepared to plunge such a large amount of money on a commodity as unknown as a racehorse astounded her. It terrified her when she realised that she had so nearly been one of those people. And that the money she had been so eagerly prepared to gamble was not even hers.

Even so, still believing that Reverse would trot up, Cassie rushed off to the Tote to place what for Tyrone would have been a token bet but for Cassie was still a considerable amount of money.

'I want a hundred-pound win on Reverse, please.'

She was the only person at the windows, everyone else having already laid their money.

'The horse's name's no good, miss. I need his number.'

'Of course you do. So sorry.'

Cassie fumbled for her racecard, then realised that she'd stuffed it in Tomas's pocket earlier on.

'The white flag is up!' the course commentator called.

'Quickly now, if you want to be on.'

Cassie closed her eyes and tried to visualise Reverse's number cloth. She remembered just in time.

'Number two. Horse number two.'

She pushed the money under the grille, and the man handed her back a clutch of tickets.

'And they're off!'

By the time she'd got back to her place in the stands, they'd run the best part of a furlong. The big grey was leading, travelling very fast. Reverse was lying handy in third, and also motoring. Three furlongs from home the second horse began to tie up, and Reverse ranged up alongside him, still travelling fast and, as it seemed from the stands, still well within himself. Even though he was riding far too short, O'Dowell had him beautifully balanced, and from the way Reverse and the grey appeared to be drawing away from the rest of the field, Cassie was beginning to regret her change of mind about the size of her bet.

Then O'Dowell went for home, a good furlong and a half earlier than instructed. Cassie bit her lip and pressed her race glasses harder to her eyes. The young horse was still striding out well, but wasn't making much impression on the grey Blazes Man, who was still a length up. A furlong out, and Blazes Man began to tire and hang away from the rails, forcing O'Dowell to pull his whip through. But he had his horse balanced again immediately, and Reverse started at last to overhaul the leader.

No one, it seemed, appeared to notice the little dark bay who was making up ground hand over fist on the rails.

Not, that is, until the two leading horses, Reverse and Blazes Man, suddenly started to stop a hundred and fifty yards from home, and the little bay shot through the ever-widening gap on the rails to pinch the race from under them, and win by two lengths and going away.

The commentator called the result, the winner being a horse called Badgerstale, and a photograph for second place.

There was, as there always is on a racecourse when a rank outsider wins, a moment of stunned silence, then a buzz as everyone consulted their papers and racecards to find out who on earth had won and how and why. Cassie stood still staring out at the track, disbelieving and confused. She didn't know whether to be relieved that her horse hadn't won because she hadn't plunged £2000 on him, or furious at the way he had been ridden.

By the time she remet Tomas she had decided on the latter.

'Of course he should have won it, Mrs Rosse,' Tomas agreed as they waited for Reverse to return. 'If the boy hadn't ridden so short, he'd never have been thrown. And the horse wouldn't have wasted all that energy bolting.'

'And then the way he rode him!' Cassie exclaimed. 'He was told not to produce him till the very last moment!'

'Some jockeys are born listeners, Mrs Rosse,' Tomas told her. 'And some are born know-it-alls.'

O'Dowell hopped down off the horse and started to unsaddle him.

'He's a good sort of horse, Mr Muldoon,' he said. 'He'll win some nice ones when he learns to settle.'

'And when he's ridden to orders,' Cassie seethed.

'He ran very green, sir,' the jockey continued, ignoring Cassie and slipping off the horse's saddle. 'He didn't really know what he was being asked till that little fellah sneaked up on the rails. Then he started to motor again.'

'He'd have won if you'd ridden him like you were told,' Cassie said, raising her voice to be noticed.

But the boy wasn't interested in her opinion. He slapped the horse on the flank, told Tomas that he really was a nice sort of animal, and then sauntered off to the weighing room.

The photograph showed Reverse to have held on to second place by a head.

'There's no point in coming second, Tomas,' Cassie said over a drink. 'Tyrone always said it's first or forget it.'

'The horse was beat, Mrs Rosse. He was beat in the paddock, he was beat on the way down and he was beat in the race. He changed his legs twice in the last furlong.'

Cassie sighed and sipped her orange juice. Tomas was right, and she knew it. She knew she would also have to learn to observe Tyrone's other hard and fast-held tenet: no excuses.

She opened her purse to get some money to buy another drink, but first had to remove the clutch of tote tickets that were littering the top of her bag.

'Get rid of these for me, would you Tomas?' she asked, handing them to him.

'I thought yous weren't going to have a bet,' he replied, taking the tickets from her.

'I wasn't. Then I thought hell – just in case. It's all right. I didn't put it all on. I only had a hundred on him.'

' 'Tis always "only" when you lose,' he sighed. 'A hundred pound buys a lot of corn.'

'I know. But I thought he was sure to win.'

Tomas shook his head and then suddenly stopped. He grabbed back the tickets he'd already stuffed in an ash tray and started feverishly leafing through them. Then he examined the other tickets in his hand.

'Something wrong?' Cassie enquired.

'You said you had a hundred pounds on Reverse,' Tomas replied.

'That's right. I did.'

'Well you didn't. You backed the winner.'

'You're crazy, Tomas! I had one hundred pounds to win on number two!'

'Reverse was number twenty bloody two!'

Cassie stopped laughing and stared at him. Tomas was grinning at her, wider than she'd ever seen him grin before.

'I saw his saddlecloth, Tomas,' Cassie told him, dropping her voice. 'I remembered his saddlecloth. You had my race card, but luckily I remembered seeing the number on his saddle cloth. Number two.'

'Twenty-two,' Tomas corrected her. 'If you'll also remember, the cloth got tucked up under one side of the girth and surcingle, so you may well, from where yous was standing, have only seen the two.'

'I did. That's all I saw.'

'The winner was number two.'

Cassie started to laugh.

'My goodness! I don't believe it! What price was he?'
'33/1.'

Cassie's mouth opened and closed silently as Tomas knocked back his fresh double whisky in one, then setting his cap right, led her off to the Tote.

'You could have won a bloody fortune!' he told her on their way. 'Savin' your presence. I didn't hear the returns, but with the favourite beat, they'll certainly not pay a lot *less* than 33/1.'

Cassie wondered how in a field of only eight runners, there was one such long-priced horse. Tomas explained that he was the first runner from some new man's yard, and that the small and unfashionably bred horse looked like a toast rack in the paddock, and went down to the start on three legs.

'Sure 'tis a wonder he wasn't a hundred to one the way he looked.'

They stopped at the late pay out window while Tomas carefully counted out all the tickets for horse number two.

'I haven't my glasses,' he said to the man behind the grille. 'What do you pay on the winner?'

'Don't tell me you're the one with the tickets?' the official replied with a huge smile. 'I was told 'twas a lovely little brown-haired woman with dancin' eyes.'

'Just tell me what you're paying, Romeo,' Tomas replied good-naturedly.

'£9 to a 2/6d dividend.'

'That's 72/1!' Tomas whispered reverentially to Cassie. 'Jesus you're a rich woman!'

'All the money was for number twenty-two, and for number five,' the Tote official explained. 'There wasn't even a forecast anywhere coupled with number two. How many tickets d'you have now?'

Tomas spread the slips in front of him, and grinned.

'I'd say we have them all,' he replied.

Chapter Eighteen

On the evening of 29 June, one major worry receded from Cassie's mind: Josephine recovered her appetite. For her supper, a detail Cassie was never able to forget, she ate a bowl of chicken noodle soup, four slices of lamb, five roast potatoes and two helpings of trifle.

Her mother made no comment on this change of events, but took it all in her stride, treating this historic moment like an everyday occurrence. She did, however, manage to wink unnoticed at Erin and put a finger to her lips, just in time to stop Erin making one of her famous remarks.

And it was all due to a horse.

Or, to be a little more exact, a pony. It was Josephine's seventh birthday and Cassie, shortly after her miracle win at the Curragh, had been trying to decide what to get her. With the money she had won, the bank had been repaid, the final creditors satisfied, Claremore was safe, and there was even just under fifteen hundred pounds lodged safely in Mr Flannery's keeping. So Cassie determined to buy her daughter something really wonderful for her birthday.

Erin had suggested clothes, but Cassie informed her crisply that she'd be getting a whole bunch of new clothes anyway, now that they were solvent.

'No,' Cassie explained, 'I want to make this birthday a day she'll never forget as long as she lives.'

It took Sheila Meath, Josephine's other godmother, to suggest the perfect present of a pony.

'Why didn't I think of that!' Cassie cried.

'Because you've had other things on your mind, my dear,' her friend replied. 'It hasn't exactly been a time to see things clearly.'

Sheila also supplied the animal: a perfectly schooled first pony, with a shiny black coat and the temperament of a St Bernard. On the morning of Josephine's birthday, Cassie opened the french windows of the drawing room and made Erin stand holding the pony just outside them, with the curtains closed. She led her daughter downstairs and into the room, where there was a little pile of presents by the fireplace.

'Gracious me,' Cassie had said. 'You'll never see what you've been given for your birthday with all those drapes still drawn!'

'Curtains, Mummy,' Josephine had gravely corrected her. 'You say curtains. Not drapes.'

'OK. So be an angel, would you, sweetheart? And draw the *curtains*?'

There was a long moment of total silence when Josephine saw what was revealed behind them. It was as if she couldn't quite believe what she saw. She stood staring at the little black pony, who at once started to walk towards her, with Erin barely able to hold him back. Then she turned and hugged Cassie, and ran to the pony, who was now actually in the drawing room, putting her arms round his neck and hugging him tight.

'A pony,' was all she said. 'A pony, all of my own.'

Mattie, whom Cassie had in her arms, clapped his hands and hooted with laughter when he saw the pony walking round the drawing room.

'Come on, Josie!' Cassie said. 'Let's give your brother first ride!'

And placing Mattie in the saddle, Josephine took the leading rope and led her brother round the lawns, with Cassie keeping a firm hold on him.

'That won't have done much for his asthma,' Erin sniffed afterwards.

'It won't have done him any harm either,' Cassie

507

retorted. 'In fact if you ask me, it'll probably have done him the power of good. Fresh air, and a bit of an adventure. I've been thinking that we probably mollycoddle Mattie too much.'

'Never!' protested Erin. 'Sure 'tis a wonder he's still alive! He's that finely wove!'

Nevertheless, despite Erin's protestations, Cassie started adopting a less restrictive régime as far as Mattie was concerned, allowing him to play with the pony, putting the toys back in his nursery, and for good measure, letting Josephine and her blanketed bed in there too.

She did this not just on her own initiative, but under the guidance of Sheila Meath, whom she discovered was a firm believer in alternative medicine.

'Half of what the doctors tell you, my dear,' she would say, 'is sheer nonsense. A little boy like that. He can't possibly go through life dust-free! This kind of early isolation only makes things worse later on. The doc you've got to go and see is old Jimmy FitzStanton out in Killiney. He might even recommend putting Mattie on the box.'

Sheila wouldn't elaborate any more, saying if she did, she'd be bound to get it all wrong, and only muddy the water. Instead she made an appointment for Cassie and Mattie in a fortnight with Jimmy FitzStanton.

In the meantime, there were horses to be trained, and now even more urgently, new owners to be found.

'And how do yous intend goin' about that?' Tomas asked her one morning as he was making up some linseed mashes.

'I'm going to say a novena to St Jude,' Cassie replied with a grin.

'A novena to St Jude is right,' growled Tomas. 'I can't think of a greater lost cause.'

'Just you wait and see, Doubting Tomas,' Cassie said. 'Just you wait and see.'

On the ninth day of Cassie's novena, Reverse ran his second race of the season at Navan. It was a very moderate race, and the horse won as he liked, although the official distance was only half a length.

'He idled soon as he hit the front, sir,' Dermot Pryce's deputy jockey told Tomas after the race. 'But there was no point in knocking him about. He's too good an animal.'

Tomas and Cassie had a quick drink to celebrate their first win of the year, and when they returned to the horsebox, they found a message stuck under one of the wipers. It was a small white visiting card, from someone called Peter Brandt. On the back was a handwritten message that the writer would be delighted if Mr Muldoon and Mrs Rosse would meet him in Jury's hotel that evening for a drink at eight o'clock.

They barely made it home again before it was time to turn round and head back to Dublin. As it was they were twenty minutes late.

'That is, I understand,' said Mr Brandt, 'of little moment in Ireland. I start to worry when people are a day late.'

He offered them seats and called the waiter over, ordering champagne.

'I hope you like champagne,' he enquired.

'I just love it,' Cassie said quite truthfully.

Tomas remained silent, having been saving his thirst for a large John Jameson.

Cassie studied their host as he carefully lit a large cigar. He was about forty or forty-two, she guessed, not that tall, long-faced with dark eyes and perfectly even teeth. He was also Swiss. Or at least he was resident in Switzerland, according to his visiting card.

'I saw your horse win this afternoon, he said, carefully blowing out his match. 'My congratulations.'

'You were at Navan?' Cassie said with some surprise.

'He'd hardly have seen it win now, would he?' Tomas muttered, 'if he'd been at Wexford.'

'I like horseracing,' Brandt replied. 'And I am here on a holiday.'

The waiter poured the champagne, and Herr Brandt raised his glass in a toast.

'To more victories.'

'This is very civil of you, I'm sure,' Cassie said, enjoying the first glass of champagne she'd had in nearly two years. 'But if you'll pardon me, I'm sure you didn't call us all the way in to Dublin just to drink our health.'

'Pardon me,' Brandt replied politely. 'I forget how busy you must be. No, no. No, I asked you here for drinks so that we might talk business.'

Tomas forgot about his longing for a large whisky, and pulling his jacket down, sat more upright in his chair.

'Mr Muldoon. It is a very simple request. I would like you to buy me some racehorses.'

'You would, would you?' Tomas replied affably. 'Well now, that all depends on how many.'

Brandt was visibly impressed. So was Cassie, but for opposing reasons.

'Your yard is full, yes?'

'We have some vacancies. How many horses were you thinking of buying? And what sort?'

'Six horses. All handicappers.'

'You don't want any youngsters?'

'I want six handicappers. And they must be ready to race in a month. Six weeks.'

'You'll want them all to be winners too, no doubt.'

'Of course.'

Tomas turned to Cassie, suddenly desperate for her advice. But Cassie was staring in bewilderment at Brandt. She saw from the look in those dark, cold eyes, that the man was serious. And that the man meant business.

Brandt produced his cheque book, and opened it neatly in front of him on the table. Then he produced a gold fountain pen from his inside pocket and carefully removed the cap, before staring at the nib to make sure it was quite clean.

'How much do you have to spend?' Tomas replied.

'I have half a million pounds,' Brandt informed him.

'But you will make me even happier if I am not forced to spend it all.'

'You won't need a tenth of that.'

'Thank you. But what I would like you to feel is that you have the money to make people sell you good horses which otherwise they would not perhaps sell. I will write you a cheque for £250,000, and we can negotiate further monies, or anything unspent, when you have concluded your business, yes?'

Brandt started writing the cheque, and Tomas looked at Cassie, who was already looking at him.

'Mr Brandt?' Cassie asked. 'May I ask you something? Why Claremore?'

'I liked the way your horse won today,' Brandt answered, still writing.

'That's not the only reason, I feel sure,' Cassie persisted.

'No, it isn't, Mrs Rosse,' Brandt replied, putting his gold pen away as carefully as he had taken it out. 'I went round your yard yesterday when you were all on the gallops. I saw how many empty boxes you have. Which is good. Because the trainer I want has to be hungry.'

'He's nuts,' said Tomas on the drive home. 'Either he's nuts or I'm dreaming.'

'We can't both be dreaming, Tomas,' Cassie said, looking at the figures on the cheque as they passed under the street lamps.

'Then he's nuts. Completely doo-lally.'

'Where will we look for the horses?'

'We'll cross that little bridge, Mrs Rosse, if that cheque you're so busy holding isn't made of rubber.'

'And if it isn't?'

'Maybe you could manage another novena or two. For it's going to be no easy task, I can tell you. Finding six handicappers. We don't want to be buyin' horses that have shown their ability, for they'll be humpin' bloody great weights, savin' your presence. So we'll be looking for the ones due to win off low weights. And how in the

name of all that's holy are we meant to recognise them?
Sure if I could do that I'd never be drivin' around in this
poor old excuse for a motor car, now would I?'

He shook his head.

'Jesus God. Six handicappers, and they've all got to
win. I'd sooner find six pins in a cow byre.'

The cheque was duly honoured, as Cassie knew it would
be, and Tomas and she both set to work reading the form
books and racing papers until the small hours of the morning. By the time Cassie set off for Killiney with Mattie for
their appointment with Jim FitzStanton, they had offered
on three horses, and been refused on two. The one they
had purchased, for at least two thousand pounds more
than it was worth, belonged to a very shady garage owner
in Tipperary, who was just about to go out of business and
was very glad of the windfall. The horse was a five-year-
old Tomas had seen run at Wexford at the end of May,
when he had considered the horse unlucky to lose.

'Ah, 'twas the jockey,' the garage proprietor had
explained. 'Christ, sure the bugger needs holdin' up, but
not until after all the others have weighed in?'

The horse was a big sort, and would be well up to carrying weight if and when the time came. But at the moment,
having not yet got his nose in front, he had not come to the
handicapper's attention, and was still running off low
weights.

'He needs feedin', that's all,' Tomas said when the horse
arrived. 'You'll be lookin' at a different class of horse by
the time he's tucked into a week or so of old Tomas' square
meals.'

Otherwise they were not having much luck.

Happily, the reverse was true as far as Jim FitzStanton
went. Admittedly Cassie thought initially that she was in
the hands of a crank, when this enormously tall man with
a shock of white hair and schoolboy spectacles sat her
down and started to ask gently but searchingly about
Cassie's mental and emotional state. Cassie laughed

nervously at first, unwilling to answer these questions seriously, lest she should unstop the floodgates. Then they both sat in silence for a while, staring at each other, while Mattie fidgeted and coughed.

FitzStanton then called through to his wife on a rather makeshift intercom, and asked her if she wouldn't mind looking after the little boy for a few moments. Cassie was loath to leave Mattie in the care of strangers, but when Mary FitzStanton came in, all her worries evaporated. She was the sweetest and kindest-faced woman she had seen since she had left the convent. Mattie at once delighted in her company, and within minutes Cassie could hear him laughing and chattering away nonsensically outside the door.

'Now then, Mrs Rosse,' FitzStanton said. 'It's better for you to tell me about it. But if it makes you feel better, I do already know about your grief.'

He smiled at her, and far from breaking down as she feared she would, Cassie found herself smiling back.

'The point is, Doctor, you do understand that Mattie is an adopted child?'

'Yes yes. Quite, I do indeed. Sheila Meath told me all about it. But him being adopted – that doesn't stop Mattie being affected by your emotional and mental state. Far from it. He might be even more receptive to this kind of trauma, because he's adopted. So let's talk about it, if we may. How you are and how you have been. How he is, and how he has been. And please don't be afraid of becoming upset. You will find you will be able to come to terms with your loss more easily, if you allow yourself to grieve freely and openly. My guess is that you would rather be damned than allow anyone to see you cry.'

Cassie stared up at him, astounded.

'That's crazy,' he told her, with a gentle smile. 'Completely daft. You feel sorrow, anger and fear. Resentment perhaps, I'm sure. It's natural. It's only natural. And if you don't give proper vent to your emotions, they disappear, only to pop up somewhere else. And probably so

513

well disguised you wouldn't even know what it was that ailed you. Or – what ailed somebody else.'

He continued to talk to her for well over two hours, but during this time, comforted as she was by his compassion, Cassie felt no inclination to weep, or to reveal her emotions in any way. She was trying to make the past something which she need not yet contemplate, a closed door from which she could run away, far away, far enough away that if and when it did ever suddenly swing back open Cassie would be so distanced from it that she would hardly be able to recognise what lay beyond.

As far as Mattie went, FitzStanton explained to her that as a homeopath, to him her son's symptoms were what he called 'positive phenomena', meaning that they indicated that the body was making a strong attempt to restore the balance.

'We homeopaths see symptoms as part of the cure, do you understand? Not as part of the disease. We don't bother with trying to find the cause of the disease inside the body. Now this may sound a little odd to you, but when it works, it really works. So what I'm going to do with young Mattie here, is first make him *worse*.'

He winked at Mattie as if it was all a tease, and Mattie grinned. But Cassie knew the doctor to be in earnest.

'What I'm going to try and do is find a remedy that will match the reaction his body is having to the disease, and in fact increase that reaction, in the hope that the symptoms will intensify and then, please God, fade away as the disease fades away. I shall send you some powders in the post, and you must give them to Mattie here in the exact order they are numbered. And if you will have faith with me, you must continue until the course of powders is finished. After that, we'll meet again and see how we all got on. In the meantime, if you have any worries, or if you want someone to talk to, I'm here. And if I'm not here, Mary is.'

*   *   *

The powders arrived three days later. Cassie did as requested and gave them in the stated order to Mattie, who at the time was quite wheeze free. The duration of the course was eighteen days. By the ninth day, Mattie could hardly breathe.

Erin woke Cassie at three in the morning with the news, and at once Cassie picked up her mattress and eiderdown and transferred them to her son's bedside.

'Aren't you goin' to take him to the hospital?' Erin hissed at her, as Cassie settled herself on the nursery floor. 'Sure the child's half-dead.'

Cassie was out of bed and into the corridor with Erin on the end of one arm before Erin knew what was happening. She closed the nursery door so that Mattie couldn't hear their conversation.

'The sooner you learn to control yourself, Erin Muldoon,' she warned the girl, 'the better! Your histrionics and your wild panicking don't do Mattie any good! It was the same with Josephine! Fuss, fuss, fuss! These children are growing up neurotic!'

'Ah 'tis no wonder with a mother who's always out ridin',' Erin replied sullenly.

'Out riding?' Cassie hissed. 'Out riding! You think that's what I'm doing, you stupid girl? You think I'm just going out riding! Now you go off to your bed, and I'll explain a few home truths to you tomorrow. And I want no more of your hysterics, do you hear?'

Erin looked at her, then turned slowly on her heel and started to mooch back to her room.

'And for God's sake stop sniffing, Erin!'

'Ah sure nothin' that I do is right!'

'And for God's sake don't start crying!'

'Jesus, Mary and Joseph, aren't I only tryin' to do the best I can?'

'Then stop crying, and stop sniffing, and go back to your *bed*!' Cassie urged.

Mattie was sitting propped up on his pillows when

Cassie came back in. He smiled at his mother, but his discomfort was all too plainly visible.

Cassie sat on his bed and held his hand.

'OK, Tiger?' she asked. 'Let's see this one off together, shall we?'

'Yes,' Mattie whispered.

'You don't want to go to that horrid old hospital, do you?'

Mattie smiled at her, and shook his head.

'OK. So we'll find this kitten in your chest, and we'll tell him not to be such a naughty old kitten, won't we?'

Cassie rubbed her little boy's back gently and settled him more comfortably on his pillows. Then she read him Peter Rabbit six or seven times to try and get him to sleep, but the wheeze was too bad, and whenever he started to drop off, he was woken violently awake by another bout of coughing.

'Listen,' said Cassie softly. 'Is there anything really special you'd like?'

Mattie looked up at her, his big dark eyes ringed with grey.

'I'd like to sleep in your bed,' he answered.

'That's easily done,' said Cassie, turning back his covers. 'It's a bit small, mind. We might both fall out.'

'In your big bed.'

Cassie hesitated, and caught her breath when she realised what Mattie meant. He wanted to sleep next door. In the big bed. In Tyrone's and her double bed.

'Please.'

'It'll be awful cold.'

'*Please.*'

'OK,' she said. 'I'll go and fetch a couple of hot water bottles.'

In the kitchen, while the kettle was boiling, Cassie, her teeth chattering, but not from the cold, desperately searched for the bottle of cooking brandy she knew was in the cupboard, and poured herself a large shot. She looked at the glass of amber liquid. For a full minute she stared at it. Then she threw it away down the sink. After that, she filled two hot water bottles, and returned upstairs.

For a moment she stood staring at the locked door, at the door of a room she hadn't been in since Tyrone had been killed. Erin had been in, to dust and clean, but the door had always been relocked, and the key placed on top of the lintel.

Cassie reached up and, finding the key, opened the door. She paused before she switched on any light. What would the room look like? Would it be an old friend, the face a little worn but still easily recognisable? Or would it now look back at her as if they were strangers?

She closed her eyes for a moment, then walked to the bedside and switched on the light.

The room was still the same.

It was so much the same that the pain in her heart was suddenly so acute that it filled her chest and her throat and she felt she was going to die. But she had to be brave, she must be brave. No one was going to see her cry. No one, not even her son.

And her resolve didn't weaken. Not until she folded the bedspread back to put the two hot water bottles in the bed and plump up the pillows upon which Tyrone had rested his beautiful, wise, mad head and found his pyjamas, folded as neat as ever, where he had always left them, under the covers. Then suddenly with a massive sob, her tears started to flow unchecked as she fell on her knees, hugging his pyjamas to her face, and rocking backwards and forwards as she sobbed her aching heart out.

After some time, she didn't know how long, Cassie stopped crying, and remembering her sick son next door, turned on the other bedside light, and going to her dressing table, wiped the tears from her eyes and cheeks with some tissues, and put a token dusting of powder on her face. Then she went next door to collect Mattie.

She carried the little wisp of a child into their bedroom and tucked him in under the covers on the side furthest from the door: the side where she herself had always slept.

She brushed the hair from his eyes, and kissed his brow, before going round the other side of the bed and turning back the covers. Then she got into the side of the bed where Tyrone had always slept and, pulling his pillows around her face, settled into the shape of his body which he'd left behind him on the mattress.

Between them, Tomas and Cassie finally found and bought Herr Brandt's required number of handicappers. Only one was purchased at the sales, and that was the one Cassie bought on her own.

Tomas's eyes nearly popped out of his head when he saw what she'd brought home.

'Jesus Christ 'tis a milk pony!' he exclaimed. 'Where the devil did you find that thing? Or perhaps it's the next pony for your daughter?'

'It's only because he's small, Tomas,' Cassie replied calmly. 'You're all such snobs about small horses. Remember Battleship who won the Grand National? He was only just over fifteen hands. Petite Etoile was what you'd call a pony; and she didn't do so bad either, right? Winning the 1,000 Guineas and The Oaks. Small can also be beautiful, you know.'

'He's not even beautiful,' Tomas snorted. 'He's a head on him like a mule.'

'There's nothing wrong with his conformation though,' Cassie argued. 'He's got a nice deep chest and really nice quarters.'

'His quarters look better than they are, Mrs Rosse, because he's dip-backed. What's he called, anyway?'

Cassie laughed, and pulled the horse's ears.

'The Donk,' she replied.

'Good,' said Tomas. 'At least he has one thing right about him. His name.'

The Donk had run three times that season and the best he'd achieved was a distant sixth in a ten-horse race over west in Listowel. But Cassie had noticed that the year before he'd been finishing pretty close up to some fairly useful horses, although never actually winning his race. She'd also noticed that his grand dam had produced six winners, four of which were very useful handicap horses. There was also firm evidence of speed on his sire's side, although nothing fashionable. Which was why Cassie got him so cheap.

'I am not interested in their breeding please, Mrs Rosse,' Brandt told her on the telephone from Geneva when she rang to give him the latest news. 'All I want to know is when they are running. You will kindly keep me informed as to your plans.'

'He'd be the ideal owner,' Tomas said, 'if only he wasn't a Kraut.'

'He's Swiss, Tomas,' Cassie retorted. 'You know dam' well he's Swiss!'

'I know he's got a Swiss passport,' Tomas replied. 'And there's plenty of 'em, too, with South American ones.'

'But you like the Germans! You helped them during the war!'

'We do not like the Nazis, Mrs Rosse. And we were neutral during the war. You wouldn't find a man in Ireland who liked the Nazis.'

'Herr Brand is *not* a Nazi.'

'Not now, maybe. I'd not be sure about what he once was.'

But whatever Tomas felt about Cassie's new owner, and however little he considered her latest equine purchase, he still paid the same amount of attention to The Donk and fed him up as well as he did all the other horses in the yard.

Within three weeks of his arrival, such was the improvement in the little horse that it was decided to run him the following Thursday in a mile-and-a-half handicap at Limerick.

'He'll not win,' Tomas said, categorical as always, 'but he's the sort who'll come on for a race. And we'll be able to get the measure of him against the horses with some form. For there's three or four entered who've won a few races between them.'

Cassie rang her new owner at the weekend and discussed their race plans.

'Will he win on this Thursday please?' Brandt asked her.

'We don't think so for a minute, Herr Brandt,' Cassie replied. 'But we'll sure find out how good or bad he is, because he's not far off ready.'

'Good. Then we will please speak after the races.'

The little horse travelled badly on the long journey to the races, and was awash with sweat when they finally unboxed him. Tomas took one look at him and stated that whatever outside chance the horse might have had he'd lost travelling, so it was just as well he wasn't fancied. In the pre-parade ring, however, the horse calmed down, and was walking round nice and easily, beginning to look about him and take an interest in things – so much so that by the time they had him saddled up he was up on his toes.

'All right, old lad,' Tomas said, squeezing the wet sponge in the horse's mouth, 'gently does it. You're only here for an easy.'

Liam led him round, and the little liver chestnut looked a picture of health in the bright sunshine. But he was friendless in the market, opening at 16/1 and drifting to 25/1 by the time the horses were cantering down to the start. By the time they were galloping back in earnest towards the winning post, The Donk was fifteen lengths in the lead. When they passed the post, he'd increased his lead to twenty lengths, and was easing up.

His win was greeted with total silence. Cassie was the only person to be heard shouting him home. Even Tomas was grim-faced as the little horse was led into the winner's enclosure. All around, baffled racegoers were seen to be consulting their race cards in an effort to identify the runaway winner.

'I thought I told yous to give him an easy,' Tomas muttered at the jockey as they unsaddled the horse together.

'And didn't I do just that, sir?' the boy answered. 'I'd him bowling along nicely fourth or fifth, then he suddenly took hold and there was no stoppin' him. I never even asked him. If I'd asked him, sure he'd have won the race before as well!'

Then with a cheery grin, the boy disappeared to weigh in.

'Jesus,' was all Tomas could say over his drink. 'Jesus.'

'Anyone would think we'd lost instead of won,' said a still elated Cassie. 'Tomas, that's a very good horse!'

'You noticed,' Tomas replied, draining his drink. 'I dare say the handicapper did, too.'

It was a quiet journey home. Tomas hardly said a word, while Cassie worked out the repercussions of the win. The race had been worth barely £300 to the winner, and none of them had even had a token gamble. The handicapper was present at the races, and so having witnessed the ease of The Donk's victory with his own bare eyes, there was precious little chance of The Donk racing off seven stone seven again in the foreseeable future.

'There's only one thing for it,' Tomas finally announced. 'If he eats up tonight, we'll run him again Saturday, for he's still in at Naas, and again next week, before the new weights is published.'

Still, Cassie thought as they turned into Claremore, tired and fed up with Tomas' belly-aching, still at least the owner will be pleased.

'Mr Brandt? This is Cassie Rosse, I have very good news for you.'

'Yes, Mrs Rosse?'

'Your horse won today! The Donk! Your first runner and he comes home your first winner!'

There was silence from the other end of the line.

'Mr Brandt? Herr Brandt, are you still there?'

'I am still here, Mrs Rosse. Yes.'

'Then perhaps you didn't hear me. I said—'

'I am still here, and I heard most well what you said.'

'Aren't you pleased?'

'On the contrary, Mrs Rosse. What price was this horse please?'

'He started at 25/1.'

Another silence. Longer.

'Mr Brandt?'

'Mrs Rosse. When I asked you what chance this horse would have, you expressed no confidence.'

'That's right, Herr Brandt. Tomas said—'

'It is of no interest what Tomas said. If this horse was not going to win, you must understand, Mrs Rosse, the horse should not then have won.'

'I don't understand.'

'I think you do, Mrs Rosse. When you say a horse is not going to win, then that horse will not win. Not if I am not backing it.'

Silence. This time from Cassie as she realised the implications of Brandt's remark.

'Mrs Rosse?'

'Herr Brandt.'

'You will run the horse before the weights go up, and you will tell me where and when. And the chances.'

'I can't do that, Herr Brandt, until I know what's declared. Who the final runners are.'

'Once you know that, telephone me immediately.'

The line went dead. And so did a little bit of Cassie. Had Tyrone ever stopped any of his horses? She just couldn't imagine him doing so. And yet if certain owners only wanted their horses to give their true running when they were 'on', how could he have escaped so doing?

She asked Tomas.

' 'Tis easy. Mr Rosse would never have owners the like of that, Mrs Rosse,' Tomas replied. 'Every horse which ran from here went to the races to do his job.'

'So what do I do, Tomas?' Cassie asked. 'I want all my horses to run on their merit.'

'Then that's exactly what you do, Mrs Rosse.'

'Herr Brandt will take his horses away.'

'Then let him.'

'Right,' Cassie grinned. 'Now go on showing me how you make up feeds.'

The Donk ate up every oat the evening they returned from Limerick, and the next morning, so it was decided to run him again at Naas on the Saturday. Even with his five-pound penalty he'd only be carrying seven stone twelve pounds, and Cassie and Tomas agreed to put the same boy up on the horse who rode him at Limerick, since he was an apprentice, and was still claiming the full seven-pound allowance. So in actual fact The Donk would only be carrying seven stone five. If he ran as he had run two days earlier, on the form book he was home and hosed.

Herr Brandt was informed the horse was fit and running, but not that he was a certainty. Cassie simply said what she had always heard Tyrone say on such occasions, that the horse was thrown in at the weights, and should run a big race. Herr Brandt in return informed her that he was 'on'. For her part Cassie did not tell him that even if he wasn't, the horse would still be asked to win.

He would be asked seriously, too, because the race on Saturday was an altogether more competitive and valuable affair, which had attracted a big field. Word was out on the Claremore horse, however, and he started at 7/2 joint favourite with the second top weight, trained by Mick Ward, which had won its last three races. The Donk dwelt at the start, coming out of the stalls almost last, and was badly boxed in on the rails six furlongs from home. Through her glasses Cassie saw that the little horse had his ears back and was obviously hating being shut in. She wanted to scream at the boy to pull the horse out there and then so as he could get a clear run before it was too late, but instead the boy was hard at work with the whip, which only made the little horse lay his ears back even more and drop further off the pace. Then as the field swung into the straight, the horse immediately in front of him suddenly tired, dropping back so fast that The Donk's young jockey had to snatch his horse up and swing him wide to avoid running into the tiring horse's heels. The moment he did so, and The Donk saw daylight, the little horse got hold of his bit and started one of his what came to be famous charges. He stuck his neck out and flew past the field on the outside, catching Mick Ward's horse at the distance, and going on to win from him by three lengths.

It was a sensational finishing burst and as the horse was being unsaddled, the racing press flocked round Tomas to find out more about the little horse. Cassie retired tactfully to the bar and set up their usual drinks: orange juice for her, and a large John Jameson for Tomas.

'Word has it you've a nose for a horse,' Sheila Meath said on finding her at the bar.

'Word has it I'm lucky,' Cassie grinned.

'What on earth inspired you to buy such a dreadful-looking animal?' Sheila asked.

'He had the eye,' Cassie answered. 'Tyrone always said forget the size of bone, forget the length of pastern, forget the depth of girth. When it comes down to it, and you're wondering yes or no, look in its eye.'

'He was crazy, your husband, you know,' Sheila sighed. 'Completely crazy but as usual absolutely right.'

The Donk won one more race before the handicapper caught up with him. Rather than break the little horse's spirit by making him carry too much weight, Cassie ran him once more and unplaced under top weight, before putting him away for the season, with the intention of moving him up in class the following year. Of Herr Brandt's other five horses, three of them won their appointed races, one began to break blood vessels, and the other turned out to be a squib, showing all at home on the gallops then funking it on the track. Even so, Cassie and Tomas were well pleased, and the owner had obviously placed and landed some healthy wagers because there had been no further complaints from Switzerland.

In fact very little had been heard from Switzerland at

all. Now whenever Cassie rang up to give Herr Brandt the required information, she always got his secretary, and Herr Brandt was always away on business. At first Cassie hadn't given his absences a second thought, but when Mrs Byrne informed her that not one of Herr Brandt's training bills had yet been paid, Cassie became anxious.

'I'm sure I'm quite probably worrying unduly,' she told Tomas. 'But it all seems so contradictory – a man who's prepared to hand you more or less a blank cheque to buy horses, and then doesn't pay his training bills.'

Tomas shook his head and continued to weigh out the feeds. 'Didn't I tell you he wasn't to be trusted?' he said. 'Them Germans. Sure they're either at your feet or your throat.'

'He is not a German, Tomas,' Cassie contradicted. 'He is a Swiss national.'

'And sure I'm a Dutchman,' Tomas muttered inconsequentially.

Cassie rang Switzerland, but now got no answer at all from Herr Brandt's number. When she tried again the following week, the telephone had been disconnected.

It was Sheila Meath who spotted the paragraph in the foreign news and called Cassie.

'Isn't Herr Rudi Brandt that mysterious owner of yours, Cassie?' she asked. 'Your enigmatic Swiss?'

'Yes,' Cassie answered. 'Why? Do you know something that I don't know?'

'Do you know he's been arrested?' Sheila enquired. 'Page five in today's *Times*. "Swiss financier held on currency charges." '

Cassie found the item in the newspaper, but discovered little else. Herr Brandt was an international financier, which as Tomas laconically pointed out, covered a multitude of sins, and the implication was that he had been smuggling currency. Bail had not been granted, and he was at present languishing in a Genevan gaol awaiting trial.

'Technically speaking,' Tomas informed Cassie, 'his horses are yours, in lieu – as I believe they have it – of his non payment. At least they are under the rules of racing.'

'Horses don't pay bills, Tomas. Owners do. And anyway, Tomas, as far as the rules of racing go, any agreement trainers have with their owners has no real standing in law. I can't sell a defaulting owner's horses without it being legally agreed by both parties.'

'Ah, who'd be a trainer?' Tomas sighed. 'Sure only fools the likes of us.'

Herr Brandt was finally released on bail, while awaiting trial for smuggling gold and other currencies. All his assets were frozen, except for his racehorses, which were duly sent to the sales in order to realise some of the capital Herr Brandt was going to need in order to finance his defence.

Determined to buy back The Donk, Cassie sold two yearlings she had bought, and the one remaining piece of her own jewellery. Because of the improvement in the little horse's form, she had to pay over ten times what she had paid for him only a matter of months ago, but even though Tomas thought she had now completely taken leave of her senses, Cassie believed in the little horse so much that she considered it money well invested.

Tomas had the last laugh however. He found a paragraph on the Brandt case in one of the more popular newspapers which exposed the plaintiff's father as having been a colonel in the German SS.

Chapter Nineteen

Niall Brogan needed just ten minutes in order to confirm Cassie's worst fears.

'You're right, it's a tendon,' he said, coming out of Reverse's stable. 'That's him done till next year, I'm afraid.'

'I pulled him up real easy today,' Cassie told him as they walked over to the office. 'Canter, trot, walk, just like the book says.'

'There's nothing to blame yourself for, Cassie,' Brogan assured her. 'Horses is legs and legs is racing.'

Even so, Cassie needed the shot of whisky she poured out for her vet and herself in the office. Reverse was without doubt a potential Classic horse, probably the best animal ever to have been at Claremore.

'He was due to run in the Beresford and the Dewhurst,' Cassie told Sheila Meath over dinner that evening.

'That's racing,' Sheila replied.

'So everyone keeps telling me,' Cassie smiled. 'But it doesn't make the disappointment any easier to bear.'

'True. But then rumour has it that the O'Brien youngster's going to take all the beating. Oddly enough, that's by Northern Dancer as well.'

'You mean Nijinsky? Sure, I've heard he's something other, that horse. But then the way Reverse won last time out at Leopardstown . . .'

Cassie drifted off into a reverie, while Sheila eyed her across the table.

'I think perhaps it's a blessing in disguise, young lady,'

527

she announced. 'Because if you ask me, it's high time you had a holiday.'

Sheila had been right as usual, Cassie recalled as the taxi sped them both into the heart of Paris. Before she had gone to bed that night she had taken a long, hard look at herself in the mirror and realised what a toll the last two years had taken on her. She had, as Tomas would have said about one of her horses, run up a little light. The reflection she saw in the mirror was no longer that of a young and softly curvaceous woman. Instead she saw a gaunt, skinny creature, with dark rings under her tired eyes.

Tyrone would not have liked her the way she was now.

'One thing I can't stand is a skinny woman,' he used to tell her. 'Women are meant to be loved and admired. You can't cuddle up to all skin and bones.'

Then she'd got into bed and considered Sheila's proposal that they left Tomas in charge and took themselves off to Paris for the week of the Prix de l'Arc de Triomphe. Why not? she thought, as she settled her weary body into Tyrone's side of the double bed. Why not? Sheila was right. If she tried to keep going like she was, there was really every chance of her cracking up. She knew that was true, and was beginning to face up to the fact. Now that Mattie was so much better under Doctor FitzStanton's care, it would be perfectly possible to leave him for a short while. He hadn't had a single wheeze since his last course of powders, and every time Cassie looked at Josephine, she seemed to have sprouted another inch, she was growing so fast. She just loved her pony, and was out of doors in all weathers riding him.

'It really would be much the best thing,' Sheila Meath had advised her over dinner.

'I'm quite sure, Sheila,' Cassie had answered. 'But so far there's just been so much to attend to.'

'So much you've wanted to attend to,' Sheila had corrected her. 'You can be brave for too long, you know. And you really have been. Everyone is quite in awe of your fortitude.'

'Really?' Cassie had smiled in return. 'Oh boy. They should see me at lights out.'

Paris was exhilarating. Tyrone had always promised Cassie a second honeymoon in Paris, but it had inevitably been deferred because of the horses. Cassie hadn't minded. It seemed they had so many years ahead of them still, Paris could wait till it was mutually convenient. Fate had sadly decreed otherwise.

Instead she was seeing it for the first time with her great friend Sheila Meath, who was far more than an adequate substitute. Sheila knew the beautiful city from when she was a child, and had subsequently lived there for five years when she was first married, her late husband having been in the Diplomatic Corps.

'Which means you can show me the real Paris? I wouldn't want you to show me the real New York if I came to America! I'd want to see the most famous and beautiful bits of your capital. Not the parts which are like every other major city in the world: the endless suburbs, the ghettos, the slums, the ugly new houses and flats. Paris is just the same, you know. It isn't all the Champs Elysée and the Bois de Boulogne.'

So Sheila showed her all the things Paris had to offer, and Cassie fell head over heels in love with the most beautiful city she had ever seen.

'I can understand now why they say when good Americans die they go to Paris,' Cassie commented.

'Absolutely. It's a place you can never forget,' Sheila agreed. 'Wherever you go for the rest of your life, it stays with you. Hemingway rightly calls it a movable feast.'

By the end of the week, on the eve of the big race when they dined with some of Sheila's old friends who lived in a large apartment in the 16e Arrondissement, Cassie, according to Sheila, was at last beginning to look her old self. Not that she felt it. Inside she was still awkward in the company of married people, awkward and lonely, still a bit one-legged, as she thought of herself. Certain questions had to be deftly side-stepped, so that her widowhood was not shown to have made her one of life's walking wounded. Instead she tried to be lively, interested and interesting, the way she had always been when Tyrone had been around.

The only moments when Cassie felt exposed were when men would compliment her on her looks, which due to the happy time she was having in Paris, were rapidly returning. At moments like this, Cassie would suddenly drop her eyes and become tongue tied, feeling that any response she made would be an infidelity against Tyrone's memory. Unfortunately, her silence would be misconstrued as simple demureness, and instead of discouraging attention, it invariably had the very opposite effect.

But she was learning to cope. And at the pre-race dinner, Cassie discovered that it was actually possible to enjoy herself quite wholeheartedly in civilised and elegant company without any untoward feelings of remorse.

The company was also good the following day at Longchamps, where there were many Irish gathered to vociferously support their country's representative in the most valuable race run in Europe. To their immense delight, after a thrilling contest the Irish horse Levmoss won, beating the gallant English mare Park Top, with Lester Piggott up. A typical Celtic roar greeted the McGrath horse as he returned to be unsaddled, and it wasn't long after that the champagne was flowing in the bars.

Cassie and Sheila Meath had met up with some old friends from home, including Willie Moore, who had invited them to a celebratory party in their box.

'I'd a nice touch,' Willie told Cassie as they stood overlooking the scenes below them in Longchamps' spectacular tree-lined paddock. 'How about yourself?'

'Let's just say Sheila and I have more or less paid for our vacation,' Cassie replied happily.

'I was sorry to hear about Reverse,' Willie said. 'He'd the makings of a very useful colt. But tell me, one of my lads said old Celebration had also broken down?'

'I'm afraid it's true, Willie,' Cassie answered. 'After his last win at Phoenix Park, Niall discovered he'd a hairline fracture of the nearside cannon bone. So I'm retiring him to stud. He'll be standing next year, down the road, at Major Parker's. I'm not selling him, of course. We're coming to an arrangement.'

'Very sensible, because you'll do well by him,' Willie told her. 'He's a grand stamp of horse.'

Somebody touched her arm to attract her attention, and Cassie turned to find herself face to face with a tall, balding and bespectacled Frenchman.

'You will not perhaps remember me,' he began.

'Of course I do,' Cassie interrupted, her cast-iron memory for faces as usual not failing her. 'We met at Leonora's. It must be three years ago.'

'Nearly exactly three years ago,' the Frenchman replied, half-bowing. 'Jean-Luc de Vendrer, in case your memory for names is not as extraordinary as your memory for faces.'

'You make champagne,' Cassie recalled.

'And you refuse to talk about your children.'

De Vendrer smiled at Cassie's amazement, and raised his glass.

'To our reacquaintance.'

'Right.'

They drank, and when she looked up from her glass, Cassie found the Frenchman looking her right in the eyes. He asked her if she was in Paris long, and she told him about her week's vacation. He was studiously delighted with her enthusiasm for the French capital, and enquired if she had spared any time for the French countryside.

'Not on this trip, alas,' Cassie told him. 'We're returning to Ireland on Tuesday.'

'Could I perhaps tempt you to dine with me tonight?'

'Tonight I'm afraid is all booked.'

531

'But of course. In light of this sensational Irish victory. Lunch tomorrow then?'

'I'm meant to be shopping with my friend Sheila.'

'Shoppers need to eat.'

'OK,' Cassie found herself agreeing. 'Lunch tomorrow would be lovely.'

De Vendrer carefully wrote down the address where she was to meet him, then excusing himself left the party, which, as he explained with good humour, was becoming a little too boisterous for someone who had backed the losing horse. He wished Cassie well until tomorrow.

When he had left, Cassie looked at the address he had given her. It simply said 'Lasserre'.

The one word was quite sufficient for the cab driver, who drove Cassie to the famous restaurant on the Avenue Franklin D. Roosevelt at breakneck speed. Cassie had conceded to Sheila's pleas to treat herself to at least one Paris original, and had bought herself a beautifully tailored Chanel suit, in white wool, bound with a navy blue edging. She had also bought herself a Paris hat.

De Vendrer was waiting for her outside, standing by the door studiously reading a folded-over copy of *Le Figaro*. He discarded the paper, kissed Cassie's hand and complimented her on her looks as he held the restaurant door open for her.

'But how clever to have had something made for you while you were here,' he said, after Monsieur Rene Lasserre had greeted them personally and shown them to their corner table.

'That's very gallant, Monsieur de Vendrer,' Cassie replied, 'but I bought this costume off the rack.'

De Vendrer pretended not to understand. Then when Cassie explained that the suit was not tailormade, he shrugged and said that this was not possible.

'If it is,' he added, 'then you must have the perfect figure. And as for the hat . . .' He kissed the tips of his closed thumb and forefinger, closing his eyes. 'Perfection.'

'You have probably never eaten food anywhere near as good as this, yes?' de Vendrer enquired.

'I have never eaten food one tenth anywhere near as good as this, Monsieur de Vendrer,' Cassie replied. 'I really didn't know there was food this good this side of Paradise.'

'René will appreciate that. You must tell him. And please. If we are to be friends, you must call me Jean-Luc.'

'And you must call me Cassie.'

'Ah *bon*. Then we are to be friends.'

De Vendrer raised his glass and drank to her. Cassie looked down at her food.

Afterwards they strolled by the Seine, while Jean-Luc entertained Cassie with stories concerning the various bridges which spanned the river. He took her round Notre Dame, which Cassie had only seen from the outside with Sheila, and then all the way up the famous steps which led to the Sacre Coeur.

'This is rather like the Taj Mahal,' he explained. 'It should really be seen first time by full moonlight. But since you are here for so little time, alas you must see it by day.'

'It's still awfully beautiful,' Cassie said. 'Even by an October sun.'

'Like yourself,' Jean-Luc said, before taking her arm and leading her to a small café overlooking the square, where they had coffee and cognac.

'Is there a very urgent reason for your immediate return?' he politely enquired. 'I do have a reason for asking, I assure you.'

'I have to get back to my children. And horses, I'm afraid,' Cassie answered. 'The season's not quite over yet.'

'Ah. And when do your horses run again?'

Cassie drank some coffee and felt herself blushing.

'They don't,' she admitted. 'Maybe one goes at the end of the month, but what with one thing and another, and with which I won't bore you, we're already roughing them off.'

She looked back up at him.

'That means getting them ready for the winter.'

'I understand. So why not stay an extra week. At my expense. And get yourself ready for the winter?'

The invitation seemed too good to refuse. Sheila Meath was most certainly in favour.

'A week at his château, my dear?' she exclaimed. 'Why if I were you, I should leap at the chance. Already you're looking quite a different girl to the pale little thing you were when you arrived. An extra week of luxury in a château in the Loire valley will do you nothing but good.'

Cassie was finally persuaded when Sheila volunteered to move into Claremore and keep an eye on things until she returned. Cassie thereupon called Jean-Luc and accepted his very kind invitation. He expressed his delight, and told her that he would collect her the following morning and together they would drive down to his country home.

Her first view of the château took her breath away. Cassie had thought the drive up to Claremore was pretty impressive, but it was nothing compared to the poplar-lined road which seemed to run for miles after Jean-Luc's Bentley had passed by the gate lodge and through the stone-pillared gates. Cassie had also thought that Claremore was some house, until she saw Jean-Luc's ancestral home.

'This has to be the most beautiful house I've ever seen,' Cassie gasped as the Bentley made the final sweep up the drive, revealing through the windscreen the enormous château.

'It is certainly considered one of the most beautiful houses in France,' Jean-Luc replied gravely.

'Is that right?' Cassie asked, leaning forward to gain a better view. 'It's such a wonderful colour. I've really never seen anything like it. How would you call that colour?'

'I would call that colour,' Jean-Luc replied, 'the colour of history.'

Cassie smiled and turned to see if Jean-Luc too was smiling. But he wasn't. Instead he was polishing his glasses carefully on a perfectly spotless linen handkerchief.

As she walked in through the great door and into the tapestry-hung hall, Cassie was suddenly and surprisingly glad she knew Leonora. If she hadn't known her, she would never before have stayed in a place of comparable size, with an army of servants, enormous corridors, and the sort and size of furniture which could neither fit nor ever look at ease in an ordinary-size house. If she had never stayed on Long Island, or spent so much time at Derry Na Loch, she might well have been intimidated by the opulence of her new surroundings, and a staff ready to cater to her every wish.

Jean-Luc introduced Cassie to his housekeeper, and then excused himself, having first said how much he was looking forward to seeing Cassie for drinks in the salon before dinner. He made his farewell as if he was leaving on a short journey, and the manner of his departure was the same; as if they were both going to go their quite separate ways until later that evening, when they would rendezvous, perhaps to discuss the adventures which had befallen them in the interim.

The housekeeper appointed Cassie a personal maid, a young bashful girl called Celine, who spoke a little English, and who led her up flights of stairs to her own suite of rooms, followed by a young boy who struggled with Cassie's unmatching luggage.

'*Alors, m'moiselle,*' the maid said as the boy carefully deposited Cassie's luggage on the floor by the end of her bed, 'you want Celine unpick you?'

'I like to do my own unpacking, Celine,' Cassie smiled. 'Thanks anyway.'

'Monsieur de Vendrer, he say please be ready for seven.'

Celine flashed a beguiling smile at Cassie, then pushed the young boy out ahead of her through the door, leaving

Cassie to wander through the suite of rooms, which consisted of a drawing room with a log fire burning in the grate, a bedroom with a superb antique four-poster, also with its very own log fire, a maid's room and two bathrooms. Cassie smiled to herself and wished Erin was with her. She'd have gone round exclaiming at everything, and telling Cassie to look at this and to look at that. She would have gasped audibly at the tapestries, the fine furniture, the paintings and the brocades, and then she would have clucked her tongue and expressed her firmly held opinion that it was very wrong for one person to have all this.

Cassie laughed at the thought then sat down on one of the two ornate antique sofas. They were both painted in the palest of greys, upholstered in faint pink and cushioned with feathers. As she sat, Cassie felt what exhaustion there still was left in her system beginning finally to fade away as she realised that there was no getting up at the crack of dawn to go and ride work, and that she could sleep in as long and as deeply as she wished. She leaned back, kissed the palms of both her hands and blew the kiss to the enormous drawing room.

After she had luxuriated in the huge bath, she changed into a long black velvet skirt and a sequinned top. She studied herself anxiously in the ancient looking-glass, and hoped Jean-Luc would not be disappointed. Then she frowned at herself and wondered why she should be so concerned. After all, they had only just met. Or rather, re-met.

He was waiting for her in the salon, an enormous, but beautifully proportioned room, filled with wondrous furniture and paintings. He was dressed formally in black tie, and a pair of evening slippers, the fronts of which were hand-embroidered with swans, their necks intertwining – the same motif Cassie had seen embroidered into the corner of one of the tapestries in her bedroom.

'I hope you do not mind,' he said in greeting, 'but we shall be dining alone.'

Cassie said that was fine, thinking that it would give

them a better chance to get to know each other, while her eyes roamed the room, looking at the treasures which filled it. Jean-Luc pretended to ignore the apparent inspection, and asked for her comments on the champagne they were drinking.

'It's the best I've ever tasted,' Cassie said simply.

'Good,' Jean-Luc nodded in return. 'You are an excellent judge. This is my very best vintage. I shall send you back to Ireland with a case or two.'

Cassie smiled in gratitude but didn't protest. Tyrone had always expressed the opinion that if someone made you a good offer, take it.

Jean-Luc indicated a chair for Cassie, then sat down opposite her. On the table where she placed her glass, she noticed some photographs. Three of two young girls, charming, smiling and pretty as pictures, and two of a very beautiful woman. She looked from the photographs to Jean-Luc, who was once more carefully cleaning his spectacles. She felt herself colouring, and just hoped the blood wasn't going to rush to her face. For some inexplicable reason she had simply assumed Jean-Luc not to be married.

'Are these pretty girls your daughters?' she asked him, seeing him look up at her.

'Yes,' he replied.

'And this?' Cassie half asked, turning the picture of the beautiful woman to her.

'My wife.'

Cassie stared at the picture and knew that she had turned bright red. She prayed that since Jean-Luc was seated from her at such a distance, and that the light was low in the room, he couldn't see the colour of her embarrassment.

'I'm sorry,' Cassie suddenly blurted out.

'Why?' Jean-Luc enquired politely.

'Because I really didn't know you were married,' Cassie replied quite truthfully.

'I'm not,' Jean-Luc answered, 'and neither, alas, are you.'

537

Turning the photograph away from her once more, Cassie looked round at Jean-Luc and saw him studying her earnestly through his round spectacles.

'You're not married?' Cassie enquired hesitantly.

'No,' Jean-Luc said with more than a touch of melancholy. 'Not any more. Alas we are both of us quite alone.'

Then he looked down at his hands, and studied the thumb of his right hand as it slowly rubbed the palm of his left. Tragedy seemed to hang in the air, Cassie thought. She must consider carefully what she said.

'I'm really sorry. I simply didn't know,' she began.

'How could you?' Jean-Luc answered, still not looking up. 'There was no reason you should.'

'Did you know about my husband?'

'Of course. I read it in the newspapers.'

Still his thumb caressed the palm of his other hand.

'I can't think why I didn't ask you in Paris whether or not you were married.'

'Perhaps because I didn't want you to. You seemed to be so happy. You were enjoying your day. The very last thing I wish is for me to spoil it by mentioning our sadnesses. Perhaps too, for you, as it is for me, the memory it is still most painful. I was always advised in these matters, by my mother, never to enquire. People will talk about their sadness, she said, only when they are ready to do so.'

'Are you ready to do so, Jean-Luc?'

'I think so, yes. And you?'

'I think maybe I am, too.'

'Good. Then let us talk over dinner.'

They dined in the smaller of the two dining rooms. On their way to table Cassie saw the more formal of the two rooms where it was obviously possible to sit forty or fifty people at the main table. She was therefore very glad her host had chosen the more intimate room for just the two of them. They dined by candlelight, and the food was exquisite.

Throughout the meal they talked of their individual

sorrows. Jean-Luc knew much more of Cassie's than she of his, because they had friends in common, and because Tyrone's tragic accident had received international news coverage. Cassie found herself able to talk quite freely of her feelings, and as she did so, part of the burden seemed to be lifting from her shoulders. Jean-Luc listened intently, making only the chance and always pertinent comment.

'Grief instructs the wise, remember,' he said at one point. 'Sorrow is knowledge.'

'I think that's probably true,' Cassie agreed. 'I know my friend Sheila Meath would go along with that. She keeps telling me that people who conceal their grief never find a remedy.'

'Your friend is right.'

'What about your wife?' Cassie asked.

'I lost my wife almost three years ago,' Jean-Luc replied, once more removing his glasses to clean them systematically. Cassie noted how big and sad his eyes were without them. 'We had been married for ten years, and when she was gone, I really thought that I too would die.'

'I know,' Cassie said, 'I know exactly.'

'But life is here to be lived,' Jean-Luc continued. 'To weep excessively for the dead is to insult the living.'

Jean-Luc carefully replaced his spectacles and stared at Cassie through the candlelight.

' "Sadness flies on the wings of morning and out of the heart of darkness comes the light," ' he said.

'That has to be one of the most beautiful things I've ever heard,' Cassie sighed, shaking her head slowly. 'Really.'

'It is beautiful, Cassie, because it is true. We must be aware of our sorrows, but we must not bury them away. Sorrow is one of the vibrations that prove the fact of living.'

Cassie looked back at him through the flickering candlelight. He was so intellectual, and so sensitive-looking, with his high forehead, those enormous liquid dark eyes, and his delicate, sensitive hands.

'Do you play the piano?' she asked.

'Yes,' he replied, 'I do. Why?'

'I thought you might,' Cassie smiled in return.

He played to her after dinner in the music room: Chopin's Nocturne No. 2 in E flat major, Opus 9, and Liszt's Consolation No. 3. He played as well as any amateur pianist Cassie had ever heard, with an exquisite touch and a pleasant lack of unnecessary *rubato*.

Then as they sat by the fire drinking their coffee and Armagnac, Jean-Luc asked Cassie what she would like to do during the short time she was staying.

'If I may presume,' he said, 'perhaps it would be a good idea if I did not burden you with social entertainments. I think perhaps – or I guess, as you would say – that maybe a long and quiet rest would do you much good.'

'Thank you,' Cassie answered gratefully. 'You know, after dealing with people all year, day in day out, I wouldn't care if I didn't see another living soul all week.'

'I'm afraid that you will be seeing me from time to time, alas.'

'On the contrary, Jean-Luc. I shall look forward to your company.'

That night, as the moonlight poured in through her open window, Cassie slept the first deep and untroubled sleep she had slept since her beloved Tyrone had been taken from her.

Celine knocked on the door at half past eight the following morning, and in answer to Cassie's call, wheeled in breakfast on an old mahogany trolley. Then she brought Cassie her wrap, put it round her shoulders, and plumped up her down-filled pillows for her, before disappearing with a smile to go and run a bath.

Cassie sat up and looked with undisguised pleasure at the coffee and rolls, the curls of butter lying on ice and the bowl of homemade apricot jam. It had been a very long time since she'd enjoyed the luxury of breakfast in bed. She had really almost forgotten what it was like not having to scramble out of bed and into a pair of old riding breeches before grabbing a lonely cup of instant coffee in the kitchen on her way out to ride work.

The maid returned from running the bath to enquire in her wonderfully fractured English if there was anything else Cassie required, before leaving her in peace to eat her breakfast and stare at the view outside her windows. Jean-Luc had told her she could stay in bed all day if she wished, but Cassie considered that would be a precious waste of golden moments. So she finished her breakfast, bathed, then dressed in her best slacks and dark blue cashmere polo-neck sweater.

As she sat brushing her hair at a window, looking out over the perfectly cultivated gardens and grounds of the château, she wondered if what she was looking at was real, if life could actually be like this, like the vision she was looking at, like the dream she was in. And if this sort of life really was possible and did exist in actuality, what then would it be like? Would she hate it? Cassie wondered. Would she grow quickly bored and long for the discipline of hard work once more? Or was it actually possible to live such a life and be happy?

If it was, she would never have to get up first thing every morning, knowing that, whatever the weather, she would be out in it, either riding or supervising her string at work, while the late winter winds and rains toughened and cut deep lines into her once soft skin. She wouldn't have to keep her weight down, so that she could still ride the best of her young horses without causing them unnecessary strain or hurting their still unmade backs. She could get up at her leisure, then be driven into town to shop idly, and have a gentle lunch outside a café with a girl friend, while they watched the world go passing by. She could go out to parties and stay late dancing, secure in the knowledge that she could lie in the next morning under perfectly laundered linen sheets, propped up on swansdown pillows. She could relax; she could be free;

she could be a woman; she could return to humanity.

It was a perfect October day as she and Jean-Luc strolled through the grounds. He told her the history of the château and of his family, and asked her if she would like to visit the vineyards after lunch. Cassie said she would be delighted, and then in answer to his gentle inquisition, found herself telling him the story of her young and unhappy life. He listened most attentively, nodding sometimes, and at others making peculiar French interpolations when he considered some chapter of incidents particularly shocking.

By the end of their walk, as he led her back into the château for lunch, Jean-Luc stopped for a moment, and holding her by the elbow, looked directly in Cassie's eyes.

'Good,' he said. 'I see now that you are in especial need of care and attention.'

The longer she was at the château, the more relaxed and happy Cassie became. Jean-Luc became very serious on the matter of her well-being, and after three days declared himself well satisfied with the progress his houseguest was making.

'When you arrive,' he told her, 'still you look like a woman in mourning. You wore your sadness like a mantle. No – please, I know you were doing your very best not to let anyone know your grief, but it was in your very aura. Now, you are more at peace. You have tranquillity. And this is good.'

'It has to be this wonderful place, Jean-Luc,' Cassie replied. 'This wonderful place, and you.'

Jean-Luc nodded seriously, and very carefully took Cassie by the arm.

'Thank you,' he said. 'I am so very glad that you said that to me.'

That afternoon, the fourth day of her stay, he took Cassie walking through the typical deep woodland of the Loire valley. The leaves were just on the turn and in the clear October sunlight the trees were a blaze of autumnal colours.

'You're very privileged to live here, aren't you?' Cassie asked him. 'I mean, this has to be one of the most heavenly places in the world.'

'I do not consider it to be privileged, Cassie,' Jean-Luc answered gravely, 'to live anywhere without someone to love.'

Uncertain how to take that remark, whether it was reflection upon the loss of his wife, or whether it was intended as an introduction for Cassie to enter the next stage of their association, she wandered ahead and stood on the banks of the river. After a moment, Jean-Luc came to her side and put his arm through hers.

'I'm not at all sure, Jean-Luc,' Cassie said, 'that I'll ever be able to love anyone ever again.'

'No, no,' he argued. 'That is not what you mean. What you mean is that you will perhaps never be able to love anyone in quite the same way ever again.'

Cassie watched the river flow past, flattening the reeds and racing round the stones. It was like life, slip-sliding past her, seemingly going faster and faster the longer she watched it go. Then she turned to Jean-Luc.

'Do you really think that's what I mean?' she asked him.

'I am quite sure,' he replied. 'Like I am that there are many other ways to love.'

He smiled at her, then stroked her hair very gently, finally tipping her face up towards him with his long, slender fingers.

'You are a very beautiful woman,' he said, before kissing her. He kissed her as if he had been kissing her all his life, and then, taking her hand, he led her away from the river and back towards the far distant château.

Somewhere in the woods behind them a single bird began to sing. It was not a nightingale.

Jean-Luc had finally fallen asleep, his head turned away from Cassie, but one hand still holding hers. The sheet barely covered him, and Cassie looked first at her own

543

naked body, and then at the body of the man lying naked beside her. She waited for the shock wave to hit her, the shock of revulsion and the remorse that she must surely feel. But she felt nothing. Nothing at all.

But then she hadn't felt very much when they had made love. Jean-Luc had done nothing wrong; in fact he had been very sensitive and gentle. Without a further word he had led her upstairs and into her bedroom, where kissing and caressing her with quiet passion, he had undressed her, and taken her to bed. He had been attentive and imaginative, and Cassie hoped that she had been the same. But it had all been dream-like, a distant experience which seemed to be cocooned within an echo. She knew that a man, someone, was making love to her, and she knew that she was making love to him back. She felt his kisses, his hands on her body, his body against hers, and she felt him inside her, strong and urgent. But the more passionate he became, the slower seemed the motion of her mind. Reality receded from her; it was almost as if someone else other than she, Cassie, was experiencing the encounter.

And now he slept. Cassie looked at him, eyes fast closed, a half-smile on his face. She drew the sheet up over the rest of his slim and still very athletic body, and then quietly moved away from him, to turn on her side and stare at the wall. For a long time she thought about what she had done and wondered why it all seemed to lack any significance. Then she suddenly realised that the reason why she felt no remorse and no guilt was because she felt nothing; and she had felt nothing because she still only loved Tyrone. She could only have felt guilty for what she had done if she had fallen in love even halfway with the man lying asleep beside her.

She lay on her back and stared at the ceiling. All in all, she thought, Tyrone Rosse was a quite impossible act to follow.

She was woken from a deep sleep by Jean-Luc making love to her again. As she realised where she was and what was happening, Cassie panicked and wanted to stop him. But he seemed to misinterpret her struggles and her cries for passion, and turning her face roughly to him with one hand, kissed her so hard that she could feel blood in her mouth. Then still kissing her fiercely, he started to make violent love to her.

When he had finished, he turned on his back and lay in silence. Cassie turned to him, strangely puzzled and bewildered, the taste of her own blood still on her lips, silently searching for an explanation. Jean-Luc raised himself up on one elbow, smiled at her, stroked her hair gently and kissed her cheek.

'Are you not hungry?' he whispered, lying back and stretching both his arms in the air above him. '*Mon Dieu* – after love like that, I am.' He turned and stroked her hair again. 'And what about you, *ma petite*? Are you not hungry too?'

'I hadn't really thought about it,' Cassie said, putting a finger to her bruised lips.

'I will send down for a little love feast,' he said, getting out of bed, and walking naked across to the house telephone.

Down his back, Cassie could see red marks where she must have torn at him with her nails. She suddenly felt very confused. As a person, he was so kind, so solicitous. So why had she tried to stop him making love to her again? Why had she cried out and pleaded with him to stop? Why had she clawed in desperation at his back? And why had he paid her no heed? Had her fierce resistance only excited him all the more? Reality was now returning to her, sternly and sombrely, as Jean-Luc reeled off in French the recipe for what was obviously his favourite after-intercourse picnic. Cassie pulled the bed-sheet up protectively under her chin and watched him as he put down the telephone.

'I have sent for champagne of course,' he said as he walked back to the bed. 'And some little mushroom pies the chef makes, very small, very delicious. And some salmon. Salmon is always so good after making love.'

Jean-Luc got back into the bed and smiled at her. Cassie moved slightly away from him and, excusing herself, picked up her wrap and went and locked herself in the bathroom, where she ran herself a hot bath in which she lay soaking until she heard the maid arrive with the trays of food.

Cassie knew that the telegram she had rung and instructed Tomas to send to her, requesting her immediate return to Claremore, would not arrive until morning, so she still had to survive one more night. As she dressed for dinner, delaying her arrival downstairs until the last possible moment, Cassie decided her best tactic was to behave as if nothing had happened – nothing, that was, to upset her. She had been very frightened by the sudden violence of his lovemaking, but she blamed only herself. She had encouraged him into her bed by not discouraging him, and the reason she had not discouraged him was because she wanted someone to make love to her. She wanted to know what had happened to her feelings. She wanted to know if she could survive the experience; and if she could, she would know that she could recover from her most terrible loss, and with time on her side most probably she could be capable of rebuilding her life.

And until the second time he had made love to her, in a way that for some reason had frightened her, she had found Jean-Luc most attractive, gentle, intelligent and amenable. But she only blamed herself. She blamed herself for her ignorance. She knew that a lot of men liked to make love roughly, without always first making sure their passion was being reciprocated, just as she was quite well aware that within the confines of a bedroom and a relationship, many women liked to be symbolically raped. But she and Tyrone hadn't had a relationship like that. Their lovemaking had been passionate, frequent and, above all, fun. It had never been unnecessarily nor unexpectedly violent.

Then perhaps Jean-Luc hadn't asked her if she wanted to be raped because he had simply assumed that her manner had suggested she might be the sort of woman who would enjoy it. It had to be entirely her own mistake, Cassie finally decided, fastening up the neck of her silk blouse, and no real fault of his at all. She should simply have told him that she didn't like what he was doing and then, no doubt, being a man of such sensitivity, he would have stopped. Tyrone had always said that in life you only got what you asked for.

When she went downstairs in search of him, he was not as usual in the salon. Instead, hearing voices and laughter coming from across the hall, she turned and went in to the library.

Jean-Luc looked up in surprise as she entered, and for a moment Cassie thought she saw a look of anger in his eyes. But it passed so quickly that she thought she must have been mistaken. There was another man there, dressed in a pair of worn cord trousers, old tennis shoes, and a thick blue fisherman's sweater. Jean-Luc introduced him as Georges Boutin, a painter friend of his from the town.

Georges was older than Jean-Luc, and much bigger too; a bear of a man, with wild grey hair and laughing blue eyes. He took one look at Cassie, kissed her hand, and went off into a stream of rapturous French to Jean-Luc. Jean-Luc smiled and laughed politely while he listened to the tirade of compliments concerning Cassie, while Cassie smiled and tried to get a quiet look at one of the canvases which Boutin had brought with him. But they all were turned away, with their painted faces to the wall.

Boutin saw Cassie looking at the backs of his paintings, and immediately picked one up. But Cassie was watching Jean-Luc, who visibly stiffened, and said something quickly and quietly to the painter in French. Boutin ignored whatever it was Jean-Luc had said and twirled the canvas round dramatically for Cassie to view.

It was an oil, stunningly painted and conceived, of two naked women in bed, kissing.

'Yes?' he shouted, roaring with laughter. 'You like?'

'Very much,' Cassie replied. 'Yes I do.'

Boutin picked up another bigger canvas and turned that round for Cassie to inspect as well.

'*Et alors!* And this?'

The second one was of three naked people. A man, who looked suspiciously like Boutin himself, lying with two girls. Not peasant girls, but two beautiful, sophisticated-looking women, both making love to the man.

'I don't like that one as much,' Cassie informed him.

'Too *vulgaire, peut-être?*' Boutin asked, knocking back a large brandy. 'A little too real for the American fantasy, yes?'

'No,' said Cassie. 'It's just very badly painted.'

Boutin stared at her as if she had struck him on the face. Jean-Luc seized this opportunity of turfing him out of the study, having collected the remaining four or five canvasses.

The painter was still staring at her as he was dragged out through the door. Cassie helped herself to a glass of champagne, while the painter's angry roars receded across the vast hall, finally to be silenced as Jean-Luc slammed the huge front door.

'My apologies, Cassie,' Jean-Luc said on his return. 'He is a drunken oaf, but at times a very fine painter.'

'Do you buy much of his work?' Cassie asked.

'Only the ones which interest me,' her host replied. 'Now if you would like to come in to dinner?'

Over yet another superb meal Cassie reconsidered her feelings, particularly in light of her host's quiet and caring attentions. So he'd been a little over-enthusiastic maybe, second time round. And sure, he'd ordered up that love feast like it was a thrice-weekly occurrence. But maybe he and his late wife had always had little love feasts. Maybe this was just a return to the good old ways, in celebration of Jean-Luc himself being able once more to make love, rather than part of a normal après-seduction routine. And as for the paintings, Jean-Luc was a Frenchman. Frenchmen were renowned the world over for their interest in art, and in women. So what more natural than good paintings of naked women, erotic or not?

And then there was his lifestyle. The way he lived at his glorious château was so effortless, and the very easiness of the existence constantly seduced Cassie; so much so that she was dreading her return to Claremore and its demanding routine. As she sipped an exquisite Chablis, Cassie seriously wondered what marriage would be like to this strange, elegant and serious Frenchman; and what her children would make of living in this wonderful house, which was like something out of one of their fairy-tales. She suspected they would love it as much as she would, and that Jean-Luc would most likely make a very sensitive and responsible step-father. And she, Cassie, would help run this great house, and perhaps become a famous hostess. She would certainly be rich enough to have her own racehorses, and somebody else to train them.

'You are dreaming,' a voice said. 'Please tell me what you dream about.'

She woke up and looking through the candlelight saw Jean-Luc smiling at her.

'Perhaps you are dreaming of what the night has in store, yes?'

Cassie smiled but said nothing. Because underneath she wasn't smiling at all, as she realised that if they were both beginning to entertain serious feelings for each other, which Jean-Luc had certainly indicated that he was doing over dinner, then she realised she was going to have to do a little more homework to find out if they really were compatible, and that the afternoon's violence had not been a sudden aberration.

'Please, I would like you to come to my bedroom tonight,' he whispered as they climbed the stairs hand in

549

hand. 'You have not yet seen my room, and I have some very fine works of art in there.'

'Isn't this a little late in the day to be inviting a girl to see your etchings?' Cassie laughed.

'No,' Jean-Luc replied very seriously. 'I think on the contrary.'

She understood what he meant when she saw the room. Dominated by a huge oak four-poster bed, it was like an art gallery, with practically every inch of its walls covered with erotic prints and paintings. Jean-Luc led Cassie round the room by the hand, talking her through his collection of erotica in much the same manner as Sheila Meath had taken her round the Louvre. He indicated with particular interest certain line drawings, which he considered witty, but which Cassie thought were nothing short of grotesque. In fact there was nothing on any wall which Cassie would account to her liking, with the exception of one magnificent painting by Georges Boutin of a naked young girl spreadeagled across the bed in her sleep. The rest of the collection ranged from the oddly bizarre, to the openly sadistic.

'I don't understand how you can sleep with paintings like that in your room,' Cassie said, indicating a particular canvas.

'Because it is not only erotic,' Jean-Luc explained, standing back to look better at the picture, 'but also a particularly fine example of religious sexuality. Paintings such as this illustrate the artist's freedom to show with impunity highly sadistic and therefore very erotic scenes under the guise of religious art. As I am quite sure you are all too well aware, sadism has often found a great ally in the Church.'

He smiled and walked on, stopping a moment later in front of a large and handsomely painted watercolour.

'Perhaps this will be of greater appeal to you,' he said, but without a smile. 'Woman as the horse.'

Cassie looked round at de Vendrer curiously.

'Are you showing me these in the hope of shocking

550

me?' she asked. 'Because if you are, you're in no way succeeding.'

'But of course not, *ma petite*,' he replied, wandering away to stare at another watercolour. 'I have a profound interest in sensuality and the erotic. Do you not share this?'

'I can't in all honesty say that I do,' Cassie replied calmly, refusing to be drawn into argument. 'I think that eroticism is very important, and most enjoyable – in the right hands. And as far as art goes, it obviously plays a major role. But actually, what really turns me on is love.'

Jean-Luc turned round, visibly disconcerted for the very first time. It was as if Cassie had waved garlic at a vampire.

'I suppose you think only uncivilised people satisfy their sexual instincts without love,' he replied, unable to keep the chill from his voice.

'Well yes, as a matter of fact I do,' Cassie said.

'Then in light of today's events,' Jean-Luc countered, a smile returning to his face, 'that must mean you have fallen in love with me.'

'Really?' Cassie enquired very coolly. 'I don't recall saying that I was satisfied.'

There was a moment's silence while Jean-Luc regarded her from behind his round, brass spectacles. Then he smiled broadly and kissed the tips of two of his fingers.

'Bravo!' he said. '*Formidable*! You are an infinitely more fascinating woman than I first gave you credit for!'

He moved towards her and taking her by one arm, stood her in front of another set of pictures hanging in an alcove. Cassie regarded them in silence, although the content of this set of pictures upset her more than all the others.

'*Alors*,' said Jean-Luc, lowering his voice to a whisper. 'I thought something along these lines could provide a most interesting evening.'

'This is what you would like?' Cassie enquired carefully.

'No,' Jean-Luc replied.

And bending down to whisper in her ear, he told her at length what he would really like.

Cassie was forced to listen, so strong was his hold on her. She glanced fearfully back at the bed with its enormous four posts, which were apparently going to play a key part in the proposed events. He then moved behind her, and taking her by the other arm, pushed her slowly but inexorably to the bed. Cassie struggled, but the scholarly-looking Jean-Luc was a deceptively strong man.

Then suddenly she was free, as releasing her, he pushed her down on to the bed. Cassie lay there, refusing to show the fear she was feeling. Instead she smiled up at the man standing above her, who was beginning to undo his shirt and tie.

'Now what?' she enquired coolly.

'You just lie there, *ma petite*,' he whispered. 'I will not keep you waiting long.'

He walked away from the bed towards a door in the wall. Rather than let him see that she was watching him closely, waiting for the chance to escape, Cassie lay back on the pillows and stretched out. Jean-Luc looked back at her once, then opened the door and disappeared into the small room within.

Before he half-closed the door behind him, Cassie had time to see that the room was a closet, cupboards within cupboards with a light which came on as the door was opened. From that information alone, Cassie deduced that there could be no window in there, and no other door. Not if the closet was built into the thick walls of the room.

And unbelievably there was a key in the door. In her side of the door. Holding her breath, and biting her lip to stifle the scream she felt coming, Cassie slid off the bed and tiptoed to the cupboard.

'Please God,' she prayed. 'Please God don't let the key be stiff!'

It wasn't. It turned easily and almost silently in the lock, the moment Cassie slammed the door completely shut. Cassie leaned for a moment with relief against it before Jean-Luc started pounding on it like a madman from within, forcing her to run as fast as she could to the main bedroom doors.

They were all locked.

Cassie had neither seen nor heard Jean-Luc turn the keys. He had obviously used the conjuror's theory of distraction, and locked them both in while Cassie was taking her first and privately appalled look at what hung on the bedroom walls. Now they were both imprisoned, he in his closet, Cassie in the bedroom. If it wasn't so terrible it would be funny.

Her prisoner was hammering loudly on the door and shouting in French from within. But the door was very heavy, and the walls twice as thick, so his voice was distant and muffled. Even so, fearful that with his seeming brute strength he might be able to break the lock, with a superhuman effort Cassie dragged a large chest of drawers from along the adjoining wall, and pushed it hard up against the door. Then she started desperately searching for the door keys.

But there were none. Jean-Luc must still have them on him, because a very thorough search revealed nothing. There was no other way out, the windows of the room opening out only on to the sheer and blank walls of the château.

Then she remembered the house telephone.

'Celine?' she said, when her maid answered the second call. 'This is Madame Rosse. I'm afraid something very foolish has happened, and Monsieur has locked us both in his bedroom and mislaid the key.'

The maid didn't understand at first, but after about Cassie's fourth or fifth attempt to explain, she announced that she understood, and would come up that minute with the pass key.

While she waited, Cassie quickly undressed and put on

one of Jean-Luc's robes, which hung along with his silk ties and shirts in another closet in the walls. She wanted the maid to assume it was quite a normal night, if, she thought wryly, such a thing was possible under this particular roof.

'Is this the only pass key?' Cassie asked, easing Celine back into the corridor as the maid opened the main door, anxious for her not to become aware of her master's muffled shouts of rage.

'Because if this is the only pass key,' Cassie continued, shutting the main door behind her, 'I'd better hang on to that. There are a few other locked doors round here, you understand.'

She smiled and winked at the girl, who smiled blankly back at her, having failed totally to understand what Cassie was saying, which was exactly Cassie's intention. By the time Celine might have been having any second thoughts, the key was safely in Cassie's hands.

'Thank you so much!' she whispered, waving the key at her. 'Sorry to have gotten you out of bed!'

Then she shut the door and waited long enough for the maid to have got back all the way again to the servants' wing before making her final escape. While she was waiting, she looked around the room, anxious to leave her host something by which he would remember her. Then she recalled seeing a pair of scissors in one of the dressing-table drawers, when she had been searching for the keys, and fetching them, she went into the other wall closet where she had found the robe, and cut every single one of his silk neckties neatly in half.

She locked all the doors of her host's bedroom suite on her way out, before returning to her own room to collect her belongings and to get dressed. It was now after midnight, and she imagined there would be little chance of summoning a taxi from the nearest town, particularly in her schoolgirl French. Then she remembered that in both Leonora's houses, all the keys to the garages and cars were kept on a board in the kitchens. So she tiptoed downstairs, across the hall and through the pass door which she knew must lead, just like Claremore, to the domestic offices.

There was no sign of any keys in the kitchens. Nor in either of the small rooms leading off, which were obviously butlers' pantries. But further along the corridor leading away from the kitchens, Cassie found the estate office, and hanging on the wall was a board of numbered and labelled keys. Under Garage One, she found and took the set of keys for Jean-Luc's Bentley. Tyrone for a short time had owned a similar car, so at least Cassie reasoned she would be familiar with the controls. Then she let herself out of the heavily bolted back door, and made for the garages, which lay on the opposite side of the courtyard to the stable block.

The garage doors, being on the outside of the block, opened away from the stables and straight on to the back drive. Once Cassie had refamiliarised herself with the car, she held her breath and pressed the starter button. The engine fired at once, and almost inaudibly. As far as Cassie could tell from a long backward glance in her driving mirror, no lights came on in the stables nor in the servants' quarters as she slowly drove the car down the grass verge of the back drive. Within a couple of minutes she was safely out of sight of the château, and within five she was on the road to the nearest town.

She knew she would have to abandon the Bentley in the town because its loss would invariably be discovered long before Cassie made Paris or the coast. So as soon as she reached the town, Cassie determined to hire another car before continuing on her way.

The proprietor of the only garage she could raise at that time of night was not as keen as Cassie was, however, that she should continue her journey at such a late hour. He became considerably less stubborn once Cassie had offered him a more than generous commission on the deal, and finally offered to rent her a much abused Renault at an exorbitant rate.

Cassie paid without a murmur, anxious to be on her way. While the garage proprietor was filling the rented car with petrol, she collected the Bentley from where she had left it on the corner and parked it on the garage forecourt.

When she alighted from the car, Cassie found the proprietor's humour had worsened.

'You are from the château, *madame*?' he asked darkly.

'I have been a guest at the château, *monsieur*,' Cassie replied.

The proprietor nodded, then spat vehemently on the ground.

Cassie paused for a moment in the loading of her luggage.

'You don't like Monsieur de Vendrer much either?' she asked.

'*Madame*,' the old proprietor replied. 'Were there to be another revolution tomorrow, de Vendrer would be the first to visit Madame Guillotine.'

'He's none too popular round here then, I guess.'

'He is filth, *madame. Salot.*'

The proprietor spat once more on the ground, then looked at the handsome car standing parked on the forecourt.

'I was rather hoping I could leave this car of his here,' Cassie ventured. 'So that maybe they could collect it tomorrow.'

'You are in a hurry to leave the château,' the proprietor replied, more as a statement than a question.

'Yes,' Cassie agreed.

'Then by all means please leave the car here,' the proprietor said, suddenly smiling. 'It will suit me very well. I can hold it against the monies Monsieur owes me. He still does not pay me for his wife's garage bills.'

Cassie threw her last case in the back seat of the Renault, and looked sharply up at the old Frenchman.

'You did say his wife's garage bills?'

'*Oui, madame*. They are outstanding since March.'

Cassie straightened up, and stood holding on to the top of the car door.

'His wife died three years ago, *monsieur*.'

'His first wife killed herself three years ago, *madame*. He married again three months later. Everyone loved his first wife. So sweet. So gentle. But –'

He shrugged, and relit the butt of his yellowing Gauloise.

'But what, *monsieur*?' Cassie enquired.

The proprietor raised his eyebrows, shrugged again, and tapped his head once to denote madness.

Cassie gripped on to the car door even more tightly, and looked back over her shoulder anxiously, as if the shadow of the château still loomed behind her.

'This new wife – bah!' the proprietor continued. 'What can you expect?' he shrugged. '*Elle etait une* go-go girl!'

'Where is she now? She wasn't in residence at the château.'

'Abroad. The West Indies. Always abroad. Madame de Vendrer, she does not like the rain.'

He held one hand up to the night sky, from which indeed heavy rain was now starting to fall. Cassie shivered and got back into the car.

'Thank you, *monsieur*!' she called over the engine as she started it up. 'And if I were you, yes – I would keep the car! Lock it away in your garage, until that bastard pays you what he owes!'

The old man nodded and waved once before disappearing back inside his premises. Cassie put the car in gear and drove off round the town, looking for the Paris road.

She had called de Vendrer a bastard, she recalled as she headed north-east through the now torrential rain. As an insult, she had called him the very thing that she herself was, and of which she was no longer ashamed. Yet when she wanted to call someone so terrible as Jean-

557

Luc de Vendrer something appropriately insulting, the first word that had sprung to her lips was 'bastard'.

She smiled grimly to herself, wiping the windscreen with her hand to try and clear the mist. Neither the heater nor the demister worked, but Cassie didn't care. She could take her time now, because she was free.

He had been so plausible, she thought as she drove. He had been so sensitive and, initially, so gentle and attentive. And he had played the tragic widower so well! Damn him! Cassie thought, banging the steering wheel, damn him to hell and twice over! He had simply set about seducing her for want of something better to do, and in order to do so, had pretended to be in the same state as his victim, bereft and still in grief. And she had fallen for it, totally – hook, line and sinker. As she drove through the rain on the long road to Paris, she ended up cursing herself more than him, for being such a gullible fool, such a compliant and unsophisticated idiot.

Later that day, as she sat waiting for her flight to be called at Orly airport, Cassie read in the newspaper that Celebration's old trainer Willie Moore had retained for the next season one of the most highly thought of American jockeys for his rapidly expanding string. The name of the particular rider was Dexter Bryant.

Chapter Twenty

Dexter Bryant's start to the next season was nothing short of sensational. He won first time out at the Curragh on one of Willie Moore's promising two-year-olds, and out of his next twelve rides had four more winners – a strike rate of almost 2½ to 1. The knockers had all been standing by as usual, ready to forecast the Yankee's undoubted failure, according to them due to his totally unsuitable style of race riding. But even though he rode too 'flat', and held his whip in that faintly absurd upright fashion universally favoured by American jockeys, those observers with open minds could see from Bryant's first few rides in public how beautifully balanced he got his horses and how tenderly he rode all the youngsters.

Cassie saw him again face to face for the first time in the weighing room at Leopardstown. She was standing talking after the last race to Dermot Pryce, who happily now was fully recovered and riding again, when Dexter came out of the changing room. Cassie excused herself from Dermot for a moment, and intercepted Dexter before he reached the main door.

'Hello Dex,' she said. 'How are you?'

Dexter turned as if surprised, but Cassie could tell from the look in his eyes that he had already both seen and recognised her on his way out.

He touched his hat with a finger, as if he was still wearing his race cap, and smiled politely.

'Mrs Rosse, ma'am,' he replied. 'Why how good to see you again.'

'Congratulations on your success, Dex. You're certainly making them sit up and take notice.'

'Thank you, ma'am. And if I may say so, I was awful sorry to learn about Mr Rosse.'

'Yes,' said Cassie. 'I still miss him terribly.'

'I'm sure you do, ma'am,' Dexter replied.

'You must come to Claremore, Dex,' Cassie offered, looking at the handsome boy who had now become an extremely handsome man. 'I'd love you to see the house. And the yard.'

'That would be a pleasure, ma'am,' he said. 'Now if you'll excuse me, Mr Moore is waiting for me with some of his owners.'

Dexter touched his hat again and went, watched by Cassie. He wasn't nearly as short as most other jockeys, she noticed, standing a good three to four inches over her. But he was very slender, slim in hip and leg, and without a visible ounce of spare flesh.

Cassie also noticed that when he had walked out of the weighing room and she had caught her first close sight of him, her heart suddenly missed a beat.

The start of the new season for Cassie was one of mixed fortunes. Reverse, seemingly recovered from his troublesome tendon, ran in the Gladness Stakes at the Curragh, which was won by the O'Brien hotshot as forecast. Dermot Pryce pulled Reverse up two furlongs out, as he felt the horse 'go' under him. When Niall Brogan got to look at him, it was discovered that he had 'done' his other tendon.

'This often happens, you know, Cassie,' her vet told her. 'While the horse is recovering from one bad leg, the good leg takes all the strain. In fact it takes too much strain, and instead of the bad one going again, the good one goes.'

'So what's the prognosis?' Cassie enquired.

'Do you want the bad news, or the bad news?' Brogan asked her. 'You fire or retire.'

Cassie didn't believe in firing horses, considering the heat treatment archaic and painful to the horse. She also considered it only a short-term measure – an opinion gleaned from Tyrone, who considered a fired horse afterwards to be at least a stone inferior to what it was before the operation.

'I don't understand what a stone inferior means, Ty,' Cassie had asked him when Tyrone had first explained.

'I don't mean in the animal's bodyweight, Cassie,' he'd told her. 'I mean in his ability. Say if he'd been running off the eight-stone mark in a handicap, a "fired" horse afterwards you can safely call a seven-stone horse still running under eight.'

Tyrone had firmly believed in nature's cure: rest, rest and more rest. So Cassie followed suit, and turned Reverse away into the summer pastures, with the intention of standing him at stud the following season. Tootsie, however, had wintered well, and had grown into a nice sort of four-year-old, and ran a very promising third first time out. The Donk had come back into training looking like he always did, as if he should be pulling a milk cart, but within eight weeks had won a valuable mile and three-quarter cup race at York.

'We'll have to start thinking about the Gold Cup now,' said Tomas when they'd all returned to Claremore. 'This fellah looks an out and out stayer to me.'

Cassie was delighted, having taken a big risk in buying The Donk back. But after his win at York, it looked as though her reinvestment in the little horse was rock solid.

Other than that, except for a nice two-year-old she had bought cheaply for the ever-patient Joe Coughlan, Claremore had only ten others in training, and all, so it seemed, moderate animals, without a win to their names. With a complement of only fourteen horses in the yard, it promised to be a tough season.

Particularly after Leonora returned to the scene.

She had taken all her horses to England after Tyrone had died, where she had placed them with a fashionable

Newmarket trainer, before disappearing to wherever the jet set was jetting. Every now and then Erin would read out some scandal from one of the gossip pages of the newspapers about the ex-Principessa, who had briefly re-married and then quickly divorced again, but soon she seemed to have faded from Cassie's life – so much so that now Cassie barely gave her old adversary another thought. Her indifference was greatly helped by the fact that in the yard all talk of Leonora or her horses was forbidden.

But then Leonora decided to return to Ireland. After her first divorce, due it was rumoured to what she knew about certain of her husband's less salubrious 'romances', Leonora persuaded Franco to let her keep Derry Na Loch. This concession meant little to a man of such vast wealth, who had in all honesty looked upon the great house as a very occasional residence, despite Leonora's perverse liking for what Franco considered to be a damp and priest-ridden little island.

Worse, Leonora returned with a dozen horses, six of them new, and the other half dozen all useful performers, which she put in training with a very dashing and highly social young Anglo-Irishman called Henry FitzGerald, whose stables were in Kildare. When she saw the strength of Leonora's string, Cassie wasn't unduly fussed. Leonora had six two-year-olds, and Cassie had only one, so there was very little chance that their paths would ever cross in races for young horses; and since Cassie nursed no overly ambitious plans for any of her older animals, with the exception of The Donk, while Leonora was as always bound to want her horses to be seen in all the smart races at all the right tracks, she hoped that Ireland was going to be a big enough place for both of them that summer.

But the more you know your enemies, the less you understand them, as Tomas was at pains to point out as, time after time, he and Cassie discovered that Leonora's horses had been left in against theirs in minor races at second-class tracks. At first Cassie thought it merely coincidental that when she decided to give James Christiansen's horse Moviola his first chance of winning in an insignificant race at Thurles, Cinema Short, winner already for Leonora and her new trainer of a good race at Leopards-town, was declared a runner. He duly trotted up, and Moviola, only three-quarters fit, toiled in ten lengths second, the winner making him look like a selling plater.

One week later the same thing happened when Cassie and Tomas, having cleverly placed Tootsie in what was usually a moderately contested conditions race, found Leonora's Phoenix Park winner Kutchicoo left in at the declarations. Leonora's filly received weight from Cassie's filly, being a three-year-old, as opposed to Tootsie who was four. Kutchicoo was also a very big placid sort of filly, and a front runner, whereas Tootsie was lean and nervy and had to be held up for a late run. Kutchicoo led from start to finish and Tootsie never got in a blow. To rub salt into the wound, Dexter Bryant rode the winner.

By the end of May, Cassie had become well aware that a campaign was being fought. Wherever Claremore went, so did Leonora. Even when they went racing as far west as Galway and Listowel, it was odds-on that Leonora would not only have a runner, but a runner in the same race. Cassie never saw her at the races, only her trainer Henry FitzGerald, who always greeted Tomas and her politely, wishing them good luck and a sporting contest. Invariably his representative had all the luck and won the usually one-sided contest.

Even when Leonora's horses didn't come in first, they still beat Cassie's, so much so that not only the humans but the horses themselves started to become dispirited. In desperation, Cassie devised a plan where she would enter the Claremore runners all over the place, and keep it a total secret between Tomas and herself and her owners as to where the horses were actually going to run until the last minute, eleven o'clock on the day before the race.

But still Leonora couldn't be shaken off. By some miracle, she and Henry FitzGerald always chose the same races as Cassie and Tomas.

'Miracle my backside,' snorted Tomas, 'savin' your presence. We're being spied on.'

'How?' Cassie challenged. 'Even if Liam, or Tony, or the new lad Derek, or even Mrs Byrne wanted to inform on us, they couldn't, Tomas, because they don't *know* we're running until we actually declare the horses. And by then it's too late. So either it's you that's telling Leonora, or it's me.'

'Sure you know dam' well 'tis neither of us,' Tomas growled, lighting up another of his interminable Sweet Aftons.

'So who in hell can it be, Tomas?' Cassie asked helplessly. 'We're being well and truly taken apart here!'

'I've a very good idea,' Tomas replied calmly, 'you just leave this to me.'

Cassie would have done well to have stood by Tomas' advice, but for some reason best known to herself – probably sheer rage, she decided afterwards – Cassie determined on bearding the lion in its den. Or in this case, the tigress.

She called uninvited on Leonora at Derry Na Loch.

The butler, a different man from before, younger and openly arrogant, kept Cassie waiting in the large marble hall. By the time Leonora wandered downstairs, yawning, some thirty minutes later, Cassie's temper was almost at breaking point.

'I'm not used to being kept waiting this long,' she found herself saying.

'And I'm not used to people calling uninvited,' Leonora replied, as she walked on past her and into the drawing room.

'I wasn't sure you'd see me,' Cassie said to Leonora's back.

'Why's that, Cassie?' Leonora asked, turning to her and closing the doors. 'Do you have something catching?'

She smiled and stubbed out her cigarette, immediately lighting another.

'Anyway,' Leonora continued. 'How are you? You've got awful thin. Drink?'

She unstopped a decanter and looked quizzically at Cassie who shook her head.

'Of course not,' Leonora answered for her. 'Far too early for Miss Goody-Two-Shoes.'

She poured herself what looked from the dark amber colour like a very large brandy, yawned once more, then stretched herself out on the sofa.

'For God's sake do sit down, Cassie,' she said. 'You look as though you've come to deliver an ultimatum.'

'I've come to ask you what in hell you think you're playing at,' Cassie replied, refusing to sit.

Leonora screwed her mouth to one side and looked up at Cassie.

'You really should put on some more weight, you know,' she countered. 'Men don't like skinny women. Tyrone couldn't stand them.'

'There was only one woman Tyrone couldn't stand, Leonora. And that was you.'

As soon as she'd said it, Cassie wanted to bite her tongue. This was just the sort of cat fight she did not want to get into. But Leonora chose to ignore the remark, preferring to smile at Cassie enigmatically, before lighting yet another cigarette from her barely half-smoked one.

'So you want to know what I'm playing at, do you? My, but you must have seen an awful lot of B-pictures when you were a kid.'

'You're making a fool of yourself, Leonora. Chasing us round all the second-and third-class racetracks with your first-class horses.'

'These aren't my first-class horses, honey,' Leonora smiled. 'The horses I keep on this godforsaken island are my second-class horses.'

Cassie was bested. She stared at Leonora, not knowing

what to say. Leonora kept smiling for a moment, then she clicked her tongue.

'Say. Don't tell me you've become a bad loser, Cassie McGann?' she asked mockingly.

Cassie sat down and stared for a long time at the painting over the fireplace without having the slightest idea of what it looked like.

'You don't have to do this, Leonora,' she said finally and quietly. 'This isn't your living. You don't know what it's like, hanging in there by your fingernails, trying to survive and keep hold of everything you have left. Which in my case is just my family and my way of life. It's a game to you. Sending your horses out against mine to win a few hundred pounds in prize money. It's like you standing on the corner of O'Connell Street, dressed in your silks and your furs, playing a fiddle and trying to fill your mink hat with pennies. It's just a game to you, that's all. Because nothing depends on it.'

'Oh but you're wrong, sweetie, it does,' Leonora replied. 'An awful lot depends on it. What depends on it is beating you.'

'So you're not going to call it a day?' Cassie said.

'A day?' Leonora frowned in reply. 'A day? Why, Cassie McGann, as far as I'm concerned, it's barely dawn.'

She eyed Cassie, then finishing her brandy in one large gulp, got up to help herself to another.

'OK,' said Cassie, standing up. 'If it's war you want, suits me. But let me just tell you one thing before I go, Leonora. You're going to live to regret this. Your bloody-mindedness – you'll live to regret it. I'll make sure of that.'

Something in Cassie's tone wiped the smile off Leonora's pudgy face. She paused by the drinks table for a moment, then darted in between Cassie and the door.

'I've been drinking, honey,' she said, with a far too obvious change of tone. 'You've really got to pay no attention at all to old Leonora when she's been drinking.

In fact I haven't just been drinking, sweetheart, I'm smashed.'

Gripping one of Cassie's arms with a heavily bejewelled hand, Leonora tried to steer her reluctant guest back to her chair.

'Listen,' she continued. 'This is just terrible. Do you know that? At each other like this after all the great times we've had together. Stay to dinner. Why don't you stay to dinner? You stay to dinner and we can talk over all those great times we've had together. I'm so bloody bored, Cassie McGann. So bloody *bored*. Jesus – besides you, there's no one in Ireland that I *like* any more!'

Cassie, staring at her vaguely smudged lipstick, the whiteness of her skin, and the nicotine which was fast beginning to stain her teeth and her fingers, thought it was probably nearer the truth that there was no one in Ireland who liked *her* any more.

'Come on,' Leonora pleaded, tightening her grip. 'Stay for dinner. It'd be fun.'

'I don't have the time, Leonora,' Cassie said, shaking herself free of Leonora's grasp. 'I have work to do.'

'You look as though you could use a square meal.'

'We eat just fine at Claremore, thanks all the same.'

'What you mean,' Leonora said, her mood once more on the turn, 'is you look after yourself.'

'I ride out every morning, Leonora. Even if I wanted to, I can't afford to get fat.'

Leonora looked at her with unconcealed dislike then did her best to hide it with a smile.

'I've got an even better idea, Cassie,' she said, once more getting herself between Cassie and the door. 'Listen. Suppose I came back to you. Suppose I left Henry FitzGerald and brought my horses back to you. How about that? I come back to you and you'd be top of the pile again! Just like that! OK? I'd really like that.'

The bejewelled hand was on her arm again, as Cassie stopped to consider what she was saying. More than anything in the world she needed good horses and rich owners in her yard, and Leonora would be the perfect answer. She was greedy enough to want to go on buying horses until she won a Classic, and she was quite rich enough to do so. If Cassie played her part right, she could even buy the horses for Leonora, with a book full of blank cheques. And what did she have to do in return? Nothing, except train her horses. Train her horses and sit and be bored by a tiresome drunk; there was no Tyrone any more, and no marriage to be endangered by a beautiful, voluptuous and unscrupulous blonde.

'You haven't got the horses, Cassie,' Leonora was saying. 'You need good horses, and plenty of cash. I've got both those things. And in spades.'

There Cassie stood, high on the hill, with the racing world spread out before her, and Lucifer at her elbow.

Once again she shook herself free of a devil's grasp.

'Thanks for the offer, Leonora,' she said finally, 'but the answer's no. I wouldn't accept a horse from you if you were the Queen of England herself. But if you want a contest, boy, you're on.'

'Jesus Christ, Cassie!' Leonora laughed. 'You've got a stable of mules, baby!'

'I may well have, Leonora,' Cassie answered, 'but what I've also got is time. And a long, strong suit in patience. I don't care if it takes till the end of the century. I'll beat you where and when it matters. Because that's what's great about racing, Leonora. What's great about it is that for people like you, with all your rotten millions, first past the post is the one thing you just can't guarantee buying.'

'Christ – you were always horse-mad,' Leonora said, turning back once more to refill her glass. 'Horse bloody mad. But Jesus look at you! Look at you, you're falling apart at the seams! You're crazy. You know that? Completely crazy. I mean, Christ. Who'd ever have thought you'd end up as you have?'

'I haven't ended up, Leonora,' Cassie replied, pausing by the door. 'On the contrary, I'm only just starting out.'

Cassie left, and as she crossed the large marble hall, she heard the crash of a brandy glass breaking against the door she'd closed behind her.

Tomas was waiting impatiently for her when she returned to Claremore.

'We're home and hosed, Mrs Rosse,' he said, wiping his hands down the front of his trousers as Cassie poured them drinks. 'Didn't I tell yous to leave it all to me?'

'I only wish I'd listened, Tomas,' she answered, handing him his whisky.

Tomas ignored her, and took a deep draught of his John Jameson.

'I found our spy,' he announced.

Cassie looked up, hoping against hope it wasn't anyone in their yard. Her greatest fear was that it might be Mrs Byrne, who she knew needed the money.

' 'Tis a woman,' Tomas said, 'and wouldn't you know it?'

So it was Mrs Byrne, Tyrone's and now her own trusted secretary, the only other person privy to their confidential information. Cassie groaned inwardly and sat down.

'Shall I tell you how I knew?' Tomas said, wiping the back of his hand across his mouth. 'Be her shoes. Dear Christ, she's always had a weakness for new shoes, to the despair of her husband, and you should have seen the pair she had on her today! They must have come from Brown Thomas's themselves!'

'I never noticed Mrs Byrne was wearing new shoes,' a bewildered Cassie replied.

'Mrs Byrne?' Tomas spluttered into his glass. 'Mrs Byrne? Have yous taken leave of all your senses? Mrs Byrne indeed. Sure I'm talking of old Rosie McGinty in the Post Office!'

Cassie stared at Tomas, then got up in silence and refilled their glasses, while Tomas sat quietly chuckling in his chair behind her.

'Of course,' Cassie said, getting there. 'Rosie Red-Ear, as Tyrone always used to call her. The listener-in.'

'And wasn't the Guv'nor right? That old biddy hasn't missed a word anyone's said on the phone round here since I don't know when!'

Tomas went on to tell Cassie that it wouldn't have taken a lot of money to persuade Rosie to reveal which horses Claremore intended to declare and on what courses, gleaning this information whenever Cassie had telephoned the respective owners to discuss the matter. The content of all these conversations would be invaluable, because Cassie always took great trouble to keep her owners fully informed of the plans she had for their horses, and exactly how good their chances were.

'And all for the price of a few pairs of shoes,' Cassie commented wryly.

'It'd be for a lot more than just shoes,' Tomas replied, 'you mark my words. Because her husband's a terrible weakness for the bottle.'

'So how are we going to stop her, Tomas?' Cassie asked, 'short of moving house.'

'Ach, she'll not be doin' it again, don't you worry,' Tomas replied, draining his glass. 'Her son has a poteen still over in the valley, and as I said to Rosie on leaving, she'll not want the police getting to hear of it, now will she?'

Tomas grabbed his old cap and was gone. Gone too, was Leonora's information service. Cassie smiled and finished her drink.

As soon as she'd found that Willie Moore was not running his best three-year-old against Moviola the following Saturday at Gowran Park, with Dermot Pryce sidelined after an accident in the starting stalls, Cassie rang Dexter Bryant and offered him the ride. As luck had it, she beat Henry FitzGerald to it and Dexter accepted, albeit somewhat cautiously.

'Why not come over and ride him tomorrow morning

570

at work?' Cassie asked. 'I'm a great believer in jockeys getting the feel of their horse before the race.'

'OK, ma'am,' Dexter replied. 'I'll be there.'

'You can ride him second string,' Cassie said. 'Then maybe you'd like to stay on and have some breakfast.'

Moviola pleased Dexter on the gallops, and the jockey expressed himself happy to have been offered the ride. But, his eye, he confessed, was really more taken with the way The Donk worked.

Over breakfast of fresh orange juice and lightly scrambled eggs, Cassie told him the story of the little horse and Dexter made it plain that he'd be more than interested in riding him. If Pryce was still on the injury list, Cassie told him, he could have first refusal.

But although Dexter showed great interest in riding the few good horses Claremore had, he still remained very polite and reserved in Cassie's company.

'I thought perhaps you wouldn't be speaking to me,' Cassie suddenly said, deciding to take the bull by the horns.

Dexter looked up at her in genuine surprise.

'On the contrary, ma'am,' he replied. 'I thought the shoe would be on the other foot. After the trouble I got you in.'

'After the trouble I got *you* in.'

'You didn't write the note, ma'am.'

'You've been riding for the person who wrote that note, Dex,' Cassie told him. Dexter regarded her blankly. 'You didn't know Kutchikoo belonged to Leonora Von Wagner?'

'That wasn't the name on the race card, ma'am,' Dexter replied.

'It wouldn't be, Dex. Of course, she's been married and divorced twice since you knew her as Miss Von Wagner.'

'Mr FitzGerald rang up and offered me a spare ride.'

'You can bet your life it wasn't Mr FitzGerald who thought of offering the ride to you.'

Cassie grinned and poured them both some more black coffee.

'So we're still friends, then, Dex?' she asked, genuinely hopeful.

'Sure we are,' Dex smiled in return. 'You bet.'

'OK. So now maybe, please God, you'll stop calling me ma'am.'

Rosie 'Red-Ears' was then persuaded to pass on to Leonora, for a modest sum of money, the contents of Cassie's transatlantic telephone call to Townshend Warner that night, when he was informed where Moviola was running and what his chances were. Cassie didn't tell him whom she'd booked to ride, following Tomas' slightly unethical suggestion of not declaring Moviola's jockey until she reached the course. Leonora took the bait, however, and left Kutchikoo in the same race in the hope of rubbing Cassie's nose in it. She wasn't at the meeting, but Cassie could tell from Henry FitzGerald's expression when he saw Dexter Bryant's name given out as Moviola's jockey in the announcement of runners and riders for the fourth race that the news had flapped the normally unflappable young man.

There was no doubt at all as the race progressed that Dexter's riding was improving Moviola immeasurably. Normally a strong-pulling horse, Dex got him settled nicely in the middle of the field, but on the outside of the pack where the horse liked to be. Then while the other riders were all busy jockeying for position three furlongs from home, he simply shook the horse up and rode him out with just hands and heels. Kutchikoo was produced with a flourish verging on the violent by Tommy Dwyer, a seasoned campaigner known for his hard driving finishes. But Moviola had flown, and won easing up by four lengths, with Kutchikoo going nowhere fast back in sixth.

'He's a nice horse, sir,' Dex said to Tomas, as he dismounted. 'Too smart for this company I'd say. And certainly good enough to pick up a nice race cross the Channel.'

Then with a touch of his cap and a smile to Cassie, he went to weigh in.

'Well?' said Cassie to Tomas over the winning drink.

'You're beginning to sound the spit of his late self,' Tomas replied. 'Well indeed.'

'He's in for the Waterford at Ascot,' Cassie continued. 'The worst thing that can happen is he could lose.'

'True enough,' said Tomas, picking up his glass. 'But first things first. Let's drink to this afternoon, because that was a rare old race, and a rare old bit of tacticalisin', too. So here's to you, Guv'nor.'

Tomas raised his glass and slid a sideways look at her. Cassie raised her glass in return, but was quite unable to form a reply. It was the first time ever Tomas had acknowledged her as the Guv'nor.

'You must have had a bet,' Cassie finally said, modestly thinking that had to be the reason.

'I didn't have a penny laid out,' Tomas grinned in reply. 'Not a brass farthin'.'

'So when will you get your licence to train, do you reckon?' Dexter asked her later over dinner.

'Who knows?' said Cassie. 'This year, next year, some time, maybe never. It's a bit, I imagine, like being a suffragette.'

'Aren't there quite a few ladies training like you?' he asked. 'With their head lads holding the licence?'

'Sure,' Cassie answered. 'Trouble is, there aren't any girls in the Turf Club.'

They were eating in the kitchen of the house, which over the past years Cassie had managed to transform from a room which had looked like a medieval dungeon to a warm and comfortable country-house kitchen. She had stripped the old dressers of their dark green paint, removed layer after layer of grease-soaked wallpaper until the handsome stonework below was once again exposed, lifted the rotting straw matting from over the fine big flagstones, and torn out the terrible old black

573

kitchen range, which took for ever to cook even the sim-
plest meals. Now in their place was a handsome Aga, and
the fireplace, freed from hobs and stoves and hanging
kettles and pans, was now once again in use as a practical
fireplace. The room was now so warm and welcoming
that during the winter months the family hardly ever
moved out of it.

'Mummy,' said Josephine, 'I don't understand what
you meant when you said in America they were feeding
horses on nuts.'

'Ask Dex,' Cassie said, taking away her daughter's
clean plate, 'Dex knows all about how they feed their
horses back home.'

While Josephine moved along the bench to sit closer to
her new hero, Cassie gently reprimanded Mattie for
feeding Brian under cover of the table.

'But he's so hungry, Mummy!' Mattie protested. 'He
really is hungry!'

'Brian is always hungry,' Cassie replied, pushing the
enormous dog's snout away from her son's plate. 'Brian is
a professional scrounger.'

Josephine was listening earnestly to Dexter as he
explained that the 'nuts' in question were not the sort of
nuts Josephine imagined – peanuts, or cashews, or wal-
nuts even, but a different way of feeding concentrates to
horses, in the shape of little pellets.

'I always imagined you only fed nuts to cattle,' Cassie
said, beginning to dole out the homemade ice cream.

'Not any more,' Dex told her. 'Most of the big studs, as
well as the main yards, they're all using 'em. They combine all the necessary proteins, carbohydrates, vitamins
and roughage a horse needs to get and stay fit. You're
serious when you say you don't have 'em over here?'

'I've heard of one or two people in England using some
sort of racehorse cubes,' Cassie replied. 'But no one over
here, no.'

'Believe me,' Dex replied, 'tomorrow you'll all be
feedin' 'em.'

Cassie was intrigued. Even with Tomas' great skill as a feeder, she was still finding that certain of their more highly strung horses, once they were oated up, became very nervy and started picking through their feed, discarding the ingredients in their mangers they didn't like, and leaving them at the bottom, despite the added 'enticers' of molasses, sugar-beet pulp and sliced carrots. If these nuts were a success, if you really could feed them to your whole yard, she thought, firstly it would eliminate any fussy eating, and secondly, it must be highly cost effective.

'There's only one problem as far as I see it,' Dex told her. 'They make some horses very loose. Their droppings, you understand. Which is why Mr Fines, whom I was with for ten years, when he began using them, he mixed 'em with good quality bran, and kept all his horses on Canadian hay. And that used to do the trick. They never dropped nice and firm, like they do on oats, but it did prevent any protein wasting, which as I'm sure you know, is the bane of the feeder's life.'

Dexter's all-round stable knowledge greatly impressed Cassie, and since she was always in the market for ideas, she sat questioning him and listening to him in front of the drawing room fire until long into the evening.

'Mr Fines must be some trainer, I guess,' she said, pouring them both some more coffee.

'He taught me everything I know, Mrs Rosse,' Dexter replied. 'I really owe it all to him.'

'How was it starting out?' Cassie enquired, settling herself back down on the floor by the fire.

'You mean after I left the Von Wagners?'

'Yes. I guess I do.'

'Tough. I guess I pushed brooms and muck barrows in about half a dozen yards before I finally got taken on by Mr Fines. It was tough there at first, too. I mean you really had to earn your rides, and the failure rate – boy, that was some failure rate.'

'You made it,' Cassie smiled.

'I was never not going to make it,' Dex answered.

'Sure,' Cassie agreed. 'You were the most determined person I'd ever met.'

'I was only as determined as you were, Mrs Rosse.'

'You still are, I'd say. And whatever happened to Cassie?'

After that, Dexter rode for her whenever Willie Moore didn't claim him. Since Willie and Cassie were such close friends, Willie would ring her well in advance and tell her his plans, and when Dex would be free. Leonora's horses, even though on paper so vastly superior, were a very distant third best. Dex even managed to coax a couple of firsts from Claremore's no-hopers, one of them winning a good handicap at Naas and attracting the eye of a bloodstock agent who was looking for potential hurdlers. An offer was made for the horse via Tomas, and a good four-figure deal was concluded soon after, to the delight of the owner who had paid only £300 for the animal. Claremore made its percentage, and the horse went on to win three of his six novice hurdles.

Before that, Dexter rode Moviola into a close-up fourth place in the Waterford at Royal Ascot, and finally got Tootsie's nose in front in a nice race at the Curragh. The Donk unfortunately coughed the week before Ascot and had to miss the Gold Cup, for which he'd been quietly fancied, but was aimed instead for the Goodwood Cup. Best of all, as far as Cassie was concerned, Joe Coughlan's undying loyalty was at last rewarded when Dex brought home Casablanca, Joe's expensive new two-year-old, the easy winner of a very good nursery at Navan.

But even with these victories, there were just not enough horses at Claremore to make ends meet comfortably. With costs rising almost daily, Cassie needed more like thirty horses in training to keep the books out of the red. And she needed more winners: not that she was ever going to get rich on a trainer's winning percentage, but because winners attracted more winners, like bees to the honeyjar. She was determined moreover to keep her yard 'straight' and not have to rely on gambling on her own horses' chances.

'You're probably too honest for this game, Cassie,' Dex laughed over their now weekly kitchen dinner. 'That's probably why they've kept you ladies out for so long.'

'Don't tell me you're a stopper,' Cassie retorted.

'I just ride to orders,' Dex answered, still smiling, but intending his answer seriously. 'I'll tell you one thing, though. I don't bet.'

Cassie excused herself and got up from the table. 'Time for the children's story,' she said.

'Sure,' said Dex, finishing his coffee. 'Mind if I come and listen?'

They both sat on Josephine's bed while Josephine read Mattie 'The Quangle Wangle'. Then just as Cassie was about to read 'The Open Road' from *Wind in the Willows* to her daughter, Josephine came up with a better suggestion.

'Could Dex read to us tonight please, Mummy?' she asked.

'That's up to Dex, Josie,' Cassie replied. 'Maybe if you ask nicely—'

'She's already done that, Cassie,' Dex said, picking up the book. 'Do you want this? Or shall I tell you one of my very own stories?'

It was no contest. A Dexter Bryant original won hands down. As he sat on Mattie's bed with Josephine sitting listening on his knee, one arm round his neck, and the thumb of her other hand stuck firmly in her mouth, Cassie pretended to busy herself tidying up the nursery. Now and then she would sneak a look at the expressions on her children's faces, as they listened in total enchantment to Dex's story about a flying horse, and remembered how Tyrone would sit just like that on Josephine's bed, holding her in just the same way, while he told her stories of Snaggletooth the wicked old witch and Balmy Barney from Ballydehob.

577

Dex finished his story and both the children put their arms round his neck and hugged him goodnight.

'Those are a great couple of kids, Cassie,' he told her as they returned downstairs. 'You don't know how lucky you are.'

'Yes I do, Dex,' Cassie replied. 'That's the one thing I don't need reminding of.'

Tomas, for all his apparent irascibility, was also a good listener, and attended Cassie long and hard while she sat him in the yard office and propounded her theories about feeding concentrates.

'You mean we should change our ways, Guv'nor,' he said evenly. 'Throw away the knowledge of centuries, and take up with some new-fangled and practically untried and tested method.'

'It's not so new fangled, Tomas,' Cassie reasoned. 'They've been on the market for some time now. And there's no reason why a properly balanced nut—'

'Nuts is about the size of it,' Tomas muttered, pulling out his battered packet of Sweet Aftons.

'OK – cubes, if you'd rather,' Cassie replied.

'Oats is what I'd rather,' said Tomas.

'Come on, Tomas, bear with me. A properly balanced cube or concentrate could contain everything the horse needs. In one form of food.'

'Ach,' said Tomas dismissively, waving out his match, 'there's nothing wrong with the way we're doing it.'

'Look. I'm not trying to revolutionise feeding methods, Tomas. Feeding methods are being improved all the time. Why – you're always working on some magic new formula yourself! And that's my point. Because I'm not suggesting we start feeding cubes to our horses. What I'm suggesting is we make our own cubes. Or rather concentrates. And since everyone says you're the best feeder in Ireland, I'm suggesting we make them from *your* feed recipes.'

That effectively silenced Tomas. He took a draw on his

cigarette, removed a piece of tobacco from the end of his tongue, and then after a moment started to nod his head.

'We need money, Tomas,' Cassie continued. 'If we're going to make Claremore into one of Ireland's top training establishments, which we are, make no mistake, we need capital. Because we have to modernise.'

'Modernise what?' Tomas asked, raising his bushy white eyebrows. 'Sure didn't himself see to all that? With all them brand new boxes? And the indoor school? And the covered gallops? What else needs modernising?'

'The gallops need re-laying. And we need an all-weather gallop, too. We need heat lamps in the boxes, we need one of these mechanised horse walkers, electric groomers, yard vacuums, better transport, foaling boxes, some sort of security system, and –' here Cassie held her breath and said a silent prayer – 'I want to put in an equine swimming pool.'

Tomas nearly swallowed the stub of his cigarette. Then he stared up at Cassie as if she was certifiable.

'An equine swimming pool indeed,' he repeated.

'An equine swimming pool,' Cassie reaffirmed.

'What about an equine snooker table, Mrs Rosse?' Tomas asked. 'And an equine tennis court?'

'I'm serious, Tomas,' Cassie assured him.

'Sure I know you are,' Tomas answered. 'That's what worries me.'

'OK, you can think what you like. But believe me, this is the way racing's going. I've listened to Dexter Bryant, and it's like everything else. What we have back home in America, you have over here tomorrow. And if we're going to climb to the top of the pile, Tomas Muldoon, we're going to have to be first in a lot of other fields before we are going to be first past the only post that matters.'

'And which post might that be, Mrs Rosse?' Tomas enquired.

'The one that lies at the end of one and a half miles of undulations on Epsom Downs, in Surrey. The Epsom Derby.'

* * *

579

'How much will you be requiring, my dear Mrs Rosse?' Mr Flannery asked her, leaning as far across his desk as he decently could to catch the pungent aroma of Cassie's scent.

'As much as you'll lend me, kind sir,' Cassie smiled, carefully crossing her legs, and allowing her skirt to hitch up some more.

It was a last desperate effort by Cassie to obtain full capitalisation from one source. She had tried some of Tyrone's old connections, including Townshend Warner. But he, her likeliest bet, had just suffered a heart attack, and was in intensive care in a Houston hospital. Joe Coughlan had been willing to mortgage his house, his business and his one good racehorse in order to help her, but Cassie would have none of it. She wanted a clean loan, with a reasonable rate of interest. The last thing she wanted was her most loyal owner risking his all for a scheme which could well fail completely.

So she had turned finally to 'Old Flann at the bank', albeit highly reluctantly. She knew she would have to go a lot further than just smile at him for the size of the loan she was after, and while she was dressing to go out and meet the loathsome man for lunch, she suddenly wished for a little of Leonora's worldliness and sexual wisdom. Having only ever known Tyrone and, very briefly, Jean-Luc de Vendrer, she knew she was gauche and naïve for a woman of her age when it came to dealing with men, and more particularly, with what men wanted. And even more particularly in an age where men were finding it easier than ever to get what they were after, with women ever more eager to supply it. The Sixties had been the decade of staying loose and letting it all hang out. Even Princess Anne had jumped on the stage of the Shaftesbury Theatre in London, and joined in the dance at the end of the first nude musical *Hair*.

Not that Mr Flannery had witnessed the spectacle, but nonetheless, Cassie suspected, he was well aware of the changing sexual climate, even in Ireland. Her fears were justified, when all through lunch he rubbed his knees against hers under the linen-clothed table, and kept dropping his napkin for a very obvious peep up her skirt. He worried endlessly through the meal at how lonely Cassie must be without a man in that great house of hers, and hinted several times that for him there was a big and important promotion in the offing, to a post which would be greatly enhanced by the addition of a wife.

And now back in his stifling office, he was asking Cassie if she would like to remove her jacket, and while Cassie dallied as to whether she should or not, he all but ripped it off her. Cassie was wearing a thin silk polo-neck sweater under the jacket of her suit, which showed off her perfect figure. Flannery ran a finger round the inside of his stiff collar and remarked how remarkably fit Cassie kept herself.

'But back to business,' he reminded himself out loud. 'Back to business. You already have your eye on some premises, so you say.'

'I've been looking at Peacock's Mill, on the outskirts of Athy,' Cassie told him. 'Mr Muldoon heard they were considering selling it.'

'Mr Muldoon I feel sure will give us good advance warning of the end of the world,' Flannery replied, smirking. 'Yes? Yes?'

'If I offered on it, lock, stock and barrel, I think we could get it for fifteen thousand. We'd need another ten grand to get it right for our purposes, and say an initial float of five.'

'You'd be looking for a loan, then, of thirty thousand pounds.'

'That's about it, Mr Flannery.'

'A secured loan.'

'I guess it would have to be.'

'Secured against Claremore.'

'That's my only collateral.'

'And Claremore stands you now at let us say—'

Flannery pressed the fingertips of both his hands together and did his best to look roguishly at Cassie.

581

'Let us say um – eighty? Eighty-five?'

'I'd say nearer one hundred and twenty-five.'

'Equine establishments are not everyone's cup of tea, alas, my dear Mrs Rosse.' Flannery got up and walked round the room, ending up behind her. 'No, no. Equine establishments really are not everyone's cup of tea. However,' he said, coming forward behind her. He placed his hands on both of Cassie's shoulders, his fingers reaching down as far as they dared towards her breasts.

'Although I might well get admonished for my foolhardiness, they do say that a well-known emotion is blind, yes? Yes? And so, because of my – my *belief* in you, my dear Mrs Rosse, I am prepared to grant you this loan, against a charge on Claremore. And at an interest of only three and a half per cent above base rate.'

'Three and a half per cent?' Cassie exclaimed, using her apparent dismay to turn in her chair and dislodge Flannery's hot pudgy hands, which were slipping ever further towards their target.

Flannery leapt back as if shot. 'Most people, I have to tell you, Mrs Rosse, would think twice of lending such a sum against such dubious collateral.'

'Perhaps in that case, just to make sure, I'd better go ask some of these other people,' Cassie said, rising and collecting her jacket.

Flannery stood between her and the door.

'I will lend you all the money you need, Mrs Rosse, at one and a half per cent above base—'

'Yes, Mr Flannery?'

'I have a very charming cottage in Kinsale, recently purchased, with a remarkable view of the harbour. I would be more than honoured to entertain you there as my guest, let us say this weekend?'

Cassie did up her jacket and tugged it down into shape. Then she looked at the smooth and white-faced man who stood in the way not only of the door, but of her future. 'You'd like me to go to bed with you, would you Mr Flannery?'

Flannery coloured crimson, and his chin began to tremble. 'That wasn't quite what I said, Mrs Rosse,' he answered.

'It was what you meant, Mr Flannery,' Cassie countered.

'I could let you have the money at base rate. With no extra interest.'

'In return for a weekend in Kinsale.'

'It really is a most charming spot. Are you at all familiar with it?'

'Only by reputation, Mr Flannery. What about the charge on Claremore?'

Flannery took his handkerchief out of his top pocket, and passed it once across his brow. 'I'm afraid I would still have to insist on that. Yes, most certainly,' he replied.

'Sorry,' Cassie said curtly. 'No deal.'

'It's the rules of the bank, Mrs Rosse.'

Cassie leaned forward, and putting a finger under his wobbling chin, tickled him mockingly like a baby.

'What about you, Flanny-boy?' she half-whispered. 'Don't you have any capital?'

'Nothing like the amount you require, Mrs Rosse,' he gasped.

'But what do *you* require, Mr Flannery?' she continued. 'If I can give you what you want, don't you think you could give me what I want? Or do you think that I should charge you interest too?'

'I'm not quite sure of what you mean by that, Mrs Rosse.'

Cassie smiled at him, then taking him by one of his fat, moist hands, led him back to the chair where he was sitting and pushed him down into it.

'I mean if you want me to come over, then you borrow the money against your collateral from your bank. And lend it interest-free to little Cassie.'

She leaned right over him, one hand on either arm of the chair, until her face was a matter of inches from his.

583

She had undone her jacket again, so that the objects of his earlier desire now hung tantalisingly close to him, and he became almost suffocated by her scent.

'Well?' she said, her eyes glinting mockingly. 'What do you say, *sexy*?'

'Yes,' Flannery gasped up at her, now completely in her thrall. 'Yes, yes of course. I don't see why we couldn't come to *some* sort of mutually amicable arrangement. Yes, yes. Why not? Why not indeed?'

Cassie looked at him, at the sweat that was beginning to shine on his unlined white forehead and the fine mist which was starting to cloud the lenses of his black wire glasses. Then she flicked his tie out from under his vest, and gave one of his cheeks a good, hard pinch.

'Good,' she said, standing up. 'After all, if you expect favours from girls, then I think girls should expect some favours back from you, don't you?'

She did her jacket up, collected her purse, and went to the door.

'What about the weekend?' Flannery stuttered, scrambling to his feet.

'I'm really not too sure,' Cassie said, going to the door. 'I think I need a second opinion on it.'

She threw open the door and called out into the bank.

'Excuse me, everyone!' she cried. 'But Mr Flannery wants me to go on a dirty weekend with him in return for lending me some money at three and a half points over base!'

Flannery made a desperate attempt to shut his office door, but Cassie had her foot firmly wedged in it.

'I reckon that represents a pretty lousy deal, don't you?' she asked.

The employees, all of whom she knew from Erin loathed Flannery as much if not more than Cassie did, began to laugh, some of them out loud, while several girls roared back their support to Cassie. Cassie grinned, clenched her fist in the air, and removed her foot from the manager's door, leaving the crimson-faced Flannery to hide himself away within. Then she walked to the nearest counter to audible applause from some of the girls, and bidding the teller good afternoon, withdrew all her remaining funds and closed her account.

Outside in the street, in full sight of the still wide-eyed employees, and also the now ashen-faced Flannery who was watching from the side of his office window, Cassie let all the air out of his car tyres before getting into her own car and driving off back to Claremore.

'If I had the money, I'd sure back you,' Dexter told Cassie that evening as they sat on the terrace of Claremore drinking wine.

'I don't think I'll have much trouble actually raising the money, Dex,' Cassie answered, 'though thanks for the thought. No, I guess the catch is whether the gamble will pay off.'

'What America does today—' Dexter ventured.

'We're talking Ireland here, Dex,' Cassie interrupted with a grim. 'What America does today the Irish will think about doing next century. And only think about, remember.'

She poured them both some more wine, and for a moment they sat in silence and watched Josephine jumping her pony in the home paddock below them.

'That kid's a natural,' Dexter said.

'She wants to be the first girl to win the Grand National,' Cassie replied.

'You mean she doesn't know Elizabeth Taylor has beaten her to it?'

Cassie laughed, then drank some wine. 'Of course, there's no reason why we shouldn't go international, I suppose,' she said, changing the subject back. 'We don't just have to think of selling our concentrates here in Ireland. We could compete directly in the whole of the British Isles. And not only that, I reckon we should really be aiming for the private owner, and livery yards, rather than just racing. Trainers are ultra conservative, you know, particularly in Europe. They still swear by oats. Whereas to the ordinary owner, who doesn't grow his own fodder, and has to rely on his corn merchant, ready-made cubes and concentrates must be becoming very attractive alternatives.'

'You sound as if you're rehearsing a sales pitch there, Cassie,' Dexter said.

'Maybe I am, Dex,' Cassie answered. 'I've a meeting at the Bank of Ireland Monday morning.'

Early on Sunday evening a dark blue chauffeur-driven Bentley Continental pulled up outside Claremore, and Leonora got out. Cassie received her at the front doors, and stood with her on top of the steps outside.

'Aren't you going to ask me in?' Leonora enquired.

'I'm really not sure,' Cassie replied. 'I wasn't expecting you.'

'OK,' Leonora sighed. 'So I was in a foul mood when you called uninvited. But that doesn't mean that you have to behave as badly as me.'

Cassie smiled and stepped aside. The one thing she admired about Leonora, Cassie thought as she followed her into the house, was her ability to wrong-foot her opponents.

'I love this house,' she announced as she swept into the drawing room, 'but Jesus Christ you could do with Billsy.'

'Who or what is Billsy?' Cassie enquired.

'Who or what is Billsy indeed,' Leonora echoed, flopping on to a sofa. 'Don't you *ever* leave the stable yard? Billsy is Billsy Deane, lover. Only Ireland's top interior designer. He's going to do Derry Na Loch as a set of pleated tents.'

Cassie stared at Leonora as if she'd taken leave of her senses, then decided not to venture any further into what was for Cassie uncharted territory.

'Drink?'

'I don't arrive at this time of day to take tea, sweetheart.'

Leonora started to cough, and then lit another cigarette, as Cassie poured them both a drink.

'What did you arrive at this time of day for, Leonora?'
Cassie asked.

'I heard you needed money,' Leonora replied, putting
her gold lighter away in her purse.

'I don't need money.'

'OK. If you want to split hairs, an investment then.'

Leonora shook her fringe out of her eyes and stared up
at Cassie. After a moment she followed the look with her
frosty little smile.

'Word travels,' Cassie said.

'Nowhere faster than in Ireland,' Leonora answered.
'The word is you want about fifteen grand.'

'About,' Cassie agreed cautiously.

'That's peanuts,' Leonora said. 'I can let you have that
now.'

She reopened her purse and fished inside for her
cheque book.

'Wait up,' Cassie said. 'What's the big hurry?'

'It sounds like a hot number, that's what,' Leonora
replied impatiently. 'And like all very rich people, I
enjoy making money. What are the banks quoting you?
Because I'll undercut them by a point, and I'll only take
twenty per cent of your gross once you're in profit. How's
that for starters?'

'I don't want your money,' Cassie replied. 'So you can
put away your bank book.'

'Oh for Chrissake don't start coming all proud again!'
Leonora retorted. 'I'm not doing you any favour, goddammit! This is business!'

'That's why I don't want your money,' Cassie told her,
getting up and walking over to a window. 'If it was a
favour, I really might have considered it. After all,
money is only money. But we couldn't do business
together. You must be crazy.'

'Of course I'm crazy,' Leonora agreed. 'I've been crazy
since the day I was born. And who do I have to sleep with
to get another drink round here?'

Cassie refilled Leonora's glass, while Leonora

impatiently stubbed out her half-smoked cigarette and at once relit another one.

'But I'm not crazy, Leonora,' Cassie said. 'Which is why we couldn't do business. Why should I give you twenty per cent of my idea for the loan of a few thousand? The bank will lend me the money, and I'll only need pay them back the interest.'

Leonora stared at her, twisting her mouth sideways as she did so, and biting the inside of her lip.

'Sure,' she replied after a long moment, 'but business isn't just money. Business is who you know. And nobody knows my new husband better than me.'

'Sorry,' Cassie smiled. 'I've forgotten what your new husband does.'

'He makes a lot of money,' Leonora said. 'And one of his sidelines, well it's more of a hobby really.' She drew on her cigarette and blew the smoke into a thin stream up towards the ceiling before looking back into Cassie's eyes. 'One of his hobbies is a firm called UFM. United Fodder Merchants. They make animal feedstuffs.'

Cassie held Leonora's gaze. She'd thought there had to be something other than sheer profiteering behind Leonora's offer. Lesser people profiteered. Leonora took you over before you were even on the market.

'Sorry, Leonora,' Cassie replied, still holding her look. 'No deal.'

'OK,' said Leonora, looking away and putting out her cigarette. 'Get buried then.'

Cassie walked to the door and opened it. 'And now I'm afraid you'll have to go,' she said. 'I've guests this evening.'

Leonora collected her purse and rose. 'Sure,' she said with a smile as she walked past Cassie. 'I know.'

Dexter Bryant was among Cassie's close friends who had been invited for an informal kitchen supper that evening.

'Did Leonora know you were coming here tonight?' Cassie asked him during the meal.

'Yes,' Dexter nodded. 'As a matter of fact she did.'

'How?'

'Because she wanted me to go to dinner with her tonight at Derry Na Loch.'

One of the assistant managers of the Bank of Ireland, a Mr Tuohy, listened most sympathetically to Cassie's request on the following day, and indicated that the bank would be only too pleased to offer her facilities for the loan, provided a charge was secured on Claremore. The loan was to be over three years, and a weekend in Kinsale was not part of the package.

Tomas pretended to be indifferent about the whole affair, merely expressing the opinion that Cassie had to be out of her mind to think such a hare-brained scheme could succeed.

'Listen,' he told her. 'If the Lord God had intended horses to eat nuts, he'd have given them a pair of nutcrackers.'

But later it came back to Cassie from one of the lads that Tomas was warning them all to look out to whom they were talking, because in a couple of years' time he was going to be a multi-millionaire.

After a closely conducted survey, and a properly organised business analysis, Peacock's Mill was deemed to be an ideal property, and the bank was informed that Mrs Rosse intended to bid for it at the auction, to be held in the first week of August. At the same time, samples of certain concentrates had been brought back for analysis from America by a bloodstock agent friend of Cassie's, and laboratory tests were being conducted on Tomas' feed recipes, in order to see if they would make up satisfactorily into what was finally to be known as the Claremore Concentrate.

Meanwhile, The Donk's cough which he had prior to Ascot, and which had meant his withdrawal from the Gold Cup, had not developed and he was back in full work during the Royal Meeting itself. In preparation for

589

his main target of the season, the twenty-one-furlong Goodwood Cup, he took in another mile-and-three-quarter race at Leopardstown which he won more or less as he liked. Dermot Pryce, it now seemed, was sadly and permanently sidelined, so once again Dexter Bryant was on board. After the race Dex was of the confident opinion that the little horse would take all the beating at Goodwood.

'There's no outstanding stayer this season,' he told Cassie in the bar afterwards. 'And at one and three quarter miles, the little fellah's still only cantering.'

'But will you be able to ride him, Dex?' Cassie asked.

'I'll think about it, Guv'nor,' Dex grinned, 'if you say please.'

Cassie did say please, but that was all. She found herself still very fond of Dex, who had grown from a boy full of determination and purpose into a man of dedication and also of great natural charm and warmth. Cassie knew that he found her attractive as well, but before there had been the chance for any romance to flower, Tomas had nipped it smartly in the bud.

'This young man of yours, Guv'nor,' he'd started one morning after the second string had returned from the gallops.

'I don't have any young man, Tomas,' Cassie had replied, over their mugs of tea in the office.

'The way he looks at you with them googly eyes of his, I'd say *he* thinks you do.'

Tomas had glanced at her, as he relit the stub of the Sweet Afton he'd tucked away behind his ear.

'If you're referring to Dexter Bryant, Tomas—'

'Sure I'm hardly referring to Sean Connery now, am I? I'm just sayin' that he'll stop listening to you the moment you start listening to him, that's all.'

'Meaning?'

'Meaning precisely that, Mrs Rosse. There's no benefit to be had crossin' the line, you know. Not in a racin' yard.'

'I have no intention of crossing the line as you call it!' Cassie had replied, more than a little curtly.

'You'd be as well not to,' Tomas had finished, 'not if you want him to keep ridin' you winners. A man keeps his ambition just as long as he keeps his pants up.'

It was the nearest Cassie had ever come to losing her temper with Tomas. And only because she had known he was right.

Even so, however much she protested, Cassie found it increasingly hard being alone in Dex's company, although she seemed almost wilfully to fly in the face of providence by still continually inviting him to eat dinner with her children and herself in the kitchen at Claremore. She made it her excuse that she wanted to prove to herself how strong she could be.

But on the Sunday before the big Goodwood meeting, the temptation almost proved too strong. Cassie had thrown a lunch party and Dexter had been amongst the guests. And he had lingered behind, ostensibly to play with the children. Cassie didn't even know that he was still there until all her other guests had gone and she saw Dexter riding up the drive on Bouncer, with Mattie on his saddle in front of him and Josephine on her pony beside him. It was such a pretty sight that for a moment Cassie stopped helping Erin clear up and stood watching the party ride slowly up to the house with a smile on her face. Dex was teasing them both, and Josephine in particular, so much that by the time they pulled their horses up below the terrace, Josephine was quite pink from the giggles.

'I've been fired!' Dex called up to Cassie. 'Jocked off! Young Mattie-boy's riding The Donk in the Goodwood Cup!'

'And Dexter and I are going to get married!' Josephine shouted. 'Tomorrow!'

'My oh my!' Cassie laughed. 'Tomorrow? I'll never get the invitations out in time!'

'It's going to be a very quiet affair!' Dex called up. 'Just you and Mattie and the horses!'

591

After they'd helped Erin bathe them, and read them their stories, Cassie and Dex tucked the children up in bed as if they were their very own. Josephine gave Dex an extra long kiss and hug, and told him not to be late for their wedding.

Cassie was still laughing downstairs with Dex about the children before she realised that she was in his arms. Then her laugh stopped as she saw how seriously Dexter was looking at her.

'Dexter,' she said. 'Dex.'

But it was too late. He had kissed her, and even though she quietly protested when he stopped, he simply kissed her again.

'I've been dying to do that, Cassie, ever since I saw you again,' he whispered. 'I've been dying to do that in fact for over twelve years.'

'Dexter, please,' Cassie said, trying to find the strength to push him away from her, to refuse him any further contact.

'It's OK, Cassie,' Dex reassured her, 'it's really OK. I could see how you were feeling as well. I could see you were feeling just the same as me.'

'I don't know how I'm feeling, Dex!' Cassie protested, almost indignantly, as she finally managed to prise herself out of his arms. 'I'm sorry, but it's just not fair.'

'What isn't?' he asked her. 'You kissing me? I don't find that unfair. What I find unfair is all those years we missed. All that time gone by.'

Cassie sat down on a sofa and looked up at the serious-faced Dex. He was wearing exactly the same expression he had worn all that time ago when he had climbed into her bedroom on Long Island.

'Dex, I've been married since then,' Cassie told him. 'You must try and understand. I've been married, I've had babies and I've lost my husband. A man I loved deeply. I'm just not the same girl you knew in America.'

'Sure you're not,' Dex replied. 'You're even more marvellous. I know I'll never understand what you've been

through, but you mustn't expect me to. I love you for
what you are now. For what you are to me. That's how it
is, Cassie. You're still the most wonderful girl I've ever
met.'

Cassie looked up at him, as Dexter smiled and sat
down beside her. 'You can't, Dex,' she said. 'You
mustn't.'

'I can't? I mustn't what, Cassie?'

'You mustn't fall in love with me.'

'It's a little late for that, Cass.'

He smiled at her sweetly and took her hand in both of
his.

'Dex, I don't know what I feel. I don't know how I feel.
I don't even know if I feel. If I still can have feelings. I
know that I like you tremendously, that you make me
feel warm and that I love being with you. Beyond that, I
don't know how I feel. Really.'

'It's OK, Cass. We've plenty of time.'

'It's not a question of time, Dex.'

'What is it then?'

Cassie fell silent, looking at how serious he had
become.

'You mean I'm not good enough for you?' he said without malice, just with a sort of innocent curiosity.

'That's not what I mean at all,' Cassie replied.

'I guess maybe it is,' Dex replied. 'Jeeze – I'm still such
an idiot. You know that? I keep forgetting how different
things are! How much everything's changed'

He got up and started to pace the room. Cassie
watched him anxiously.

'Or rather not changed,' he continued. 'No – it's my
fault, Cass! It's OK! You see I forget things like how you
are now, what you are, where you are, and what I am,
and where I am. You see, you see – I keep seeing us, you
and me, I keep seeing us as we were. The way we were. A
boy and a girl, that's all. But now you're Mrs Rosse,
widow of a famous trainer, getting pretty famous in your
own right, and I'm a professional jockey who works for

people like you. That's what you mean, isn't it? That's what it's a question of, right?'

Cassie looked up at him, but was unable to keep her eyes on him, unable to bear looking at the pain on his face. So she just looked down again and shook her head, even though she knew and he knew that he had spoken the truth.

Dex knelt down beside her and took her hand again.

'I'm sorry, Cass. I really didn't mean any of that,' he said.

'Of course you did, Dex. And there's nothing for you to be sorry about. I'm the one who should be sorry,' Cassie replied.

'You mean sorry for letting me get involved with you?'

'I mean sorry I can't love you back. It's not to do with where we both are, and what we are. It's too early for me, that's all. It's still too soon after Tyrone. I nearly made a terrible mistake in France, and—'

'And you don't want to make another, that's understandable.'

'You're not a mistake. But I could be, Dex. Because I don't know who I am yet. I really do need a little more space. And a little more time.'

She looked up at him, and tried to smile. But found it impossible.

Dex smiled instead and stroked her cheek lightly before rising. 'Listen,' he said. 'I'd best be hitting the road. I have to ride work tomorrow for this very strict lady trainer.'

Cassie rose after him, and took his hand, to stop him leaving quite yet. 'Please forgive me, Dex,' she said. 'Please. It's just time. That's all I need. Time.'

'I guess that's all any of us need, Cass,' Dex replied. 'And I guess it's the one thing none of us ever gets enough of.'

Then he squeezed her hand and was gone.

Things looked good that week. The weather was fine, The Donk was popping out of his skin, and the Goodwood Cup appeared all over bar the shouting, there being only four other entries, all of whom strictly on form let alone on Cassie's timings were held by her own horse.

And the fact that he was her horse and not anybody else's added a different dimension to the whole race, because if The Donk won, the winner's prize money, which that year had risen to over £20,000, would all come back to Claremore.

'I haven't even had a bet,' she told Tomas as they saddled him up for the race. 'There's no point, is there? Not if he's going to win all that lovely prize money.'

The only worry Cassie had that week had been over Dex. He had turned up to ride work on the Monday, and was his usual sweet and charming self. But on Wednesday he was oddly taciturn, and on the morning of the race, when he was due to walk the course with Cassie and Tomas, he didn't show up at all. When Cassie returned to her hotel, she found a message of apology from him, saying he'd developed a cold, and had overslept because of the medication he'd taken.

And when he'd walked into the paddock to mount up, Cassie was appalled by how pale he looked.

'Are you all right, Dex?' she asked, as he arrived by her side for his race orders.

'I'm OK, really,' he replied. 'Don't worry. It's just a bad cold.'

'You don't sound as if you've a cold,' Tomas said.

'I've taken some of those cold capsules,' Dex said, checking his horse's girths. 'You know, the ones which dry you right out.'

'It's a pity you didn't walk the course,' Cassie complained. 'It gets awful confusing out there in the country.'

'I've been through it with the other jocks, Guv'nor,' Dex replied. 'Dozens of times. No problems. Now. Shall I make all? Or hold the little horse up for a burst?'

'Against this field you go on,' Cassie instructed. 'The going's just right for him, after the overnight rain, so jump him off in front, and make them come after you.

595

Give him a blow coming up the hill, and don't worry if they start coming at you. They'll be crazy if they do when they're climbing, but that's what we want. Let them think you're beat, then three out, kick him on again, and let's see what he's got in the locker.'

The Donk went down to the start with his head in his chest, and his ears pricked. On the way past the stand, he gave a good-natured buck, to show his well-being, and then settled down to enjoy his canter. He was the clear favourite at 5/4 against, the next horse in the market being the Ascot Gold Cup runner-up, Preface, at 2/1, and drifting. By the time they were off and running, the Claremore horse was even money.

Dexter did exactly as bid, jumping The Donk off first in a field where no one was anxious to make the running. After two furlongs he had poached a ten-length lead before the horses behind him realised how easily he was going. As they turned away from the stands, and out into the country, Dexter had him fifteen lengths clear and going sweetly. Of his four opponents, two were already apparently being tailed off, one of the back markers being Preface. Running along the back of the course, before the long climb up to the final straight, the field was well strung out, with The Donk if anything increasing his lead. Judging from the buzz in the grandstand, the race was over bar an accident.

Indeed, The Donk was now in what appeared to be an unassailable lead, knowing his stamina, as he and Dex approached the point on the Gold Cup course where it criss-crosses with the other part of the racecourse, and where there is a sweeping turn off to the right which to all intents and purposes, and to a jockey who doesn't know the course, would appear to be the final turn back to the grandstands stands, and home. Which it isn't.

Yet Dexter took it. Approaching it, he had taken a long look over his shoulder at the field strung out behind him, and seeing his nearest rival hard at work over fifteen, maybe twenty lengths back, had then turned front again, and obviously mistaken which running rail to follow. He swung the little horse to follow the first rail on his right, which led in fact back into the country, and as he did so there was a mighty shout from the stands as the crowd realised the favourite's mistake. But by the time Dex had realised it, the others were past him and gone straight ahead up the hill, on the correct route for home. Dexter pulled the little horse up, and through her glasses Cassie saw Dex sitting back on his saddle and pushing up his goggles. Then he kicked The Donk on and cantered slowly for home.

There was a Steward's Enquiry, and at it, Dexter Bryant was fined and warned for taking the wrong course. As soon as the horse was safely in his stable, Cassie announced to Tomas that she was returning to her hotel, and Tomas announced to her that he was going to get legless. Neither of them had bothered asking Dexter for an explanation. There was no point. The race had been run and lost.

Leonora offered Cassie her version of events when she caught up with Cassie in the owners' and trainers' car park.

'Wasn't that a crazy thing to do?' she asked. 'Though I have to believe it wasn't entirely a mistake.'

'What do you mean by that, Leonora?' Cassie asked. 'I hope you can back up any accusation you may be about to make.'

'It's just that Dex was at dinner with me the night before he left for England,' Leonora replied, fishing in her purse for yet another cigarette, 'and we got talking old times. You know how it is.' She smiled over the flame of her lighter as she lit her cigarette.

'And I may be wrong,' she continued, 'but I doubt it. Because I got the distinct feeling, darling, that Dexter Bryant was just a little piqued, shall we say, when he learned that the little prank when he climbed into your bedroom and ended up getting fired was *both* our doing.'

Cassie looked at Leonora, feeling a hate in her heart

which until then she had not realised it was possible to feel.

'You know that isn't true, Leonora,' she replied, icily calm. 'You know perfectly well you wrote the note.'

'Did I, darling?' Leonora said, frowning, and replacing her lighter in her purse. 'Did I really? Well, well, well. My *memory*. You're right. Maybe I really ought to stop drinking.'

She smiled, and then walked away to her limousine, where her chauffeur was already out and waiting by her door.

It was one defeat Cassie found very hard to take. She had tried very hard to follow in Tyrone's footsteps, and not pin all her hopes on the results of one race but this time she had failed. She was bitterly disappointed.

'It's only racing, Cassie McGann,' Tyrone had always said whenever she tried to commiserate with him. 'One horse loses, another one wins. One horse wins, another one loses.'

But she knew that this race had been different. This race should never have been lost and, worst of all, she knew it hadn't been. The race had quite deliberately been thrown. And all because of a falsehood.

Leonora's one falsehood had spoilt a thousand truths. That was the way with lies. Cassie's relationship with Dexter was now ruined irrevocably: he would consider Cassie to have been the liar, and not Leonora, so subsequently everything which Cassie might say to him, however truthful it was, would always seem to Dexter another possible deception. Such was the art of a deliberate liar like Leonora; she proved the old saying that, with skill, the smallest amount of lying can be made to go the longest possible way.

'Listen, Guv'nor,' Tomas had said to her one morning, after listening to a very unaccustomed outburst of resentment from Cassie. 'We've a saying in Ireland – and very suitable it is in this instance – that lies are always the jockeys of misfortune. So never yous mind for now. Liars don't get to look God in the face.'

'Neither, I hope,' Cassie added bitterly, 'do two-bit jockeys who pull horses.'

Dexter certainly never got to look Cassie in the face again that season. She was so hurt that he had doubted her and believed in Leonora instead, and so inconsolably angry that he had thrown the greatest race she had ever had a chance of winning, that Cassie went out of her way to cut and snub Dexter at every conceivable opportunity. She was also privately furious with herself for allowing such an intimacy to arise between them. Tomas had been right as usual. In situations such as this, there was just no crossing the line.

Worse was to come. Cassie had been reliably informed that she was the only serious buyer for Peacock's Mill, and yet at the auction for the property, just as the Mill was about to be knocked down to her for precisely the indicated reserve, another party entered the bidding, and within a couple of minutes the property was out of Cassie's reach. She had been forced to bid far too high for it anyway, since the bank had only agreed to lend twelve thousand for the initial purchase, but she had stayed with it till the bidding reached nineteen and a half. It was finally sold to the representatives of Sir Robert Ando, the owner of United Fodder Merchants Ltd, and the most recent husband of Leonora Von Wagner.

'Jesus, Mary and Joseph,' Tomas seethed, as they drove slowly home. 'What the bloody hell did you ever do to this woman? Savin' your presence.'

'What did I do to her?' Cassie echoed.

'That's what I asked you, Mrs Rosse,' Tomas repeated. 'What in the name of all that's holy did you ever do to her?'

'I beat her at tennis,' Cassie replied. 'That's all I ever did to her: beat her at a game of tennis.'

After weeks of searching and negotiating, they at last found another mill. It had vacant possession, and little wonder, Cassie thought when they first saw it, because it had fallen into total disrepair. Its state did however enable them to purchase it privately for less than half the money she had been prepared to lay out for Peacock's Mill.

'There you are!' Tomas crowed as they walked round their new property. 'What did I tell you about setbacks?'

'That they're often blessings in disguise,' Cassie replied wearily. 'Except I'm not at all sure how much of a blessing this place is going to be, Tomas. We're going to have to rebuild the whole damn thing from the ground up.'

'From little acorns . . .' Tomas said, lighting another Sweet Afton.

'Boy,' Cassie said. 'With you around, who needs a dictionary of quotes?'

Leonora finally added insult to injury when, shortly after Cassie had purchased her derelict property, she learned that Leonora's husband was busy knocking down Peacock's Mill with the intention of developing the site as a housing estate.

'The next thing your father will be telling me,' Cassie informed Erin over tea, 'is that bad luck always comes in threes.'

'And so it does, Mrs Rosse,' Erin replied, cutting Mattie's toast into fingers and covering them with honey. 'Just as babies always bring good luck, so bad luck always comes in threes.'

The third blow was a little longer in coming. Joe Coughlan's new horse, a two-year-old flyer called Casablanca, won the valuable Athos Stakes at Phoenix Park at 12/1 against, and with the proceeds of the biggest tilt he'd ever had at the ring, Joe Coughlan ordered Cassie to buy him a decent yearling.

'I was thinking I might copy Tyrone and go over to America looking,' Cassie told Sheila Meath one day when she went over to see her young horses. 'Combine a bit of business with pleasure. I don't suppose you feel like another little holiday?'

Sheila accepted with alacrity, and Cassie knew she would be glad of more than just her company, because Sheila was one of the best judges of young horses in Ireland, and everything Cassie was learning about the points of the horse she was learning from her. They arranged to fly over after the Doncaster Cup, for which The Donk stood his ground.

He was second favourite in the pre-race betting – hardly surprising since it was considered he hadn't exactly had much of a race at Goodwood. The horse which had won the Goodwood race was favourite, but an uneasy one, and Cassie and Tomas were in no doubt who would finally start favourite on the day.

Particularly since Cassie, leaving nothing to chance this time, had secured the services of one of the top English jockeys. The little horse travelled well, and was full of beans on the day before the race when Cassie herself gave him a spin on the town moor. But on the morning of the race, he seemed a little uneasy, dull in the eye, and for him oddly disinterested in his food. By twelve o'clock he was down in his stable, and in great distress.

Niall Brogan, who whenever possible travelled with Cassie for all the important races, saved his life by his prompt attention and medication. But he was in no doubt whatsoever, even before he had run tests, that the horse had been doped, and in even less doubt as to by whom.

'When I see the effects of dope on a horse, Cassie,' he said as he left The Donk's stable, 'that's when I pray to God for the day of the Tote monopoly. You can count your lucky stars the little fellah's still alive after what they've shot into him. But I very much doubt if you'll ever get him to the races again.'

Cassie sat with the little horse all day and half the night nursing him. Niall Brogan had sent their travelling head lad into the town to buy half a dozen inflatable mattresses, which between them all they managed to get under the stricken horse for support; because until he was strong enough to sit up, or even rise, there was a very real danger the horse would die, since horses cannot breathe properly when completely prostrate for long periods.

At one o'clock in the morning he suddenly half sat up, and once he was up and kept in that position, helped by a rebuilt wall of the inflatable mattresses, Tomas took over the nightwatch and sent Cassie back to her hotel bedroom.

By morning, the horse was on his feet and nibbling at his hay, and after a thorough examination of him, Niall Brogan told Cassie he was out of danger, and that she could leave for America as planned, and that Tomas could ship the little horse home quite safely the following day.

When she arrived back at Claremore that evening, to pack for America and say goodbye to her children, Cassie found a telegram awaiting her, informing her that Mary-Jo Christiansen's great-uncle James, Cassie's favourite owner, had, aged eighty-one, died peacefully in his sleep.

Chapter Twenty-One

Mary-Jo's mother met Cassie at Pittsburg airport. She was late, and arrived in a more modern but just as ramshackle version of the never-to-be-forgotten family station wagon. Cassie was waiting for her as the Oldsmobile drew up, and Mrs Christiansen, apparently barely a day older, peered out of the driver's window, looking for her guest.

'I'd have recognised you any day, Cassie,' she said as they stood embracing in the heavy rain. 'You're just as cute as you always were.'

'How are you, Mrs Christiansen?' Cassie asked.

'Helen,' came the reply. 'I guess you're old enough and big enough to call me Helen now. And come on. Let's get in the car before we drown like rats.'

On the long drive back through the incessant rainstorm, Cassie caught up with all the family news. Mary-Jo was in Africa, safe and well when last heard of; her two youngest brothers were both married with two children each and fine jobs; while Frank, the eldest, now in his early thirties, was something of a financial prodigy, as he had already been made a full partner in the firm of stockbrokers where he had worked since leaving Yale. He too had got married, to the daughter of a Texan million-aire, but his beautiful bride of only eighteen months had been tragically killed in a hit-and-run accident in New York.

'Sometimes I think he won't ever get over it,' Helen Christiansen said as she turned off the main highway. 'It's over eight years ago now and, like I said, his life's one great big success – as far as his career goes. But it all goes into his work. That's where all his purpose goes. He never goes out and enjoys himself. He just comes home weekends, eats and rests up, then back to the money market.'

Cassie looked at the blur of rain-drenched landscape, and was reminded of her own solitary existence. But she at least had the wonderful consolation of her children.

'I'm sorry, Cassie,' Helen Christiansen said suddenly out of the silence. 'I did't know what I was saying. That was hardly very tactful of me.'

'On the contrary, Helen,' Cassie replied, 'you've got to talk to somebody about these things. And who better than someone who knows about it first-hand?'

She said this without bitterness, or without the slightest hint of recrimination. Helen Christiansen turned to her and smiled gratefully as they stopped at an intersection.

'How is it with you now, Cassie?' she asked. 'Is it any easier?'

'A little,' Cassie told her. 'I guess one day, like they say, I'll wake up and say, OK, life has to go on. But at the moment—'

She fell silent, turning to her window again and wiping the mist away with the back of a gloved hand.

'If I hadn't got the kids,' she added finally, 'I don't think I'd have made it.'

'James said you were the bravest girl he'd ever known,' Helen said.

'I was very lucky to have known James,' Cassie replied.

'Sure,' said Helen. 'I guess we all were.'

Back at the farm after the funeral, Cassie remet all Mary-Jo's brothers, and their wives and children. The years seemed to have done nothing to the Christiansen boys. They were all freckle-faced and wide-eyed, and full of positively tangible energy. Pete, the youngest, who still looked as though he'd put a frog in your bed, had married a suitably mischievous professional violinist; while Bill, always mad for the girls, had captured the prettiest girl in the whole of West Virginia – according to Bill – for his bride.

'You look great, Cassie,' Bill said to her. 'But really. Then I always did say you were far and away the prettiest of Mary-Jo's friends.'

'I'll bet you said that about all Mary-Jo's friends,' Cassie replied with a smile.

'You must be kidding! Have you forgotten Holly Arnold?' Bill laughed. 'Even with her braces on, she still looked like a horse!'

'You want to take it easy there, brother,' Pete advised him. 'Horses are Cassie's great love, remember?'

'She sure brought a lot of fun into Great-Uncle James's last years through the horses he had with her and her husband,' said a gentle voice from behind her.

Cassie turned, and there was Frank, the eldest of the boys, as serious and as freckle-faced as ever.

'Hello, Frank,' Cassie said, suddenly feeling rather shy in front of a man with whom she shared unspoken sorrow. 'How are you?'

'I'm fine, Cassie,' he replied, 'and you look just terrific.'

'I've just told her that,' Bill informed him with a grin, and at once Cassie was right back where they'd always been, right from the moment they'd all tumbled out of the family wagon after that first trip back from Locksfield station.

'You go flirt with your own wife,' Frank said good naturedly, 'while I take care of our guest.'

They picked up the pieces so easily that it seemed as if it was just last week when they had last seen each other, not over twelve years ago. Frank knew all about Cassie's business affairs, as he had helped run the financial side of his great-uncle's racing interests in the last years of his life.

'He was real sorry he never made it over to Ireland to see you both,' Frank told her. 'He was just crazy about your husband. When he first met him here, they sat up all night with a bottle of Jack Daniels, and kept the whole house awake with their laughter. I was just devastated when I heard what had happened to Tyrone.'

'I'd quite forgotten you'd met him, Frank,' Cassie said, finding herself so much at ease in the warmth of Frank's candour.

'Sure I did,' Frank replied. 'I was home the weekend Tyrone was here. He seduced us all so much, I nearly got back on the goddam plane to Ireland with him.'

'I'm afraid that was Tyrone all over,' Cassie agreed. 'Can you imagine what it was like being courted by him?'

'Crazy, I guess,' Frank said. 'Come on, let's go walk round the farm.'

They walked, and as they walked, they talked. And the more they walked, the more Cassie found herself able to discuss her life with Tyrone in a way she had not discussed it, not even with her closest friend Sheila Meath, since the day Tyrone had died. She told Frank stories about their life together, their joys and their triumphs and their disasters.

'This is great, you know,' Frank said at one point. 'I mean you were so lucky. You seem to have had a marriage in a million.'

'I know it, Frank,' Cassie replied. 'If that doesn't sound smug.'

' 'Course it doesn't, Cassie. Marriages like yours are made in heaven. So it's nothing you can pride yourself on. I guess we'd have had a marriage like that as well, Susanna and I, if she too hadn't gotten killed. She was a wonderful girl. You'd really have loved her, Cassie. Just everyone did.'

They were standing leaning on the paddock rail, over-looking the field where Cassie had so often stood with Mary-Jo, watching Prince growing up. She fell silent, and stared at the unknown horses which now grazed in front of her, swishing their tails at the last of the flies, and occasionally stamping a hindleg in anger as one of them managed a bite.

But Cassie wasn't silent because she was sad at her

606

memories, but because for the first time since she had lost Tyrone she had talked about him with joy, and a new kind of love, a love which was based on the exhilaration of having loved and been loved by such a wonderful person. It was as if the door behind her had finally closed, and another door had opened ahead. Tyrone was still beyond that door, which now swung open in front of her, but now she saw him quite clearly in sunshine, and no longer in a vale of tears, as a strange sense of euphoria settled over and within her.

She turned to Frank, who was chewing a long blade of grass, and staring into the far distance of his own memories.

'Frank,' Cassie said. 'I'm not sure how to say this. I'm not sure if it will even make sense.'

'Listen,' Frank interposed. 'You don't have to bother saying it, Cassie. Not if you're feeling the same as I'm feeling right now.'

'It's as if I've just turned a very big corner, Frank,' Cassie ventured. 'That's the only way I can describe it.'

'Me too,' Frank nodded, and then turned to smile at her. 'My feelings exactly.'

They flew back to New York together, easy in each other's company like the old friends they now were.

'Some day soon,' Frank said, somewhere over Pennsylvania, 'I'm going to have a couple of racehorses, and you're going to train them for me.'

'That's fine by me, Frank,' Cassie answered. 'But wouldn't you rather have them race over here?'

'Then what excuse would I have to come and see you?' he smiled. 'Problem is, I don't have that sort of money personally. And it's not exactly the sort of venture I feel I could persuade my somewhat model-T partners to invest in.'

'They'd be wrong, you know,' Cassie told him. 'Any moment now bloodstock is going to take right off.'

'Maybe you got something there, Cassie,' Frank

nodded thoughtfully. 'There are always new markets for growth. Anyhow, till the time I can nudge the old fogeys into investing in equine equity, I guess I'll have to keep dreaming.'

'Do you invest in small businesses at all?' Cassie asked him, quite directly.

'Sure we do,' Frank said. 'All the time. If they have the right sort of growth potential.'

'Then how would you like to invest in me?' she enquired.

Frank turned and looked at her. 'I can't think of anything that would give me greater pleasure.'

For the rest of the journey, Cassie explained about her and Tomas' plan for food concentrates, and about the various aspects of marketing them. Frank listened attentively and asked some probing questions. Luckily, Cassie had employed a go-ahead firm in Dublin to do the market research, and their findings had been highly encouraging.

On the taxi ride into Manhattan, Frank told Cassie he would give the matter his maximum attention, and promised her an answer before she left America.

In New York, before flying down to Kentucky where Sheila Meath was already taking a preliminary look at some young bloodstock, Cassie called Gina and got her answering service, which informed her that Gina's name was now Meryl Hope, and that she was busy working on Danny Browne's latest film *I Know Where It's At I Just Don't Know When*, but if Mrs Rosse would like to leave a message, the answering service would make doubly sure Miss Hope got it. Cassie left the number of her hotel, and a message to say that she'd be in New York until tomorrow only, and could they meet.

When she returned from a shopping spree and lunch with Frank Christiansen, Gina had returned Cassie's message, inviting her to dinner that evening at her new apartment on East 50th Street. Cassie arrived dead on seven o'clock, only to find, according to the Philippino maid who opened the door, that Gina had been delayed on the shoot. The maid took Cassie's coat, and showed her into the vast living room of the expensive apartment, where sitting incongruously on a black leather sofa, amongst all the mirror and chrome, was Mrs Roebuck.

Cassie could hardly believe her eyes. She had intended to visit Westboro Falls before leaving for home if time allowed, but here was all that mattered in Westboro Falls come to New York.

'I told Gina to say nothing,' Mrs Roebuck said, as she got slowly to her feet. 'I thought we could surprise each other. My, but you look pretty!'

Cassie kissed her gently, before leading her back to the enormous sofa where they both sat down. She had already noticed from Mrs Roebuck's hands and gait the stranglehold her arthritis had taken on her. In fact, despite her expensive new clothes, and her beautifully coiffured hair, Mrs Roebuck was no longer the twinkling-eyed and spry little lady from Cassie's childhood. Her face still shone with goodness, but it had grown fat and puffy from, Cassie guessed, the drugs the doctors were pumping into her to try and ease the pain.

'It's a wretched thing, sure,' Mrs Roebuck told her without complaints. 'They gave me these steroids, but I didn't like 'em. OK, the relief from the pain was great. But I got all fat – look! And started to grow hairs like a gooseberry! So now they're treating me with the steroids I make myself. But personally speaking, Cassie, I'd rather they just left me alone.'

Mrs Roebuck carefully folded her swollen hands and smiled round at Cassie. In the old days, she'd have patted her on the knee, or maybe pinched her cheek, but now all she could do was smile. Even so, when she did, the old twinkle came back in her eyes.

'How's Westboro?' Cassie asked. 'I was going to come and visit you on my way back from Kentucky.'

'Well I'm just glad I saved you the journey,' Mrs Roebuck replied. 'You wouldn't recognise the place.'

She went on to tell Cassie how the town had changed

beyond all recognition, particularly over the past five years, since the military had arrived.

'Something to do with our defences,' Mrs Roebuck explained. 'All top-secret, but we could all see the huge holes they were digging in the ground.'

Then as her arthritis worsened, and she could do less and less for herself, Gina insisted that her grandmother should move in with her at her New York apartment, and saw to it that she got the best treatment available for her condition. Mrs Roebuck had dallied, but the choice was either that or a retirement home.

'You mean your own family wouldn't have you?' Cassie asked in amazement. 'Your son and his wife weren't prepared to take you in?'

'My daughter-in-law was, Cassie,' Mrs Roebuck smiled. 'That's the funny thing. Jeannie was all for it, but it was my son who said no. He said he had to think of his own marriage and his own life first, and I quite agreed with him.'

Happily Gina had done so well modelling, and now also as an actress, that she was rich enough as well as kind-hearted enough to have her grandmother live with her. Mrs Roebuck said she loved New York; she found it invigorating, and all the people Gina brought home were such fun that she didn't miss Westboro Falls one bit. But Cassie couldn't help feeling as she stole the occasional look at her that despite her beautiful cashmere sweater, her fine wool skirt, and her handmade shoes, Mrs Roebuck would still actually have been happier in her old apron sitting in front of her favourite stove back in New Hampshire, military or no military.

Gina arrived back home an hour and a half late, looking more beautiful than ever, even though, as she put it, she was dressed down.

'That's the look right now, Cassie,' she said with a grin. 'When you've made it, you got to look as if you're back on social security.'

And Gina had certainly made it. Having earned a small

fortune as one of New York's top models, she'd then been offered a couple of parts in nothing movies, which she'd accepted, and made something of; so much so that Danny Browne had offered her the second lead in his new movie on the strength of her performances.

'You have to meet him, Cassie,' Gina told her, as they sat down to a superb lobster dinner, prepared and served by Gina's Philippino couple. 'He's even shorter off-screen than on, about five one, that's all. He's amazingly serious, worries about his health and inhales cold water up his nose three times a day. He also wants me to marry him.'

'And will you?' Cassie asked, scooping out the very last bit of her lobster.

Gina glanced quickly down the table at her grandmother, then laughed, covering Cassie's hand with hers.

'Can you imagine me Jewish?' she said. 'I mean I love the guy, I love Jews, I'd even learn to cook kosher. But you know as well as I do: once a Catholic . . . I'd never make it past first base.'

'But he wants you to change your religion?' Cassie persisted.

'He's just as willing to change his,' Gina told her. 'But it's his family. They get a little heavy on the subject.'

Mrs Roebuck excused herself shortly after they finished eating and got up, ready to go off to her bed.

'I'm leaving first thing in the morning for Kentucky,' Cassie told her. 'So I guess I won't see you till my next trip.'

'You won't see me at all if you leave it another ten years,' Mrs Roebuck told her.

Cassie took hold of the old lady by her shoulders and kissed her warmly on both cheeks.

'Goodnight, Mrs Roebuck,' she said.

'Goodbye, Cassie darling,' Mrs Roebuck replied.

Cassie watched her go slowly off to her bedroom, helped by Gina's maid. She knew, like Mrs Roebuck did, that it was most probably the very last time they would see each other, and as Mrs Roebuck's bedroom door closed, so another door shut behind Cassie.

Then Gina poured her some more wine and Cassie came and sat beside her on the huge leather sofa, where they talked long past midnight, about everything that had happened to them, their old friends, their new friends and both their present lives.

'Your grandmother told me Maria's married with three kids,' Cassie said. 'Isn't that great?'

'She's married an accountant, Cassie,' Gina replied, 'and she's bored suicidal. Do you know what he does when he gets home in the evening? He dusts. And then goes round checking that all the ornaments are straight, that they're all just as he left them the evening before. If I were Maria I'd push him over a cliff. Trouble is, there's no real point in killing him, because the guy's dead already.'

There was a short and awkward silence, while Gina glanced at Cassie and then hurriedly poured her some wine.

'OK,' Gina said. 'I had to say something wrong sooner or later.'

'You haven't said anything wrong,' Cassie reassured her.

'I haven't?'

'Not a thing. We can't sit here all evening talking like the old friends we are without once mentioning Tyrone.'

Gina smiled in relief and sat back, pulling her legs up under her. 'Thanks,' she said. 'So do you want to talk about it?'

'Not really,' Cassie replied. 'It's one of those things, you know, Gina. When you've lost somebody and you want to talk about it, nobody asks you. When you're beginning to come good again, as we say in racing, and you don't want to talk about it, everyone asks you.'

'I'll bet,' said Gina.

Even so, Cassie found that she did want to talk about it. Simply because ever since talking to Frank, she now found it easier to talk. So she told Gina what she wanted to know about her life with Tyrone, and about her life after Tyrone. Since her visit to the Christiansens, it was as if the major part of the burden had finally been eased off her shoulders.

'It's a terrible and confusing thing, grief, you know, Gina,' Cassie tried to explain. 'In a way you can't bear to think about the person you've lost, because the pain's just too much. And yet in another way, you don't want to stop thinking about them, because whenever you do, you feel you're being unfaithful to their memory.'

'You've just got to start thinking about yourself, I guess, Cass,' Gina reasoned. 'From the way you talk about him, there's no chance you're ever going to forget him. But you can't spend the rest of your life looking over your shoulder.'

'That's right, Gina,' Cassie replied. 'I think that finally got home to me yesterday in Locksfield, Pennsylvania.'

The trip to Kentucky proved not only pleasurable, but productive. Cassie established some useful new contacts and found a nice yearling for Joe Coughlan; and was persuaded by Sheila Meath into buying a winning mare by a son of the great Mahmoud, who was in foal to a stallion called Sir Jack. The mare was only for sale because of the bankruptcy of her owner, a heavy gambler who had finally lost his all at the Las Vegas gaming tables.

'What do I need another one for?' Cassie complained, as they made arrangements for the mare to be flown back to Dublin. 'I've still got my lovely old Gracie.'

'You'll need to establish more bloodlines, that's why,' Sheila replied. 'Unless you want to interbreed and end up with a lot of dotty horses. Anyway, this is a damn good-looking sort of mare, and I wouldn't be at all surprised if she didn't throw a rather nice foal.'

At the end of a pretty exhausting and hectic week spent dashing around the beautiful country that makes up Kentucky, Cassie and Sheila had half a day to spend in New York before flying back home. Sheila went off to have lunch with her old friend the British Ambassador, while Cassie was taken out to dine by Frank Christiansen.

'Do you want the good news or the bad news first?' he asked her over cocktails. 'The bad news is we can't agree on the amount you've asked for.'

Cassie did her best not to look as crestfallen as she felt, while Frank studied her earnestly over his Martini.

'Any particular reason, Frank?' she asked.

'Heap good reason,' Frank replied. 'We think the figure's too small. No, don't laugh—' he said quickly, as Cassie looked up at him in surprise. 'I'm actually being serious. The money you're after is the sort of money our firm spends on towels for the director's washroom. The model-T guys think you're small potatoes if you come cap in hand for anything under let's say a hundred grand. Which is what I said your base-line figure was.'

'I don't need a hundred thousand, Frank,' Cassie frowned. 'I just need enough to get things going.'

'You've got a hundred thousand,' Frank replied, 'and you're going to need every cent of it. You don't sell automobiles by just putting a set of tyres in the showroom. People want to see the whole damn car. And they want to try it out. It'll be the same with your concentrates. Buyers won't come looking for them. They'll want to see them everywhere. They'll want free samples. They'll want to pick up their horse magazines and see full-page advertisements. And they'll want to see them succeed first, before they feed one ounce of it to even the kid's pony. So you're going to go find someone who needs some money – no I don't mean bribe money, I'm talking sponsorship money – and Claremore Concentrates is going to back 'em. And if this stuff's as good as all your reports say that it is, sooner or later you'll pick a winner and there you go.'

'It's as easy as that,' Cassie said.

'It's as hard as that,' Frank replied, 'and that's why we're starting you off with a hundred grand. I also know you're right. I think equestrianism – is that right – I think equestrianism is going to be a mighty big growth area. In ten years' time, we won't even recognise the market.'

614

Cassie finished her drink and looked at Frank. 'What are the provisos?' she asked, with a grin, remembering the offer of a weekend in Kinsale. 'I'm not sure I like provisos.'

'There is a proviso,' Frank nodded, 'but I don't think you'll find it objectionable, Cassie. The proviso to this deal is that you make us both a million, and with the proceeds I get to own a Derby winner.'

'The first part of the proviso, Mr Christiansen,' Cassie replied, taking the offer of his arm in to lunch, 'is one hell of a lot easier than the second.'

The first part wasn't easy either. As predicted, few of the racehorse trainers wanted to know about any more fancy foodstuffs which might be coming on the market, even though in pure dietary terms the Claremore Concentrate was probably vastly superior to the old-fashioned and haphazard way most of them fed their animals.

'Look here,' one particular purple-faced and weather-beaten old trainer in Lambourn, Berkshire, had told their sales rep, 'I've been feeding horses since before you were born. There's not a thing you can tell me, and there's not a thing I don't know about it.'

'Very well, sir,' the young man apparently had replied. 'What is the fibre-value and protein content of oats as compared with our racehorse cubes, and which vitamins are essential for the proper welfare of the horse's muscle structure?'

The trainer had failed to answer either part of the question not only correctly but at all. The young man had also failed to get an order.

During the whole of the first racing season that Claremore Concentrates was on the market, the sales analysis showed that only eight per cent of all professional trainers had tried the new concentrate, and that only five per cent decided to use it regularly. However, of the five per cent who remained loyal, three per cent all recorded their best ever number of winners in one season, and none of the five per cent experienced any equine digestive

615

problems at all throughout the year. While it was hardly an auspicious market launch, the few portents that showed were all positively good ones.

On the other hand, the private market showed a much healthier reaction to Claremore's product than the professional sector. Owners of small yards standing hunters or just riding horses at livery found their concentrates more economical, easier and more satisfactory, as did private owners with family horses. The Claremore Standard Horse Mixture, which contained in one bag a carefully balanced mixture of all the basic foods, minerals and vitamins a riding horse in ordinary work needed, was an instant success, and indeed kept the company afloat while the sales force tried desperately to get more than a foot in the commercial door.

'Sure they'll never take to this stuff over here, let alone in England,' Tomas had prophesied. 'They'll suspect it for bein' too American. It's like the food I hear yous eat over there. Sausages in bread rolls covered in ketchup, and them hamburger things. That sort of food'll never catch on this side of the Atlantic.'

'What we need,' Sheila had advised, 'is what your American friend said, a rider: someone who'll feed their horse on nothing but your foodstuffs, and then go and win some dam' great event on the TV.'

'I'll do it!' Josephine had volunteered. 'I'll ride Blackstuff, and win a class at Ballsbridge!'

'I'm sure you would,' her mother had agreed. 'But maybe first of all, Josie, we should start off aiming just a little bit lower.'

'OK,' Josephine had agreed, jumping down from the table. 'But when you're ready for us, you just say the word.'

Cassie had sat in silence for a little longer over their last glass of wine, before suddenly banging her fist on the table.

'Dammit, Sheila!' she said. 'We're doing it the wrong way round! What we should do is first of all announce what we're going to do, and then set about doing it!'

616

'The longer you live in this crazy country of ours,' Sheila had replied, 'the more Irish you become.'

Cassie had explained her plan, and as she did, Sheila Meath's eyes grew wider and wider. They would simply announce in their advertisements that Claremore Concentrates produces winners and that in the forthcoming season, to prove the value of their revolutionary foodstuffs, they would feed and sponsor an event horse to win an important event.

'You don't want much,' Sheila had muttered darkly. 'What's it to be? Badminton? Or somewhere really important?'

'Look,' Cassie had reasoned, quite unreasonably, 'it doesn't matter if the horse comes nowhere. We'll have tried our best, the horse will have tried its best, and we'll have had what's known as value publicity. The public will soon forget our boast. In fact I'll bet you my very bottom dollar, whatever wins the event we're aiming for, a month after it's over nobody'll be able to tell you the name of the horse. But they won't forget the name of Claremore Concentrates.'

Sheila had looked at her long and hard.

'Mr Rosse left more than a little bit of himself behind in you, young lady,' she'd said. 'Now I suppose all you want me to do is go and find you the horse.'

'Yes please,' Cassie had answered. 'We'll advertise for the rider.'

It was on the face of it a madcap scheme. But like a lot of long-priced gambles, it paid off, although not in quite the way Cassie had envisaged it. Sheila Meath had a cousin with a very good intermediate event horse, now without its rider due to a fall out hunting. Cassie advertised for a proven rider who needed guaranteed sponsorship, and from over two hundred hopeful replies, they selected a short-list of twelve to be interviewed, finally choosing a young English girl called Mary Taylor-Walker, who was the cognoscenti's tip for the top. Everything went according to plan; the initial advertising campaign attracted due attention, and then the horse came third in his first intermediate two-day event. In the next three events, he was never worse than eighth, and never better than fourth, but expectations of achieving the win which had been announced in advance were high, particularly as both horse and rider were improving all the time.

The plan was to win at Norlands Park, Worcestershire, in October, the last month of the eventing season, and it very nearly paid off. Going to the third stage of the two-day event, the cross-country, the horse was lying in joint first place with two others, and was favourite to emerge the final winner, due to his proven superiority over his closest rivals. But three quarters of the way round the course, running uphill to a one-stride double, a dog ran out across the horse's path, and either the horse or the rider lost concentration, resulting in a fall which happily was considerably less serious than it looked. It did, however, put paid to the horse's chances not only of winning the event, but of winning within the season, as predicted.

Cassie and Sheila had come over from Ireland to watch, and there was a certain amount of rueful banter in the bar when they realised their hopes were gone.

'Come on,' Sheila finally said. 'After coming all this way, we might as well go and see what wins the bloody thing.'

Amanda Holford's up-and-coming horse Without Equal duly won, being the only one of the leading four horses to finish within the given cross country time. Cassie was surprised to see the rider grin at her after the presentation, as she had never met the girl.

She did shortly afterwards, as she and Sheila were walking back to the car park. They heard someone running up behind them, and when they turned, hearing someone call out, saw Amanda waving at them to stop.

'Sorry,' she said, as she caught them up breathlessly, 'but I had to speak to you before you disappeared back to Ireland.'

618

'Really?' said Cassie. 'What about? Oh – and well done, by the way.'

'Thanks,' Amanda said, with a supremely cheerful grin. 'And hard luck you. Still, as they always say, someone's bad luck is your good luck. And actually in this case, someone's good luck is also your good luck.'

She grinned happily at them both once more, waiting quite deliberately to be asked to explain.

'OK,' Cassie said, catching the pretty girl's infectious grin. 'How come?'

'Well,' Amanda explained, 'you see I shall probably be looking for a new sponsor next season, and I wondered whether you might be interested.'

'Oh,' said Cassie, somehow without reason hoping for better things, 'well now that all depends, Miss Holford.'

'Mandy,' said the girl, taking off her riding hat, and undoing a mane of blonde hair. 'Sorry – what does it depend on?'

'A lot of what my partner describes as model-T guys sitting in their boardroom the other side of the Atlantic.'

'Really?' Amanda asked with another cheeky grin. 'Well I shouldn't worry too much, because I should think they'll be rather pleased with you when they hear.'

'When they hear what exactly, Mandy?' Cassie enquired.

'Oh,' Amanda replied. 'Only that I've been feeding Without Equal on Claremore Concentrates all season.'

Interim Two

'And that was the beginning of your long and I believe happy association with Amanda Holford, yes?'

The tall man with the shock of prematurely white hair stopped taking notes for a moment and stared up at Cassie, who was standing looking at a framed and signed photograph of Mandy winning the world-famous Badminton Three-Day Event on Without Equal.

'It also marked the turning point,' Cassie replied. 'And quite by accident.'

'I see that,' the man replied, smiling.

'Our sponsorship of Mandy, and her meteoric rise to the top – well, you can imagine what that did for our bags of horse food.' Cassie replaced the photograph and sat down opposite her interviewer. 'Of course as far as eventing went, Mandy had *carte blanche*,' she continued. 'I knew nothing about it whatsoever, although I know a lot more now. Sheila Meath looked after that side of things. As far as Claremore was concerned, the success of our feeds meant financial independence. It also meant we could turn this place – and I'm speaking technically here – into one of the finest training establishments in the British Isles. Having the facilities that we have now didn't make me a better trainer, of course. But it did mean I could do the very best by the horses people sent me. And it also meant that prospective owners were greatly encouraged when they first visited Claremore because they realised they'd get value for their training fees. You'll see why when I take you around. We even

have our own laboratory for analysing blood samples –
for analysing anything.'

'Forgive me, but in the words of the great Duke
Ellington, it don't mean a thing if you ain't got swing.
And you certainly seem to have it.'

'The boys in my band certainly do.'

'I think it has to be more than that, don't you? All the
great trainers, they've all had a special empathy with
horses. What do you think it is?'

'Luck,' Cassie replied. 'Luck, an open mind and above
all patience.'

'You certainly were patient when it came to them
handing out ladies' training licences.'

Cassie shook her head and smiled. 'Not really. I could
have got my licence earlier, but I was told there was no
point in rushing these things.'

'Who by?'

'My head lad, Tomas. Tomas Muldoon. I had to wait
till he said I was ready. Or rather, to put it in his precise
equine phraseology, until I'd come good.'

'Which was when?'

'After we'd won the Gimcrack at York for Joe
Coughlan. With the horse Sheila Meath and I found on
that trip to Kentucky. He was a great big horse, even as a
yearling. And when he arrived here, no one thought he'd
stand training, he was so burly. And Tomas thought we
shouldn't even race him as a two-year-old. But I thought
the opposite: that racing would fine him down and take
the weight off his legs. I don't really like racing my two-
year-olds early. But this horse had such a lovely action
that I didn't think he'd jar himself up, so I made a kind of
exception. The horse was kind of exceptional, too, finishing unbeaten as a two-year-old. And that's when Tomas
thought I'd "come good".'

Her interviewer noted this, then pointed his pen at
the firescreen. 'This quite charming tapestry screen,'
he said, 'with this logo. Does it have any special
significance?'

621

'The "logo",' Cassie replied, 'was my husband's coat of arms. And the words were his motto.'

' "Compassion, Commitment and Celebration". Aren't those also the names of three of your best known horses?'

'Yes, that's right they are. Not forgetting Graceful Lady. Graceful Lady was our foundation mare, and Celebration our foundation stallion.'

Chapter Twenty-Two

November, 1985

Frank Christiansen met Cassie at Washington airport and drove her into the city. Over dinner, they discussed the chances of Frank's horse Ready Steady in the following day's big race, the Washington International at Laurel Park.

'I've spoken to Liam already,' Cassie told Frank, 'and he says the horse didn't travel too well. Which is odd, because he's flown water I don't know how many times, and never turned a hair.'

'I think maybe he'll find the track a little sharp for him anyway,' Frank said. 'You say he needs every inch of a mile and a half. And Laurel Park's more like one mile three.'

'Listen, whatever happens to your horse, Frank,' Cassie replied, 'it's worth it to see you.'

They had become lovers three years after they had re-met at James Christiansen's funeral. Frank had arrived over in Ireland for his first visit ever and had fallen in love with everything he saw, including Cassie.

'Actually no, that's not strictly true,' he'd said with a frown as they'd walked the hills above Claremore. 'I couldn't get you out of my head after I saw you again in Locksfield.'

'You had quite some effect on me too, Frank,' Cassie had replied. 'And all to the good.'

They'd flown over to England to see Amanda win the International Three-Day Event at Burghley; then, since Frank was anxious to see a little of England on his trip as well, they had driven across Yorkshire and up into the Lake District where they had booked in for one night at Sharrow Bay Hotel, and ended up staying three.

It was the perfect place and setting for a romance to flourish, set as it is idyllically on the Ullswater lakeside, with both the dining and drawing rooms overlooking the water. The food was the best Cassie had eaten anywhere outside Lasserre's, and unequivocally the best Frank had eaten, period. They didn't stay in the main part of the hotel, sleeping instead in a charmingly converted old farmhouse which belonged to the proprietors, situated a mile or so from the hotel, on a hill overlooking another part of the great lake.

The decision to become lovers was made by Frank. 'I've booked us into a double room,' he'd told her with a boyish grin, as they drove through Cumbria. 'I hope that's OK.'

'I'd have been mighty miffed if you hadn't,' Cassie'd answered.

And so they'd spent a blissful four days in the September sunshine, eating, sleeping, walking and making love. Cassie knew it wasn't the passion that she'd had with Tyrone, but she also knew that a grand passion was something she was no longer looking for. When Frank had once expressed some concern at his adequacy as a lover, compared with 'the Great Man', as he had affectionately dubbed Tyrone, Cassie kissed him and told him not to look for comparisons. He was totally different from Tyrone, which was one of the reasons most probably, she argued, why she loved him. And the way Cassie loved him and the things she loved him for were also different.

'Don't keep looking over my shoulder, Frank,' she'd told him. 'I stopped doing that when I met you.'

Marriage was only mentioned once. It was on one of Cassie's frequent transatlantic trips, when they were driving down to visit Frank's mother and father.

'They asked me after your last trip what the game plan was,' Frank had said.

624

'Meaning if we were going to get married?'

'I guess.'

'What did you say, Frank?'

'I said nope.'

'Without even asking me?'

'Do you want to get married?'

'Nope.'

And that was the only time it had been mentioned.

Until now, as they lay in bed in Cassie's hotel suite, Cassie on her side studying the form for the big race, and Frank on his back, hands behind his head, studying the ceiling.

'Do you think maybe we *should* have got married, Cassie?' he asked out of the blue.

'Nope,' said Cassie, turning the pages of her notebook.

'Don't you reckon it would have worked out?'

'I don't see how it could have worked out. I wouldn't have given up my job for anything, and neither would you. Why should you? Why should I? And believe me, Frank, this has been a hell of a lot better than most marriages.'

'I guess my mother would have liked it.'

Cassie closed her notebook and turned herself back to Frank. She stroked his cheek with the backs of her fingers.

'Your mother, Frank Christiansen,' she said, 'couldn't care less. What matters to her, and I know 'cos she told me, is that you're happy. So there.'

Ready Steady was unplaced in the International, beaten not by the Atlantic crossing, as was first feared, but simply being found wanting for speed, as Frank had guessed. But he was far from disgraced, running on well at the end into sixth.

'Another mile and a half and he'd have got there,' he joked to Cassie as they walked back from congratulating their horse and jockey.

Cassie laughed, then stopped in her tracks when she saw a face in the crowd.

'Frank, will you excuse me?' she said. 'I'll meet you

back up in the stands.' She lost the face for a moment, and then she saw it again, as it turned and suddenly stared at her out of the crowd ahead, realising it was Cassie and that she was in pursuit.

'Dexter?'

Cassie had finally caught him before he could slip past a crowd thronging a gate in the rails.

'Dexter!' she called. 'It's me! Cassie Rosse!'

Dex stopped and turned, having nowhere left to go. Cassie stopped in her tracks as she saw him close to. He was only a year or so older than she was, but now it looked more like fifteen.

'Mrs Rosse,' he said, tipping a non-existent cap, and grinding a cigarette out under his heel.

'I thought it was you, Dexter,' Cassie continued, recovering most of her composure. 'How are you?'

'I'm OK, Mrs Rosse,' Dexter answered, looking down at the long-dead cigarette. 'How are you?'

'We can't talk here, Dex,' Cassie said.

'*You* want to talk to *me*, Mrs Rosse?' Dexter asked, sounding over deliberately surprised.

'I'd like to, yes,' Cassie replied. 'Come up to our box and have a drink.'

Dexter laughed and lit another cigarette. 'That's very kind of you, Mrs Rosse,' he said, blowing the match out, 'but if you knew me now, that's the last thing you'd ask me to do.'

Then Cassie saw it – in his red and watery eyes, on his face where the veins had broken and in the yellowing of his skin.

'Come on, Dex,' she urged him. 'Make it a cup of coffee then.'

'I couldn't, Mrs Rosse,' he told her, trying to slip away from her in the crowd, 'not with the sort of people who'll be up there. Anyway, I don't need a coffee. I need a drink.'

Cassie grabbed him by his sleeve just before she lost him.

'And I need to speak to you. Come to my hotel before dinner. Please. I'm staying at the Belmont. It's very important that we speak.'

'Sure,' Dex nodded, before pulling himself free and disappearing once again in the mêlée of racegoers.

Frank and Cassie were sitting in the hotel bar having a drink after dinner, when a man in a plain blue suit came up to them.

'Mrs Rosse?' he asked. 'I'm sorry to trouble you, ma'am, but I'm Security, and there's a guy outside who says you're expecting him.'

'Thank you,' Cassie said rising. 'I'll come at once.'

'Mrs Rosse,' the man warned, following her closely, 'this guy is *very* drunk.'

'So is the guy at the end of the bar,' Cassie informed him, indicating a dark-suited business man who was making a nuisance of himself.

At first she couldn't see Dexter, then as she stood on the sidewalk, thinking perhaps he'd had second thoughts and run, she saw him in the shadows, leaning sideways against a wall. She went and touched him on the shoulder, but he was barely sensible.

Frank and she walked him back into the hotel lobby between them, their arms round his back to prevent him from collapsing. The man in the blue suit caught them up as they pressed the button for the elevator.

'Excuse me, Mrs Rosse,' he said, 'but I have to ask you what's going on here? I'm afraid we can't allow people in this kind of condition in the hotel.'

'It's OK, really,' Cassie replied as the elevator doors opened. 'This man is a friend of mine. I'll take care of him.'

Together she and Frank undressed Dex and bathed him and put him to bed where he slept, hardly moving, until ten o'clock the next morning. Frank was out bying him some fresh clothes when Dex finally awoke.

'Hi,' said Cassie. 'Care for some breakfast?'

'I don't understand,' Dexter replied, rubbing his face and eyes.

'All will come clear, don't worry,' Cassie told him. 'You're in good hands.'

Dexter looked round the luxurious room, then back at Cassie. 'Have I died or something?' he asked.

'I hope not,' Cassie laughed. 'Because if you have, I have too.'

She rang room service for some breakfast, and then sat down in an armchair while Dexter got his bearings.

'Do you remember coming to the hotel?' she asked.

Dexter shook his head. 'I just remember seeing you on the racecourse.'

'You were in a pretty bad way last night.'

'That's the way it goes most nights.'

'Most nights for how long now, Dex?'

He looked at her, then reached for his cigarettes which Cassie had left by the bed. 'Most nights since Goodwood, I guess.'

He didn't eat any breakfast; just drank a lot of black coffee and smoked about half a pack of cigarettes. Cassie didn't ask him anything, preferring Dex to come to her. One thing she had most certainly learned training horses was to be patient.

Frank returned with some boxes of clothes, which he left in the drawing room of the suite, before going back out on some business. Cassie assured him everything was fine, and asked him to make sure he was back in time for cocktails before dinner.

She left Dexter to get washed and shaved while she fetched the new clothes Frank had bought. Then while Dexter was still in the bathroom, Cassie put through a couple of calls to trainers who were friends of hers, and for whom Dexter had ridden. They told her only what she already suspected. After that ill-fated season, when Willie Moore had refused to renew Dexter's contract for the following season, disgusted with Dexter's riding of The Donk and further infuriated by his retained jockey's increasing insobriety, Dexter had flown back to America to continue his career back on home ground.

But he began drinking more and more heavily, and as a consequence developed a weight problem. He started to lose rides because of his increasing weight, and races because of his addled judgement. Within a space of five years he went from the top of the pile to the bottom. Since his last ride in public, over eight years ago, he had odd-jobbed round stables, picking up whatever menial work he could get, in order to finance his drinking.

'Do you have anything to drink, Mrs Rosse?' a voice asked her from the bedroom doorway.

Cassie put the telephone down and turned round. Dex was washed and clean shaven, and dressed in the new clothes they'd bought him. But he still looked terrible.

'I really do need a drink,' he said.

'No you don't, Dex,' Cassie answered. 'What you need is help.'

'Sure,' Dex nodded slowly. 'But first I have to have a drink.'

He looked round the suite, but could see no bottles. Cassie had locked them all away. He went over to the drinks fridge and looked inside, but there was only Diet Coke and Perrier.

'OK,' he said, pulling on his new sports coat, 'I guess it'll have to be the bar.'

He went to the door.

'You don't have any money, Dex,' Cassie said.

'No problem,' he replied. 'I'll put it against your room.'

'I've already warned the bar.'

'Then I'll have to go drink someplace else.'

Dexter slipped the safety chain off the door and unlocked it.

'That's fine by me, Dex,' Cassie told him. 'But you walk out of here now, and I reckon you'll be walking away from the last chance you're likely maybe ever to have.'

'You offering me a chance?' he asked, stopping with his back still to her.

'I'm offering you the chance of a chance,' she answered.

'What's the deal?'

Dexter still didn't turn round, almost as if he was afraid to look Cassie any more in the eyes. 'You don't owe me anything, Mrs Rosse.'

'I owe you an explanation about Leonora.'

'I know you didn't write that note, now. It's OK. You're off the hook.'

'Then why did you believe I did?'

He paused once more by the half-open door, and then he shut it, leaning his head against it for a long time before replying. 'You quite sure you don't have a drink, Cassie?' he asked.

Cassie sent down for some more black coffee instead, while Dex sat silently in a chair, staring at the carpet. Then he sat slowly back and rested his head on the back of the chair.

'I've wondered every goddam day of my life since then,' he suddenly said, 'why I finally chose to believe her and not you.'

'Leonora's a very seductive person,' Cassie replied, pouring him some more coffee. 'There's many the time she's had me believing things she's wanted me to.'

'Sure,' Dex agreed. 'But I'll bet she never seduced you in quite the way she seduced me.'

Cassie stopped drinking her own coffee and slowly put down the cup. It actually hadn't occurred to her that Leonora and Dexter might have been lovers before the Goodwood race. But that, she decided, would of course make perfect sense. She had turned Dex down and Leonora had been waiting in the wings. She guessed that in fact Leonora had anticipated that Cassie would reject Dexter, and had timed her strike to perfection.

'Did she tell you about the note before or after she got you into her bed?' Cassie enquired.

'Oh after!' Dexter replied, laughing for the first time since they'd re-met. 'We were lying in that huge round

630

bed of hers, with that mirror behind it, and she was leaning on my chest with both her elbows, and her chin on her fist. You know? And she smiled, and said how she'd always fancied me, and how you'd hatched the plan to get me up to your room because she and you had a bet you wouldn't lose your virginity before you went back to school. And that all the time you were both laughing behind my back.'

'Oh Dex,' Cassie said sadly. 'Isn't it odd how people always find lies easier to believe than the truth? Why didn't you just come round the next day and ask me? Instead of throwing the race. And ruining your career.'

Dexter breathed in deeply, and with visibly shaking hands lit another cigarette.

'Christ, I've never wished for anything harder in all my life, Cassie,' he said. 'But I was infatuated. Really. And it happened just like that! You have no idea what that woman is like, believe me.'

'I think I do,' Cassie replied.

'Not in bed you don't,' Dex answered shortly.

It was as simple as that. The secret of the world was knowing a few tricks. And if the few tricks you knew were the right tricks, men would forfeit empires.

Or deliberately take the wrong course in a vital horserace.

It wasn't anything to do with who wrote the note or who didn't, Cassie decided. Dexter Bryant had tasted of the lotus.

'That offer of help still valid?' he asked sarcastically. Looking up, Cassie found him staring at her, reading her mind. 'Or has it suddenly been rescinded?'

'It's ridiculous, isn't it?' Cassie said. 'Life, I mean. I should have let you make love to me. God knows I wanted you to, but I'd been warned off. Told not to cross the line. Because I was told if I did, you wouldn't listen any more to what I had to say to you as your guv'nor. And what happens? I do the right thing, supposedly, I don't go to bed with you, and you pull my best horse in his finest hour. You throw a race which would have put the name of the little horse on the Goodwood Cup forever. All because I did the "right thing". Dear heavens, talk about the famous road to hell.'

Availing himself of the ensuing thoughtful silence, Dex got to his feet and brushed the ash off his new coat.

'For the record,' he said going to the door, 'what was on offer in the offer?'

'The chance to ride as first jockey for Claremore,' Cassie replied.

Dexter didn't even get as far as turning the door handle this time.

'You're crazy, Cassie,' he said, wheeling round. 'Jesus Christ – look at me. Look. I'm all washed up.'

'What you are, and what you want to be, Dexter Bryant,' Cassie told him evenly, 'is entirely up to you.'

It took three months to dry Dex out, four weeks of cold turkey and eight weeks of recuperation. But the patient, left in Frank's care in a clinic in New York, never wavered in his determination, nor weakened in his ambition to succeed. By March, he was off cigarettes as well as alcohol, and Frank had him pounding the pavements and working out daily in the gym. The plan was that if there were no setbacks, as soon as Dex was three parts fit, he was to fly over to Ireland and take up residency in the stable-lads' hostel, to ride work for two months only, after which a decision would be made as to if and when he could again ride in public.

Dex's only quarrel with the plan was that it was too conservative.

'Listen,' he told Cassie when she came to say goodbye at the clinic. 'You save all the mid-season horses for me. I'll be fit for Royal Ascot.'

Because she had stayed on until Dex was through the worst part of his rehabilitation programme, as the clinic euphemistically called it, this was the longest Cassie had been away from Claremore for years. However, with a fit and strong Mattie away working and finding his feet in Australia, and Josephine showing all the signs of becoming a successful actress in London, she was now able to stay away longer when necessary, without the dreadful feelings of guilt she had always suffered whenever she had been forced to leave her children while they were still growing up.

Even so, she still missed Claremore.

Dick Slattery, a tall serious lad from the village, who acted as Cassie's manservant, chauffeur and handyman, was hovering on the top of the steps, waiting for sight of the car as Cassie swept up the now smoothly tarmacked drive.

'Quick now, Mrs Rosse,' he said, taking her luggage from the car, 'sure isn't Tomas waiting to see you in the study?'

'Nothing wrong with any of the horses, I hope?' Cassie asked, hurrying up the stairs.

'I'll say not,' Dick replied, holding the front door open with one of his huge feet, 'the horses is all fine, thank God.'

Tomas was on his feet when Cassie came into the study, anxiously pacing the room.

'It's Erin,' Tomas told her, his baby face suddenly looking old and lined with worry. 'The girl's disappeared.'

'When, Tomas?' Cassie asked simply. 'When and how?'

' 'Tis all right, Mrs Rosse, she hasn't herself murdered yet. She left a note three days ago saying she was gone, but we've no idea why or where. And her mother's half-cooked with anxiety.'

The police found her easily enough, in a small boarding house in Wexford. Or rather they didn't find her, so much as Erin came to their notice. After she had been gone for five days, the landlady of the boarding house into which Erin had booked herself, as a Miss Smith, slowly became suspicious of her, explaining as she

633

did subsequently to the police that what had aroused her curiosity was the fact that the poor lady in question spent all her days shut in her room sobbing, as she chose to put it, 'quite laudably'.

Tomas fetched Erin home but failed to extract a reason from his daughter as to why she had run away. She had simply wept all the way from Wexford to Wicklow. Cassie went up to Erin's room to see if she could do any better. She'd had to deal with similar emotional upsets with Erin before, notably when Mattie was sent away to Switzerland for two years because of his health, and when Josephine was first sent off to boarding school. Erin had wept and sobbed for a week each time, and Cassie had quietly but firmly had to talk her down.

This time, however, Erin was apparently deaf to her questions. Whenever Cassie spoke to her, however quietly and gently, Erin would just raise the level of her sobbing until Cassie would have had to shout over it to make herself heard. Finally, Erin's hysteria became so worrisome that Cassie called in the retired Doctor Gilbert's successor, Doctor Ryan.

'It's most probably the menopause, Mrs Rosse,' the rather earnest young doctor told her, after he'd administered a sedative.

'Erin's barely forty,' Cassie replied. 'Don't you think that's a little young for the change?'

'Unmarried middle-aged girls, Mrs Rosse,' Dr Ryan replied, tut-tutting his tongue, 'there's no saying what sort of arguments they get into with their bodies.'

'I don't think it's the change,' Cassie said, showing him to the door.

'Ah well now, fair's fair, Mrs Rosse,' protested Doctor Ryan. 'And I don't tell you what's going to win the Derby.'

Cassie thought Erin was pregnant.

Of course there was no way Cassie could voice her suspicions to Erin's mother or father, although from the way Mrs Muldoon had taken to weeping into her pinny in

634

the kitchen, Cassie thought she'd already guessed. Tomas as well, for he now went about his business in the yard with a frown on his previously unlined old forehead all the while. Erin stopped crying publicly, but from her red eyes every morning at breakfast, it was perfectly obvious how she had spent the night.

When they were alone one evening, as Cassie was sitting in the drawing room holding one of Erin's interminable skeins of wool while Erin sniffed and wound the wool into balls, Cassie decided to go for broke.

'OK, Erin,' she said, 'I'm sure you'll tell me it's none of my business, but exactly how pregnant are you?'

Erin's jaw literally dropped open and she stared at Cassie idiotically.

'It's going to show sooner or later, you know,' Cassie continued, her arms out in front of her, holding Erin's wool.

Erin got out of her chair and snatched the wool off Cassie's hands, stuffing it back into her knitting bag.

'Erin,' Cassie sighed. 'You're going to have to tell somebody sooner or later, sweetheart. And if you are pregnant, it's going to be better in the long run if we deal with it now.'

'God help me!' Erin suddenly said, bursting into a flood of tears, 'God help me but I'm three months gone already!'

'So what are you going to do, Erin?' Cassie asked patiently.

'I'm goin' to kill meself! That's what I'm goin' to do, Mrs Rosse!'

'No you're not, Erin. Don't be such a foolish girl. For goodness sake stop crying and take hold of yourself.'

Pulling an already soaking hankie back out from her sleeve, Erin blew her nose noisily and did her best to stop crying. But she found it difficult, because every now and then when she withheld a sob, her body would rock and she'd emit a sound like a giant hiccough.

'I might as well kill meself, Mrs Rosse,' Erin mumbled. 'Because if I don't, me father will.'

'Of course he won't, Erin,' Cassie reassured her. 'Your father's one of the kindest men I know.'

'Not when it comes to illegitimate babbas he's not.'

Erin knew her father better than Cassie did. Cassie found this out when she sat Tomas and his wife down in the drawing room to explain their daughter's predicament. Tomas listened in silence throughout, while his wife buried her face once more in her apron. When she was finished, Tomas nodded his thanks and rose to his feet.

'Come along, woman,' he said to his wife. 'And stop bawling like a banshee.'

Cassie didn't like the look on Tomas' face at all.

'What are you going to do, Tomas?' she asked.

'That's no concern of yours, Mrs Rosse,' he answered very formally. ' 'Tis a matter between a father and his daughter.'

'What are you going to *do*, Tomas?' Cassie repeated.

'He's going to larrap her!' Mrs Muldoon screamed, 'that's what he's going to do! He's going to larrap the hide off her!'

'Oh no you're not, Tomas Muldoon!' Cassie warned him, putting herself between him and the door.

'Indeed he is!' Mrs Muldoon cried. 'And a good thing too, the hussy!'

Tomas stood looking at Cassie patiently, while she barred his way out of the room.

'Tomas,' Cassie said, 'you raise one hand against that girl – what am I *talking* about! She's not a girl! She's a forty-year-old woman!'

'She's still my daughter,' Tomas answered.

'And this is not the Middle Ages any more!' Cassie shouted. 'Your daughter is not a little girl to be put over your knee and – and larrapped! She's a grown woman, Tomas! She's forty years old! And she needs your love! And your understanding!'

'Her mother said it for me, Mrs Rosse,' Tomas replied calmly. 'She's a hussy. And she's having a bastard child.'

Cassie looked at Tomas, but this time it was Cassie's eyes that were dancing in flames.

'Sit down, Tomas,' she ordered. 'And you, Mrs Muldoon. Sit down both of you. While I tell you what life can be like when a parent rejects you, and how it is to be what you call a bastard child.'

The dialogue had its required effect. Erin, while not exactly welcomed back unconditionally into the bosom of her family, was at least spared the threatened 'larapping' from her father, although Cassie had been more than inclined to believe that the lashing would have been from Tomas' tongue rather than his belt. And Erin was to be allowed to remain at home, on the condition that she kept her 'shame' hidden from the village.

'But I'll have to go to Mass!' Erin had protested. 'I can't miss going to church so I can't!'

But her mother apparently was insistent. If necessary Father Patrick could come to the house and hear Erin's confession, and most likely administer the sacrament as well. But otherwise Erin was to remain confined until her child was born. Anyone asking after her would simply be informed that Erin was unwell.

'I'm not altogether sure that's the best plan, you know,' Cassie advised Tomas. 'People are bound to discover the facts later.'

'Let them,' Tomas replied. 'They'll have no proof.'

'There'll be a baby, Tomas! For everyone to see!' Cassie argued. 'Isn't that proof enough?'

'There will not be a baby,' Tomas told her. 'For the moment it's born, she's to have it adopted.'

Cassie knew that was a forlorn hope. Erin was far too maternal a woman to give away the only child she was likely to have. Also, from the conversations Cassie had already had with her, it was obvious that Erin loved the father of her baby, although even the threat of death itself would not have dragged his name from her.

But Cassie also knew it was an equally forlorn hope to argue with Tomas once his mind was set. So instead she

637

determined to let the storm abate, which it already was showing signs of so doing, and to adopt what Tomas himself would have called 'the long view'.

Besides which, Tomas' health had suddenly started to cause considerable concern. Tomas was a strong man, even in his early seventies, who thrived on hard work. Stress was an unknown word to him, for whenever he had a doubt or a worry he would always talk it out, and he religiously maintained that the day he stopped working with his beloved horses would be the day he died.

But he had been a lifelong heavy smoker, a habit which Cassie had tried without success to get him to break when they first started working together. And now, with the additional worry about Erin, he was smoking more than ever and Cassie would regularly hear him coughing desperately, early in the morning when he started work.

So now she found herself nagging him to go and see a specialist in Dublin. After all, he could afford the best advice, because thanks to Claremore Concentrates, he was now a rich man.

'Ach – doctors,' Tomas would reply disparagingly. 'Sure if we're goin' to get better, 'tis the good Lord who'll see to it. So why should the doctor take me money? Anyway, if I had to see someone, which I don't, I'd rather see Niall Brogan. A vet can't ask his patient what's wrong with him like doctors do, now can he? Ah no. No, a vet – he's got to *know*.'

Mrs Muldoon was predictably defeatist in her attitude when Cassie counselled her.

'You might as well try teach an elephant the piano as get Tomas Muldoon near a doctor,' she'd sighed. 'And like as not yous can't get an old dog to learn new tricks, neither can yous get him stop his old ones. Besides, he's had his three-score years and ten now, Mrs Rosse. So what harm's a few more old cigarettes goin' to do him?'

They certainly didn't improve his health, Cassie noticed with even more concern, as she saw throughout

the cold of January and February how much more difficult Tomas was finding it to catch his breath. But he
would neither ease up in his work, nor go and see any
doctor – not even the local GP, Doctor Ryan. Cassie often
teased him about how his wealth hadn't affected his lifestyle one iota, and that he was still the same Tomas
Muldoon who had greeted her on the steps of Claremore
twenty-five years ago.

'I hope to God I am, Guv'nor,' he'd reply. 'For sure 'tis
only money.'

Then sooner than they both knew it, it was the foaling
season. Claremore now boasted several useful brood
mares, all the producers of winners, but the best line was
still from Cassie's original foundation mare, Graceful
Lady, who had eventually died eight years earlier, aged
twenty-five. Her first-born, Celebration, had proved a
successful sire without ever quite achieving the top rank;
but, when mated with the daughter of the mare Sheila
and Cassie had returned with from Kentucky fifteen years
earlier, had produced a very good colt whom Cassie had
named Compassion. She liked the young horse so much
that she kept him for herself. The gamble paid off: the
horse won ten races for her, from distances of six furlongs
to a mile and a half, victories which included a major
Derby Trial and the Prix Ridgway at Deauville. He
proved to be ultra-consistent and so easy to train that
Compassion had been kept racing until he was six, when
he was retired to stud. Cassie and Sheila then managed
to buy a Northern Dancer mare privately before the
Saratoga sales one year, and brought her back to
Claremore to be covered by Compassion. The first foal
the mare threw was a filly born with deformed hocks,
but second time around she foaled normally and produced a strapping dark bay colt which was immediately
christened Commitment, to complete the trio.

Commitment went on to win six high-class races,
before topping off his brief and brilliant career with a
runaway victory in the Irish St Leger. He then took up

stud duties at Claremore, remaining in Cassie's ownership despite several huge offers, most notably from the Arabs. One of the first mares he covered in his first season was a bay six-year-old called Summer Visitor, who was a daughter of the late James Christiansen's useful horse Moviola, which he had left Cassie in his will. Summer Visitor had also proved herself no slouch, winning three times, including the Yorkshire Oaks, when a three-year-old, and the Prix du Cadran at Longchamps when five.

And now her time had come round to foal. Despite the hi-tech state of Claremore, with its resident vet and fully trained staff, Cassie still insisted on foaling each and every one of her mares personally. The only thing that had become easier about the process was that all the foaling boxes were now covered by a highly sophisticated close-circuit television system, so that at least when Cassie and Tomas were waiting for the mares to start they could do so in the comfort of their own homes.

Summer Visitor started showing the usual signs of discomfort which precede giving birth about half past seven one cold February night; and by ten past twelve she had thrown a rather lanky bay colt who seemed to start growing the moment he struggled to his feet.

Tomas sat back on his haunches as the colt found out where the milk supply was, and watched while Cassie tidied up the mare, and put down some fresh, dry bedding.

'Jesus,' he sighed, 'I don't know why I bother to get out of me bed.'

'No, neither do I, Tomas,' Cassie replied, still checking everything was right with the mare.

'You seem to know how to do it all well enough.'

'I had the very best of teachers.'

'I could have stayed in me bed, readin' me book. Still. You're a long time dead.'

He lit another cigarette, and started to cough. Cassie looked round at him anxiously. For one brief moment she saw the young Tomas crouched on his haunches, leaning against the wall, just as he had when they were waiting for old Gracie to give birth. And then she saw her dear old friend grown suddenly old. And tired.

'You'll have trouble with that boyo,' he said to her, when he'd recovered his breath. 'He'll be all leg for the first two years.'

Tomas' first-sight judgements were usually infallible. Off-hand, Cassie couldn't remember one of his early prophecies which hadn't come true.

'He's nice and straight even so,' she said, appraising the newly born colt. 'And he's got a very bright eye.'

'You and your eyes,' Tomas sighed. 'What good's a pair of bright eyes if the rest of the bloody thing's all leg? Savin' your presence.'

Cassie laughed, and helped Tomas to his feet.

'We'll take our time with him, Tomas,' she said. 'Like we do with them all. Patience, right? And yards and yards of it. Now come on, let's go and wet the baby's head.'

It was the last foal they were to welcome into the world together, and the last bottle they'd crack in celebration.

'To Celebration,' Tomas had said, raising his glass. 'In celebration.'

And they had drunk together to the funny old mare with the club foot that Cassie had bought as an impulse buy, and to her first-born foal who had reshaped both their fortunes.

The next morning when Cassie arrived at the yard to supervise work, Tomas was absent.

'He's been took to the hospital, Guv'nor,' Liam the deputy head lad told her. 'He was very bad in the night, and Mrs Muldoon called an ambulance.'

Why the hell hadn't she called her? Cassie wondered as she deputised Liam to lead out the string and conduct the morning's work, leaving Cassie to drive at top speed to the hospital. The thing Tomas dreaded most was the hospital, particularly the local one, which he had christened Scutari, after one of Florence Nightingale's most infamous infirmaries.

She found him there in a bed already in the cancer

641

ward, surrounded by the terminally ill, with Mrs Muldoon seated by his bed, her head lying on the covers, buried in both of her hands.

Tomas looked at Cassie beseechingly.

'Get me out of here, Guv'nor,' he whispered. 'This is no place for a man to meet his God.'

They had him back home by teatime. At his request, Mrs Muldoon and Cassie carried his bed into the living room of the new bungalow he had built on the site of his old cottage with some of the money from the horse feeds, and remade it in front of the french windows so that he could lie looking out at the garden and the sweep of the fields up to Claremore. He seemed to rally once he was back home, and Cassie and Mrs Muldoon hoped and prayed that the terrible suffocating attack he had suffered in the night was the result of too much whisky and too many cigarettes after the birth of the foal, and not anything more serious.

Then Doctor Ryan arrived two days later when Cassie was between visits, and apparently told Tomas that he had a terminal dose of what he called 'the smoker's disease'.

Cassie was furious when she discovered what he had done, and called the doctor from Claremore when she got home that evening.

'What in hell was the point in that, Doctor Ryan?' she demanded. 'Tomas Muldoon's no fool, you know. He understands that he's dying, but it has done incalculable harm telling him so!'

'Mrs Rosse,' Dr Ryan replied nervously, 'it's only fair that a patient nowadays should know his prognosis—'

'Nowadays?' Cassie interrupted. 'What makes us so much better nowadays that we can come to terms with our mortality at the drop of a hat? I'd really like to hear your thinking. When I left Tomas Muldoon yesterday, he was at peace with himself. He was absorbing what he knew and was coming to terms with it. Your matter-of-factness has removed his last shred of dignity, his chance

642

to rationalise what's happening to him. He didn't need to hear all that, you know. He didn't need you to lay on the guilt about his smoking. OK – so he's got lung cancer.'

'He's got considerably more than lung cancer, Mrs Rosse,' the doctor replied.

'I guess you found it necesary to tell him that as well?'

'Patients have every right to know exactly what's wrong with them.'

'Did Tomas ask you?'

Doctor Ryan hesitated.

'Not perhaps in so many words, no.'

'What did he say?'

'He said – he said is it bronchitis? I wouldn't have been doing my job if I'd lied.'

'Maybe not, but you'd have sure as hell have been a Christian. What else did you tell him?'

'He asked should he see the priest.'

'Yes?'

'And I said great heavens no. No no. No, I told him he'd got at least four or five weeks.'

Cassie replaced the receiver disbelievingly and went and sat by the fire. Her new dog, a large Bearded Collie called Bunbury, came and laid his head on her knee, which he did whenever he felt his mistress was sad.

'Everybody's going, Bunbury,' Cassie said, stroking his head. 'They're all going or gone. Sometimes it does seem an awful short journey, doesn't it? And all for what? What do we become? If we're lucky, a fond memory maybe.'

Cassie visited Tomas every day, twice a day. She sat by him, and read to him for the first few days, but as he grew more weary, she took a small piece of tapestry she was making and sewed by his bedside. Mrs Muldoon made endless tea which neither of them drank, and ushered in a seemingly non-stop stream of Tomas' friends from the village and vicinity who had come to bid their old friend farewell. All came bravely smiling, and none with the word goodbye. Instead they recalled a moment shared, a good time had, a laugh remembered. Tomas smiled at them all, and nodded, now barely able to speak although still fully conscious. Cassie made sure there was a private nurse to help Mrs Muldoon take the best and the most proper care of him, and see that he was kept shaved and washed, for Tomas was the most fastidious of men, and could never bear to be seen untidy.

He slept most of the time now, occasionally waking and staring for a moment to see who was near him. Doctor Ryan had seen to it that his last days were as pain-free as possible, but in such a short span of time Tomas had grown painfully thin, and could find little comfort, even once they propped him up with air cushions.

'I feel like one of our old horses,' Tomas had whispered to Cassie one day as she and the nurse turned him. 'Though one man I'd give anything to see walk in here would be old Niall Brogan with his gun.'

Then one morning when Cassie went to visit, she found Tomas sitting out in his favourite chair, wrapped in several sweaters, a dressing gown, and thick white woollen bedsocks. He smiled as best he could as Cassie came in, and Mrs Muldoon drew her aside.

'He's asked to see Erin,' she said. 'He asked especially. And he wanted you here, too.'

Erin came in, and stood awkwardly by the door.

'Go over to your father, child,' her mother ordered. 'He can hardly speak to you from there.'

Erin went to her father's side, and after a moment, with great difficulty, Tomas turned his head to her and signalled slowly with a finger for her to bend down. As her face reached his, he took her hand in his frail grasp, and whispered to her for several minutes. Cassie watched and saw the tears fall unchecked from Erin's eyes, down on to her and her father's clasped hands. Then Tomas kissed her on her cheek, and raised his other hand slowly to her hair.

Mrs Muldoon clicked her tongue and shook her head, but when Cassie glanced round at her, she saw the old woman's eyes were quite blinded with tears.

Tomas pointed slowly at Cassie, and beckoned her over. 'Let's have a drink, Guv'nor,' he whispered barely audibly in her ear as she bent over. 'A drop of the creature.'

Cassie poured them all a whisky.

'He likes his with a drop o' sugar in it now, Mrs Rosse,' Mrs Muldoon said. 'And a little bit of water.'

They put his drink carefully in his hand, and Tomas looked down at his glass for some time, before raising his eyes and looking at the three women standing before him. Then he lifted his glass as high as he could and held it out to them all.

'God bless you,' he said.

When they'd drunk their whiskies, Mrs Muldoon took Tomas's still-full glass, and sat with his hand in hers. Cassie leaned over and kissed Tomas' smooth brow, but he was barely conscious. As she left, she just caught sight through the french windows of the nurse and Mrs Muldoon lifting his painfully thin body back into his bed, before Erin drew the curtains.

The telephone rang by Cassie's bed at half past two. It was the nurse to say that Tomas was dying.

Cassie dressed as quickly as she could and drove to the bungalow. Father Patrick was administering the Last Rites while Erin and Mrs Muldoon knelt silently by the bed. Cassie dropped to her knees beside them.

By four o'clock Tomas had gone. His breathing had become slower and slower, and more and more shallow, until suddenly he opened his eyes once, almost as if in surprise, and then with what sounded like a deep, deep sigh, he died.

Cassie sat in the kitchen staring at her clenched hands, while Mrs Muldoon and the nurse laid Tomas out. Erin was opposite Cassie across the table, sitting rocking backwards and forwards slowly, and keening. There were no tears now on her face, or in her eyes. She just rocked herself and gently moaned.

Dawn was breaking when Cassie left the bungalow.

She walked back to the house, choosing to leave the car behind her, as she needed the air, and the space and time to think. There seemed to be no one now, with Tyrone long dead, and her children away growing up abroad. Now Tomas was gone, she had no real company. Together, once Tyrone had been killed, Tomas and she had nursed their crumbling empire and rebuilt their fortunes.

And now there was no one with whom Cassie could 'shout 'em home'.

He wouldn't be there in the yard later that morning, nor on any coming morning, measuring out the feeds and checking the welfare of all the horses with her. He'd just be a space where someone used to be, a gap in a life that went on. There'd be no wise man beside her in the Land Rover as they bounced their way along the gallops, alternately cursing and praising the lads as they galloped their horses up and past them. No one beside her in the grandstand any more, putting his race glasses down three furlongs out and telling her they were done; or not even bothering to watch the race at all, so supremely confident was he that 'they'd take all the beatin' '. No one to lead the horse in with her afterwards, and pull at its ears, and run a thankful hand down its neck before skilfully throwing the sweat sheet over the sweating animal and telling Liam to lead him away. No one to drink with in the bar, in victory and in defeat. No one with such a hope in his heart and such a love of life that he had to disguise it all behind a constant stream of pessimism. No one called Tomas in her life any more, except as a memory. No one called Tomas Muldoon.

She stopped halfway to the house and looked up above her at the grey early morning sky. More than ever she knew what she had to do, and above all, she knew now that she would do it, because she could do it. She made a fist of one of her hands, and holding it high above her head as she walked on to the house, hoped and prayed that Tyrone and Tomas were both watching.

Chapter Twenty-Three

By the middle of April, Dexter Bryant was in residence at Claremore and back riding work. Cassie had done her best to ensure that his return to Ireland was as discreet as possible, but somehow the story was leaked, and the more popular press ran some pretty lurid 'Riches to Rags and Back Again to Riches?' stories. But the staff kept the reporters out of Claremore and well away from the subject of their present attentions, and pretty soon Dexter Bryant's return was yesterday's news.

So far, Dex was as good as his word. He hadn't touched a drink since he entered the New York clinic, and he was three quarters of the way to being match fit. The most remarkable and the most touching part of his return was that he refused any of the special treatment which was initially offered him, preferring instead to work in the yard alongside the rest of the lads, and to sleep in their hostel rather than alternative accommodation more in keeping with his previous standing.

'Look,' he explained to Cassie. 'These guys I'm working with – they're not at the bottom of the heap. They don't know what life's like down there. I do. I've actually come to and found myself lying on the sidewalk with my face in the gutter. You don't get a lot lower, you know. So if I'm going to get back on top, I'm not asking any favours. More than anything, it wouldn't be fair on the rest of the guys.'

So Dexter stood in line. And because he did, the other lads, most of whom had resented his return as it would

647

lessen their own chances of getting any free stable rides, accepted him with good grace. He was given three horses to 'do', and was expected to ride whatever his name was against on the following day's exercise board. In fact his life was the same as any of the other lads in the hostel, the only difference being that when their day was done, and they wandered off into the village to drink and gossip in O'Leary's, Dex would stay behind, and spend all his free time reading up form, so that if and when he rode again in public he would know precisely what he was racing against.

He was made no exception. At first, Cassie kept a watchful eye on him, just in case he suddenly found himself out of his depth now that he was in strange waters. But she soon relaxed her vigilance when it became perfectly apparent that the jockey was as determined as ever he had been to get back out on the track and start bringing home the winners.

By the end of May, Dexter was back riding the two-year-olds in their gallops. One morning Cassie put him up on a notoriously difficult and strong-minded colt belonging to Peter Sankey, the property magnate. She herself was riding a three-year-old winner belonging to the same owner, and elected to school the younger horse alongside hers.

As soon as Dex vaulted lightly up on the two-year-old, the horse changed its manners. Where only a minute earlier he had been plunging and rearing round the yard as one of the lads tried to hold him ready for Dex, he now walked round calmly and sweetly as if he was ten years old, not two. Dex stroked the young horse's neck with one hand, and gave a pull at one of his ears.

'How shall we go, Guv'nor?' he asked Cassie, as they left the yard in twos.

'He's a puller,' Cassie told him, 'and he'll have your arms out of their sockets if you give him the chance. So I want you to get him to settle. If you can, which I kind of doubt, get him to tuck in behind me for the first couple of furlongs, and for the last two pull him out but *don't* let him go on.'

'You got it!' Dex called back with a grin, as his horse decided to try and take off before he was told.

But Dex had the measure of him, and rode him precisely to Cassie's instructions. Cassie had quite deliberately set him what was an almost impossible task, since the horse he was riding had carted everybody on the gallops, and would almost certainly take hold once they were cantering and pull his way past Cassie.

But it had to be done, if Dexter was going to make it back properly to the big time. There would be no point putting him up on the more temperamental of Claremore's good horses if there was any doubt about Dexter's nerve. As they started trotting their horses out, Cassie could see that behind Dex's natural good humour and apparent confidence, there was tension in his eyes and round his mouth, as he felt the strength and determination of the young horse under him. By the time they reached the point where they were to start work in earnest, all the banter had stopped.

Cassie deliberately let the other horses go off in pairs first, as she knew this would be a further test of horse and jockey. Her own mount was pawing the ground and trying to turn in circles, in an attempt to unsettle Cassie so that she might lose her contact with him, allowing him to take hold and bolt off after his stable mates.

Dexter's fiery two-year-old, on the other hand, was standing like a mounted policeman's horse on point duty. Cassie eyed horse and jockey surreptitiously, and swore to herself that if Dexter dropped the reins the youngster was so relaxed he'd just probably put his head down and start grazing.

'OK!' Cassie suddenly called. 'I'm going to kick on, Dexter! And you follow after a count of five!'

She set her horse off, and for one awful moment Cassie thought the horse had taken hold, which would ruin the whole experiment. Then she got him back, and cantering nicely, just as she heard the dull thunder of Dexter's horse who was now following on behind her. Cassie sat as still as she could for two furlongs, then took a look over her shoulder. Dex's horse was tucked in half a length adrift and going as sweet as you could wish.

'We'll go on now!' Cassie shouted back to Dexter. 'Three quarter speed! But don't let him go whatever you do!'

Cassie kicked on and immediately her horse started galloping just below racing clip. She heard Dex's horse quickening as well, and as he loomed alongside her the horse looked sure to run off, so fast was he travelling. But Dexter had him, and the moment they were racing neck and neck, he just dropped the horse so that the animal relaxed and was perfectly content to remain in company, rather than head at full speed for the wilds of Carlow.

Dexter didn't look anywhere except ahead through the horse's ears. Neither did Cassie, but she could sense and feel the unity of the two galloping horses.

'Well?' she asked Dexter, after they'd pulled the horses up carefully, and had turned them to walk home.

'Great,' said Dex, ruffling the horse's mane. 'I'd say this young fellah's about ready to race.'

'OK,' Cassie replied. 'And I don't think he's the only one.'

Erin went into labour the evening before Dexter's first scheduled ride in public. As she sat comforting her, and waiting for the midwife, Cassie wondered once again what Tomas had whispered to his daughter just before he had died. Naturally she had never asked, since it was something between father and daughter, and Erin had never volunteered the information. But remembering the tears that had fallen, Cassie was sure that they had finally been reunited.

By nine o'clock, the baby was fully engaged, and the midwife had still not turned up. So Cassie prepared to deliver the child. Erin, contrary to her normally tearful

650

and timid character, was a model of courage and fortitude, never complaining as her birth pains grew worse and worse. But by the time the midwife did finally arrive, full of apologies for her wretched car breaking down, Erin had bitten practically clean through her bottom lip.

Just before she was delivered, as the top of her baby's head became visible, Erin clutched Cassie's hand and gave one loud scream, so that for a moment Cassie thought Erin was going to die.

And then a few moments later, with one good slap from the midwife, another heart began to beat independently, and another brand new life was born.

'It's a boy,' Cassie said to Erin, as the midwife cut and knotted the cord. 'It's a little baby boy.'

Then Erin started to weep, but for once they were tears of pure joy, as her baby was placed gently in her arms.

'Ah God so it is, Mrs Rosse,' Erin cried. 'Will you look at the little devil? A little baby boy.'

Cassie looked at the tiny child in Erin's arms, its eyes tightly shut and its little body swathed in a blanket, and knew that the baby would never leave its mother's side.

'Have you thought what to call him, Erin?' Cassie asked.

'God help us,' Erin replied, without taking her eyes off her baby. 'Wasn't that one of the last things my father asked me? He said if the babba was a little boy, would I ever call him Padraig Tomas Tyrone? Savin' your presence of course, Mrs Rosse.'

The future of the baby was debated by Cassie and Mrs Muldoon long into the night. At first Erin's mother would not hear of the baby remaining at Claremore.

'Perhaps among other things,' Cassie suggested, 'Tomas also requested that Erin might keep the child if she so wished.'

'He was a sick man, Mrs Rosse,' Mrs Muldoon answered. 'Sure he'd have said anything to make his peace with his Maker.'

'I don't think that's strictly true,' Cassie argued. 'You know better than I how much he loved his daughter. Maybe we ought to ask her.'

'You'll do no such thing, Mrs Rosse,' Erin's mother replied, 'with the greatest respect, of course. I'm her mother, and as far as this matter is concerned, what I say goes.'

'Mrs Muldoon,' Cassie sighed, beginning to lose patience, 'Erin is over forty, and the mother now of a child herself.'

'Of a bastard child,' Mrs Muldoon answered, defiantly.

'And she's still not saying who the father is,' Cassie continued, ignoring the challenge.

'Sure the child swears she'll never betray the father. At one time I thought she was all for claiming it as a virgin birth.'

'OK,' said Cassie, 'then here's what I suggest. I suggest that I adopt the baby, which will give it the respectability you want. I don't know who knows or who doesn't know Erin's "guilty secret", but all we simply have to say is that I'm adopting another child. And Erin can bring it up as her own. Which won't be any great problem because your dear daughter has brought up both my children as her own anyway.'

Cassie smiled at Mrs Muldoon, as she remembered Erin's fierce possessiveness. She particularly remembered the almost physical tug of war they'd had when Josephine first went away to school.

'And maybe, who knows?' Cassie continued. 'Rather than give the baby away, this way perhaps you'll get to love your first grandchild.'

Mrs Muldoon looked up at Cassie, startled. It was fairly obvious from her expression that this was the very first time she had viewed Erin's baby as being related to her.

'Mary, Mother of God,' she whispered, fumbling for a handkerchief in the pockets of her pinny, 'sure I've nothin' against the baby. He's the sweetest little child and I've nothin' against him at all. It's just – it's just the shame, Mrs Rosse. The shame.'

'There's no shame in a baby being born,' Cassie told her. 'The pity would be if you remained ashamed.'

Dexter had his first public ride for Claremore later that day, riding the Peter Sankey two-year-old he had galloped so successfully. It was a big field, of twenty-one runners, and the horse finished third, beaten two lengths and half a length, after running very green.

The punters clapped him into the unsaddling enclosure as if he'd ridden the winner.

'He's a good sort,' Dexter told Cassie, as he pulled the saddle off the horse, 'but I think he'll appreciate a longer trip.'

'I think you're right,' Cassie replied, 'and well done.'

When she got home, Father Patrick was waiting in the drawing room to see her.

'I stopped by to see Erin,' he explained. 'I rang her mother to see how she was, and I heard she'd been delivered.'

'Erin's fine,' Cassie told him, 'She was very brave, and she's delighted with her little boy.'

'Yes indeed,' the priest agreed, 'I went to see her, and the baby. And yes indeed. They both seem to be doing very well.'

Cassie took a quiet look at Father Patrick. He was normally so energetic and forthright, yet this evening he was sitting on the edge of his chair, nursing his whisky and staring immovably at the carpet.

'Is something the matter, Father?' she finally asked him.

'Well not really, no, Cassie,' he replied. 'I can hardly in all honesty say there's anything the matter. I've been very lucky to have been the PP here for so long. I always think that the powers that be must have overlooked me, because really I should have been moved on long ago.'

'They're moving you on?'

'Yes, I'm to go to South America next month.'

'Just like that?'

'Next month. As you say. Just like that.'

He took a drink of his whisky, then carefully put his glass down, still averting his eyes from Cassie.

'To come to the point, Cassie,' he said after a silence, 'Erin's mother explained your plan for the child, and I would like to compliment you on its excellence.'

'Thank you, Father Patrick,' Cassie replied, smiling at the formality of the praise.

'Indeed while you were at your business this afternoon, I understand that Mrs Muldoon explained your offer to Erin, and subject to your confirmation of it, I have a feeling the young woman in question will be only too delighted to avail herself of your very great kindness.'

'I like children, Father. And with both of mine now all but grown up, I shall enjoy having a baby around the house again.'

'Even with your full life?'

'There's always room for a baby.'

Father Patrick finished his whisky, but declined the offer of another, preferring instead to get up and pace the room in silence for a while. Then he sat down again, and asked if he could after all perhaps have that second whisky.

Pouring his drink for him, Cassie could only put the priest's restlessness down to his sudden foreign posting. She gave him his whisky and then sat back down opposite him.

'This is going to sound ridiculous, coming from me,' Cassie said to break the silence. 'But is there something particular you want to talk to me about, Father?'

The priest rubbed one hand wearily across his eyes, frowning as he did so; then he looked directly at Cassie for the first time that evening.

'I'm the father of Erin's child, Cassie,' he said.

Oddly enough, Cassie thought, as she tried to remain composed and not look as thunderstruck as she felt, oddly enough she had put Father Patrick on her mental list of suspects, only to strike him off as an utterly ridiculous notion. Firstly, he was a man above suspicion, free from the usual tattle-tales which apparently follow most priests in Ireland from parish to parish; and secondly, he was such an utterly handsome and virile man that Cassie couldn't help thinking somewhat uncharitably that if he was indeed to fall from grace, then the object of his temptation would hardly be the timid and bashful Erin Muldoon – even though in the last two years, as Cassie had noticed, Erin had grown quite extraordinarily religious, going to church on practically every conceivable occasion. But still Cassie had rejected as absurd the idea of Father Patrick as a real-life father.

'I know what you're thinking, Cassie,' Father Patrick said, interrupting her thoughts. 'You're wondering why poor quiet little Erin Muldoon? Well there's your reason. Poor quiet Erin. I felt sorry for her, and she felt sorry for me. She was never out of the church. Always there with a helping hand, or a ready ear. And odd as I'm quite sure it will seem to you, we fell in love. It wasn't just a sexual encounter, you understand. The irony is we only made love the once. Which perhaps is a little unfair of the Fates. But then, if you sup with the devil . . .'

He drank some more whisky, then carefully brushed some invisible hairs from his jacket.

'I thought of leaving the priesthood,' he continued, 'and of marrying Erin. But I'm a man of a certain faith, Cassie, and I still really do believe that the love I have for Christ is greater than the love I could have for anyone else. And I think Erin is mindful of this fact. So I requested a posting in South America.'

Cassie looked up at him, surprised for the second time that evening.

'That's right, Cassie, I requested the posting. Now of

655

course, by telling you all this, I'm throwing myself
entirely on your mercy. You could well think me a
despicable sort of fellow, and see that I was defrocked.
Or you could tell Erin that I asked to be sent abroad,
rather than as she sees it, as an act of God. And I offer no
defence except the love that I have for God, and in miti-
gation of my sins, that by knowing my child, my son – is
in your safekeeping, I can devote the rest of my life to the
propagation of Christ's word.'

Father Patrick stared at Cassie unblinkingly, not
challenging her to make a decision, but simply and honestly just awaiting her verdict. Cassie knew the man well
enough to realise that if she gave him the thumbs down,
he would merely accept her finding and abide by it without further argument. But Cassie also knew that she was
in no position to judge a fellow human being's behaviour,
besides considering that Father Patrick's one slip from
the path of righteousness was not going to turn one of the
most passionately devout men she had ever known into a
heinous sinner.

'I hope you keep safe and well in South America,
Father,' she said, rising and extending her hand in farewell. 'We shall all miss you greatly.'

'I shall miss you all greatly as well,' he replied, gripping Cassie's hand firmly in his own, strong hand. 'I
know my son will grow well in this house, because you're
a very exceptional person, Cassie Rosse, and a wonderful
mother. All I ask is that you say nothing of this to Erin.'

'If you'll absolve me in advance,' Cassie replied with a
smile, 'I haven't seen you since Sunday.'

'I think God would forgive you most things, Cassie,'
Father Patrick said, collecting his hat. 'Thank you. And
may God bless all here.'

Cassie watched him as he got on his bicycle and rode
off down the drive and out of her life. She guessed that he
would never come back from South America, which was
why he had chosen to go there; somewhere where there
was still very real danger for a Catholic priest to live and

656

work, somewhere where he might easily die for his faith and atone for his one surrender to temptation. And as she closed the front doors on him, she recalled the days when she was new at Claremore and how she and Father Patrick would argue hammer and tongs about the Church's teachings as far as babies and a woman's role in the world went, and how shocked the young and freckle-faced Erin had been that Cassie should argue with a priest.

And now she was to be the adoptive mother of his child. She smiled to herself as she went back into the drawing room, at the thought of how much Tomas would be enjoying the irony.

By late summer, both Cassie's new offspring were growing apace. Padraig Tomas Tyrone was the bonniest boy baby, as handsome as his father and as open-faced as his mother. Erin was as proud as anything of him, although she had to reserve her most outward displays of emotion towards her child for when she was at home behind the closed doors of Claremore, because it was made known very quickly that Mrs Rosse was in the process of adopting another child.

The Nightingale, however, was growing a little too quickly for Cassie's and Sheila Meath's liking.

'I'd be tearing my hair out, wouldn't you, Sheila?' Cassie asked her friend one day as they stood looking at the colt chasing round the home paddock. 'I'd be at my wits' end if I was trying to get him ready for the yearling sales. Look at him. He's such a lanky brute.'

'And more than a little lop-sided,' Sheila added. 'I wouldn't be surprised if he's still a maiden at three.'

'By the look of him,' Cassie added, 'I wouldn't be surprised if he's still a maiden at five. I just wish he'd stop growing so goddam *fast*.'

Even so, as they stood watching him cavort round the paddock, there was something rather special about the colt, something quite indefinable. So much so that the two

657

women found it hard to drag themselves away to go and look at the other youngsters, the ones who actually were destined for the sale ring.

'It's when you look at some of these others,' Sheila said, 'that you can see how exceptional Nightie might be.'

'He's got a bit of presence, hasn't he?' Cassie agreed.

'I'd almost go so far as to say he's got star quality,' Sheila replied.

'If only he'd stop growing upwards and grow a bit more outwards,' Cassie grumbled.

Sheila turned and looked at her and raised an eyebrow. 'I don't suppose you've ever thought of changing your name to Tomas Muldoon the Second, have you?' she asked.

Frank came over for the Goff's sales, and Cassie bought two yearlings on his behalf.

'You're the perfect owner,' Cassie told him over dinner afterwards. 'I wish there were more like you. Even with all the races your horses have won you now, you've never pressurised me into running them when I advised you not to, or complained when they got beat when they should have won.'

'Jeeze, it's a sport, Cassie Rosse,' Frank laughed. 'The day you take this game seriously is the day you stop enjoying it.'

'That was Tyrone's philosophy totally. And when things start to go wrong, sometimes I have to remind myself not to forget it,' Cassie replied.

Frank stayed over for a week, and he and Cassie picked up the pieces just where they'd left them a few months earlier, just as they always did. But as the time approached for Frank to take his leave, Cassie noticed a change in his mood.

'Don't tell me you have something you want to discuss with me as well,' she laughed over their farewell dinner *à deux* at Claremore. 'It seems to have been that sort of year.'

'Why yes, I guess I do, Cassie,' he replied, looking up from his cheese. 'Is it that obvious?'

'Frank, we go back a long way now.'

'Sure, but even so. A woman's intuition, I guess?'

'Maybe. What's on your mind?'

'Cassie. I want to get married.'

'Frank,' Cassie answered, looking at him through the candlelight. 'Sometimes I'd give an arm to be your wife.'

'But you won't, Cass.'

'I can't, Frank.'

'Right. That's why I want to get married.'

'You have someone in mind?'

'Cassie. There's only one person I ever have in mind. You know that. But we've been through this. You're here, in Claremore, and you're here to stay. I'm over there, in New York, and I'm there to stay. Period.'

'Maybe I should take out a licence to train over there.'

'You'd hate it. This is you. This place.'

'OK, Frank. So maybe you should come and work over here. Or better still, not work over here.'

Frank came round behind her chair and eased it out for her as she rose. Cassie took his arm as they walked through to the drawing room.

'I couldn't not work, Cass,' he said. 'You know that. And I couldn't work over here. Dublin isn't New York, however charming it may be. I'd be bored by the middle of the first week.'

'Why do you want to get married, Frank? It's really not been on your agenda before.'

Frank swilled the brandy in his glass and inhaled the aroma. 'You'll find this a little crazy, Cassie,' he replied. 'But I'm jealous. I want to have children. Seeing you with little Padraig, I get broody. Really. Obviously it's an urge I've been sublimating.'

'I've never seen you sublimating,' Cassie smiled, resting her head on his knee. 'You only have to see a TV commercial with a baby in it, and your chin starts to pucker.'

'Go to hell,' Frank said with a broad grin. 'Is that right?'

'I shall miss you, Frank,' Cassie told him later when she lay in his arms. 'This year I'll have lost two men that I loved.'

'We'll still be friends, Cassie. Nothing can ever destroy what we have.'

'What we have had, Frank,' Cassie corrected him. 'So I guess you'd better make love to me one more time before we kiss each other goodbye.'

They made love more than once that last night, both of them reluctant to think this was the last time they would be in each other's arms. Then they slept a little before dawn broke, and when the light woke them, they made love again, gently and sleepily, before falling back to sleep, Frank lying behind Cassie, his arms circled round her waist.

When she woke up eventually, Frank had gone. Cassie hadn't even heard the car leave for the airport. She sat up in bed, clutching the sheets round her naked body, while the tears ran silently down her face. Everyone she knew was going. It was as if the world about her was changing its blood.

The good thing about that summer had been the renaissance of Dexter Bryant. He had ridden his first winner two weeks after his initial ride at Naas, and since then had slowly and steadily increased his tally for the season to a respectable fifteen. Two of these had been for Willie Moore, who, on Cassie's prompting, and on the evidence of his own eyes, had offered Dex the odd but good spare ride.

There had only been one worrying moment. Dexter had been put up on what the racing papers liked to call one of Claremore's 'hotshots', a three-year-old filly called Scarlet Ribbon who had run promisingly enough in the Irish 1,000 Guineas to indicate she would be one to follow in the immediate future. Cassie placed her well in a stakes race at the Curragh, and the punters went for the horse as if she couldn't be beaten. But the ground had come up very hard and the filly, quite unable to act on it, trailed in last, at 1/3 on.

From the stands of course it looked as though Dexter had left his effort far too late, and when he found he couldn't get the filly into the race, had simply dropped her out. So by the time the jockey was walking the horse back to be unsaddled, the crowd were in an ugly mood. Dexter was given 'the bird', and as well as the verbal abuse he was subjected to a barrage of beer cans, lighted cigarettes and saliva. Clearly very shaken, he left the racecourse immediately he had changed and failed to return to Claremore that evening.

By eleven o'clock, as Cassie was preparing to go to sleep, someone telephoned anonymously and said Dexter had been seen drinking in Dublin. Cassie told him to mind his own business, read some more of her book, then turned off her light and went to sleep.

When she arrived at the stables in the morning, the first person she saw was Dexter, mucking out one of his horses. Cassie said nothing to him about his disappearance until after the horses had all been exercised, when she summoned him to her private office in the new block.

'Do you want to talk about it?' Cassie asked him as she poured them both some coffee.

'There's nothing to talk about, Guv'nor,' Dex replied.

'You were seen drinking in Dublin.'

Dexter looked up in surprise. 'Who told you?'

'The caller didn't give his name. But it sounded suspiciously like your arch-rival Terry Doyle.'

'I wouldn't be surprised, Guv'nor. He's backed Scarlet Ribbon, and pretty dam' heavily, too.'

'I can't trust you with my best horses, Dex, if you drink. You know that.'

'Sure I know that,' Dexter replied easily, with a smile. 'And the day I take a drink, that's the day I walk away from here.'

'Nobody would have blamed you after yesterday.'

'I would have. I'd never have forgiven myself if I'd

weakened because of a few lousy punters talking through their pockets. I sure wanted a drink. In fact I can't remember the last time I wanted a drink so badly. But I got over it.'

'How, Dex?' Cassie asked.

'You're not going to believe this,' he replied, grinning. 'I went to a bar.'

'And that's how you got over it?'

'You spend all evening in a bar, by yourself, Guv'nor, without drinking. My therapist in New York used to make me do it all the time. It's a very salutary experience. Watching people losing their minds.'

Cassie finished her coffee, and got up, ready to return to work. 'As soon as the ground comes right, we'll run Scarlet Ribbon,' she said, before letting Dex go. 'And you'll ride her.'

'No I won't,' Dexter replied. 'I'll win on her.'

They waited nearly two months before they ran the filly again, rather than risk another dismal performance on the wrong going. Finally the ground came right for a good race at Leopardstown, and Scarlet Ribbon duly 'obliged', winning as she liked from a high-class field, with Dexter easing her up as they passed the post. The punters had gone for her again, returning her the even money favourite. But this time as the filly was led back in to be unsaddled her jockey was given a hero's ovation.

'If you can treat those two imposters just the same, right?' Dexter said with a grin to Cassie *en route* to weighing in.

'You got it,' Cassie replied.

The Nightingale wasn't broken in until November, which was much later than Cassie normally liked to break her horses, but because he was still so ungainly and awkward, she left the first part of the young horse's training till what she considered to be the last minute.

Sheila Meath did the breaking, as she always did with Claremore's best and most promising yearlings. Both she and Cassie were surprised at how easily Nightie, as he was known in the yard, accepted someone on his back. He showed no resistance or resentment; in fact he seemed visibly to enjoy the procedure.

'Then he's always been a bit of a bright fellah, this one,' Cassie remarked to Sheila, watching Liam quietly riding the young horse at a walk round the indoor school. 'You said yourself he's a thinker.'

'If you can do with this chap what you did to that other heavy-topped youngster you had,' Sheila replied, 'he could make up into something quite extraordinary.'

'If he takes to training,' Cassie concluded thoughtfully, 'I won't race him till late summer. That other big horse, he was much better furnished altogether by his first Christmas. Nightie looks as though he's going to take a lot longer to grow into that damn great frame of his.'

And so Cassie took it slowly and patiently with the big dark horse, allowing him the first four months of the following year to develop in his own good time. While her other two-year-olds were learning how to canter, she was still working Nightie on the lunge, building up his sides, quarters and neck. Then she walked him out herself on the roads, nothing but roads and hills, for another four weeks before he was allowed near the gallops.

Dex was given the job of introducing the horse to the canter, so that Cassie and Sheila could watch him from the ground. They were both sadly disappointed.

'That's the scratchiest action I've seen in a long time,' Cassie said as they watched the horse pull up. 'He's not using himself at all.'

Dexter confirmed their suspicions, saying that the horse had worked like a pony.

'We'll just have to wait and see what he's like when he gallops,' Cassie said. 'If he gets to use those quarters of his properly, we could still be in business.'

The good thing about the horse was that he was not growing so fast upwards any more, and had begun to grow sideways. In fact, by the end of May he was an altogether better shape; so much so that although at the canter he was still as unimpressive as ever, it was decided to give him his first serious piece of work, to see if there was any noticeable difference at the gallop.

Again Dexter rode him, alongside the best of Claremore's two-year-olds, a horse called Sixth Heaven, who had come to hand early and won his first race on the bridle. Cassie was by herself that morning, as Sheila was down with a heavy cold, so she hacked up the gallops on Bouncer, and sat waiting for the horses to come towards her.

It was a warm morning, and there was a haze hanging over the grass as the first two horses came shimmering into view. They were Sixth Heaven and The Nightingale. Cassie held her lightweight miniature race glasses up one-handed and watched them approach. At once she felt a surge of excitement as she saw how the big dark bay was working. At the gallop he was a totally different animal, stretching out in front to cover the ground while tucking his hind legs well under him to give him full impulsion. Dexter was sitting quite still, not asking the horse to do anything except work half-speed. But the horse was merely idling beside Sixth Heaven, who was almost at full stretch just to keep pace with the newcomer. By the last furlong, Dexter was fighting a losing battle to keep his horse from striding away up the hill.

'You didn't take him on, Dex, did you?' Cassie asked as the jockeys brought the horses back past her for their debriefing.

'No way, Guv'nor,' Dex grinned. 'I tell you, this horse is something other. That was only second gear.'

The decision then had to be made when to race the horse. Cassie was in the extraordinary and enviable position of owning the horse as well as training it, so she had only herself to listen to as to when it should run. Herself and Sheila Meath, of course.

'You're on a hiding to nothing, Cassie,' Sheila told her.

'If the horse isn't quite ready, if he needs a race, you'll only have yourself to argue with. To my old eye, provided there are no setbacks, he looks as if he'll be plenty ready for the Renvyle Stakes in July.'

There were no setbacks. The horse improved so much with every bit of work Cassie got into him, that the word was already out about him. He looked a picture in the paddock before the race, and by the time he was going down to the start, he was contesting favouritism. But obviously the punters weren't so impressed with his unimpressive action as he cantered past the stands, and by the time they were under orders, The Nightingale could be backed all over the ring at 5/2, and in some places at 3/1.

He won, as Dex afterwards described it, doing handstands. The race, run over six furlongs, was over the minute the jockey asked the horse his first serious question, two furlongs out. Dex picked the horse up and asked him to go, and that was that. He won so easily that he was headlines on every racing page the following day.

'Cassie's Private Jet Streaks Home' was one of the more popular headlines.

The *Irish Times* put it somewhat more decorously. 'Claremore reveals potential Classic Hope', it stated. 'Home-bred horse looks ideal Guineas type.'

What pleased Cassie most of all was that she knew there was still lots of room for improvement in the big-framed horse, and that if she planned his career correctly, and if the horse was as brilliant as he appeared, there was indeed every chance that he could shape up into the Classic hope she had always dreamed about and prayed for.

Dex was in no two minds about The Nightingale.

'This is the best horse I've ever sat on,' he told Cassie when they reran the race over and over again on the video.

'See the way he quickens? He's devastating. Those other horses, the ones all struggling behind him like selling platers. Those are all everyone else's Classic dreams.'

665

After he'd won his next race in much the same manner, strolling away from a very high-class field, Cassie received a telephone call from one of the top international bloodstock agents, who informed her he'd been instructed to offer her half a million pounds for the horse.

'Sorry, John,' said Cassie. 'He's not for sale.'

The phone rang again shortly before midnight.

'Three quarters of a million, and a twentieth of the syndication at stud.'

'I love you, Johnnie, but goodnight,' Cassie told him, and hung up, switching the telephone on to automatic answer.

Cassie ran him once more successfully in the Dalkey Stakes before sending him over to Newmarket for the most prestigious two-year-old race at the end of the season, the Dewhurst. She sent him over not only to win, but to get his first taste of air travel, of being away from home, and to get his first sight of the track where the 2,000 Guineas was run. She knew it was one thing to pick up races at home, but quite another to pick them up on a raid. Particularly at Newmarket.

The Dewhurst is invariably a high-class race, and a hotly contested one. This year's was no exception, with seven of the eight contenders all being talked of as Guineas contenders. Between them, the eight starters had won seventeen races, and over one and a half million pounds in prize money.

Of the eight runners, five were owned by Arabs, one by the Englishman Peter Sankey, and one by the Aga Khan.

The money paid for seven of the eight runners lumped together came to over five million pounds.

The horse which had cost his owner-breeder nothing except for his food and lodging, won by six lengths.

Immediately after the race the big four bookmakers all made The Nightingale even-money favourite for the first of the next season's Classics, the 2,000 Guineas, and when the Free Handicap was published, The Nightingale not unsurprisingly was top-rated.

The second-rated horse, a grandson of Mill Reef called Millstone Grit, was a non-starter in the Dewhurst, due to a twisted hock. Owned by a Mr Charles C. Lovett Andrew, he was also unbeaten in three races.

The Nightingale was retired for the season, roughed off and sent to winter in north-east Italy.

Josephine, on the other hand, came home for Christmas from Italy, where she had been filming the location work for a television movie, due for transmission in the spring. Every time Cassie saw her, she just couldn't believe how she had managed to give birth to such a beautiful girl.

'Everyone says I'm the spit of you,' Josephine would tell her, whenever her mother complimented her on her looks.

'Nonsense,' Cassie would reply. 'If anything, you've your father's good looks.'

She was slightly taller than Cassie, but with her mother's perfect figure. Her long hair was now dyed pure blonde, which Cassie privately disapproved of in principle, although with Josephine's perfect peaches-and-cream complexion, Cassie had to admit that the total effect was quite stunning.

'Anyone else coming to stay for Christmas this year?' Josephine enquired on the drive back from the airport.

'Just family,' Cassie replied.

Her daughter looked round at her sharply. 'Family?'

'Sure. I thought we'd have Christmas by ourselves for a change,' Cassie continued.

'OK,' Josephine replied, 'I'd like that. Just the two of us.'

'Just the two of us,' Cassie agreed, 'and Mattie.'

Her adopted son was due home five days before Christmas. According to the very occasional letter from Australia, it seemed that the experiment of sending him to the other side of the world was paying off. Mattie was working hard, learning a lot and enjoying himself.

It had been a difficult decision for Cassie to make,

because of Mattie's asthma, which had suddenly returned with a vengeance during his adolescence, despite the ministrations of Dr FitzStanton. Cassie had been told by the homeopath that this was a fairly normal development with asthmatics, and that it was also really make or break time.

'It's now partly a mental battle, you see,' he had explained with his usual care and patience. 'Mattie has to make a conscious decision as to whether or not he's going to beat the disease. And if we all engage in a very positive approach, and treat him as if he's a quite normal chap, rather than one requiring kid-glove treatment, the chances are we can persuade him that he's going to be able to lead a perfectly normal life, provided that he takes proper care of himself.'

So Cassie followed this advice through, sending Mattie to a normal school and allowing him to engage in whatever activities he wished to. And like so many other asthmatics, such was his determination to overcome his disability that he became a very good all-round sportsman, excelling particularly and surprisingly at athletics. Cassie and Josephine were always delighted with his successes, particularly when they remembered how as a little boy he could barely run across the nursery without an attack of 'the wheezles'.

He was, however, no scholar, and although the thing he wanted to be more than anything else in the world was a vet, he failed to achieve the necessary academic qualifications.

It was Sheila Meath who suggested the trip to Australia.

'His passion is for animals, that we know,' she'd told Cassie. 'Particularly horses, and that you didn't know.'

'No, I didn't,' Cassie had agreed, somewhat surprised. 'I knew how he'd set his heart on becoming a vet, but he's always adopted a rather take-it-or-leave-it attitude as far as horses in particular are concerned.'

'Yes, but for goodness sake that's only a smoke screen, Cassie,' Sheila had continued. 'When they were growing up, it was always Josephine who was going to be the horsey one, winning the Grand National, or jumping for Ireland in the Olympics. Mattie deliberately took a back seat there, because of his health. And now of course he won't tell *you* what he really wants to do, because it just looks as though he's jumping on the band wagon.'

'You're telling me he wants to train?'

'More than anything. But more than anything, he wants to train independently.'

And so it was arranged that Mattie should go and learn the ropes with one of Sheila Meath's many relatives who were dotted all around the globe. This particular nephew was one of Australia's most successful trainers, but such was Sheila's persistence that he was soon persuaded to take Mattie on as a trainee assistant, with the proviso that there'd be no favours, and Mattie would have to start where everyone else did: at the bottom.

Mattie had found it hard at first, which was really the whole idea of the exercise. He rang home constantly during the first three months, and although he never said so in as many words, it was perfectly obvious that if Cassie had weakened, or hinted that if it was too much for him he could bale out and come home, Mattie would have been on the next plane. But Cassie held on. Even though it broke her heart to hear how brave her son was being while obviously so lonely, prompted by Sheila she just pretended that all was for the best, and fed him bromide after bromide over the phone about distances and absences and character-building.

'I don't know how I'd have handled it without you,' Cassie told Sheila. 'Not having had parents in the accepted sense, I guess I find it harder than most trying to do the best thing.'

After six months the telephone stopped ringing, and it was as much as Cassie could do to get a letter back from him. Sheila, however, got the odd 'confidential' report from her nephew, and although never a man to squander praise, it was perfectly apparent that young Mattie was earning his stripes.

And now he was coming home, and the plan was for just the three of them – Cassie, Josephine and Mattie – to spend the central days of Christmas happily together once more as a family.

And so they would have done had it not been for Leonora.

Cassie had all but lost touch with Leonora. When last read of, she was divorced and back on the international circuit. She knew that Leonora was still buying blood-stock however, since she had seen pictures of her at the Newmarket Highflyer Sales, and heard that Peter Carroll, a top bloodstock agent, had been commissioned to buy her some yearlings. At dinner one night, someone tried to bring Cassie up to date with the latest news of Leonora's marital adventures, but Cassie showed no interest whatsoever and immediately changed the subject to matters of more immediate concern.

Had she not been quite so resolute, she would have learned that Leonora was back in Ireland, and that her latest marriage would greatly affect Cassie's personal future and the closely guarded security of her family.

On 20 December, Cassie and Josephine drove out to the airport to meet Mattie. Looking for someone casually dressed and crumpled, which was Mattie's normal appearance, they both missed the tall and elegant young man who walked nonchalantly through customs and ambled up behind them.

'You waiting for someone, girls?' said a broad mock-Australian accent behind them.

Cassie and Josephine wheeled round startled, only to be confronted by Mattie's bronzed and smiling face.

'Good God!' Josephine laughed as she hugged him. 'I thought you'd come back with corks on your hat!'

Mattie grinned, kissed his sister and then turned to his mother.

Cassie smiled and did her best, but for one of the very

few occasions in her life, her tears got the better of her as she embraced her handsome son.

'Oh Christ,' Mattie sighed. 'Don't start going all wet, Mum. I've only been away two years.'

'I know,' Cassie said, 'but it seems like ten.'

They drove straight back to Claremore, where Cassie had arranged a small drinks party in honour of her son's return, and then dinner for just the three of them.

When they arrived at the house, it looked as though one of the guests had got the time wrong and arrived early, because there was a metallic-black BMW coupe already parked at the bottom of the steps.

'I don't recognise it,' Cassie said, going on into the house ahead of her children who were being playfully assaulted by Bunbury. 'I wonder who it is?'

Dick hurtled too late towards the front doors to open them, but Cassie as usual just beat him to it.

'I see we have a visitor, Dick,' Cassie said, taking off her hat and coat.

'We have that, ma'am, so we do,' Dick replied, sliding finally to a standstill on the polished floor. 'Isn't she waiting for you this half hour in the drawing room?'

'I don't recognise the car,' Cassie told him.

'You'll recognise your guest,' Dick answered, fishing in his pocket and producing a visiting card.

Cassie looked at the card and frowned, momentarily as unfamiliar with her guest's name as she was with her mode of transport.

Then just as Dick closed the drawing-room door behind her, she made the connection.

Leonora.

She was standing with her back to Cassie, examining a new painting over the fireplace as Dick held the door open for Cassie. Even from Leonora's rear view, Cassie could see the improvement. She had lost a lot of weight since they last met, and her blonde hair, grown long again, fell in shining coils around her shoulders. Then she turned round and waved one hand at Cassie, a hand free of the eternal cigarette.

'Hi,' she said.

'Hello, Leonora,' Cassie replied, quietly astounded at the physical change which had come over her adversary. She looked ten years younger. Gone were the beginnings of the bags under the eyes, and the flesh under the chin; gone too the crow's feet and the pouching of the cheeks. The only tell-sale sign of her age and her former habits were the tiny perpendicular creases above her upper lip.

'Don't tell me you've given up smoking?' Cassie asked.

'How did you know?'

'This has to be the first time since we were kids I've seen you without a cigarette, that's why.'

'I have given up smoking,' Leonora replied, putting a hand on Cassie's shoulder and kissing the air near Cassie's face, 'I have given up drinking, I have given up snorting, and now with my latest marriage, it appears I've also given up sex.'

She stood back and smiled at Cassie, then slowly tossed back her mane of blonde hair, perfectly aware of the astonishment and, she hoped, envy her appearance was causing Cassie.

'You've lost a lot of weight, too,' Cassie added.

'And you've gained some,' Leonora replied, sitting down on a sofa without being asked, 'which is no bad thing.'

Cassie checked her own appearance briefly in a mirror on one wall, before turning back to Leonora.

'Don't you ever ring to say when you're calling, Leonora?'

'I did, but you were at the airport, darling.'

'You could have called yesterday. Or this morning.'

'Jesus – you're so goddam proper, Cassie darling! Life is too blasted short! I only decided to drive to Cork at lunchtime, so I rang you from the car, and when that strange butler of yours told me you'd be back late afternoon, I thought I'd stop by. Why ever not? It's been an age since we met.'

Cassie looked at Leonora, then pointedly looked at her watch.

'What Dick obviously neglected to tell you was that I have guests, Leonora, so I'm afraid I can't ask you to stay.'

'Darling, I have to be in Cork two hours ago, so even if I wanted to, I couldn't possibly. I just thought since you were on my way I'd stop and say Hi. And tell you we're going to be at Derry Na Loch for Christmas, and that you simply must come across sometime for dinner.'

'Must I?'

'Certainly. I want you to meet my new husband before he dies.'

Leonora gave a great hoot of laughter and picked up a copy of *Harper's*.

'Christmas is all booked, Leonora,' Cassie replied calmly. 'So even if I wanted to, I couldn't possibly.'

Cassie moved towards the door, hoping that Leonora would take the hint. But Leonora remained seated on the sofa, flicking through her magazine.

'I didn't know this was your required reading,' she said. '*Pacemaker*, or *Sporting Life*, sure. But fashion and society?'

'That's Josephine's,' Cassie replied.

'Yes? That who you were meeting at the airport? No, of course not. I saw Josie in Brown Thomas's yesterday.'

'I really do have to go and change,' Cassie replied, opening the door.

'OK, darling,' Leonora sighed, throwing the magazine down, and getting to her feet. 'What are you doing New Year's Eve? I'm giving a real old-style bash – pink champagne, dance bands, fancy dress, balloons, "Auld Lang Syne", the lot. I'd love you to come. All of you. Josie, Matt – whoever you have staying. How about it?'

The hairs on the back of Cassie's neck started to stand up, and Cassie couldn't understand why. She hadn't

673

mentioned that Mattie was home, so Leonora couldn't possibly know. Unless Josie had told her. Yet her daughter would most certainly have mentioned seeing Leonora in Dublin if they had talked, but she hadn't, so that ruled out that possibility. So why would she mention Mattie's name as if she already knew he was home? Dick couldn't have told her, otherwise Leonora wouldn't have asked who she was meeting at the airport.

From this sudden attack of unreasonable anxiety, Cassie knew instinctively that Leonora was here for a purpose, that she was once again up to something malicious. Cassie was absolutely sure of it. But try as she may, Cassie could not for the life of her imagine what it could be.

Then Mattie walked into the drawing room, and Leonora threw the match on her carefully prepared bonfire.

'Jesus Christ,' she drawled, opening her eyes as wide as she possibly could, as she stared at the tall and now strikingly handsome young man who stood before her. 'Jesus Christ, Cassie, I just don't believe it. For God's sake will you look at Mattie? It's Tyrone!'

Chapter Twenty-Four

'I wonder why Leonora thought I looked like Da,' Mattie had mused later that evening when they were alone.

He had known he was adopted since he was a child, when Cassie, as she had agreed with Tyrone when they were planning his adoption, had carefully explained his parentage to him.

'She's crazy, that's why,' Josephine replied. 'Mind you, it's not altogether crazy, because I have actually heard that some adopted children do grow to look very much like their adoptive parents. This man who plays the lead in this series I've just done, for instance, David Kaye. His son's also an actor, and he's the image of his father. And he's adopted.'

'Do you think I look like Da?' Mattie asked his mother.

'No,' Cassie lied. 'Not one bit.'

'I mean I think it would be great if I did,' Mattie said.

'I don't,' his mother answered bluntly.

Mattie had frowned at her, knowing as he did how much his mother had loved his father. But Cassie had changed the subject to Mattie's Australian adventures, and he soon had his sister and his mother helpless with laughter as he regaled them with accounts of his life down under. And as long as she laughed, and listened to her son talking, Cassie was able to put aside for the moment thoughts of Leonora's quite deliberate act of provocation.

But when Mattie and Josephine had finally gone to bed, still laughing and talking all the way up the stairs, Cassie was left alone with her terrible doubt.

She had often thought Mattie looked remarkably like Tyrone, but had always dismissed the notion as fanciful. As the boy grew, friends would often remark on the extraordinary similarity between Josephine and her adopted brother, but again, Cassie had been able to explain away such comparisons as entirely whimsical, believing that people saw only what they wanted to see.

But then as she sat staring into the dying fire, she remembered things long put out of her mind. For instance, Tyrone had introduced Mattie's mother to her: it was Tyrone who had brought Antoinette to Claremore.

He had stood with his back to her that day when he'd told her the purpose of the girl's visit, carving some more meat from the sideboard.

'She's pregnant,' he'd said.

'Not by you,' Cassie had replied.

No, not by Tyrone. Tyrone had denied it. And Tyrone never lied.

'She says we can have the baby.'

Which of course would be the most natural thing in the world. Tyrone gets a pretty young girl pregnant, the girl doesn't want to have the child, Cassie had just lost a child and couldn't have any more children without endangering her health, so what better than to offer to adopt the child, while pretending it to be somebody else's?

Particularly since the man whose child it was rumoured to be had gone off to find himself by smoking dope somewhere in India.

Particularly since the letter produced at the final adoption hearing, supposed to be from the alleged father and intended to discredit Cassie, was proved to be fraudulent, and was itself discredited.

So there was no proof, no real and actual proof that Gerald Secker had in fact been the father of Antoinette's child.

'All I need is a blood test,' Cassie told Sheila Meath on the telephone, well after midnight.

'What you need is your head examined,' Sheila had

growled in reply, angry not at being woken, but at Cassie's irrational concern. 'Of course Tyrone wasn't the father. And besides, it's perfectly true that adopted children grow to look like their adoptive parents. Look at Seamus O'Connor's two youngest. They're the spit of him, yet they're both adopted.'

'Fine. That makes sense, provided the adoptive parents live long enough. Tyrone died the year we adopted Mattie. Seamus is still very much alive. I could understand it if people thought Mattie looked like me. But they don't.'

There was silence at the other end of the telephone.

'It was just a chance remark, Cassie.'

'Leonora doesn't make chance remarks. Look, Mattie's got Tyrone's eyes, Sheila. The same long upper lip. He's even got Tyrone's hands.'

'That's just the way you see it. To me, he doesn't look like Tyrone. And more importantly,' Sheila added, 'he doesn't *behave* like Tyrone.'

'But it's all so perfectly feasible,' Cassie persisted. 'Everything tallies. Tyrone could easily have been the father. He did a lot of business with Alec Secker, the man Mattie's mother was working for at the time.'

'I remember Alec,' Sheila said. 'He moved over to England shortly afterwards. Somewhere in Berkshire.'

'Ty spent a lot of time at Alec's place.'

'It seems to me it's almost as though you *want* to believe it, Cassie,' Sheila sighed.

'Of course I don't!' Cassie replied. 'It's just that so much points to the possibility. But if I could just get a blood test.'

'You must know Mattie's blood group, surely?' Sheila asked. 'And what group Tyrone was.'

'I need to know the mother's,' Cassie replied. 'And even more importantly, the alleged father's.'

'If I were you, Cassie,' Sheila advised, 'this is one sleeping dog I'd leave well alone.'

'You're not me, Sheila,' Cassie answered. 'That's the whole point.'

'You're not going to change anything now, Cassie. And even if Tyrone had been the father, is it really so terrible? It just means you've got him in both your children.'

'It means more than that, Sheila. It means if it's true, Tyrone did something he had sworn he had never done ever in our whole life together. It means he lied to me.'

'He wasn't George Washington, my dear.'

'He was my husband, Sheila. And he swore by the truth. And if he told me a lie about Antoinette, what other lies mightn't he have told?'

What other lies indeed? Had he in fact told Cassie the truth about Leonora and himself in the south of France?

Sheila did her best to dissuade her, on the telephone that night and in person the next day. But Cassie was not to be deterred. She explained that in the clear light of day it wasn't so much that she was determined to prove Tyrone a liar, but the very opposite. She was determined to show Leonora to be the deceiver. And so obsessed was she with achieving her ambition that she quite failed to see the real motive for her adversary's malefice.

Alec Secker had no idea where his son was, and cared even less. He informed Cassie of this perfectly pleasantly when she visited him in his beautiful manor house outside Wantage, explaining how he and his son had always failed to get on since the boy was kicked out of Eton, and once Gerald had started this drugging nonsense, as he called it, he had washed his hands of him completely.

'God knows what his mother would have made of all this,' he sighed. 'But of course as you know, Liz-Anne died giving birth to Gerald's sister.'

'And you really have no idea at all of where your son might be?' Cassie reiterated.

'If he's still alive,' Secker replied evenly, 'I should imagine the Far East somewhere. But frankly, I should think he's long since dead.'

'I'm sorry.

'Yes. Well. That's how these things are.'

Alec Secker got up to pour them some more drinks, more as a punctuation, than from a necessity.

'But you remember the girl all right?'

'That Antonia girl, you mean?'

'Antoinette actually, Alec. Antoinette Brookes.'

Yes, he remembered the girl all right. A tall, very pretty girl, but somewhat remote.

'At one time, I had hopes for her and Gerald,' he recalled. 'Seemed to be just the right sort of girl for him.'

'Gerald was pretty keen on her too, right?' Cassie asked hopefully.

'I don't know so much about that,' Alec replied. 'What I do know is that she wouldn't give him a second glance. Hadn't a moment in time for him.'

'Are you sure? After all they moved in the same sort of set. Went to the same parties.'

'Not as far as I knew they didn't. No, they moved in two entirely different worlds. Gerald's was the fast Dublin young. But Antoinette – that wasn't her scene at all. Much too unsophisticated. No, no, no. Besides that, she was far too busy knocking off some wretched woman's husband.'

Cassie called Sheila from her hotel room, if only just to hear her say that she had told her so.

'Well I did, Cassie,' Sheila grumbled, 'you're just going to ruin all those years of happiness and for what? You're not going to be able to prove one damn thing. Now get on the next plane home, and forget all about it.'

'I'm not coming back until I've found Antoinette,' Cassie replied. 'We were friends. She'll tell me the truth.'

'How do you know?' Sheila asked in desperation. 'How do you know she'll tell you the truth? And if she does tell you anything, how will you know that what she tells you is the truth? If she was having an affair with Tyrone, why should she tell you now? And if she tells you she wasn't, will you believe her?'

Cassie sidestepped the question and took a sip of her

brandy. 'Alec Secker didn't know his son's blood type.'

'What's Mattie's?'

'AB, rhesus positive.'

'And Tyrone's?'

'AB, rhesus positive.'

'You're halfway home.'

'To prove paternity, Sheila, or the opposite – non-paternity, I guess you'd call it – you have to have samples from the child and both the living parents, in order to identify in detail what the experts call the agglutinogens. It's not binding anyway. You can't get a positive ID like fingerprints give you from blood groups. Proof's only conclusive if the samples differ. That's to say you can prove that someone *isn't* the child of particular parents. Rather than that they are. That's why I'm going to have someone find Antoinette.'

'But you know she's the mother,' Sheila argued.

'Sure I do,' Cassie replied. 'And she knows who was the father.'

There was no difficulty at all in locating Antoinette Brookes, now Mrs Bill Canford-Percy, the wife of a gentleman farmer and Master of Fox Hounds in southwest England.

'She'll be only too pleased to see old friends,' her rather deaf mother had told Cassie on the telephone. 'She needs all the visitors she can get these days.'

Cassie set off to visit her, assuming from her mother's remarks that Antoinette was probably suffering from the usual loneliness which afflicted certain women when they were uprooted to live in the deepest parts of the countryside. Cassie's theory was given more credibility when on arrival Cassie discovered the remoteness of the Canford-Percys' residence. It was a huge, bleak Victorian mansion, set at the end of a long unmade road five miles from the nearest village in a little known part of Somerset.

Her mother opened the door. Inside, the house was just like Claremore had been when Cassie first moved in.

'Bill's sorry to have missed you,' Mrs Brookes said as she led Cassie along a dark corridor towards a small room at the end. 'But he's off shooting somewhere.'

'I don't know your son-in-law,' Cassie explained. 'I only know your daughter, and that's from over twenty years ago.'

Mrs Brookes stopped and stared up at Cassie in the gloom.

'Twenty years ago, did you say?'

'That's right, Mrs Brookes.'

'Humphrey and I were in Baden-Baden, I think, twenty years ago.'

Mrs Brookes stared at Cassie once more, as if she was going to add something more, then deciding against it, opened the door of a small, over-heated sitting room.

By the fireplace, in a wheelchair, sat the quite unrecognisable figure of Mattie's mother.

'Someone to see you, Piglet,' her mother said. 'A friend from the old days.'

Then she turned and put a hand on Cassie's arm.

'I'll go and make us all some tea,' she said, and went, closing the door behind her.

The woman in the wheelchair didn't move. Looking at her, Cassie doubted that even had she wished to do so, she would not have been able. Her head was bent at right angles to her chest, so that her chin rested on the top of her sternum, and even through her thick cardigan and the shawl round her shoulders, Cassie could see the very visible deformation of her spinal column. Her legs were covered with a blanket and her hands lay uselessly crippled in her lap.

'Antoinette?' Cassie asked quietly as she sat down opposite her. 'Antoinette? Can you hear me?'

Antoinette didn't move. Cassie got out of her chair and knelt down directly in her eye line.

'Can you see me?' she asked.

The eyes were the only part of the woman that moved in reply. They moved up and down in their sockets.

681

'Can you hear me?'

Again the eyes moved up and down.

'Do you recognise me?'

This time the eyes moved from side to side. Cassie then sat on the floor, where Antoinette could clearly see her and explained who she was, and from where they had known each other. When she finished, she asked Antoinette if she understood and remembered. But the eyes didn't move.

Cassie explained again. More slowly, and in even simpler terms. But the eyes still didn't move.

'You don't remember who I am?' Cassie asked once more.

The pale green eyes stared back at her, almost as if they knew her well, then moved slowly once, from side to side.

The mother came back into the room with a tray of tea, just as Cassie was picking herself up off the floor and sitting back in her chair.

'That's it,' Mrs Brookes said, putting the tea tray down. 'Having a good talk about the old days.'

Refusing the rather dubious-looking scones, but accepting a cup of greyish tea, Cassie asked Antoinette's mother how much her daughter remembered. She had to ask twice and raise her voice considerably to get an answer.

'How much does she remember?' Mrs Brookes replied. 'Everything. Absolutely everything.'

'She doesn't remember who I am,' Cassie ventured.

'She remembers everything from yesterday like it was today,' the old lady continued, not in direct response. 'I'll ask her what we heard on the radio, I'll say was it "Woman's Hour"? Yes, she'll say. And it will have been.'

'She can talk then?'

'Or was it "The World At One", perhaps. Or "Morning Concert". You can't catch her out.'

'But can she talk?' Cassie said, raising her voice once more, almost in desperation.

Mrs Brookes looked at Cassie over her teacup, which she then put carefully down on a table.

'No,' she replied. 'No not really. Not in so many words.'

Antoinette remembered nothing except the events of the day before. Locked in that once beautiful head, now bowed permanently over her chest, was the truth Cassie sought, but which Antoinette could never reveal to her. Cassie moved her chair nearer and put her hands on Antoinette's.

'She probably won't be able to feel that,' her mother said. 'But she can see it all right. She says everything with her eyes. Tell her all about the times you had together. She'd like that. She does love her visitors.'

She could hardly talk about the times they'd had together in front of a mother who had known nothing of her daughter's child. So Cassie started to tell her all about Claremore instead.

But Antoinette's mother must have sensed something, because Cassie had hardly begun to talk, when the old lady put a hand on Cassie's arm.

'Nothing about horses, mind,' she said. 'You do know that, of course. Being an old friend.'

So it had been the result of a riding accident, Cassie concluded, as she sat talking about nothing in particular, to someone who had no idea at all who she was. And the more she talked, the more she became aware of the irony that the creatures to whom she had dedicated her existence, were responsible for the death of her husband, and by some frightful accident now prevented her from finding out the truth about her son's paternity.

She stayed with Antoinette until well into the evening, spending the last hour listening to a play on the radio, because she could feel the woman's unspoken need for Cassie to delay her departure. Finally, when Antoinette fell asleep, her mother rose and nodded to Cassie.

'That was very kind of you,' she said as they walked to the front door. 'Most people find ten minutes quite long enough. And it will give us both so much to talk about tomorrow.'

'Was it a hunting accident?' Cassie enquired, observing

all the sporting prints and the fox heads on the walls.

'It was a hunting accident,' Mrs Brookes replied. 'The second year of their marriage. She jumped a hedge blind, which dropped eight foot on to a main road. Jumped right into the path of an oil tanker. Never really liked hunting, you know. But of course, Bill . . . His father had been MFH, and his father before him. Terrible business altogether. Saddest of all, poor girl lost the baby she was carrying as well. I often think, if only they could have saved her baby.'

The old lady looked up at Cassie and smiled at her so sweetly that Cassie wanted to gather her in her arms and tell her that there was a baby of her daughter's, that he had been a beautiful baby, an angelic child, and that now he was a full-grown and handsome young man.

Instead she returned the smile, shook Mrs Brookes by the hand, and walked away back to her car in the pouring rain.

Sheila had been right. Nothing had been gained from it. Cassie knew this the moment she crossed back over the threshold of Claremore and embraced her children.

'Oh my God,' Mattie groaned. 'You'd think she'd been away for years. Instead of a few days.'

But the children were well used to Cassie's absences, as much as they were to her emotional reconciliations.

'What were you doing anyway?' Mattie asked. 'Buying?'

'No,' said Cassie. 'Looking.'

'And did you find what you were looking for?'

'No, Mattie. I didn't. But then that's not always such a bad thing.'

But if Cassie was doing her best to put the troublesome matter out of her mind, someone else was not.

Leonora called one morning early in the New Year.

'Sorry you couldn't make it to my party,' she said down the telephone.

'It wasn't a question of couldn't, Leonora,' Cassie replied. 'More one of wouldn't.'

Leonora ignored the put-down.

'There were lots of interesting people there,' she continued blithely. 'Not ones who can only talk pasterns and fetlocks, and who's out of what by whom. I mean really interesting people.'

'Sure,' Cassie replied. 'The sort of people who talk about who's having who, and with whom.'

'Gracious me,' Leonora laughed mockingly. 'Don't tell me at last you're developing a dirty mind. I'll tell you who was at the party. A guy who was in Thailand with Gerry Secker.'

Cassie waited a moment before replying.

'Why should I want to know that?' Cassie asked evenly.

'Oh because I heard tell you were looking for Gerry.'

'Who told you?'

'You won't find him,' Leonora replied. 'He's dead.'

She put the telephone down before Cassie could ask any further questions. For one moment, Cassie was tempted to pick up the telephone and call Leonora back at once, to demand an explanation. Then she realised that would be playing right into Leonora's hands, so instead she called Bunbury and took him out for a long walk up the hills.

As she walked, with the dog running ahead of her up the track, barking joyfully with the sheer exhilaration of being alive, Cassie decided to put any further thoughts as to Mattie's parentage from her mind. She knew that Leonora was out to worry her, and although she had no idea at all as to why, she determined to let the question of whether or not Tyrone had fathered Mattie remain unanswered. In one way she saw it would be better if he had, because at least Cassie would know what sort of person her adopted son's father had been. He would have been the man she loved, and not a rather unpleasant, selfish and wayward young blood; Mattie at least would have the blood of Tyrone coursing through his veins. And if that indeed was the fact of the matter, Cassie knew it was one with which she could learn to live, and eventually for which she most probably would grow thankful.

But could she learn to live with the fact that Tyrone had lied to her? That was something with which, however long and far she walked her beloved dog, Cassie could not yet come to terms.

Towards the end of February, The Nightingale returned from his Italian winter holiday. He had wintered well, and when Cassie supervised the horse's unloading, she was once more grateful that Tyrone had gone to school on the wisdom of the great Vincent O'Brien, who had first pointed out the efficacy of sending top horses away for the worst of the winter. He'd gone on record as saying that the Italians had been sending their horses to Pisa for generations, and because of the mild Mediterranean climate, with none of the debilitating cold winds suffered by Ireland and England, horses did tremendously well out there.

And The Nightingale, once they got his rugs off, proved no exception.

'He looks as if he'll be ready to race by April,' Mattie said, running his hand along the horse's neck and quarters. 'And I'll tell you something else, Ma. This is quite some horse.'

Josephine had returned to England to publicise the launch of her television series, and Mattie was now officially the assistant trainer at Claremore. It had been agreed between mother and son that Mattie should stay on to gain the necessary first-hand experience of training in Ireland before setting himself up on his own.

Over dinner that night, both delighted with Nightie's well-being, the plan for the big campaign was discussed. If the horse came easily to hand, then it was agreed he should have just the one run before going to Newmarket for the 2,000 Guineas.

'If you take in the English rather than the Irish 2,000,' Mattie said, 'you do know that means a head-to-head with Millstone Grit?'

'We're going to have to take him on sometime, Mattie,' Cassie replied.

'We'd win our own 2,000 with the horse in gumboots.'

'If Nightie's as good as I think, then I want him to do it the traditional way. The English 2,000, the Epsom Derby, the King George and Queen Elizabeth, and then either the Leger, or the Prix de L'Arc de Triomphe.'

'Anything else you'd like for Christmas?' laughed Mattie.

'This isn't for me, Mattie,' Cassie answered. 'You know who this is for.'

And as she looked across the kitchen table at her son, she found herself looking into her late husband's eyes.

March for once was mild and warm, so spring was early, and all the horses that had wintered abroad came to hand early as hoped. By the end of the second week. of the month, Dexter, who had now moved out into a cottage on the edge of the village, arrived to start riding The Nightingale at work. He was more impressed than ever with the big horse.

'OK, so we're really in business, Guv'nor,' he told Cassie with a cheerful grin, as he vaulted lightly off the horse on the gallops, to allow the youngster a pick of fresh grass.

'Did you ever doubt it for a moment?' Cassie asked, walking round the horse, checking his legs.

'Some of the horses,' Dex replied, shaking his head, 'they're one-year wonders. You know that as well as I do. Brilliant two-year-olds, and they just don't train on. But this fellah – boy. I'm just dying to press the go button.'

'I don't want you to do that yet, Dex,' Cassie told him. 'We're going for the Gladness, not the Ascot Guineas Trial, and if he's the horse we think, I don't want to see it. I want him to win cleverly.'

'You don't want to show your hand,' Dexter nodded. 'OK.'

'No,' Cassie finished. 'It's not that I don't want to show my hand. It's an early April race, and I don't want you raiding the locker. I want the horse to have an easy race, so that he thinks, great, racing's still a nice experience. I've seen a lot of really good three-year-olds lose interest just like that, because of one tough race that came that bit too early.'

Just over two weeks later, Cassie began to get the measure of the opposition. Millstone Grit started firm favourite for the Ascot 2,000 Guineas, and galloped home in record time, slaughtering four other English-bred Guineas hopes. Excuses were made by the beaten horses' connections that their animals were still backward, but as Cassie, Dex and Mattie could see from the videotape of the afternoon's racing, the only reason all the other horses lost was because they were beaten by an exceptional animal.

'Just when it was looking so goddam easy,' Dex sighed, watching the slow-motion replay. 'He galloped them stupid.'

Cassie looked at her stopwatch and the notes she'd made.

'His split timings are pretty interesting,' she told them. 'They bear out exactly what you say about galloping them dead. He does all his best work early on in the race, and in fact his last furlong is one of his slowest. But by then he's got 'em all ringing the undertaker. He could come home turning somersaults.'

'Ssshhh,' said Mattie. 'They're just going to talk to the trainer.'

The interviewer introduced Jonathan Keating, a tall and very debonair man, who affected an ultra-laid-back image, but in fact was one of the turf's few real geniuses.

'Well, Jonathan,' the interviewer started, 'it looks as though you've got a really good one here.'

'Yes, it does, doesn't it?' Keating answered, with a smile.

'How good?'

'How long's a piece of string, Julian?'

The interviewer grinned, but was well used to Keating's apparently flippant approach.

'He looks good enough to win a Guineas to me,' Julian Wilson replied.

'Then perhaps you should take out a training licence,' Keating told him, poker-faced.

'Seriously.'

'He was a very good two-year-old, and now he looks as if he'll make a very good three-year-old. He'll certainly have a go for the Guineas.'

'With The Nightingale as his most serious rival, I suppose.'

'The Nightingale and the French horse, Pastiche. And you can't rule out Never Mind. If ever a horse was purpose-bred to win a Guineas, it's him.'

'What about the Derby?'

'Let's get Newmarket out of the way first, shall we?' Julian Wilson thanked Millstone Grit's trainer and turned back to the camera.

'If Jonathan Keating gets any more laid back,' Mattie said, 'he won't be able to get up in the morning.'

'Who does own Millstone Grit?' Cassie asked, looking for the newspaper. 'I guess I've become a typical trainer. I never look to see who the owner is.'

'A fellow American,' said Dex, flicking open another Diet Coke. 'Whatsisname.'

'If you both stop talking,' Mattie complained, 'we might actually get to hear.'

'. . . who's here today to see her horse win, without her husband,' Julian Wilson concluded his introduction to the winning owner, 'who's abroad in the Middle East on business.'

'Jesus,' Mattie hissed, forcing Cassie to look up as the camera cut to a beautiful woman standing by the interviewer. 'Jesus God – look! It's Leobloodynora!'

The tape stopped there, as Cassie had left it timed only for the big race. Mattie wound the tape back a little way until he found the single of Leonora smiling as she was introduced. Then he froze the frame to a still, and leaning forward covered Leonora's smile with one hand.

Over his hand, Leonora's grey-blue eyes stared at them coldly without one iota of warmth.

'I'd say the eyes have it,' Mattie said, turning to his mother with a grin. 'Wouldn't you, Guv'nor?'

Cassie stared at the unmoving image of Leonora, and once again felt her blood chill. Leonora was the owner of Millstone Grit. Or rather she must be the co-owner with her husband, because in the pictures Cassie had seen of the horse in the sporting press, she had failed to recognise the owner's colours.

Leonora owned the now co-favourite for the 2,000 Guineas.

Leonora owned the only horse which on paper Cassie knew was capable of beating The Nightingale.

As Cassie continued with the preparation of her own horse, she occasionally wondered why Leonora hadn't raised the subject when she had visited Claremore before Christmas, or when she had telephoned Cassie in the New Year. Perhaps she assumed that Cassie already knew, and was waiting for Cassie to mention it. Whatever the reason, Cassie knew the omission was quite deliberate. Leonora was far too skilled a card player to miss any chance of a bluff, a double bluff or a finesse.

Her ploy may well have been intended to worry Cassie, to shake her confidence at a vital moment. But in fact it had quite the opposite effect on her rival, who became only more determined to succeed.

'It's been rather like shooting in the dark up till now,' Cassie told Mattie as they watched Nightie's last piece of work before his first race of the season. 'But now I can see what's in my sights—'

Cassie smiled, while her son looked round at her.

'I thought it was the Derby that was in your sights?' he asked.

'It was. And it still is,' Cassie replied. 'But this has kind of altered things somewhat.'

'You mean it's no longer "just a race"?'

'You got it, Mattie. This isn't "just a race" any more. This, to mix my metaphor, is a whole damn new ballgame altogether.'

The Nightingale thundered past them, nostrils flared and ears pricked, and with Dex perched in perfect balance on the horse's withers.

Cassie and Mattie's watches clicked to stop, and they both looked at the times.

'Wow,' said Mattie.

'You said it,' Cassie agreed. 'And that's still only three-quarter speed.'

The going was perfect for the Gladness Stakes, the sun and April breezes just sufficiently drying out the worst from the showers which had fallen earlier in the week. The field of ten runners included all the best of the native Guineas hopes. Once again the big horse went down very scratchily to the start, but this time, the 'whisper' being so strong about the Claremore hot-shot, the punters weren't to be denied, and The Nightingale started the 4/6 favourite. Dex rode the race absolutely to his orders, keeping the big fellow loping along on the outside, well free of trouble. For those in the stands who'd put their money where their mouths were, it must have looked for a moment that the jockey had left it too late, because there was a very audible gasp from the packed crowd as the leaders kicked for home, with the odds-on favourite still idling half a dozen lengths adrift. Then inside the distance Dex just shook up the big horse, and in a matter of a few strides it was all over, The Nightingale getting up and winning by three quarters of a length.

Not a lot of so-called experts spotted the ease with which the big dark horse won. They had already fixed in their mind's eye the facility of Millstone Grit's Ascot victory and the distance by which he had achieved it, and so consequently, although the *Telegraph* called Nightie's win 'clever', and *The Times* reported that 'Cassie Rosse's big horse seemed to win as he liked', the consensus of opinion was that the horse looked idle, and was unlikely to stay with the blistering gallop Millstone Grit was sure to get at Newmarket. As a consequence, Millstone Grit was installed as favourite at 5/4 for the Guineas, with The Nightingale available at 11/8.

Only *Sporting Life* read the Curragh Race accurately.

After the way the Claremore horse strolled home at the Curragh, it's no longer a question of who's going to win the 2,000 Guineas, but who's going to come second. The Nightingale played with a very high-class field, and when Dexter Bryant simply shook the reins at him, the big horse at once lengthened his stride and strolled away from Bless Me Father and Levitation, who were both all out at the post.

The reporter then went on to discuss the time of the race, which was only half a second outside the Curragh record for seven furlongs, and concluded very confidently that The Nightingale would win at Newmarket at the beginning of May 'with one leg tied behind his saddle'.

The home money started to pour in for the Irish second favourite, and Cassie, although her security system was, she hoped, second to none, took the precaution of hiring extra guards and dogs, to keep away any unwelcome visitors from the yard. Every move the horse made was now done under carefully arranged surveillance and protection, even though at Claremore they were in the fortunate position of not having to leave the estate to get to the gallops, since both the turf and the all-weather strips were safely contained within Claremore's stone walls and high fences.

Nonetheless, two lads stayed awake in shifts outside Nightie's box, and the close-circuit television never slept either.

As it happened, it wasn't The Nightingale who went wrong before the Guineas. The day before the big race,

Millstone Grit went down in his box with what appeared to be an attack of colic, which as the public afterwards learned, posed an enormous problem for Jonathan Keating, his trainer. Under the rules of racing, no medication can be administered to a horse the day before a race, and in order to relax muscular and intestinal spasms of a horse suffering from colitis, it is necessary to inject an antispasmodic drug. So Keating was faced with a set of unenviable choices. He could hope it was just a mild attack and do nothing. If that hope proved valid, the horse would recover quickly and by himself, and be able to race the next day. He could do nothing in the hope that it was indeed a mild attack, be proved wrong, and lose his best horse with a twisted gut. Or he could inject the horse, thus ruling out the possibility of the horse dying, but also of the favourite being able to run in the Guineas.

He wisely chose the better safe than sorry path, and had his vet inject the horse. As it happened, it was a bad attack of colitis, and it took more than just an antispasmodic drug to save him. It took all the skill of one of Newmarket's top vets and the faithful round-the-clock attentions of the horse's devoted lad.

The punters, however, did not see it that way, and the eleventh-hour withdrawal of the favourite was not taken well. Jonathan Keating was subjected to some terrifying verbal abuse on his arrival at the course and, deciding in disgust to miss the race and return immediately to his home, was then knocked unconscious by a full and flying beer can. He was rushed off to hospital where they had to put eight stitches in the wound to his head.

There were also reports in all the morning papers of a full-scale row between Leonora and Keating, the former accusing the latter of ill-considered thinking and over-hasty action with regard to the treatment of her horse. Keating was reported as telling Leonora she could always take her horse elsewhere, and the latest rumour buzzing round the course was that was exactly what Mrs Charles C. Lovett Andrew intended to do.

693

Mrs Charles C. Lovett Andrew was also highly noticeable by her absence from the racecourse.

Happily, The Nightingale had journeyed well, and was so relaxed when Liam pulled him out of his stable on the morning of the race that it might have seemed that the horse had been in Newmarket all his life. Dex rode him in a gentle exercise canter and the big horse worked as he always did, easily and sensibly.

'You can count your money, folks,' Dex said as they put the horse up for his breakfast. 'There's nobody going to beat my fellah.'

On the way to the parade for the race, the French horse played up and, breaking ranks, aimed a kick at The Nightingale before his jockey could pull him back into line. The kick, which, had it landed might well have broken one of Nightie's' legs, missed the Claremore horse by inches, thanks mainly to Dex's quick reactions. But the incident unsettled the Irish horse and he started to sweat up profusely, which was most unusual for a horse already renowned for his extraordinarily mature temperament, so much so that by the time the horses were being led out in alphabetical order, The Nightingale was beginning to shake almost uncontrollably. Rather than upset the favourite perhaps irrevocably, Dexter, gambling on nothing worse than a heavy fine, pulled his horse out of line and cantered him slowly down to the start prematurely.

'What in hell is he doing?' Cassie asked Matt as they watched the incident from the stands. 'Does he want us to lose the race before it's even run?'

But fortunately for Dex, the French horse was now behaving so badly, rearing and plunging in the middle of the course, that all the other horses had broken line and were making their way to the start in any order they liked.

Cassie swung her glasses back down the course and focused on her horse. With great relief she saw Dex had cooled him right down and was walking the last two furlongs to the starting stalls. By the time all the runners had reached the start, and the roll was being called, Nightie's ears were pricked again, and Dex was quietly stroking his neck, talking to him all the while.

'I don't think I can watch,' Cassie told her son, putting her glasses down.

'Girls,' Mattie sighed.

Cassie picked her glasses back up.

'They're under starter's orders!' the commentator announced, 'and they're off!'

The Nightingale was drawn two off the rails on the far side of the straight mile. He was so fast out of the stalls that Cassie saw that Dex had to take a pull at him to settle. But the horse was such a sensible animal that he at once took note of his rider, and dropped back to settle near the rear of the tightly bunched field. The French horse Pastiche, who had caused all the trouble, was taking them along at a rattling good gallop, which was sure to find out those horses who didn't genuinely get the trip. There certainly could be no excuses for it being 'a funny sort of race'. All the horses and jockeys concerned knew they were in a proper contest.

Pastiche dropped away three furlongs from home, and at the Bushes, Pat Richards set Never Mind alight, and the horse responded by lengthening and going two lengths clear. Biopic, the quietly fancied third favourite, set off in pursuit, with Cimeno, one of the outsiders, matching him stride for stride.

Dex, meanwhile, was lying about sixth, two off the rails, and apparently blocked behind a wall of three beaten horses.

Then coming into the dip, The Nightingale appeared as if by magic in the centre of the course, Dex having smoothly switched him out from his cover and shown him daylight. As soon as he shook him up, The Nightingale knew he meant business, and for the first time in his life slipped into top gear. The result was sensational. The sudden acceleration, coupled with the big horse's enormous stride, made the leading three horses, who only one second before would have appeared to have had the finish between them, look as though they were treading water.

The Nightingale swallowed them up, with Dex riding him out only with hands and heels, to win by 2½ lengths.

Cassie asked her son to lead the horse in, but he refused, as did Josephine, who had been excused from rehearsals for her new play and had arrived two minutes before the 'off'. And so to tumultuous cheers from the punters, and a positive avalanche of Irish hats in the air, Cassie Rosse from Westboro Falls, New Hampshire, led in Claremore's and her own first Classic winner.

'What a race,' Brough Scott said to her on television shortly afterwards.

'What a horse,' Cassie smiled.

'Is he the superhorse everyone is saying he is, Cassie?'

'Ask me that after Epsom, Brough, or at Longchamps in October.'

'You think he's that good, do you?'

'From the way he won today,' Cassie replied, 'I'll be lucky if I ever have another horse half as good as this fellow.'

'And of course he's homebred, just to make the fairy tale complete.'

'He's homebred and made, absolutely. And I don't think you've seen the best of him yet.'

Brough Scott paused as he consulted a slip of paper he'd been handed off camera.

'Hills go even money for Epsom, and the Tote 5/4,' he told Cassie.

'I'd take the 5/4, wouldn't you?' Cassie smiled. 'You won't get that on the day.'

'Will he handle Epsom? He's a very big horse.'

'They're always either too big or too small, aren't they? Until they win. And then they're just right. He'll handle Epsom. I'll make sure of that.'

The last remark passed unnoticed by everyone, except the staff at Claremore. They knew its significance, and they knew, like their Guv'nor, that Nightie would handle Epsom all right.

Because Cassie, an unconventional woman in a conventional man's world, did not always respect the orthodoxies of her profession. When Tyrone had been alive, she had always been bombarding him with questions about certain training practices she privately considered either archaic or just downright illogical.

'Why, for instance,' she had often asked him, 'if people aren't certain their horses will stay say seven furlongs or a mile, why don't they school them seriously over that distance instead of waiting till they race in public and wasting the punters' money when their horses run out of steam?'

'Because that's what we call leaving your race on the gallops,' Tyrone had sighed.

'Nonsense,' Cassie had countered. 'It's simply because it's the way you've always done it.'

So when her time had come to take control of Claremore, and whenever she had a horse in her care she wasn't sure would get a certain distance, she would have a mixed gallop with some of Willie Moore's string, having converted Willie to her way of thinking.

'Look,' she'd told him, 'if you want to race them over seven furlongs, gallop them over seven. If you want to race them over a mile and a half, gallop them over a mile and a half. You don't have to take them racing clip. Take them the same speed as you normally work them. Three quarters speed. And the ones who are going best at the end are going to be the ones who are going to get the trip best on the course.'

So far, with the exception of the rogue horses who never did any work at home, saving it all for the races, Cassie had proved herself right. When she announced that a Claremore horse got a mile and two, it invariably did. And she never once used as an excuse for a horse of hers that got beaten that it was because it didn't get the trip.

'Horses get bored too,' she'd told Tyrone. 'They

shouldn't be standing in all day. Arkle used to help round up the sheep on the farm. Old Pat Sullivan told me he used to hack his horses five miles to the races and win on them. We're too soft on our lot. They're mollycoddled. They should all be doing more. Toughening up. Keeping their minds open.'

And so her horses swam, and were turned out in the paddocks on warm afternoons, and were exercised twice a day, the more uppity ones having half an hour on the lunge or the horsewalker besides their twice-daily constitutional. And if they were fit, they raced as often as possible, the only proviso being that they had to have the ground they liked.

'I've seen too many good horses being ruined by being made to run on the firm,' she told Mattie. 'Your father wouldn't do it, and neither will I. Claremore horses don't race on concrete.'

By the same right if any of her horses were to run at Epsom, then they had to learn how to gallop down hills.

Hills were one thing Cassie did not have to construct at Claremore, for she was surrounded by them. What she did do, though, was create a Tattenham Hill and Corner in County Wicklow. And oddly enough, although it was perfectly visible to the eye of any visitor, invited or uninvited, the long-railed drop Cassie built down the side of the hill behind the house itself rarely raised any curiosity whatsoever.

Tomas had called it Herself's Folly, and when Cassie had broached the idea to him, had suffered one of his minor fits of apoplexy and asked her if she wanted to break all her horses' legs or what?

'If they're going to break a leg coming down hill, Tomas,' she'd answered him, 'I'd rather they learned not to do it at home.'

'Dear God in heaven,' Tomas had sighed. 'You're becoming more Irish than the Irish.'

'What I mean,' Cassie had continued, 'is that people don't think twice about running their horses at tracks with severe gradients, like Epsom, and Lingfield, and Cheltenham over the jumps. And yet they think you're crazy if you propose schooling a horse at racing pace downhill. You wouldn't go out hunting on a horse that couldn't gallop downhill.'

'I wouldn't go out hunting,' Tomas replied. 'You need a plate in your head to follow hounds.'

'Mark my words, Tomas,' Cassie had warned him. 'When and if I ever have a runner in the Esom Derby, the one thing we're going to be sure of is that he can handle the track.'

And so The Nightingale, who'd already been introduced to Claremore's version of Tattenham Hill, was given two very serious schools along the rise of the hill and down its long left-handed slope.

He handled both outings perfectly. Dexter kept the horse perfectly balanced, the first time making him run down the hill on the rails, with the other horses in front and to the side of him, and the second time making him hit the front as they came off the final bend.

'The only thing we can't re-create,' Cassie said at the daily debriefing, 'besides the crowds, and the funfair, and that amazing, crazy atmosphere, is the camber of the straight. You've ridden it, Dex, so you know it. But what we've got to watch out for is tired horses inside you rolling off the rail and coming across the course because of the camber. We have to be on the rail, or one or two off it at most. And we mustn't be more than eight of the pace coming off that last bend. I'd prefer to see you make your run up on the rails, but if they shut you out, you're going to have to sail for home a lot earlier than old Nightie's used to. You get something taking you on the inside who starts to tire and he'll carry you over to the grandstand.'

The three of them, Cassie, Dex and Mattie, ran the race in their heads a thousand times. They examined every eventuality, and at the end of each session, they always came to the same conclusion.

'Given you don't get hopelessly boxed in, Dex,' Cassie

recapped, 'which if that happens on a horse like Nightie will be your own goddam fault, because he has the speed and dexterity to get you out of *anything*, then the only way you get beat is if Millstone Grit poaches too big a lead. Now he's an out and out galloper. He's going to make it all from the moment those stalls fly open, till the moment he passes the winning post. He's going to try and gallop your speed out of you – blunt you, psyche you out of it. And remember – a horse like that can easily break the spirit of his rivals. If he comes into the home-straight eight, ten lengths clear, my money will be on him to beat us. That horse doesn't stop galloping. You watch that video of Ascot. He's easing up. Joe Peters drops his hands two hundred yards from home.'

'Your friend's running Millstone's stable companion as well,' Dex said. 'Now why's that? He's a no-hoper, and he sure can't be in it to make the pace.'

'No,' Cassie answered thoughtfully. 'He's running to stop us winning.'

But that was Leonora's last resort. Her next move was intended to have a far greater and a more immediate effect.

It started with a telephone call.

'Hi,' she said to Cassie one week before the Derby. 'I'm real sorry about your horse.'

Cassie took a deep breath and kept her voice as calm as she could. 'There's nothing the matter with my horse, Leonora,' she replied.

'Not according to you there isn't, darling,' Leonora drawled back. 'But there is to me.'

'What?' Cassie asked.

'Oh,' Leonora replied lightly. 'Just the fact that he's running in the Derby. That's what I'm sorry about.'

'Sure,' Cassie said, about to hang up, 'but I guess this is just one of the cases where we'll have to let the best horse win.'

'Not my thinking at all, sweetheart,' Leonora purred. 'So why don't I pop on over to see you and we can have a little chat?'

'You're banned from here, Leonora. My staff have been

700

given explicit instructions to stop you entering Claremore.'

There was a short silence, during which Cassie could hear the click of a lighter, and the inhalation of a cigarette.

'Too bad,' said Cassie. 'Started smoking again, Leonora?'

'Listen, Cassie Rosse,' Leonora replied, in a complete change of mood. 'If you know what's good for you, you'll get your ass over here. Because it concerns your goddam horse. And that spoilt little brat of an adopted son.'

The telephone went dead. And so momentarily did Cassie's feelings. Then she walked slowly to the door and called Mattie.

He answered immediately, coming out of the study where he'd been watching the video.

Cassie looked at him and smiled, before collecting her car keys from the hall table.

'I have to go out, Mattie,' she told him. 'Don't wait up.'

Leonora was by herself in the drawing room, drinking. She glanced at Cassie, then poured herself another brandy.

'At least you had the good sense to come,' she said.

'You have something to say to me about my horse,' Cassie replied, 'and apparently about my son.'

'Sit down,' Leonora snapped.

'No thanks,' Cassie answered.

'Do as you like,' said Leonora, crossing to a large deeply cushioned sofa and collapsing on to it, still clasping her drink. 'Do cartwheels.'

She shook back her long blonde hair and sighed, staring up at the ceiling.

'Well?' Cassie said.

'That's what Tyrone always used to say,' Leonora remembered, still staring at the ceiling. 'Well.'

Cassie bristled with rage at the impertinence of Leonora reminding her of what her husband used to say. But she knew that to show one moment of anger was to lose

701

the initiative in whatever game it was Leonora was now playing.

'I haven't got all evening, Leonora.'

'Jesus Christ, Cassie. You're one great long boring cliché.'

'Just get to the point, Leonora. What about my horse?'

'He's not going to win the Derby.'

'We'll see about that come next Wednesday.'

'You didn't hear what I said, Cassie sweetheart. I said your horse isn't going to win the Derby. And do you know why he isn't going to win it? Because he isn't going to run in it.'

Leonora slowly pulled the edge of her blonde fringe aside with the third finger of one hand and regarded Cassie from under half-shut eyelids.

'There's nothing wrong with The Nightingale.'

'No, darling. But there's going to be.'

'Who says?'

'I do.'

Cassie held Leonora's gaze, and herself together, although inside she was sickened near death with fear.

'If you do anything to The Nightingale—' Cassie began.

'I'm not going to do a thing, sweetheart,' Leonora sighed. 'You are.'

'And what am I going to do?'

'You're going to withdraw him.'

Leonora threw her cigarette away into the empty fireplace, and got up to pour herself another drink.

Cassie stood in silence as she tried to work out why Leonora should imagine Cassie would withdraw the ante-post favourite. It was such an absurd and ridiculous contention that Cassie knew Leonora must have good reason.

'OK,' she said, sitting as casually as she could on the arm of a chair, 'let's hear it, Leonora.'

'Well,' Leonora replied, coming back to the sofa where she was sitting. 'It's all very simple. If it wasn't for you, for your horse rather, this would be my Derby. It probably will be anyway, but I want to make quite sure. And the only way I can make quite, quite sure, is to remove the only horse capable of beating mine. Which is yours.'

Leonora smiled, a pretend sweet-little-thing smile, and lit up another cigarette.

'There are fourteen other runners in the field, Leonora. Anything can happen in a horse race.'

'Sure, honey. I'm just trying to minimise the risks. And all things being equal, as they say, without The Nightingale, I win. Pillar to post.'

'So what if you do?' Cassie said, rising. 'The Nightingale runs.'

'In that case, you poor thing, you'll never know.'

Turning back, Cassie found Leonora watching her with an almost idle curiosity.

'What won't I know?' Cassie asked, dreading and half anticipating the answer.

'You'll never know who was the brat's father,' Leonora replied. 'And you'll never know the truth about your husband and me.'

'Which of course if I pull my horse out of the Derby, you'll volunteer – quite truthfully – just like that.'

Leonora threw back her head and gave her famous hoot of laughter.

'Sometimes you're such a silly bitch, Cassie. You don't think I have proof? You think I'd expect you to take your horse out on an idle promise from someone like me? Jesus.'

Leonora stretched and once more got up from her sofa, strolling across to a bureau with a deliberate insolence. She unlocked the desk.

Cassie remembered another desk unlocking, and another secret being revealed.

Leonora took out from the bureau what Cassie knew she must take out. A letter. Cassie remained standing where she was, refusing to plead for information. Leonora laughed and flapped the letter at her, all but half a dozen paces from where Cassie stood. Still Cassie said nothing. Leonora squared the letter up in her hands and turned it so that Cassie could see the writing. The writing was unmistakably Tyrone's.

Cassie could have snatched it easily. She could have taken it from Leonora's hands in a second. She was fit and fast, and Leonora was drunk and slow. But she didn't move, because she knew the letter wasn't in the envelope.

'I'm disappointed,' Leonora told her. 'I really thought you'd try to grab it. I guess I should have credited you with a little more intelligence. Because of course you're right. The letter isn't in the envelope. The letter is with my lawyer. Along with all darling Ty's other letters.'

'I'd like a drink please, if I may,' Cassie said, more to buy time than anything.

'Sure you do,' Leonora said, pouring her one. 'If I were in your shoes, I'd want half a dozen.'

Leonora handed Cassie a brandy, and then walked away from her back to her seat. Cassie stood and drank the brandy, then put down the empty glass.

'You propose that I should take my horse out of the Derby in return for some letters my husband wrote you.'

'You got it? Full marks, McGann!'

'Who's to say there's anything of import in them?'

'Who's to say why he wrote to me?' Leonora smiled again, her smile fast becoming a leer. 'You're after the truth, Cassie sweetheart. The truth about Mattie. And the truth about your husband and me. You're in a gambler's profession. So I guess you're just going to have trust to old Lady Luck. Like all those poor saps do who bet on your nags.'

Cassie picked up her handbag. 'No deal,' she said, turning for the door.

'What do you mean!' came a scream from behind her. 'No deal!'

'Exactly that. The Nightingale runs.'

Leonora ran round in front of Cassie and got to the door first. 'I'll see you in hell!'

'Do that. But I'm not taking my horse out.'

'Surely to Christ you're not worrying about the stupid punters, are you!'

'I'm just thinking about one person, Leonora. One person only. And that's why the horse runs.'

'I'll let the newspapers have the letters!'

'OK.'

'They're all about our affair! And Ty's affair with Antoinette! And how unknown to you he's the father of your adopted child! Jesus – they're so sensational they'll have to print extra editions!'

'I really have to go, Leonora. Now get out of my way, before I throw you out of it.'

'See sense, you stupid bitch! Take your goddam horse out of the race! Or I'll make your family a laughing stock!'

Cassie looked at her, at the desperation on Leonora's face, at the hate in her eyes.

'It's too late, Leonora,' she said. 'Tyrone's dead.'

'And what in hell is that supposed to mean?'

'It means you couldn't get him to love you when he was alive, and you're certainly not going to get him to love you now he's dead. Not even in make-believe. Tyrone loved me. Sure, you loved him, and I guess he was most probably the only man you ever really have loved. But he'd never have fallen for you. Or for your tricks. He thought you were ridiculous. He thought you were pathetic. He used to laugh about you.'

'You're lying!' Leonora screamed. 'You're a filthy, lying, stupid bitch!'

'Sure I am,' Cassie said. 'But the horse still runs.'

'He'll lose! I'll see to it that he loses! My horse will knock the shit out of him!'

'On the contrary.'

'You want a bet?' Leonora was staring at Cassie with mad, drink-reddened eyes. 'I said, you want a bet!'

'I heard you the first time, Leonora.'

'My horse will beat yours any day of the week!'

Cassie looked at her a little longer, then shrugged.

'In that case, why all the fuss to make me withdraw him?'

705

'For Christ's sake, I told you! To make mine a certainty!'

Cassie looked at Leonora, spread-eagled absurdly across the door, then walked back into the room.

'I'll make you a bet, Leonora. And you know what that is? I'll bet you anything you like to name there's nothing incriminating in these letters you say you have.'

'You'll only get to find that out if you ever get to read them!' Leonora hissed.

'That's true,' Cassie agreed. 'But if you want to make a bet, then that's mine.'

Leonora remained leaning against the door for a moment, then came back over to the drinks table.

'You fancy betting the letters on the result of the Derby?' she asked.

'OK,' Cassie shrugged. 'If that's how you want it. The Nightingale wins, I get the letters.'

'And if Millstone Grit wins? What do I get?'

'You get to win the Derby.'

'Come on, Cassie McGann. I'm not kidding. I don't want prize money. I'm a millionairess ten times over. I want a side stake.'

'You want something more than winning the Derby?'

'You bet I do. You said you'd bet me anything I liked.'

Cassie looked at Leonora, who was standing with her back to Cassie, drinking another large brandy.

'Did I?'

'You said – your words – "I'll bet you anything you like there's nothing incriminating in these letters." You going to stand by that? You're that confident?'

'Sure I am,' Cassie replied. 'Why? What do you have in mind?'

Leonora turned round and slowly smiled.

'Claremore.'

As Cassie drove home, with the roof down on her BMW 325 convertible, she felt oddly calm about her decision. If, or rather when, The Nightingale won, then she would have achieved her heart's ambition, and fulfilled her posthumous promise to Tyrone that she would win the Derby for him. She would also get custody of the letters, although she now firmly believed there was nothing incriminating in them whatsoever. Leonora's desperation had made her sure of that. And if her horse lost, and there was always that possibility, however remote, she would also lose Claremore. But then if The Nightingale lost, she would have lost everything anyway, everything she had built on the result. So there would be no more point in staying on at Claremore. She would have failed in her task. She would have failed herself. Worst of all, she would have failed Tyrone.

But then The Nightingale was not going to lose.

She stopped her car on the top of a hill high above Claremore and looked down at the estate below her, at the beautiful house, its stone glowing in the warmth of the evening sun, at the immaculate stable yard, the gallops stretching across the fields, and at the blue mountains rising far in the distance. It was a dream come true. Almost. But without The Nightingale being called first past the post that following Wednesday, it would all have been in vain. This was a once-in-a-lifetime opportunity.

Then she remembered two other things; the brilliance of her horse; and the strength of Tyrone's credo.

'To my mind there's only one way to achieve immortality on the turf,' Tyrone had maintained. 'And that's by winning the Derby. Not a derby, small "d" derby. But the Derby. The Epsom Derby. The daddy of them all. You can forget all the other Classic and Group I races. The horses people remember are the ones that win at the Epsom Derby.'

For a moment though, as Cassie looked down again at the beautiful house below her, and remembered all the work which had gone into its restoration, and the establishment of Claremore as one of Europe's top racing yards, she thought she must have taken complete leave of her senses, to risk it all on the result of a horserace, albeit the Epsom Derby. Had she done it in a do-or-die attempt to

707

escape finally from Leonora's thrall? She had seen in Leonora's eyes when she had turned round how much she meant it, how much she wanted Claremore. And she had realised as she was driving home why it was. Because Leonora wanted to be her, to be Cassie. Why, she had no idea. But that was how it had been, since they first met at the Academy. She had pursued and persecuted Cassie remorselessly, because even with her great wealth and her stunning beauty, Leonora, the girl who had everything when they first crossed paths, was jealous even then of Cassie, the girl who had nothing.

Which was why Cassie knew deep in her heart there was nothing incriminating in those letters, nothing which would prove Leonora's allegations of an affair. And if there was something in them which established Tyrone as Mattie's father, then that was something with which Cassie would have to learn to live. She had already in her heart forgiven Tyrone any trespass, and with God's help she knew she could eventually forgive any possible deception.

Even so she wished he was there by her side, to put his strong arm around her, to cheer her and make her laugh, and give her the strength to hold out. It was all very well, she thought wryly, being a woman in a man's world. But you were still a woman.

And then she heard it. From the quiet of the still dark green woodland far below her, rose a bird song of such immeasurable richness, of such variety and vigour, that the world and time stood quite and utterly still, and the clouds fell away from the face of the rising moon, as the air was filled with the deep and unforgettable throbbing of a nightingale's song. Then the note changed to a long-drawn-out and wonderfully plaintive piping note; and as it did so, Cassie looked up to the darkening blue of the night skies above her, and thanked God for making sense of her madness.

Interim Three

High on the Epsom Downs, the camera has stopped rolling, and the crew are packing their equipment away into various cars, busy talking about the merits and demerits of their present modes of transport. But the interviewer is far more interested in the pluses and minuses of the contenders for the following day's big race.

'Off the record,' he asks the pretty woman by his side as they stroll back down Tattenham Hill, 'is Millstone Grit your only real worry?'

'I hear Never Mind has improved several pounds since we beat him at Newmarket,' the woman replies. 'And I don't know a great deal about Paul Lestoque's horse, En Vas, except he doesn't appear to be bred to get the trip.'

'Strictly speaking, on a line through Russian Defector,' the interviewer points out, 'who beat En Vas at Chantilly, but who finished out the back door himself at Chester behind Daringdoo, the French challenge looks held.'

'Operanatomy ran a good trial at Lingfield, but his times weren't anything to write home about.'

'And he didn't beat much,' the man agrees. 'So really it's a two-horse race?'

The woman nods her head. 'If they both get a clear run.'

The man stops and digs his heel into the turf. 'If it stays like this, the going should be perfect.'

'Ideal,' the woman replies. 'Nightie should bounce off this.'

'How is the big fellow?' the man enquires. 'How did he travel?'

'Touch wood, he's one hundred per cent. And he travelled fine. The great thing about him, John, is his temperament. He's so relaxed. The more I travel him, the more amazed I am what a nice nature he has. And except for that incident in the parade at Newmarket, nothing seems to bother him.'

'That's what you want really, isn't it? If we're talking about horses getting the trip, a relaxed horse, with a great big stride like your chap, is a much better bet than a highly strung animal with a short, choppy action.'

'Sure,' the woman smiles in reply. 'Not that he wins a lot of friends going down to the start.'

'Sir Ivor was just the same,' the man tells her. 'Used to go down like a seaside pony. And you think your horse will handle this hill?'

'I know he will.'

They walk down the rest of the famous hill and round Tattenham Corner, deep in conversation like the old friends which they are.

The man laughs as he relates a story. 'After Nightie's very first race last year, I got 66/1 about him for tomorrow's race. The bookie's been after me ever since to reduce my wager.'

'I sure hope you'll be wearing your armour-plated vest when Nightie gallops up the straight tomorrow,' the woman laughs in reply.

Then she stops just before the final bend runs out and looks up the course, at the long climb to the winning post.

'This is where we want to be,' she says, standing two or three horse widths from the rails. 'Maybe fourth or fifth, with Millstone Grit no more than six lengths up, and bang in our sights. Dex will give him a steady here, make sure he's got the big chap balanced, and then kick on.'

'As far from home as this?' the man frowns. 'You surprise me.'

'We're going to surprise them all,' the woman replies, suddenly very determined. 'Nightie is going to bury 'em.'

Chapter Twenty-Five

Everything went entirely to plan, until the evening of the race itself. Part of Cassie's carefully conceived arrangements included stabling Nightie a few miles from the racecourse proper at a private yard in Esher. This was no reflection on Epsom's highly efficient security, but simply in recognition of the amount of money Cassie's horse had been laid to lose. Rather than take the slightest chance of the favourite being got at, Cassie had elected to keep the horse secretly and under a round-the-clock surveillance in the totally secure private stables of one of her wealthy British owners. Such was her diligence, it had even been somewhat controversially decided to return Nightie to his lodgings outside Esher after his pre-race 'blow' on the Tuesday, and to transport him finally to Epsom early on the morning of the race itself.

Mattie had considered this last decision as over and above the call of his mother's duty, and told her so.

'OK,' Cassie had replied, 'just go ask your great hero, Vincent O'Brien. He always used to stable his Derby runners away from the course.'

'Not the night before the race, Ma.'

'Maybe not, Mattie. But the difference between Vincent and me is Vincent's not a woman.'

Cassie even took her turn keeping vigil outside the favourite's stable on the Tuesday night, but the hours passed without incident, and by the time Nightie was loaded into the horse transporter at dawn the next morning with his precious legs carefully bandaged, and his feet

711

freshly shod with his racing plates, the party from Claremore breathed a corporate sigh of relief.

All except Cassie.

'Come on, Ma,' Mattie teased her as they sat up front in the cab. 'Ease up! He's home and hosed!'

'I'll ease up when I'm good and ready, Mattie,' Cassie answered shortly. 'For a start, when we get to the course.'

Her worries were not unfounded. They had barely travelled two miles from the yard at Esher when a builder's pick-up truck suddenly shot out from a side turning and forced Liam who was driving the box to stand on the air brakes.

Cassie was out of her seat and through into the back of the lorry in a flash.

'What's the damage, Frank?' she asked the lad who was already peering anxiously over the partition.

'I think he's fine, Guv'nor. It certainly threw the old fellow forwards right enough, but the knee pads'd take care of that.'

The horse happily seemed completely unbothered by the emergency stop, and was good-naturedly trying to chew his way through the lad's wind-cheater. Cassie stroked the horse's neck, then having satisfied herself the horse was standing all square, told Liam to drive on.

It wasn't until they arrived at the course and unloaded Nightie they saw the actual damage.

'He's spread a plate, Guv'nor,' Liam said as soon as he saw Frank lead the horse down the ramp.

'Let's just hope that's all he's done, Liam,' Cassie replied, lifting the now stationary horse's off-foreleg, where sure enough the lightweight racing shoe had come half adrift from the animal's hoof. 'Hand me the pincers, quickly Mattie.'

'I'll go and find the farrier,' Liam said, while Mattie rummaged in a tool box.

'No you won't, Liam,' Cassie replied, easing the racing plate to one side of the hoof. 'You'll call Mr Brogan. The horse has pricked his foot.'

Even before the shoe was removed completely, the damage was clearly visible, in the shape of a tiny but angry red mark on the bottom of the foot.

'Damn,' said Cassie quietly. 'Damn, damn, damn.'

'Will he not be able to run then, Guv'nor?' young Frank asked, barely able to keep the tears from his eyes.

'He'll run if I have anything to do with it, Frank,' Cassie replied. 'Now what we need is Mr Brogan, like I said. And a van load of ice.'

Liam opened the cab door and reached inside for the mobile telephone.

'What will we want the ice for, Guv'nor?' the now ashen-faced Frank enquired.

'To pack that foot of his, that's what we want the ice for, Frank. We're going to have to freeze this foot of his solid and hope and pray for the best. Now lead him off to his box, and stop looking as though it's the end of the world. We've got to give the impression that nothing's the matter.'

Frank led the horse away, doing his best to look carefree, while Liam raised Niall Brogan at his nearby Surrey hotel. He arrived within half an hour, and after an initial examination of the injury, gave the horse absolutely no chance of running.

'As we all know,' he said, 'this is the leg the horse leads with. If there is even a suspicion of pain here, he won't stretch out. He's not going to risk himself. Particularly a great long striding horse like this fellow.'

'So what do you advise, Niall?' Cassie asked.

'Withdraw him,' the vet answered. 'Rather than have him disappoint the biggest racing audience in the world, and probably do himself more harm, I'd withdraw him, and we'll have him one hundred per cent for the Irish Derby.'

'I can't withdraw him, Niall,' Cassie replied.

'Can't, Cassie? Or won't?'

'Both, Niall. Look. I won't run the horse if it's going to harm him. But we've a good few hours before the off.

Over seven in fact. And if we can get the inflammation out of his foot, and the foot stays cold for two hours before the race, I'll run him. On condition that if Dex thinks the horse is feeling it at all on the way to post, he'll be ordered to withdraw him. How's that?'

Niall chewed the inside of his lip thoughtfully, and shook his head.

'It's a hundred to one shot, Cassie. There's a fair amount of heat in that hoof already.'

'I know. But that's your responsibility, Niall,' Cassie answered shortly. 'Mine is whether to race the horse or not. This isn't the first time this sort of thing has happened. What about the winner of the '87 Guineas? Don't Forget Me? This is more or less precisely what happened to him. So let's go to school on that, right? They did it with ice, and that's exactly what we're going to do.'

'Where in hell do we get ice from at this time of morning?' asked Mattie.

'That's for you to find out, Mattie,' his mother retorted. 'And not now! Yesterday!'

In response to the urgency in his mother's commands, Mattie doubled off to see if there was yet any sign of the caterers, while Niall and Cassie attended further to the horse's hoof.

'You'll need more than ice, Cassie Rosse,' her vet informed her gloomily. 'You're going to need a bloody miracle.'

By now it was half past eight. By nine o'clock Niall had cleaned and cauterised the nail-prick in the sole of the horse's foot, and a few minutes later Cassie stood holding the damaged hoof up while Liam kept a cold hose playing constantly on the wound.

Once again, the big horse's temperament was his salvation. He stood as quietly as could be, munching some hay, while the three of them took it in backbreaking turns to hold his up-turned hoof.

Jonathan Keating's head lad was the first to suspect that there might be some trouble with the favourite. On his

714

way back from Millstone's Grit's box, he noticed the steady trickle of water coming out from under the door of The Nightingale's stable.

'Everything all right in there?' he enquired, popping his head over the door.

Niall Brogan stood up at once and tried to block the lad's view of the proceedings, but in vain.

'Nothing wrong with your horse I hope, Mrs Rosse?' the lad said.

'Nothing whatsoever, thank you,' Cassie replied, leaving it at that. But the lad went on his way unconvinced and it wasn't long before all sorts of rumours that all wasn't right with the favourite began to circulate around the stables.

'The best thing is to issue a statement,' Cassie said, playing the cold water on the horse's upturned hoof. 'Otherwise there's just going to be one almighty panic, and we'll have the press all over us. So let's nip it in the bud now, and hope that'll take the pressure off.'

Niall Brogan agreed, and Cassie dictated a short statement to him while holding The Nightingale's leg up. The statement simply said that the Derby favourite was a little sore on the sole of one foot, due to an old injury when he'd struck a stone on the gallops at home. A further bulletin would be issued if it was felt necessary at midday, but as things stood, there was no doubt about the horse standing its ground.

'That's not true, Cassie,' Niall pointed out.

'As far as I'm concerned it is,' Cassie replied.

Shortly afterwards, when Mattie arrived with the first consignment of ice, packed tight in two large coldbags which he'd scrounged from Niall's nearby hotel, there was still no sign of the press as he showed his pass to Security and entered the stable block. Liam and he put the horse's leg in a large round feed bowl and packed ice all around it, as high as the fetlock joint.

'He's not going to stand still in that all morning,' Niall prophesied gloomily.

'He won't have to,' Mattie replied. 'I rang a racing chum in Newbury, who's bringing across one of those special boots. You know – a Jacuzzi boot.'

'Newbury? Christ – that'll take hours, Mattie. And by then it'll be too late.'

'It won't take hours, Niall. This chap's got his own helicopter. And he's already on his way.'

Mattie's friend landed in the middle of the course thirty-five minutes later, and within another quarter of an hour Nightie was standing quite happily with one leg laced into an ice-filled special boot.

'A Jacuzzi boot indeed,' Niall Brogan muttered half to himself as Cassie and he went in search of some coffee. 'I just hope the horse doesn't develop herpes.'

'If you had your way,' Cassie laughed in reply, 'you'd still be blowing medicines down horses' necks with a blowpipe!'

'You've little chance even so of leading in the winner.'

'What are the current odds?'

'It was a ten-to-ninety chance against at nine o'clock. I'll give you forty-sixty now.'

An hour and a half later the chances had improved to sixty-forty, when Niall took the boot off the horse's hoof for the first time, and after drying the hoof thoroughly and allowing the horse to stand and move around its box unencumbered for ten minutes, could find no heat in the foot. Cassie then issued a final statement to say that any crisis there had been with the favourite had now passed.

When Cassie returned to the horse's box, she found Mattie had disappeared to collect more ice by helicopter, and Niall Brogan sitting on the upturned feed bucket reading *Sporting Life*.

'Only *The Times* opposes you,' he said, showing Cassie the table of Experts' Selections.

'*The Times* and my vet,' Cassie answered.

'Your vet has an open mind,' Niall replied. 'I have to admit I'd have given you no chance at all, even at ten o'clock. But now—'

'Well?'

'Eighty-forty.'

'I'll drink to that,' Cassie said.

'Now there's an idea,' Niall Brogan agreed.

And leaving Liam, Frank and Mattie in charge, they headed for the nearest racecourse bar.

The day was going to be a scorcher. The mist which had blanketed the course at dawn, had long since lifted, and the sun was shining down from a cloudless sky. Cassie had been so concerned she hadn't for a moment noticed what sort of day it was going to be.

'They're predicting a record attendance,' Niall told her as he poured them their first glass of champagne. 'Your fellow's a bit of a star already it seems.'

'I just hope he won't let them down,' Cassie said, thoughtfully enough to make Niall look round at her.

'Hello,' he said, 'and what's happened to the famous Rosse confidence?'

'It's perfectly all right when I'm with the horse, Niall,' Cassie replied. 'But as soon as I'm on my own, it's down tilt.'

'In that case,' Brogan said, pouring some more wine, 'time for another attitude adjuster.'

Brough Scott came up to her, as dapper and debonair as ever.

'Mrs Rosse,' he said with a frown, 'I hope what I'm hearing about your horse isn't true.'

Cassie turned and greeted him.

'On the record, or off, Brough?' she asked.

'Off the record for the moment,' he replied. 'Though maybe if you're in the mood a little later, Cassie, you might like to say hello to my hundred and one million viewers.'

'Off the record, he spread a plate in the lorry this morning and pricked his foot. And Niall thought he'd done his chance. On the record, the horse runs.'

'Is he sound?' Scott asked.

'I won't – correction, I wouldn't be running him otherwise,' Cassie replied.

'Can I use this in my run-up?'

'Why not save it until after he's won?'

'Fine,' Scott said, with a grin. 'In that case, if there are no further setbacks, can I grab you for a pre-recorded interview say in one hour? You know where we are. On that little lawn in front of Members'.'

Cassie agreed, and Brough Scott left to continue his field work.

'I like that guy,' Cassie said. 'He speaks as he finds, and I think that's most refreshing. So much of racing is such lip service. Now I'd best go and change, I suppose.'

Brogan followed her out of the bar with the half-drunk bottle of champagne under one arm.

'You'll never get to Esher and back in time now,' he told her.

'I've got my clothes with me. I can change in the weighing room. John Meredith's an old chum of Tyrone's. He said it'd be OK.'

Having brought her case with her from the stables, Cassie hurried over to the weighing room. She now felt cautiously optimistic. There was still an hour and a half before the first race, and three hours altogether before the Derby. And the horse's foot was still as cold as ever. Keeping her fingers crossed, she hurried up the steps of the weighing room and in through the doors.

The first people she saw inside were Jonathan Keating and Leonora. Leonora's husband apparently had talked her out of her rash threat to move Millstone Grit, although judging from the look of heavy boredom on her trainer's face, he'd have been the last person to object had Leonora carried her warning through.

Leonora was wearing a dress and matching coat of brilliant red, topped off with a stunning picture hat in the same colour, banded in white.

Cassie was still in her slacks and old baseball jacket.

'Well,' said Leonora, spotting her, 'if it isn't the ex-favourite's owner and trainer.'

'I don't have time to stop and bitch now, Leonora,' Cassie said, 'I have to change.'

'Why?' Leonora laughed. 'Things gotten so bad you've taken up race riding?'

'I'm sorry to hear about your horse,' Keating said, with genuine concern and sympathy.

'There's nothing wrong with my horse, Jonathan,' Cassie replied, stopping on her way to the Clerk of the Course's office.

'I heard he'd pricked his foot.'

'Maybe he did, but there's nothing wrong with him now.'

'I'm glad to hear it,' Keating replied. 'Good luck, if I don't see you before.'

'Thanks, Jon,' Cassie said. 'You too.'

She turned and continued on her way, but not before she'd heard Leonora laughing and saying purposefully loudly that horses with pricked feet don't win Derbies. Jonathan Keating, it appeared, agreed with her.

Cassie checked with John Meredith if it was still all right for her to change there, and in order to find out exactly what the favourite's chances were, he personally escorted her to the room reserved for lady jockeys, where he left her to change into an outfit Josephine had persuaded her to have made, which matched her racing colours perfectly; a simple silk dress in a claret colour, and a beautifully tailored half coat in light grey, with a matching claret border. Her hat was a pillar box, in claret with a grey tassel. She examined herself in the mirror and decided that as usual her daughter had shown exemplary taste.

As she walked back into the weighing room, she bumped into Dex.

'Mr Brogan said I'd find you here,' he said, dumping his bag on a bench. 'What gives?'

Cassie walked him out of anyone's earshot and explained the situation. Dex listened without interruption, and when Cassie had finished, asked what the chances were of getting the horse to post.

'They're improving with every minute,' Cassie told

719

him, 'And if every minute could only be a hundred seconds long today, we'd be home and dry.'

'And you're really serious about me withdrawing him if I think he's feeling a little tender on the way down?' he asked her.

'Absolutely. It's only fair on the public. Whatever you do, he mustn't come under starter's orders.'

'It's going to be awful difficult to know if he's feeling it,' Dex warned her, 'with that funny old scratchy action of his.'

'I know what this means, Dex, believe me,' Cassie replied. 'But I have to have your word.'

'You've got more than my word, Guv'nor,' Dex told her. 'You know that.'

After Cassie had recorded her pre-race interview with Brough Scott, she and Dexter hurried over to the stables to see what progress the patient was making. They were enormously cheered to see the horse out of his box, and being walked up and down the yard by Liam, under the watchful gaze of Niall Brogan.

'You want the good news or the bad news, Mrs Rosse?' he asked her.

'I'll take the bad,' she replied, the prayers flying out of her and up into the sky.

'The bad news is I was wrong,' Brogan said, poker-faced. 'The good news is you weren't.'

Cassie flung her arms round Niall's neck and kissed him.

'That's the first time I've been kissed by a trainer,' he grinned, 'and you're not home and hosed yet.'

'Dear heaven!' Cassie laughed. 'Is every Irishman descended from the same tribe as Tomas Muldoon?'

The horse was put back up in his box, with the ice-packed boot laced once more on to his foot for good measure, while Liam and Frank started their labour of love in getting the horse ready. The time was flying by now, with the horses for the first race already making their way across to the pre-parade ring. Cassie rushed back up to the pre-parade ring, where she was due to meet Josephine, who had just arrived with a party of friends from the theatre. Cassie told them of the dramas, and as they were actors, she couldn't have had a more appreciative audience. Cassie finally told her daughter that as far as she was concerned Josephine would win Best Turned Out, kissed her, asked her to look out for Sheila Meath, and left to go and saddle up her horse.

Mattie rushed out of nowhere and caught her up on the way to the saddling boxes.

'He's firming up now,' he told his mother breathlessly. 'I got him at evens an hour ago, but you can't do better than 4/5 on now. I reckon he might even start at 4/6.'

'He won't be the housewife's choice, and that's for sure,' Cassie said. 'Not at that price.'

'No,' Mattie agreed. 'They all seem to be going for Never Mind. He's 7/2. Four points in since yesterday.'

But once they caught sight of The Nightingale being led round the pre-parade ring by Frank, all their worries about the opposition faded. He was strolling round completely relaxed, as if standing for hours in an ice-filled boot was something he did every day. Cassie signalled Frank to bring the horse in to be saddled, and she and Liam went quietly and efficiently through their familiar routine.

'Another notch more your side, Guv'nor,' Liam called, as the girth was done up.

'And remind me to tell Dex to check his girths twice at the start,' Cassie muttered.

'You always do, Guv'nor,' Liam grinned, straightening the number cloth. 'It's engraved on your memory.'

'Tell them, tell them, and then tell them again,' Cassie replied. 'That's what my husband drummed into me. And you know what an old windbag Nightie is,' she added, throwing the surcingle over the saddle. 'As soon as he sees his girth he blows himself out.'

Frank fixed on his own arm band, bearing the number of the race, and the horse's name, as Cassie ran a final check over her charge. As she did, Liam squeezed a sponge in the horse's mouth, and then crossed himself as

721

the horse was led away to the main paddock. Cassie and Mattie both dwelt for a moment, watching the big horse amble off, then Mattie took his mother's arm and escorted her off to the nearest champagne bar.

'There's nothing more you can do now, Ma,' he told her, 'except worry. And you might as well do that with a glass in your hand.'

Mattie bought some champagne, and they stood drinking it in front of a television set.

'That man,' Mattie sighed, staring at the outrageous figure who was giving the viewers the latest news from the ring. 'He's something else, but I'm not at all sure what.'

'The favourite is hardening all the time,' the commentator told the camera. 'There was a time you could get evens earlier on, but now The Nightingale, or Nightie to his fans, is 6/4 on, friends! This looks like being the first odds-on Derby favourite since Sir Ivor, if my memory serves me right! And now I'm told he's 7/4 on! Well that leaves all you housewives out, right? 4/7 The Nightingale, and there'll be some singing all right tonight in Ireland if that one wings it home! 5/4 against Millstone Grit, you can get 6/4 in places! 6/4 Millstone Grit, 7/2 Never Mind, 5/1 Russian Defector and Four To A Barre, both grandsons of the great Nijinsky! 6/1 the French horse En Vas, 8/1 Operanatomy, and there's been hard interest for this one since this morning, when he opened at 14/1! 8/1 Operanatomy and 9/1 bar the rest! For my money, you can bar the rest! Because as far as I'm concerned, if The Nightingale comes down Tattenham Hill backwards, he's still going to fly home first! Over to you, my noble lord!'

'Jesus God, that's all we need,' Mattie sighed. 'It's worse than being tipped by Wogan.'

Cassie handed Mattie her glass of champagne, unable to drink it. Mattie knocked it back and then followed his mother out and towards the paddock. The horses were still being led round, with Liam standing at the owners and trainers entrance, nervously watching his charge. The Royal party arrived and made their way into the centre of the parade ring, followed by a deputation of smartly dressed owners and trainers.

'I've often wondered in cases like yours,' Mattie said to his mother, as they watched The Nightingale stroll past them, 'who gives the orders to who? Does the trainer tell the owner? Or does the owner tell the trainer?'

'All I have to say at a time like this,' Cassie replied, 'is thank God you're here to keep me laughing.'

Josephine just made it to the centre as the jockeys in their brilliant silks were filing in to find their connections. Dex arrived and tipped his cap, then stood idly chatting to Mattie and his sister while Liam adjusted the girths, and Cassie gave the favourite his final check.

'Jeeze, but doesn't he look like the winner?' Dex grinned as he patted the horse's quarters.

The Nightingale certainly looked the pick of the paddock, bulging with highly tuned muscle, and his dark coat supple and gleaming. And while several of the others were beginning to sweat up considerably on this hot June day, Nightie was still as cool as ever.

'Remember, Dex,' Cassie said, 'if he stumbles, changes his leg, tip toes, if he does anything on the way to the start that makes you suspect he's not sound, you're to withdraw him.'

'You got it. Now what about the race?'

'We've been over that enough, wouldn't you reckon?'

Dex grinned as he stood ready to be legged up.

'Just keep your eye on Leonora's second string, Second To None. Believe me, she'll do anything she can to stop you.'

Mattie legged Dex up, and the jockey glanced over to the unprepossessing chestnut which carried Leonora's second colours.

'They've certainly put the right man up,' he said to his connections. 'Nick Franklyn would ride off his mother.'

Frank led the favourite away, and Cassie noticed with some pride that the Royal party seemed to have eyes for no other horse. She also noticed that Leonora was having some long last words with the sallow-skinned jockey who was about to be legged up on her second string. He nodded, and then with a leg up from one of the lads, walked his horse on to join the others.

The parade passed without incident, although several of the horses were beginning to sweat profusely from the heat and the tension, most noticeably Major Robert, Whizz and, unsurprisingly after his antics at Newmarket, Pastiche. The horses then turned and started to canter back in order past the grandstands. This, as far as Cassie was concerned, was the make or break point. She put her race glasses up and watched The Nightingale closely as Dex stood up in his irons and asked the horse to canter away from them. She watched in total silence as the horse cantered past the winning post and round the top bend, until he pulled up at the point where the horses file across the Downs to the start.

'Goddammit,' she said. 'Goddammit.'

'What is it, Ma?' Mattie asked, whipping round to her in surprise.

As far as he could remember, he'd hardly ever heard his mother swear before. And now she was not only swearing, she was standing with tears visibly in her eyes.

'What's the matter, Cassie?' Sheila Meath enquired, putting her hand on Cassie's arm.

'Nothing,' said Cassie, fighting for control of herself. 'Nothing at all. The bloody old horse is sound.'

The horses only had to walk now, before they reached the starting stalls, across a long track over the Downs to the far side of the course. As they did, the bookmakers eased some of the other fancied horses half a point or so in a last desperate attempt to hedge against the red-hot favourite. But the serious betting members of the public weren't to be fooled, and by the time the horses had reached the starting stalls, The Nightingale was 1/2 everywhere.

'He'll cane the bookies if he wins,' Mattie gasped, as he rushed back from the rails to where the Claremore party was in the stands.

'When he wins, Mattie,' Cassie said. 'Now there can be no possible "if" about it.'

'Where's Josie?' Mattie asked, looking about him.

'Being sick,' one of her friends replied.

'Great,' said Mattie with a grin, as a white-faced Josephine returned. 'Here comes the girl who was going to win the Grand National.'

'They're going into the stalls,' Cassie announced, watching closely through her glasses. 'Nightie looks as if he's fallen asleep.'

One of the outsiders, Busybee, started to make trouble, whipping round and refusing to be led up. Most of the others were in by now, including the favourite, who was standing quite still and relaxed, even though the horse two berths away was trying to get up. The handlers got the blindfold on Busybee, and turning him once to disorientate the horse, soon had him installed.

They were all in.

'They're under starter's orders!' came the announcement.

'They're off!'

The break was perfectly even, though Cassie noticed that The Nightingale was one of the first out. Dex had him settled in a matter of strides, while one of the outsiders, a maiden called Washdown, decided, as is so often the case, to try and make a name for himself by winning the race from the front. By the time the field had swung right-handed towards the woods and up the hill away from the start, Washdown had bolted into a three-length lead.

This, thought Cassie, isn't going to suit Millstone Grit at all, and she swung her glasses back to the rest of the field to pick up Leonora's horse who, sure enough, was running now in second. Sweeping her glasses back further she found The Nightingale lobbing along in about tenth, on the left of the field so that he could pick up the rails as the field swung back across the course to head for the top of Tattenham Hill. Two in front of him, and already being scrubbed along, was Second To None.

By the time they reached Tattenham Hill, Millstone Grit had swallowed up the early tearaway and was beginning to stretch his field. Pastiche, running a much better race altogether than he did in the Guineas, was four lengths away in second, just ahead of another Irish horse, Quare Hawk. Then came En Vas, Never Mind, Russian Defector, Major Robert and Sing Your Song. The Nightingale, whom Dex had steered nicely on to the rails, just where he wanted to be, led the second group of horses, with Second To None now dropped back into the place behind him. Cassie could see her horse was still cantering, while the others were being really pushed along to go the scorching gallop set by the leader.

'This is crazy,' Mattie announced. 'He just can't possibly keep this pace up!'

'He did at Ascot,' Cassie replied, 'and he's half the runners beat already.'

As they started the long, steep drop down the hill, and as Millstone Grit increased his lead to a good ten lengths, the beaten horses started quickly to drop back. Pastiche was seen to be doing his best to stay with him, but Quare Hawk fell away tamely, burned out by the breakneck pace. Never Mind and En Vas passed him and went in pursuit of the leader, followed by Russian Defector and Major Robert. Sing Your Song lost his rhythm, quite obviously hating the notorious undulations of the famous course, and started to veer across the track.

Halfway down the hill, The Nightingale was still idling at the front of the second group, Dex sitting still as a mouse, with a double handful of rein.

Then as Millstone Grit led the field at full gallop towards the final part of the bend, Dex made his first move, easing The Nightingale slightly away from the rails as directed by Cassie in order to keep his horse perfectly balanced as they lined up for home.

As he did so, Nick Franklyn, having kept Second To None still in touch by running him at full stretch behind The Nightingale, drove his horse up through the gap which Dex had left on the inside, whipping his horse as hard as he could on every stride. Cassie swung her glasses on to Leonora's second string, just in time to see her jockey kick Second To None away from the rails and straight across The Nightingale's path.

It was a suicidal manoeuvre.

An almighty gasp went up from the stands as the crowd saw Dex, in order to avoid a serious collision, snatching the favourite up. In the moment of doing so, he lost half a dozen lengths, and his perfect attacking position.

'We're stitched!' Mattie shouted. 'The bastard's buried us!'

And as a wall of beaten horses started to fall back across The Nightingale's path, it certainly looked as though the day was lost. But Cassie never stopped believing. She knew how fast The Nightingale could fly, and she focused her glasses back on Dex and watched as he got the horse balanced again in one moment and waited for another opening.

The field, led a good six lengths by Millstone Grit, swept off the final bend and into the straight, The Nightingale at the back, with only four behind him. As they kicked for home, Cassie watched Dex pick his way skilfully through the ruck of beaten horses, on a horse which she saw hadn't even been asked yet for his effort. Pastiche, En Vas, Operanatomy and the weakening Never Mind were now the only horses between The Nightingale and the leader, who was still galloping remorselessly for home. Bill Langley, Millstone Grit's jockey, took a good look over his shoulder as he passed the three-furlong marker, and obviously seeing no sign of the favourite, gave his horse one good slap and kicked him on for what looked from the grandstands now like a certain victory.

And then Dex, boldly switching his horse to the outside of the field, asked The Nightingale for his effort, and when he did, the effect was so devastating that the crowd seemed to hold its corporate breath for one split second, before unleashing a roar that must have been heard up in London. Because The Nightingale flew. He flew like an arrow past Never Mind, En Vas, and Pastiche, making them look like handicappers. And still Dexter hadn't touched him with the whip. He had just sat down on to his horse and asked him to go. Only Operanatomy stood between The Nightingale and Millstone Grit now, who was still four lengths to the good as they passed the two-furlong marker. Operanatomy's jockey was extremely busy, trying to keep his obviously beaten horse straight and running. But he was fighting a losing battle, and the horse started to roll away from the rails, right across the flying favourite's path.

'Not again!' Sheila cried. 'I just don't believe it!'

Cassie prayed for Dex to keep his head. She prayed to Tyrone. She prayed to Mrs Roebuck. She prayed to Mary-Jo. He mustn't snatch his horse up again, she told them. He must let the other horse come right across him and keep galloping, so he doesn't lose his vital momentum.

Her prayers were answered. While others might have lost their heads seeing a horse veering so violently across their track, Dex kept his, gambling on the horse keeping rolling. Operanatomy did just that, and as he fell away cross the course towards the stands, Dexter now asked The Nightingale seriously to go after Millstone Grit, who was showing no signs of stopping.

Nonetheless, when The Nightingale turned on the tap, the leader suddenly looked lead-footed. In one moment of blinding acceleration, The Nightingale made good the four lengths' difference between the two horses, and by the furlong post was at the leader's quarters. Bill Langley was hitting his horse on every other stride, but Dexter never went for his whip, riding the favourite with hands and heels only. In another few strides, the horses were even, neck and neck for just a split second, and for that one unbelievable second, The Nightingale suddenly seemed to idle, to hover alongside his adversary, rather like an eagle would before swooping on his prey.

Then Dex just shook the reins at him, asking his horse to go for the kill, and in a couple of strides the race was over.

As The Nightingale swept contemptuously past Millstone Grit, the vast crowd roared even louder, exhilarated and utterly astonished by the incredible speed of the big horse. In all her years of racegoing, Cassie had never heard a volume of sound like it. It engulfed her like a tidal wave, as people all around her forgot their dignity and started to jump up and down in sheer excitement. Millstone Grit, who only moments before had victory almost certainly in his sights, now suddenly collapsed like a burst balloon, conceding second place to the unconsidered Whizz, who came with a late rattle out of the pack.

But there was no doubting the winner. From an apparently impossible position as the field turned into the straight, The Nightingale had sped through the field like a bullet, passing horses who were still not spent, until he picked off the leader as if he was a seaside donkey. Yet as he now passed the winning post the horse hardly seemed extended. Two furlongs from home there must still have been a six to seven lengths' difference. A furlong and a half there were two. Half a furlong later, at the distance, they momentarily matched stride for stride, and then with that one shake of the reins, history was written. The Nightingale strode the last hundred yards up the hill to win his Derby in a new record time by four lengths.

As Dex eased him past the post, as Cassie had hoped that he would, as Cassie had dreamed that he would, as Cassie had prayed that he would, she covered her face with her hands, and then after a moment raised both her arms to the sky.

'I told you that I'd do it for you, Ty!' she cried, laughing up at the clear blue beyond. 'Didn't I tell you that I'd do it!'

And then with an arm tightly round each of her children's shoulders, Cassie went to lead her hero in.

Aftermath

Jonathan Keating was one of the first to congratulate Cassie.

'Good stuff, Cassie Rosse,' he said with a grin, 'but you should have won by a distance.'

'That's OK,' Cassie replied. 'Four lengths will do just fine, thanks all the same, Jon.'

She didn't remember much else, not in clear and logical detail. The euphoria was too great. The Nightingale was cheered all the way back from the post to the unsaddling enclosure, and Cassie was besieged with reporters, and rushed from pillar to post to be interviewed by the media.

She remembered her visit to the Royal Box, and the genuine delight of the Royal party at The Nightingale's victory.

She remembered Dexter Bryant's unabashed tears of joy as he unsaddled his hero and then hurried off speechlessly to weigh in.

She remembered The Nightingale hardly blowing as Liam threw a sweat rug on him, before the sponsor's blanket was draped over his back and the photographers moved in.

But most of all she remembered the man who met her at the entrance to the bar at the foot of the Members' Stand.

She was standing talking to Sheila Meath, who was still laughing with delight at Nightie's historic victory, when she noticed a man in black top hat and tails watching her. For a moment Cassie thought this was something she was going to have to get used to that day, since her face had already appeared countless times on the course television sets all afternoon.

Then something in the man's eyes, she wasn't at all sure what, made her look again, and as she did, he smiled at her and raised his top hat. Cassie half-smiled back and then continued talking to Sheila.

A moment later the man was at her side, doffing his hat.

'Excuse me, Mrs Rosse,' he said, 'but may I also offer you my congratulations?'

Cassie turned and thanked him, taking in the man and trying to place him. He was in his early forties, very good-looking, and somehow well known to her.

'You won't remember me,' he told Cassie, in direct contradiction to what Cassie was feeling. 'Although we have met once or twice. On the course in Ireland.'

'You'll have to forgive me,' Cassie began. 'Obviously the nature of my job—'

'I fully understand,' the man interrupted courteously. 'But I just had to come and say well done, because I don't think I have ever seen a better Derby winner.'

'That's very kind of you,' Cassie replied. 'I think maybe the horse can take his place with five or six of the post-war best.'

'He did it in record time.'

'Equal record time, He equalled Mahmoud's 1936 record of 2 minutes, 33.8 seconds.'

'That record was suspect,' Mattie interrupted. 'It was hand timed, Ma, as against today's electrically timed races.'

'OK,' Cassie agreed. 'But I guess until someone goes faster, Mattie, that record still has to stand.'

Mattie grinned then took the rest of the Claremore party back into the bar for more champagne, leaving Cassie with the stranger.

As he went, Cassie looked from her son to the man standing in front of her, and then back at the receding figure of Mattie. But the bell still didn't ring.

'Allow me to introduce myself,' the man said, 'I'm Anthony Wilton.'

'Hello, Anthony,' Cassie answered, shaking the man's offered hand.

'You might remember me better as Gerald Secker,' he added, carefully wiping the crown of his black top hat.

Cassie stared at him unbelievingly.

'You're dead,' she gasped.

'Yes I was,' he agreed. 'To all intents and purposes. But how did you know?'

'Someone told me. Someone was talking about – about your family, and I was told you were dead.'

'I was left for dead, but it's a very long story. And I'm sure you don't have time to stand and listen to it now.'

Gerald smiled at her, and began to make as if to move away.

'No – wait,' Cassie asked him. 'I may not have time, but I'll find it. Why have you changed your name?'

'That's all part of the story, Mrs Rosse.' Are you sure you want to hear it?'

'First just answer me one or two questions. Your name. Why did you change it?'

'I had a terrible row with my family,' he replied. 'Have you met my father? He had a terrible temper.'

'Had?' Cassie asked cautiously.

'He died a month ago. From a stroke.'

'I had no idea,' Cassie told him. 'Please accept my condolences.'

'Thanks,' Gerald replied. 'But I assure you, there was no love lost. I work abroad, you see, in America. In the wine trade. And I only came back to England when I heard about my father, to clear up the estate.'

'You said you had a row with him.'

'Yes,' Gerald said, then smiled. 'I got a girl into trouble, and he somehow got to hear of it. I was a thoroughly bad lot then, I'm afraid—'

'This girl,' Cassie enquired. 'Was it in Ireland? Was it a

girl who was working for your father? A girl called Antoinette?'

Gerald Secker stared at Cassie, and then nodded.

'How did you know?'

'That doesn't matter,' Cassie said. 'You got her pregnant? I mean you're sure it was you?'

'I'm afraid so, Mrs Rosse,' he replied. 'I was her first. And I didn't behave very well. I took off for India, and in fact to all intents and purposes dropped out for – well, I suppose ten years.'

He smiled at Cassie, almost timidly, as if he thought she was going to scold him. He smiled just like Mattie did, almost timidly, when he thought Cassie was going to scold him.

Cassie suddenly took his hand and shook it warmly.

'Mr Secker,' she said.

'Mr Wilton,' he smiled. 'Tony.'

'Tony,' Cassie continued. 'I can't tell you how glad I am to re-make your acquaintance. Why don't you come and drink a celebratory toast with us?'

'I'm sure I've taken up far too much time of yours already, on a day like this,' he replied.

'On the contrary,' Cassie said. 'You've made my day.'

She took him into the bar and introduced him to her party. Anthony and Mattie took to each other immediately, and within no time at all were exchanging horror stories of working and living abroad.

Josephine took her mother aside at one point and asked her who the stranger was.

'Just a friend of your father's,' Cassie told her.

'How funny,' Josephine replied. 'I was just thinking how like Daddy he looked.'

Cassie stared at her, then started to laugh.

'What's so funny?' Josephine asked.

'Nothing,' Cassie replied.

Leonora was nowhere to be seen. She had apparently left the course immediately the race was over, not even staying to see her horse unsaddled in third place.

And although there had been a legal arrangement effected over their wager, Cassie was made to wait an unduly long time before the letters were finally handed over.

There was nothing of any interest in them whatsoever. Just as Cassie had suspected.

Altogether there were thirteen letters, all of which Tyrone had written to Leonora during the period she had kept her horses with him. The content of the correspondence was entirely about horses Tyrone intended to buy for her, or horses he did not intend to buy for her. Being a scrupulous record keeper, and never knowing exactly where his flighty owner might be from one minute to the next, Tyrone had taken the precaution of putting down on paper every transaction made on behalf of Leonora.

There wasn't a trace of affection or romance in one word of one letter. Neither was the subject of Mattie's paternity ever mentioned.

The bluff with the letters was the last shot of a desperate woman. And she wasn't waving, Leonora was drowning.

Sometimes, if she awoke at night, Cassie would lie staring into the darkness and wonder what would have happened to her if The Nightingale had been beaten.

And then she would smile as she remembered Tyrone's old dictum, which he would repeat to her over and over again in a tone of mock resignation whenever Cassie proposed a supposition.

'My dear child,' he would say, often resting his forehead on the edge of the table to emphasise his point. 'With the help of an "if" –'

'I know,' Cassie would finish. 'With the help of an "if" you might put Ireland into a bottle.'

Epilogue

'What was Dexter's view of the race?' Cassie's shock-white-haired interviewer asked her.

'Dex maintains he won unextended,' Cassie replied. 'That the horse had so much in hand, he could have picked Millstone Grit off if he'd been thirty lengths adrift coming into the straight.'

'He was ten lengths off the pace at Ascot, right?' the journalist continued. 'When he turned for home in that notoriously short straight, and still won the King George VI by two and a half lengths.'

'And the St Leger by fifteen.'

'I'd like to have seen that. I hear it was his greatest performance ever.'

'No,' Cassie disagreed. 'The Derby was the one that mattered.'

'More than the Champion Stakes? More than the Arc?'

'More than anything you could possibly imagine.'

'And you resisted the temptation to sell him on to stand at stud in America?'

'Sure. I reckoned it was time an Irish success stayed in Ireland.'

Cassie finished her champagne, and smiled at her guest. 'Now then,' she suggested, 'how about going to see the object of your admiration in the flesh?'

'I guess I'm doing that right now, Mrs Rosse,' the man answered.

'Nightie'll be having his run out right now,' Cassie

said, ignoring the flattery and rising from her chair. 'He looks a picture, you'll see.'

'I'd be delighted,' J. J. Buchanan answered. 'And thank you for your time.'

'It's been my pleasure,' Cassie answered, walking to the door, and holding it open. 'And while we stroll down to the home paddock, I'd like to ask you a few questions, *Mr* Buchanan. Like why you changed your name from Joe Harris Junior? And whether you were really going to propose to me the night my mother died?'

Then taking Joe's arm, Cassie walked him across the hall and out through the front doors of Claremore, into the afternoon sunshine.

THE END